Nicola Thorne is t[...]wn novels which includ[...]et, *Bird of Passage* an[...]ch *Innocence*, *Yesterd*[...] *A Place in the Sun*).[...]ne *Gold*. Born in Sou[...]E. She lived for many[...]her home in Dorset.

By the same author

The Girls
In Love
Bridie Climbing
A Woman Like Us
The Perfect Wife and Mother
The Daughters of the House
Where the Rivers Meet
Affairs of Love
The Enchantress Saga
Champagne
Pride of Place
Bird of Passage
Champagne Gold

The Askham Chronicles:
Never Such Innocence
Yesterday's Promises
Bright Morning
A Place in the Sun

NICOLA THORNE

Never Such Innocence

This edition published by Grafton Books, 1999

Grafton Books is an Imprint of HarperCollins*Publishers*
77–85 Fulham Palace Road,
Hammersmith, London W6 8JB

First published in Great Britain by
Granada Publishing 1985

ISBN 0-261-67181-2

Printed and bound in Great Britain by
Mackays of Chatham PLC, Chatham, Kent

Eight lines from 'MCMXIV' reprinted by permission of Faber and Faber Ltd from *The Whitsun Weddings* by Philip Larkin.

CONTENTS

Never such innocence
Never before or since,
As changed itself to past
Without a word – the men
Leaving the gardens tidy,
The thousands of marriages
Lasting a little while longer:
Never such innocence again.

From *MCMXIV*
by Philip Larkin

PART I

1898: For Queen and Country

CHAPTER 1

On a hot April day in the year 1898 Lady Askham sat on the verandah of Shepheard's Hotel in Cairo viewing with detachment the people passing by. The flotsam and jetsam that filled the busy Sharia Kamel Street was certainly worth her attention, had her thoughts not been elsewhere. They were centred on the situation between her daughter Melanie and Harry Lighterman, a subaltern in the Lancers, who, clearly, were in love. Harry was personable enough; educated, elegant, well-mannered despite the misfortune of having a grocer (although an enormously wealthy, ennobled one) for a father.

Lady Askham had come to Cairo not only to see her younger son Bosco, also in the Lancers, but to view his colleague more carefully. Hitherto her acquaintance had been brief because Bosco was a popular young man with a number of friends, most of whom he paraded from time to time at the family's homes in Wiltshire and London. The extent of her daughter's infatuation with the young lieutenant of such dubious ancestry had emerged only gradually; by a series of letters which Melanie was exchanging with someone in Cairo who was not her brother and which aroused her mother's discreet curiosity. Then one day the full import of the clandestine correspondence burst upon the family when Lord Askham had a letter from Harry asking for his daughter's hand in marriage. Whereupon Dulcie Askham was abruptly despatched to Cairo, with Melanie and her sister Flora in attendance.

Below her in the street, dog carts jostled with bicycles, donkeys and stately Victorias filled with impatient, elegantly dressed Europeans who seemed by their imperious gestures to feel they should have right of way. Egyptian fellah women in blue gowns and black veils, eyes darting curiously about, their mouths concealed, sauntered along clutching bundles or babies or both. Turbaned Bedouins in their striped *kufeihs* stood around exchanging gossip of the desert, and native government clerks hurried about on their business dressed incongruously in oversized European suits and on their heads the red tarbush.

Suddenly through the throng three familiar figures emerged and ran lightly up the steps of the verandah pausing, out of breath, by Lady Askham's chair. Bosco and Harry were wearing white suits and cream straw hats and Melanie, her auburn hair loose, looked extremely youthful in a white muslin dress with a round neck threaded with a velvet bow, and elbow-length ruched sleeves. She carried a beflowered straw hat which she placed on the floor as she threw herself into a chair beside her mother.

'Oh Mama, how we have run!'

'But why, darling? You're all so out of breath.'

'There has been the most marvellous victory at the Atbara, Lady Askham.' Harry respectfully removed his hat, but remained standing. 'We are nearly at the walls of Omdurman.'

'It's quite sure we'll be going, Mama.' Bosco, also taking off his hat, sat next to Melanie, flicking his fingers for the native waiter serving tea on the far side of the terrace.

'But aren't there enough troops there already?'

'They're raising a second British Brigade and our regiment of cavalry will supplement that of the Egyptian Army. The Grenadiers are definitely going but the Fusiliers are staying behind. They're furious.'

The way Bosco chuckled convinced his mother that he saw it all as some kind of harmless game. But then this was typically Bosco who never took anything very seriously.

'But darling, people are being *killed*.'

'Mostly Dervishes, Mama. Our casualties at the Atbara are reported very light. It will be the first time our regiment has seen action for nearly twenty years. I shall be so lucky!' Impulsively Bosco seized his mother and hugged her while laughing, protesting, she tried to wriggle free.

'Harry and I would like to get married, Mama,' Melanie announced abruptly in the brief pause that ensued. 'Papa did say "yes" if you approved. Didn't he?'

Dulcie Askham kept one gloved hand on Bosco's arm and stared at her daughter.

'You mean here? Now?'

'At once, Mama, in case Harry and Bosco are sent off to the front.'

'But wouldn't you prefer to wait until they return, and have a proper wedding in England?'

'We were going to ask you anyway, Lady Askham,' Harry said quietly, 'before we heard the news. It isn't sure we'll all be going, but the rumours are rife. Melanie would like to stay out in Egypt with me whatever happens.'

'But Melanie is only nineteen. I thought an engagement, maybe.' Dulcie, her voice trailing away, looked to Bosco for help. 'Then, after a year . . . why, you scarcely *know* each other.'

'Better than you think, Mama . . .'

'Oh Mama, they're in *love*.' Bosco smiled. 'Let them marry in haste and repent at leisure.'

'There'll be no repentance, I assure you.' Melanie looked for confirmation to her beloved, glancing severely at her brother who went on, as if he hadn't been interrupted:

'Let them get married at the British Agency by special licence.'

'In church I should hope,' Dulcie burst out.

'Ah, then you agree?'

Harry and Melanie linked hands and Dulcie felt uneasy but helpless as she gazed at the loving pair – so innocent, so full of trust.

'I . . .'

'Lady Askham.' A young man, accompanied by a young woman, had silently approached her and Bosco, seeing him, rose and took his arm.

'Mama, this is Adam Bolingbroke. I told you about him and his sister Rachel. She and Flora have already met.'

'How do you do?' Peering upwards Dulcie Askham saw a grave-looking man of about Bosco's age, also dressed in a white suit and carrying a hat. Beside him stood a tall, smiling girl with ash-blonde hair visible under a straw boater with a broad green ribbon. Her dress, also green, had a long straight skirt and a simple bodice with a broad white collar and three-quarter-length sleeves. Dulcie extended a hand to the girl and then to the man who bowed over it.

'Flora mentioned you'd been together to the Mohammed Ali mosque. I'm pleased to make your acquaintance. Do sit down and have some tea.'

'And where is Lady Flora today, Lady Askham?' The girl's exceptionally low musical voice was quite charming.

'She went to the Museum of Antiquities. I think she thought she might see you there. Where are you staying, Miss Bolingbroke?'

'At the pension of Madame Königner near the Place de l'Opéra.'

'Are you there *alone*?'

'Yes, quite alone, but perfectly safe, I assure you.'

'I can't think it suitable for a young girl on her own in Cairo,' Dulcie said reprovingly.

'Oh, my sister is well able to take care of herself, Lady Askham,' Adam Bolingbroke intervened. 'She is a seasoned traveller.'

'Really?'

'She came through France and Germany by coach, pausing where she wished to sketch and sightsee. She is quite used to travelling alone.'

'Not like my closely chaperoned sisters,' Bosco winked at Melanie.

'Lady Flora seemed to me a very independent spirit.' Rachel Bolingbroke gave Dulcie a look she didn't much care for, one that contained the implicit suggestion that she was over-protective. There and then Dulcie took an instinctive, irrational dislike to the newcomer; it would take her years to try and analyse why. Rachel Bolingbroke was too tall for prettiness but her face, arresting, rather bold, had the look of a rather handsome boy. With her striking light blue eyes and firm chin, Dulcie could quite see that she and her own headstrong daughter Flora would have much in common. Given the chance Flora would like to take herself all over the continent of Europe too, chafing as she constantly did against the chaperonage of her mother. In Cairo she slipped away alone as often as she could to visit places of interest, although she was always accompanied by one of the hotel dragomen.

As the others chatted over their perfectly served English tea the word 'marriage' interrupted Dulcie from her reverie.

'That's delightful.' Rachel's melodious voice had a warm note of genuine pleasure. 'How romantic.'

'It isn't agreed yet.' Dulcie carefully poured herself a fresh cup from the silver pot. 'I have to telegraph Melanie's father. I know he will be very disappointed the wedding is not to be in England when he could give his daughter away. I still hope they may have patience. I'm sure it's what Lord Askham would wish.' But looking at the couple, hands entwined, Dulcie had a conviction that her hope was in vain. She turned her head. 'You too are with the Lancers, I understand, Mr Bolingbroke?' Blond, like his sister, but rather pale beside her tanned, healthy face, he appeared a shy young man who had scarcely spoken, being content to drink his tea and study the street.

'Only on a short term, Lady Askham. I find the army life is not really to my taste and hope to purchase myself out when the campaign in the Sudan is over. To do so now might seem like cowardice.'

'Adam is a splendid horseman.' Bosco spoke with enthusiasm.

'He looks like a professor not a soldier,' his mother said and Adam inclined his head.

'I took my degree in Cambridge and was intended for the law but, being undecided, my father suggested a short spell in the army instead. As the Lancers, then the 21st Hussars, were being sent to Cairo I agreed.'

'And would you too like to see action?'

'Nothing I should like better. We grow very idle here in Cairo, though of course I have as much a passion for antiquities as my sister.'

'Something, alas, I don't quite appreciate.' Dulcie shook her head.

'My mother is a very modern woman. She misses the social life of London – the teas, the parties, the balls.' Melanie managed to tear her eyes away from Harry to smile at Adam.

'But Cairo with its large English colony is exciting, too, don't you find, Lady Askham?' Rachel enquired pleasantly. 'The dances, gymkhanas, the opera, the plays in the Ezbekieh theatre? I know my brother and his fellow officers are constantly in demand as escorts to young English girls either out here visiting their families, or seeing the sights.'

'I don't know what the girls would do without the military,' Dulcie agreed. 'I hear they call the rash of young officers "scarlet fever". As for social occasions, there is no lack of them. Certainly since we came to Cairo we have made a vast number of interesting acquaintances. I hope you and your brother will dine with us one night, Miss Bolingbroke.' Dulcie signalled to Bosco and got up. 'Would you escort me, dearest, to the telegraph office? I would like to send that wire to your father.'

'Oh no, let *us* come with you, Mama!' Tugging at Harry's hand Melanie rose. 'I want to be sure you send it.'

Escorted by a dragoman Harry and Melanie accompanied Lady Askham to the telegraph office not far from the hotel. She spent a long time composing her wire and did not show it to the betrothed couple before she sent it, which caused Harry some concern, but Melanie would not have expected such a gesture from her mother who had not yet grown used to the idea that her daughter was an adult.

Afterwards Lady Askham expressed a wish to rest and so returned to the hotel with the dragoman leaving Harry and Melanie a precious hour or so on their own.

They decided to walk from the telegraph office along the Mouski, one of Cairo's main thoroughfares which, until a few years ago, had been protected by overhead matting as a shade from the sun. Now, thanks to the influence of the English occupation and Cairo's growth as a cosmopolitan capital with an influx of foreigners of every description, it had taken on the aspect of a modern street with glossy bars offering American cocktails; jewellers; pharmacies and dress shops that would rival Bond Street or the Rue de Rivoli; and large stores full of cheap goods surmounted by PRIX FIXES notices.

The Mouski, however, was still exciting, still oriental enough for a European. The old *dokkans*, recesses in the walls, remained with the seat, or *mastabah*, of the proprietor level with the floor, offering a variety of goods – spices, silks, carpets and embroideries, brasses, jewellery and silver – on shelves stacked from floor to roof. In various narrow streets off the Mouski were the old bazaars, little changed since medieval times, some of which were also full of cheap imported goods, but where occasionally a genuine bargain could be found for which the purchaser might haggle with the bearded, turbaned shopkeeper who would offer, as an added inducement and free of charge, sweet Turkish coffee, sherbet and perfumed cigarettes to complete the deal. There was a slipper bazaar protected from the sun by yellow and red lattices and awnings where the *mazd* could be bought, together with almost every kind of informal footwear made of fur, wool, silk, animal hides or wood.

There was a brassworkers' lane, where the craftsmen still embellished, in full view of the public, coffee trays, jugs, bowls and dishes using techniques perfected hundreds of years before by their forefathers. There were bazaars, their motley displays open to all, devoted to scents, copper, coffee, tea, turquoises and other precious and semi-precious stones, jewellery, tents, carpets, praying mats, swords, spears and a variety of whips, including the sinister *courbag* made of rhinoceros hide from the Sudan.

In the street known as Khan Khalil (parts of which were still covered), there was the Turkish bazaar and it was in one of the small shops here that Harry bought Melanie a pendant made of amber suspended on a pretty gold chain and, there and then, hung it around her neck while the old Turkish shopkeeper looked on with approval and offered the couple coffee and some Turkish Delight.

Harry had declined to bargain for this pendant, this token of his love, but he accepted the strong black coffee served in tiny cups and also a Turkish cigarette for himself to go with it. The Turk spoke no English but smiled and nodded as Harry gave him to understand they were to be married.

'Soon, we hope,' Melanie, her eyes full of love, looked up at Harry and he bent and swiftly kissed her cheek.

'You look so lovely, my darling. The amber matches your hair.'

'I want to buy something for you, Harry. I know, a cigarette case.'

'But Melanie . . .'

They finished their coffee and hurried along the narrow street of the Khauchand looking into shops selling brass, copper and silverware. Their hands were lightly clasped as they pushed along the street past the mass of humanity: Europeans, some in helmets and puggarees despite the heat, ladies in town attire with large hats and carrying parcels as though visiting friends in Knightsbridge; soldiers in red uniform; Arab women swathed from head to foot in the black *habbeh*, beggars holding out their hands for *baksheesh* and bright, dirty children scampering ahead openly begging. One had to be careful not to trip over them.

Suddenly Melanie stopped and drew Harry towards a stall, well back in a shop, gleaming with polished gold and silverware.

'There!' She pointed to a slim elegant case of a design that looked unmistakably English. She reached for it but the trader swiftly scooped it up and rubbed it carefully with the sleeve of his flowing robe.

'Very precious,' he said, looking at his reflection with satisfaction. He flicked it open and inside were two elastic bands, and a little tobacco fell out as though it had already been in use.

'Where is it made?' Melanie enquired.

'Here,' the trader looked around. 'It is made in Cairo.'

'London if you ask me,' Harry hissed over her shoulder.

'How much is it?'

The trader held up ten tobacco-stained fingers.

'Ten pounds! It's a fortune,' Harry protested.

'Do you mean ten English pounds or Egyptian?' Melanie enquired.

The trader threw back his head and laughed, showing a mouthful of gold teeth. 'Pounds, pounds,' he said, 'Egyptian pounds.'

'The same as an English pound. I'll take it.'

'Darling, that's a fortune,' Harry protested. His amber pendant had cost less.

'If it *is* English silver it's worth it. Besides I want you to have it.'

The trader was about to wrap it up but Melanie took it from him and presented it to Harry, kissing him as he had kissed her.

'Wear it for me all your life, my darling.'

'Close to my heart.' Harry took out a packet of cigarettes which he put carefully into the case.

'I'm so happy,' Melanie took his hand. They both thanked the trader who salaamed and touched his forehead, then they sauntered slowly back the way they had come towards the busy Mouski.

'I'd like us to be alone this evening,' Melanie sighed. 'Mama always seems to think I should be chaperoned.'

'We must do what your mother wants, dearest, else she will prevent me marrying you, as you are under age.'

She had never held Harry's hand for so long before, his strong fingers gripping hers. She felt so proud to be with him, tall as he was with straight black hair brushed well back from his forehead, and a full moustache which emphasized his military appearance.

Melanie loved Harry, or thought she did, what she knew of him. She had at any rate loved the drama of their distant courtship. She didn't care about Harry's parents, his background, his lack of a family tree because above all she longed to be married, to have the status enjoyed by her mother which gave one the freedom to please oneself. Her mother was very independent and she wanted her independence too.

When she'd come out to Egypt it was not with the

thought of actually being married to Harry *there*. But then a few days ago he'd suddenly suggested it and all at once it seemed the most immediate, most important and necessary thing to do. To be married in Egypt! Was there anything more glamorous a girl could wish? Bosco and Flora entering into it with excitement had helped. She had never stopped to think whether she was doing the right thing and, as she felt his fingers lying alongside hers, his arm occasionally protectively round her waist to guard her from the jostle of the crowd, his assurance when he hailed a cab along the Mouski to take them back to the hotel, the relief with which she sank down beside him in the plushly upholstered seat, she couldn't possibly be detached enough to wonder whether she were doing so now. But she clung on to his warm hand, fingered the amber stone which lay at the base of her throat, and watched the busy exciting streets as the little horse-drawn carriage bowled along.

In the course of the ensuing week, as details emerged of the victory against the Emir Mahmoud, Dulcie became more and more fearful of her son venturing to that bleak and hostile desert hundreds of miles from Cairo and civilization. The Emir's *zeriba*, or encampment, had been on the banks of the Atbara river, an important confluence with the Nile and, for a fortnight before the onslaught by the Egyptian, Sudanese and British troops, his followers defending it had been forbidden to venture away from it. Consequently when, after appalling slaughter, it was overpowered by the army, the sight of the carnage and the accompanying smell was as bad as anything yet encountered in this desert war, the attempt of the British to avenge the death of General Gordon thirteen years before and to deliver the Sudan from the evil of Mahdism and the occupation of the Dervishes. The blazing sun beat down upon the corpses of men and animals all in an advanced state of putrefaction. The debris of the sojourn of 8,000 men, women and children who had been cooped up in this small area of ground added to the scene of indescribable horror. Three thousand Dervishes were reported killed for a loss of five British officers and fifty-six men killed, and over 400 wounded.

For days the boats bringing back the wounded to the military hospitals in Cairo and Alexandria were arriving at Boulak, the landing and embarkation port for Cairo, to be met by members of the newly formed Royal Army Medical Corps and the Queen Alexandra nurses. The combined British and Egyptian force which took part in the operation had numbered nearly 15,000 men. Now the survivors of Atbara were put into summer quarters – those officers who were able, making the journey to Cairo or Alexandria for leave. The Sirdar, Sir Herbert Kitchener himself, proceeded to Abadia on the Nile to wait for the rise of the river in order to complete his conquest and the overthrow of the Mahdi's heir, the fearsome Khalifa Abdullai.

As the boats unloaded their wounded and the grisly stories circulated round Cairo, bringing the war in those far-off parts so perilously close, Dulcie longed for the calm, phlegmatic comfort of her husband who would cocoon her with the security, the normality she was used to. In all their twenty-five years of married life together – Dulcie herself had been Melanie's age when she married – she had never had to make a decision for herself, or do anything unpleasant without the support and constant reassurance of her helpmeet. The Askhams, born in the middle of the century, were strong believers in the firm Victorian values based on the example and home life of the dear Queen whose Diamond Jubilee they, with the whole country, had celebrated so joyously the previous year, the year Bosco had gone to Egypt.

The Earl of Askham was the possessor of one of the

oldest peerages in England, his family tracing its ancestry back to shepherds keeping sheep in the dales of Yorkshire in pre-Conquest times. The family name was Down and it was a succession of enterprising Downs who progressed from shepherding to the acquisition of land and, finally, the service of the monarch in about the twelfth century. A Sir Thomas Down had served in the wars in France with Henry II, and his descendants and those of the King were to be connected until Edward III conferred on one Sir John Down the barony of Askham in the County of Wiltshire. It was Elizabeth I who made Admiral, Lord Askham an earl in gratitude for his services in the acquisition of territories overseas with Sir Walter Raleigh before that adventurer fell from grace.

The current Earl of Askham, Frederick, was the tenth holder of the title. His elder son Arthur was Viscount Gore and his daughters and his younger son Bosco bore the family name of Down.

Gathered together for the wedding of Melanie a few weeks after the scene on the verandah of Shepheard's Hotel the family presented an attractive picture – a combination of high breeding, good looks and cleverness.

The Downs shared a strong family likeness; each one looked unmistakably related to the other although only two of the women were strictly beautiful, Dulcie and Melanie. The looks that made her mother and sister so attractive to men had evaded Flora due to some unhappy alignment of features. She was not ugly, she could indeed look very attractive; but she took little care of her appearance, screwing her chestnut hair into a tight bun and wearing gold-rimmed spectacles which her mother, anxious to turn her fledgling goose into a swan, opined that she did not need.

Chestnut hair and pale skin was the colouring of the female members of the family and, in addition, Melanie had natural highlights that in certain circumstances – in the sun, or a well-lit room – made her hair flame. The proportions of their faces varied: Melanie's the most exquisite, Flora's the least-favoured, and Dulcie's just about classically perfect with high cheekbones, large blue-green eyes and an attractive disposition of the mouth that, in her, could at times appear haughty.

Melanie's nose was slightly retroussé, her mouth wide and good-tempered. Everything about her seemed delicate, precious, like a porcelain figurine.

For her marriage she had chosen white silk, her gown loose-fronted and gathered at the throat, with large sleeves ruched at the elbows and long white gloves. On top of her massed curls sat a piece of accordion-pleated lace forming a large bow.

The ceremony in May at the English church of All Saints in the Ismailiyeh quarter was attended only by the members of Melanie's family present in Cairo, apart from the groom to whom Bosco was best man. It was a short ceremony according to the Prayer Book without music or hymns and when it was over the small gathering, including the newly married couple, left together in two hired carriages for the short drive to the Hotel d'Angleterre nearby where a reception for over a hundred people had been arranged.

CHAPTER 2

It may well be asked why so many were gathered to celebrate the wedding of two people most of them scarcely knew and some didn't know at all. A small party of officer friends of the groom plus the few civilians the Askhams had got to know during their brief sojourn in the capital might have been thought more appropriate for the occasion. However, to think that is to forget how important the presence of the wife and daughters of an earl was to the English community which virtually governed Egypt. As soon as Lady Askham had taken residence in Shepheard's Hotel it became a social cachet to leave one's card; an achievement to persuade her to grace the many dinner-parties and social occasions which formed part of the life not only of the immigrant population but of other members of the diplomatic corps, the French, the German and the Americans, to name the most important, and wealthy Cairenes too.

It was therefore unthinkable that the marriage of the daughter of such an important man should not be commemorated by those exiles at present residing in Cairo. So many presents and letters had arrived at Shepheard's Hotel, bouquets of flowers and expressions of regard once the engagement was announced, that Lady Askham, in despair, had soon decided that however quiet the ceremony a reception there must be. But who to organize it? She herself was so busy not only making calls and receiving visits, shopping, sightseeing and attending dinners but giving some thought to the welfare of Melanie after her marriage; where would she live, what would she do when her mother and sister returned to England? So houses and apartments had to be inspected, prospective staff interviewed and a whole host of arrangements made for the time when she would indeed be a married woman but possibly on her own, with a husband several hundred miles away in the desert.

The person to whom Dulcie turned, who knew and was known by everybody in Cairo, who arranged lavish balls, parties and entertainment for the wealthy, was one Achmed Asher. Mothers called upon him to arrange entertainments or escorts for their daughters; dowagers asked him to arrange their soirées and young, full-blooded officers persuaded him into their confidence when they wished to make the acquaintance of ladies for whose services there was a fee.

Achmed Asher was a celebrated Cairene about whom very little was known except that he was the product of a marriage between a low-born Egyptian woman, a *fellah*, and an English diplomat who had been asked to resign from the service after his *faux pas*.

No one could quite remember when Achmed Asher had established himself on the Cairo social scene or how. He was suddenly seen at parties and khedival and diplomatic occasions; at the races, the gymkhanas, and military entertainments; at the opera, the theatre and at small intimate parties where the guest list was jealously restricted. How did he get there? No one knew exactly, but there he was speaking, as required, fluent English, French, Italian, German and a smattering of Spanish in addition to Turkish and his native Arabic, entertaining countesses, sheikhs, Polish princes and American millionaires, impressing everyone by his urbanity, his charm, his knowledge of Egyptian antiquities. In an instant he could arrange a trip up the Nile visiting all the places of interest from Luxor to Aswan, an excursion into the desert to see the ruins of Memphis or the tombs of Apis, a party at Shepheard's, the Continental, or in a private apartment belonging to an Emir, overlooking the Nile. Whatever the event, whatever the occasion, Achmed Asher, plump, bald and usually wearing a loud English check suit and a red tarbush would usually be there smoking a fragrant Egyptian cigarette in a long amber holder and exuding his own peculiar brand of *savoir faire*.

Naturally the Countess of Askham had no sooner set foot in Cairo than Achmed's card arrived and in no time at all he was drinking tea with her ladyship on the terrace of Shepheard's explaining not only everything that went on in the street below but who, at the many tea tables scattered about, was sitting with whom; who was married or not married, as the case may be, to whom, and who exactly *was* who, from Oriental potentates bent on conquests and the *demi-monde* to Australian sheep farmers showing their families the world on their newly made fortunes, or Austrian engineers working on the great barrage in the delta of the Nile which was helping to irrigate Egypt's arid soil.

There was Achmed accompanying her ladyship to the Sultan Hassan Mosque, or arranging her trip to the pyramids at Gizeh and an overnight stay at the Mena Hotel. There were people introduced to her ladyship through the good offices of Achmed, people who wanted nothing more than a handshake, a cup of tea with a real English countess. Of course when the question of Melanie's wedding came up, Achmed not only arranged the hire of the luxurious *dahabeih*, on which the pair would honeymoon while drifting down the Nile, but the reception at the Hotel d'Angleterre with the finest French wines from E. J. Fleurent in the Halim Buildings, delicacies from Congdon & Co in the Sharia Kasr en-Nil, and cold meats from Abbitt's English Stores in the Mouski.

It was Achmed in his best check who flew down the steps of the terrace of the Hotel d'Angleterre to fling open the door of the carriage containing her ladyship and the bridal couple.

'Just in time, Lady Askham. Everyone is waiting.'

He bowed low over her hand, shook hands with the groom and kissed the hand of the bride, made his obeisances before Flora and Bosco who was already feeling the heat in his military uniform and was tugging at the neck of his high stiff collar.

'I think champagne, chilled, Achmed.'

'Of course, Lieutenant Down, honourable sir, please come this way.'

At an imperious flick of his wrist servants waiting at the top ran down the steps to escort the bridal party to where, carefully parted on two sides with a wide aisle down the middle, stood the assembled guests who started to applaud as Melanie and Harry slowly walked along the red carpet to a raised platform on which there were chairs and a long table containing silver ice-buckets of champagne, gleaming crystal glasses, an assortment of fish, meats, delicacies and bowls of exotic fruits. Prancing ahead of them, leading the clapping, Achmed, head inclining to the left and right, eyes darting all over the place to make sure that no one was there who shouldn't be, that everything was in order, reached the dais indicating the chairs for Lady Askham, then the bride, her sister, the bridegroom and the best man.

The clapping continued for some time until, at a sign from Achmed, standing to the back of the bridal party, it stopped as abruptly as it had begun. Achmed then appeared in front of the dais, his feet dancing excitedly about on the priceless Persian carpet, motioned for silence and, with a gracious little speech, congratulated the groom on his good fortune and welcomed the people assembled before asking them to pray silence for Lieutenant the Honourable Bosco Down who would propose a toast to the fortunate couple.

Bosco, still perspiring in the heat, his thirst unslaked, made a very brief speech and then gladly seized his glass raising it towards Lieutenant Harry Lighterman, 21st Lancers, and his wife, the Lady Melanie Lighterman.

As he was speaking the white-coated, white-gloved waiters circulated with trays full of glasses of freshly poured champagne. By the time he'd finished, a few surreptitious sips had been drunk, because of the heat, but enough was left for glasses to be enthusiastically raised as 'to the bride and groom' echoed sonorously around the assembly of diplomatic and military personnel, consular officials, English residents, their wives and daughters who had come over for the winter and were on the point of going home; a sprinkling of Cairene bankers, businessmen and their wives who had forsaken the dress and customs of the harem in which they had been reared, spoke French at home and bought their clothes in Paris; and that international flotsam and jetsam of society – the rich, displaced and the dispossessed, those exiled for one reason or another and those who preferred to live abroad – who made up the population of any large cosmopolis.

Bosco, on his second glass of champagne, had shaken hands with a dozen he didn't know and half a dozen he vaguely did. Everyone had processed past the wedding group for the exchange of handshakes and the expression of best wishes. Then they gathered in their own familiar groups, the diplomats talking diplomacy, the military discussing the campaign in the Sudan, the businessmen the state of the Bourse or the meanness of the Caisse de la Dette, the international body controlling the finances of Egypt since the British occupation. The women, gorgeously attired, chatted to one another about the dress shops in the Mouski or whispered about the most recent scandals in Cairo. Then, of course, there were the inevitable members of both sexes, young and not so young, who were looking for little adventures with one another, whether they were bored wives in search of diversion or young girls seriously looking for a mate.

'*Dearest* Lady Askham.' Madame Nadia Hassim, a dusky vision in flowing purple, heavily bejewelled, swept up to where her ladyship was holding court to an assortment of diplomats and a sprinkling of military men. 'Did I not tell you Achmed was a treasure?'

'Achmed is remarkable,' Dulcie submitted her cheek to a peck from one of Cairo's leading hostesses, 'and it is to you I owe all this!' She gestured vaguely at the crowd, most of whom were now sitting at small tables industriously attacking plates piled with food. Madame Hassim had sleek black hair covering her ears, a heavily powdered face and thin, pencilled eyebrows which flared over her ringed black eyes, adding to the impression she gave of perpetual motion. She made a point of befriending all the leading British ladies whether permanently in residence or merely visiting Cairo, and regarded Lady Askham as her finest conquest to date.

'Lady Askham, would you care to join a little excursion that Achmed is organizing into the desert to view the ruins of Bedreshayn and Sakkara, the relics of all that remains of the great city of Memphis? We are to travel by donkey and spend the night in a tent! Needless to say not one tent but many and all luxurious.' Madame Hassim, whom it was hard to imagine either on a donkey or at ease in a tent, gestured to where Achmed was talking on intimate terms to the senior English diplomat who was deputizing for Lord Cromer, the Consul-General having sent his apologies owing to the recent death of his wife.

'That sounds perfectly splendid, Madame Hassim,' Dulcie said warmly. 'When is it to be?'

'When you wish, but quite soon before the weather gets too hot. Would that suit you?'

'Perfectly.'

'I'll arrange it then.'

'Are *men* not included, Madame Hassim?' Bosco glanced at the rich Cairene who gave him a flirtatious glance.

'Lieutenant Down, how honoured would I be to think you might even consider accompanying us. Of course men are invited. I just spoke to Lieutenant Bolingbroke and his clever sister.'

'Ah!' Fora looked around with interest. 'Have they said "yes"?'

'They are certainly interested. Mr Bolingbroke said it depended on what was the disposition of his regiment.'

'Is it not hot in the desert at this time?' Lady Askham looked anxiously at Captain Crystal of the Royal Horse Guards who now served with the Egyptian Army.

'Cool at night, Lady Askham. Practically *freezing* in a tent. If I were Madame Hassim I would stay at the Mena House Hotel. It is a mere two hours across the desert by donkey or sand cart and the hotel will provide you with a picnic luncheon.'

'Captain Crystal is spoiling my little party!' Madame Hassim wailed. 'You can be sure, dearest Captain, that Achmed will provide only the best where the Countess of Askham is concerned. And, of course, you will be there to protect her.'

'Who else is to be of the party?' Frowning, Bosco lit a cigarette. 'I must say it sounds like a lark.' Bosco turned to Adam Bolingbroke who, at the sound of Madame Hassim's shrill voice calling his name, had joined the group. 'Adam, we are just discussing a foray into the desert. Is it sure you'll be there?'

'I said to Madame Hassim we were not certain of our movements. My sister is very keen.'

'Your sister has turned quite a number of heads.' Major Dean, another devotee of the Countess, stroked his moustaches appreciatively and looked to where the tall form of Rachel Bolingbroke could be seen chatting to an

American archaeologist, Mr Garkenstein, and his daughter. 'She is practically a guide book in herself, and my young officers are charmed to be her escort when they get the opportunity.'

At this information Bosco looked at Rachel Bolingbroke as if seeing her for the first time as someone other than his friend's sister, a chum. Women often became interesting when one knew that other men admired them. For his taste she was too tall, of insufficient beauty and too cerebral. Today however she had chosen a simple gown of bleached muslin dotted with tiny flowers, with a high neck and long transparent sleeves. She wore a small headpiece in preference to a hat which showed to advantage her fair hair, and she carried a plain white bag and gloves in her left hand while in her right she twirled the stem of her empty glass, her eyes gravely regarding the eminent explorer of Egyptian ruins.

As if aware of Bosco's gaze Rachel suddenly looked at him and he walked towards her, his arms half extended in greeting. Smiling at her companions, she turned away and met him halfway across the room.

'I hear you are going to the desert with Madame Hassim.'

'Oh, has she invited *you*?'

'I invited myself, when I heard you were going to be there.'

Rachel Bolingbroke didn't blush as most girls might in the circumstances, but regarded him gravely, her clear blue eyes disconcertingly direct.

'I don't believe you, Mr Down. You're a flatterer. But if your sister Flora were among the party, I'd be interested.'

'You mean you're not interested if *I* go?' Bosco took her by the elbow and steered her towards the group formed by his mother who now reclined in a gilt armchair, thoughtfully procured by the ever-vigilant Achmed, while the party draped themselves round her, the younger men squatting on the platform at her feet gazing up at her as if she were some votary goddess. Madame Hassim sat on one side and Flora, rather amused and looking detached from it all, sat on the other.

Flora was quite used to the way young men gravitated towards her mother rather than to her, or her prettier sister. It was a sort of game that many society women played, a kind of imitation of medieval courtly love. In London Lady Askham's soirées were famous not only for attracting eminent politicians, distinguished men and women of letters, doctors, lawyers, diplomats, but also the younger element, the main criteria for which were wit and good looks rather than wealth, titles or accomplishments. Dulcie Askham always had a coterie of special men friends who hung around her drawing-rooms, frequently took tea with her alone and wrote her passionate letters. As there was never just one particular young man no comment was made about the moral propriety of her life or, if there was, it was whispered and not voiced in public, certainly not within earshot of her family. For Dulcie Askham, as for a number of other leading hostesses, there was safety, certainly security, in numbers.

'What do you think of Madame Hassim's plan, darling?' Lady Askham beckoned to her son as he stood at the edge of the circle still chatting to Rachel. 'Do you think it would be safe to go alone into the desert?'

'We won't be alone, Mama!' Bosco replied. 'There will be quite a party. We shall be armed to the teeth, ready to attack any Dervishes who have strayed all the way from the Sudan, any marauding Bedouins.' As though his right hand held a sword he suddenly and dramatically plunged it towards the heart of Cardew Crystal who sat at Lady Askham's feet looking adoringly up at her. Cardew drew back in mock alarm as Dulcie put a hand protectively on his shoulder; but the two young men remained staring at each other as if the duel were not imaginary but real. Eyes fixed, they remained thus for some seconds while the little group surrounding the unexpected drama remained silent, a silence accentuated by the hubbub on the terrace. Then Captain Crystal, still flushed, got up and dusted the skirt of his red coat while those around Lady Askham drew back as though expecting a scene.

Bosco, Flora saw, was quivering and she quietly got up and put a hand on his arm.

'Do put your sword back in its scabbard, dearest. Please no fight, even a pretend one, on your sister's wedding day.'

'There's no question of a fight,' Captain Crystal quickly recovered his poise and stroked his pencil-thin moustache. 'Bosco and I are the best of friends. He was just demonstrating what he would do to any Dervish who assaulted his mother.'

'Or *anyone*,' Bosco said. 'Dervish or . . . Egyptian Army,' he added quietly.

'Your mother would come to no harm from anyone I know in the Egyptian Army.' Captain Crystal bowed stiffly to Dulcie and withdrew. Simultaneously the other witnesses to the incident, which indeed was only momentary but seemed to last minutes rather than seconds, regrouped themselves, leaving her just with Bosco, Flora, Rachel and Madame Hassim who had watched the scene with amusement.

'I believe your son is jealous of your conquests, Lady Askham. I must say you have captured many hearts.'

'My mother is a practised flirt,' Bosco said tersely. 'She is never happy unless she has a dozen young men under thirty swooning with love for her.'

'Bosco!' Lady Askham looked sharply at her son and Flora quickly intervened.

'Bosco doesn't mean to *sound* jealous, Madame Hassim. He is simply protective of Mama as a good son should be. It was all a joke.'

'It was *not* a joke,' Bosco looked threateningly at the back of Captain Crystal, who was trying to saunter with as much dignity as he could through the throng now thinning as goodbyes were made on the terrace. It was nearly four o'clock and the bride and groom had retired to change. 'I do wish Crystal would leave you alone, Mama. I don't think it is seemly the way he attends upon you at all times of the day or night.'

'Never the night, dearest boy,' his mother said lightly, but her beautiful eyes seemed to Rachel, who had been closely observing the scene, tearful. 'And Flora's right, you *are* jealous, you dear, silly boy. Why, Captain Crystal is only a *little* older than you. If anything I regard him as another son. Now pray, Bosco, let us have no more of these dramatics. I can't tell you how embarrassed I felt, and what I shall say to dear Cardew when he calls again – *if* he does.'

As she spoke there was a commotion by the entrance to the terrace and the bride and groom appeared with Achmed hovering in front, his hands extended once again as though in an imitation of a clap. Obediently taking its cue polite applause broke out in the company and Dulcie, thankful of the chance to close the subject, got up and went over to her daughter and new son-in-law followed by those remaining who continued to clap, smiles more firmly fixed because of the quantity of champagne they had consumed.

Melanie had chosen blue for her trousseau: a well-cut godet skirt with a short basque jacket over a narrow waistcoat with a stylish white stock at the throat. On her head a beaver hat with a box crown and a curved brim decorated with feathers, added to the rather sporty effect of her ensemble which came from one of the elegant new French dress shops in the Mouski to which Madame Hassim had introduced her. Harry was in civilian dress: a white alpaca suit, white shirt with stiff collar and a regimental tie, and in his hand he carried a white Panama hat. He looked very correct, very handsome, proud and happy.

Dulcie threw out her arms, enfolding her daughter, while Harry shook hands with Bosco and the senior male members of the party. Then he waited for his bride to take leave of her mother, gently putting a proprietorial hand on her waist and looking at his watch.

'We'll be late, dearest.'

'All the time in the world, Mr Lighterman,' the attentive Achmed assured him. 'The *dahabeih* will await your command. Everything is ready.'

'Dearest girl.' Dulcie gazed at Melanie, kissing first one cheek then the other and squeezed her again. 'Take *every* care. I wish Achmed were coming with you.'

'Mama, we have about eight servants to say nothing of the crew.'

'And me,' Harry said throwing out his chest.

'Have the loveliest time, and don't go too far down the Nile.'

'Only as far as the First Cataract, Lady Askham. The water is not yet high enough to pass over it. We plan a leisurely journey there and back.'

'Madame Hassim said that if you all go into the desert maybe we could join you on the way home.' Melanie still clung to her mother and it was observed that there were tears in her eyes which she dabbed with a white cambric handkerchief.

'Oh, that would be heaven!' Dulcie, gently unclasping her daughter, looked at Bosco. 'What a lovely end to the honeymoon. Can it be arranged, Achmed?'

'It is already in hand, Lady Askham. You have only to wish . . .' He kissed his fingers and looked up as something invisible appeared to float in the air.

Harry looked disconcerted but said nothing as Melanie embraced her sister and brother, threw her arms round

Madame Hassim and shook many hands and then, her husband by her side, paused dramatically on the top of the steps leading down to the street where her carriage decked with flowers and with a uniformed Arab driver and postilion waited. She held her bridal bouquet high in the air, glanced round her and then, as the young women shrieked, hands outstretched, and ran forward, called: 'Catch,' aiming at Flora. But Flora missed and, instead, it landed right at the feet of Rachel Bolingbroke, the only woman who remained where she was, whose hands had not been extended.

As she stood looking at it Bosco raced forward and, kneeling, picked it up and presented it to her, looking at her as if making a proposition.

Everyone smiled, Melanie laughed, kissed the tips of her fingers and, taking her bridegroom's hand, raced down the steps towards her future, while Rachel reached reluctantly for the wilted flowers she obviously had no wish to accept.

As the sun set beyond the cluster of palm trees at the water's edge, its last rays seemed to jettison rockets of fire which flamed upwards in the opposite direction to the vanishing halo. For a moment the rays splashed outwards casting a momentary ethereal, blinding glow over the whole landscape, blazing across the huge expanse of the Nile which looked, from their tiny boat in the middle, like a vast never-ending sea, a mile wide and disappearing north and south into eternity. In the distance the city of Cairo, its myriad of domes and minarets basking in that fierce fiery moment, seemed aglow. Then, just as suddenly, the sun sank completely. All that was visible – the long low lines of the desert, the clusters of palms, the animals grazing on the greensward at the water's edge or plying across the sand shepherded by a solitary Bedouin, the city itself surmounted by its majestic Citadel – were silhouetted against a long band of sapphire blue which appeared on the horizon merging into one rose-tinged and blending into the dusky opalescence of the encroaching night sky. A light breeze sprang up and the slow *dahabeih* moved a little faster as the tall lateen sail billowed and the tired oarsmen moved thankfully towards the shelter of the bank and a safe anchor for the night.

This was the last leg of the homeward journey, one that had taken Harry and his bride six hundred miles as far down the Nile as the First Cataract beyond which it was deemed, at that stage, unsafe to go. They had left the boat at Aswan in order to visit the islands of Philae and Elephantine, with the ancient tombs opposite cut into the rock face of the west bank, and the old Coptic convent of St Simeon. For a while, after a week spent on the water, it had been nice and restful to spend two days in the comfort of the Grand Hotel with its superb view of the Nile hedged in by huge rocks and boulders at the foot of the cataract.

Not that their water home lacked comfort, on the contrary. Painted in a brilliant white, it was low in the water with a sharp nose and a raised stern atop which there was a poop where the steersman kept ever-vigilant watch day and night. Inside the salons, two for sleeping, a sitting-room and a dining-room, contained fine furniture of the kind that might be found in an English home together with books, pictures and even a piano. Outside, the lateen sail sloped from bow to the uprising stern which contained the living quarters, awnings, cushions, comfortable divans and chairs for the guests to survey the scenery as the heavy flat houseboat made its way along the water, sometimes becalmed until it was aided by one of the steam tugs which plied busily along the waterway for such a contingency.

To look after such guests as were aboard, seldom more than six, in this case two, were fifteen crew members including a cook, a Syrian waiter and six oarsmen. There were quantities of good food and wine aboard, much of the former – turkeys, hens and pigeons, even a fat lamb – travelling alive in a boat attached to the stern until their demise was required.

As darkness spread and the stars came out the Nubian Reis of the boat, Mustapha, put an old brown coat with an Arab hood over his blue day garments and red fez as a sign that the sun had set, a time when all Arabs and Egyptians wrapped their heads. Touching his forehead and breast with two fingers he salaamed to his English guests, important friends of Effendi Asher.

'Is all as you wish, Effendi?' he enquired in his broken, carefully rehearsed English. 'We will soon anchor for the night.'

'Everything is perfect, Mustapha.' Harry, sitting upright in a cane chair and smoking a cigar, glanced at his wife. 'Is there anything you would like, my dear?'

'I'd like my dinner soon.' Melanie laced her hands round the back of her head as she reclined on a divan, her feet bare, the *mezd*, Turkish slippers, neatly paired by her side on the deck. 'We have to make an early start.'

'I will alert Ibrahim to your demands,' Mustapha bowed again and withdrew towards the galley from which emanated the customary delicious smell of cooking.

'I think it's that lamb,' Melanie said sniffing the air. 'I didn't notice it in the boat today. The sight of those poor live creatures waiting to be killed for us has almost marred my holiday.'

'It is the only way we can be sure of fresh untainted food,' Harry said in the flat, patient voice he used when describing interesting ruins to her as though addressing a child, or a person of feeble understanding. 'I would rather they were brought alive than dead otherwise, in this heat, they would be bad by now.'

'Yes, it is very hot.' Melanie apathetically wafted a fan which a thoughtful mother had tucked into her baggage.

'Thank goodness for the cool of the evening. And how *foggy* it was this morning, Harry, almost like an English winter.'

'Yes.' Harry screwed up his nose thoughtfully, his blue shaven cheek gleaming in the light from the lamps a sailor had lit along the deck. He put out a hand attempting to clasp one of Melanie's, but hers remained firmly linked in her lap.

'Our last night alone, my dearest.'

'Thank heaven,' Melanie said. 'I am dying to see Mama, Flora and Bosco. I mean being alone too long is too much of a good thing, don't you agree, Harry?' She looked rather sharply at him as if affecting not to see the hurt in his eyes.

'*I* have enjoyed myself alone with you, Melanie, and, who knows, it may be the last time we shall be together.'

'What do you mean by that, Harry?' Melanie guiltily drew round her the warm cashmere shawl which her maid had thoughtfully brought out from her cabin just moments before the sun went down. 'We shall have years and years alone together.'

'Well, maybe.' Harry threw back his head and looked at the stars. He was a saturnine man, dark-haired, dark-jowled with a deceptively aristocratic air. He looked at least thirty, Melanie thought, maybe thirty-five although he was the same age as Bosco, twenty-two. There was something old about Harry that had attracted her in the first place, attracted her less now that she knew him better. He acted old, he was cautious and careful in his ways. He lacked the joyous spontaneity that the Askhams as a family had always shared. Her mother had warned her about this as she had cautioned her about many other matters most of which, nay all, she had ignored in her blind determination to grow up, to be married.

'You *don't* think we'll have many years together, Harry?' Melanie inclined her head, a wry smile on her lips. 'Why is that?'

'The war, my dear. I thought there would have been a wire for me before now.'

'You mean a skirmish. That's all Bosco says it will be, *if* you go.'

'You almost sound as though you would be glad if I went.' Harry tipped the stub of his cigar over the rail of the boat and on the surface of the dark water he could see its light abruptly extinguished as it floated away.

'Well, Harry, if it's what you want I should be glad. I suppose it's why you became a soldier, after all. Of course I know you'll be all right and won't be killed. Hardly any officers die, Bosco says.'

'You sound as though you want my death.'

'That is an absurd thing to say, Harry! A cruel thing. I only married you three weeks ago, after all.'

Was it a mistake? Melanie wanted to add, but even she, used to the outspokenness of the Askhams, didn't dare. In the dusk the other differently-sized craft on the river, lit by lanterns fore and aft, jockeyed for position as they weighed anchor for the night. In the distance the lights of a steamer headed south, carrying passengers bent on sightseeing or, maybe, soldiers destined for Wadi Halfa where they would embark on the military railway built across the desert the previous year by Kitchener's men to ferry troops to the front line.

The unspoken question seemed to hang in the air between them. The honeymoon had not been the long-dreamed-of event they'd both hoped for. Melanie, vivacious, used to a frantic pace, had been bored with the leisurely drift down the river in the sole company of a husband content to view the passing scene or read a book; fretful at all the ruins, each similar to the one before, which Harry enjoyed not only seeing but lingering over. They'd had too many misunderstandings, too many arguments in three short weeks, for a supposedly happily married couple.

As Ibrahim the waiter appeared outside the galley, gazing towards them, Harry reached for the book lying on the chair he'd occupied beside Melanie, Appleton's *Nile Journal*, and marked the open page with a leather bookmark. In the dim lamplight he looked careworn and sad, yet it was not a sight that moved his new bride. For the failure of the honeymoon, their lack of understanding, she blamed not herself but him.

'It's time to change,' Harry said, gesturing to Ibrahim that he had seen him. 'I think dinner is nearly ready.'

'Do we *have* to change, Harry, for the last evening?' Melanie, drowsy and comfortable, feeling lazy despite the charged atmosphere, lay back in the divan trailing her fingers upon the deck, luxuriating in the daring delight of bare toes.

'My dear, what would the natives think?'

'Does it matter? I suppose it does to someone like you.'

'What do you mean by that, Melanie?' Harry stiffened, rose and shut his book sharply on the bookmark. Then he turned to face her, leaning against the rail, the book under his arm.

'Oh, Harry, don't let's quarrel. As you say, it is our last night.'

'Still I would like to know what you meant by "someone like me".' Harry tried to sound imperturbable. 'Why does it matter to me and not you?'

Melanie wriggled her toes. 'I didn't mean it to sound like that.'

'You mean someone who's not a born aristocrat?'

'Well, you're not an aristocrat at all, are you?' Melanie sat up and languidly draped her arms round her legs. 'Yes, I suppose I did mean that, though it was a nasty thing to say and I'm sorry. I am saying hurtful things today, and I don't mean to. I'm used to people around me all the time, Harry. Lots of people. You must try and understand. What I meant was that things like that matter less to us because . . .'

'Because *what*, Melanie?' Harry, in an attempt to stifle his trembling, took from his new case a cigarette, which shook in his hand as he lit it.

'Let's forget it,' Melanie sighed and looked at the violet-coloured sky twinkling now with a myriad of tiny stars. The Orient really was magical. On a night like this she could easily imagine the Wise Men seeing the star that led them to Bethlehem. Something she'd found difficult before.

Harry leaned his elbows against the railings, his long legs stretched out before him, and gazed at his shoes. 'I think it's important that we don't. If we are to understand each other, if we are to live together for ever, as we hope, we must be straight with each other. You know that the one thing that stopped me proposing to you was the fact that you were the daughter of an earl.'

'It didn't stop you for long, Harry.'

Melanie closed her eyes, aware of the bitterness in her voice. Was all her disappointment, her dissatisfaction with the past three weeks creeping up on her now? Reason told her to be careful, but impulse had a stronger pull. Harry seemed to treat her as something unreal, not a person. Someone to be looked after, treasured, cosseted and then treated in a rather horrible way at night, like an object. Whereas she could not forget this the next day, Harry could. When he was not making love to her he loved her. He told her so all the time, but showing her was different. It didn't seem like love to her at all.

When she opened her eyes, aware of a presence near her, it was to see Harry leaning over her, and in his eyes was something of the savagery she saw every night before he blew out the light, grasping her without love or tenderness but with a bestial sort of need. She felt it was not only assault but an insult to her as a woman. Three weeks of it was almost too much to bear; but tomorrow there would be Mama and Flora and Bosco, her close family, to meet the boat at Bedreshayn for the visit to Sakkara. Oh, happiness to be with her loved ones again!

Harry grasped her by the shoulders and shook her. 'What are you saying, Melanie? That I married you for your position? Is that what you're saying? The last thing I wanted was to marry the daughter of an earl. I wanted you. I loved you. I *hesitated* to ask you because of who you were. I told my father about my doubts.'

'I don't expect he had many.'

Melanie flinched as he hit her, slapping her twice across the cheeks and then gazing at her with eyes almost blinded by rage. When he stood up she lay there staring at him, not touching her cheeks, not moving, but staring.

'No gentleman would behave like that, Harry,' she said after a while. 'It simply proves my point. Blood will out. Your family is not well-bred and neither are you. Mother always said blood will tell and it does. My mother was right.'

'Did your mother try and stop you marrying me?' Harry got out his handkerchief and, as though the fire and anger had gone out of him, slumped into the chair next to the divan and mopped his brow.

'Of course she cautioned me. That's why she flew over here. But as you know I took no notice of Mama. She didn't think you were an inferior class or anything, she's too well-bred to suggest anything of the sort. But she did say we didn't know each other and we didn't. We didn't know each other at all, Harry. Mama should have warned me what marriage was like.'

Harry put his handkerchief back in his pocket, his hands too to conceal their trembling. His whole body was trembling with anger, frustration and desire. He had known very little about love on his marriage. Indeed his first experience, insisted on by his brother officers before his marriage, had been with a prostitute in Cairo. It had been rough and brutal and he knew no other way. He had been a virgin for far too long and someone as inexperienced as Melanie, who yet expected him to know, couldn't help him.

She still stared at him, lying where he'd hit her – no tears as he'd expected, but just a haughty anger. How well he knew that Askham haughtiness now.

'What *shall* we do, Melanie?' he pleaded. 'We have only been married three weeks. People will expect to see us tomorrow happy and joyful.' Harry threw himself on the deck beside her and tried unsuccessfully to cradle his head against her bosom. 'Oh Melanie, please forgive me. I'm sorry I hit you. I'd rather you wept than that you looked at me like that. Let us go straight on tomorrow and finish our honeymoon alone. We can go to Alexandria, to Port Said . . .'

'No!' Melanie got up so abruptly that Harry lost his balance and fell over on the deck, hitting his chin on the hard wooden planks. For a moment he lay face down, not stunned but more humiliated than he had ever felt in his life. The situation had got grotesquely, hopelessly, out of control. As the husband he had expected to keep the upper hand, but he'd never had it. He felt the low-class, bad-blooded heel she thought him.

As he slowly raised himself he saw that Melanie had risen too and was standing in front of him looking down at him, not making the least attempt to help him. He got to his feet, rubbing his chin, attempting to straighten his jacket and his crumpled tie.

'I *am* sorry,' Melanie said in an artificial voice. 'I really didn't mean that to happen.'

'You couldn't help it.' He grasped her hand. 'Melanie, can we start again?'

'Out of the question.' She coolly put her hand out of

reach. 'Mama is expecting us at Bedreshayn. The donkeys are ordered. Madame Hassim will be so angry.'

'We are just two people.'

'It will be my last chance to be with my family before we disperse.'

'But Melanie, I am your family now and I might soon go away too.'

For answer Melanie went towards the rail of the boat and looked longingly towards the shore.

CHAPTER 3

The following morning as the little boat skimmed towards the shore from the *dahabeih* the sight of Madame Hassim's party waiting to greet it on the sandy beach was unmistakable. There was an assortment of donkeys and camels piled high with baggage, an army of blue-robed Arabs scurrying about, and a number of well-dressed men and women gathered around the elegantly attired person of Lady Askham seated on an upholstered wicker chair under a large striped parasol, a hand shading her eyes as she peered through the lifting mist which obscured parts of the still waters of the Nile. Behind them on the bank a collection of mud huts and dusty palm trees constituted the shabby little village of Bedreshayn which, it was difficult to believe, had once been the site of the great city of Memphis, thirteen miles wide, founded by Menes the first mortal king of Egypt and, for short periods, its capital.

At the sight of the skiff frantically propelled across the water by four sweating oarsmen Lady Askham and her coterie rose and vigorously waved with mixed exclamations of excitement; a donkey brayed in alarm and a supercilious camel slowly arched its neck and peered curiously in the direction of the commotion at the water's edge. The checkered figure of Achmed Asher, tarbush slightly askew on his domed head, pranced excitedly about, the inevitable list in his hands which, even as the boat drew near, he was consulting as if checking a timetable, his large silver repeater watch in his hand.

As the boat drew up on the beach and was pulled on to the sand by two Arabs urged on by Achmed, Melanie scrambled out and flung herself into the arms of her mother who had walked forward as the boat approached, treading carefully on the soft sand, holding aloft over high buttoned boots a beige linen skirt. One hand steadied her beige felt hat around which, to secure it from the wind and the hazards of the journey, was a light gossamer veil tied beneath the chin.

'Oh Mama, Mama.' Melanie's head sank on her mother's bosom and fleetingly Lady Askham reflected to herself that her newly married daughter seemed as glad to see her as she had been eager to depart. The scene had a feeling of *déjà vu* and she glanced anxiously at her daughter's pale face noting how little it seemed to have been affected by the sun, trying to persuade herself that she had not, in fact, heard a sob stifled on her maternal breast.

'There, dearest,' she said, her voice heightened by a note of anxiety, pressing her powdered cheeks against Melanie's puckered eager lips. 'There, there.' Memories of the nursery returned when this, the youngest and the most excitable of her children, used to rush and greet her as though only the presence of her mother could protect her from some frightful childish superstition, some ghastly primitive fear.

Harry remained by the boat giving instructions for the removal of their baggage contained in its stern and occupying the whole of a second boat, which had once contained the now massacred poultry brought along to feed them. Finally he turned with some appearance of nervousness to greet those assembled on the shore, hats removed by the men, hands outstretched in welcome.

Bosco was the first to step forward, and then Flora who seemed uncertain as to whether to kiss him on the cheek or shake him by the hand. Still with an arm round Melanie, Lady Askham turned and planted a soft kiss on his proffered cheek which, however gracefully intended, was nevertheless an awkward and embarrassing gesture because of the frantic way her daughter still clung to her. Was it with happiness or relief? Sadly Dulcie Askham feared the latter.

Achmed, busy with his list, giving orders for Lady Askham's chair to be put back on the camel from whence it had come, began to make shooing gestures towards the gawping *fellaheen* from the village who, grouped up on the bank in various attitudes of wonder, threatened to impede the passage of the procession he was now desperately trying to put together. Madame Hassim, sensibly and uncharacteristically attired in a riding habit of grey tussore silk with a white helmet also secured with a veil, came forward and made her presence felt by embracing Melanie, reluctantly parted from her mother, in her own enveloping hug.

'Lady Melanie, how *ravishing* you look! I can see the trip has suited you down to the ground.' Madame glowed with subtle oriental meaning.

'It really was lovely, Madame Hassim,' Melanie assumed the air of languid Askham patronage with practised ease. 'We have seen so many marvellous things and – ' as Achmed came obsequiously forward she took his hand, 'it was all so beautifully arranged, the *dahabeih* comfortable to perfection, the food sublime.'

Lady Askham watched her daughter's recovery with satisfaction, reflecting that if the Askhams easily gave way to emotion they just as quickly recovered their composure which was where breeding showed, which was more than one could say for Harry who continued to look nervous and rather shamefaced. Achmed bowed, kissed Melanie's hand and then with an elaborate gesture offered it to her husband as though he were performing a second marriage ceremony. Harry accepted her hand rather clumsily, tucked it under his arm and walked with his bride towards those who still waited to greet them. There were Adam

Bolingbroke and his sister Rachel, in addition to the Askhams, a journalist from Cairo, Adrian Hastings, who was on his way to the Sudan to write about the war, Lord and Lady Duplessis, also not long married, who had wintered in Egypt and were to return with Lady Askham and Flora. Finally there was Miss Grace Plomley Pemberton who had shared a governess with the two Down girls until she had been sent to Switzerland to be finished by her father Sir Salter Plomley Pemberton, whose family had a lineage almost as long, though not quite as noble, as the Earl of Askham.

As thirteen had been considered an unlucky number at the last minute, and despite the strong objection of Bosco, the name of Captain Cardew Crystal, Royal Horse Guards, Egyptian Army had, at the last moment, been included in the list.

The party had left Cairo early that morning by train to gather at Bedreshayn and had only arrived an hour before at the tiny station surrounded by the narrow mud-walled alleys of the village. In fact half of the male force of the village was now part of the retinue. The party was met by Achmed who had preceded them by several days in order to make his preparations, engage the camels, the donkeys, arrange for the transport of tents and cooking equipment, candles and acetylene bicycle lamps for exploring the underground tombs, and ensure that all the Antiquities Passes required by the Antiquities Department had arrived for the tourists from the Museum of Egyptology in Cairo. From the station to the beach was a short walk though they had to make their way through the throng of scantily clad villagers who, accompanied by their hens, goats and dogs, had gathered early in the expectation of a spectacle, Effendi Asher's activities having been the source of no little interest for days.

The villagers felt their hours of waiting were worth while as Lady Askham, still covered by her parasol, and

Madame Hassim mounted chairs which were hoisted palanquin-fashion on to the shoulders of eight stalwart Arabs and borne solemnly off the beach. They were followed by the rest of the party on the backs of docile donkeys who passed their whole lives ferrying tourists to the Colossi of Rameses II and the Pyramids and tombs of Sakkara beyond.

Bringing up the rear were five baggage-laden donkeys, two dog carts piled with tents and chairs, and three camels on the hump of one of which there was a long ornate Chippendale table, its four feet sticking grotesquely up into the air like some solemn, propitiatory offering to the gods of Ancient Egypt.

This parade, one of the most curious seen by the villagers of Bedreshayn for many a long day, and they saw quite a few, was followed for some way by those reluctant to lose sight of the spectacle, through the palm groves flanked by fields of corn and clover which in their unexpected beauty and colour seemed like a beautiful pall cast over the grave of the once great city of Memphis. On they went past glassy pools towards that hot arid stretch of desert where Moses as a boy had lived in the palace of his grandfather, and where stood one of the oldest monuments in the world: the pyramid of Sakkara built 3,500 years before Christ.

It was not the weather for sightseeing despite the cool of the chambers in the pyramid of King Onnos and the hundreds of yards of vaulted passages in the tombs of Apis, the sacred bull of the god Ptah. The lunch taken in the garden of the house of Mariette, the famous French Egyptologist who discovered the Apis tombs, brought some relief from the heat. Lady Askham and Madame Hassim preferred to spend the afternoon there chatting to Lady Duplessis and Captain Crystal, to both of whom monuments to the dead were of little interest. The younger members of the party led by Flora and Rachel clambered about the pyramids and the Mastabas of Ptah-hotep and Ti. But Madame Hassim, Lord and Lady Duplessis, Lady Askham and her ever-faithful swain preferred to make their way to the point midway between the Step Pyramid and the pyramids of Gizeh and Abousir where the camp was to be made for the night on the edge of the green valley which spread out from the Nile, framed by palm trees and surrounded by the yellowish-grey expanse of the desert.

The camels and dog carts had gone ahead and when the advance party arrived a small colourful encampment had sprung up within sight of the river on one side and, in the distance, the pointed minarets of the alabaster Mohammed Ali Mosque in Cairo, glowing like a chimera, reminded the travellers that they were not so far from civilization after all. Rugs had been strewn on the ground upon which had been placed an assortment of comfortable chairs and divans and the long table from the camel's back. The sleeping quarters were already up, individual tents furnished with rugs, campbeds and basins, and jugs already full of the cold clear water from the Nile.

The adventurers were greeted by Achmed, sweating profusely, who showed them to their tents where Egyptian maidservants were ready to help them change, although Lady Askham pronounced herself ready for a rest.

When she emerged the sun was beginning to set beyond the pyramids and tombs of Sakkara and the rest of the party was straggling across the desert towards them, even the hardy donkeys seeming weary. By this time smells of cooking pervaded the sweet desert air and spirals of smoke from many pots cooking away over braziers spiralled towards the pink-hued sky.

Looking at the sunset Melanie recalled the previous evening alone with her husband on the *dahabeih*. The sight of her mother waiting to greet her filled her with nostalgic memories of home, and she stumbled from her donkey, once more hurling herself into those dear familiar arms.

'My darling,' Lady Askham put her lips tenderly to her daughter's hair. 'I think we must have a little talk.' In the distance Harry was chatting to Mr Hastings and the inexhaustible Bosco, Flora, Adam and Rachel were pretending to have a race on their weary mokes to see who could be the first to base.

Dulcie drew Melanie into the cool of her tent, a lamp blazing on the small brass table beside her campbed, and sat her down, noting her pale tired face.

'Is all well, Melanie?'

'How do you mean, Mama?'

'The way you keep on rushing into my arms makes one think. Even at luncheon you didn't sit near Harry. Have you quarrelled? I noticed the nasty bruise on his chin.'

'He fell and hit himself on the deck. Mama, I have been *three weeks* alone with Harry.' Melanie bent her head, her fingers kneading her handkerchief into the palms of her hands. 'It is a long time to be alone with a man.'

'But he is your *husband*, dearest. You have vowed to spend your life with him. You were so anxious to marry him.' Lady Askham had changed into a costume of terracotta moiré silk with a short jacket and a pleated chiffon vest with a high neck made of Brussels lace, against which was pinned a large cameo brooch that she had inherited from her mother, Lady Kitto. This she fingered nervously as she bent trying to see her daughter's face more clearly in the lamplight. 'Have you found that you no longer love him, Melanie? Did something happen?'

She was a woman who seldom grew agitated, whose feelings were kept firmly in control, but now even she felt a tremor of alarm.

'Harry is not as I thought he was, Mama. I don't think we did know each other well enough.'

'I did try to warn you, dearest.'

'You were right, Mama. I wish I had taken your advice.' As Melanie burst, not unexpectedly, into tears, her mother gently sat next to her and cuddled her as she had when she was a small child.

'My dearest girl, there are things one does not talk about, and I sometimes wish one did, things that are not discussed even between mothers and daughters. If you are talking about – relations between husband and wife I can assure you that the shock of this passes.'

'But why did you never say *anything*, Mama?' Melanie's tear-stained face was accusing.

'Because my mother never said anything to me. It is something all we women have to endure, but all I can say is that with a gentle and understanding man one can soon get used to this – suffering that is inflicted on women.'

'I will *never* get used to it with Harry.' Abruptly Melanie drew away from her mother and dried her eyes, vigorously blowing her nose. 'It is not only that. He is a very cold man, very precise and rather boring. He is trying to teach me things all the time. Those ruins drove me mad. After three weeks with him I felt I couldn't endure a moment longer.'

'You looked rather mad when you came flying towards me this morning, I must confess. Even Cardew Crystal commented on it.'

'What else did Cardew Crystal say?' Melanie enquired hotly. 'Honestly, Mama, I don't know how you can stand the constant presence of that man!'

'My dear, he's rather sweet!' Dulcie Askham looked surprised. 'What on earth do you object to about Captain Crystal?'

'It's almost as though he's in love with you!'

Her mother patted her hand and gave a mysterious smile which, seeing they were in the land of the Sphinx, was not inappropriate.

'He's not *in love* with me, my dearest. It's not like that at all. I am almost twice his age! Like you, he is missing his mama. You know, my darling, we do not necessarily grow old when we grow up. Just a moment ago you reminded me exactly of how you used to be as a little girl, and Cardew is a bit like Bosco and Arthur when they were fourteen or so.'

'Is that all?'

'Of course it's all, dearest child.' Lady Askham got up and peered at her face in a little mirror that had been skilfully hung on the drapes of the tent. 'I think we should join the others now. I must say I think this excursion was a mistake, far too tiring and really this,' she looked around, 'though comfortable is not at all the sort of thing one is used to. But for the sake of Madame Hassim we must at least pretend to enjoy ourselves and be grateful that we are returning to Cairo tomorrow.'

'Both Achmed and Madame Hassim have gone to an enormous amount of trouble.'

'Oh enormous, and it is all quite splendid. I'm sure it will be fun; but a day is enough, that's all I am saying. Now my little girl,' Lady Askham sat down again and took Melanie's hot hand in hers which had remained cool, as though on a winter's day in the heart of the English countryside. 'You are an Askham and we Askhams are people with character who can endure all manner of things. Your father and I thought you should not marry Harry, he is not of our kind, but you have. You modern girls will have your way, thinking you know best. Bosco likes Harry and he certainly loves you – I have observed him frequently during the day gazing at you. He may progress quite far in the army, who knows, and you will see many interesting things maybe in India or further abroad. I am quite sure that once life has returned to normal – honeymoons are never normal, my dear; in many ways they are a cursed convention – you will see your husband in perspective as the good, devoted man I'm sure he is. He is really quite a nice person, yet solemn, as you say. He is also wealthy, Sir Robert assured us of that, and in addition to the settlement your father made on your marriage you will never be in need. Husbands are quite expendable creatures, my dear; once you have borne a child or two, you will see. You can enjoy yourself very much with the many women friends you will make, army wives like yourself, and maybe an admirer or two as well. You know I have always liked young men, and they me. I am sure you will be no different from your mother.'

'Is that why you always have men around you, Mama? Because you and Papa don't get on?'

'But we *do*, you dear old thing! You know your father and I are *devoted*. But he has always been a busy man and I will not pretend the early days of our marriage were easy. It is true that a girl, any girl, marries someone who is almost a stranger to her. At least you had *some* moments alone with Harry. I never had any with your father. We always met closely chaperoned and then, suddenly, we were completely alone together, as you and Harry have been. I know what you have endured, believe me. One is cast alone with a stranger who one loves, but still doesn't know. But if the Lancers go to India you can be sure of lots of fun there and you will soon forget these first, miserable days, my poor pet.' Lady Askham swooped and kissed her and patted her hair. 'There, do spend a few moments in front of my mirror then go and change. Don't forget Harry might be sent to the desert and you will soon be all alone again. How will you like that?'

And not waiting for a reply Lady Askham swept out, stopping to exclaim when she saw the scene that confronted her. In the middle of the circle of tents the long table was now laid with a white damask cloth and set with silver which sparkled in the light of the many candelabra. A string of turbaned Arabs bore from the cooking quarters great platters of food: steaming chickens, whole pigeons, roasted turkeys and an entire lamb, cooked in garlic and spices. There were bowls of rice, a variety of steaming vegetables, fruit, cakes, sweetmeats, cheeses and silver buckets full of iced champagne.

Everyone had now changed, not into evening dress but into something different from what they'd worn during the day. The men were smoking, had glasses of whisky in their hands and the women sat or reclined, looking up towards the men as though they were at some exotic party in an exclusive part of Cairo. Jewels blazed at the throats and on the wrists of Madame Hassim, Lady Askham and Lady Duplessis, and Miss Plomley Pemberton had on a large choker of pearls that looked to be worth half her family's considerable fortune.

Apart from the candles in the candelabra there were sconces in the ground containing lighted torches whose incense-laden fumes mingled with the rich cooking smells circulating in the air, whetting the appetites of all present. The sky now was quite dark and the crescent moon shone upon the pyramids of Sakkara and Abousir and, in the distance, Gizeh, casting black shadows on the sand. Overhead the black fronds of the palm trees swayed in the warm breeze that came from the Nile.

As Lady Askham emerged from her tent, the largest in the group, Harry came anxiously over to her.

'Is Melanie all right?'

'Melanie is perfectly fine,' Lady Askham said, taking his arm with a familiar gesture. 'She's been telling me about the wonderful time you had.'

'Oh!' Harry looked at her with relief, but something in his taut face told her he doubted the truth of what she had said.

'Harry, I do absolutely *pine* for the smallest glass of wine. Do you think one of those buckets . . .' She had only to indicate the table for Achmed to rush forward, glass in hand. He had changed into a black suit with which he wore a black bow tie that made him resemble a waiter, an observation made by Bosco to Flora and which, had he known it, he would not have appreciated.

'I anticipate your every wish, dear Lady Askham. Tell me, is everything as you like it? Your tent comfortable?'

'Achmed, it could hardly be more perfect.' Lady Askham sank into a chair swiftly vacated by Flora. 'I shall remember this day and the night in the desert all my life. I only hope,' she looked down anxiously, 'there are no little things crawling on the ground.'

Achmed waved his hands reassuringly. 'Everything is covered with rugs, your ladyship, and, in any case, the desert sands are quite free from such creatures as you refer to. It is the purest, best air in the world out here and you need have no fears for your health or that of your family and friends.'

'I assure you, Lady Askham, Achmed chose this spot with the greatest care,' Madame Hassim seemed to see in the words of this doyenne of great hostesses an implied criticism of herself, and Dulcie hastened to reassure her.

'My dear Madame Hassim! Can I not see that with my own eyes? And this feast! I don't believe that Maxims could have produced anything as remarkable.'

'It will be served from the table in Arab style as soon as your ladyship is ready.'

'Oh! Squatting on the floor?' Lady Duplessis, who had gone to great care with her appearance so as not to be eclipsed by an older, but more celebrated, rival looked crestfallen.

'Oh dear me no, my lady.' Achmed, almost overcome by having a countess and a baroness in the same party, had started to perspire again despite the cool of the evening. 'You may sit where you are.'

'But there are not enough chairs to go round.'

'We men squat on the floor,' Bosco said showing an

example. 'This is the way we will soon be eating in the real desert.'

'If we go,' Adam observed beside him. But the war seemed very far away and no one took him up on it.

Lord Duplessis too thought he had a right to a chair. He was after all ten years older than his wife and almost a contemporary of Lady Askham. He was a rather portly man who had found the day particularly trying because of the heat, although he was interested in antiquities. He now wished he had not been persuaded by his young wife on such a madcap scheme.

Finally everyone sat more or less according to taste, the younger men on the floor and all the women on chairs or, like Madame Hassim, occupying divans. The servants served the food meticulously and by nine o'clock the main part of the meal was over, and guests were still preoccupied with fruit and finishing the wine as the servants cleared the table as swiftly and expertly as they had laid it. Dulcie had shared the conversation during the feast with Captain Crystal and Adrian Hastings, a rather shy young man, an acquaintance of Madame Hassim, who knew no one else and felt rather out of place. Flora, Rachel and Lord Duplessis made a compatible trio being interested in ruins. Melanie, with Harry on the floor at her feet, ate in a silence that could have been companionable or not, occasionally exchanging a word with Adam Bolingbroke who also perched close to her. Bosco occupied himself entirely with Grace Plomley Pemberton who had proved something of a fellow spirit, being irreverent during the day about the sights they were seeing and game for a diversion or lark whenever the opportunity arose. Achmed bustled obtrusively about and it is doubtful whether he ate a morsel, being somewhat unsure of his status in the gathering.

'What a very strange assembly,' Adam observed to Melanie after Harry had suggested bridge, Lord and Lady

Duplessis had joined and Madam Hassim made up the four, finally finding her niche for the first time that night, while Achmed went off to supervise the cleaning up. Flora and Rachel suggested a walk and Bosco and Grace agreed to accompany them. Melanie felt too tired and Adam stayed by her side, while Lady Askham and the devoted Captain sat drinking black coffee and exchanging compliments. Adrian Hastings disappeared into his tent and emerged later with a book with which he lay on a divan some distance from the bridge players.

'In what way is it strange?'

'Well, don't you find it an odd assortment of people?'

'Do you mean by the inclusion of Achmed and Madame Hassim and Mr Hastings whom no one knows? Otherwise I find it quite natural.'

'Oh no, I don't mean that at all, God forbid. I'm just wondering what we all have in common.'

'Well, we're all English, except for . . .'

'But half are interested in ruins and half aren't and I don't think anyone really relishes camping in the desert at all. Do you?'

'I think it's rather fun,' Melanie said. 'We can sleep in a proper bed for the rest of our lives.'

She looked quite sharply at Adam, and he thought that, though beautiful, she was a strange girl and, perhaps, rather unhappy. This opinion was reinforced when she said abruptly: 'How well do you know Harry, Mr Bolingbroke?'

'Not particularly well. Nor Bosco either, really. They keep a different kind of mess from me.'

'I'm surprised Harry's a friend of Bosco's. They can't have a thing in common.' Melanie looked at the figure of her husband hunched over the cards in his hand and Adam followed her gaze.

'I don't know your husband that well, but he's liked in the regiment.'

'Is he? I just wondered.'

Adam thought it a curious conversation, as though they, relative strangers to each other, were talking about someone they both knew even less well.

'I'm sure you'll be awfully happy together,' he said awkwardly.

'Oh, I'm quite sure we shall.' Melanie, sounding unconvinced, sat back on the divan and folded her hands in her lap with a look that to Adam, perplexed by this unexpected exchange, seemed disturbingly like resignation.

In the desert the four who had gone for a walk were on the point of returning, Flora and Rachel in front and Bosco and Grace Plomley Pemberton behind. Flora and Rachel, studying the pyramids in the moonlight, had discussed the fact that mathematics had shown how, in six hundred years, their position had demonstrated that the axis of the earth had not changed one iota in its direction.

'Your brother seems much taken by Miss Plomley Pemberton,' Rachel observed glancing back and pulling her shawl firmly across her shoulders because, now that they had left the protective encirclement of the camp, it had grown chilly.

'My brother is taken by a lot of ladies, I'm afraid.'

'He has a good deal of charm,' Rachel nodded.

'But not for you?' Flora glanced at her enquiringly.

'Oh, I don't think Mr Down and I have anything in common, Lady Flora.'

'He seemed to pay you a lot of attention the day Melanie was married.'

'I think he was being kind.'

'I think, like me, you underrate yourself, Miss Bolingbroke.'

'Why should you think that, Lady Flora?'

'Because I think we're similar, are we not? Do you not

think that by now we know each other well enough to use Christian names?' Flora smiled as Rachel nodded her assent.

'I would have thought you had a good deal of self-confidence – Flora.'

'Maybe it is the result of being an Askham. We Askhams have to put on a good front.'

'Is your mother's apparent self-confidence a front? I must say I feel quite in awe of her.'

'Oh no, that is entirely natural. I have never known her for a moment not confident. It is very reassuring.'

'Yes, it must be.'

'Are your parents alive, Rachel?'

'My mother is dead. Adam and I have a father. Otherwise we are quite alone.'

'It must seem strange. We have such a large family.'

'*That* gives one confidence.'

Flora stopped and looked at her. 'Do *you* lack confidence, Rachel? I wouldn't have thought so. After all you have travelled all over Europe by yourself. I think that a very confident thing to do.'

'It is not quite the same as self-confidence, though, is it? I find it perfectly natural to travel alone and yet in front of strangers I am shy.'

'I say,' Bosco called cheerily from behind. 'You girls are going in the wrong direction.'

'So we are.' Flora had been so immersed in their conversation that she only now realized that the lights from the camp were almost out of sight. Bosco and Grace were about fifty yards away from them to the right of the pyramids.

'Do you intend to wander across the desert?' Bosco caught up with them and Flora saw that Grace's teeth were chattering with cold. Perhaps out of vanity, a desire to show off her admirable figure, she had declined to put a shawl over her thin muslin dress when the walk was suggested. 'If so you had better take some breakfast. Although of course Miss Bolingbroke is quite used to travelling alone.'

'Not in the desert, Mr Down.' Rachel looked at him pointedly and Grace giggled and rubbed her cold arms.

'We were just talking about confidence and self-confidence,' Flora said tucking an arm into Bosco's. 'Rachel said that Mama . . .'

'We were just talking about Madame Hassim,' Bosco began to rub Flora's hand. 'I say, you're cold, like Grace.'

'What about Madame Hassim?'

'Where is Monsieur Hassim? Or is Achmed her lover?'

'Bosco!' Flora withdrew her arm, shocked, and looked anxiously at their two companions.

'We weren't saying it at all,' Grace protested, blushing so deeply it was even obvious in the moonlight.

'We were. We were talking about Madame Hassim.'

'But we never said that . . .' Grace couldn't bring herself to pronounce the word.

'Do *you* know anything about Monsieur Hassim?' Bosco looked at his sister.

'I think she's a widow. I don't know why but I do. I don't even know why she asked us all on this trip. It must have cost an absolute fortune – all the tents, the food . . .' she gestured towards their goal. 'As for Achmed, I think he's . . .'

'Yes?'

'I don't think he's married.'

'Do you think he likes men?'

'Bosco, I wish you'd stop talking like this. You're just trying to shock our companions.' Flora looked at him with sisterly disapproval.

'Well, I don't know about Grace,' Bosco replied slyly, 'but I'm sure Rachel isn't shocked.'

'Why shouldn't *she* be shocked?' Grace had a rather high voice, now aggrieved. 'I'm not shocked at all.'

'Ah, but Rachel has seen the world, Grace.'

'I have only been to Europe alone, Bosco.'

Rachel walked on ahead, but Grace hung behind, petulantly wanting Bosco's attention. Flora felt a little tired of her brother's flirtation with these two girls. Whenever Bosco was with women there was always tension. But she knew he liked Rachel. Bosco, the flirt, seemed to enjoy frank talk with a woman who didn't flirt back when she answered him. In fact Bosco's attitude to Rachel was quite different from his manner towards Grace. Maybe he thought of her as one of his sisters, a sport.

Yet, of the two, Flora preferred Rachel to Grace who had always been rather feeble in the nursery, always in trouble and complaining, and had now turned into a simperer obviously with her eyes on all eligible men.

'I hope that Crystal fellow has gone to bed when we get back,' Bosco said as the lights of the camp became brighter.

'I don't suppose he has for a minute. It wouldn't be a very manly thing to do, would it?' Flora glanced at her brother. 'And for heaven's sake, Bosco, don't make a fuss. You know that Mama just likes to be surrounded by men.'

'Young men,' Bosco corrected. 'Why men at all? Why not women? Is your mother constantly surrounded by young men, Grace?'

'Good heavens no!' Grace said primly. 'My father would never allow that.'

'Then why does mine? I don't like it, I can tell you.'

'There is no harm in it, Bosco. Mama is a very beautiful woman who likes admiration,' Flora said, trying to sound reasonable. 'Papa is too busy to do it all the time. Some women are like that. Ettie Grenfell is a terrible flirt too and she is such a close friend of Mama's. It seems to me there are some London hostesses who expect that sort of thing, but it doesn't signify anything.'

'Is *your* mother a flirt, Rachel?' Bosco called after Rachel who turned back.

'My mother is dead.'

'I'm sorry. Of course I knew that. Would you object if she were?'

'We didn't move in those sorts of circles, Bosco. My brother and I are as far removed from the aristocracy and society as it is possible to be. We simply don't understand what it is about. Before I left England I had scarcely ever been to London and know nothing of society.'

'How lucky you are,' Flora sighed. 'I hate it and yet I am expected to be part of it. Melanie loves it and has now cut herself off . . .'

She stopped abruptly and Bosco, seeing her hesitate, jumped in. 'Melanie hasn't cut herself off from society at all. Harry is a good fellow.'

'But he's not exactly society as we mean it. Nor are his parents.'

'You sound awfully snobbish, Flora old thing.'

'I don't mean to be,' Flora said precisely, reminding Rachel a little of Adam who was rather meticulous and careful in his speech. 'I don't mean to be snobbish at all. That is the last thing I mean to be, I assure you. I don't like society. It bores me. All I am saying is that Harry's mother is not in society, and it might not be to Harry's taste either.'

'I wonder what Mel was talking to Mother about? She was a long time in that tent.' Bosco looked speculatively from his sister to Rachel.

'She was telling her about her trip. She told us.'

'Well, maybe Mel's not happy, but Harry is a very good man.'

'Why should she not be happy?' Flora looked warningly at Bosco who either missed her glance in the poor light or wished to ignore it.

'She doesn't *look* happy, does she, for a new bride? Do you think she looks happy, Rachel?'

'It's hardly my business.'

'Do you think she looks happy, Grace?'

'It's certainly none of mine,' Grace said nervously. 'But I think what you say about society is quite true. One should not marry out of one's social circle, of that I am quite convinced.'

'How exactly do you define social circles?' Rachel enquired acidly and Flora was about to intervene when she saw a figure walking leisurely towards them from the camp with his hands in his pockets.

'It's Adam,' Bosco said. 'Maybe he thinks we're lost.'

They quickened their pace and Bosco called to ask if anything were amiss.

'Nothing,' Adam replied. 'What should be amiss? There is a small card party and, finding myself alone, I decided to come and find you.' He looked appreciatively round him towards the outline of the pyramids brilliantly lit by the moon. 'It *is* beautiful here, isn't it?'

'Where's Melanie?' Flora gazed past him as if expecting to see her sister.

'Lady Melanie went to bed.'

'And Mama and Crystal?' Bosco could never mention his name without sounding derogatory.

'I don't know where they are. I think they went for a walk. I thought maybe they were with you.'

'No, we haven't seen them. Your sister was just about to deliver a lecture.'

'Was she? What about?' Adam looked with amusement at Rachel who was scuffing the sand with the heels of her shoes.

'She doesn't approve of the suggestion that people should marry within their own social group.'

'I was suggesting it was a very difficult thing to *define*,' Rachel said defensively.

'We were talking of Harry.' Bosco smiled mischievously at Adam. 'I think he has no taste for society and that will make things difficult for Mel.'

'You didn't say *he* had no taste for society,' Grace corrected, 'but that his parents don't move in the same social circle as yours.'

'Or yours.' Bosco tilted his head and looked at her.

'Harry's a good fellow,' Adam insisted. 'I think he'll make Lady Melanie a capital husband.' He thought of his own curious conversation with Melanie.

'Did you not observe the bruise on his chin?' Bosco glanced up at the sky as if seeking an explanation. 'I wonder if they were in a fight?'

'Bosco, what a thing to suggest,' Flora caught hold of his arm. 'You're really being quite outrageous tonight.'

'I'm not *suggesting* it, I merely wondered. He has a really nasty ugly bruise that looks quite fresh.'

'Surely from a fall.' Adam linked his arm through his sister's and drew her ahead of the others, whispering, 'Don't get into an argument with them.'

'I wasn't arguing. Flora I like, but that other girl stands for everything I detest.'

'Including flirting with Bosco?'

'I have no interest in your friend, Adam. That should be quite obvious to you.'

'It's obvious to me that he quite likes you.'

'*And* Miss Plomley Pemberton. I think your friend likes all ladies.'

'He does have that reputation. Best steer clear of him.'

'I have no intention of doing anything else, I assure you. I doubt if, after we leave Cairo, I shall ever see him again especially if you leave the army. I wish you would, Adam.'

'Why?'

'Because you're not really happy. I can tell. It's not the life for you. When I see your brother officers, people like Bosco and Captain Crystal, I don't know what you find in common with them. I wish you would take up the law like Father and do something useful in society.'

'The army is not useful?'

'I suppose it has its place, but not for you.'

'I'm thinking about it anyway,' Adam said with a sigh. 'If we have any action I'll seriously think of it after that.'

When they got to the camp it was a strange, incongruous sight to see the green baize bridge cloth over the table with the four players, their faces silhouetted by the light of the lamps, bent over their cards. It looked like a scene from a London drawing-room transported to the desert. Behind Madame Hassim, Achmed sat smoking his pipe, his face for the first time that day not showing signs of strain. From the camp there came no other sound except for the quiet calls from the players. Those servants who were part of the party had curled themselves up in the desert by the cooking site, and the others had returned to their villages walking the few miles back to snatch a few hours of sleep before it was time to set out again.

Adrian Hastings, reclining on a divan, was either thinking or asleep and, as the party from the desert arrived, the four players threw their cards into the middle of the green baize square and Harry began to gather them together.

'Another rubber? Mr Hastings, do you play?'

'I fear not, Mr Lighterman.' Adrian, roused, sat up rubbing his eyes. 'I think I dozed off. Ah, Lady Flora. Did you enjoy your walk?'

'It's a perfect night. Has my mother gone to bed?'

'I think your mother and Captain Crystal went for a walk. They asked me to join them but I felt sleep overtake me. I'll turn in for the night.'

'It's time we all went to bed.' Lord Duplessis stiffly got up and poured himself a drink from the decanter of whisky that stood on the end of the table.

Everyone else changed positions and a solitary servant, who remained out of sight but on duty, came forward at a click of Achmed's fingers and began to clear the table. Lord and Lady Duplessis then said goodnight and disappeared into their tent, and Madame Hassim and Achmed put their heads together as though they were doing calculations which made Flora again wonder who was paying for all this.

'I think we should all go to bed,' she said and looked at Rachel with whom she was sharing a tent. Bosco was in with Adam, the couples had their own tents and Lady Askham, Adrian Hastings, Madame Hassim and Achmed had tents of their own.

'I'd like to see where Mama is first.' Bosco went to the edge of the encampment and looked in the direction they had come.

'They went the other way,' Adrian pointed towards the valley of the Nile.

'They should certainly be back now,' Bosco glanced angrily at his watch.

'Mama is quite able to take care of herself, Bosco,' Flora said gently. 'Don't make a scene.'

Without replying Bosco strode past her and disappeared in the direction indicated by Adrian Hastings, who shrugged his shoulders and went into his tent after wishing them all goodnight.

Rachel stared at Adam who wondered if he should go after Bosco. She shook her head.

At that moment Harry emerged from his tent, a puzzled look on his face.

'My wife's not here. I thought you said she had gone to bed, Adam?'

'She said she was going to bed,' Adam looked nonplussed.

'Has anyone seen my wife?' Harry's voice rose.

'Are you sure she's not there?' Flora glanced through the flap of the tent and Madame Hassim got up and began agitatedly to peep into the tents she knew were unoccupied.

'She knows her own tent,' Harry said crossly and then, lifting his head, bellowed: 'Melanie', his voice echoing across the desert.

'*Please* don't get hysterical, Harry,' Flora looked as though she felt his action undignified, and Adam and Rachel exchanged worried glances.

'Maybe you *should* go after Bosco,' Rachel said.

'We must have a search party.' Harry was now frantic. 'Lady Askham and Melanie are missing.'

'*And* Captain Crystal,' Achmed fretfully rubbed his hands together.

'He can look after himself. Who cares about him?' Harry was pacing about, first one side and then the other. He went to the far side of the encampment and bellowed again, while poor Madame Hassim, drooping with tiredness, sat down and mopped her brow despite the fact that the night was by now quite cold.

'I think *everyone* should go to bed.' Rachel tried to keep the appearance of calm though she was far from feeling it. 'Lord and Lady Duplessis had the right idea and it *is* late . . .'

'You go to bed, Rachel,' Flora said firmly. 'We'll wait up for Melanie and Mama, and I suggest that anyone who doesn't wish to go to bed does the same. We don't want the whole party disappearing into the desert.'

After Melanie had gone into her tent she sat for a few moments on the narrow campbed next to Harry's looking towards his with distaste. She felt restless and not at all tired as she'd told Adam. She was disturbed by the sight of her mother and Captain Crystal disappearing out of sight. There was something rather clandestine about their behaviour even though they'd asked anyone who wished to, to accompany them. She wished now she had. The tent was hot and oppressive and she felt need of air. The thought of sharing this tiny enclosure with her husband was abhorrent and now she was sorry they'd come. She had revealed too quickly to her parent the fact that she was unhappy. For a moment she'd forgotten she was an

Askham. Askhams weren't supposed to show feelings in public.

She went to the flap of the tent and looked over to the four playing bridge, behind them Achmed smoking his pipe and over in the corner Adrian Hastings fast asleep. She stood outside the tent looking up at the violet sky but no one noticed her. If she went after Adam he'd lead her to Bosco and Flora in the desert. Taking a quick decision she slipped away. Away from the brightly lit encampment, on one side the path led to the desert, on the other to the valley. She guessed Rachel and Flora would have wanted to see the pyramids by moonlight. She could see them now ahead of her, dimly etched like the small triangular bricks that one played with as a child on the nursery floor. She was about to take the path leading to the pyramids when she saw two figures entwine themselves beneath a palm tree in the glade leading to the river, two figures become as one.

For a moment she felt that they must be strangers and then she knew that there were no other tourists camping nearby, nobody for several miles. Maybe it was her brother and . . .

Fearful of prying she was about to turn back towards the camp when curiosity got the better of her. Like a robber, she stole furtively along the path keeping well to the shadow of the palms. The feeling of fear was overwhelming too; but also something else. It was rather thrilling. It was thrilling to feel so alone, so free and so frightened. Always protected, chaperoned and accompanied wherever she went, it was a very liberating, if terrifying, feeling to find herself alone on the edge of the desert.

Any minute now she expected Bosco and his companion to emerge from the trees. Who could it be, Rachel or Grace? And if he were with one of them where were Flora and Adam who had set out not twenty minutes before? And why were they going in the direction of the river and not the pyramids, which the two intellectual ladies of the party were so intrigued by that their indefatigable explorations during the day had made it twice as tiring as it need have been.

As for Bosco he was a disgrace. If he'd compromised Rachel or Grace . . . she shuddered and hurried forward until she came to a quiet pool in a moonlit clearing, protected by the dark fronds of the palms so that it had a curiously phosphorescent effect. She was about to enter the clearing when she discerned two figures sitting at the base of one of the palms. They were not embracing but they sat very close together and, although from where she was she could not be sure, she felt it certain that the man had his arm around the woman's waist.

And that woman was her mother. The man, of course, was Cardew Crystal.

Melanie felt such a commotion in her breast, such lurching of the heart that she thought she would faint and she sat down on the grass, her back half turned to the couple whose very intimacy made one seem an intruder. Anyone prying on that scene would be called a snoop. She sat breathing hard, painfully, for a few moments not daring to look again, and she was about to try and crawl away when someone came crashing through the trees and, with horror, she saw her brother Bosco leap into the clearing. With a roar like a lion he dragged Captain Crystal to his feet giving him simultaneously such a blow on the jaw that he hurtled backwards several feet and fell into the pool, which perhaps saved his life.

Lady Askham jumped up screaming, and then she saw Melanie who, mesmerized by the scene, had risen and walked like a somnambulant into the clearing.

'Save him!' Dulcie Askham shrieked, pointing to the sodden man struggling in the pool. 'There could be crocodiles.'

'Nonsense, Mother, there aren't any. I wish there were.'

Bosco ran to the edge of the pool and stood gazing in, as if uncertain whether to let him sink or go to his aid. It was a very small pool, only yards across and, as he hesitated as to what to do, Lady Askham running to the edge knelt down and stretched vainly for the hand of the poor floundering man who seemed just about to go under for the third time.

'Bosco! Melanie!' she urged in a voice resonant with authority.

'Leave him, Mother. He can swim.'

'It's not whether he can swim or not, Bosco,' Lady Askham said threateningly. 'It is a question of whether or not he is *able* to do so after your unwarranted attack on him.'

'Unwarranted?'

'Kindly assist him out of the water immediately.'

She pointed imperiously towards the struggling figure by which time Melanie had joined them and, lying on her stomach, reached for a hand while, reluctantly, Bosco got on his knees and, being taller, was able to grasp the other. Cardew Crystal was propelled through the water and hauled on to the bank by four strong arms, aided, as he emerged, by Lady Askham who grabbed his shoulders and helped to lay him tenderly on the ground.

'Oh Cardew, are you all right?'

'Of course he's all right, Mother.' Bosco, upright now, stared at the man lying on the ground, clenching his fists.

'You could have killed him, Bosco.'

'I wish I had.'

Mother and son stared at each other while Melanie mopped at Cardew's face with her shawl and pronounced him not very much affected by his ordeal. Cardew lay staring up at the sky for a moment then sat up groggily and lurched unsteadily to his feet, shaking the water from him like a dog.

'Blast you, you rotter,' he snarled at Bosco.

'*You* rotter,' Bosco shook his fist at him.

'Gentlemen,' Lady Askham said quietly. 'I do beg you both to cease this charade immediately. Bosco, you had no right to attack Captain Crystal like that.'

'You were lying on the ground with him.'

Lady Askham looked shocked, her lips rounding in an indignant 'O'.

'I was certainly *not* lying on the ground with Captain Crystal. We were merely sitting at the base of the tree and discussing Socrates.'

'Crystal knows nothing of Socrates, Mama! I'm sure he never heard of him.'

'Well, he has now.' Dulcie looked tenderly at the soaking warrior. 'I was discussing the Platonic theories of the universe and their Socratic interpretation.'

'Balderdash.'

'My dear Bosco, if you continue in this manner I shall feel like giving you a hiding. You are like a jealous little boy.' His mother shook a chiding finger at him.

'You were kissing him, Mother.'

'That is a perfectly disgusting thing to say! Cardew, I do apologize,' she smiled at the drenched figure which, in the chill night air, had started to tremble whether from fear or cold it was impossible to tell. 'Captain Crystal and I are friends, Bosco, nothing more.'

'Melanie can say you were kissing.' Bosco turned on his sister but his mother intervened.

'Melanie is too much of a lady to stare, I'm sure.'

'I didn't see anything,' Melanie said which was true. She certainly thought their position indicated that they had been kissing or were about to kiss, and she had definitely seen them entwined among the palm trees. But, as her mother said, she was a lady and, above all, an Askham. Certainly no lady, or Askham, told tales on their mother or saw things they were not supposed to see.

'Now Bosco,' his mother was still gazing at Captain

Crystal with tender concern. 'I want us all to go back quite normally, as though nothing had happened.'

'Mother, the man's soaking wet!'

'And say,' his mother continued as though he had not interrupted, 'that we were *all* walking – the four of us, you understand – and poor Cardew missed his foot and fell in the pool.'

'He'll have a black eye tomorrow, Mother.' Melanie felt almost light-headed, veering between laughter and tears, unsure which would win.

'No matter. That will have come from the accident. I want us all to be perfectly calm and British, and go right back to the camp . . . Goodness, here they are now looking for us, rushing along the path as though the house were on fire. Goodness, what a fuss, what a curious night this is!'

As the sun rose across the Nile Melanie lay pressed under her husband, biting her lips so that she should not scream. She thought of her mother and Captain Crystal, and she couldn't understand how any woman could take any pleasure in what she was going through now. Had her mother and Captain Crystal ever . . . the thought was as horrific as her ordeal, but it somehow helped a little to neutralize the agony of this intimate, fleshly contact with Harry. Then he rolled off her body, and she quickly covered herself with a sheet so that he should not attempt to look at her as he sometimes did, to see her shame in the light. Harry always looked a little abashed after he'd treated her in this way – she didn't call it making love – as well he might. But he never asked how she felt. Never had and probably never would. He got into his own bed, turned his back on her and soon she heard the customary sounds of deep sleep. The peace of the wicked.

She hated the sensation when Harry had been with her. It was revolting and unclean. She got up and splashed water in the basin, washing herself as she usually did to remove that horrible trace of himself that Harry had left behind.

Her lawn nightie felt clean and pure after the experience and she got back into bed and lay with her arms behind her head. She didn't know how she could endure this much longer.

She didn't think she'd slept at all. By the time they'd got back, soothed Madame Hassim – who promptly had hysterics at the sight of the near-drowned Captain and felt her party was in ruins – told all those lies, cleaned Cardew Crystal up, said more goodnights and gone to bed it was nearly one o'clock. Harry had tried to make love then – the beast, but she'd told him she was too tired. He didn't seem to care whether she were tired or not when he woke her up with his caresses later on. Perhaps he didn't think she'd notice.

From outside she could hear the sound of the servants as they scuttled about preparing for breakfast and an early start before the sun was too high. There was the smell of something that seemed like roast mutton and it made her feel slightly nauseous.

What would happen to her with Harry? She longed for him to go back to the army. In a way, and although she could not admit it to herself, she longed for him to be killed.

CHAPTER 4

The baggage, kitbags and equipment had been loaded into the train and the horses forced, with a great deal of kicking and protesting, into the cattle trucks. The 21st Lancers, for the first time forsaking their blue uniforms for khaki, in sun helmets and *Stohwasser* gaiters and decked with water bottles, knives, tent pegs, canteen-straps, swords and carbines – so that they called themselves Christmas trees – paraded for inspection by the Colonel. As the band played Auld Lang Syne they began to embark on to the train while all those relatives and friends who had been watching the scene rushed forward seeking their men.

Bosco had quickly secured seats near the window and, with him, Harry jammed the window frame keeping all others at bay. It was easy to see Bosco's tall figure despite the crush, the unremitting monotony of khaki drill uniforms. Dulcie Askham, Flora, Melanie and Grace Plomley Pemberton were only one of a number of little parties who had gathered at the station near the Abbasiya barracks to say goodbye to their men. Many of the families of the troopers were openly weeping, but the Askhams set the tone for the wives and relations of the officers by being notable for the brave front they put on it all – as though it were a time for rejoicing rather than gloom. They made it an occasion for smiles and laughter rather than tears.

It was indeed surprising how many English there were in Cairo that July and August for the departure of the battalions of the Egyptian Army, the Rifle Brigade, the Grenadiers, the Howitzer and Maxim Batteries, the 5th

Fusiliers and the Lancashires who would make the journey by rail to the Atbara camp where the forces of Kitchener were gathering. Part of the journey was to be made by rail, the rest of it by Nile steamer, and then by marching or riding through the desert. But throughout the weeks the platforms had been crowded, not only with the English but with Egyptians and the ebony faces of the Sudanese families who had come to bid their loved ones adieu.

But this day, 2 August 1898, was for the 21st Lancers – nearly four hundred men, their servants, water carriers, horses, vets and sundry equipment.

For weeks since the command had come, the troops had been training and getting themselves and the horses to a peak of fitness. The large troop horses the regiment had brought with it from India were exchanged for the lighter Syrian and Arab stallions, more suitable for the terrain where they were to fight. The Lancers were eager for battle, anxious to lose the derisive motto that someone had given them: 'Thou shalt not kill' because, for thirty-four years, the regiment had never seen action except for guarding the lines of communication in the Gordon Relief Expedition of 1884–5.

When they could get away Bosco and Harry came to Shepheard's where the womenfolk were staying. The customary round of parties and dinners continued and, except for the feeling of excitement as fresh troops arrived from England, their colourful uniforms briefly embellishing the streets, it was difficult to imagine that an expeditionary force in the south was preparing to try and extinguish once and for all the evil force of Mahdism from the Sudan. To avenge once and for all the shameful, lonely death of General Gordon in the grounds of his residence at Khartoum.

Bosco bent down to take his mother's hand, kissed it and momentarily the laughter ceased and he looked solemn.

'Take care, Mama.'

'I take care! Dear boy *I* am not the one who is going to fight the Dervishes. I hear they are terrifying savages. *You* take care.'

'As long as we get a battle, Mama, I have no care of anything.'

Next he gave his hand to Flora and she pressed it convulsively, her heart too full, suddenly too moved to speak. The last time they had seen him off had been at Southampton when he was going to join the regiment in Egypt to perform ordinary garrison duties and not take part in a war. Now he was actually bound for the front. War no longer seemed to her a glorious thing, but something to be feared even though Mahdism had brought shame upon England in Gordon's dreadful death and the failure of his countrymen to relieve him in time.

After Flora, Grace reached up to take his hand, trying to give the gesture something of the intimacy of a sweetheart rather than a mother or sister. She was not yet a sweetheart, but she would like to have been. She had soon perceived that to fit in with the Askhams a good deal of subterfuge was necessary – barracking, chaffing rather than sincerity and any attempt at romance. Just now Lady Askham, despite the noise and confusion, the smoke that billowed along the platform covering them all with specks of soot as the stokers stoked the engine, had been telling a long amusing story that had convulsed them all with mirth. But for her, Grace, the minutes ticked by depriving her of the chance to say all the things to Bosco she would like to have said: 'write', 'remember me', 'please come home safe'.

Instead she stared at him, speechless, and as her eyes filled with tears he said: 'I say, steady on, old girl,' and gave her a large dirty white handkerchief to wipe them while Lady Askham stared at her disapprovingly and Flora, embarrassed, looked away.

'Take care,' she blurted, returning his handkerchief

while Lady Askham smiled and Bosco gave her a broad, chum-like wink.

'That's a good pal,' he said. 'Take it easy now.'

A whistle blew and Harry gave his hand to his mother-in-law, his sister-in-law and then his wife who smiled at him bravely in true Askham manner.

'I know you'll be all right, Harry.'

Harry patted his heart. 'I have my shield to protect me.'

'Your what?'

'The case you gave me before we were married.'

'Oh.' Melanie dropped her eyes as though reminded of happier days that she would sooner forget. Yet since the camp and her unfortunate lapse she and Harry had managed to avoid giving the impression of an unhappily married couple. For one thing she saw to it that they were hardly ever alone together which made the pretence easier, because Melanie had always been happy in crowds and the constant presence of her mother and sister made her feel secure.

'Goodbye Harry, Bosco.' Rachel Bolingbroke quietly appeared through the smoke. 'Adam asked me to tell you he is seeing to his horse which has gone lame.' She pointed towards the rear of the train where the whinnies and snorts of protesting horses could still be heard above the din.

'I hope he doesn't miss the train, the blighter!'

'No, he is on the train with his servant and the vet trying to treat the animal.'

Her arrival prevented Harry from saying anything more to his wife though he still pressed her hand, reluctant to relinquish it.

There was a sudden blast from the engine and the train jolted and moved forwards, propelling along with it those who still clung to the hundreds of hands extended from the windows. Melanie was half dragged along too.

'Let go, Harry. Let go!' she called, but Harry hung on to her because he felt that if he let her go she'd fall and be crushed by those who were being drawn along too. Then the train stopped as abruptly as it had started and some did fall to the ground, some cried and some laughed. Some looked at the clock. The wait was getting on everyone's nerves.

Lady Askham moved with her customary dignity the few paces to where Bosco and Harry's carriage now stood. She saw the sudden look of anger on Melanie's face as she tried to wrench her hand away.

'Harry, you're hurting!'

'I didn't mean . . .' anxiously he leaned half out of the window.

'You did – let go, I tell you!'

Harry abruptly let her hand fall and she rubbed her wrist, feeling tears smarting from her eyes.

'Was it as painful as *that*, darling?' Dulcie Askham's glance was sarcastic.

'He half pulled my arm out of its socket.'

'I'm sure he didn't mean it. Do smile nicely, darling. Don't let his last memory of you be of a quarrel.'

But it was too late. A whistle blew and the crowd surged back as the train suddenly started to move again. One or two still clung to extended hands. Babies were raised for a last glimpse of their fathers. As the train drew out Dulcie caught a glimpse of the commandant, Colonel Martin, and gave him a gracious wave while Grace continued to monopolize Bosco, both to his embarrassment and the evident annoyance of his mother who had wanted to be the last one to touch him.

Careless of her dress Grace pressed herself against the dirty surface of the carriage.

'Dearest Bosco, take *care*,' she hissed and again he answered with a nod and a broad wink while glancing apologetically at his mother.

‘’Bye, Ma, have a good trip home,’ he shouted. ‘Regards to Father and Arthur.’

‘Of course. Have an absolutely *splendid* time, dearest boy.’

Dulcie stepped back still smiling with approval at her boy: the brave insouciant soldier she expected him to be. His father would be pleased. Without relaxing her smile she glanced witheringly at Grace. All this sobbing and clinging was no good at all and Grace, abashed at last, swiftly withdrew her hand, understanding that she had gone a bit too far.

‘Sorry, Lady Askham,’ she murmured but her words were lost in the noise of the wheels.

Bosco stood back and, smiling broadly, blew kisses at the ladies. Then, suddenly, he seemed to catch Rachel’s eye and, putting both hands to his mouth, touched the fingers of each and blew the kisses straight at her. Confused, caught unawares, Rachel raised a hand and waved.

‘Come back safe,’ she called suddenly, the last one, after all, to address a word to him.

For a moment the platform was a sea of raised hands, handkerchiefs, caps, scarves and umbrellas until the train became minute on the horizon and disappeared from sight.

Despite all the people who still remained the platform looked empty and some of the women who had stayed brave gave in to tears. But Lady Askham and her party, dry-eyed, moved with dignity to the exit where the carriage in which they’d arrived awaited them.

‘Can we give you a lift, Miss Bolingbroke?’

‘That would be very nice, Lady Askham.’

‘How did you come?’

‘I came by the tram. It was only a short walk from there.’

Lady Askham shook her head. 'Now what will you do alone in Cairo, you poor child?'

'She is not alone, Mama, she has us.' Flora looked at Rachel kindly.

'Yes but . . . no family.'

'But Miss Plomley Pemberton has no family either.'

'That is different. She's staying with us,' Lady Askham said, as if to be one of the Askham party were an assurance of safety and acceptability. 'And when we return to England she will be going too.'

'When will that be, Lady Askham?'

'As soon as we have Melanie settled. Melanie is the problem at the moment.'

Melanie had been a problem for quite some time to her mother who was well aware of the unsatisfactory state of the marriage, ever since the camp and its debacle the following morning with the abrupt departure of Captain Crystal without a word of explanation, though to those who knew the truth none was needed. Lady Askham had then viewed the plans for the day with some distress, especially as she had not had a wink of sleep all night because of the disasters of the evening when she had been so indiscreet as to jeopardize her standing with the children – something she had often skated near to before, but never actually done. So she had decided to return forthwith to Cairo, too, and the Duplessises and Adrian Hastings wanted to return with her. It was really too hot, they all explained. Madame Hassim was devastated at the collapse of the party – a sumptuous luncheon picnic having been planned in another picturesque spot. Achmed also felt that the expedition had been a personal failure for him despite Lady Askham's protestations to the contrary. She insisted that he must not blame himself because Captain Crystal had fallen accidentally into the water, and neither she nor most of the party had slept, unaccustomed as they were to hard campbeds in the middle of the desert.

The younger element who still wanted to explore had gone on by donkey to the Gizeh pyramids and the Sphinx and from there, after dining at the Mena House Hotel, they travelled back to Cairo by a special late train.

Madame Hassim and Achmed, after seeing one party back to the river and the other on to the pyramids, had remained behind to clear up the camp and, presumably, to commiserate with each other at the disaster that had overtaken them: failing to please Lady Askham. Such failure, even if it wasn't their fault, would get around and do their reputation as people who could achieve the impossible – and often did – no good at all.

Now that Bosco and Harry had indeed gone, no one knew for how long, maybe a month, maybe more, Lady Askham decided to return at once to England. It was unendurably hot in Cairo, the summer being at its height, and she had no wish to stay a moment longer. Sitting on the verandah of Shepheard's that night before dinner she addressed the problem to her daughters and Grace, who had attached herself to them as inextricably one of the party. They were surrounded as usual by the throng of fashionable Cairenes, and from all nations the customary sprinkling of socialites, diplomats, army personnel, explorers and Egyptologists, all behaving as though there were no war in the desert fifteen hundred miles away. White-coated waiters moved capably among the tables dispensing tea, coffee and drinks while the sun slowly sank beyond the Citadel which dominated the city, its guns still watchfully trained across the broad thoroughfares and narrow streets in case of insurgency.

'Tomorrow I am going to Cook's to book our passages home.' Lady Askham placed her glass of lemonade on its saucer and looked at Melanie. 'Now what are *you* going to do, my dear?'

'Come back with you, Mama.'

Her mother, bracing herself for an argument, sat back nonplussed while Grace gave a little gasp and leaned forward.

'Shouldn't you stay here and wait for your husband?'

'What good am I doing in Cairo? As soon as Omdurman is taken they will get leave and come home.'

'Very sensible,' Lady Askham approved. 'That's settled then.' Secretly she'd been hoping that's what her daughter would say. Opposition, however, came from another side.

'I would like to stay here, however, Mama.' Flora spoke quietly. 'Rachel Bolingbroke says there is room in her lodgings for me.'

'Oh, I couldn't possibly leave you behind.'

'Why not? You could Melanie.'

'That's different. Melanie is no longer in my care.'

'But neither is she in Harry's if he's not here.'

'She is a married lady, though.' Lady Askham decided to deal promptly with this insubordination. 'You are not.'

'But Rachel . . .'

'I care not what Miss Bolingbroke says or does. She may think it seemly for unmarried women to flaunt themselves abroad unescorted. I, most decidedly, do not. She had no right to make such a proposition to you. She is, it seems, a law unto herself and is not my concern. You are. Your father would be horrified if I were to return to London with Melanie, leaving you behind.'

'I am three years older than Melanie, Mama. Rachel is merely twenty-one. I think it is time I made my own decisions. I will stay here, whatever you say. In fact I have already arranged to take the room next to Rachel and as soon as you leave I shall move into it. It is all decided.'

'Then why did you not say so before?'

'Because I knew that you would make a fuss.'

'Please come to my room, Flora. I wish to speak privately with you.'

Majestically forbidding, Lady Askham rose but Flora remained where she was, slightly paler than usual but her eyes gazing unfalteringly at her mother. 'Please forgive me, Mama, if I don't come with you. My mind is quite made up.'

'What will you do for money?'

'I have sufficient funds.'

'Did Bosco give you money? Did he know of your plans? Really, Flora, I feel betrayed by my own children.' Lady Askham sank back heavily into her chair and at that moment Achmed Asher, resplendent in yellow-and-black check, a pearl lodged neatly in the centre of his striped cravat, his red tarbush with a black tassle centred correctly on his head, wended his way between the tables inclining himself obsequiously in front of her.

'My lady!'

'Achmed!' Lady Askham beamed at the sight of him, thankful for some diversion however temporary. Later she would return with fresh stratagems to deal with the rebellious Flora. 'What a pleasure to see you.'

'I hope so, Lady Askham, I hope so.' Achmed looked grave and declined Lady Askham's offer of a drink. 'Is there somewhere we might talk, your ladyship, in private?' He looked meaningfully at her three companions.

'Oh dear, is something the matter?'

'Nothing, I'm sure, that can't speedily be settled.' Lady Askham thought Achmed not quite his usual urbane self. His demeanour was rather strange, even forbidding.

'Can't we talk here, Achmed? My daughters and Miss Plomley Pemberton . . .'

'I would prefer it alone with your ladyship.'

'Very well.'

Resigned, slightly curious, Dulcie got up and, telling Grace and her daughters to wait for her so that they could go in to dinner together, led the way across the verandah into the hotel where, off the lobby, she found a small writing-room, temporarily deserted.

She sat down and gestured for her visitor to do the same. 'Now Achmed, I am very busy and rather fraught. My son and son-in-law left for the desert today. I have a thousand things to do. What is it exactly that you wish to say?'

'It is about my bill, I regret, your ladyship.'

'Your *bill*. For what?'

'For the excursion into the desert.'

'You expect me to pay for *that*?' Dulcie's astonishment drove her angry thoughts about Flora from her mind. 'I understood we were the guests of Madame Hassim.'

'I think there was a misunderstanding, your ladyship, which I deeply regret.'

'In what way was there a misunderstanding? There was no misunderstanding as far as I was concerned. Madame Hassim asked us to join her party. You should see her about the bill. It was not a thing I would have dreamt of undertaking myself. It was so unwise, in that heat. She, you, should have known better.'

'I realized that, Lady Askham. It was a considerable ordeal for me too. Weeks of work, preparation and . . .' he flicked his fingers, at the same time drawing out his handkerchief to mop his brow, as if the very memory were painful. 'It was not really appreciated, Lady Askham.'

'I'm sorry,' she said stiffly, feeling a little unkind.

'Madame Hassim assured me, however,' Achmed continued, tucking his handkerchief back into his breast pocket, 'that she *asked* you if she should organize an outing and that you said "yes". Accordingly she has told me to present my account to you.' With a deft, rehearsed movement Achmed extracted an envelope from his pocket and presented it with a flourish to Dulcie who sat on the edge of her chair, her familiar composure temporarily deserting her. She took the envelope, swiftly opened it and gazed at the contents.

'Two hundred pounds!' she exclaimed. 'Is this a joke?'

'Far from it, your ladyship.'

'But it is outrageous.'

'It was a very expensive undertaking. It includes the train fares to Bedreshayn and back,' he added helpfully.

'My dear man, I can't possibly pay this.' Lady Askham rose and waving the paper in front of her like a fan began to pace up and down the small room.

'Perhaps funds from England . . .'

'I don't mean I *can't* afford to. I *shan't*. Two hundred pounds for a day and night. It is perfectly absurd. As for my asking for it – why, had that been the case I would have discussed it with you. I would never undertake a business transaction without knowing the cost. Half the people there I hardly knew. Lord and Lady Duplessis, that journalist . . .'

'Mr Hastings.'

'I never met him in my life.'

'Captain Crystal . . .' Achmed looked at her insinuatingly.

'He was to make up the numbers. Madame Hassim asked me to suggest a name.'

'Quite.'

Achmed paused but Lady Askham stared at him without a word. It was, as they say, a silence pregnant with meaning. As if he had scored a point Achmed continued quietly: 'It was an expensive undertaking, approved by you, I was sure, Lady Askham – so I understood from Madame Hassim. The food alone cost a fortune, the hire of the camels, all the servants, the tents had to be purchased outright and were resold with difficulty, at a loss . . .'

'But that's not the point, is it, Achmed? How can you expect me to pay for something I never wanted in the first place? I shall summon Madame Hassim at once . . .'

Achmed threw out his arms in a despairing gesture.

'Madame Hassim is not here . . .'

'She soon will be. I'll send a servant to find her immediately.'

"I mean she's not in Cairo, Lady Askham.'

'Then where is she, pray?'

'No one knows. Some say Paris, some Lisbon.'

'You mean she's fled?'

'Apparently Madame Hassim has not the means I thought she had. I have now made enquiries.'

'Then you should have made them before.'

'She wished to impress you . . .'

'She has certainly done that.'

'Oh, Lady Askham, if you only knew what distress this has caused me.' Achmed wrung his fat little hands desperately together. 'I have had sleepless nights. I knew it would come as a shock to you, but I am badly out of pocket. Look, dearest madam, I could reduce this bill by five per cent but no more. There – shall we say £190, Lady Askham?'

'Not a *piastre*,' Lady Askham said firmly. 'Not one piastre will I pay for something I did not wish and did not enjoy. It was a ridiculous thing to do in the heat of the summer. It also lost me the friendship of Captain Crystal . . .' Dulcie, speaking impulsively, realized at once she'd made a mistake.

'Ah,' Achmed suddenly looked cunning. 'Yes, that was a pity. For the Captain to be pushed into the pool.'

'He was not pushed, he fell.' Lady Askham paused and gazed at him imperiously, resuming her seat.

'I understand there *was* some altercation, Lady Askham. One of the servants . . .'

'Snooping, I suppose.'

'Happened to see . . .'

'Oh, this is blackmail, is it, *Mr* Asher? Lord Cromer will hear of this.'

'Oh, I hope not, my lady,' Achmed went on, twisting his hands. The backs were white, but the palms were pink with perspiration as though indicative of his true state of mind. 'If it should ever come to the ears of Lord Askham . . .'

'If *what* should come to the ears . . .' Dulcie felt an ominous ringing in her own ears and sat down abruptly.

'I have a full account from the servant of the events that took place that night, Lady Askham, supported, I might say, from other sources.' Achmed paused mysteriously. 'It is said that you and Captain Crystal . . .'

Dulcie held up a hand to silence him. 'I am well aware what happened that night, Mr Asher. I was walking with Captain Crystal, and was soon joined by my son and daughter. In the moonlight Captain Crystal lost his footing and . . .'

'Oh, that wasn't what I heard at all, I regret to inform your ladyship. But if my bill is settled promptly, or a promise is made to settle within a few days, no more will be heard of the matter.'

'Then it *is* blackmail,' Dulcie said contemptuously. 'We Askhams, I'm afraid, do not stoop to blackmail. Besides, do you think people will believe the words of yourself and a servant against mine?'

'I'm sure your ladyship would prefer that nothing where heard at all,' Achmed replied unctuously. 'Rumour can be an ugly thing and I believe that Captain Crystal has not been exactly discreet among his colleagues in the Egyptian Army. He was very mortified indeed.'

'Then he is decidedly *not* a gentleman,' Dulcie said airily. 'I doubt whether people would believe his word either.'

'But I'm sure your ladyship will not wish to put it to the test. I assure you I will call at once at the office of the Consul-General and lodge a complaint if my bill is not paid. And if it is, I can promise you . . .' Achmed put a finger to his lips as though sealing them.

'You're a hateful, horrible little man, Asher.' Dulcie

rose and stood over him. 'I should have known you had no class, none at all, yet some say your father was a diplomat. Very strange. I see now that you worm your horrid little self among the English, extorting money from them by making up gossip of a malicious kind. I wonder how many others have suffered like this? There is not a word of truth in what you say.'

'Then you have no worry, Lady Askham,' Asher sat comfortably back in his chair, folding his arms against the buttons that strained across his paunch to keep both sides of his jacket together. 'Yet I must have my money. Defaulting on payment owed is taken very gravely in Cairo where the British have set such high standards, done so much to get rid of corruption. Even if the matter is concluded to the satisfaction of your ladyship I'm sure that quite a few tales will travel back to England. So many of the English are returning there now . . .' Asher waved a hand towards the window as if saying farewell to departing ships and regarded Dulcie with an expression that was a curious mixture of servility and contempt.

Dulcie took a deep breath. 'I will have the money for you to collect at the hotel tomorrow, Mr Asher. I do not owe it, but I will pay it as I see you are consumed with malice. Please leave a receipt with the clerk at the desk, and kindly ensure that I never see your face again. And please understand I have no intention of yielding to further blackmail. Say what you like. My son will soon be returning from the desert and I hate to think what he might say or do if he knew about this. Especially do. He would probably wring your neck. If he were here now it would be a *very* different story, I can tell you. I notice that you waited until he'd gone before you presented yourself and your odious demands, and yet the picnic was over three weeks ago . . .'

Achmed looked insolently at Lady Askham, his face for once unsmiling. He remained there for some time, tapping his hand on the polished surface of the writing table long after she'd turned her back on him and left the room.

Ever since he'd read his mail on their arrival at the depot which stood at the confluence of the Nile and Atbara rivers, which was as far as the railway went, Adam Bolingbroke noticed that Bosco had been out of sorts. Instead of cheering him up his letters, or a letter, depressed him and he lost his customary ebullience which was so greatly appreciated by the men in those trying conditions.

It had taken them eleven days to get to the River Atbara where the last battle against the Mahdists had been fought in April. The train from Cairo to Khizam took twenty-four hours, followed by nine days on a Nile steamer and finally thirty-six hours on the desert railway built by Kitchener the year before from Wadi Halfa to the Atbara. All through the rough, wearisome journey Bosco could be depended upon to cheer everyone up, to crack the right note of levity at a trying moment, to laugh whenever disaster threatened or their spirits were in the dumps. But since his letter that morning he had not been his usual self at all – he had looked withdrawn, thoughtful, even angry.

The 21st Lancers were encamped in an old mud fort by the side of the river, a remnant of the engagement the previous April. Since that time a small township had grown up on the old mud village of Dakhila and had become an important staging post for the expeditionary force. The whole of the 2nd British Brigade had passed through on their way to the south. A number of personnel engaged in transport or railway maintenance, who lived there permanently, had built themselves substantial dwellings, and the Sirdar had an imposing house by the river. There were also two large hospitals, unfortunately always full because of the effects of heat and disease if not of actual battle. In addition there was a long line of mud rooms, known as Harmony Row, belonging to various officials and a veritable street occupied by itinerant Greek merchants, maybe the sons and grandsons of those who had supplied the British Army in the Crimea over forty years before. These enterprising traders sold everything from cigarettes to fountain-pens and willingly accepted cheques drawn on London banks.

But more than anything the encampment represented a huge depot both for food, ammunitions and other essential supplies with which to provision the troops for up to three months. Part of the success of Kitchener's campaign had been in logistics; ensuring that the necessary things were in the right place at the right time.

Ever since their arrival the Lancers had been occupied in greeting old friends, reading their post, obtaining supplies and exercising their horses who were cramped and stiff from nearly two weeks in confined, uncomfortable conditions.

By nightfall on 15 August the men were able to relax and it was then that Adam, out for a stroll, came upon Bosco sitting on an upturned box outside his tent rereading the letter which had seemed to upset him.

'Bad news?' Adam flopped on the ground beside the tent and started filling his pipe.

Bosco made as if to crush the letter in his hand, then smoothed it out again carefully over his knee.

'I need this for evidence,' he said gritting his teeth.

'Can you talk about it, old man?'

Bosco looked at Adam as though engaged in a strong debate within himself as to what he should do.

'It's absolutely nothing.'

'If you want to talk about anything . . . in the letter. Only too willing to help.'

Bosco Down was unused to sharing confidences. Few things ever stirred him enough to make him feel he needed help. He skimmed quite happily over life's surfaces and was seldom in distress. He looked at Adam, his kind, thoughtful face shadowy in the light of the paraffin lamp. They really hardly knew each other. Adam was a loner, Bosco one of the boys, yet, since their sisters had become friendly, a sort of camaraderie had grown up between them. Bosco now almost regarded him with affection, as a brother. Who better than a brother in whom to confide the problem pressing on his mind? He linked his fingers across his knees and as he spoke the veins swelled on his neck and forehead as though he were labouring.

'It's that fellow Crystal! You know who I mean?'

'The bloke that was with us in the desert? He's in the Egyptian cavalry.'

'The one who was always around my mother.'

'What has he done?'

'He's here somewhere,' Bosco looked up as though expecting to see his enemy walk through the trees. 'I mean, somewhere in this force. I hear he came down with the cavalry.'

'But what has he done?'

'He . . .' The knuckles of Bosco's linked fingers were white. 'He compromised my mother.'

'Good Lord, the bounder!' Adam leapt up and tapped his pipe out on the heel of his boot. 'Is that what the letter's about?'

Bosco nodded. 'Mama's been blackmailed by that villain Achmed. He knows I pushed Crystal in the pool the night of the picnic.'

'I think we all knew that,' Adam said quietly. 'We guessed.'

'Did you?' Bosco's voice scarcely rose above a whisper.

'You all looked so dishevelled, unhappy, agitated, and then Crystal disappearing at first light. It was obvious there'd been a row.'

'Well, this little . . .' Bosco shook the letter passionately, 'asked my mother for money to pay for the trip. When she wouldn't – she thought she'd been asked as a guest – he threatened to tell Lord Cromer – nay, any English person in Cairo who would listen and plenty would, I can tell you – that my mother and Crystal were paramours . . .'

'Which is not true . . .'

'Of *course* it's not true.' Bosco dashed one fist into the other. 'She does flirt, I will admit, and I caught her flirting that night. I was angry. But they are not . . . lovers.' Bosco could hardly give voice to the word. 'The fact is that Crystal has put it about they were.'

'Are you sure?'

'Of course I'm sure,' Bosco tapped the letter. 'Mama said he told all the Egyptian Army, according to Achmed. She was forced to pay up – two hundred pounds, I ask you, almost my year's allowance from my father – and get away from Cairo as soon as she could. She took Melanie and Grace with her and left Flora behind.'

'I thought it would have been the other way round.' Adam looked behind him to where other Lancer officers were drinking in a clearing by the side of the swift-rushing river. Among them was Harry Lighterman who had been drinking rather a lot since he left Cairo, not that he'd been alone. There was so little to do to relieve the tedium of the long journey through the arid, barren desert.

'No, Melanie is Mama's girl, always has been. She was too young to marry. Flora yearns for independence.'

'Then she should get married too.'

'Ah, but Flora doesn't want to marry. She thinks it's exchanging one tyranny for another.' Bosco looked at Adam and smiled. 'Like Rachel, I reckon. She's staying with her.'

'Yes, it's in my letter from Rachel. I hope you don't mind.'

'I don't mind, but Mama is in a great old state about that too. In fact it is a very unhappy letter from Mama. It's why I've felt depressed all day. I feel so angry, yet I don't know what to do.'

'Come, let's have a drink.' Adam put a hand on his shoulder. 'The boys are well ahead of us.'

Bosco hesitated and then, folding the letter, tucked it into his pocket.

'If I see that Crystal I'll kill him. I will. He won't need any Dervish to do it.'

As they got to the clearing their fellow officers were getting to their feet. In the middle were a few empty whisky bottles and glasses and Bosco and Adam were greeted with some derision as they approached. Gesticulations were made with empty arms.

'Too late. All gone.'

'We're just going to Harmony Row. There's sure to be a party.' Harry put an arm round Bosco's neck and lurched against him. 'Old chum,' he added.

Bosco looked at Harry and saw that although he wasn't completely drunk he wouldn't need much more to make him. He was worried about Harry's drinking, the determined way he uncorked a bottle and poured, regardless of the hour of day. On the boat he'd begun soon after breakfast.

They never talked about the reason for Harry's increased drinking, because he hadn't been such a drinker before. Bosco thought it had to do with Melanie. But they couldn't talk about it because gentlemen didn't discuss that sort of thing, especially if the woman in question was a sister of a brother officer. Gentlemen were meant to suffer in silence: to play the game.

The drinks were plentiful in Harmony Row. The residents were always glad to see men who had come from the north, to exchange gossip about Cairo and London with the latest news from the troops in the south. Fresh bottles were sent for from the Greek bazaar which stayed open as long as the troops were awake and it was nearly midnight when Harry, Bosco and Adam returned to the camp.

Because of the long march the following day neither Adam nor Bosco had drunk much, but a fresh supply had tipped Harry right over and he was slung rather inelegantly between his two brother officers on the way back, an arm round the neck of each. They took Harry to his tent and laid him on his blanket on the floor helping to remove his boots.

'You'll have a hell of a head tomorrow,' Bosco said. 'That was a bit of injudicious drinking.'

'Isn't all drinking injudicious?' Harry slurred the words. 'I've never drunk so much in my life before.'

'Then why now, old man?'

Bosco sat on the floor beside him while Adam squatted by the flap of the tent.

'Why not?' Harry chuckled and winked in the gloom. 'Nothing else to do.' He paused and then continued. 'Besides, a man likes to feel a man.' He unbuttoned his shirt, baring his chest, and thumped it. 'Your sister, Bosco, old boy, never made me feel a man. She hated me, Bosco.' Harry put a hand on Bosco's arm and gave him the leering smile of the inebriate.

'Oh, that's not true, Harry!'

''Tis, 'tis,' Harry waved a finger in the air. 'Has she waited for me in Cairo to come back? No. Did she write me a letter? No.'

'No letter from Melanie? Well, she's gone back to England, you know. I'm sure one's on the way.'

'I *know* she's gone back to England. Everyone in the regiment knows that. That's all I heard today as they read their letters. "Did you know, old boy, that she has gone back to England?"' Harry sounded close to tears.

Guiltily Bosco felt the letter crumpled in his pocket. 'I'm sorry, Harry. I should have told you myself. I was

. . . well, there were things in Mother's letter that upset me. I was out of sorts myself today. Too bloody out of sorts to notice anyone else.'

'Your sister doesn't love me.' Harry patted his shirt pocket and closed his eyes. He fumbled for something, and producing the cigarette case Melanie had given him for their wedding, held it up. 'I said I'd wear this next to my heart for ever.' For some time he gazed at it then, suddenly, he kissed it, his eyes filling with tears. Then he flung it as far as he could across the ground, closed his eyes again and appeared to sleep.

Some time later, after turning him on his face in case he was sick, Bosco and Adam left the tent.

The following day, after the Lancers had struck camp and started their journey south, an Arab servant found the cigarette case in the scrub grass and gleefully sold it for fifty piastres, or ten English shillings, to a Greek trader.

As dawn broke on 2 September it became clear that the arid plain below the Surgham Hill was thickly covered with brown men in their white, brightly patched *jibbas*, the sign of a follower of the Mahdi, now long dead and buried in the tomb which topped the town of Omdurman dimly visible beyond them. The Mahdi's follower, the Khalifa Abdullai, had amassed an army of about sixty thousand men, more than double the number of the troops of Kitchener waiting in their formations on the other side of the hill at Egeiga, in a crescent beside the river. The Dervish throng was interspersed with the flags of the Emirs who led them: green, white and red, and in the centre flew the sacred black banner of the Khalifa himself, surrounded by the members of his own tribe, the Taisha.

It was a formidable sight confronting Bosco and his comrades who had been sent on reconnaissance, as they gazed through their field glasses. Slowly, like a swarm of ants, the mass began to move to the throbbing sound of drums, and the wail of thousands of human voices chanting the *ombeya – La Illha illa llah wa Muhammad rasul ullah*, there is only one God and Mohammed is his prophet – rose up to greet them, chilling in its frenetic intensity.

'God, what a sight!' Bosco let his glasses fall and gazed excitedly at Harry standing next to him. 'What hope have we against them?'

'Guns,' Harry said grimly fingering his revolver, and the bullets of his bandolier strung across his chest. 'The modern weapons of war.' As he spoke the Dervish cohorts began to fan out, one towards the army drawn up by the river, one towards the Karreri Hills to their left, and a smaller one towards the heights on which they stood.

'I hope you're right,' Bosco said, and suddenly a bullet ricocheted off a stone in front of them. 'The blighters have seen us. Let's go,' and they stumbled for their horses, making their way quickly back to the *zariba*, the thicket of thorns which was the only protection the British and Egyptian armies had between them and the frenzied Dervish mass, most of whom were armed merely with primitive spears, some carrying antiquated rifles and some of them on horseback.

When the small detachment of Lancers reached the *zariba* the field guns had already opened fire, and the news was that the rest of the cavalry, the Egyptians and the horse artillery under the command of Colonel Broadwood, threatened by the advancing Dervish hordes in the Karreri Hills, had disobeyed the Sirdar's orders to return. Instead, they were creating a diversion by attempting to get the Dervishes away from the army and the beleaguered Camel Corps, whose fleet-footed beasts were yet too clumsy and slow for the Dervish horsemen. The gunboats ranged on the Nile behind the *zariba* opened fire and, as the mob appeared over the horizon, the first British rifle shots were fired by the Grenadier Guards to be taken up all along the semicircle, only two men deep, which had been drawn up the day before as part of Kitchener's plan.

For a time it had seemed there would be no fight after all, that the Khalifa might remain in Omdurman, challenging the troops to flush him out, or desert it altogether and flee south by the river. But now there was no mistake. As the fire of the Guards was taken up by all the battalions along the line – the Warwicks, the Highlanders, the Lincolns, the Egyptians and the Sudanese – battle had indeed been joined. On both sides there was a mood of exhilaration in the air.

Once on low ground by the river Bosco and his companions joined the other squadrons of Lancers who waited, hoping for the order to go into action. Up to now they had made only a few sorties, like the one to the Surgham Hill, and their wish was to add glory to the regimental banner devoid of military honours. As he stood watering his horse, listening to the din of the battle behind him, Bosco felt an exultation in his blood that swept away all the exhaustion from the march across the desert to this spot, the two nights that he and most of his comrades had lain sleepless, fully dressed in case of a surprise attack. Not far from him now the Sirdar sat mounted on his white horse, bovine and impassive, surrounded by his aides, issuing brief staccato orders as the huge advancing wave of men, careless of their own safety, threatened to engulf the defenders of the *zariba*. Recklessly they hurled themselves forward, and white banners fell only to be quickly seized and borne aloft again by comrades eager to die for the honour of the Prophet. It was a stirring, even awesome sight and there was not a man behind the *zariba*, even if he hated him, who did not admire the courage of his enemy.

The carnage wreaked among them was terrible. Many had scarcely time to fire a single shot. The shells from the artillery and gunboats caused great holes in their ranks as white-clothed bodies were flung into the air, falling in severed pieces upon the ground below. Those missed by the shells were found by the bullets as the well-trained troops, armed with the world's most modern rifles, directed their deadly line of fire right into the enemy ranks. Yet still they came, an endless, seething mass in a great brown tide.

Bosco was about to mount a biscuit tin obligingly provided by one of the gunners, the better to survey the holocaust, when there was a diversion from the right and two cavalry officers from Broadwood's troop galloped up to the Sirdar to report on the position of the cavalry squadrons in the hills.

The Sirdar was angry with Broadwood whom he had ordered to return to the *zariba*, and he listened impatiently as the two men explained what had happened. Then he pointed peremptorily over to the Lancers waiting beyond the hospital tents and turned towards the thinning Dervish ranks.

Bosco remained on his box, his face stern, his attitude rigid. As the cavalry officers rode up and dismounted one of them stumbled and, almost falling against him, looked up to apologize. Bosco stared into the face of Cardew Crystal, whose approach he had observed. For a moment the two men glared at each other, then Cardew put out a hand.

'Hello, Down, I heard you were here.'

Bosco ignored the outstretched hand and Crystal said nervously: 'No hard feelings, Down. This is war.'

'It is war,' Bosco said coldly and was about to step down and walk away when there was a commotion in the front and a leading Emir, his pennant trailing, urged his horse towards the firing line, straight at the mouth of the cannon, as though he would take it alone, or, maybe, by the power of prayer and help from on high. For a moment it was as though the entire allied force held its breath and then the Emir, his body riddled with bullets – perhaps he was already dead but carried forward only by the fearlessness of his horse – raised his sightless eyes to heaven and fell with his banner to the ground.

Seeing him lying there the remaining Dervishes also fell to the ground, stretched out among the dead and those too hideously wounded to move but who were trying, even in their death throes, to take one last shot at the enemy.

The Sirdar put up a hand calling loudly: 'Cease fire, please! Cease fire! Cease fire!' and then he observed to those close to him, for he was a parsimonious man, 'what a dreadful waste of ammunition.'

'It's all over,' Bosco looked dejectedly at Cardew as the firing ceased, 'and it's only eight-thirty in the morning.'

Pockets of fire continued following the Dervish retreat, claiming more victims, but the *zariba* had been saved and the bulk of the enemy frontal attack decimated.

'I say, Down, I know what's the matter, can't we call a truce?' Cardew persisted as the Lancers, deprived of a fight, looked morosely at their horses tranquilly drinking from the river. 'I meant no harm, you know.'

'My mother had to leave Cairo because of you.'

'I heard about that. It was no fault of mine. I never breathed a word to a soul.'

'Yet everyone knew about it. People said you boasted about your conquest. Hardly an honourable thing to do, was it?'

'You made an ass out of me, Down.' Cardew abandoned his excuses.

'Well, you've made an ass out of *me*.' Bosco tried to walk away as Cardew grabbed his arm.

'I meant no disrespect to Lady Askham. I wish you could believe it.'

'I wish I could too,' Bosco said, turning his back and,

going up to his horse, took the reins from his servant just as General Gateacre, Captain Brooke and others of the Sirdar's staff came galloping up towards Colonel Martin. For a few moments there was some animated talk, the staff officers waving their arms in the direction of the desert and the Surgham Ridge. Suddenly alert, tense with anticipation, the Lancers watched the officers ride back, then they turned as a man to their colonel who was already leaping on to his horse.

'We are to go after them. We are to clear the way between the *zariba* and Omdurman. The Sirdar orders us to do this in the absence of the cavalry.'

There was a cheer from the Lancers who sprang on to their horses festooned with water-bottles, tins of bully beef, picketing gear and saddlebags, and made their way across the field of carnage that had just been committed in the name of the Queen. But their eyes were not on the bloodstained ground, the masses of dead, the wounded attempting to crawl towards the water, but on those who were disappearing beyond the Surgham Hill only half a mile away.

The great plain between the Lancers and Omdurman was marked with small parties of wandering Dervishes, some on horseback and some on foot, all looking aimlessly around for their lost leader, the Khalifa, who had remained out of sight during the frontal attack. It was so hot that the air seemed distorted with mirages, some of the Arabs appearing to walk on the water and some in the air. Bosco wiped his eyes and adjusted the strap of his helmet, his heart beating with excitement. Yet it still seemed impossible to envisage any sort of action with this pathetic, unresisting mob. He was riding with Harry and Robert Grenfell, one of his best friends in the regiment with ideas and tastes similar to his own, scion of a noble military family like the Askhams and the Kittos. Bosco grinned at Lieutenant Grenfell as each officer's troop fell in behind them, and their ways parted. Then to his fury Bosco observed that Cardew and his colleague from the Egyptian Cavalry were also riding with the Lancers, and he called out to Adam just behind him: 'What's that fellow doing here?'

'General Gateacre told him they could ride with us. Look ahead, Bosco,' Adam urged, spurring his horse. 'Don't let anger distract you from the main task.'

As Cardew slipped over to the left out of sight, Bosco wiped the sweat off his face and continued towards Omdurman where the flattened top of the Mahdi's tomb, shelled by the gunboats the day before, seemed like a beacon. Surely the day was theirs? To his right Harry rode at the head of his troop, and Bosco raised an arm in salute at his brother-in-law who, having recovered from his binge at the Atbara, had hardly had a drop to drink since, and had never once referred to the evening.

When they reached the Surgham Ridge, on which they'd stood only two hours before, they found it unoccupied; but that several thousand Dervishes were fleeing towards Omdurman, and a message was sent to the Sirdar to ask for instructions. As they waited a few shots rang out from snipers still lodged on the Surgham Hill forcing the regiment to scatter.

As the heliograph in the *zariba* began to flash, the signaller took down the message, reporting to Colonel Martin: 'Advance, sir, and clear the left flank. Use every effort to prevent the enemy entering Omdurman.'

Murmuring with excitement those Lancers who had left their horses remounted and Colonel Martin ordered two patrols, one under Lieutenant Pirie and the other under Lieutenant Grenfell, to reconnoitre the ground ahead which, from where they were, appeared smooth, and to scatter the small straggling parties of Dervishes in their way.

Catching its master's mood, Bosco's horse stamped

impatiently and he stroked its flank, ignoring Cardew Crystal who stood near him.

'I detest that fellow,' Bosco observed to Adam who stood with him. 'Why does he hang around us? He's no business riding with the Lancers. The flag of this day is ours – not his. Mark my words, one day I'll have a fight with him.'

'Look out, Grenfell,' Colonel Martin shouted as the snipers in the rocks turned their attention from the bulk of the regiment to the advance parties. Grenfell turned and galloped back to report that the ground ahead looked as safe as the way they had come. But Lieutenant Pirie had more spectacular news. About three-quarters of a mile to the south-west lay a ditch, or *khor*, which was full of Dervishes lying in wait and armed to the teeth.

At this information a thrill of apprehension ran through the regiment as Colonel Martin gave the orders to advance. Four hundred horsemen with their lances waving in the breeze, their revolvers or swords at the ready, formed into lines of squadron columns and trotted forward for about three hundred yards into a mass of Dervishes who immediately fell to their knees and started firing.

Bosco's horse reared and he saw Lieutenant Sykes's horse fall under him. Two of the troopers ahead rolled off their horses and lay on the ground. The noise of musketry and returning fire came from all around as Bosco drew his revolver and fired into the mass of war-like Arabs taking aim.

It soon became clear that there were only two courses left: to retreat or to charge. Colonel Martin had no doubt. Raising his sword he cried: 'Right wheel into line.'

Behind him seventeen-year-old Trumpeter Steele, the youngest man in the regiment, sounded his bugle and the sixteen troops of Lancers, plus the two members of the Egyptian Cavalry, who had come for the ride and hardly bargained for this, formed a galloping line and began to charge, their helmets forward to protect their faces from the gunfire and the burning dust, carried by the pounding hooves, that rose from the desert. On either side the Arabs continued to fire away until struck down by sword or bullet and, raising his head, Bosco observed that the retreating Dervishes as they drew nearer to Omdurman and refuge were but specks on the horizon.

Bosco dug his spurs into his horse's flank, aware of the men and animals whizzing past him, the cries of the wounded Arabs ringing in his ears when, suddenly, a new and horrifying sight confronted him. A crowd of several thousand Dervishes, hidden behind the main body of the enemy, sprang up from the narrow ditch in the ground, banners aloft, and, with blood-curdling yells, drew back their spears and prepared to hurl them at their enemy. It was an ambush.

The collision between galloping horses and stationary men was as forceful as it was violent and a roar of anger and fury went up from the Lancers before they began to topple in the fray. They had run into an ambush.

Several men fell from their horses, some remounted and fell again and the riderless horses galloped on, adding to the mêlée and confusion with their frantic whinnying. Bosco saw Lieutenant Grenfell fall and was about to go to his aid when Harry passed him hanging half off his horse which had taken fright and was beyond the control of its rider. Harry's right leg was caught in its stirrup, his left was loose and his body tilted sideways as he clung to the reins desperately trying to regain his seat. Seeing his predicament a mounted Dervish was pursuing him, taking swipes at the luckless rider with a long curved sword.

Bosco dug his heels into his horse and pelted after Harry, the horse running lengthways along the *khor*, over fallen bodies dead and alive. He fired his revolver at the Dervish but his aim went wide and he realized he would have to close in and tackle him directly. He put back his gun in its holster and moved his mount to the Arab's side, just managing to deflect his next aim and knocking him sideways. Harry, meanwhile, tried again to right himself given this respite, and the Arab turned furiously upon Bosco who grappled with him, knocking the sword out of his hand.

Suddenly his own mount went from under him, carried away by fear and the lack of firm hands on his reins, and Bosco found himself clasped by the Arab who swung him along preparing to dash him to the ground. Bosco kicked savagely with his spurs into the horse's flank and the injured animal screamed and bucked, causing its rider to slither off it backwards taking his attacker with him. For a moment Bosco and the Dervish lay locked in an embrace like lovers, then simultaneously their hands moved to each other's throats and each began to squeeze. Harry, meanwhile, had righted himself and managed to calm his steed and was frantically circling the interlocked pair trying to take aim at the Arab, but not daring to fire in case he hit Bosco.

Just then both men uncoupled, the Arab reaching for the knife in his belt and Bosco for his revolver. They acted together, the Arab plunging his knife into Bosco's side as Bosco fired, taking half the man's face away. As he fell back one staring eye was still fixed on his killer, while he weakly stabbed Bosco's body again.

'Quick, Bosco,' Harry shouted, leaning down, extending a hand. 'Take it, take it. You saved me, now save yourself.'

Bosco clenched his stomach and with his other hand reached up towards Harry who began to pull. But just then Harry's clasp slackened and he fell forward, a smile of triumph frozen on his face. A bullet fired from the front had entered his chest just above the heart and he toppled over on to Bosco who lay under him knowing, by the awful stillness, that Harry was gone. He gently pushed

Harry aside and sat up, his clothes soaked with the blood of the Dervish, himself and now Harry. He put his arms round Harry and laid him gently on the ground looking into his open eyes for a sign of recognition.

'Harry?' he cried. 'Harry?'

Harry was still smiling, his eyes wide open, and as the blood oozed from the hole in his chest, it was the most fearsome, most gruesome sight that Bosco had ever seen. Stealthily a wounded Arab began to crawl along the ground towards them, and a few yards away Bosco saw the slain body of Robert Grenfell being hacked to pieces by a group of frenzied tribesmen.

'Leap up,' a voice called above him, and looking, he dimly perceived Cardew Crystal brandishing a sword protectively over his and Harry's body.

'I can't leave Harry,' Bosco muttered, holding on to his brother-in-law.

'Harry's *dead*, man. Hurry! Hurry, or you'll kill us both.'

'I can't, look what they're doing to Grenfell.' Bosco pointed weakly to his left as Cardew leapt off his horse, moved Harry's body roughly to one side and tried to take Bosco in his arms.

'Don't think I care a fig about you. I'm only doing this for your mother, you know.' He bent again to try and lift him by the legs.

At those words a vivid memory of Cardew and his mother, in each other's arms at the base of the palm tree by the pool, briefly invaded the terrible scene of carnage around him and, seized by a strength he didn't know he had, Bosco frantically clasped Cardew's hand.

'What did you say, Cardew?'

'This is no time for talk!' Angrily Crystal tried to wrench his hand away, but Bosco, despite his weariness, held on to it, preventing his escape.

'Let me go, Bosco! I tell you. You'll kill us both.'

Perhaps he meant to. Bosco looked into Crystal's eyes, but at that moment he knew he couldn't kill a fellow officer, an Englishman, no matter what he'd done. Still he didn't remove his hand and, with an exclamation, Crystal let his legs fall. He was about to turn and remount his horse when the wounded Dervish, who had crawled so painfully after Bosco, took aim at Cardew, thrusting his spear into his stomach as he bent over Bosco, spattering Bosco's body with a fresh gush of blood.

An astonished look came into Cardew's face. He stood upright, both hands clutching at the spear which he withdrew causing a fresh effusion of blood, intestines and offal. He sank to his knees, as though praying, and then with a groan lay sideways, his feet curled up like a baby.

'You've done for me as I said you would, Bosco, blast you,' he whispered, his accusing eyes still wide open with shock. 'Should have steered clear of you. You've killed me too.'

Tenderly Bosco drew Cardew's head on to his lap, his eyes filling with tears. He cradled him as he died, whispering in his ear that he was sorry, sorry, sorry. He knew his own end was not far off and he sat there resignedly awaiting his last moment, giving what succour to his dying companion he could.

It was then that Adam and Bosco's sergeant, who had come to look for him, found them.

The heat of the charge appeared to be over as the Lancers streaked away into the desert in pursuit of the enemy on the other side of the *khor* which was now full only of the dead, and screaming wounded horses and men.

His sergeant got off his horse and knelt by Bosco's side, feeling the pulse in Cardew's neck.

'Leave him, sir, he's gone,' he said gently. 'Let us help you now.'

Bosco, still clinging to Cardew, pointed to Harry.

'He's dead too, sir. Best save yourself.'

'I can't leave them, don't you see,' Bosco said weakly. 'I have to go with them.' He buried his face in Cardew's matted hair and began to weep as Adam and the sergeant gently prised him away, and took him to the other side of the *khor* to save him from the mutilations of the enemy and let him die in peace.

PART II

1899–1904: Pax Britannica

CHAPTER 5

Askham, with its village of warm stone houses clustering round its gates, formed a small self-contained community which had scarcely changed for centuries. The family at the Hall remained the same, their numbers varying through the years though the Askhams had never gone in for really large families. In the eighteenth century one of the earls of Askham had fathered thirteen children from two wives, but that was the most that had ever been produced. In their progeny, as well as the husbanding of their fortune, the Askhams were temperate. As a race they planned everything with care, and if there were one or two high-fliers and black sheep, some profligates and ne'er-do-wells, as there are in most families, certainly noble ones, there were always sufficient sober, thoughtful and clever Askhams to ensure continuity and consequent prosperity.

Most of the people in the village worked in the big house as their mothers and fathers had before them, as their sons and daughters would after them. In true feudal fashion the villagers felt that they were part of the family, that the family was part of them. They worked in the kitchen, in the laundry, in the garden, in the estate workshops and on the farms, in the stables and, as gamekeepers, in the extensive Forest of Askham which, like the village and the Hall had grown and matured over the centuries from small beginnings.

And then when Bosco Down came home so wounded from the River War they nursed him, helped him and prayed for his recovery in Askham parish church where so many of his ancestors were buried.

Bosco had nearly been buried there too. The spear that almost killed him perforated the wall of his stomach, piercing his liver and his spleen. The massive haemorrhage he sustained was sufficient to cause his death twice over, yet he lived. His comrades had staunched the blood on the field, and hurried him to the hospital station near the river from which he was transported by steamer to the hospital on the Atbara near where he had camped only a few days before. For days he lay in delirium hovering between life and death, and several times he nearly joined the corpses laid out for burial in the mortuary.

But somehow his will to survive prevailed, and in time he became strong enough to make the rest of the journey to Aswan where the hospital boat *Mayflower*, manned by the Red Cross, transferred him to the military hospital at Abbasiya in Cairo from which he had started on his journey together with his brother-in-law whose body now remained behind.

Graves were dug for Harry, Cardew Crystal and Lieutenant Grenfell and others who had fallen in the battle next to the river. There was a solemn funeral and the bugles played the last trump. Then the army marched away, leaving the neat cemetery surrounded by the unburied skeletons of the Dervish dead, the ruins of the *zariba* so valiantly and successfully defended on that September day.

By February 1899, when Bosco lay in a downstairs room of the house where he was born, surrounded by the love and care of his family, the graves were probably long since covered by the shifting desert sands so that no trace of them, except for the occasional crooked wooden cross, remained.

Bosco couldn't remember when he'd really started to notice things again, to realize he was alive. He thought it was the time that Flora walked into his room in the Abbasiya hospital, cool and wholesome in a blue silk dress carrying a large bunch of flowers, but he couldn't be sure. Time, and the passage of time, had so little meaning for him then. He remembered bits of the Atbara, fragments of Aswan before he was put aboard the *Mayflower*; but that sight of Flora, her face sheltered under a broad straw hat, looking, he thought for the first time, beautiful, was the most powerful memory he had.

It was Flora who helped him get well, who was with him when he started to walk and who sat in his room for the best part of every day reading to him and, on his behalf, writing the letters home to his mother and father that they never expected to receive again. Dulcie had wanted to come out to be with him, but the common sense of Flora prevailed. Flora, as well as Bosco, became much stronger during that time – he physically, she mentally. In his suffering and in her reaction to it, in the strength she gave him, she seemed to have found a purpose in her life.

It was Flora who brought him home and it was Flora who sat by his side on this wintry morning reading as he slept. But Bosco was not really sleeping. He lay with eyes half open in that state between dreaming and waking, and from the dream, which had been about the desert, he peeped out on to the skeletal trees of Askham Forest and the misty whiteness of a snow-laden English sky. He yawned and Flora, perceiving he was awake, put down her book and reached for his hand lying on the white coverlet of the bed.

Bosco slept only fitfully, never for long. Sometimes he was awake all night and slept through the day as though the time mechanism of his body had not adjusted itself to being well again, as though he were still half dead. He didn't like being alone at night and often Flora, or his servant Charles, dozed on the couch in his room to pacify and comfort him when the terrors of his dreams, his waking nightmares, overwhelmed him and he cried out for help – help in the desert, in that awful trench full of the heaving, twisted bodies of horses and men.

'Did you sleep well?' Flora enquired gently, pressing his thin hand.

'I dreamt about the desert, but it was not a bad dream. For once it was peaceful.' Bosco smiled and reached for the glass of water by his bedside. 'I *am* better, you know, Flora.'

'You are much, much better.'

'But in my mind.'

'That too.' She smiled encouragingly.

'I've been the most fearful coward, Flora.'

'Darling, you haven't. They wouldn't have given you a medal for being a coward.'

'I don't mean then, though I didn't deserve the medal. I mean now. My fears, my dreams . . . I seem to spend my time reliving that awful day wondering how I could have saved Harry and Crystal. I caused the death of them both.'

'That's not what Colonel Martin and your brother officers said. They said you tried to save Harry, and then refused to leave the bodies. You had to be dragged away. That was scarcely the behaviour of a coward. They'd hardly recommend a coward for the DSO.'

So much of what had happened was confused in Bosco's memory that the actual details of the action were blurred. It was as though, by his dreams, he was trying to fit it all together again like the pieces of a jigsaw puzzle. He felt he'd never know the truth. Some men had ridden through the charge completely unscathed, and whether the whole episode, which only lasted a few minutes, had been a success or a failure was still a matter of debate. The Lancers had lost as many men as the Dervishes. It didn't stop them going on into Omdurman, which anyway was taken by the British without a fight after the Khalifa had fled. Whether or not it was a strategic success, the charge entered the military annals as a heroic, historic occasion. Two other officers were awarded the Victoria Cross and the Sirdar himself saw the regiment off when it went back to the Atbara, the only one to which he gave the honour. Like their brother officers of the 17th Lancers, who immortalized themselves at Balaclava in the Crimea, the 21st had earned themselves a niche in history.

There was a knock at the door and Dulcie popped her head round. 'Ah, I see you're awake, dearest. And how is my boy today?' She glided towards his bed, ignoring Flora, and sat down by his side, her cool hand on his brow. 'Did you sleep well?'

'I slept very well last night, Mama.' He glanced at Flora. 'The angel by my side.'

There was a good deal of rivalry between his mother and Flora. In his well moments he enjoyed playing one against the other. Flora clearly had the upper hand because she had been with him longest, but as soon as they came home their mother asserted her personality to dominate the sickroom. One thing, however, she didn't like was missing her sleep, so night-time duties were happily relegated to Flora.

Dulcie, fresh now, fragrant, youthful – looking beautifully coiffeured as always, dressed in a pretty pink woollen two-piece with a cashmere vest just visible beneath five long rows of pearls – was prepared for day duty. She looked dismissively at Flora whom she had never quite forgiven for defying her wishes and staying on in Egypt.

'Charles will shave Bosco and prepare him for the day. Why don't you take a rest, dear? Your poor eyes will be quite weak with all this reading.'

Bosco sat upright in his bed. 'Mama, today I'm getting up. I feel very much better. I'm getting up, getting dressed. I'm well.' Each day Bosco had got up for a few hours, but he always remained in his dressing-gown.

'Do you think it's *wise*, dear?' his mother said doubtfully. 'Doctor Fraser said . . .'

'Doctor Fraser said that when I wanted to get dressed I

might,' he tapped his head. 'He said my only illness now was in the mind.'

'What rot that is, Bosco. There's nothing wrong with your mind. You have nightmares, who wouldn't after the harrowing experience you went through? I know I'd never sleep again.'

'He still feels Harry's death, Mama . . .' Flora lowered her eyes, 'and that of Captain Crystal.'

'But you tried to *save* their lives,' his mother said impulsively. 'Captain Steele saw you throw yourself against the Dervish who was about to kill Harry.'

'But Harry died and Crystal had no need. He should have got a medal, not I.'

'Ah, poor Cardew . . .' The mention of his name was still sufficient to bring a flush to her carefully powdered cheeks. It was rather like uncovering a family skeleton. The fact that no one talked about it made it worse. Those who knew didn't dare, and those who didn't couldn't. Cardew Crystal was spoken of like any other brave soldier who'd died in the field, with respect, unemotionally, but with an added reverence because Bosco said he'd saved his life. No one but Bosco, however, had seen enough to corroborate this. 'Oh, I had a letter,' she said quickly, glad to change the subject, and producing a crumpled envelope from her cardigan. 'The Bolingbrokes would like to come and see you.'

'Adam is back?' Bosco sat up excitedly.

'Yes, with that extraordinary sister of his. She wants to visit too.'

'Oh Mama! How lovely.' Flora jumped up and put out her hand for the letter. 'When? May I see?'

'Whenever it suits *us*, of course,' her mother said tersely. 'I would suggest tea on . . .'

'Mama, you can't just invite them to *tea* when they come all the way from Bath.' Flora scanned the page.

'You don't want them to stay, do you, dear?'

'Of course we want them to stay, don't we, Bosco?'

'But not while your brother's unwell and Melanie . . .'

'Mama, I'm better. Seeing Adam again will make me even more so. Melanie is quite well too. Pregnancy is not an illness.'

'I don't know what you see in those Bolingbrokes,' Dulcie said abstractedly. 'They're not at all our kind of people.'

'He saved my life, Mama. Aren't you grateful for that?'

'Of course I'm grateful to Mr Bolingbroke though I understand a number of men came to your aid. You're exaggerating in your impulsive, generous way.'

'Without Adam I'd be dead. Like Harry and Crystal.' Bosco's face assumed that familiar, haunted look his mother knew so well and he slumped back on his pillows. 'Please invite him to stay.'

'Whatever you wish, dearest, but with Melanie near her time do you think it really a good thing?' Dulcie appealed for help to Flora.

'I think it would cheer her up too, Mama.' Flora's tone was matter-of-fact. 'After all we have no fears for Melanie.'

Dulcie sat heavily down in the chair next to Bosco's bed. '*I* fear for Melanie, poor creature, a mother with no husband to care for her, no father for her child.'

'But she has us. She has her youth.'

'Melanie is sad too,' Dulcie produced her handkerchief and gave a sniff. 'Sometimes I fear for her more than for poor dear Bosco.'

'There's no need to fear for Melanie nor for me, Mother,' Bosco said, feeling suddenly agitated. 'We both have our family. In this she will be more fortunate than many a young woman widowed in the war. The Lightermans have provided for her well . . .'

'It's not the *money*,' Dulcie removed a speck of invisible dust from her skirt. 'It's having them as *relatives* that worries me. Grandparents of the same child. Do you realize we'll *never* be free of them?' She looked wanly from Flora to Bosco. 'They will have a right to see Melanie and her baby for the rest of their lives. Oh, the pity of it! That Melanie should be so briefly married, and unhappily, to such an unsuitable man. If it hadn't been for him Bosco would not have been so severely wounded and . . .'

'Harry tried to save my life, Mama, and lost his own. I would have tried to save Harry whether he was my brother-in-law or not. I really don't like to hear you speaking of him or the Lightermans like this. They have been kindness itself to Mel and me. Nor do I like the way you speak about the Bolingbrokes. You must realize, Mama, that the days when we didn't mix with people like that are gone. Long gone, and best forgotten. This is a new age.'

'And frightening too,' his mother said. 'One doesn't quite know where one is – not like the old days.'

Rachel Bolingbroke sat nervously on the edge of her chair, a teacup in her hand. On one side of her was Adam, also not at ease, and opposite, as though ranged against them, the Askham family seemed to resemble the bulwark of the Establishment, as unfamiliar as, and slightly more fearsome, in Adam's opinion, than a row of Dervishes.

Seen in their natural, familiar environment, the four members of the family they knew seemed to bear little resemblance to the people they'd met in Cairo; the soldier Adam had fought with so bravely, and the enthusiastic Egyptologist with whom Rachel had shared lodgings during those hot, frightening months when she'd gone daily to the hospital to visit Bosco.

For days they'd debated whether to accept the invitation at all. All they had intended was to stop by for tea and then stay at a local hotel. Looking at them now, both wished they'd stuck to their original intention. Not that the Askhams hadn't been kindness itself; Flora actually running down the steps to greet them, throwing herself into Rachel's arms as the carriage sent for them arrived at the imposing portal of Askham Hall, itself almost a mile away from the main road.

But now, by chance or forethought – Adam wasn't sure which – the Askhams sat on one side of the fire burning in the grate of the massive drawing-room, the Bolingbrokes on the other. The sofa itself was vast and could have taken six more people, at least, and on an identical piece of furniture opposite them, similarly richly upholstered in pink-and-oyster brocade, sat Lord and Lady Askham with their daughter Melanie and ranged on chairs on either side were Bosco and Flora. Between them was the tea table that seemed to have the significance of a dividing line between two opposing formations drawn up for battle.

Which was a ridiculous idea. Adam shifted uneasily, teacup in one hand, plate, on which reposed a solitary iced cake, on his knee. Maybe it was that the Askhams seemed to wear smiles that were fixed rather than genuine; although there had been nothing insincere about the welcome of Flora and Bosco who, still limping, had waited for them at the top of the staircase that seemed to go on for ever from gravelled driveway to porch.

Melanie looked very much changed which was not unexpected as, besides her widowhood, she was nine months pregnant, her bulk concealed by a cleverly cut maternity dress which hung directly from a frill at her throat in long flowing folds. Next to her Lord Askham seemed the very quintessence of the aristocratic Englishman, his blood almost wholly empurpled by centuries of aristocratic inbreeding. He was a very large man lengthwise, not fat, but his bulk was considerable. He wore morning suit because he had travelled down from London, having spent the forenoon at the House of

Lords. He had a very long, lined, well-set face with bushy eyebrows over humorous contented brown eyes, and a thick full moustache, like Lord Kitchener, though this was greying now as was his hair, thick and curly at the sides, brushed straight back and rather sparse on top.

All in all the tenth Earl of Askham looked what he was – powerful, rich, formidable, a ruler, a judge of men.

Next to him, Lady Askham wore a tea gown in palest green with an elegant bell-shaped skirt embroidered at the hem, and full bishop-style sleeves, ending in tight folds of lace over hands which were neatly clasped together on her lap. The Bolingbrokes were, of course, quite used to seeing Lady Askham thus poised and beautifully dressed; but in her own home, in the proximity of her Lord, she appeared more gracious, not quite so formidable as she had when holding court on the verandah of Shepheard's Hotel in Cairo, or at her daughter's wedding party. As his lordship was the stereotype of what he was expected to be, so did his wife seem the embodiment of Victorian propriety – feminine, grand and, in the presence of her husband, just a little docile. In the warm security of Askham and all it stood for, the naughty world of flirtations, dalliance, of the sordid little Achmed and the scheming Madame Hassim, of blackmail, seemed very, very far away.

But Bosco and Flora were the same, smiling and friendly across those acres of space, if a little tongue-tied as people are when time has passed since they last saw one another.

As tea was served by a cohort of well-trained servants – each with his or her function, whether it was to carry trays, set the tiny tables by each person, pour the tea or hand round sandwiches and cakes – the talk had been about Bosco, his journey from Cairo and his slow recovery. There was a brief mention of Captain Crystal, very brief, and then a rather longer discussion of Harry and his bravery, a tribute to the fallen hero, the dead husband, the father of Melanie's unborn baby. Melanie had sat, taking very little part in the conversation as though it had nothing much to do with her, looking ahead of her towards the fire.

'Shocking business,' Lord Askham said resting the saucer of his teacup uncomfortably on his massive knee. 'Very sad and very shocking.' He sipped his tea and then brushed the back of his hand against his moustache, finishing with an expert flourish on either side. 'I feel if I'd been there they would never have married at all.'

'Oh Papa,' Melanie jerked her head away from the fire. 'You know that's not true. What had to be had to be.'

'It didn't *have* to be at all, my dear. I'm not saying you didn't love Harry, I know you did,' he looked behind him to make sure that all the servants had departed. 'I'm just saying the marriage was too hasty, unwise . . . and now . . .' His glance rested sadly on the concealing folds of her dress.

'Dearest, you did cable your permission,' his wife's tone was placating, accompanied by a bright smile at the Bolingbrokes. Her husband was the only person in the world she found more formidable than herself and, in public at least, she always addressed him with just that right note of deference expected of an obedient wife.

'I relied on your good judgment, my dear. I wonder now just how good it was.'

'*Pas devant les enfants*, please, Fred,' Dulcie whispered loudly, looking at Melanie. 'It's all over now, sadly. I don't wish our guests to think we are quarrelling.'

'But Rachel is like a sister to me,' Flora looked fondly at her nervous guest. 'I'm sure she doesn't mind this family talk at all.'

'Not at all,' Rachel murmured and Bosco smiled at her and crossed his legs, swinging back in his chair.

'Harry was a very sound fellow, Father, and I'm sure Mel is tired of this talk.'

'I'll go up and lie down for a while anyway,' Melanie rose awkwardly to her feet. 'I slept very badly last night.'

'Shall I come with you, dearest?' her mother looked at her as one woman who has borne children looks at others who have yet to undergo the same misfortune.

'Oh no, Mama, it's quite unnecessary, and please nobody bother to get up.'

As the men started to rise they sat down again; only Bosco went to the door and opened it for her, kissing her on the cheek as she passed.

'Bad business,' her father shook his head after she'd gone.

'Don't start again, Fred, please,' Dulcie intervened, but Frederick Askham continued as one used to having his way.

'She doesn't even mourn him. He has left her with nothing but sorrow.'

'I'm sure the baby will give Lady Melanie much happiness,' Rachel murmured and Bosco looked at her gratefully.

'We shall all love the little fellow, or girl, whatever it is. We shall take it to our hearts.'

'And you, Miss Bolingbroke, when did you come home?' Lady Askham held out her hand for her husband's cup. 'I was telling Lord Askham all about your adventures.'

'I came home with Adam. He is to leave the army.'

'Oh?'

'I never meant to make a career of it, Lady Askham, merely a year or two.' Adam looked apologetic, as though he somehow had to account for his behaviour to these people.

'Sickened by the war no doubt.'

'I meant to leave it anyway; but, yes, I did find the slaughter disgusting and also unnecessary. We should have sent the Khalifa an ultimatum once we had shown him the strength of our guns. It was like a massacre.'

'Those Dervishes needed a good hiding.' Lord Askham looked at him sharply. 'Don't tell me they didn't get what they deserved. That Mahdi fellow was detestable, you know, an out and out rogue.'

'In his day he was a true patriot, sir. He was against the exploitation of his people by the Egyptian slavers.'

'Before our time, of course,' Lord Askham nodded. 'But after the British took over in Egypt all that slavery business stopped – well, in most cases. If the Mahdi was once a patriot, a zealot for reform, he soon changed his tune and became cruel, blood-hungry and a lecher to boot. The Khalifa, his successor, was no better. And his followers became just like their masters, committing the most awful atrocities against innocent people.

'Oh no, they had to be wiped out after what they did to poor Gordon.' Lord Askham looked solemn for a while. 'Funny fellow though he was; bit of a fanatic too.'

'Yet, though primitive, the Dervish was a brave fighter, sir, the bravest men I ever saw or ever thought to see.'

'Savages have no feelings,' Lord Askham drained his cup and placed it on the small table in front of him, as though having the last word. 'I believe it is a scientific fact that they do not actually have the physical sensitivity that we civilized people have.'

'You mean they don't suffer, sir?' Adam tried hard to keep the anger out of his voice. 'They don't thirst? I saw them myself, with the most frightful wounds, crawling piteously towards the Nile.'

'Like animals. An animal wants water too. You need have no worries about the feelings of the savages, my dear fellow.'

'You weren't actually there, Father.' Bosco, carefully listening to the exchange, uncrossed his legs. 'I don't see how you can possibly know what you're talking about. I've told you a thousand times how really brave the Dervishes were. They earned the admiration of the entire

British Army who saw them. To say they have no feelings is absurd.'

'Dearest, please don't be rude to your father,' Dulcie smiled placatingly at Bosco. 'I know you're not quite yourself, but . . .'

'But I *am* myself, Mother. I am also tired of Father talking as if the only people in the world with any feelings were the British. He looks down upon every soul who has the misfortune to be born south of Dover.'

'My dear boy,' his father's tone was condescending, 'I'm taking into consideration the fact that you have been very unwell. In fact it's a miracle you're here today with us at all. We know that, and we are grateful for it. I was kept fully informed of the situation in the Sudan, not just for one campaign but for the two years before it ended. I assure you I know what I'm talking about. So kindly don't argue with me or attempt to tell me my business.'

'It's a business you know nothing about directly, Father! Running wars from behind a desk!' Bosco jumped up and went to stand in front of the fire, his hands behind his back, his chin thrust out before him. Lord Askham, in a long life devoted to public service, was accustomed to concealing his emotions. His noble features scarcely ever changed colour, as they did now, going from natural white to an unhealthy shade of red. Visibly and painfully he tried to regain his control of himself while his wife swiftly intervened:

'Dearest Bosco, please don't provoke your father. It must be very embarrassing for Mr and Miss Bolingbroke.'

'I wish you'd call us Rachel and Adam, Lady Askham. After all, I know Flora so well.' Rachel was grateful for the interruption.

'Ah yes, and you and she lived together in Cairo.' As Lord Askham's customary *sang-froid* returned, he seemed to study his guest with interest. 'And whereas I'm sure it was an experience for Flora, it is not one I'd wish her to repeat. I am not in favour of unmarried women alone abroad, I must tell you that in all honesty, Miss Bolingbroke. In fact I think all women do well to travel with an escort or chaperone. Abroad can be a very dangerous place. When my wife and daughters went together I could not think that any harm would come to them.'

'And none came, dear.' Dulcie looked at him sweetly. Even after the passage of time she could never quite rid herself of the fear that he would hear about Crystal and the odious Achmed.

'None came?' Her husband returned her glance indignantly. '*None* came, you say? Yet my daughter returns home, briefly and unhappily married to a man unworthy of her, and expecting his child, while my elder daughter remains behind, by herself. A circumstance I utterly deplored. And yet you say you came to no harm. I tell you, my dear, it will be a long time before I allow any of the female members of my family to travel abroad unescorted again!'

'Father, you talk like an old flibberty-gibbet. First the Dervishes and now women. I can't think what our visitors will think.'

'You really are distressing your father and us, Bosco dear,' Dulcie said looking at him warningly. 'You're not yourself.'

'In that case I'll go,' Bosco said abruptly. 'I'll see you all at dinner.'

As he walked quickly from the room Lord Askham avoided looking at him and Dulcie slipped a hand in his.

'He's far from well. The war still preys on his mind . . .'

'I think it preys on the minds of us all, Lady Askham,' Adam said quietly. 'We saw sights that day I never in my mind thought to see and can never forget. I really am sorry that we have intruded. We meant just a courtesy call, not to take advantage of your hospitality. Please let us go tonight to a hotel . . .'

'My dear Mr Bolingbroke,' Dulcie looked shocked. 'I wouldn't *dream* of such a thing. You must think us the most inhospitable family in the world and I assure you we are not always like this, at sixes and sevens.'

'Of course you'll stay. What nonsense,' Lord Askham said peremptorily. 'We have a little party tomorrow night – in honour of my eldest son and his new fiancée. They'll join us later. You're here for the weekend. Now – what do you say tomorrow to a little hunting, Mr Bolingbroke?'

'I'm afraid I don't hunt, my lord.'

'Don't hunt?' Lord Askham looked aghast. 'You have *never* hunted?'

'I'm afraid not.'

'We've no horses you see, Lord Askham,' Rachel smiled apologetically. 'We are used to a very different style of life from this.'

'If you can ride you can hunt,' Lord Askham ignored her. 'You're a cavalry officer, aren't you?'

'I've no clothes for hunting, sir.'

'You can borrow Bosco's clothes. Good sport.' Lord Askham tenderly stroked his moustache. 'My son Arthur hunts and so does Frances, the gel. If you can ride you can hunt.'

So the matter was settled.

CHAPTER 6

The Master of the Askham hunt raised his stirrup cup and toasted those – family, visitors and servants – gathered on the steps of the Hall to see them off. The pink-coated male members of the hunt and the ladies in black riding habits clustered round him as the servants moved among the hunters collecting the empty glasses.

Adam sat uncomfortably upon a huge roan. It was not that he felt awkward on a horse, but he had never hunted before and although Bosco's hunting clothes fitted him he felt uneasy in them. There had been a good deal of chaffing and laughter as Bosco helped him dress, but Adam hadn't joined in the fun, nor had he appreciated the well-meant advice to keep his eyes on the fox because the horse knew the route backwards. Condensed breaths from horses, dogs and humans formed vaporous clouds in the air which hummed with excited voices, laughter, the yelp of hounds and the pawing of horses as they awaited the signal to be off.

As he waited to one side of the gathering, Rachel gazed anxiously at Adam from the steps and raised a hand encouragingly to cheer him on. Lord Gore raised his hat to his mother and joined his father, the Master, as the hunters grouped themselves around the pack and the huntsmen put their horns to their lips. They all set off at a brisk trot down the drive towards the great ornate iron gates a mile away. Certainly it was a pretty sight, the pink and the black, the mottled colours of the hounds and horses outlined against the wintry, frost-covered landscape and the dark green of the firs in the forest beyond the lake.

Arthur Gore's fiancée, Lady Frances Crewe, galloped off with the rest, but Melanie couldn't and Flora didn't hunt. Lady Askham often hunted, but today she had many things to do for the small party she was having in the evening in honour of Frances and Arthur who had recently decided to marry. Bosco wished to hunt, but the doctor thought he was still too weak and should have some gentle practice in the saddle before he started chasing after foxes. He stood watching them thoughtfully until they were out of sight.

'Cheer up,' Flora said, linking her arm through his.

'I'm quite cheerful, but Adam looked none too happy. He's been blooded, poor fellow. Well, better the fox than a pack of Dervishes.'

'I thought he did look awfully nervous,' Flora followed his gaze. 'I don't think you should have forced him to go.'

'I didn't force him. Father wished it and, as we know, Father's wish is law.'

'I wish you wouldn't argue so much with your father.' Dulcie took Bosco's other arm as they walked back into the house. 'It upsets him. You know, he *does* know such a lot about things, and is a close friend of Lord Kitchener.'

'He doesn't know about Dervishes, Mother, and we do. I can't have Father constantly telling me my own business. He thinks I'm a child.'

'Then you'll have to learn, my dear, to curb your temper because as long as you are part of this household your father must and will have the last word. He was very upset last night.'

'I'm sure Adam will enjoy himself.' Rachel hurried along behind them. 'He's just a trifle nervous, never having hunted. But he is an excellent horseman.'

'He has to be blooded.' Bosco turned to her. 'You should have gone too.'

'I can't even ride.'

The Askhams exchanged those secretive, family

glances, making Rachel once more feel an outsider. Even Flora who didn't hunt rode well, and her unwitting connivance reminded Rachel of their status in this closely knit family whose friends and acquaintances were all like themselves. Adam, correctly dressed and mounted, looked nevertheless rather absurd, the stranger in unfamiliar surroundings.

'I'm going to see Mel,' Bosco announced going towards the broad staircase which led from the vast tiled hall, branching halfway so that the first floor could be approached from two sides.

'Shouldn't you rest, darling?'

'I *am* rested, Mother. I wasn't at breakfast and I'm told Mel wasn't either. Don't keep on about this, just because I can't hunt.'

'Doctor Fraser said . . .'

'Doctor Fraser wants his fee . . .' Bosco looked angrily back at her. 'I'm quite better and next week I'll be riding.'

'Very well, then. I must go and see Mrs Daintry who wants to discuss the seating plans for tonight. I wonder what time the Lightermans arrive?'

'The Lightermans are coming?' Bosco looked surprised.

'Just for the night, for the party. I could hardly not invite them. Besides they are very anxious to see you. I believe they want to go to Omdurman to see the place poor Harry died.'

'Well, I don't want to talk about it,' Bosco said, and vanished up the stairs.

Rachel and Flora went into the drawing-room, from the bow windows of which they could see the tail end of the hunters as they reached a turn in the drive.

'I do hope Adam *will* be all right,' Rachel said. 'I feel a bit nervous about him.'

'Oh, you mustn't be,' Flora steered her firmly away from the window. 'Would you like a walk in the park?'

Suddenly to be out of doors, away from this huge

enveloping house, seemed attractive and Rachel went upstairs to fetch her coat.

When she came down Flora awaited her. She was warmly enveloped in a cloak with a hood and looked rather like a peasant which made Rachel in her coat and tight-fitting felt hat feel a little too female, even overdressed. It was quite obvious to her that whatever one did at Askham Hall, whatever one said or wore, was bound to be wrong. Either you dressed one way and the family dressed another, or you said something and the family said something else.

'You're very confident, aren't you,' she remarked to Flora as they followed the path between the rhododendron bushes that led down to the lake. 'I admire that.'

'I?'

'Your family.'

'You mustn't be put off by my father. He always acts in front of people, but by himself he's terribly sweet. He and Bosco have always aggravated each other, and now he feels very guilty that Bosco was so badly wounded.'

'But why would he feel guilty?'

'Because Bosco didn't really want to go into the army. It was always decided that he should, and he had no choice.'

'You mean he couldn't choose for himself?'

'Not really. He was named after our uncle, Bosco Kitto, my mother's brother who covered himself with glory in the Ashanti campaign, and the talk was always of Uncle Bosco and how our own Bosco would be like him.'

'Well, he has. He got a medal. Your father should feel very proud.'

'But had he died like Harry what would he have felt then?'

'What any parent or widow feels – remorse, grief, certainly pride. But I don't see how anyone can blame himself if a full-grown adult makes a choice. Bosco could always have said "no".'

'Oh, but he couldn't. I don't think you understand.'

They came to the lake and stood silently for a moment looking at it, and upon the house beyond. They could hear the horns of the hunt, though it was going in the opposite direction across open fields and away from the forest; but the sound was carried a long way over the still air. Rachel sighed deeply.

It was so peaceful: the still water, the clear sky and the crackle of their feet on the crisp, frost-covered leaves as they began to skirt the edge of the forest. A family of mallards sailed pompously across the lake, breaking the surface with a wash the ripples of which fanned out to the water's edge on either side. Several seagulls, driven inland by the weather, dived low over the water and on the far bank a thick spiral of smoke rose through the trees as two of the estate's gardeners heaped forkfuls of fresh, damp foliage upon a pile of burning leaves, producing a rich, pungent smell.

From where they stood the house rose above them as though on a hill although, in fact, the lake was in a dip in the ground between Askham Hall and the forest. It was difficult to imagine now, gazing at the vast eighteenth-century mansion built of white Chilmark stone, that it had once been a tiny hunting lodge used by the first Barons Askham in the fouteenth century. Gradually it had evolved into a large Tudor house built of red brick interlaced with beams. The whole had been pulled down by the architecture-crazy sixth Earl who had engaged James Wyatt, a rival and contemporary of Robert Adam, to construct a building on strictly neo-classical lines with an orthodox central block, a huge plain portico facing on to the gravelled drive and side pavilions attached to it by colonnades.

At the back of the house, on which they were now looking, a terrace ran the entire length from east to west. A flight of steps led to a smaller terrace, below which were the sunken gardens and then the field of scrub and grass –

covered with daffodils in the spring – which swept down to the lake.

As Rachel gazed upon the whole harmonious structure, she thought that the large windows seemed almost like wise old eyes gazing dispassionately down upon these modern women poised on the edge of a new century. On all sides of them were the different cries of birds as they flitted in and out among the trees, beneath the eaves of the roof, interrupted occasionally by the sound of the horn growing ever more faint as the hunt moved beyond the village.

Rachel was the first to break the silence and, taking up a small stone, threw it into the waters of the lake disturbed only slightly by the wash of the ducks which had reached the far end. 'It must be magical to belong to a place like this. It must influence one's life.'

'It does influence one's life,' Flora replied. 'Not always for the best, though, beautiful as it is. You asked me why Bosco went into the army. Well, he had to, because Arthur as the heir will inherit all this, and the lands and the money. For Bosco it was either the church or the army. It has always been like that with younger sons. As for Melanie, she wanted to be married to get away from this. Funny, isn't it? You see in a way we've all been stifled to death – that is, three of us have, not Arthur. He is an Askham through and through. He sits for the Borough of Askham in Parliament and he is at home here as my father was before him and his father before that. The elder sons have always conformed but the younger children have often been rebels, like us. My father knows that and thinks he can keep us by bending us to his will. All we wish to do is flee. Rachel, I wished to talk to you alone today because when Bosco is quite better I want to live in London. I wondered if we could share with each other as we did in Cairo? Maybe we could take a small house in Marylebone or Mayfair – I would pay the best part, of course, and . . . would you like that?'

Rachel looked at her friend, her eyes anxious, behind gold-rimmed spectacles which were misted over with the cold winter air. 'I am going to live with Adam.'

'Oh, I didn't know.'

'You didn't know he was leaving the army?'

'He really does mean to?'

'He has begun the process of buying himself out. It will be very costly for our father who wishes him to read for the Bar. We in fact have seen a house near Gray's Inn, in one of those little streets on the other side of Lamb's Conduit. But why can't you stay with us?' Rachel put a hand on her arm excitedly. 'Oh, that would be such fun.'

'I don't know that my mother would allow it. She is frightfully old-fashioned.'

'You mean because of Adam?' Rachel laughed. 'But you would be chaperoned and we would have a maid. Surely she wouldn't object to that?'

'Well, I haven't told her any of this yet, of course. This may make it a little bit harder. She would prefer me to live in our town house, because Father and Arthur are there most of the week, and she sometimes too. But I shall resist that.'

'But what will you do, Flora? Have you thought about that? Won't you be bored in London with nothing to do?'

'I shan't be doing nothing,' Flora said rather sharply. 'I intend to do a higher degree, become a Doctor of Philosophy of London University. I have already filled in the papers and with my Cambridge degree they will gladly have me. I intend to pursue Egyptian studies and, hopefully, will go again to Cairo in the winter. Maybe you will come with me?'

Rachel grimaced. 'I have to work. My father can't support Adam and me.'

'Work? What work will you do?'

'You know Mrs Fawcett?'

'The leading suffragist? I've heard of her.'

'She is finding me office work to help the movement. So I'll be working in something I like.'

Flora frowned. 'Goodness knows what Mama will have to say to that!'

When they returned to the house it was to find it bustling with activity as the great dining-room was set for dinner and the upstairs drawing-room made ready for a reception afterwards to which local people were invited.

Because Melanie was imminently expecting her baby and Bosco not quite recovered from his injury, Dulcie had not had the large house-party she would have normally entertained for such an occasion, and the numerous guest rooms on the second floor remained closed. The fifty servants who ran the house had seldom known such little entertaining, but many idle hands were occupied in polishing, scrubbing, varnishing, mending and restoring the priceless family furniture and treasures. No servant, certainly those with a long family association with the house, would have dreamt of slacking: they felt for Askham Hall more than mere duty. Most of them were bound by ties of close affection, even love, such as they might have for their own homes and so they put into the house something of themselves, something that would hopefully be shared by their children and their children after them.

The house was a reflection of their pride, and the family simply an extension of their own hopes and aspirations. Now with Lady Melanie a widow and expecting, and Mr Down a wounded hero, the entire staff, like the rest of the family, were content to bide their time to wait for their recovery.

A light luncheon was served in the small dining-room where the family, when they were alone, sometimes dined quietly. Bosco and Melanie were already there when Flora and Rachel arrived and Lady Askham was looking anxiously towards the door because the routine of the house was precisely timed.

'I'm so sorry, Mama,' Flora breathlessly slipped into her seat. 'We went an awful long way.'

'It was such a heavenly day for a walk,' Rachel added. 'Forgive us, please.'

'Certainly you are forgiven,' Dulcie smiled graciously and rang the bell. 'Tell me, Miss Bolingbroke, how do you like Askham?'

'What can one say, Lady Askham? It is enchanting. How many rooms are there in the house?'

Dulcie sat back as the door opened and the servants bearing dishes entered, and made a pretence of counting on her fingers. 'I think there are about two hundred; but no one has counted for a long time. My husband's grandfather was a very keen builder and made a few additions that now no one ever uses, to the west side overlooking the conservatories.'

Rachel admitted that she hadn't even seen the conservatories, and glanced at Melanie who seemed to be enjoying a private joke with Bosco.

Seeing her expression Melanie rapidly composed her features.

'We have never seen them either,' she said, 'that's why we were laughing.'

'You mean you haven't seen parts of your own home?'

'I certainly can't recall them.'

Although it was supposed to be a light meal the luncheon consisted of soup, main course, dessert and cheese. Bosco had a glass of beer and the ladies drank water poured from crystal jugs into tall glasses engraved with the Askham crest. Looking at the table it was hard to think that this was a casual meal because there was a full setting of silver apart from a number of plates, glasses, condiment sets and, on the sideboard, enough tureens, entrée dishes and plates to feed a party three times as large. Certainly in her small home, Rachel reflected, this would constitute the main meal.

They were waited on by the under-butler, two maids and a footman – the steward and the butler being engaged in supervising preparations for the evening in the great dining-room next door.

There was nothing in the Askham household, Rachel decided, that wasn't done on such a scale and in such proportions as to make someone like herself and Adam feel that they came from the very lowest stratum of under-privileged society. In her own home they had a cook and two maids and she often baked the bread and nearly always assisted in some aspect of the housework. She was an able needlewoman and did all the darning and mended all the clothes.

Luncheon was soon over and the servants swiftly cleared away to set the table again for those who were expected to partake of a buffet collation after the hunt. Lady Askham went off with Flora to oversee some arrangements, Melanie and Bosco to their respective rooms to rest and Rachel was about to go into the library to select a book to read – having been assured that she could be of no help to anyone – when she saw a lone horseman dressed in hunting pink gallop up the drive and, dismounting, run breathlessly up the steps and hammer on the door.

The footman who was on permanent duty in or near the hall rushed to open the door and Rachel remained by the library door, her curiosity aroused.

'Fetch Lady Askham or Lady Flora,' the rider gasped. 'One of the hunters has met with an accident.'

The man removed his black top hat and came into the hall while the footman ran towards the servants' quarters to find out where her ladyship would be. Black-coated servants began dashing in and out of the hall going from one room to another and up the stairs and in a moment, it seemed, one arrived with Lady Askham and Flora discovered in some nether part of the building.

'Why, Andrew,' Lady Askham said, recognizing the hunter as one of the servants. 'Whatever is the matter?'

'A gentleman has fallen and broken his leg, Lady Askham, maybe his back. His lordship says he mustn't be moved and begs your ladyship to send a coach for him at once. Someone else has gone for the doctor.'

Dulcie raised both hands to her cheeks. 'My goodness, whoever is it?'

'It's the gentleman as has never hunted, my lady. He fell over the big fence between the paddock and the meadow. I think his name is something "broke".'

'Bolingbroke,' Rachel cried, running into the hall. 'Oh take me to him quickly.'

'Yes, Captain Bolingbroke, ma'am. He's in a bad way, I'm sorry to say. Are you his wife, ma'am?'

'His sister.'

Dulcie was immediately in control of the situation.

'You, dear Miss Bolingbroke, and Flora take the largest carriage which is very comfortable and I will follow in the Victoria to make sure that poor Adam is returned swiftly to the house. Dear me, how unfortunate! And on this day of all days.'

The buzz of conversation and the sound of music stealing in through the half-open window seemed to accentuate the quietness of the room where Adam lay. Only his laboured breathing occasionally caused Rachel to walk from the window and gaze upon his face, ghost-like in the yellow light of the lamp by his bedside. The anxiety of all those hours since she had seen him lying like a corpse on the frost-covered ground, his leg bent grotesquely under him, had taken their toll. Despite the knowledge that his only injuries were concussion, extensive bruising and a compound fracture of the femur, she felt unable to join the revelries taking place below.

Doctor Fraser was already there when the little party from the Hall had arrived and, for a time, there was some concern because no one knew how long he'd been unconscious. He hadn't been missed from the hunt until he was found by an advance party on its way back, and could have lain there in the bitter cold for at least an hour or maybe two. The doctor had travelled back in the carriage with Adam and Rachel and by the time they got to the house all was in readiness for the reception of the injured man: water-bottles in his bed and four stalwart servants standing in the hall to carry him upstairs.

Their arrival had coincided with that of Sir Robert and Lady Lighterman and the latter, who had been a nurse, insisted on helping the doctor despite her finery, and together they had set his leg.

By nightfall Adam had recovered consciousness and, as the guests began to arrive, the doctor had pronounced his patient quite out of danger and had gone to see Melanie who had complained of pains during the afternoon.

Anyone else but Dulcie Askham would have been overwhelmed by the day's disasters – Adam brought back unconscious from the hunt and her daughter complaining of labour pains – just when she was expecting a hundred people for an evening party, to say nothing of the members of the hunt to be fed as they drifted disconsolately back, having failed to find the fox. But no, Askham Hall was geared to accommodate any emergency large or small and the huge staff went about their duties with the precision of the complement of a British man o'war, which was sometimes what her ladyship thought the Hall resembled – a large well-maintained battleship ready for any event, short of sinking.

Thus while maidservants ran up and down the stairs with hot water and dressings, while the doctor set the injured man's leg, and a contingent prepared for a similar service in case Lady Melanie's labour should continue, others quietly continued with their preparations in the large dining-room and the great reception room upstairs where the guests were to be entertained. A small orchestra which had travelled from Winchester was even tuning its instruments when at last Doctor Fraser left and the first carriage drew up in the drive.

The kitchen staff, the French chef, his assistant cooks and the various minions and scullery maids had been busy from early morning; fetching and preparing the game from the store in the yard; the beef, turkeys, tongues, chickens and hams from the cold larder; cleaning and cooking the vegetables, dressing the salads and mixing the puddings in great round vats.

In the still room the still-room maid had for days been preparing her jams, jellies, custards, minces and aspics with which, in the bakehouse, the master baker and his assistants got to work early on the day itself. From early morning they were kneading the dough for bread and rolls which were formed into intricate shapes before being baked in the hot ovens. The final decorations were put on cakes, and the fillings provided by the still-room maid, into tarts, pies, flans and tiny savoury canapés.

During the day, as well as breakfast and tea, they were to serve a small luncheon for the family, a buffet for the hunting party, a full dinner for thirty in the dining-room and a cold collation for the hundred or so people expected for the evening reception. The wines, selected days before by the butler, had been fetched from the cellar by the cellarman, and champagne had been put into coolers filled with ice from the large icebox.

Gardeners had spent the morning bringing in shrubs and fresh flowers from the hothouse – camellias, carnations, gardenias with assorted greenery to adorn the tables and fill the large vases in the drawing-room, and the housekeeper and her staff had spent hours arranging them.

Doctor Fraser had declared that Melanie was in no imminent danger of producing her offspring and had departed for London where he was to attend a dinner given by his old hospital. Adam was left in the care of his sister and the hospitality of Lady Askham who, in addition to everything else she had to think of that day, had done her very best to get Rachel to come down to dinner.

But Rachel's humiliation was now complete. In twenty-four short hours both she and Adam had dismally failed to keep up the standards expected by the Askhams. Lord Askham had not once sent to ask after him, showing, by his singular absence of curiosity, exactly what he felt about an officer of the cavalry who was incompetent enough to fall off his horse.

Rest, Doctor Fraser had said. Adam must not be moved from his bed for at least a week and, pressing her face once more against the cool window-pane as she looked upon the beautiful park drenched in moonlight, Rachel felt close to tears.

As she studied her reflection in the window-pane she saw not one face but two; there was a footfall behind her, a hand on her shoulder.

'How is he?'

'Bosco! I didn't hear you come in.'

'I came on tiptoe. Why, Rachel, you're crying.'

His finger brushed her cheek and he let it linger, his eyes gazing into hers. The gesture was immediate, intimate, embarrassing, and she brushed his finger away, taking a step back. In his evening dress Bosco looked very splendid, yet his attraction to her was not overpowering, being too unsubtle, suggestive and reminiscent of the fact that he found all women attractive, not just herself.

'Why did you do that?'

'Do what?'

'Brush my finger away?'

'Need you ask why? I'm weary, that's all. I feel upset and also unhappy about what's happened here.'

Bosco reverted to his brotherly role and sat on the end of Adam's bed.

'My dear girl, you couldn't help it. It could have happened to anyone, even Father.' He folded his arms and smiled. 'There, he's upset you, hasn't he? He doesn't mean to be callous, you know. He just doesn't like being put out. But he *did* send me to ask how you and Adam were.'

'Did he?' Rachel searched his eyes.

'Yes, I said I was coming to fetch you to dance and have a glass of champagne and one of the maids is going to sit with Adam.'

'I couldn't possibly leave him.'

'But you can. Now slip along to your room and put on a nice dress and then come back and get me. I'll sit with Adam until the maid arrives. Go on, now, it's decided.'

He gave her a friendly push towards the door and she felt that if she refused it would only add to the misery she felt already.

When, half an hour later, Bosco led a transformed Cinderella into the drawing-room the heads of the couples dancing, of the ladies sitting at one side and the gentlemen standing at the other, turned curiously towards them. Rachel's evening dress was of blue taffeta with a tight-fitting bodice, a low décolletage, short bulbous sleeves and a flowing skirt flounced and trimmed with lace. She wore long white gloves fastened with tiny buttons, and her fair hair was brushed high above her forehead with a bun at the nape of her neck. No one knew who she was and there was a murmur as the more polite got on with their dancing, and the heads of those sitting out drew close together in earnest speculation. The members of the small orchestra tinkled away impervious to everything but their contribution to the gaiety of the evening, and slipped into a number by Strauss.

'Do you waltz?' Bosco murmured into her ear, placing an experienced hand round her waist and drawing her into the centre of the floor.

'As badly as I do everything else.'

'You underestimate yourself. I hear you're a wizard on Egyptian antiquities.'

'It's not quite the same thing as waltzing to Strauss.'

Bosco threw back his head and laughed joyously into her face. 'I like you a lot, you know, Rachel. Did you know I liked you so much?'

The movement helped Rachel to keep her composure, not to betray her gaucheness by a girlish blush.

'I didn't know you liked me so much, no. I didn't think we had much in common.'

'Oh, but we have,' his arm tightened round her waist. 'We both detest humbug and I think you see a lot of it here. But it's not really humbug, it's tradition . . .'

Now she did blush and swirled vigorously to try and conceal her discomfiture.

'I don't think it's humbug here at all. It's perfectly beautiful. And your parents are most gracious to us . . .'

'Besides, you're a good talker,' Bosco interrupted her. 'I'm awfully attracted to intellectual women. You know I love Flora, and she is a true bluestocking.'

'I do, it's true, feel like a country cousin here,' Rachel said rather abjectly. 'We're quite out of place.'

'You make far too much of it . . . Ah!' He stopped by a couple who were about to leave the floor. 'Have you been properly introduced to my brother's fiancée – Lady Frances? She was the first to give succour to poor Adam. Actually my leg is quite paining me. I hope you don't mind if we stop.'

'I'm glad. I mean I'm not glad your leg is hurting, but I'm a very indifferent waltzer.'

'Frances, Rachel wants to thank you for looking after Adam.'

Lady Frances, her arm through that of her fiancé, smiled regally at Rachel.

'How is poor Captain Bolingbroke?'

'He's sleeping. The doctor gave him a draught. He's just bruised and shaken and his leg is broken in two places.'

'Thank God for that. I thought he was dead.' Lady Frances shuddered and a similar spasm passed over Arthur Gore's impassive face.

'I too. I couldn't believe it when Andrew told me he was missing. We were too busy looking for that wily old fox. Frances was absolutely splendid,' Arthur confided to Bosco. 'A real Florence Nightingale. I didn't know you had it in you, my dear.'

Frances looked gratified. 'Oh, we Crewes can turn a hand to anything. I must say, Miss Bolingbroke, you look very fetching. Is your gown from London?'

'Bath,' Rachel said. 'Actually I had it made before I went to Egypt.'

'Egypt, of course,' Arthur snapped his long, practical fingers. 'I was trying to remember how Bosco and Flora knew you.'

How could they possibly *know* someone like us? Rachel thought, following the pair in front through an arch into the next room where refreshments were laid on a long low table by the window behind which stood watchful servants dressed in the Askham livery of green and gold. Dotted around the room were small tables laid with plates, knives and glasses and each one decorated with a colourful posy in a small crystal vase.

'Champagne, I think,' Bosco drew out chairs for the ladies as footmen hurried over, and Rachel and Lady Frances sat down. 'Rachel, you haven't eaten, I know. Would you like to choose or shall I select something for you?'

'You choose,' Rachel was glad to sit down even though she had hardly been on her feet. A terrible weariness seemed to overwhelm her as she looked at the elegant, well-dressed couples sauntering in from the next room and watching the crush slowly gather at the buffet table, at ease in these sumptuous surroundings.

The walls in both rooms were hung with tapestries, scenes of battle and portraits of Askham ancestors in civil or military garb, or in robes of state, the ladies and children beautifully dressed and posing against sumptuous drapes or sitting in garden glades, bathed in golden sunlight. Both ceilings were decorated with intricate three-dimensional plasterwork: lozenges, quatrefoils, rectangles and octagons filled with flowers, foliage and hunting animals, at the centre of which was an Askham heraldic device picked out in exquisite colour. There were enormous chandeliers hanging from each ceiling, aflame with thousands of tiny lights, and brightly lit sconces on the walls, Askham Hall having been one of the first great English houses to be wired for electricity.

Normally there were Aubusson carpets on the floors, but these had been taken up in both reception rooms to facilitate the dancing in one, and to protect the priceless carpets from the imprint of pointed tablelegs in the other.

'I don't think I've ever seen so much food and drink,' Rachel remarked as the footman uncorked the champagne and poured it into tall fluted glasses. 'The kitchen must be busy the whole time.'

'You should see their really big parties,' Lady Frances said. 'This is just a tiny affair on account of Bosco's injuries and Melanie, poor dear.'

Lady Frances sighed as though deprived, yet managed a wan smile as her fiancé raised his glass to her and Bosco reappeared followed by a footman carrying a huge tray of plates of food which he proceeded to lay before them: fish in aspic, tongue *en gelée*, cold beef, salads and freshly baked bread with little pots containing swirls of butter.

'We'll have a really slap-up party in the spring,' Arthur said draining his glass.

'When is the wedding?'

'At St Margaret's in the summer. We had to choose a time when the Prince and Princess of Wales were free, so their programme more or less decided the date.'

'Oh, why?' Rachel spread her napkin over her lap.

'Because he's my godfather.' Lady Frances looked astonished that someone should apparently be ignorant of this important item of information.

'I see.'

'He's my godfather as well,' Bosco put a canapé into his mouth, 'so when I get married do I have to choose a date to suit him too?'

'Of course,' Lady Frances looked surprised. 'He'll be very hurt if you don't, the sweetie.'

'But Arthur's godmother is the Queen. Is *she* not going to attend your wedding?'

'You know the poor dear Queen is too old to do anything like that,' Arthur said irritably. 'We shall go and see Her Majesty when we return from our honeymoon and get her blessing.'

'Ah, Miss Bolingbroke, there you are! I just sent to enquire after the patient. Is someone with him?'

'One of the maids, Lady Askham,' Rachel replied. 'He was sleeping when I left.'

The men got up as Lady Askham advanced upon them in a swirl of voile, the colour of champagne, with bows and flounces over an underdress of pleated silk, her chestnut-coloured hair done *à la grecque*, leaning on the arm of a young good-looking man. Rachel noticed that Lady Askham still eschewed her Christian name, maybe because she genuinely forgot but more probably to emphasize her status as someone whom the family did not consider a familiar.

'This is Major Tidy,' Dulcie drew her escort forward. 'He is in the Buffs. Like Rachel he scarcely knows a soul.'

'Except *you*, Mother,' Bosco said pointedly, getting up and offering her his seat.

'Darling, *you* know James!' His mother flashed him a meaningful smile and took the champagne Arthur held out for her. 'James is going to stay the night because he forgot to book into a hotel. James, we've got the teeniest little house-party here because we have two invalids – now, unhappily, three – in the house.'

'I hope I'm not putting you out, Lady Askham.' Major Tidy sounded very formal. He had black sleeked-back hair, a neat moustache and an open, rather vacuous-looking face. He reminded Rachel, just a trifle, of Captain Crystal.

'My dear, we shall all enjoy having you. Fred will want you to hunt with him tomorrow. We had the most frightful accident today.'

And she began to tell Major Tidy, who had obviously only just arrived, all about Adam and his fall. In the distance Lord Askham was sitting at a table with two pretty women and another man, just as though they were two couples, and Flora, looking attractive without her spectacles, her hair elegantly coiffeured with a 'doormat' fringe, was talking earnestly to an elderly couple who had been there when they came. Seeing them, Flora came over.

'Darling, do you know James Tidy?' her mother cried. 'He's with the Buffs.'

'How do you do?' Flora looked resigned, politely holding out a hand.

Major Tidy bowed, the footman brought another chair for Flora, and Rachel thought how extraordinary it was that Lady Askham should invite to a party in honour of her son and his fiancée a man no one knew. Yet few, as far as she could tell, seemed to consider it in any way exceptional, although she sensed the hostility of Arthur and Bosco who stood glowering on the edge of the circle, drinking champagne, glasses clenched in their hands.

Flora asked about Adam and Frances told her once again how she'd found him and the fright they'd all had.

Lady Frances Crewe was a tall young woman with a rather brittle sort of beauty – dark eyes and jet-black hair. She could either smile with great brilliance or bestow on those present a rather sour, superior expression in the manner of one trying hard not to notice an unpleasant smell. She wore one of the most daring evening gowns in the room with a very low décolletage, and her long thin white neck seemed to stretch from her body like the stem of a very tall flower. Lady Frances was very rich, considered most supercilious, even by connoisseurs of *hauteur*, and altogether a good match for Arthur Gore who shared many of her qualities.

In appearance her fiancé was as unlike Bosco as it was possible for brothers to be. He was tall but very thin, whereas Bosco, also tall, was sturdily built, like the polo and rugby player, the sportsman he was. Arthur had the long, serious face of his father, without the lines, and was cleanshaven. Bosco was cleanshaven too, but everything about him seemed open and friendly: wide forehead, strong broad nose, sparkling humorous eyes. They both had the blue-green eyes and dark chestnut hair, inherited from the Kittos, which Dulcie had bequeathed to all her children. Arthur's was brushed straight back, Bosco's had a side parting, military-style. Finally, Bosco invariably looked cheerful and reasonably contented, even when he was ill, whereas Arthur had the look of one constantly on his guard in case someone infringed his dignity.

During the supper interval the room filled up until all the tables were taken by women in beautiful ballgowns and men in evening dress with decorations. Bosco, Rachel noted, wore his DSO and the medal that had been struck for the Sudan campaign, and Lord Askham had a whole row that he had collected over the years, mostly for being who he was rather than for any particular merit. One or two men wore military evening dress (which was considered a little affected by those in the know) and a few were in hunting pink, the formal dress of the Askham Hounds.

At a given signal a cake was brought in and Bosco made a gracious speech congratulating his brother on his good fortune in securing the hand of Lady Frances Crewe for a bride. The Crewe family lived nearby, indeed they shared land boundaries with the Askhams, and Lord and Lady Crewe were there with three sons and a daughter, the others being married or living abroad.

Lady Askham looked as poised and gracious as ever and, for the speech, James Tidy had somehow been relegated to the back of the room, while she sat next to her husband surrounded by her family and that of the bride-to-be.

Rachel couldn't help thinking of Melanie's wedding as she listened to Bosco, only there could hardly have been a greater contrast between this well-dressed English county set in magnificent surroundings and the hot verandah of the Hotel de l'Angleterre with its colourful, cosmopolitan crowd.

There was another contrast too. The Askhams, sitting with the Crewes as though posing for a family portrait, smiles of approval on their faces as Bosco extolled the virtues of the bride, were so much happier at the engagement of their eldest son to one of their own sort than of his younger sister who had chosen to marry beneath her. Sir Robert and Lady Lighterman even now sat apart, a couple who stood out by the singular fact that they were unknown in society, that Lady Lighterman had never been presented at Court and that, no matter how many millions of pounds Sir Robert had, he would never, ever be one of them.

Melanie had married beneath her and now she was paying for it. For not only did she expect a child she didn't want by a man she had only briefly loved; she had to face the fact that her name was Lighterman as well.

'I should get back to Adam,' Rachel whispered to Flora after the health of the engaged couple was drunk and the string orchestra, refreshed from its labours, struck up in the gilded drawing-room once more. Couples began to saunter back and Lord and Lady Askham, their family duty done, separated. He rejoined the lady he'd been dancing with and Major Tidy appeared, as if by magic, at her ladyship's side.

'Do come down again if you feel like it. I do hope you find him well,' Lady Askham called as she passed Rachel then, seeing someone, stopped. 'Oh, Sir Robert, have you met Miss Bolingbroke? She is the sister of the unfortunate victim of this morning's accident and is just about to return to his bedside.'

'We met this afternoon.' Sir Robert looked like a comfortable family grocer, rather Pickwickian, with a bald head and a red cherubic face. He bowed over Rachel's hand. 'My wife assisted in the setting of the poor captain's leg.'

'She was very good. I am much indebted to her.'

Rachel smiled once again at the small, round little woman tricked out now in a purple ballgown bearing an unfortunate resemblance to a tent, and sparkling like the window of a Bond Street jeweller. But beneath her uncomfortable veneer, which had been foisted on her by her husband's position, Mabel Lighterman was a capable, good-hearted woman with a sort of earthy charm acquired in her days as a nurse at St Thomas's Hospital after Florence Nightingale had started to reform the profession.

'We didn't talk about Harry,' Sir Robert's rheumy eyes

looked mournful. 'I know you met him in Cairo. One of the last to see him.'

'Yes, I saw him off.' Rachel, thinking of Adam, felt suddenly bereft of words and squeezed Lady Lighterman's hand. 'I'm *so* sorry. He was a fine man.'

'Fine,' Mabel nodded, as if her memory of her son were distanced now. 'Might we have the pleasure of looking in on the Captain before we leave tomorrow?'

'Please do, if he's well enough. I'll see you at breakfast. Goodnight.'

Rachel looked around for Bosco just in time to see him, glass in hand, escorting a pretty lady back to the dance floor. She didn't mind. Such people as Bosco, treating flirtation as mere sport, were always bent on another conquest. Frances and Arthur followed him and Lord Askham, his hand round the waist of the nubile young woman, was ushering her in the same direction that his wife had also taken with Major Tidy. The orchestra was playing a selection from *The Merry Widow* and as the empty glasses and plates jostled together, the army of footmen swept round collecting them on to trays. She exited quietly and climbed the stairs towards Adam's room feeling guilty that she'd left him for so long. The long corridor was in darkness save for dim lights at each end. Quietly Rachel turned the handle of his room, stole inside and bent over his bed.

'He wanted some water, miss,' the maid said, getting up. 'I gave it to him and he went back to sleep. He's been very peaceful.'

'Thank you,' Rachel replied. 'Do you think I might just go and change and then I'll relieve you?'

'Please, miss,' the girl sat down again and resumed her knitting.

Rachel's room was at the far end of the corridor, quite near Melanie's and, as she passed, she wondered if she should look in and see how she was. She tapped upon the door and, as she listened, she heard a loud groan. Throwing open the door, she saw Melanie rolling on the bed, hands clenched to her stomach, her face drenched with sweat.

'Get someone, please,' Melanie called. 'For God's sake, get someone quickly. I thought no one would come. There's something wrong with the bell. I knew this afternoon this was going to happen.'

Rachel flew along the corridor, down the stairs and back into the ballroom where the waltzing couples reminded her of Thackeray's description of the ball before Waterloo.

Lady Askham was in the middle of the dancing throng, closely partnered by Major Tidy. Flora sat out chatting to the same elderly couple Rachel had seen her with before. Rachel whispered in her ear and Flora got up abruptly, in the middle of introducing them as her uncle and aunt, and went over to her mother, whispering in hers. Her mother gave her vague, rather remote smile as though to assure everyone that everything was perfectly all right, then she said something to Major Tidy and left the dance floor with Flora.

'Are you sure?' she enquired of Rachel. 'Doctor Fraser said . . .'

'Quite sure. She's in awful pain. She rang the bell but no one heard her.'

'Most unfortunate,' Lady Askham said looking momentarily perturbed, Rachel couldn't decide whether about the broken bell or her daughter's situation. 'Dr Fraser went up to London on an evening train. Someone had better go and see if he's back.'

Mabel Lighterman, observing the activity from a seat by the door, came over and asked if there was anything wrong.

'Nothing wrong exactly, but it seems that Melanie's baby may be imminent. Isn't it a bother?'

Mabel, who had already done her good deed that day in helping to set Adam's leg, left the room followed by Flora, Rachel and a graceful Lady Askham, smiling around at everyone to reassure them that nothing was amiss.

'I was a midwife too,' Lady Lighterman said once they were in the corridor. 'You'd better send for a lot of hot water.'

By early the following morning the family living in Askham Hall had been increased by a further member – a male child delivered by its grandmother assisted by the head carpenter's wife, who had seven children of her own, and a number of housemaids who carried up buckets of hot water, cloths, changes of linen and a small quantity of beer which Mabel Lighterman, reverting to her days when she was a hardworking midwife, found refreshing as she went about her task.

Lady Askham insisted that nothing should interrupt the party, no guests should be disturbed. While her daughter laboured upstairs to produce her first grandchild, she passed the small hours in the arms of Major Tidy and several other young men on the dance floor not only in order to keep up appearances but because she was enjoying herself, knowing, or presuming, there was nothing further she could do.

Lord Askham did his bit, partnering his guests in the waltzes, mazurkas, schottisches and gallops which the orchestra produced from its extensive repertoire. He also drank a lot of whisky because he was rather more nervous about the whole business upstairs than his wife. Arthur, Frances and Bosco supported the united family front until the final tune had been played, the weary orchestra packed up its instruments, and the last carriage had driven away down the drive.

Only Flora stayed outside her door to be near Melanie,

and Rachel cat-napped in Adam's room between visits down the corridor to comfort Flora. As unmarried women they had no place in the birth room.

Indeed the whole night long, and into the dawn, Askham Hall ran as it always did, always would, winter and summer, autumn and spring; like a well-oiled machine, with the servants fulfilling their respective functions as they had for generations to ensure that the family and their friends went about their pursuits unhindered, undisturbed.

Birth, and death, could have happened in that vast house without a soul, who didn't have to know, being any the wiser. Such was the Askham way.

CHAPTER 7

Despite the appearance of calm that Dulcie tried very hard to maintain, the control over the show of any feelings other than those generating pleasure and good temper, the days following the party were ones that she found very hard to take.

It was not that she took exception to the presence of her tiny grandson, who was a delight, but because politeness decreed that his other grandfather and grandmother should be invited to stay on in the house seeing that it was thanks to Mabel that the baby was there at all and in good health. Doctor Fraser had not returned to the village until well into the following day, when his services were no longer required, and by the time help was sent for to a village ten miles away the baby was safely delivered.

In addition, the care and attention that Adam Bolingbroke required was irksome, seeing that they had only just got Bosco sufficiently well to leave his bed; and the close friendship between Rachel and Flora was not one that commended itself to her mother at all. Dulcie felt that Bosco, now recovered enough to take an interest in female company again, seemed to pay too much attention to their young guest who, away from the heat of Cairo and with the benefit of fresh English country air to bring the colour to her cheeks, seemed much better endowed than Lady Askham had at first thought. Certainly Bosco seemed to think so. He spent much time either alone in Rachel's company or taking long walks with her and Flora in order, he said, to get his leg into marching order again.

Lady Askham would have liked to go to London with Lord Askham and Arthur to enjoy a few days in the company of her fashionable friends, to see a few of the young, or not so young, men, eminent politicians and men of letters whom she liked to entertain to tea. But she felt that politeness prevented her leaving her guests to their own devices, and at least a modicum of maternal interest and grandmotherly concern seemed required towards Melanie and her infant son.

The trouble was that everyone else in the house seemed so happy. The weather was pleasant, sunny if cold, and it seemed to her ladyship that it would be churlish to show her displeasure. So she tried very hard indeed and it was not until Flora threw her new bombshell that she was able to relax and give way to a good old-fashioned display of bad temper.

'What do you mean, *live* in London?' she stormed, after Flora, finding her mother alone in her sitting-room, had announced her plans.

'Bosco is quite well now, Mama. He will soon be rejoining his regiment.'

'And what, pray, is wrong with the huge house we maintain in St James's Square? Is there not sufficient room there for you?'

'It's not the same thing, Mama.'

'And with the Bolingbrokes!' Lady Askham continued, the mood of comparative serenity she'd been working so hard at completely fractured.

'But do you not like them, Mama? I find them very pleasant people.'

'Did they put the idea up to you?'

'Indeed they did not. I suggested it to Rachel who said she and Adam intended to live in town anyway.'

'That is a very fine reward for my hospitality,' Lady Askham sniffed. 'A nice way to repay kindness.'

'It was suggested by me, *before* Adam's accident, Mama.'

'Then please forget it.' Lady Askham resumed the

delicate crochetwork she had been engaged on before the arrival of her daughter. 'I wish to hear no more of it again. I rue the day we ever met them. Fancy any young man coming here and not being able to hunt! Your father has never got over it.'

'*Anyone* could have fallen off a horse.'

'If you ask me it was done deliberately so that . . .'

Now Flora's own temper broke, one not so easily contained as her mother's because, apart from anything else, she was so prey to frustrated hopes and ambitions that her general mood was never very calm anyway. She was constantly emotionally at loggerheads with her mother.

'Mama, what a terrible thing to say! He could have killed himself, or would that have been deliberate too?'

'Well, that's silly . . .'

'Not as silly as what you just said.'

'Maybe I didn't mean to go so far.' Dulcie snipped a bit of silk with scissors held by fingers that were beginning to tremble. 'But I do really resent them hanging around here, and those Lightermans . . .' her mother raised her eyes to the ceiling, the plasterwork of which, picked out in blue and white, with its tiny leafy pendants and coronals of flowers, was an altogether more delicate and feminine decoration than the intricate ornamentation of the ceilings of the main staterooms.

'I suppose you aren't even grateful to Lady Lighterman . . .'

Lady Askham's eyes travelled from a contemplation of the ceiling to her daughter's face and she lowered her voice as though the sound could travel through the inches thick walls.

'Were you aware that she *drank* all through Melanie's confinement? Quantities of beer were consumed.'

'I understood she had a glass or two to refresh herself, Mother, and she certainly was not drunk when I saw her after a night's work.'

'It's just the fact that she should do it at all that I find so distressing,' her mother said. 'Beer. What lady drinks beer?'

'But you've always said Lady Lighterman was no "lady".'

'That she certainly isn't and please take that note of sarcasm from your voice, Flora dear, or I shall have to send you to your room.'

'Mother, I am *twenty-four*!'

'Of that I am well aware,' her mother sighed. 'But not yet married and thus under my care, as I have pointed out to you before. Nor likely to be,' she remarked looking at her. 'Do you have to wear those spectacles all day and scrape back your hair so unbecomingly?'

'Mother . . .' Flora flopped into a chair. 'Sometimes I feel I . . . thoroughly dislike you. Also you do not have charge of me. I am of age and can please myself what I do.'

'Oh dear. Now we have a real rebel on our hands, have we? I shall have to send for your father. If I can't point your duties out to you, he will.'

'What duties, Mother!' Flora stood up again and stamped her foot. 'What duties? Does not this house run quite well without my help, or yours, or Melanie's or Bosco's? If we all died tomorrow, caught in some awful catastrophe, would not this house continue to run as well as it does now?'

'I certainly hope so.' Dulcie began to feel she had regained the upper hand. 'Not very likely, such an event, but were we to be extinguished by the hand of God – ' she looked briefly upwards again in a fleeting tribute to her Maker. 'Were such a thing to come about I hope the servants would know just what to do and how to behave. They coped very well last Saturday I must say. Not a soul knew Melanie was having a baby.'

'Great credit to you that, Mother.'

'What exactly do you mean, Flora?'

'Didn't you think your place was by Melanie's side?'

'Mine?' Dulcie looked amazed. 'What could *I* do? I know nothing about babies.'

'You've had four, Mother.'

Dulcie looked pained. 'Please don't remind me of that tiresome time, dear, one baby after another. It seemed too dreadfully unfair.'

'Yes but *four* children, Mother. You should know something about them.'

'But not how to deliver them, dear. I wouldn't know what to do. That awful woman was actually a *midwife*. I assure you I'd have been in the way. And Melanie wouldn't have wanted me there either.'

'How do you know? Melanie loves you.' Flora bent forward, her face a few inches from that of her mother.

'And I love her, but I could not help her and she knows that. Besides she would expect me to entertain the guests. You should have been there too. Several people remarked on your absence and I had to make excuses for you.' Dulcie passed a white beringed hand across her forehead. 'Do desist now, dearest Flora. I have one of my headaches coming on.' She turned her face towards the window and then, with a start, forgetting about the pain in her head, peered out. 'Is that Bosco on a horse?'

Flora went to stand by her mother and shielded her eyes against the sun.

'Yes, with Rachel.'

'But I thought she couldn't ride.'

'He's teaching her.'

'That's another thing I don't like.' Dulcie threw her needlework on to the table by her side. 'She's after him.'

'Oh Mother! She is not after him. If anything he is after her.'

'He couldn't possibly be interested in someone like that.'

'Why not?'

'Because,' Dulcie permitted that brief, disdainful smile with which Flora was so familiar to flit across her face, 'she is not one of us.'

'But Melanie didn't marry "one of us" either, did she?'

'And let's hope Bosco learns *that* lesson. Goodness knows what the Père Bolingbroke is like.'

'He's a lawyer.'

'Thank heaven for that anyway, a modicum of education even if without breeding. But you know, looking at Harry Lighterman one would never have thought he could have come from such exceedingly common stock. His face was really quite refined and his manners impeccable. Of course in the bedroom his lack of breeding showed.' Lady Askham momentarily closed her eyes. 'I will not go into it any further, but your poor sister . . .'

Flora put her hands to her ears. 'Mother, I will listen to no more of this! I can't stand it a moment longer. Sometimes I feel you're a monster!'

Then, her hands still over her ears, she ran from the room leaving Dulcie feeling so agitated that she helped herself to a small glass of sherry from the decanter she kept in a cupboard by the wall, should just such an emergency occur.

Soon the whole household was aware that Dulcie and her daughter had quarrelled and not long after that they knew why.

Mabel Lighterman tried to pour oil on troubled waters because she was perceptive as well as kind and she had long experience of dealing with all kinds of people, the very rich and the very poor. Besides, she had three children of her own.

She was such a good soul, so well-intentioned that she couldn't conceive anyone would feel about her the way Lady Askham did, especially when her ladyship was always so successful in hiding her true feelings. Indeed, from her attitude towards her anyone would have thought that Mabel Lighterman was among her closest friends.

'You have to let them grow up,' Mabel said after a distressing scene at table when Flora once more left the room, followed by Rachel and Bosco who made their excuses having finished their lunch. 'If she wants to live on her own why not?' She looked at her husband, his florid face contented after a good and exceedingly rich meal. 'Don't you agree, Robert?'

'I don't think Lady Flora should flout her mother's wishes.'

'If she likes her studies let her pursue them, who knows? She is a good sensible girl but no beauty, if I may say so, Lady Askham, not like yourself and our dearest little Melanie. She may not marry, and if she wants to live away from home, let her. Miss Bolingbroke too is a very nice, sensible girl.'

'That's what I don't like about her.' Dulcie put her hand on the table and studied her rings.

'What, that she's sensible?'

'I don't think she's a good influence on Flora.'

'But why ever not?'

'Can't you see it? I can't explain,' Dulcie said vaguely. 'Something not quite right about her. She travels abroad on her own.'

'That *is* bad,' Sir Robert agreed, helping himself to more wine. 'I know what you mean, Lady Askham.' He was anxious to be seen to be on her side.

'Well, I must confess I don't,' Mabel said gently. 'I do beg you to think again about Flora. And now I must go and see Melanie. Have you seen her and the baby today, Lady Askham?'

'Not yet,' Dulcie looked at the fob watch which hung on a gold chain round her neck. 'I thought I'd go this afternoon.'

'Come, let's go together.' Mabel smiled as she got her short, comfortable body away from the table. 'Melanie would love to see you.'

Melanie was fond of her mother but she was also hurt by her. Her mother's strength had been necessary but, in the months she had waited at home, humiliating, making her feel like some discarded object waiting delivery from a burden she didn't want.

Melanie's transformation from a happy excited young woman just out of her teens, to a disillusioned bride, and then as a widow expecting the child of a man she scarcely knew, had been so sudden that at the time it was difficult for her emotions to absorb what had happened to her. But Mother was always there: robust, sheltering, comforting. She had relied too much on her mother's strength, leaned too heavily upon her. It was as though her mother lived her life for her.

And then that night when, above all things, she needed her mother she hadn't been there. Instead there had been a plump, wrinkled, elderly lady, an apron over her fine clothes, showing a different kind of strength; helping her, supporting her and showing by her experience just how superficial and inadequate her own mother seemed by comparison. In those hours she had formed a bond with, of all people, her husband's mother; a tie that she had previously thought she could only have with her own. In the days that had passed since then the bond had strengthened and she looked forward to Mabel's frequent calls, to the long hours she spent with her and the baby when Lady Askham was somewhere else.

Her mother's brief visits reminded her of her own days in the nursery when the young children came to regard seeing their parents as an event. When, washed and dressed in their best clothes, they were taken downstairs to spend some time, never very much – maybe half an hour, occasionally more – with their father and mother in her sitting-room or, if there were guests, visits from aunts and uncles or grandparents, in one of the drawing-rooms where they felt swamped, overawed by rather grand people in huge acres of space.

But the greatest change that had happened to Melanie, which had surprised not only her but everyone close to her, was her delight in her baby, her acceptance of the role of mother which, while she was awaiting the birth, she had appeared not only indifferent to but actually to resent. She had even refused to give the baby to the wet nurse engaged for him and fed him herself, and instead of having his cot in another room she wanted it there by her side.

Flora had just left her when her mother and Mabel arrived together. Mabel bustled in, thoroughly familiar with the room and its occupants, Dulcie almost hesitantly as though she felt a stranger. And she gazed down at the baby with a rather startled expression as if she couldn't quite understand how he came to be there. Melanie sat in her large bed, propped up on pillows with her dark hair brushed over her shoulders, wearing a pretty negligée of blue muslin with a cape tied with dark blue bows. She was pale, but looked in excellent health, well rested and smiling. Mabel stooped and kissed Melanie who embraced her, but when Dulcie bent down to peck her cheek it was without the welcome of her daughter's arms.

'Melanie, we must have a name for the baby,' Dulcie sat down carefully at the side of the bed. 'We can't spend all our time calling him "it".'

'Robert,' Melanie said.

'I *beg* your pardon, dearest?'

'Robert after his grandfather. If it had been a girl I'd have called her after Mabel.' She extended a hand to her mother-in-law who grasped it gratefully, her short, podgy arms such a contrast to Dulcie's which were long, firm and very young-looking.

'Oh, that is such a sweet gesture, Melanie. Really nice. But shouldn't he be called after his poor papa?'

But Melanie had already decided she couldn't bear to have her son called Harry by his first name.

'Robert,' she said. 'Robert Harold Lighterman.'

'No Askham names?' The tip of Dulcie's nose quivered with displeasure. 'What about your brother Arthur? Or Bosco, or your father Frederick?'

'I think that would be nice, dear,' Mabel said, nervously straightening the bedclothes which were in immaculate order. 'Robert Frederick, or Frederick Robert, perhaps, out of respect to his lordship.'

'Robert Harold,' Melanie joined her hands over her flat stomach. 'I have decided.'

And Dulcie knew that her daughter, soon to be twenty-one, had indeed come of age. 'Well, it's as you say, dear, of course. After all, you are his mother. I only hope your father isn't too disappointed. His first grandchild.' Dulcie gave an exaggerated sigh. 'He will have another soon when Arthur marries Frances. I should think all their children would be given Askham names.'

'And Crewe ones. Frances will see to that. To change the subject, Flora told me she's going to live in London, Mama. Should you mind if I went with her?'

'To Askham House, of course.'

'No. I thought Flora and I might take a house in Marylebone, or even Hampstead.'

'You'd live alone together?'

'With the nurse, of course, and a servant or two. But I understand your main objection to her sharing with Rachel is that she will be living in the same house as a young unmarried man. Well, if she lives with me she won't.'

'What an excellent idea,' Mabel's comely face creased in smiles. 'You won't object to that will you, Lady Askham, or may I call you Dulcie now that we're such friends?'

'Call me anything you like,' Dulcie said getting up. 'I

have to see Mrs Daintry, do please excuse me.' And gracefully, elegantly, with a sweet, sad smile but without looking at anyone in particular, she left the room.

'Dear me, you have upset your mother. Why did you do that now? You could at least have consulted her about the baby's names.' Mabel tapped Melanie's arm.

'Why should I? She never consults me about anything.' Melanie tucked her small dainty hand into Mabel's capable fist. 'I no longer feel about Mama the way I used to. Do you know what I think she is?' Melanie stuck out her chin and looked into Mabel's eyes, but as that good woman, perhaps fearing the worst, didn't reply she continued. 'A selfish tyrant. She is persecuting poor Flora and since I've known you I realize how patronizing and offensive her attitude to me has been, sneering about Harry, disparaging me and the baby. I didn't see it before, but I do now. Flora has just been here with me and is very upset.'

Mabel put another large hand over Melanie's, encasing both. 'Now look, my dear, let me give you some sensible advice if I can. You have just had a baby. A young woman is never very rational at a time like this. It is well known.'

'But Mama has done nothing . . .'

'Your mama could *do* nothing, if you mean the night the baby was born. She was helpless to do anything for you, whereas I was qualified. Do you know in St Thomas's we used to go out at all hours and deliver the babies of the poor women who lived in the charity dwellings round about? Often I would go alone at night and not a soul there to help me. Sometimes she might be a young unwed girl, or someone whose husband was out or drunk or who had left her. Assisting you here was a piece of cake helped by all those servants, and pleased I was to do it, especially as the baby, the darling,' she looked fondly at the infant asleep in his crib, 'was my own grandchild. But what could your mother do? Nothing. She had a house full of people, and quite rightly she didn't wish to distress or upset them. They may have thought they had to go. She didn't want that, nor should you. Your father and mother are very grand people, and folks like them, like you, don't behave like us. We don't expect them to. You mustn't be hard on your mama because of that nor,' she continued hastily seeing Melanie about to intervene, 'because she didn't think Harry good enough for you. He wasn't. When I first knew his father he worked at a small grocer's shop in Brixton as an errand boy. He was sixteen and I was fourteen and at work too.

'But we both wanted to better ourselves. I wanted to be a trained nurse like Miss Nightingale and Robert was more ambitious, even then. When he was nineteen he bought that grocer's shop with his own money and in a few more years he had about a dozen. Do you know that Robert was worth a million pounds by the time he was thirty? I was ever so proud of him and still am, and he will be really glad your baby is to be named after him. Though he may seem a silly old man now, fawning on your parents and drinking a bit too much, he isn't at all. He's out of his depth here in this big house with these fine folk, and I am too. You and your baby have given us both an anchor and we love you and little Robert very much, Mel dear.'

Moved by her own words, her eyes streaming with tears, fat, emotional Mabel, who had been born and reared in the unsmart part of Brixton, embraced her daughter-in-law and after a while Melanie cried too, leaning her head on the great big motherly bosom so different from her mother's trim, well-corseted lines.

'Would you like a glass of beer?' she said, when Mabel had heaved herself up and they were both wiping their faces.

'Whatever gave you that idea?'

'I know you like it if you feel stressful.'

'But I couldn't drink a glass of beer now! It's midafternoon. Bless you, dear, for being such a kind little thing. Tell you what, I'll get the maid and we'll have a cup of tea, a nice cup together. Shall we?'

And as her daughter-in-law nodded she pulled the bell by the side of the bed, which had been mended since the night of the birth when Melanie nearly had to deliver her child by herself.

'Now then,' Mabel sat down again, once more taking her hand in hers, 'let's be practical. We have a very big house, much too big for us now that Harry has gone and our daughters are married. Do you know we have fifteen bedrooms? Well, you can have a little suite all to yourself and come and go as you please, and if Flora would like . . .'

She stopped as Melanie shook her head. 'No, Mabel, it wouldn't do. Even I can see that. If we both left here to come and live with you it would upset our parents too much. We have our own family house too in St James's Square and I think it may even have more than fifteen bedrooms, perhaps twenty. Flora and I want to be independent. We don't want to hurt our parents, and living with you would; but we want to show them we have the right to our own lives, that we don't want to be tied down. The trouble is, you see, when Bosco goes back to Egypt and Arthur gets married, Mama and Papa will be here all on their own, that's when they are here. I think Mama is afraid of that, even though she doesn't say it.'

'Very well, dear,' Mabel patted her hand. 'I think what you say is right and very thoughtful. Robert will buy you and Flora a nice little house – no, don't say anything – it will be for the baby, for his namesake.'

'Please, *dearest* Mabel, Flora and I both have money. Our grandfather left us each a small legacy and you have settled a very generous sum on me.'

'Harry would have liked it though,' once more a tear trickled out of Mabel's eye, making a lonely path down her cheek. 'Oh, I know you maybe weren't very happy with him. I can tell. Harry had never been with women, you know. He was a good boy and anxious to make his parents proud of him, and we were. I am sure that if you and Harry had had time to settle down you would have seen his qualities and come to love him, as we loved him and he loved you. You would have seen a much nicer, very different side to Harry from the one you saw.'

'I loved him at the beginning,' Melanie said emotionally, 'please don't think I didn't. But Harry *was* rough and I didn't know anything about that . . . either. I did have a shock, I'll confess . . .'

'All women do, dear, all women do.' Mabel shook her head. 'It's the sin of Eve. We all have to suffer for it.'

Melanie looked interested. 'Oh, is that what it is? I've often wondered. Yes, I'm sure that, given time, Harry and I would have got used to each other. In Egypt, with Mama, it wasn't easy. I see now what a silly little girl I was.'

'No longer,' Mabel got up as the maid knocked on the door and, because things were never done in halves at Askham Hall, arrived with a footman to ascertain Lady Melanie's wishes.

'Just a pot of tea, dear,' Mabel said. 'And a few of those nice cakes, the ones with cream and plenty of jam we had at tea yesterday.' She winked at Melanie and licked her lips mischievously. 'If you're not careful I'll be stealing your pastrycook – oh, and perhaps a few of those pastries with fresh custard in, if there are any left. You'd never have thought I'd just had a good dinner, would you?'

Adam's leg was not only fractured and his body bruised but he had been mentally shaken as well. In fact the doctor believed him to have sustained the kind of concussion that affected the brain but did not result in prolonged loss of consciousness. Accordingly Adam's convalescence was protracted and it was not until he'd been in bed three weeks at Askham Hall that he was able to get out of bed and walk about his room.

'We're a couple of cripples,' Bosco said, watching him hobbling about. 'But I think my limp has gone now. All those walks with the girls have helped, and the rides. Do you know Rachel has quite a fair seat on a horse? I can't believe she never rode before.'

'Well, she didn't,' Adam winced in pain and sat down in a chair by the window, facing his friend. 'Bosco, we'll have to get away from here soon, you know. Now that I'm out of bed I am quite well enough to travel and be nursed at home.'

'Are you not happy here?' Bosco looked disappointed.

'Of course I'm happy here, overwhelmed with kindness; but . . . when your mother asked us for a weekend she didn't expect me to stay for weeks.'

'It was hardly your fault.'

Adam looked at him but said nothing. The frosty attitude of Lord Askham made him think that at least one person thought it was. Not that he saw much of his lordship, who had visited him once for five minutes in three weeks.

'I shall miss you a lot,' Bosco said; then, after a pause, 'and Rachel. She has lifted my depression a great deal in the time she's been here. I've become awfully fond of her.'

'Depression? Why should you feel depressed?'

'Ah, why should I feel depressed?' Bosco leaned back in his chair and closed his eyes. When he opened them again that rather grim, haunted look that Adam had seen so often whenever they talked about Omdurman was there again. 'Don't you know?'

'But the battle is finished. Kitchener is now Governor-General of the Sudan, and the Khalifa is dead.'

'It's not what might happen; it's what *has* happened. Do

you never think, Adam my friend, that what I did to Crystal was deliberate? That I killed him?'

Adam leaned forwards, his hands clasped between his knees. 'My dear fellow, you most certainly did *not* kill Cardew Crystal. The fact that he tried to help you and was then killed himself doesn't deflect from your own personal bravery. You're mad to think anything else.'

'But Crystal knew Harry was dead. By lingering with Harry I caused Crystal's death and, you know, the more I think about it the more I think I meant to. There now, I've said it.'

Bosco looked exhausted, the blood drained from his face. 'That's what I dream about – not the desert, not the battle, not the charge, but deliberately causing, wanting to cause, the death of a brother officer because he made love to my mother.'

'Oh Bosco . . .' Adam left his chair, forgetting his injury, and knelt on the floor beside his friend. 'I do beseech you, don't give way to such fantasies.'

'They are not. They're real,' Bosco opened his eyes wide, as though reliving that day. 'I think I *wanted* Cardew to die. "Hurry," he said, "or you'll kill us both" and when he said that, I remember, I hesitated. I imagine I thought I would indeed die, knowing I was so fearfully wounded, and that I'd take Cardew with me. Even though I didn't spear him I killed him just as much as if I were the Dervish who did. "You've done for me, Down," he said, and as he died, looking into my eyes, I think he knew I meant to.'

'It's very far-fetched,' Adam said feeling wretchedly inadequate. 'You may have hated the man but you didn't mean to kill him.'

'By lingering with Harry, already dead, I lured Crystal to his own death. Tell me, Adam,' Bosco joined his hands as one considering a philosophical point, 'how can I live the rest of my life with that knowledge? Who will try me? What jury will judge me? To whom can I confess?'

'It's only in your mind because you've been so ill. It's an absurd idea. I felt depressed, too, lately, and that my life was useless. Here I am at twenty-four, nearly twenty-five, and still kept by my father, and for years more if I read for the Bar. If you feel useless I do too.'

'I don't feel useless,' Bosco said. 'I feel a murderer. At least you don't feel that. In my heart I have carried the knowledge of my crime, and every time I woke I hoped it hadn't happened, wasn't true. But I tell you one thing, Adam,' he shook a finger at him, 'I wanted Cardew Crystal dead, and you know the awful thing? My mother hardly remembers him now. She never even mourned him. She has gone on to another and another. She is impatient because she has to stay here when she would like to be in London flirting. It's James Tidy or Billie Hardy or Hugo Belper . . . she can't keep her hands off young men.'

'Oh, I think that's going a bit far.'

'No, it isn't. I see it all with my own eyes. I saw her with Crystal in the palm clearing in Sakkara. They *were* kissing. Why does she have to do it? Why does she have to make me kill for her?'

'Would you kill the others?'

'Yes.' Bosco clenched his fists.

'I don't know what to say,' Adam said at last. 'I don't think your mother means anything disloyal to your father, or her family.'

'I know it's a game. But it's a game I hate. It is undignified. Of course he flirts too, but somehow I don't mind that so much.'

'It's expected of a man.' Adam's tone was sarcastic. 'Frankly I feel you're too involved with your mother, Bosco. You should get away. Go back to Cairo as soon as you can and let her live her own life, even if it does seem flirtatious and silly.'

Bosco, he noticed, kept on looking out of the window as

if he expected to see something, or someone. 'There she is,' he said jumping up. 'There she is with Flora. See what a fine seat she has on a horse, Adam?'

Adam, following his gaze, saw Rachel and Flora riding, moving at a trot around the lake, towards the forest. Rachel's head was flung back and she was laughing; the shiny gold of her neat bun under her riding hat shone briefly in the sun.

'Isn't she gorgeous?' Bosco said, then he gazed at his friend. 'I'm in love with her, you know. But will she have me?'

Adam collapsed into the chair he'd previously been sitting on.

'How can you be in love with Rachel?'

'Didn't you guess? Did she say anything?'

'She doesn't know.'

'She doesn't *want* to know. She thinks I don't mean it, that I'm a flirt like Mama.'

'Well, aren't you?' Adam smiled wryly.

'Not since I knew her properly. She's so like Flora, you know, and I've always loved Flora. I felt protective towards Flora because she has always been rebellious and she is plain. But she has a beautiful mind and, if I were someone meeting her, I think I'd fall in love with that. Rachel has a fine mind and is also lovely to look at, which makes it easier.'

'Not everyone finds her good-looking. Some say she is too square and tall, her features too mannish and well-defined. You know, Bosco,' his tone became gentle, 'she is not at all like you.'

'That's why we suit.'

'She is a very intense young woman, dedicated to causes. I can't see her fitting into society or life in the army, even if you're serious.'

'I am serious. And she will fit in, if she loves me enough.'

'I don't know what to say. Have you told her this?'

'No, but I intend to before you go and if you're going soon I'd better tell her soon.'

'I don't know what your mother will say. She doesn't really approve of us, you know.'

'I know that; but then I'm not the heir and she can't possibly disapprove of me marrying whom I want.'

'Then you *are* talking about marriage?'

'Yes. The days that I have spent in Rachel's company both here and in Cairo have made me want her more than I can say.'

'I wonder,' Adam said, as if to himself, 'I wonder, can you possibly know what you're doing? All I can say to you, my dear boy, is this: please don't hurt my sister.'

Bosco turned his eyes from the window and gazed at him. 'Brother-in-law,' he smiled. 'I'll go and meet them on the way back. Tonight we may have another engagement party.'

As Adam went thoughtfully back to bed Bosco hurried down the stairs and bumped into his mother who was coming from Melanie's room.

'Ah, Mama . . . is Melanie all right?'

'Melanie is perfectly all right,' his mother looked preoccupied.

'I thought you looked agitated.'

'Well, I don't like that creature in her room all the time. Even though her perfectly ghastly husband has returned to town why do you think she has to stay?'

'Mel wants her.'

'But why? I'm her mother.'

'She's a dear old soul. Don't you like her better, Mother, truthfully?'

Dulcie didn't reply but tucked her arm into her son's as they walked down the broad staircase together.

'Adam's much better,' Bosco said. 'He's talking of wanting to go home. I'll miss him.'

'Well, he *has* been here three weeks,' his mother said, taking care to try and not show her relief. 'Although of course he is *always* welcome, as a friend of yours.'

'But . . . not yours?' They paused in the hall, Bosco staring into her eyes.

'You know I don't like them *very* much, dear. They're extremely ordinary people, the girl so frightfully silent and solemn.' Dulcie made a face that was meant to be funny.

'I think they're both extraordinary people.'

'Well, you would say that. What has got into my children I do not know. I think I have failed them. Melanie and Flora want to live alone in London together and you seem so oddly attached to that girl and her brother. Only dearest Arthur is a true Askham, doing what is expected of him and getting married to someone of whom your father and I deeply approve. Thank God he is the heir.'

'Thank God he is.' Bosco kissed her fondly on the cheek and went jauntily out of the door, taking the path down towards the lake where now he could see the girls cantering out of the forest. He raised a hand and raced down the path towards them, arriving breathless as they reached the far end of the lake to turn towards the house.

'Well, you can run well,' Flora said, bending down, her face flushed. 'Nothing wrong with your leg now.'

'My leg's fine.' Bosco looked not at her but at Rachel mounted behind them, her hands loosely on the reins. 'Had a good ride?'

'Marvellous.'

'Adam says you're going home.'

'I know. All good things come to an end.'

'Can I talk to you for a bit?'

'Just me?' Rachel pointed towards her chest, glancing at Flora who slipped off her horse.

'You can ride him back, Bosco.'

'I'd like to walk if you could take Rachel's horse.'

'Of course.' Remounting, Flora held out her hands for the bridle of the chestnut and Rachel, looking from one to the other, dismounted with Bosco's strong hand in hers. He didn't let go as she gave the bridle to Flora.

'See you back at the house, Flora. Mama's on the warpath about you and Mel.'

'We'll be gone soon too,' Flora said. 'Just as soon as we can make arrangements.'

'I'm sorry we shan't be sharing,' Rachel said regretfully, but Flora merely looked at Bosco and smiled. Then, ranging her horse alongside Rachel's, she trotted up the steep path towards the house.

'What's the mystery?' Rachel was conscious of his hand tightly holding hers.

'Don't you know?'

'No, I don't.' Rachel picked one of the dead buds off the rhododendrons as they passed and Bosco, glancing up to see if they were concealed by the bushes from the house, turned to face her. She was conscious then, as she never had been before, of his body; and the strong wave of the attraction she had always resisted suddenly felt overwhelming.

'You must know I love you, Rachel?'

'How can I know? You never told me before.'

'You must have been aware of it.'

'I thought we were friends.'

'Don't you love *me*?' He seized her arms and shook her as he gazed into her eyes demanding an answer, and the attraction and desire turned a little into fear.

'I can't let myself love you, Bosco.' Her voice shook and she moved away from him, along the path. 'How can a woman like myself expect to be loved by you, and, if you did love me, what would it mean?'

'That I would want to marry you,' he said, going after her. 'What else?'

Rachel caught at the twig of another rhododendron

bush as they passed and hung on to it. She felt that this time, this moment was crucial to her life; and yet she was utterly unprepared for it, nor did she know how to reply.

She knew she did love Bosco, that she had probably loved him in Cairo, but that she was too frightened of committing herself, too unsure of him to trust him with an emotion that he might not value, might not return. She knew his reputation.

'Have you talked to your mother?' Rachel's voice was very matter-of-fact, prosaic, and Bosco felt a twinge of anger.

'Of course I haven't talked to my mother!'

'You know she doesn't like me.'

'She neither likes nor dislikes you.'

'She dislikes. It is quite obvious that she dislikes. She didn't like me in Cairo and she doesn't like me here. Sometimes I think she actually hates me.'

'That's absurd.'

'No, I do. I imagine she thinks I'm a bad influence on your family; firstly Flora, encouraging her to be independent, and now you. I can see her looking out of the window at us often when we're walking or riding in the meadow or out here. She hovers by the library door to eavesdrop on our conversation. She thinks Adam and I are not her people, not your kind, and have you considered, Bosco, what sort of life you would have with a wife of whom your mother disapproved?'

'But I wouldn't even be here. I'm going back to Egypt, and then probably to India. I want you to come with me.'

They reached a seat by the side of the lake in the open and, although it was cold, both instinctively sat down on it. Bosco took hold of Rachel's hand, warming it. She wore a riding habit that belonged to Melanie, and the classic cut of the black outfit suited her, as did the tiny little black hat, her face half covered by a veil. She looked elegant, remote and mysterious and Bosco, who had never kissed her, scarcely ever touched her, wanted to take her in his arms and crush her. She seemed to sense his passion and moved a little away, putting space between their bodies.

'You really are serious?'

'Really.' He realized that his heart had begun to pound.

'Then I must say "no".'

'Oh Rachel . . . darling . . . why?'

'It is too soon. I'm unprepared. You gave me no hint before this. We hardly know each other, and remember what happened to your sister who married a man she scarcely knew.'

'We know each other very well. We've spent three weeks under the same roof. We know each other better now than Mel and Harry ever did.'

'We don't really know each other, Bosco. We have talked and we have read and walked, ridden together . . . but knowledge, no. That is a very different matter.'

'Then you don't love me.' His voice was flat and dejected and she suddenly felt panic-stricken as though she had mishandled this important moment of her life. She clutched him, moving, as she did, near to him again.

'Oh no, I don't say that! I think maybe I do love you. You're a very attractive, fascinating man. You know it too. But I am very wary of you because I'm not sure how sincere you are, and I think you have it in your power to hurt me.'

'But now you're hurting me!'

'Just wildly to say "yes I'll marry you" without thinking. Is that what you want, Bosco?'

'Yes.'

'Without the approval of your family or friends?'

'Yes. The one whose approval I most value is Flora, and I know she loves you too.'

'I'm not a very good dancer.'

'We shan't spend all our time dancing.'

'And I'm not a flirt . . .'

'Neither . . .' he stopped. 'That's it. Miss Plomley Pemberton.'

'*And* the ladies you danced with the night your nephew was born.'

'My dear, they're people I've known for years. Besides, I didn't love you then.'

'I don't think you really love me now. You know what I think?' She put her head on one side and viewed him with the kind of objectivity that people in an art gallery might look at a painting. 'I think you're too emotional, and you're unhappy. Something worries you terribly and I don't know what it is. Maybe it was the war, I don't know. I think you should go back to Egypt. You have been terribly badly wounded, but you're better now. I think you should go back to Egypt and face what it is you're afraid of.'

'I'm not afraid,' Bosco said quietly, marvelling at her perception.

'What is it then?'

'I can't tell you yet. I'll tell you when we're married. I want you with me to help me to face life.'

Rachel's hand stole into Bosco's and then, if he had kissed her, she would have responded. She wanted him to turn to her but he didn't, remaining locked in that unfathomable, unspeakable mystery of what troubled him.

'Bosco, I can't marry you now, but if you still love me and think as you do now, and I feel the same, let's talk again, say, in a year's time?'

'But I need you now,' Bosco said.

'I can't say "yes" now. I really can't. I have Adam to see back to health. I can't leave him with my father. I have a lot of things to think about in connection with my life. I never saw myself as the wife of a soldier. There are, also, all the other things we spoke of . . .'

Rachel turned her head, her eyes travelling beyond the rhododendron bushes, up the meadow and across the formal gardens to the windows at the side of the house which were Dulcie's sitting-room.

And there watching them, goodness knows for how long, standing by the window, was his mother, and even though she couldn't see the expression on her face Rachel knew what it would be.

CHAPTER 8

The Monday dances at Shepheard's Hotel were a popular feature of the Cairo winter season now drawing to its end. This year no threat of impending battles in the Sudan hung over the army; there were no regiments arriving, and departing, for the south; no hospital ships plied backwards and forwards up the Nile disgorging wounded soldiers to be treated at the military hospitals at Abbasiya or on top of the Citadel. Kitchener ruled in Khartoum, Cromer in Cairo. Orders flew by wire and special messengers from Her Majesty's functionaries in Whitehall. Stability, authority and discipline had overcome chaos and there was prosperity everywhere. The English, conquerors of Egypt and the Sudan, had established their unique brand of the *Pax Britannica* with which they brought uncivilized, recalcitrant nations to subjection. The railways not only ran on time, but carried ten million passengers a year and it was now possible to go all the way from the Mediterranean to Aswan in the greatest possible comfort and speed.

The hotels in Cairo, Alexandria, Luxor, Heliopolis and Aswan were full of tourists; the bazaars were packed with sightseers and shoppers, and it was difficult to get a place on a Nile steamer setting off to transport passengers to view the scenes of the major battles of the two years' campaign: Dongola, Berber, the Atbara, Khartoum, where poor Gordon had fallen, and Omdurman itself where he had been avenged, and where the shattered tomb of the Mahdi bore permanent witness to the destruction of the Dervish empire.

The army of course remained; British, Egyptian and Sudanese soldiers of every class and colour, sporting a variety of gorgeous uniforms – red, white, green, various shades of blue and the khaki of the Camel Corps and the Sudanese infantry.

But it was only the officer class who were to be seen at the Turf Club; playing golf, tennis, squash, croquet, or watching the racing at the Khedival Sporting Club at Gezira; and, of course, only the officer class attended the regular weekly dances at the Savoy on Saturdays, the Gezira Palace on Thursdays or Shepheard's on Mondays.

When Bosco returned to Egypt in May 1899 he plunged hectically into every activity that was going. His military duties were largely ceremonial and when these were over he played polo, tennis and squash; raced from the Khedival Yacht Club in Alexandria; took part in the gymkhanas at Mena House and the Helouan hotels, and danced vigorously at all the private balls and all the public dances. As a veteran of Omdurman he was very much in demand, and hostesses competed to ask him to their soirées, receptions and dinners. There was something quite frenetic about Bosco's activity and those who knew him best, and knew how badly wounded he had been, imagined that this almost punishing dedication to gaiety was a kind of thanksgiving because he was alive.

But Bosco wanted merely to forget – to forget about Rachel, to forget about the war and to try and bury the sense of guilt he carried with him wherever he went, whatever he did. He didn't feel a hero, he felt a coward; and one day, he thought, someone – a fellow officer or a member of the Egyptian Cavalry who knew Crystal – would guess the truth and accuse him of deliberately bringing about his death.

But everyone had forgotten about Cardew Crystal. His only memorial now was in the memory of his family and the mind of Bosco Down who thought that, but for him, Cardew would still be alive.

It was midnight at Shepheard's and the dancers still

twirled about the floor, the red and blue uniforms of the military mingling with the white dinner jackets of the civilian men, the colourful, fashionable dresses of the ladies. The floor was mostly full of young people. Fathers played bridge or *chemin de fer* in neighbouring rooms and the mothers sat out at the small tables looking approvingly at the military and speculated on the chances of their daughters in capturing a young officer for a husband.

In the season in Cairo – as in London, Paris, Rome or any of the great capital cities – there were a number of proposals rashly made and repented of afterwards when much delicate unscrambling had to be done; officers were quietly transferred to other regiments, usually India, and young women were packed disconsolately home. But there were some weddings too and the new young brides stayed behind to scheme and entertain and gossip and to produce offspring as their mothers had before them, following their men and the flag around an Empire, great and mighty, on which the sun never set.

Bosco was very popular with the young women, and particularly their mothers who knew he was not only a hero of Omdurman but the son of an earl. He was much fêted wherever he went, and many a matronly heart pumped a little harder when a daughter was seen in the arms of the blue-coated Lancer, so bold, brave and dashing, so tall, so very handsome – and so rich.

But Bosco was very careful not to become entangled with any young English girl with a pretty face, no fortune and a scheming mother. He danced, he chatted, he dined but he never asked a young unaccompanied woman out to dinner, or whispered endearments into her ears on the dance floor. People knew he was a flirt, but they hoped that one day he would settle down and start to take things seriously and that, when he did, he would choose their daughter. No one knew about his commitment back home, nor about his rejection, and everyone would have been amazed if they had, for what girl in her right mind would turn down a chance like that?

Bosco was wandering off to the bar, having delivered his latest partner back to her mother, when his attention was caught by an arm waved in his direction and a familiar face smiling at him. He was about to ignore it and pass on, but the owner of the face got up, unmistakable in a flowing turquoise dress dotted with tucks and bows and sparkling with sequins. She wore a sequined turban on her head and, at her throat, a treble choker of pearls was secured by a huge sparkling diamond. The strong pungence of her perfume preceded her.

'Captain Down, for I hear it is Captain now! May I congratulate you on your promotion – and your decoration.' She looked admiringly at the two medal ribbons on his chest.

'Thank you, Madame Hassim,' Bosco bowed stiffly, unsmilingly, and made as if to resume his passage between the tables, but she put a hand very lightly on his arm.

'Won't you join my table for a glass of champagne?'

'Thank you, no.'

The smile vanished to be replaced by an expression of bewilderment.

'Have I offended you in some way, Captain Down? I thought we were such good friends?'

'We were, Madame Hassim, but no longer. Please excuse me.'

'But may I not know the reason?' Madame Hassim dropped her voice to a whisper, conscious of the curious faces looking at them.

'Don't you know?' Bosco appeared surprised.

'Know what?'

'I find it very odd that you know nothing about what happened last year concerning my mother.'

'Your *mother*, Captain Down? Do you mean the contretemps at Sakkara? Oh, I have forgotten all about that, I assure you.'

'I am talking about the consequences.'

'But what consequences?' Her heavily mascaraed eyelids blinked alarmingly.

Bosco tried gently to disengage his arm from her clasp. 'Please do excuse me, Madame Hassim.'

She abruptly stood back and he bowed and continued through the room towards the bar.

'Captain Down!'

He stopped, embarrassed to see her speeding after him, her tough little face set in a determined expression. 'Please don't make a scene, Madame Hassim. People are looking at us.'

'I am well aware of that, Captain, but I am *very* upset to be treated so by you, and in public! I assure you that I have done nothing concerning your mother with which to reproach myself.'

'Well . . .' Bosco felt puzzled. He pointed to a table being vacated nearby. 'Shall we talk?'

'I hoped you'd say that.' Madame Hassim, all smiles again, draped herself on a chair while Bosco, after summoning the waiter and ordering champagne, sat opposite her clenching his fists together on the table.

'I hear you were very badly wounded, Captain Down, after covering yourself with glory.'

'No need to speak about that . . .' he waved a hand.

'And poor Mr Lighterman, *and* Captain Crystal,' Madame Hassim's luminous eyes momentarily brimmed with ready tears. 'Your family must feel very bereaved, poor Lady Melanie, your mother . . . what *was* it about your mother, Captain? You were going to tell me.'

Did she know or didn't she? Watching her face carefully Bosco related to her the events of the previous summer concerning Achmed Asher, and her own alleged part in the proceedings.

'Blackmail!' Madame Hassim threw up her plump, beringed hands. 'I can't believe it. Of *course* I settled the bill with him.'

'*You* settled the bill?'

'Of course, and as for an indiscretion with Captain Crystal, I knew your dear mama far too well. She was like a mother to the poor man who, I believe, was an orphan.' Madame Hassim's mobile features now composed themselves in an expression indicating profound sorrow. Bosco wondered, such was her versatility, if she'd ever been an actress.

'And *did* you go away?'

'Of course. I always go in the heat of our summer to Europe where the weather is not so humid. I went to Cannes.'

'Without saying goodbye to Mother?'

Madame Hassim now looked vague. 'I *think* I sent her a little note, I can't quite remember but maybe I didn't. I must confess I was a little upset at the way the desert party collapsed, the abrupt departure of Captain Crystal, the seeming ingratitude of so many others. Maybe I felt a little angry, but . . . what you suggest is monstrous.'

'Have you not seen Achmed since?'

'Has anyone seen him since, Captain Down? Have you?'

'I haven't seen him and if I had all of Cairo would have heard about it.'

'Of course.' Madame Hassim acknowledged the implication of his male prowess, his prerogative to take swift action with a thief. 'He's disappeared. Suddenly he was there and suddenly he was gone. I can't recall anyone who has seen him this season.'

'How very strange,' Bosco studied his hands. 'Did no one wonder where?'

'Oh no – in Cairo people are only curious for five minutes and then they think of something else. People used Achmed, but no one was particularly fond of him. No one knew much about him, really. But how *glad* I am I saw you, to put the matter right. The man was clearly a rogue.'

Madame Hassim finished the glass of champagne the waiter had brought during Bosco's recitation of the events and glanced over her shoulder.

'Do, *please*, come and join my party to show we are friends again. One or two of them you might know. *Please*.' She put a hand lightly enough on his arm, but he had the sensation her fingers were like grappling irons.

Bosco gave in graciously and, getting up, offered her his arm and led her back to a small table at the far side of the room where seven people were sitting, three other women and four men. There was an English couple he had briefly met before called Smythson from York, a Turkish diplomat and the rest were Egyptian. One of them was a woman of such outstanding beauty that Bosco found himself gazing at her even while shaking hands with the others. Madame Hassim introduced her as Nimet El-Said from Alexandria.

'And under my care for the season,' Madame Hassim added as an afterthought, as though any man might wonder what a woman like that was doing alone in Cairo. There were many very beautiful women in Cairo, it is true, but not many young Egyptian women of good family were allowed to congregate in public places like Shepheard's Hotel. Although most good Egyptian families had formally abandoned the harem, the harem mentality still prevailed. Women often lived in a separate part of the house from the male members, and certainly few well-brought-up young Egyptian women were ever seen out of the house unless in discreet boutiques on the Mouski or in other private houses. Madame Hassim explained this by saying that Nimet El-Said had just returned from visiting America, the insinuation being that she had been influenced by emancipated ideas.

Bosco thought that Nimet was about nineteen. She had a

smooth, smoky skin the texture of alabaster, huge tranquil black eyes that slanted just a little giving her a slightly oriental appearance, enhancing her attraction. Her jet-black hair was dressed fashionably and rather carefully, Bosco suspected, to make her look older.

Madame Hassim casually put Bosco next to Nimet and ordered more champagne while the Smythsons got up to dance, and so did the Turkish diplomat, with a woman of Madame Hassim's age, a member of the Cairene smart set.

'Do you dance?' Bosco said, still looking at Nimet, who shook her head sadly.

'Alas, not here. It is too public. Madame Hassim entertained us to dinner and we came here for a couple of hours.'

'Does your father know you're here?'

Nimet laughed and smiled at him mischievously. 'What do you think?'

Bosco saw that her feet were tapping to the music and she looked with envy at the young English and foreign girls who were enjoying themselves on the dance floor. 'But, please, don't let me stop you dancing.'

'Madame Hassim?' Remembering his manners, Bosco got up reluctantly and held out his hand, which was accepted graciously, Madame allowing him to lead her away from the table.

'I can see you're quite taken by her.'

'Who wouldn't be?'

'It's a pity she can't dance, but maybe you'd like to see her privately?'

Madame Hassim smiled at him from her bland, carefully painted face.

'How do you mean?'

'If I invited you to dinner, would you accept?'

'I could see no possible harm in that.'

'Neither could I.' Madame Hassim looked over her

shoulder to where Nimet was engaged in conversation with one of the older Egyptian men at the table. 'Her father is a very wealthy man, a sheikh, who lives in Alexandria. She is staying with me a few more days, to visit the opera and the theatre. Her father is an enlightened man, but he is an Egyptian. He wants her to be well looked after.'

'I can't understand how he let her go to America.'

'Oh, he was there too.'

'Then where is he now?'

'In Alexandria, where they live. He is one of the most important businessmen in Egypt, a friend of Lord Cromer. Everyone knows him.'

'Then I'll have to be very careful.'

Bosco thought she winked at him.

Madame Hassim's apartment was in the tree-covered Shubra Avenue which had linked Cairo with the Shubra Palace, the magnificent home of Mehemet Ali, founder of the present Khedival dynasty. But for many years it had been subject to a dispute between the members of that family and remained unoccupied, sadly falling into decay. Many of the fine villas lining the road had been turned into apartments and some had become derelict so that the area, which had once been very fashionable, had gone into decline too.

Towards the end of dinner, which consisted of European and Arab dishes served in eastern style, the diners sitting on large cushions on the floor and helping themselves from a low table in the middle, Madame Hassim asked her guests what they would like to do for the rest of the evening. There was a dance at the Mena House hotel, a short carriage drive away, or maybe they would enjoy a walk to the gardens of the Shubra Palace which, despite neglect, were still magnificent and worthy of a visit.

'As Nimet doesn't dance in public I think we should go

to the gardens,' Bosco said, looking at the silent woman by his side whose presence was so disturbing.

'I would like a game of bezique.' The fourth member of the party, Ramlah Bey, glanced casually at Madame Hassim. 'Why don't we let the young people go to the gardens and we can play bezique while we drink our coffee?'

Ramlah Bey had been one of the party at Madame Hassim's table at Shepheard's and Bosco was not quite sure of his status, whether he was Madame Hassim's lover or merely an escort. He was of an indeterminate age and class, polite, inscrutable and self-effacing. In a crowd no one would notice him.

'I'd certainly like some air,' a feeling of excitement made Bosco quite prepared to abandon caution. 'Nimet?'

Nimet had hardly spoken during the long meal, being content to listen, her exquisite head on one side, her beautiful eyes alight with interest as Bosco had been prevailed upon to give a description of the battle for Omdurman; but he never once referred to the charge, despite some prompting from Madame Hassim. With Nimet one felt that her silence was not due to emptiness, but that she was one of those rare, gifted beings who only spoke when they had something interesting to say, some contribution to make to the conversation. Clearly she was not a chatterer, which made Bosco like her all the more. The less she said the more he was intrigued by her.

'The Shubra gardens are very beautiful,' Nimet said in her low, tuneful voice. 'There is a lovely kiosk in the middle which I used to visit with my parents when I was a child.'

Satisfied, Madame Hassim clapped her hands and her tall Nubian servant entered with coffee and sherbet then, while the men smoked cigars, she lit a small pipe and sat there puffing away, her bright eyes thoughtful.

'I have a key to the kiosk,' she said, 'it was given me by

Prince Hassan, the last person to live in the palace. Since then all his relatives have been squabbling about its ownership. It's a great pity because it is one of the most beautiful residences in Cairo.'

Soon afterwards Bosco and Nimet slipped out of the apartment, down the broad stairs, once the main feature of the elegant villa which had belonged to another relative of Mehemet Ali, and into the tree-lined road. The stone villas standing back from the road in gardens, many overgrown, the palace in the distance and, beyond, the great pyramids of Gizeh all cast dark shadows in the moonlight. It was an exciting, enticing night and Bosco was powerfully aware of the slim, sensuous body of the girl walking beside him. He wanted to reach out and touch her. Instead he said: 'How long have you known Madame Hassim?'

'She is an old friend of my father's.'

'And how do you know Ramlah Bey?'

'He too,' Nimet nodded and Bosco thought she was endeavouring to be discreet.

'You must tell me about America. My brother is getting married in July and plans to go there for his honeymoon.'

'There isn't much to tell,' Nimet said.

'I suppose you were as carefully protected as you are here?'

'Not quite so carefully,' Nimet turned to him and smiled, a secret, almost conspiratorial smile which seemed to have little to do with America.

She was equally as enigmatic during their exploration of the huge palace gardens, with its wealth of tropical plants, some rising, neglected, to astonishing heights; its groves of lebbek, sycamore and orange trees casting spooky shadows across the overgrown lawns. Nor were they the only people there. So near to Cairo, yet so isolated, the spot was a favourite rendezvous for lovers and a few other couples strolled between the trees, some hand in hand. But Bosco and Nimet didn't touch.

'You must miss your family,' Nimet said, 'or do you prefer it on your own in Cairo?'

'I prefer it on my own,' Bosco was emphatic.

'You seemed to have a very good time when I saw you the other evening. You are popular with the ladies. Is there some special lady you're attached to?'

'Not in Cairo.' Bosco glanced at her.

'Maybe you're engaged to someone in England?'

'Not engaged. As a matter of fact she wouldn't have me.'

'But do you still love her? Or shouldn't I ask?'

'You shouldn't ask,' Bosco said, and carefully looking around to be sure they were unseen drew her into the shadow of a tree and took her in his arms. To his surprise she yielded immediately, returning his kiss with ardour. His hands travelled down her slim body, fingers strayed across her tiny breasts and he felt her quiver, then sigh with satisfaction as, her arms closely entwined round him, they reluctantly broke away.

'Do you think Madame Hassim planned this?' He felt shaken but elated.

'I think she realized we liked each other and wanted to be alone.'

'You wanted to be alone with me?' He gazed into her eyes and, as she nodded, he kissed her again only more deeply until his body seemed to merge with hers.

'Maybe if we go back Madame Hassim will not be there?' Nimet's translucent eyes lit up.

'Is that planned too?'

'Who knows?'

'I find myself very bewildered.' Bosco kept her hand firmly in his as they started back the way they'd come, forgetting about the kiosk, the key to which lay untouched in his pocket.

'You mean no English girl would behave like this?'

'No one that I have been fortunate to know.'

'I have been married,' Nimet said with sudden candour. 'I thought you should know that.'

'Are you married now?'

'My husband died. He only lived six months. He had tuberculosis and no one knew. My father took me to America to try and get over the shock.'

'I'm very sorry to hear that,' Bosco pressed her hand, 'but relieved too. I thought you quite experienced when I kissed you, not averse.'

'In Egypt women mature very early. I was married when I was fifteen.'

'But you can't only be seventeen now?' Bosco said incredulously, but Nimet only smiled mysteriously and said:

'Isn't it the privilege of a woman to conceal her age?'

'I don't believe you're seventeen, that's all.' For a moment Bosco was overcome by a feeling of doubt, almost fear, certainly bewilderment, as though he had embarked, or was about to embark, on a dangerous undertaking. He was aware of this same feeling of fearful yet excited anticipation he'd had before Omdurman: that one wouldn't wish things other than they were, yet didn't know how they would end. Something was warning him to be careful, but he was too excited, too headstrong, to heed it.

As he had anticipated, when they returned to the apartment they were admitted by Madame Hassim's maid who said that, after all, she and Ramlah Bey had gone to the dance at Mena House and would not be back for some time. Smiling, she showed them into a long drawing-room richly furnished and hung with oriental tapestries, and heavy oil paintings of Egyptian and European scenes. There were plaster busts on pedestals, lamps glowing on low tables, and several sofas, deep and intimate. Bosco looked round him with amazement.

'Shall I bring coffee, Effendi?'

'That would be very nice.' Bosco knew then that everything was prepared for him and Nimet to be alone together.

As soon as the maid had left he took her in his arms again and kissed her. Once more she willingly succumbed and drew him down upon a long divan that ran almost the length of one wall. Her fragrant perfume was so delicate that he could only sense it when he put his face in her hair, gently unpinning it so that it flowed loosely over her shoulders. They were still caressing each other on the couch when the maid re-entered, creeping past them and quietly putting the coffee upon the brass tray. Bosco, feeling slightly foolish, straightened up to thank her, and she inclined her old head.

'Madame Hassim asked me to tell you that if there is anything you require you have only to ring this bell and ask.' She pointed to a small ornate brass handbell on an ormolu table. 'Otherwise everything is in readiness,' and bowing again she pointed towards a door at the far side of the room which was partly ajar.

Bosco stared at her and then at Nimet, who now sat upright on the divan running her fingers through her hair, ignoring the maid who exited as stealthily as she had come.

'What does she mean?' The open door seemed like an invitation.

'I think we would be more comfortable in there. Don't you?' Without waiting for a reply Nimet rose and, taking his hand, led him across the long room, over the gleaming parquet floor covered with Shiraz carpets, and through the door that had been so enticingly left half open.

The room they entered was also sumptuously furnished; the walls were hung with silk and decorated with little gold-framed prints of scenes that, at a casual glance, looked vaguely erotic. The centrepiece of the room was a huge bed draped with a spread of the same material that hung on the walls and, again, low lamps burned, the oil emitting a slight pungent smell that blended exotically with incense smoking in a small bronze brazier warmed by a candle. The whole atmosphere was of such opulence and eroticism that Bosco felt he had walked into a dream, and would soon wake up in his hard bed in the Abbasiya barracks.

But there was nothing dream-like about Nimet, who began to disrobe with a complete lack of modesty, yet with the grace and delicacy of a dancer. Then she went to the bed and, drawing back the cover, curled up on the white sheet underneath, displaying her beautiful body without shame. She held up her arms to Bosco who quickly undressed too and, completely overwhelmed by this candour, lay beside her and embraced her.

When Bosco woke a pale light glowed behind the drawn blinds and the maid was standing by his bedside with a cup of sweet black coffee in her hands.

'Effendi,' she said smiling and bowing, exactly the same as she had been the night before, as if she had not slept. 'There is a carriage waiting for you outside. Madame Hassim thought you might have to get back to your quarters before sunlight.'

Startled, Bosco sat up, anxiously feeling the bed beside him; but it was empty and there was no trace of Nimet in the room except that faint tantalizing fragrance of scent lingering on the pillows.

'She has gone to bed,' the maid said.

'Then this isn't her bedroom?'

The maid shook her head, and through the door came the Nubian servant with a jug of hot water which he proceeded to pour into a basin on a sandalwood tallboy on the far side of the room.

'Abbas will shave you, sir, and your clothes are ironed and ready for you.'

On one of the divans in the room were the shirt, tie and white suit he had worn the night before, and beside them his underclothes were folded as though they had been freshly laundered. On the floor his newly polished shoes only waited for him to put them on.

Bosco saw that it was nearly five o'clock and reveille at the camp was at six. He got quickly out of bed and, after washing and being expertly shaven by the Nubian, left the house half an hour later, entered the Victoria drawn by two Arab horses waiting for him in the shady street outside and was taken swiftly back to his barracks. There he became immediately distracted by his duties; the exercising of the horses, the dress parade and practising for a ceremonial march to be viewed by the Sirdar.

It was thus not until the evening that he had the chance to reflect on what had happened the night before, and then he became suspicious again and wondered how he could have been so guileless, so naïve. Nimet, widowed or not, was no young untried girl but an enchantress – a deeply experienced, profoundly passionate woman. A voluptuary. But whoever she was, she had completely bewitched him and he refused to let himself be deterred from seeing her again. In fact, he was only counting the hours until he did.

That night therefore he wrote to Madame Hassim and sent the letter round by his servant; two days later he had a reply asking him to come to dinner again. But this time when he arrived only Nimet was present and, as the old maid withdrew, she greeted him rather shyly and took him once more to the divan where their lovemaking the previous night had begun.

'I wondered if you'd still want to see me?' she said, in the voice of a demure young girl.

'And why should I not wish to see you again?' Bosco felt so relaxed in her company that he was inclined to play a little game.

'I thought you might be . . . maybe a little disgusted that I was so . . . free,' she concluded, as if the effort were costing her a great deal, looking at him from her trusting, curiously innocent dark eyes.

Bosco laughed and kissed her. 'I could certainly teach you nothing. Why did you tell me the lie about being a young bride? No woman could learn so much from one sick man.'

Nimet pouted and ran her finger along the lapel of his jacket. 'Maybe I taught him something too. I think love is an art that cannot be learned. It is instinctive.'

'Not as instinctive as all that,' Bosco said, 'but I won't pry any more. When you want to tell me you will.'

But that night she didn't, nor the many nights that followed, always assuming the same pattern: a note to Madame Hassim, a small intimate dinner *à deux*, and a night of love in the large bed until he was woken, alone, as usual by the old maid, shaved by the Nubian servant and sent home in the Victoria pulled by the same two sprightly Arab horses.

One night he woke and Nimet was still with him. He lay on his back and listened for sounds he thought he'd heard in the apartment. Nimet stirred beside him and sat up, her jet-black hair cascading over her small oval breasts.

'What is it?'

'I thought I heard sounds.'

'Probably Madame returning.'

'Why do I never see her again?'

'Do you want to?'

'You always answer my questions with a question,' Bosco said. 'Is it an old Egyptian custom?'

'Maybe it's a wise one.'

Nimet leaned over him and he suckled each tiny rust-coloured nipple as though he were a baby being lulled to sleep. When he awoke again she was gone. It was like a fairy tale by the Brothers Grimm that he recalled from childhood, where the disappearing trick is part of the magical arts: and the effect on him of Nimet was magical, there was no doubt of that. It drained him of all feeling except desire for her, made him suspend all judgment and ask no questions. He wanted to take her to the theatre or the opera; to a sporting event at the Turf Club or driving in the Gizera oval, the fashionable meeting-place for Cairenes. But she said that, if they went anywhere public, Madame Hassim would have to chaperone her – they agreed that neither of them wanted that!

The Lancers were returning to England, some of the regiment had already gone, and Bosco had made an application to be seconded to the Egyptian Army where, besides an increase of pay, he would automatically be promoted to Major.

For Bosco had nothing to return to England for, and if he thought of Rachel now it was to see her only in the light cast by Nimet, and that had blinded him. One night Nimet asked him about her.

'Why did she refuse you?'

'She said we didn't know each other very well.'

'That's no excuse for not marrying. One gets to know a spouse well afterwards.'

'She didn't love me then.' Now he felt he didn't care very much.

'Was she a very high-born lady too?'

'No. My mother didn't like her; but I . . . I needed her at the time.'

'Why did you need her?'

'Why does one need a woman?' Bosco said, turning to her. But he didn't really mean that about Rachel; that he only wanted her carnally. What he wanted from her was the warmth, companionship and love that he knew Nimet couldn't give him. What he felt about Rachel and Nimet were two very different things and, had he had them both, they would have been complementary to each other. Only women never saw things like that, and he realized now why so many men he knew had mistresses as well as wives.

He and Rachel didn't correspond. Perhaps neither wanted to be the one to write first. In time Bosco came to think that his falling in love with her had been illusory, and that he had only felt that way because he had been lonely and in need: cut off from women too long because of illness. Maybe his feeling for her had been sickness too. Here in exciting Cairo, in the middle of a passionate love affair with a beautiful, mysterious Egyptian, he felt suspended from normal emotions, and thought very little either about Rachel or his family or home.

Adam, however, wrote to him a few times and Bosco replied. He missed Adam in the regiment, and Harry, and it was this absence of his two best friends that contributed to his decision to apply for a transfer from the Lancers and stay with the Egyptian Cavalry instead. But the main reason was Nimet. He couldn't bear the thought of being separated from her.

In July he was due to go home for Arthur's wedding, but after that he had decided to make his life in Egypt. He could never see an end to his affair with Nimet, but nor could he see anything more permanent with her. She seemed a companion for erotic adventure rather than a partner for life. The proposal to Rachel had been an aberration. Now he didn't plan to marry at all.

'What of the girl? Did you hear from her?' Nimet said.

'I told you we never correspond.'

'Are you sad because she doesn't love you?'

'I was, but I'm not sad now. I'm going to try and stay in Egypt to be with you.'

Nimet opened wide her lustrous, almond-shaped eyes. 'Is it possible?'

'If I join the Egyptian Army. Lots of people do.'

'Perhaps you could leave the army; or do you like the life?'

Bosco appeared to consider the question.

'I am used to it; it's the only life I know. Although I hated the battle I loved it too, except that I'm haunted now by memories of it.'

'Why is that?' Nimet said wonderingly.

'I killed a man.'

'Don't soldiers always do that in battle?'

He looked at her, uncertain whether to go on.

'I did it deliberately because I hated him. Does that shock you?'

'Was he an enemy?' Nimet sidestepped the question by, as usual, asking another.

'No, he was a friend. But he was a young man who paid a lot of attention to my mother and, to my mind, made a fool of her. I kept on saying I could kill him but, of course, I didn't think I meant it. But in the middle of the charge my brother-in-law was killed and I stayed with him, wounded myself. This other chap, his name was Cardew, came up to me and tried to save me: "Hurry," he said, "or you'll kill us both" . . .'

'And?' Nimet prompted.

'I looked at him and I imagine I thought "I don't care if he *does* die. He can come with me", and I made no effort to save myself. He was killed by a Dervish spear as he bent down to help me. That's what I have on my conscience: deliberately willing him to die.'

'Oh.' Nimet, clearly troubled, regarded him gravely and slid her little hand into his. 'Don't be sad. It's all over now. If you are meant to die you die.'

'I suppose so.' Bosco nodded and shook himself awake from the contemplation of that ugly nightmare.

'But if you stay here I suppose you can just see this affair going on for ever,' Nimet continued, rather solemnly he thought.

'For ever and ever, can't you?'

'I must return to my father.'

Bosco stared at the ceiling which was painted gold, rather like the canopy of a tent, an arched golden dome tapering away from the silken-hung walls. The pale glow of the oil lamps sent shadows dancing upon it, tiny little puffs of smoke alternating with the continuous pall of the incense burner.

'Somehow I don't believe you have a father.'

'But of course I have!' She raised herself on her arms, indignantly looking at him and, once again, he could see her shadow take life on the ceiling.

'Yes, but I mean, not in the way you said. It's all right, I don't want to know. I tell you I am very happy with things as they are, happy to ask no questions. Except – there is one question I want to ask.'

'Yes?' Her voice sounded rather timorous.

'Where do you go when you leave here?'

'To my room,' she replied in surprise.

'What is this then?'

'The guest room. My room is very tiny. Isn't it kind of Madame Hassim?'

'Very kind.' But there were still the nagging doubts.

As she lay back he slowly caressed her body and she began to twist about like a cat, relaxed, almost purring.

'You know I love you,' he whispered.

Preparations for the regiment's departure went ahead and Bosco was told that his application to join the Egyptian Army was being considered by the authorities including the Sirdar personally, who thought well of him. In a few days the Sirdar, Lord Kitchener, would want to see him and, possibly, Lord Cromer would too. Bosco wrote to tell his parents about his decision; that he would go home on leave in July and then he would come back, for good.

The next time he called at the apartment in Shubra

Street he was admitted in the usual way by the smiling maid and salaamed by the Nubian, Abbas. Bosco, however, was surprised to find himself taken not to the drawing-room, where he usually met Nimet, but to the small parlour where he had been received on the very first night he had come, now a full month ago. There, waiting for him, smoking her pipe and wearing a long white-and-gold robe, her black hair hidden by a gold turban surmounted by a huge Brobdingnag diamond star, was Madame Hassim. She looked very Oriental and rather forbidding squatting on a silk cushion on the floor, the multiple folds of her plump little face rather set and severe, the *kohl* round her eyes particularly black. She didn't get up when he entered, but motioned to a low chair.

'Will you drink coffee, Captain Down?'

'Where is Nimet?'

'She will join us shortly. In the meantime . . .'

'No, thank you.' Bosco smiled uneasily at the maid who went out slowly backwards as if she were in the presence of royalty. Maybe she thought she was.

'How glad I am to hear you are so happy with Nimet,' Madame Hassim said huskily, the fragrant smoke from her pipe reminding him of a burnt offering at the shrine of a deity. 'She is a very nice girl, is she not?'

'Very nice.'

'And you love her, perhaps?'

'Yes, I suppose I do.'

'You don't sound very sure, Captain Down?'

'Look,' Bosco ran his hand round his tight collar, 'what is this, Madame Hassim? Some form of interrogation?'

'Not at *all*, Captain Down! But the young girl *is* my responsibility. I have to answer to her father, you know.'

'I don't believe that story. Nor do I think she's so young.'

'Whether you believe it or not, it is true. Now that you have dishonoured her, how can I send her home to him?'

'What do you mean "dishonoured"?' Bosco leapt up and, standing over her, looked down at her accusingly.

'Don't you call it "dishonoured", Captain Down? Is it not the same thing in England, to make love to a young unmarried girl of good family? Would not something be required of you?'

Now all the suspicions that he had ruthlessly put to one side crowded in upon Bosco and, with them, also came a peculiar kind of dread, as though the knowledge of something he had not wished to know was now being forced upon him.

'"Good family!"' Bosco cried. 'A girl of good family behaving like a . . .' He stared at the inscrutable face of Madame Hassim and, then, the word which had always been at the back of his mind came almost unbidden to his lips. 'Like a whore,' he whispered, sinking back into the chair.

'Really, Captain Down,' Madame Hassim looked shocked, 'that remark might cost you something. Nimet El-Said is of an impeccable family. She happened to fall very much in love with you – love at first sight – as soon as she saw you. She thought then of you as a husband . . .'

'Husband?' Bosco choked on the word.

'Ah! I see you have no intention of making an honourable woman of her? Really. Did you never have any such intention?'

'Not with a woman like that.'

'I see. How disappointed Nimet will be to hear it. She said you told her you were engaged to a lady in England but were so no longer and that you loved her, Nimet.'

'But I didn't ask her to marry me.'

'. . . that you were staying in Cairo,' Madame Hassim took a ferocious puff of her pipe and continued, 'had applied to join the Egyptian Cavalry – just to be with her. I thought marriage *must* be in your mind, Captain Down.'

'Well, it isn't. I have never been engaged and I have no wish to marry. Nimet knows that.'

'I don't think she does. That is why she questioned you so closely about the lady in question. She did not wish to usurp the affections of another. She would be very, very distressed if she heard of this conversation.'

'As no doubt she will, Madame Hassim, seeing that she reports everything I have told her to you.'

Madame Hassim took her pipe in her hand and gesticulated with it vaguely about the room.

'Captain Down, what woman in love does not confide in another woman? Poor Nimet has no mother. She is sick with love of you. Maybe she did behave foolishly; but it was the action of a woman in love wishing to please a man. We Egyptian woman are hot-blooded – not like your prim English miss. I assure you, her father . . .'

'I want to see this father,' Bosco said. 'Produce him.'

'*Then* will you make an offer?'

'He doesn't exist, well, not in Alexandria, as an important businessman. I have met many well-born Egyptian women and none of them behave like Nimet. It is true she fascinates me. Or, maybe I should put that in the past tense now that I see you in your true colours. Not content with frightening my mother you now try and play the same tricks with me.'

'Whatever you say, dear Captain Down,' Madame Hassim went on, 'is of no consequence. Nor will I let my reputation be sullied. What happened to your mother is in the past and had nothing to do with me . . .'

'Which I doubt . . .'

'But the present *is* very much of consequence to me. You must either make an honourable woman of Nimet or . . .'

'Or . . . ?'

'Pay some compensation to her poor father for the distress . . .'

'But he need know nothing about it . . .'

'Inevitably he will know when the saddened girl returns to him, her reputation shattered. Such an experience cannot but leave a mark on a woman.'

Bosco jumped up again and was advancing towards Madame Hassim when she grabbed a little bell and rang it frantically. The burly Nubian entered and stood in the doorway glowering at Bosco.

'Do take care, Captain Down. I know you are a hero, but Abbas is no stranger to strong arm tactics if called for.'

'What do you have in mind, exactly?' Bosco said.

'Five thousand pounds, or marriage, of course.'

'I have not got five thousand pounds. Such a sum is a fortune.'

'But you are a very rich man. Or rather your father is . . .' Madame Hassim gave him an artful look and, seeing his expression, nodded her head, whereupon the Nubian disappeared. 'I see we are in business,' she said.

'We are not in business, Madame Hassim. I will not pay you one penny for this extortion. But as Nimet is a prostitute – although I did not know it, nor,' he looked around him, 'that this is a brothel, although I should have guessed – I will pay you whatever it is that such women require as a fee.'

'There is no question of a mere "fee", Captain Down. What you have done is very, very costly. A very large sum or, possibly, continuous payments are more what I had in mind. What is more, if you do not pay it . . .'

'Yes?' Bosco, about to leave, turned and looked at her.

'Who knows, the story might circulate round Cairo.'

'Let it.' As Bosco opened the door the Nubian hastily backed away. But the maid standing by the outer door let him out, as usual, smiling.

* * *

The Earl of Cromer, plenipotentiary Consul-General of Egypt, representative of Her Imperial Majesty Queen Victoria, and a member of the distinguished Baring family, was a red-faced man with closely cropped white hair and a white moustache. His eyes behind gold-rimmed glasses always appeared half closed and his manner, although authoritative, was relaxed and genial.

He came to the door as Bosco entered and, clasping him kindly on the shoulder, drew him to an armchair by the window overlooking the Kasr ed-Dubbara, near the great bridge across the Nile. Lord Cromer went to his desk and, picking up a silver cigarette box, offered it to Bosco and then took one himself. He had on a grey tweed suit and a striped shirt and looked the quintessence of affability. Bosco assumed he had been sent for about his posting to the Egyptian Army, although he had expected to see the Sirdar first.

'Well, Bosco, how goes it?' The Earl offered his visitor a light, and they both appreciatively blew smoke into the air.

'Very well thank you, sir.'

'Good, good. And you're quite recovered from your injuries?'

'Quite sir.'

'Good.' Lord Cromer puffed at his cigarette and leaned his head thoughtfully against the back of his chair. Then he sat upright, moving to the edge of his seat, the cigarette burning in his hand.

'You know, my dear Bosco, I am a very great friend of your father.'

'Yes, sir.'

'Of both your parents. My late wife especially was very fond of your mother.'

'Yes, sir.'

After many years of happy marriage Lord Cromer had been widowed only the previous year.

'You know I regard you and all your family with affection.'

'It is very kind of you to say that, Lord Cromer.' Bosco began to feel uncomfortable and stubbed his half-finished Turkish cigarette out in a huge circular brass ashtray.

'I am speaking to you now *in loco parentis*, Bosco, not as Consul-General in Egypt.' Lord Cromer reached out and patted his knee. 'I have recently heard a rather distressing story which concerns not only you but your mother and I sent for you straightaway in order, hopefully, that I may be reassured neither are true.'

'Yes, I see, sir,' Bosco was acutely aware of the admittedly avuncular but also penetrating stare of the great man, famous in Egypt for his probity, his pertinacity.

'Are they true, Bosco?'

'If you're talking about a Madame Hassim . . .'

'One of the most evil women in Cairo. I must say she appears to be perfectly charming; but there is another, darker side. She is an adventuress, a procuress . . .'

'Ah . . .'

'You fell into a trap, Bosco. How could you possibly . . .' Lord Cromer rose and began to pace the room. 'That house in Shubra Street is one of the most notorious brothels in Cairo. Had you never heard of it?'

'Never, sir, but I am not in the habit of patronizing brothels, and this is a matter I never discussed with my brother officers.'

'It's a wonder you didn't meet some of the others there,' his lordship muttered and Bosco remembered the noises in the night. 'I must say that neither am I familiar with brothels, my dear boy, but I feel sure I could tell a house of ill-fame from one where normal, honest people dwell.'

'I was deceived, sir, into thinking a young girl . . .'

'I know all about it,' Lord Cromer spoke tetchily, as though this were not the first case of its kind. 'In other words she bamboozled you. But how naïve of you, Bosco . . .'

'I was very naïve, Lord Cromer.'

'And now this woman . . . this creature,' Lord Cromer reached for a letter on his desk and held it towards Bosco, 'claims that you have not paid her for services rendered, that you have frequented this establishment a dozen times.'

'She asked for five thousand pounds.'

'Two hundred is more like it. Pay it, like a good chap.'

'She claimed the girl she introduced me to at Shepheard's Hotel was of good family and wanted to marry me. Five thousand was the bride price.'

His lordship snorted. 'I thought better of you, Bosco.'

'I thought better of myself, Lord Cromer. But we met privately in an apartment over dinner. I was never aware of anyone else around except the servants.'

'Ah, the private apartment,' Lord Cromer looked thoughtful, 'and dinner. Better say three hundred. The whole house is a brothel, you know. But I have heard the private apartment being used to trap guileless men before – maybe with the same lady that entertained you.'

'I cannot think of her now except with shame, but at the time . . .'

'Oh, Madame Hassim is very selective. The girl may well have been of good family, once . . . but probably they came down in the world. However, Madame Hassim would also take care of disease and . . . er . . . offspring, so you need have no fear on that score. She is a superb businesswoman and supposedly wealthy. She doesn't live there, of course, but has her own apartment overlooking the Khalig-el-Masri, the old canal that flows through the heart of Cairo, and a large villa in Luxor. But this is not all . . .' his lordship stared out of the window. 'Something about your mother last year . . . and Cardew Crystal. Not very savoury at all.'

'That's all over, sir, and Cardew is dead.'

'But did he not die with you at Omdurman?'

'Yes, sir.'

Now Bosco knew what his dread was. It wasn't about discovering that Nimet was a prostitute, or that Madame Hassim was a madam nor that his parents might get to hear about it. It was because, somehow, he had feared that finally his cowardice would be revealed.

'What a very unfortunate circumstance.'

'It was, Lord Cromer. He tried to save my life. I shall feel guilty about it for as long as I live.'

'Well, well, well . . . what a business. Very singular . . .' His lordship looked reflectively out of the window and then sat behind his broad desk. Joining his hands into a steeple he looked severely at Bosco. 'My dear Bosco, because of the affection I have for your family I will do my personal best to settle this matter. But you must leave Cairo. No Egyptian Army for you. And some money must be paid, as I say about three hundred pounds, which is over-generous but everyone knows it is a very expensive establishment, or everyone *should* know. It's probably all she wants and should shut her up. You see . . .' Lord Cromer tapped the offending letter, 'she says that if she does not receive satisfaction she will have no alternative but to write to your father. You don't want that, do you? I don't suppose she means it, but one can't take the risk. She does enjoy a certain standing among some foolish members of the English community, few of whom are here long enough to know about her. But if she did write, implicating your mother, it would be most unfortunate. Good heavens, Bosco, what silly people you were to become involved with a woman like that. I know I was away last year myself, but a word to the consular offices . . .'

'We never thought, sir. There was also someone called Achmed Asher.'

'He's in prison for embezzlement. An intimate of Madame Hassim's. Some say they are related.'

'No wonder no one's seen him,' Bosco stood up. 'Lord Cromer, I and my family *have* been very foolish. I can't tell you how sorry I am for the distress we have caused you personally. My mother's little flirtation with Captain Crystal was of the most harmless sort . . .'

'I know your mother, my dear boy,' Lord Cromer said jovially. 'All perfectly harmless. The trouble is that your father might find information like this coming from such a source distressing.'

'Very distressing, Lord Cromer. It would make him ill.'

'*And* your consorting with a notorious house of ill fame . . .' Lord Cromer held up a hand as if he could hardly bear to think of the matter. 'Anyway, now we have this in hand, Bosco. Your application to join the Egyptian Cavalry will be withdrawn, no reason given. I myself will have a word with the Sirdar – family business, something like that.'

'He doesn't know of this affair?'

'Good heavens no!' Lord Cromer laughed. 'Herbert is a man of unimpeachable integrity. He strongly disapproves of his officers resorting to brothels, though he knows it is to be expected among the ranks. Not a word will be said to him. We have our own little network of spies in Cairo, you know. We have to. I have known the Egyptians, my boy, for over twenty years and believe me you can't trust them. They are up to all sorts of monkey tricks. But we, here, know what goes on. Everything.' The Consul-General gave a smile of satisfaction at the thought that, metaphorically speaking, he had his finger on the collective Egyptian pulse. 'Now I'll settle this, Bosco. She'll have her pay-off and you may go home and never trouble us again. Is that understood?'

'I hardly know how to thank you, Lord Cromer.'

'Thank heaven for the British presence in Egypt. If

you'd been in Cairo in the days of Tewfik Pasha and got into a scrape like this you'd have been found, face downwards, floating in the Nile.'

Lord Cromer dramatically drew his finger across his throat and, putting his arm once more familiarly round Bosco's shoulder, saw him to the door.

CHAPTER 9

When Queen Victoria died at six-thirty in the evening of 22nd January 1901 everyone knew it marked the end of an era. No one alive – or very few – could recall another monarch reigning over England. She had ascended the throne as a young woman of nineteen and died an old, venerable and much-loved lady of eighty-two in possession of her faculties right to the end.

Victoria's reign coincided with a period of unrivalled prosperity in her country's fortunes. Through industry and by conquest it had cemented its lead as indisputably the greatest nation in the world, with an Empire that circumscribed the globe: from Egypt, through the Middle East and the Far East to Australia, across the Pacific to the West Indies and then over the Atlantic to South Africa where, even then, England was currently subjugating the Boers in a struggle that had become increasingly unpopular at home.

But few had thoughts of the war as the country mourned its queen, and her body was taken to be buried beside that of her beloved Albert, who had so long since predeceased her, in the mausoleum she had had erected for him at Frogmore in the grounds of Windsor Castle. Instead the nation's thoughts were with the dead monarch and her family, the elderly, bearded man who had succeeded her as Edward VII.

The Askham family, along with many others lining the shrouded streets along which the coffin passed on its way to Windsor, watched the funeral procession from a Home Office window in Whitehall. Lord and Lady Askham were there, restrained and solemn in their grief. Dulcie wore a long black coat with a black astrakhan fur collar and a neat little toque made of the same material, a veil over her face, her hands in a warm astrakhan muff. Black became her pale beauty and it suited Melanie too, Melanie so much older-looking and more dignified than the young girl who had been widowed two-and-a-half years before. But Flora looked drab in black. She couldn't carry it as her mother and sister could, and she seemed shrivelled and old as though she had been bereaved herself.

Lady Gore, Arthur's wife, appeared noble in black, even though the pallor of recent illness made her fine, disdainful features rather sharp and haggard. She had suffered three miscarriages since her marriage eighteen months before, and the anxiety and strain showed. Askhams were expected to produce heirs rather quickly. A speedy demonstration of fecundity was regarded as a necessary condition of being an Askham wife. Arthur had been born within a year of marriage, ten months to the day, and that was the sort of thing expected of women married to Askham men – a few years given to breeding in earnest and then, duty done, they could do pretty much as they pleased while their husbands grew even richer and helped to run the country.

Frances, apparently such a superb specimen of English womanhood, felt that somehow she'd failed to live up to standards, even though no one reproached her for a moment. Indeed, all the family were united in demonstrating a degree of kindness, understanding and compassion that, too, were attributes of being an Askham. One did not kick a dog when it was down. But there was, also, a certain amount of tacit sympathy for poor Arthur for having chosen a first-rate filly who, somehow, turned out to be not quite up to standard, especially as the Crewes had a reputation as prolific breeders.

Arthur looked the prosperous politician he was: heir to a great title – impassive, sorrowful, correct, an embryonic statesman like his father, or maybe a diplomat, a future Ambassador to France. A crêpe band was tied round his black top hat and his long, morose features seemed almost made for mourning. Bosco, on the other hand, in his Lancer uniform, now embellished with French-grey facings and the Imperial cypher on his shoulderstraps – 'the Empress of India's' as a tribute to the heroes of Omdurman – looked dashing and insouciant, tall, commanding, ready to give his life, as he nearly had, for Queen and country.

After the passage of the cortège the family walked from Whitehall, through the sombre crowds to their own house in St James's Square where they had arranged to entertain friends to a light collation to make up for the rigours of that sad day.

Once assembled, the Askhams received their guests with a kind of muted grief, as though the death of the Queen were a personal family affliction. And in a way it was. The wealth and privileges of the aristocracy sprang from allegiance to the Crown which had bestowed nobility on them, or their forefathers, in the first place.

Most of the people in that room, dressed in deep mourning, were more or less connected with the Royal Family either as friends, servants or, in some cases, by blood. There were a few exceptions, but not many. So they wore black as a sign, banded together, as they were, by a particular sense of intimacy with the deceased which the bulk of the population – who also mourned her – didn't possess.

There were some who *had* to be asked who had nothing to do with royalty at all, like the Lightermans, parents-in-law to an Askham and people Dulcie always felt she had to ask because Melanie felt towards them not only duty, but affection. Since she had taken up residence in Marylebone, not far from the Lightermans' substantial town house in Manchester Square, Melanie seemed to prefer Mabel's company to that of her mother. Mabel, who donned an apron as soon as she set foot in the small house in George Street in order to show the nurse exactly how to look after her grandson, how it was done in the old days when the nurses at St Thomas's used castor oil and plenty of carbolic.

Dulcie was disappointed in her daughters – she admitted it – not to them, but to many of her intimate friends. But her disappointment was compensated for by the devotion of her daughter-in-law, Frances, who was just what she had hoped her daughters would have been: dutiful, loving and respectful, obeying every wish, asking advice in all matters. Dulcie couldn't see enough of Frances and thus she took her failure to produce a living heir rather hard. It was not the sort of thing that she would have expected of a dear girl like Frances. With her striking good looks, coupled with her ability as a shot and her fine seat on a horse, her love of balls, hunts, sports of all kinds, and her healthy physique, one would have expected the babies to be appearing without any difficulty at all – fine bouncy babies one after the other, all as healthy and fit as their mother.

But Dulcie didn't despair. The couple *could* conceive, and what was a miscarriage or two when they were young and had so many years together? They had their whole lives to look forward to. And she knew that Frances, though badly stricken by her miscarriages, and very ill after the last one with blood poisoning, wouldn't give up. No matter what; she would go on doing her duty like the robust young Englishwoman she was.

Yes, Frances and Arthur, what a joy they were. Watching them now circulating among the guests in the large reception room of the first floor of the house overlooking the Square, she felt a pride in them that was lacking whenever she contemplated the fortunes of her other children. She knew she had so little control over Melanie and Flora, and even darling Bosco was a bit of a problem. He had only recently come home, having gone from Egypt to India on a year's referment to an Indian cavalry regiment that was short of officers. She had rather dreaded that Bosco might stay in India after his disappointment about Egypt, whatever that was. He had given no reason why he didn't stay there; but then Bosco always enjoyed mysteries. He didn't confide in his mother. He didn't ask her opinion on almost everything, as did dear Arthur and Frances who were quite happy occupying a wing at Askham Hall and living in St James's Square, when they were in town. Although only just home, she had hardly seen Bosco who was busy setting up a separate establishment in Duke Street, St James's; just around the corner to be sure, but quite unnecessary when he could have had his own suite of rooms at home.

But Dulcie noticed how the young women, there with their parents, some recent debutantes and some coming out this year, eyed Bosco as he circulated as though hoping against hope that the next group he approached would be theirs.

She must get Bosco married quickly, Dulcie thought, remembering with dread the awful time he told her he'd proposed to that Rachel girl who had actually had the temerity to refuse him. Refuse her son! She shuddered whenever she thought of it, and of what might have been the dread consequences had she said 'yes'! She had certainly been responsible for Bosco returning so soon to Egypt and, probably, asking for the transfer to India as well. However, it was just the sort of thing one expected of people who fell off horses and outstayed their welcome – coming for a weekend, and remaining a month. No breeding.

Happily nothing had been heard of them since they finally took themselves off, in an Askham coach needless to say. At least, she never asked if Flora saw the girl. She simply wasn't interested.

Now Hesther Savage was a nice girl. Dulcie watched her from a corner where she sat with a few cronies, by now all feeling rather tired after standing for hours either at windows or in the streets. Hesther's mother, Lady Savage, who was sitting next to her, was a childhood friend. The Savages had that kind of cosy relationship with the Askhams that the Crewes had. They were an ancient family, rich, with plenty of property scattered throughout the country and connections at court. Indeed, Lady Savage had been lady-in-waiting to the Princess of Wales, now Queen Alexandra. Suddenly Hesther Savage seemed more acceptable than ever.

'Dearest Hesther,' she turned to Amelia Savage who was gossiping to the Duchess of Quex on her other side. 'I was thinking what a beauty she has become, Amelia. I'm sorry Bosco missed her presentation. I wonder she wasn't snapped up in her first season.'

Lady Savage excused herself to the Duchess and gave her full attention to her old friend Dulcie Askham. 'Don't worry, there are plenty of eligible men around, my dear. I only hope she chooses the right one.'

'Anyone in particular?' Dulcie surveyed the dozen or so young men in the room whom she knew to be unattached.

'Archie Cuthbertson asked Edgar for her hand, but Edgar thought he hadn't enough money. His father is only a baronet and, Edgar says, parts of his estate are heavily entailed.'

'Did Hesther mind?'

'Indeed she didn't,' Lady Savage said peremptorily. 'Hesther is quite happy to be guided by her parents. She said she thought Archie was nice but dull, which wouldn't have mattered but for the lack of fortune. As I told her, I wouldn't have had half such a happily married life if dear Edgar had been the blade his father was.'

The women exchanged glances.

'Quite,' Dulcie lowered her chin, her eyes speculative. 'I think maybe I'll have a little dinner-party quite soon and invite Hesther and Bosco.' Her eyes sidled round to her friend. 'No objections there, I trust?'

'My dear, who could object to Bosco?' Amelia, a tall, angular lady who looked like a draped lamp-post in her mourning clothes, grew quite animated. She had not the beauty, the wit or the charm of Dulcie, but she was a clever woman and very accessible to the young in search of experience. Indeed, half the officers in the regiments stationed at the Palace and at Windsor were rumoured to have been introduced to their first delights of love in the arms of the second lady of the Princess of Wales's bedchamber. 'Mind you, she'd be lucky if she gets him. He has told everyone he is against marrying.'

'Oh, has he?' said his mother grimly. 'He hasn't told me.'

'Mama, we are off,' Flora, arriving unnoticed, kissed the Duchess and Lady Savage on the cheeks and squatted in front of her mother. 'Mabel is giving us a ride back.'

'Oh dear, I hoped you'd all stay for family dinner.'

'Sorry, Mother. Mabel had asked us already.'

'Really, dear, I think you might have consulted your mama, to see what plans we had. It *is* the day of the dear Queen's funeral, after all.'

'Not ask your mother!' The Duchess quizzed Flora through her lorgnette. The Duke of Quex had been dead for years and the line was now extinct due to many years of inbreeding and an insufficiency of males. But the Duchess maintained a firm grip on London society, having established standards in the eighties that those who considered themselves in society were supposed to adhere to. In fact there was a set of rules known unofficially as the Quex Rules which were guidelines to behaviour and decorum, rather as those of Lord Queensberry now governed the rules of boxing. It was clearly a Quex rule for an unmarried daughter to consult with her mother and, in the Duchess's opinion, Flora should be reminded of it.

'Your Grace knows that I have my own household now,' Flora said, quite unabashed. 'I no longer live at home and think therefore that I may make what arrangements I please.'

'My dear Flora,' the Duchess boomed. '*I* was not married until close on thirty and, until the day my father took me to the altar, I never did or thought a thing not approved of by my dear parents.'

'Indeed, Your Grace?' Flora sounded very polite.

'I see my words have no effect on you, Flora dear. I pity your poor parents.'

'Dearest Duchess, I have unfortunately become *quite* accustomed to the behaviour of my daughters,' Dulcie fluttered her black-bordered handkerchief in front of her face as though it were a fan. 'Thank heaven for my dearest Frances.' She waved to her daughter-in-law who waved back and then, excusing herself to the people she was with, came over and also kissed the Duchess and Lady Savage, both of whom, of course, had known her since she was in her cradle.

'Flora is just off, Frances dear. We will only be a small party for dinner.'

'Melanie too?' Frances gave Dulcie a surreptitious smile of sympathy.

'They are going to dine with Lady Lighterman.'

'And Bosco, Mama.'

'Oh, that *is* unsupportable.' Vexed, Dulcie got up and signalled to a footman to fetch her son which he did, bringing him from the far side of the room.

'Yes, Mama?'

'I can't have you dining with the Lightermans and spoiling our party.'

'But Mama, you didn't ask me,' Bosco said gently.

'I took it for granted you'd be there.'

'I'm sorry, Mama.' Bosco glanced at Flora. 'I've hardly seen the baby since I got home and he's with Lady Lighterman today.'

'You can see him another time.'

'I have arranged it now, Mama.'

'We're off, dearest Dulcie.' Lady Lighterman, plumper than ever, sailed across the room, Melanie's hand tucked firmly in hers. She was dressed in tightly fitting black bombazine with an old-fashioned bustle, her bright, unnaturally gold hair only partly obscured by a close-fitting hat of artificial black petals. The overall impression reminded the Duchess of women of the servant class, confirmed by the way she clutched the hand of the daughter of an earl as though she were an equal, though no well-trained servant would permit herself such familiarity. The Duchess was therefore at a loss to place her and, aghast at such a display of vulgarity, averted her eyes, though it was certainly according to the Quex Rules that Dulcie should have to introduce her, which she did as gracefully as she was able. Mabel was charmed to meet the Duchess and plomped herself next to her, uninvited, telling her that she had never met a real live duchess and briefly squeezing the august arm as though to assure herself she was real.

As the Duchess said to Lady Savage afterwards, it was certainly a great cross for their poor, dear Dulcie to bear having such a creature even remotely connected with the family.

Gradually more and more people left, most of them having neglected to refer even once to the great Queen whom they were there to mourn. Instead they had complained about the discomfort of such long hours of waiting – because it had been important to get there early in order to obtain a good view – and then went on to the trivia and gossip at which society so excelled. The men speculated about the rearrangement of the Court now that it would return to London from Windsor where the old Queen had lived, and the women about the position of the King's mistress now that he was at last on the throne.

It was this sort of conversation that both bored and disgusted Flora and she was glad to make her escape in the Lightermans' comfortable brougham in the company of her brother and sister.

When the Lightermans and their guests returned to Manchester Square, turning into the circular drive and stopping at the great double doors which were thrown open by invisible hands on their arrival, Mabel announced she had a surprise for them and looked eagerly to the upstairs window of the drawing-room.

'There she is!' she cried, taking the hand of the tiger who had jumped off the back of the coach to help her out. She puffed up the three broad stairs followed by her guests and, several minutes later, by Sir Robert who had even more difficulty, because of his increasing girth, negotiating first the steps of the brougham and then those of the house.

'Rachel!' Lady Lighterman called as soon as she was inside, and Rachel appeared at the top of the stairs, one hand on the broad rail looking down on to the circular hallway.

Bosco paused on the steps at the sound of her name and looked at Flora.

'Rachel Bolingbroke?'

Flora nodded.

'Then I must go,' Bosco made as if to turn back, but Flora put a restraining hand on his arm.

'Don't be so silly! All that happened two years ago.'

'But I remember it too well.'

'Bosco, Rachel is a particular friend of mine. It is inevitable that you shall meet.'

'Then you planned this?'

'Not at all. I knew she was coming, but I didn't plan it.' Flora marched firmly into the house followed, with some reluctance, by Bosco.

'There now,' Mabel said as Rachel, accompanied by Adam, slowly reached the hall. 'Isn't this a nice surprise? I don't suppose you two have seen each other for well . . .' she looked enquiringly from Bosco to Rachel and, then, their eyes met.

'Two years,' Rachel said.

'More or less,' Bosco attempted nonchalance.

'My, that *is* a long time, and how much has happened. You must tell us all about it, Captain Down, and I'm sure you'll be glad to see your friend Mr Bolingbroke again.'

The men clasped hands.

'You look awfully fit, Bosco,' Adam said. 'Is that the result of pig-sticking in India?'

Bosco laughed. 'I played a lot of games as well.'

'Pig-sticking always seems to me a particularly revolting sport,' Flora observed, following Mabel into a parlour off the hall where footmen helped divest them of their coats. 'Don't we look terrible all in black? Did you see any of the procession?'

'From the Mall,' Adam answered. 'We saw it all. Farewell to a great queen I say. We shall never see her like again.'

'Amen to that,' Mabel said piously. 'Now who's for a nice cup of tea?'

'This is an awfully splendid place you've got here, Lady Lighterman,' Bosco put his arms behind his back and walked around looking about him.

'All for young Bobby when I go,' Sir Robert said proudly. 'He will be a young man of considerable fortune. My daughters are married to rich men and well provided for. No, it is all for Bobby now that his father is no longer with us. His mother, too, will be well taken care of, quite independently of her son.'

'How very generous,' Flora smiled approvingly at him and put her arm through Rachel's. 'I haven't seen you since before Christmas. Tell me, how was Bath and your father?'

They walked up the stairs followed by Adam and Melanie, with Bosco and Sir Robert behind.

'How's the baby?' Adam enquired.

'Beautiful. You haven't seen him for a long time, have you?'

'I think it was October, when we came to dinner.'

'I don't call him a baby any more. He can walk.'

Just then little Robert, holding the hand of his nurse, came to the top of the stairs and squealed when he saw his mother who rushed up to him, her arms extended.

'There, my precious,' she said kissing him. 'We are all back.'

Little Robert looked at all the grave figures dressed in black with some kind of awe, stepping to one side as they passed him into the drawing-room. The sober, unaccustomed grandeur and also, perhaps, the splendid dress uniform of his uncle startled him and he burst into tears. Bosco scooped him up, holding him high above his head.

'Well, young man? What's the matter?'

Little Robert immediately stopped crying, looking with fascination at the gleaming medals on Bosco's chest.

'There, you can have it,' Bosco lowered him on to the floor and, unclasping the medal of the Distinguished Service Order, gave it to him. The little boy immediately put it in his mouth.

'Oh, be careful, Bobby!' Melanie cried kneeling beside him again. 'That is very precious.'

'He can have it.' Bosco's face was impassive as he looked sadly at his small nephew. 'It means nothing to me.'

'Now, Captain, that's a very silly thing to say,' Mabel swooped down with a rustle of black bombazine and took the shining silver from the toddler.

'I mean it. It was a medal I didn't deserve. His father should have had it. It belongs to him.'

Mabel looked awkwardly from Melanie to her husband, the medal on its ribbon still in her hand.

'Give it to me, Mabel,' Melanie said firmly and taking it went up to Bosco and pinned it on his chest, patting it as it hung in place. 'There. That's where it belongs. You can wear it for Harry, Bosco, but please don't say such silly things, and don't spoil this occasion when we're all here together, reunited after two years.'

'I'm not spoiling anything,' Bosco slumped on to a sofa as though he were suddenly weary, 'but I couldn't help thinking, today, watching all those men marching, of the ones we left behind at Omdurman, their only memorial the sands of the desert.'

'The memorial is in our hearts, Captain. *That's* where it matters.' Mabel sat next to him and patted his hand. 'Now, cheer up. We haven't seen you for a long time and you haven't seen Adam and Rachel. You must have lots to tell us. Let's all have a happy day now that we're here together, despite the death of the Queen. I'm sure she'd wish that.' Ever since Victoria had knighted her husband Mabel liked to think of her as every bit a familiar as the aristocrats they'd left in St James's Square. The Queen had said a few words to her on that occasion and Mabel thought she recognized in her a fellow spirit: a simple woman, not hoity-toity at all. She looked up as a stream of servants entered bearing silver trays upon which were teapots, cups and saucers, milk jugs and tiers of plates with beautifully cut sandwiches, cake cut in slices, or small, individual iced cakes with cherries on top. The trays they placed on tables spread out for them by the windows.

The drawing-room was a beautiful room running the

length of the house and overlooking the bare branches of the wintry trees in the Square. It had three large double French windows leading on to a balcony with a wrought-iron rail. The walls of the room were lined with silk and hung with pictures portraying celebrated people by famous artists: Reynolds, Van Dyke, Gainsborough and, more recently, Sargent who had also painted an enormous, full-length canvas of Sir Robert Lighterman in his robes as an alderman of the City of London which had a solus position at the head of the room. The long windows were framed with heavy silk curtains tied back with thick gold cords, and a silk-covered tasselled pelmet hung in an unbroken line from one end of the room to the other.

The parquet floor was covered with a huge Wilton carpet, into which had been specially woven a delicate pattern of birds to go with the silk on the walls. In each corner of the room there were large ornamental vases six feet tall filled with pampas grass and artificial flowers. Scattered about were small, highly polished mahogany tables, with cabriole legs embellished with scrolls, and decorated with dainty crystal vases of fresh flowers bought the previous day in Covent Garden. In the huge fireplace, surmounted by a marble mantel, a great fire warmed the room which had, in addition, central heating as well as electric light installed by Sir Robert when he bought the house, almost derelict, from an impoverished nobleman.

Restoring it had been his joy in his old age. He had employed the finest designers and decorators and given them a free hand. For, although he did not have portraits of ancestors of his own to hang on the walls, he was a man who put his great wealth to the acquisition of things of beauty, and this was his comfort now that his only son was dead – that and his grandson who was his sole heir. So that Bosco's mention of Harry, and the scene with the medal, had brought tears to his eyes as he dandled his grandson on his knee. The servants busied about serving tea, and

Flora wondered aloud how anyone could eat another thing.

'Oh, you'll be hungry again by dinner-time,' Mabel said, helping herself to a piece of light cream sponge. 'I must say this cold weather gives me quite an appetite.' She looked at Bosco. 'There now, dear, did that nice hot cup of tea make you feel better? You mustn't be melancholy, you know. Put it all behind you. Sir Robert and I are *proud* that our son died for his country. It is not given to many mothers to have a hero for a son.'

'Harry *was* a hero, Lady Lighterman,' Bosco said with emotion. 'And I'm sorry I made a scene about the medal. We all feel that not enough men were honoured on that day.'

'But your regiment got two Victoria Crosses in one engagement, and an honour from the Queen, for it to be known as "The Empress of India's".'

'Medals and honour never make up for friends, or lives needlessly lost. I did try and give my medal back, you know, as it was awarded to me when I was still too ill to know what was happening. But my colonel said it was an honour for the whole regiment. Thus I do, indeed, wear it for Harry, Cardew Crystal and all the other men who died.'

'That's the spirit, my boy,' Sir Robert said, yawning and handing Bobby back to his mother. 'I must confess I feel terribly weary after all that standing. I'm going to take a nap until dinner-time and you must all amuse yourselves as you please. Mabel?'

'I'm going into the kitchen, dear, to talk to Cook. I didn't have time to see her this morning. We had to leave the house so early,' she explained to Bosco. 'But how *glad* I am I saw that procession and all the kings and princes walking in it. Did you see the Kaiser? They say he is a terrible fellow, but I thought he looked rather nice and I'm always sorry for him, poor dear, because of that withered arm he has.'

'I'm not sorry for the Kaiser!' Bosco exploded. 'If we

have a war this century it will be because of Germany's expansionist policies fanned by the Kaiser.'

'But, dear, it is said he held his grandmother in his arms when she died. He must be a kindly soul to do that.'

'Well, all I can say is that the new King can't stand him. You ask my father. He knows all about it.'

The thought of asking anything of Lord Askham, who scarcely ever seemed to see anything beneath the level of his nose, terrified Mabel. She knew what the Askhams really thought of her, which was why she tried so hard to dress well and be pleasant and natural with them. But it was uphill work because she never felt at ease with them. Yet to her it was to be expected that they should despise her because of her humble origins. Mabel Lighterman remained convinced, even in the twentieth century as she had been in the latter part of the nineteenth, that people had their natural places and that whatever one did, however one strived, however much money one made, one could never get over that accident of birth that made some people common and others noble.

It amused her, however, to steal Melanie from Lady Askham. A being made entirely without rancour or malice, it nevertheless helped her to get just a little of her own back for all the petty humiliations, the disparaging glances, the patronizing tones, she was subjected to.

She heaved herself off the sofa, patting Bosco's hand yet again. 'What are you going to do, dear?'

'I'd like a walk,' Bosco said.

'But dear, it's nearly dark!' Mabel looked out of the window and saw that the lights were beginning to come on in the houses opposite.

'I can still find my way in the dark,' Bosco laughed. 'You're a good soul, Mabel, and I like you. You must call me by my Christian name, and forget about this "Captain" business. Flora, do you fancy a stroll?'

'I'm going to read in the library,' Flora said, 'I have an essay to write for next week.'

'She's *very* clever,' Mabel said admiringly, gratified by Bosco's kindness to her. 'All these books and papers. A real scholar in the family!'

'I must see to Bobby,' Melanie took him by the hand and went towards the door. 'See you at dinner.'

'I'll come with you,' Rachel quickly got up, as though afraid of being alone with Bosco, and Adam said:

'It looks as though I'm your walking companion.'

Accordingly the two men donned their hats and coats and walked up through Spanish Place to Marylebone High Street and then towards Regent's Park.

'I see you haven't got over that business,' Adam remarked, after they'd discussed trivialities and were halfway up the street.

'What business?'

'You know, about Harry . . . and Cardew.'

'I've got over it, but I don't forget it,' Bosco swung his cane towards a lamp-post. 'I often dream that Cardew leans over to me from his horse calling "Hurry, or you'll kill us both". He haunts me. Do you know, even the Sirdar got to hear about it and sent for me before I finally left Egypt?'

'Really?' Adam stopped and, in the light of a lamp, lit a cigarette.

'I'd mentioned it to Lord Cromer, and he told Lord Kitchener.'

'What happened?'

'The Sirdar was good enough to say that he'd made enquiries of people who were in the charge and no one blamed me for Cardew's death.'

'So finally, I hope, you accept that.'

'He didn't know what was in my heart, did he, Adam? That I had murder there? I couldn't tell him I murdered a man. The only one who knows that is you.'

'But you're wrong, because you didn't. Everything happened too quickly. Logically you'd never have wanted to kill poor Cardew. You'd never have done it.'

'I hesitated, and . . . Harry was dead, you see. "Leave him," Cardew said, and I didn't.'

'But it *wasn't* murder, and you must realize that, Bosco, or you'll ruin your life with all these fantasies.'

'It is ruined anyway.' Bosco quickened his pace, Adam having to walk faster to keep up with him. 'I'm rootless, you know, Adam. I don't belong anywhere or to anyone. If Rachel had accepted me two years ago I might have been a different person. Tell me, does she have anyone in her life?'

'Only the Cause,' Adam smiled. 'She is devoted to women's suffrage.'

'No, I mean to marry.'

'She is married to the movement. She constantly attends meetings at people's houses, and sits up all night writing pamphlets, then tours the country making speeches. I am rather proud of her really.'

'It's too late now anyway,' Bosco said.

'I didn't ever think you were really suited quite honestly.'

'I had the most shameful episode in Egypt,' Bosco said suddenly. 'Can you bear to hear another sordid story?'

By now they had reached the park, which was not yet closed, and they walked along by the lake which tapered into the canal at one end, broadening into a boating pond and bird sanctuary at the other. There were a few ducks and pigeons standing around with a hopeful air, waiting for food; but a mist had come down over the water, and people were hurrying home from seeing the procession or from their places of business, their heads bent against the cold. Bosco told Adam the story of Nimet and Madame Hassim, about his naïveté in thinking that a brothel was a private home, about the blackmail at the end, and the intervention of Lord Cromer.

'I was *asked* to leave Egypt,' he concluded. 'Wasn't that shameful?'

'Well, it was a bit foolish,' Adam replied after a moment, trying to digest the story. 'But then I don't know how I should have acted in the circumstances.'

'You would never have done what I did. You know I'm named after my uncle, Bosco Kitto, who was a wild man, and people, though proud of him, were rather relieved when he died honourably. I think as well as his name, I have his blood in me.'

'You're very fatalistic this evening,' Adam said. 'I think you're just a normal young man, and I'm an abnormal one.'

'How do you mean?'

'I've never been with a woman, you know.'

'Never?'

'Never.' Adam grimaced. 'It is not that I don't like them – please don't misunderstand me – but I am shy of them, and all Rachel's friends rather frighten me. So as Flora does, I too, keep to my books and learning.'

'Don't you like Flora, Adam?'

Adam looked at him curiously. 'How do you mean? Of course I like her.'

'As a wife? Wouldn't she suit? It would give me much pleasure to have my best friend married to my favourite sister. And, oh, you *are* my best friend, Adam.' Bosco caught his arm and pressed it. 'You don't know what it means to me to have someone in whom I can confide, someone who is warm and sympathetic and doesn't condemn me.'

'How can I condemn you? There's nothing to condemn. Surely no one else condemns you?'

'I don't confide in anyone else as I do in you. People *would* condemn me for what happened in Cairo, consorting with a common prostitute. I was so disgusted when I knew. I actually felt love for the woman, Adam. I was quite besotted with her. I was going to stay in Egypt for ever to be with her. Yet all the time she was deceiving me and trying to trap me and, do you know, she wrote to me after it was over?'

'Really?'

They turned around the pond at the north end, crossed the bridge and proceeded across the flat meadowland towards St John's Wood. Suddenly, out of the shadows a woman appeared, wearing a shabby coat with a tattered fur boa round her neck and a flat, crumpled hat on her head. Taken aback, they both stopped and looked at her.

'I could give you a good time, dears,' she said hesitantly in a hoarse, cockney voice. 'If you . . .' then, seized by a spasm of coughing, she bent over, clutching her coat, and they could hear the rattle of congested phlegm in her chest.

'My poor woman,' Adam, recovering himself, went up to her and put a hand on her shoulder. 'You're far too unwell to be out in this weather.'

'What can I do?' the woman gasped. 'I am not a common whore, sir. I have six children and we live in one damp basement room in Camden Town. I can't keep them no more.' She sank to the ground, her eyes filling with tears, her rasping breath forming white smoke in the bitter air. 'On the day our poor Queen, gracious lady, was buried I am reduced to this.'

Adam leaned down and helped her up. Then he took some notes from his pocket and pressed them into her hand.

'Here are a few pounds. Go back to your family and buy them food, and if you will get in touch with me at this address,' he added his card to the notes in her hand, 'I will arrange for my sister to get help for you. She is involved in charity work of this nature among other things.'

'Oh sir,' tears sprang to the woman's eyes convincing him that her story was true. 'I am an honest woman, sir. How can I thank you?'

'You'll thank me by going home to your children straight away and buying them some food. Now take care across the park because all the gentlemen here are not as well disposed as we are and, please, get in touch with me as soon as you are well.'

He patted her shoulder whereupon she grabbed his hand and kissed it. Then, with a stricken look on her face, she crushed the notes she'd been given in her pocket and, turning, hurried across the park towards Camden Town.

'You *are* a droll fellow,' Bosco said with amusement. 'She probably says that to everyone and spends the money on drink.'

'How can we know?' Adam sadly watched her thin form retreat into the mists swirling more thickly now across the park. 'I think she told the truth. But I like to trust people and, if she is lying, well, *I* have a clear conscience.'

'A common tart,' Bosco said scornfully. 'You are too kind for your own good, my friend.' Bosco linked his arm companionably in Adam's. 'I think we should turn and go home too, taking your good advice to heart, or else we may be set upon and robbed.'

Indeed the shadows shuffling through the park among the skeletal trees took on a menacing aspect and, rather than continue round the lake, they left the park by a gate leading into the road along which a few carriages, their hurricane lamps lit, had slowed to a crawl, the drivers leaning forward to peer ahead, the horses stepping cautiously.

'You were saying about this woman,' Adam pulled his scarf more securely round his neck. 'She wrote to you. And then? I must say I'm intrigued.'

'She said that her father had, in fact, been a sheikh but was now dead and, widowed and impoverished, she had been befriended by Madame Hassim and led into the path of prostitution. She said she had indeed loved me, and pleaded for my help.'

'And did you give it?'

'Certainly not! What could I do? She had brought me low enough already, and Lord Cromer's trust in me would have been jeopardized.'

'What sort of help did she want?'

'She wanted to come to England and abandon the life she was leading.'

'And what did you do?'

'I? Do?' Bosco looked at his friend in amazement. 'I thought I was the naïve one, not you. I ignored the letter, naturally. Let her find her own way to England if she will, or ask for the help of Madame Hassim. I never wish to see either of them again. About Flora,' Bosco continued as they came in sight of the welcome lights of Baker Street which would take them to Manchester Square. 'What do you say?'

'I only see her as a friend,' Adam said quietly. 'But if you talked to me about Melanie, there's something different.'

'Mel? My sister Mel? You'd take her and the baby?'

'I'd take her and ten babies,' Adam said emotionally. 'But would she take me? I have no fortune and no prospects.'

'If she loved you who cares about fortune and prospects. Besides, she has plenty. Do you know, the life that my parents live sometimes sickens me. It sickens Mel too. That's why she likes the comfortable vulgarity of the Lightermans.'

'I wouldn't call them vulgar,' Adam said sharply. 'They have a beautiful house.'

'Oh, the place is superb. But he hasn't done it himself. The Lightermans are *vulgar*, my good fellow, very nice and kind but vulgar. Mabel is horribly vulgar. But for Mel I think she has the warmth and comfort of our old nurse Hudson, warmth that my mother lacks. I like her too.'

'Vulgarity and all?'

'I see I've annoyed you, Adam, and I'm sorry. It was an ass-like thing to say. No, I do like them; they're good, honest people. I've also travelled the world, don't forget, and met all kinds of folk. I feel I've got away from my class; but my parents, my brother and sister-in-law are stuck with it. What worries them is that, if Frances and Arthur can't have live children, the title might become extinct. It frightens them to death.'

'But what about you?'

'Oh, I shan't marry now.'

'But you're not still in love with Rachel?'

Bosco didn't reply at once but continued the slow pace along Baker Street. 'I don't know if I was in love with her then. Since Egypt I'm not at all sure just what my feelings are, or if they're to be trusted.'

'She didn't think you were,' Adam said sadly.

'Maybe she was right. But you, Adam? Does Mel know about you?'

'Good gracious, no! I see her quite a bit, you know, because Rachel and Flora are such friends and she and Melanie frequently ask us to their house, and they come to ours. She is so wonderful with that child, so maternal, so full of repose. I was very taken by her when I first met her again at your house, and my regard for her has grown. To me she is a heroic creature. I would give anything to make her happy.'

'Maybe you will.'

'What would your parents say? That I was marrying her for her money?'

'Probably, but I know you're not and, if you love Mel and she loves you, and wants to marry you, I'd be the happiest fellow in the world.'

CHAPTER 10

'Adam *Bolingbroke*,' Lady Askham cried in a voice resonant with incredulity, 'to marry my daughter! It's unbelievable. Will no one rid us of that family? What have we done to deserve *this*?'

'Is it so very unfortunate, Mama?'

'I blame it on you completely, Bosco, encouraging people of that sort – middle-class, ordinary.'

'What, exactly, is ordinary, Mama? Maybe people think us "ordinary". Adam is being called to the Bar. I hear he is extremely well thought of as a barrister. He might well stand for Parliament – as a Liberal,' he added maliciously.

'Don't you think Melanie might have told us of her intentions herself? Or that *he* might have had the courtesy to ask your father formally for her hand? Has he no manners, in addition to no breeding?'

'I think they're both a little afraid of you and Father, Mama. If that's the case, you have only yourselves to blame. You have been consistently unfriendly to the Bolingbrokes and I can't, for the life of me, see why. I am sent as an emissary. Come, Mama,' Bosco got up and kissed her on the forehead. 'Aren't you pleased to have our Mel happy?'

'How can she be happy with a man like that? I find him insipid to a degree.' Lady Askham crinkled her white, unlined brow. 'I even forget what he looks like.'

'He is of medium height, Mama, with light-coloured hair, now thinning. He is not handsome, but distinguished I would say. Yes, he has a definite air of distinction. But, apart from that, he's the nicest man I know, and I couldn't be happier than to have him as a brother-in-law.'

'I think you say something like that deliberately to provoke me, Bosco. All this unfortunate business came about because of Flora, of course.'

'But I thought you said *I* was to blame?'

His mother fixed him with those imperious, yet limpid, blue-green eyes . . . eyes that had turned so many a male heart.

'Don't be impertinent, Bosco. You know quite well what I mean. Flora continues to see "that girl".'

'Well, at least I didn't marry her, Mama. You should be relieved about that.'

'I think if you had married her I should be dead now,' Dulcie clutched that part of her dress beneath which, she guessed, her heart lay. 'What your father will say I do not know. I dread him hearing it. And talking of marriage, my dear boy, is it not time you gave the matter a little thought?'

'But Frances is expecting, Mama.'

'She has never held a child yet and the doctor has confided to me that he doesn't think she can. This time he is keeping her in bed in the hope that she won't miscarry. Poor Arthur . . .'

'Poor Frances!' Bosco retorted. 'Three miscarriages, and now pregnant yet again.'

'We women know our duty, Bosco,' Dulcie said sternly. 'Even if *you* don't. Should dear Arthur and poor Frances fail to provide an heir it will be more your duty than ever to marry. I thought Hesther Savage a *very* sweet girl the night she came to dinner. Amelia tells me she is quite taken with you.'

'I find her rather calculating,' Bosco said, 'but pleasant enough. You've no idea, Mama, of the effect on a man if he knows he's sought after.'

'That's your trouble,' his mother tartly replied. 'You're too well-favoured.'

'Not by everyone. Rachel, after all, refused me.'

'That's because she knew her place.'

'Oh Mama,' Bosco got to his feet laughing. 'You do amuse me. It's because she didn't love me. I suppose you would consider such honesty deplorable in a well-bred girl?'

'I'd think it foolish,' his mother went to the window, and gazed out on to the Square. 'Why, here's your father now.'

The house was a double-fronted imposing building on the west side of St James's Square. It had four floors, an attic and a basement and was almost as wide as it was high. It contained, as Melanie had once said, at least twenty bedrooms as well as three reception rooms, a large dining-room and a small one, an extensive kitchen and a number of domestic offices. A staff of twenty servants maintained it.

It had no garden, giving directly on to the street like other houses in the Square including the one on the north corner where a number of British prime ministers had lived including the Earl of Chatham and Mr Gladstone. But at the back there was an extensive mews where the Askhams' town coaches were housed and their horses stabled.

Frances had gone to Askham Hall for her confinement where, kept to her room, she was looked after by Dr Fraser and a specialist obstetrician who made regular trips from Winchester.

It was the summer of the year of the Queen's death when Bosco made the announcement about Melanie to his mother, and the season was at its height. Dulcie adored the season and was at balls, parties and dinners every evening squired as usual by a number of young men, soldiers, diplomats and writers. One of her latest conquests was the poet Hector Lafaire whose father had been French but who lived in London and wrote in English verses of no very great moment, most of them now written for, and dedicated to, Dulcie whom he called 'My Fair One'.

My dear one is the fairest of fair
To run my hands through her hair
Oh if I dare . . .

And so on. The subject of these platitudinous lines was seldom seen at any function without Mr Lafaire hovering nearby. Bosco, naturally, hated him and went out of his way to be rude to him whenever he saw him which was quite often, because the new suitor played the part expected of him at the balls and dances, the country weekends and house-parties to which they were all invited.

Bosco, in fact, had thrown himself into the season, and was enjoying it. Despite the denials he made to his mother he did like female admiration, though he searched in vain among the young women to whom he was introduced for someone who had a little more to offer than mere looks and good breeding.

He had encouraged Adam to make his suit to Melanie, and had followed their romance with approval. He willingly chaperoned them when they dined out together, or went to the theatre and, inevitably, Rachel or Flora was one of the number too. However, it was very seldom Rachel. Either she wished to avoid him deliberately or she was, indeed, too busy; but when she did consent or could be persuaded to make up the four he felt that the evening was transformed because of her presence.

He always looked forward to seeing her, despite the ambivalence of his feelings, and his uncertainty about hers. Her manner was studied, correct and very polite, as though she were anxious to do the right thing and, if she had any feelings for him, she certainly wasn't revealing them.

About Melanie's real feelings for Adam, Bosco wasn't

sure either. She entertained his suit with some alacrity, but with no obvious pleasure. There was none of the heady, blatant love that had marked the period of her engagement to Harry.

But then Melanie had been widowed, suddenly matured and subsequently saddened by life. Who could expect a young woman to approach a second marriage with the same excitement as the first? She was older and she had a child to consider. She was in an ambiguous position because few eligible men of her age wanted a ready-made family.

But Adam had no such reservation, and if Melanie failed to blossom in their love, Adam did not. Plainly he adored her; she transformed his life and perhaps blinded him a little to her real feelings, her true qualities, as well.

The Askhams felt compelled – the way they always felt compelled to do the correct thing – to celebrate the marriage of their daughter to Adam Bolingbroke. It took place very quietly in the parish church of St Marylebone where, years before, that other earnest swain, the poet Robert Browning, was married to his beloved Elizabeth Barrett.

Only family attended the wedding and Bosco found himself once again, for the second time in three years, best man at the wedding of the same sister. In many ways it resembled the first and in many ways it was different; but the grave, unsmiling face of his mother remained the same, joined this time by similar expressions of displeasure on the faces of their father and eldest brother. Frances remained in Wiltshire trying desperately to hang on to the fragile seed within her of a future Askham. Rachel was there and Flora; the weather was again warm, but the country was different; and the party travelled not to a hotel but to Askham House in St James's Square in carriages owned by the parents of the bride.

The same people attended the reception as attended any Askham gathering and, if it lacked that spontaneous sense of joy that should inform such a happy occasion, it was because the friends of the Askham family felt pretty much the same way as her parents about Melanie once again choosing a bridegroom from an inferior class.

Sir Robert and Lady Lighterman, who had missed the wedding of their son, were there at the marriage of his widow to a man they liked. So they managed to look cheerful. Mabel had a dress of mauve tussore, with many bows and flounces, specially made for the occasion and if, with her bright gold hair, it made her look a trifle vulgar and out of place it was only what the members of the Askham set expected. She also drank too much champagne and her loud, rather coarse laugh frequently interrupted the muted, genteel tones or the braying laughter of the rest of the gathering.

But it was difficult to see how anyone could object to Mr Gervase Bolingbroke, a tall, upright gentleman of some sixty-five years who looked like the prosperous country solicitor he was. Although clearly out of place in such company, because he didn't know a soul besides his son and daughter and had only once met the bride, he could hardly have been called obtrusive in the way that Mabel was; or even her husband who liked buttonholing politicians and prosperous city gentlemen and extolling to them the virtues of thrift and free enterprise, as if they weren't sufficiently aware of these already. He would then give them his card and invite them to call on him in Manchester Square which, needless to say, they never did.

No, Gervase Bolingbroke was the very opposite: quiet, restrained, monosyllabic, wishing only to be away from this social bedrock and back in his beloved Bath. Bosco, Flora and Rachel made sure he did not lack for company, because everyone else ignored him, preferring their own little familiar cliques of people they had known since birth and saw practically every day. Adam felt as much out of place as his father, even though he was the bridegroom, and trailed after Melanie as she introduced him to the Kittos, the Lawfords, the Pooles, the Copely-Hendersons, the Frenches who had come up from Somerset, the McLaren-Buchanans who had travelled all the way from Argyll, the Tufts, the Savages, the Bulstrodes, the large family of Crewes, to whom she was related, and the number of aunts, uncles and cousins who never missed a binge like this.

Lady Hesther Savage was there with her mother and father, her sister Moira and her brother William, who was a subaltern in the Guards. She didn't make a play for Bosco; she wanted him, for once, to take some interest in her and couldn't understand why he persisted in talking to that dull old man whom no one knew. So, on a pretext of saying 'hello' to Flora she wandered across the room twirling her glass of champagne – watched anxiously by her mother who thought that girls of such young age (she was nineteen) shouldn't drink alcohol.

'Doesn't Mel look *lovely*,' Hesther pecked Flora on the cheek, her eyes swivelling towards Bosco, 'and isn't she lucky. Two husbands in three years!'

There was a little silence as waves of shock rebounded among those near enough to hear, and a few eyes were disapprovingly turned towards her.

'I'd hardly call it "lucky",' Flora said, 'to be widowed within three months of marriage.'

'I didn't mean to sound rude or cruel,' Hesther said unabashed, 'what I meant was that Mel is so attractive that she would never lack for suitors – even if this one does look a little boring,' she added *sotto voce*, but quite loud enough for Mr Bolingbroke to hear.

'Have you met Adam's father?' Bosco propelled him forward and even Lady Hesther blushed.

'I do beg your pardon. I don't know him at all. He's awfully nice, I'm sure.'

'My son is of a studious disposition,' Mr Bolingbroke said kindly. 'But I assure you he is not at all boring. Do you find him boring, Mr Down?'

'Adam is my greatest friend,' Bosco said coldly. 'You really should look to your tongue, Hesther.'

'I can't apologize enough,' Hesther hung her head.

'I'm the boring bridegroom's sister,' Rachel held out her hand. 'How do you do?'

Flora promptly intervened to try and calm the situation and made proper introductions, adding that she and Rachel were to share a house, as they had in Cairo.

'Oh, is that decided?' Bosco enquired.

'Adam and Melanie will take our house in John Street, because it is so convenient for Gray's Inn. And, yes, Flora and I do get on well together and shall enjoy sharing again.'

'How singular for two women to live alone,' Lady Hesther said, 'I must say it's a way of life I know nothing of.'

'We are quite old enough to live on our own,' Flora said smoothly. 'I have my studies and Rachel her own interests.'

'And what are they?' Hesther was curious.

'I am a keen supporter of female suffrage.' Rachel stared at her.

'Oh that,' Hesther put a hand to her mouth and giggled. 'Father says that will never happen in our lifetimes or if it does he will emigrate.'

'Where to, I wonder?' Rachel enquired. 'Many countries are beginning to feel as we do, including the United States of America. In New Zealand woman already have the vote.'

'I don't think he'll go there,' Bosco said jovially. 'Maybe to Egypt, where women have their own part of the house and are never allowed out on the streets. That should suit him, Hesther.'

He smiled at Lady Hesther who returned his smile, half hoping that his brotherly chaffing was an indication of something a little more intimate. Her hopes rose when he took her by the arm and steered her away.

'You shouldn't argue with bluestockings, you know.'

'What are bluestockings?' Her blue eyes gazed ingenuously at him.

'Clever women.'

'Oh, but I'm not clever.'

'I know.'

'Do you like clever women, Bosco?' Lady Hesther paused by a table and helped herself to a sandwich, eyeing him slyly. An alliance with his family was her mother's fondest dream and he had already been invited to the ancestral home in Devon for part of the summer.

In a far corner a three-piece string orchestra was playing strains from Brahms and Schubert and through the windows the summer air, fanned by the trees in the Square, was fragrant with the smell of flowering chestnuts. Ladies in cool dresses and straw hats talked to the gentlemen in morning dress, one or two of whom were mopping the backs of their necks because of the heat. Spying her son engaged in what looked like an earnest conversation with Lady Hesther, Dulcie excused herself to a group of people insincerely offering her congratulations, and went over to them.

'Enjoying yourselves, my dears? Hesther, how *pretty* you look.'

'But I'm not clever, Lady Askham. Bosco is just explaining to me that he likes women with intellect.'

'He's only teasing, dear,' Dulcie frowned at Bosco. 'Look at the smile on his face. You know he likes to tease. I do hope you're going down to stay with the Savages at

Strutton Cheyne, Bosco? Edgar is hoping to take you yachting in Salcombe,'

'Yachting?' Bosco looked interested. 'It depends if I can get leave.'

'I'm sure you can get leave if you really want to,' Hesther pouted. 'You're just making excuses.'

'Why on earth should he make excuses?' Dulcie fanned herself vigorously. 'Oh dear, it *is* hot despite the breeze. I can't wait to close the house up. Indeed I should have done so already if it had not been for the wedding,' she dropped her voice, as though announcing a death in the family.

'Are you going to Lady Barker's dance tonight, Bosco?' Hesther acknowledged a sign from her mother. 'I must go now, but if you are I'll see you there.'

'It depends if I can get leave,' Bosco said with that tantalizing smile. It was so easy, even pleasurable, to be cruel and break hearts.

Melanie arrived on Adam's arm and said: 'Mama, we're going to change now. We just want to slip away and not break up the party.'

'I wish they'd all go home, Mel. I want to rest before Cissie Barker's dance.' She gave Adam her bright, insincere smile. 'What a dear your father is. Is he staying in town at his club?'

'I don't think he has one,' Adam replied. 'He's staying with Rachel.'

'In that case I'll take them home,' Bosco looked towards the corner.

'That's awfully kind of you, Bosco,' Adam consulted his watch. 'Our train leaves Victoria in an hour.'

'I'll take you to the station, see you off and then come back and collect your papa.'

'But what about Lady Barker's dance?' Dulcie whined. 'I *hoped* you were going to dine with us all first.'

Bosco regretfully shook his head. 'Mama, I haven't yet

decided what I'll do tonight. Please don't try and organize me.'

'He's so *difficult*,' his mother said to no one in particular and then her expression changed as Hector Lafaire sidled up. She gave him her hand which he kissed.

'A thousand apologies for being so late, fair one. I had another engagement.'

'Sweet of you to come at all,' Dulcie pressed his hand. 'Melanie, isn't it enchanting of Hector to make the effort?'

'Enchanting,' Melanie said woodenly.

'A little present is winging its way to you, my dear lady,' Hector kissed her fingers.

'I hope it doesn't wing its way before we're back,' Melanie laughed humourlessly. 'Or it might pass the house altogether and wing its way *right* across London.'

'Cruel lady,' Hector smiled. 'I assure you this one will very firmly stop where it's meant to. And, dearest Dulcie, are we dining together with Cissie Barker before the ball?'

'Of course, Hector, and Frederick . . .' She looked vaguely around for her husband, but he had retired into another room with his cronies to enjoy a glass of brandy and a game of snooker.

Melanie kissed her mother and Adam shook her hand. Dulcie's eyes filled with tears and impulsively she held on to her daughter.

'Oh dear, I hope it's better than the last time. Adam, do be kind to my poor, little baby . . .'

'Oh *Mother*,' Bosco cried impatiently. 'Can't you ever learn about tact?'

'Tact?' Dulcie enquired, artlessly batting her eyelids, 'what*ever* is that?'

At the back of the house in John Street there was a small walled yard which, with the aid of ivy, honeysuckle and plants in tubs, had been turned into a pretty little patio. In the summer a wrought-iron table and chairs, painted white, were put outside. Here Rachel had served supper to her father and Bosco and, after the former had gone to bed, they sat chatting over coffee and brandy, Bosco smoking a large cigar.

'Weren't you meant to go to some ball or other?' Rachel enquired.

Bosco looked at his watch. 'I may look in if I have time.'

'Father liked you very much, Bosco. It was very kind of you to bring us back.'

'I wanted to. I liked your father too. I now see where you and Adam get your sterling qualities from.'

'Oh? Have I got sterling qualities too?'

'You know you have. Why are you so strange with me, Rachel?'

Rachel tossed back her head and played with a spoon that had been left on the table. It was now dark and the small lamp glowing in the window of the study looking on to the yard was its only illumination. Bosco didn't see the flush that had come to her cheeks.

'I don't feel I'm strange. I don't mean to be.'

'We must have seen each other a dozen times since I came back from India and you always avoid talking to me alone.'

'I do talk to you!'

'Yes, but not the way I mean. Not alone.'

'But what is there to say?' she said.

'We have a past together, have we not?'

'Not really a *past,* Bosco. Just an episode when you were not well.'

'Oh, that's the excuse is it?'

'It's no excuse. It's the truth. You had been a long time by yourself and there I was, a young woman. You thought you needed me.'

'I did.'

'But you didn't and you don't now. See how well you

have done without me. Besides, didn't I say that if you continue to feel the same way then we could speak again in a year's time? Well, all I heard was that you briefly came home with your regiment after a year and then went to India. I never heard from you.'

'I confess I was very confused. I didn't know how I felt. I still don't, except,' he paused and looked at her, 'that you disturb me, Rachel. I like being with you, yet how can I ever be alone with you? You seem to insist that we are always in company. Flora, Melanie, Adam, your father . . . this is the first time we've been really alone together.'

'I don't *insist*, it just happens like that.' She bent over the table as if choosing her words and he thought what a graceful line her profile offered, almost Grecian in its simplicity with her soft curly hair, little wisps out of place, and the very fine down upon her skin. 'Besides, you have never indicated that you wanted to be alone with me.'

'I thought it was your turn,' Bosco said. 'You spurned me two years ago. Don't you believe in equality between the sexes?'

'Yes I do, but do you?'

'I don't know. You'll have to teach me.'

Impulsively Bosco bent towards her and kissed her cheek and as he did she turned and their mouths met. He closed his eyes and her faint perfume had the fragrance of English heather, so far removed from the cloying erotic scent of a house in Shubra Street. He wanted to inhale her, to hold her, and ultimately he wanted to possess her.

She drew away first, her lips curving into a smile. 'Was that an accident?'

'One I planned for months.' He reached for her hand and drew her towards him again, aware, as he did, that she looked nervously behind her. 'Afraid that anyone may see? There is no one there, I assure you, no servants, and your father is tucked up in bed.'

He kissed her again and this time she yielded, but in a moment she pushed him away, freeing herself.

'I do want you, Rachel,' he persisted. 'I know now that I do.'

'You want me in what way?' She looked solemnly into his eyes.

'I don't know how I want you, except that I do. I planned this for today. I planned to bring you back and be alone with you. That's why I didn't tell my mother I would go with her to dinner. I wanted to see you more than anyone.'

'Even Lady Hesther?' Her tone was arch.

Bosco gave a short, derisive laugh. 'I can have Lady Hesther any time I want.'

Rachel rose sharply and walked a few paces towards an ornate bust of some mythical deity, made of Parian-ware. It was now badly cracked and stained by the weather and must have stood in the courtyard since the semi-translucent porcelain became fashionable in the middle of the last century.

'Oh, I see.'

Bosco sprang up, going to her side, putting an arm round her.

'That was a terribly coarse thing to say. I didn't mean it. I'm talking like a trooper. What I meant was . . .'

'That you have any number of young women after you and can pick and choose.'

'But I choose *you*, Rachel,' he tried to take her in his arms again, but she held back, her face strained as she looked up at him.

'Bosco, I am a woman of twenty-four years. I am not a young girl angling for a mate, or a conquest.'

'I know how old you are and I know who you are and what you are. We are now almost related, as your brother is my brother-in-law. Did you think of that?'

'Yes, I did.' Rachel curved her hand over the worn head of the statue. 'I feel, also, that we have a troubled relationship which we can't quite resolve.' She sat down and folded her hands on her lap. She had changed after coming home and wore a pleated white blouse and a long straight black skirt. She looked, Bosco thought, earnest and dedicated, certainly an attractive woman with a mission in life apart from finding a husband. One of the new breed, such as Flora was. 'You once asked me to marry you, Bosco.'

'And you refused.'

'Yes,' she nodded and paused, as if choosing her words with care. 'I will not say that there were not moments when I regretted my decision deeply, but time convinced me that I was right. You never wrote to me, you never sought to see me again when you came back, only briefly I know, to England. And now you turn up out of the blue and expect to re-enter my life as though nothing had happened. What do you expect me to make of that?'

Bosco sat down again in the chair he had vacated next to her, his chin on his chest.

'I am extraordinarily attracted to you, Rachel, but, it is true, I don't know what I want. I did want to marry you, but I know I didn't write or try and see you again. I realize now how this hurt you – I didn't really think you cared – and that explains your attitude to me. I was very foolish. I am a foolish man. Your brother has just married my sister. I'm glad of that because he is my dearest friend; but I just can't suddenly announce my intention to marry you.'

'You certainly can't,' Rachel said coldly, 'because I do not consent.'

'Well then . . .' he saw the haughty, smouldering glow in her eyes. 'What do you want?'

'I think we shouldn't see each other,' she said at last. 'I mean, we're bound to meet when Flora and I share a house, when Adam is living here in this house with Melanie. But we should confine our meetings to formalities.'

'I think that's silly,' Bosco tried again to take her hand, but she shook hers away.

'Please don't, Bosco. I feel you're playing with me.'

'I assure you I'm not. But you say you don't want me to propose?'

'Would you?' she challenged him and, as he didn't reply, she went on. 'Whatever would Mama say? Why, it might give her a heart attack.'

'Yes, it might,' he said seriously, 'and I'll admit I'm not being very brave. I'm not very brave. The effect on my mother and father would be quite shattering, even though they would be gaining an incomparable pearl for a daughter-in-law.'

'Even though they don't realize it.'

'Quite,' he agreed. 'My mother does wish me to marry, but not you.'

'Someone like Lady Hesther Savage.'

'Someone like her would be very suitable from my mother's point of view,' Bosco agreed. 'But I don't love her and I think, in fact I'm sure, I'm beginning to love you again. Can you understand that, Rachel? Can't you help me?'

She closed her eyes, aware of her own emotional tremor. The effect this man had on her was too ridiculous, too disturbing. She resented it. He was, after all, a sort of aristocratic gigolo who delighted in his good looks and his effect on women. She was quite sure they were not suited to each other, that his attraction for her was because he was very male and good-looking. It was purely carnal. And he, in turn, was attracted to her because she was the only woman he had not been able to conquer merely by a nod of the head.

But he had, oh yes he had. If he knew how many nights

she had lain awake thinking of him, longing to hear from him, reading Adam's letters from him, and then to learn, a year ago, that he had come back to England and gone abroad again, without trying to see her . . . Then she had hardened her heart, and meant to keep it that way.

'No, no, no, Bosco,' she thumped her clenched fist on her lap, 'I will *not* let you upset me again. I will not.'

'I upset you before?' His eyes gleamed with hope.

'Of course you did! You think I am made of stone, that I was impervious to you? I wanted you to love me and to be sure you loved me, but I was right – you didn't. And that mother of yours . . . her face today at the wedding. You'd have thought it was a funeral. You'd have thought Adam was some kind of pariah instead of the nicest, straightest man on earth, and clever. Does your mother not feel proud that he came first in the Bar finals in the whole of England? Is that not an achievement?'

'I have told her time and time again . . .'

'But it has no effect because we Bolingbrokes are nobody.'

'I've assured her that with a name like Bolingbroke you must at least be related to the kings of England . . .' Bosco tried to introduce a note of levity, but he failed. She continued to regard him with a kind of hauteur that made him feel he was the one without background. 'Well, anyway, yes I did have a difficult time because it was I who told her that Adam and Mel wished to marry. And, yes, she would have liked Mel to marry someone else. He has no money, or very little, and she has a small fortune . . .'

'Adam would never . . .' she said scornfully.

'Oh, I know! And how hard he will work to prove it. But there you are, that is Mama. I love her but in a way I hate her too. And did you notice that French poodle, the latest in her line of conquests . . .' Bosco's face contorted with rage.

'He seems very harmless to me. I wouldn't worry about

your mother, Bosco. If I were you I'd worry about myself. Why you need her approval, why you're frightened of her, because you are. Do you want me to be your mistress? Is that what you're suggesting?'

'Rachel . . .' Bosco slumped back on his chair, his face grey.

'Oh, isn't it shocking that I can talk like that? But men do have mistresses – who are not suitable for them to marry. A friend of mine, a very well-educated girl, is the mistress of a married peer. He keeps her in a little house in St John's Wood and visits her every week. They can never be seen together in town and her life is lonely and rather frightening. Why does she do it?'

'Why?' Bosco gazed at her.

'Because she must love him, I suppose. She must get some pleasure from it.'

'But I wouldn't keep you in a little house. You have one already,' he smiled. 'It would be a meeting of equals. These are modern times, Rachel. You tell me you're a modern woman. Well?'

Rachel looked at him in amazement. 'I do believe you're serious,' she said slowly.

'When your father goes you'll be alone in the house for quite some time. I mean, I shall only be a sort of relation visiting to keep an eye on you. In *loco fratris*, so to speak . . . in your brother's place . . . Well, what do you say?'

He held out his hand to her again, and, this time, she took it.

'I'll think about it,' she said.

CHAPTER 11

'It's just the same as before,' Melanie said bitterly. 'Why is this all men want?'

'My darling, it's perfectly natural,' Adam said with a kind of desperation, moving away from her body beside him on the bed and then lying straight with his eyes towards the window, drenched with perspiration. It was very hot in Paris and the windows were open, but still there was no air. The next day they were taking the train for Vienna and the Austrian Tyrol, and he hoped the weather would be better then.

Had it been a mistake to come to Paris for the honeymoon? Melanie had seemed to welcome it but in an apathetic way that had, at the time, surprised him. She had left all the arrangements to him. Now she seemed to have as little interest in the honeymoon as she had in the preparations. They went vigorously sightseeing every day; dined with some style in the evenings; went to the theatre or a cabaret in Montmartre – the opera was closed – and then had a small tussle in the bedroom every night. One could hardly call it making love.

Is this what had been the matter with her marriage to poor Harry? If it was, did her mother know and, if she did, why hadn't she told Melanie something about it or, more importantly, told him? Yet Melanie had had a child; she was no shy young virgin, but she had a shy young virgin's ways. She was coy, nervous, unwilling . . . plainly frightened. All Melanie wanted to do was to go to bed and sleep. Adam decided to let her sleep and turned his back to her. Yet he felt frustrated and he felt angry. All his adult life he had desired this. For two years he had yearned for her, and now it was a disaster – both Melanie and the experience of love itself. His eyes open, he stared at the outlines of the furniture in the room, brightly lit in the moonlight. It was a hotel well beyond his means, as was the scale of the honeymoon, but the whole thing was a wedding present to him from Bosco, with strict instructions not to let Melanie know. More and more he felt gratitude and veneration for his friend.

He felt Melanie's finger running along his back. 'Don't be cross.'

'I'm not cross,' he said.

'You are.'

'I'm disappointed,' he turned towards her, still lying on his side. Their noses almost touched.

'Well, we can't do it every night.'

'We don't do it every night!'

'I just wish you wouldn't get into bed and expect to make love. It should be spontaneous.'

'But I do love you spontaneously!' He put a hand to her cheek and even this slight gesture made her draw back.

'But you can show it in other ways.'

'How?'

'You can be more jolly during the day. You're frightfully solemn, Adam. I don't think we should have chosen a sightseeing honeymoon. The last one was a disaster too.'

'You paid no interest in what we did. You told me to make what plans I liked. I thought Paris would be exciting,' Adam said angrily. 'And, please, don't spend your whole time comparing this honeymoon to the last one. It's awfully unpleasant for me.'

'I can't help it, if it's the same.'

Adam angrily jumped out of bed and put on his dressing-gown, tying the cord tightly round his waist. 'It's not the same. I'm not the same man! He's dead. He was killed at Omdurman. I was his friend and I saw him . . .'

'Adam, now you're being ghastly.' Melanie sat up and

hugged herself, looking at him mournfully. 'I know all *that's* not the same. But you're rather serious, like Harry was – why, we spent all day yesterday at that awful Louvre Museum – and you do seem to want to make love every night. Harry did too, and every morning. Thoroughly nasty. He loved antiquities, like you do, and then, every time we got into bed . . . Only I must say he was worse than you.'

'How?' Adam demanded, thoroughly roused, leaning over her. Perhaps his curiosity had in it an element of prurience, too, wondering how Melanie was with another man.

'He was quite cruel and violent, actually. You just try and then you give up. He didn't give up. You're more of a gentleman. I like you better.'

'Thank you.' Mollified, Adam sat on the bed by her side. 'You know, I feel thoroughly wretched. I feel that we . . . don't understand each other now, Melanie, and we did before. I thought we got on beautifully before. Now it's rather awkward. There's a funny kind of restraint.'

'It's because of this,' Melanie said petulantly. 'This thing that you all want and we women don't. I think it's perfectly horrible, if you want to know.'

'Then why didn't you tell me before?' He leaned over and gazed into her beautiful face, now looking so young and vulnerable, so desirable. Above the low line of her nightdress he could see the crest of her bosom – her full, peerless bosom glimpsed fully just once, just that and no more. No nudity. Melanie wouldn't permit it.

'How can one *talk* about a thing like that?' Melanie put a hand over her breast as if perfectly aware of his thoughts. 'I did think you were different from Harry, not so passionate. You never caused any trouble before. I knew you'd want to do it once or twice – well, now you have. But who wants to talk about it beforehand?'

'Don't you think I'm any good as a lover?' Adam demanded.

'I think that's rather a vulgar thing to ask, Adam. I wouldn't really know. I only had Harry before and he was worse than you, so perhaps you are all right. I mean I don't really understand about this thing, do you? How it works? I suppose it's absolutely necessary for babies, but it is frightful.'

'Don't you enjoy it at all?'

Melanie shook her head. 'Do you?'

'Of course I do.'

Even now he remembered the feeling of sheer rapture when he had first entered her, however clumsy he'd been and however unwilling she, though she had not appeared quite so unwilling then. After all, she knew what to do and helped him to do it. As it were, she showed him the way because, as a celibate man, he'd had no idea. It was rather like marrying an experienced woman who then changed her mind and became timid and virginal.

'Why were you so nice to me the first time then?' he demanded.

'Well, we had to get it over. It was obvious to me you had no experience.'

'Did you expect me to?'

'Oh no!' She shook her head. 'Harry hadn't either. Bosco told me you had no experience and that I must be nice.'

'Oh, did he?'

'It was really sweet of him, because I didn't know. Needless to say he's had a lot.' Melanie smiled as though, paradoxically, she were rather proud of him. Though why it should be all right for her brother but wrong for her husband he couldn't say.

'So you *can* talk about it sometimes?'

'Only with my brother and he brought it up. He likes you a great deal. I think he loves you, in a way.'

'Look, I love him too,' Adam said thickly, 'but if you can talk about it with him why can't you with me? I'm your husband.'

'But you weren't then.'

'Well, I am now.'

'And we're talking about it.' Her logic seemed irrefutable. 'Darling, I think we should go to sleep,' Melanie said, patting him like a dog she wanted to pacify. 'Do calm down. I promise you another try later on and I won't make a fuss – when we're in Austria,' she added quickly, remembering Harry and those awful early mornings.

'Thank you,' Adam quietly removed his gown and crawled humbly back beside her.

The next day they went to Vienna and there they saw all the sights. They ate strudels and tortes full of cherries and cream and drank the hot chocolate for which Vienna was famous. They went to the opera, which was open – it was now September – and they did everything it was possible for a sightseeing tourist to do. But they didn't once make love and Adam saw how, once this tension was removed, this nightly attempt on his part to complete the marital act, she blossomed, she became happy and gay, a good companion, a delightful energetic young woman. Once again she was the vibrant person he'd admired and with whom he'd fallen in love; the woman, in fact, he would like to have made love to every night. But, in order to keep her like this, happy and pleasant during the day, he had to resist taking her in his arms. Instead he confined himself to a chaste kiss on the brow, which she returned with that comforting 'good dog' pat.

'Happy day,' Melanie would say, turning her back on him and snuggling her head against the pillow. 'Thank you, darling.'

'I do love you,' Melanie said, 'you can see that. I love you a lot more than Harry.'

'Is that because I don't . . .'

She leaned over the table and put a finger on his lips. They were sitting in the beer-garden of an inn high in the Tyrolean Alps, eating würst and drinking out of tall glasses filled with sparkling amber-coloured lager. They looked very happy and the few envious eyes gazing at them thought how wonderful it must be to be young and so in love – maybe newlyweds, maybe lovers? They walked a great deal in the mountains, Adam carrying the bag with their lunch picnic on his back. High into the mountains and through the thick black forests they walked, hands sometimes entwined. There was always a lot of laughter and gaiety.

'Why must you always talk about "it"?' she said, removing her finger.

'I don't always talk about "it". I've never referred to "it" since Paris. But I would like to do "it" again,' he reached for her hand, trying to make light of the whole thing. 'You see, I love you so very much and that's how I can show you I love you.'

'It's a funny way to show it,' Melanie thoughtfully shook her head. 'I can't understand it at all.'

But that night she did let him show how much he loved her, in the way he wanted. She made it easier for him by lubricating herself and guiding him into her moist, welcome interior. He was so astonished by this unexpected eroticism and the feeling was so ecstatic that he slumped immediately on her body, and she lay there for some time until, when he didn't move, she said: 'Are you sleeping or have you finished?'

'Finished,' Adam said thickly, easing himself away from her. 'I'm sorry. I'm not very expert.'

'Well, it's what you want,' Melanie said. 'You can do it as quickly as you like. I don't mind. It's just this nasty messy business afterwards I hate.' And she got out of bed, as she had before, to go to the lavatory and then wash herself carefully, as if she wanted no part of him to remain inside her.

When she came back he put his arm across the bed for her to lie on, and leaned his head against hers.

'Thank you,' he said. 'You've made me very happy. There is just one thing, Mel.'

'Yes, dear?'

'If you wash, and that, afterwards . . . well, I don't know much about it, but . . .'

'But what, Adam?' she turned enquiringly to him.

'It would be nice for us to have a baby.'

'Oh, we can have a baby any time.'

'But doesn't . . . all that have to stay in . . .'

'Oh, Adam, don't be so vulgar,' Melanie removed his arm from under her back. 'You *don't* have to talk about it all the time, you know. You spoil everything. We had such a nice day and now this.'

'I'm sorry.' Adam felt himself blushing with shame and remorse in the dark. He had lost the pleasure of her warm body close beside him by irritating her. 'And thank you again.'

'We'll have babies, don't you worry,' Melanie said forgivingly in a tired voice, her duty done. 'I know all about that. Now just go to sleep, you silly boy, and we'll have another nice day tomorrow.' She kissed him quickly on the cheek and turned her back on him.

In a moment she was fast asleep. But Adam lay awake for a long time, conscious that part of him was only half satisfied, only partly happy; and wondering if this were to be the pattern of their married life, henceforth and for ever more?

Adam and Melanie were abroad a month and when they returned home they settled into the house in John Street now vacated by Rachel. They had a cook, a nursemaid for Bobby and two maids, but no carriage and no manservant and Lady Askham thought it was a terrible way for her daughter to begin newly-married life. The first marriage, to a soldier, couldn't really count as a proper one in the sense that she couldn't have expected Melanie to settle in Egypt in the manner she would have in London.

Had Harry lived, Dulcie had no doubt that he would soon have left the army as his father wanted him to. A substantial sum of money would have been settled on him to provide a suitable house with full staff in the manner to which an earl's daughter was accustomed. Sir Robert had promised her as much before the marriage. Harry would have no need to work unless he wanted to. Or maybe he could have dabbled in politics or something suitable to the state of a gentleman – certainly not trade.

One would have thought that the law presented itself as a suitable profession but, no, Dulcie wasn't satisfied. She didn't like Adam and she didn't like his family, and that was that. She proceeded, by constant insinuations and hovering about the small Bloomsbury house, criticizing this and that, to try and make Melanie discontented with her life style. She was forever inviting her to spend a few quiet days at Askham Hall – as though she had a hectic life – to be in the company of her sister-in-law. Besides, she said, the country air was *so* much better for Bobby.

It was thus that gradually Melanie, previously in the company of Flora, became more and more under her mother's influence and, in time, she began to resemble her.

Like Dulcie Melanie was a beauty and, like her, she was vain and easily bored: she enjoyed the attention of men. She liked clothes and amusing herself, and she spent a lot of money on both pursuits. It was her own money, and Adam couldn't criticize her for spending it. He was only too aware of his inability to provide sufficiently for her.

So, very soon after the honeymoon the newly-married couple were beginning to diverge, to go their separate ways, much sooner than people would have expected. A child or two, Melanie thought, to please Adam and then she'd be on her own and be able to do as she liked, as her mother always had.

Adam had joined chambers in Gray's Inn presided over by Sir Arthur Paget QC and Mr Roger Huntingdon-Strayne QC who were two of the most capable barristers in the Chancery Bar, and shared a very high opinion of Adam. He was given briefs where others were passed over, devilling for his masters. When he wasn't in court he was poring over his books, either in the small study overlooking the backyard of the house in John Street or in the library of Gray's Inn. Often when he got home late Melanie was out, either in St James's Square with her mother, in George Street with Flora or at one of the many other, more substantial houses belonging to young marrieds like herself, with rather richer husbands.

But no criticism or sign of discontent with Adam ever came from her lips. She praised his skill at the Bar and spoke of him with every sign of affection and love. Besides, he was such a devoted stepfather to little Bobby who, however, spent a lot of time with his grandparents in Manchester Square because there was so much more space for the toddler to play in, to say nothing of the loving care of Mabel and the two nurses specially employed to look after him.

Within six months Lady Melanie Bolingbroke had emerged from being a rather insecure, embittered war widow to a fashionable, attractive, much sought after young matron of twenty-three years. It was as she had wanted. She even had one or two admirers in the style of her mother, but was warned by that great lady about this.

'You mustn't encourage Lieutenant Ashby, dear, though I can see he is attractive and so very handsome in his Guards' uniform.'

'Oh Mama, it's quite innocent!'

'I know it's perfectly innocent, dear, but people will talk.'

Melanie glanced at her slyly and Dulcie said, with admirable aplomb, 'I am a *lot* older, a mother of grown-up children *and* a grandmother. Talking of which, dearest, is there any sign of . . .' she gazed insinuatingly at a point somewhere in the centre of Melanie's anatomy.

'You mean, am I expecting a baby, Mama?'

'Well yes, dear, if you put it crudely like that.'

'No I'm not, Mama.'

'I don't know why you have to be so direct,' Dulcie complained, going to the window and looking on to the lake, for Melanie was spending a few days at the Hall. 'It's one of your less attractive qualities. You lack, I don't quite know how to put it,' she waved an elegant hand in the direction of the lake, 'finesse.'

'Well, Mama, in the roundabout way you put things I often don't know what you're talking about.'

'Is everything all right in that . . . quarter?' Lady Askham's eyes once again fixed on the same spot until Melanie felt uncomfortable and folded her hands across her trim stomach. 'I remember . . . with poor Harry . . . his demands distressed you so much.'

'With Adam, it's quite the opposite.'

'Oh?' Lady Askham looked startled. 'Is that a good thing?'

'For me it is, yes.'

'My dearest,' Lady Askham said delicately, 'one has one's obligations, you know. One may not like or enjoy them, but . . .' she cast her eyes on the floor. 'Besides there *is* the question of children . . .'

'Oh, we will have children, Mama, don't worry about that. When we want to.'

Melanie gave her mother a charming smile and, excusing herself, left the room before there could be further interrogation, to pay a visit to her sister-in-law whose confinement was expected daily. Doctor Fraser was on hand and so was the eminent obstetrician in Winchester ready to pack his bag and summon his carriage at a moment's notice. From the moment her pregnancy was confirmed Frances had spent most of her days in her room, resting if not actually in bed.

'I ask myself is it worth it?' she asked Melanie, sighing as she took her sister-in-law's hand.

'Of course it's worth it! Arthur must have an heir.'

'It's not even as if Arthur were especially attentive; he's not. I feel he regards me rather as a cow waiting to calf – someone to be kept in a shed and visited daily. Only, with Arthur, it's weekly. I wish he'd married someone else.'

'Oh, dearest, don't say that,' Melanie gripped her hand and sat on the chair next to the chaise longue pulled up to the window with a view of the lake. 'Arthur has so much to do, now that Papa is older and with this slight heart condition. The estate, Parliament, various interests in the City . . . all kinds of things, and he knows you're well looked after.'

Frances appeared unconvinced. 'Believe me, it's a terrible trial to spend all one's time lying down. I was such an active woman. I tell you, Mel, I can't go through this again.'

'Perhaps you won't have to, if it's a boy.'

But Frances had a girl, born not very long after this conversation took place. She had a quick, easy labour and an almost painfree delivery executed by Dr Fraser without any help from the obstetrician. The baby was small and delicate, and was baptized Dorothea Antoinette Clare after her mother, her grandmother and Dulcie whose second name was Clare.

Dulcie took rather a dim view of her name being so far down in the line of precedence, but she was consoled by the fact that a daughter was not nearly as important as a son. In truth, a daughter was quite useless and, looking at the little thing in the arms of Frances's sister Charlotte, a wave of sorrow and pity for the poor unwanted creature, born after so much travail, seemed to flow from her. For it was absolutely plain that neither Frances nor Arthur were pleased with their production.

The Honourable Dorothea Down was christened in the village church at Askham in April 1902. Had the baby been a boy the ceremony would probably have been held at the Queen's Chapel of the Savoy in the presence of royalty, because the baptism of a future earl of Askham was an event that royalty would naturally be expected to attend. As it was, only a sprinkling of London society thought it worth while to travel to Askham for the event. Naturally, all the family came. It was, in fact, the first full family gathering since the marriage of Adam and Melanie the previous summer.

Frances and Arthur had stayed at Askham since the birth because Frances's baby was only very small and rather delicate, and Frances herself felt depressed at her failure to produce an heir, to say nothing of the thought of trying all over again. Now at the ceremony she looked far from well, Rachel thought, and, indeed, the general mood was one of subdued mourning for the son that might have been. It was odd how the Askhams could make normally joyful occasions into mournful ones – like Melanie's wedding and the christening of Dorothea. But that was the price paid by those who didn't play the game. Something that both Frances and Melanie understood quite well.

The Crewes, when foregathered together, were a very jolly lot. There were so many of them and they spent almost all their waking hours pursuing some vigorous sport or other, so that their hearty laughter and frequent allusions to outdoor topics soon dispelled the gloom.

'Never mind, old girl,' Frances's eldest brother, Viscount Normington, slapped her on the shoulder. 'You'll soon be up on a horse again.'

'I have every intention of being on a horse again.' Frances gave that brittle smile which few remembered seeing so often before she'd married Arthur. 'I'm certainly not spending another year in bed.'

Arthur flushed and, turning to his uncle, Lord Kitto, remarked that there were rumours that Lord Salisbury would soon retire. Arthur was very involved in politics, and his prospects for the future, and had accordingly spent very little time with his wife as she lay in an upstairs room, overlooking the beautiful Forest of Askham. It was not something that Frances meant to forget; and she repeated her statement at the small family dinner that night held in the Hall after all the bustling, jolly Crewes had gone, shouting to one another from their respective carriages as they bowled down the drive.

'It's not the sort of thing we talk about at dinner, my dear,' Arthur looked at his mother for confirmation.

'You're still a little shaken, dear,' Dulcie said trying to please both. 'In time . . .'

'I want Frances to come to America with me this summer,' Arthur said. 'She'll soon get over it.'

'*And* leave the baby I sacrificed so much to have?'

'My dear, the nurses will look after her,' Melanie volunteered. 'She can play with Bobby.'

'Are *you* off somewhere this summer, Adam?' Dulcie always looked as though she had to steel herself for a moment before speaking to her son-in-law.

'We thought we might go to Switzerland.'

'Oh, did we?' Melanie said sharply. 'First time I heard of it.'

'Dear, we were only talking about it last week.'

'Did we? I forget.'

Adam wanted to go to Switzerland because, remembering the Tyrol, he thought the relaxing air might help his wife to be in the mood to conceive. If she guessed this was the purpose she wouldn't go.

'Salisbury resign?' Lord Askham had apparently been brooding on what Arthur had said that afternoon. 'No, he won't abandon the reins.'

'He will, Father. Arthur Balfour is all set to take over from him.'

'Oh good!' Dulcie clapped her hands. 'A.J. is such a dear.'

'Yes, but would he make a good prime minister?' Lord Askham growled. 'He's far too "precious" for my liking.'

'Oh, dearest, how too unkind,' Dulcie lowered a petulant lip. 'You know he's *awfully* able.'

'I think I agree with Lord Askham,' Adam said nervously. 'He doesn't care a rap about the common man.'

'Does *anyone* care a rap for the common man?' Arthur replied and Lord and Lady Askham laughed at what they took to be a witticism, while Bosco scowled and Rachel riposted:

'Yes, Adam does and I do.'

'It was just a joke,' Arthur said uncomfortably.

'But is it not a very usual way of talking in the circles you frequent, Lord Gore?' Rachel's eyes rested on him.

'Of course not! Of *course* we care for the common man. This country has grown great on his labours.'

'Exactly, but we don't do enough for him or his family. The social legislation in this country is nonexistent. We have no proper welfare or social insurance system, and the operation of the poor laws is a disgrace. I am connected with many charitable undertakings and I know. But charity is not enough; nor should it be necessary. That is what I blame Lord Salisbury and his government for, not the fact he's an old man.'

'Bravo,' Bosco tapped his hands together, his eyes alight with mischief, as he looked at Rachel's flushed face. 'Speech. Speech!'

'You were asking for trouble, Arthur,' Flora chided him gently. 'As soon as women have the vote Rachel will stand for Parliament.'

Dulcie hurriedly rang the small silver bell before her on the table. 'Oh please, I beg you, no politics on this happy day. No agitation, no feminism,' she clasped her brow. 'My poor head can't stand it and too much argument makes Lord Askham ill.'

'But, Mother, if we have politicians in the family,' Bosco drawled amiably, 'they must be prepared to defend their policies. *I* have never heard that a Lords' debate made Father ill. I agree with Adam and Rachel.'

'You would,' his mother said. 'That comes as no surprise to me.' She looked up at the butler summoned by the bell. 'Serve coffee in the drawing-room, Wakeford, and put out a table for bridge. Lord Askham and Lady Melanie might like to make up a rubber.'

'I'll play,' Arthur said. 'Frances?'

'I may as well.'

'Adam is going to stand for Parliament at the next election.' Bosco, determined to press his point, leaned over the table and tapped it. 'We will have more politicians in the family.'

'You must let me sponsor you,' Lord Askham already had his cigar case out as Dulcie got up from the table signalling to the ladies.

'I don't think you'd sponsor him, Father.' Bosco was enjoying himself.

'He's not one of these Liberal fellows, is he?'

Adam cleared his throat. 'I *do* support the Liberal cause, Lord Askham.'

'And I support the Labour Party,' Rachel said. 'Keir Hardie is the most impressive politician I have ever met.'

'Well, thank God there's no likelihood of him or his cronies ever running the country.' Lord Askham, his face red, reached over for the port dismissively and Rachel reluctantly got up and followed the ladies from the room.

'Must you be so provocative, dear?' Lady Askham passed her a cup as they waited for the men in the drawing-room. 'I mean, do you get pleasure out of doing it deliberately?'

'Have I offended you *again*, Lady Askham?' Rachel took her coffee, staring boldly into her ladyship's eyes.

'I must say you do seem singularly successful at it.' Dulcie gave her a specially patronizing smile, one that she usually reserved for servants and estate workers who had performed some menial service. 'I grant it must be very boring for you to be in a household where the old-fashioned values, and a view of life that places an emphasis on beauty and order, prevail.'

'Oh *Mama*!' Flora said crossly. 'You're needling Rachel. How can she reply to that when she's a guest in your home?'

'Oh, she does remember that?' Dulcie gently, smilingly, placed a cup on the table beside Flora.

'Of course she remembers it! Has she not a right to her own opinion?'

'Of course she has, but I think that when your father and brother support the present administration, in both Houses of Parliament, it ill becomes a guest in this house to approve of someone like that horrible little man Hardie, who is set on destroying all that we hold dear.'

'But Lady Askham,' Rachel tried hard to control her tone of voice, 'I don't mean to distress you, believe me; but there are too many people in this country in poverty for someone with a social conscience to endure the complacency of the Tory government.'

'The electorate seem satisfied with it.' Dulcie sat down, slowly stirring her coffee.

'The election was mainly to support the Boer War. Women are not enfranchised, nor are many of the ordinary men, who do not qualify.'

'I am sure *they* are best without the vote because they have had no experience of responsibility. As for women,' Dulcie gazed at her mildly, as though she were explaining a difficult point to a small child, 'we can wield enough power without the vote. I'm sure I never felt I needed it. I am quite content to let men run the country so long as we run the home – and them!' She glanced at Frances and Melanie who smiled at her approvingly, while Flora leafed through a magazine she had found on the sofa next to her, the discussion evidently boring her. Her mind dwelt largely in the ancient world where everything, at least seen in historical perspective, seemed so ordered, so calculable. Yet, as a woman in academic society she was fully aware of ill-informed discrimination, and had recently come round at least to looking at women's issues from Rachel's viewpoint.

Every time she tried to get on to some expedition she found that all the interesting jobs were given to men; while the women acted in a clerical capacity, being considered fit only to draw objects and then catalogue them, rather than taking part in the excitement of discovery.

'As you are not married, Miss Bolingbroke' (Lady Askham persisted in calling her by her surname, even though her brother was a member of the family) 'you possibly are not aware of the power of the woman in the home. It is *we* who shape the politicians.'

'I am quite well aware of this argument, Lady Askham, but I am unconvinced by it.'

'And the spectacle of women walking in processions and making fools of themselves is horrific,' Frances observed. 'At least it horrifies me. It demeans our sex.'

'How?'

'Because it is so undignified. I think a woman should be a creature to be reverenced, not laughed at.'

'Lady Gore, you really have a very odd idea . . .' Rachel began hotly, but at that point the door opened and the men strolled in smoking large cigars and calling for a game of bridge or snooker.

As soon as she decently could Rachel said goodnight and went up to her room.

For a long time she stood at the window gazing out at the scene, inhaling the real beauty of Askham and its surroundings as she had three years before. But even then her views were changing. Even then its beauty had a question mark over it. Was it right that so much should be enjoyed by so few? Bosco said it was, but then Bosco belonged here and Adam, the compromiser, thought you could keep the old with the new.

These were exciting times for Rachel. She felt busy and fulfilled and she was really not deterred, scarcely even annoyed, by the tittle-tattle, the uninformed criticism of the women downstairs.

She undressed slowly, unpinned her long hair and brushed it, put on a linen nightgown and got into bed to read. She could hear the house settling down around her as all its little cogs and wheels fitted into their respective places. She heard a board creak and low conversation as Melanie and Adam passed her door on their way to bed and then, eventually, the light outside her door went out. She waited.

When the great house was finally still as though all the occupants were asleep – the master and mistress, the children of the house, the guests, and the servants: the women sleeping upstairs in the attic and the men safely tucked away in the basement – there was a tap at Rachel's door, whereupon it immediately opened. She sat up as Bosco crept towards her with the stealth of a burglar, and put out her arms for him. He sat on her bed and clasped her, giggling into her shoulder.

'I feel like a naughty boy.'

'You *are* a naughty boy,' she looked at him with mischievous eyes. 'What *would* Mama say?'

'But it's nice like this,' he said undoing his robe and slipping into bed beside her. 'Thank goodness all the beds in this house are so big.' He snuggled up to her and started to kiss her urgently, as though impatient of words.

Later as the moonlight transformed the room into daylight they lay together, talking.

'Your mother does hate me, you know.' Rachel, replete with the careless satisfaction of lovemaking, was on her back, her arms behind her head. 'Why does she dislike me so much?' Glancing at Bosco she sat up, supporting her head on her hand. 'It can't *just* be because of class. I mean, we're not aristocracy: but neither are a lot of her friends.'

'She thinks you're dangerous,' Bosco said.

'Has she told you that?'

He shook his head. 'No, but that's the reason. She senses it, and she's right.' He reached up and stroked her face. 'You are a *very* dangerous woman, Rachel Bolingbroke, not only a feminist, a supporter of that awful Keir Hardie, but a trapper of men. Look how you ensnared me.'

'I did no such thing!' she replied indignantly. '*You* ensnared me.'

'Well, I may have laid the trap but you fell into it eagerly enough.'

'Who would blame me?' Rachel adopted a wheedling, mocking tone. 'A plain, unwed virgin of twenty-four dazzled by a handsome soldier. It's the classic case of Beauty and the Beast.'

'You mean I'm the Beast.'

'No, *you're* Beauty.' She, in turn, stroked his head. 'You are very beautiful, Bosco. Classic. Of course you know how women admire your looks. You're terribly vain.'

'I'm not! And men admire yours.'

'No, I'm no beauty. I know that.'

'You're extremely good-looking. I think if you'd allowed more men to admire you in the past you would realize just how attractive you are. But you're formidable and it puts them off. Like Flora. If she let down her hair and put away those glasses she could be very attractive. Do you know she has an excellent figure? Quite voluptuous. Why is it that you intellectual women must hide your charms?'

'From being women, you mean? Ah . . .' Rachel sank back on the bed again. 'I've wondered about that too, especially since I knew you. I think we're very aware of the injustices towards women in the world and, as men are mainly responsible for them, we are frightened of attracting them or being attractive to them physically. Mrs Pankhurst is quite a beauty you know, and so is Christabel. But Sylvia *is* a wee bit like Flora.'

'Except that Flora isn't a feminist,' Bosco said, 'despite living with you for nearly a year.'

'She is becoming more so. She has discovered how prejudiced the academic world really is towards women; she can't get a job worthy of her talents on any of the expeditions. She can't get a degree from Oxford or Cambridge.'

'But she has a degree.'

'Yes, theoretically she has the degree. She passed the exams but she can't be awarded the proper degree by either of our major universities which is why she's doing her higher studies in London. The last time the question of admitting women to full degrees at Cambridge was defeated the undergraduates had bonfires to celebrate it. The more you think about it, Bosco, the more wicked it is.'

'I don't think about it,' Bosco tried to draw her towards him but she resisted him.

'*That's* what I really object to about you. I love you and yet there are things about you I positively dislike. This intense masculinity, for instance; this insistence on sport and games; this pretence that women's rights don't matter. You heard your mother and Frances tonight.'

'They have their point of view. It's their right to say what they like as much as it is yours.'

'But they're conditioned by men and don't realize it.'

'Don't let's argue,' Bosco said in a whisper. 'We don't have very long together and hardly ever spend a night in the same bed. You say my mother hates you. She'd hate you far more if she knew about us.'

'She'd hate me far far more if I'd married you when you asked me, and it was perfectly legal. That's the irony.'

'Do you want to get married?' Bosco said suddenly.

'*I* don't think about that. Let's not think about it.'

'We must talk about it some time, darling.'

'But not now. Look, Bosco, we get on so well. We love being together like this. We love the secrecy, if you like, of this relationship. Sometimes I'm walking in the street or working in the office and, quite suddenly, I think: "Bosco's my lover." I feel quite transformed and an extraordinary feeling of happiness takes over. I feel a special, privileged woman, sorry for everyone who isn't me. Would I feel like that if we were married? Did the two married couples here lead you to think tonight that they were very happy?'

'Melanie and Adam?'

'Frances and Arthur.'

'No, I must say neither did. Melanie and Adam are certainly a most extraordinary couple. They hardly ever see each other and don't appear very harmonious when they do. Yet I know he adores her. I'm so disappointed because I love them both. Did Adam ever say anything to you?'

Rachel shook her head. 'He never would. But when we're out with them I always feel they're unsuited. I never really did think they were right for each other. The whole thing surprised me. They're so completely different.'

'Flora would have suited him better. I told him.'

'But Mel's a beauty. I know why Adam fell in love with her. You can't control your emotions to suitable people, Bosco Down.' She pointed a finger at him knowingly.

'Oh yes?' he said and, pulling her towards him, began to caress her completely naked body.

When she woke in the morning Bosco had, of course, gone. It amused her to lie there thinking of him because he was almost like the lover in a novel who left at dawn. She knew nothing about Bosco's past loves except that he had had them; but if that was the reason he showed the skill and tenderness he did then she didn't mind, as long as he hadn't them still.

They had become lovers in the summer of 1901 shortly after the conversation in the backyard of the house, while Melanie and Adam were still abroad. It was not a sudden spontaneous thing, but something they planned and talked about beforehand, for many weeks, rather like one plans a wedding. They didn't want to regret it with hindsight. For Rachel, to take a lover was a serious business, as serious as marriage, and to her, it was a kind of marriage with duties and obligations, despite the absence of vows. They had pledged themselves to each other for a period, length unspecified, to see how it worked and whether two people with such opposite temperaments and characters could ever plan to enter the more solemn state sanctified by church and law.

It had worked better than Rachel had thought it would, and now Bosco was talking about marriage again and telling his parents. Yet still she hung back. Why?

A timid knock on her door interrupted her thoughts and as she called 'Come in' Flora entered, already dressed.

'I hope you don't mind me coming in like this,' Flora approached the bed rather timidly, Rachel thought, and perched on the edge of a chair a good distance away from the bed.

‘Of course not.’ Rachel propped herself on her pillows. ‘I was just about to get up.’

‘I hope your maid looks after you well.’

‘Oh, very well! It’s luxury I’m not used to, a proper ladies’ maid. Really, Flora, when I think of the comfort you live in here and our dear little house in town I wonder you can exist.’

‘I don’t mind at all, I assure you,’ Flora sounded deliberately offhand. ‘I can live quite happily in both worlds. I can live in the desert in a tent.’

‘You’re lucky, because I would find living in this way very difficult.’

‘Is that so?’ Flora looked at her keenly and then dropped her eyes. ‘Rachel, I shan’t be going back to London with you because I thought I’d stay with Frances for a few days. Mama is very worried about her.’

‘Oh why? Is she not better? I did think she looked pale.’

‘She talks of going home to her parents.’

‘Leaving Arthur?’

‘Yes, for a time anyway.’

‘Is this because of the baby?’

‘It has something to do with that whole problem. Their anxiety to have a son has upset their relationship. Arthur is apparently very persistent in his demands, rather thoughtless, and Frances says she can’t endure the thought of another pregnancy, not yet.’

‘Oh dear, I *am* sorry to hear that, although I can’t say I blame her.’

‘She says she is missing out completely in the life she loves, and is used to. She is a very active woman taking part in hunts, gymkhanas and so on.’

‘I could see that from her family,’ Rachel smiled. ‘They reminded me of a pack of hounds, all braying together.’

Flora nodded agreement. ‘Luckily they’ve all a lot in common. Arthur has never actually been quite like that. He is more intellectual, and was a scholar at Eton. I’m afraid my siblings don't seem to choose very complementary partners.' Once again her eyes lingered on Rachel. 'Bosco, for instance . . .'

Hearing his name unexpectedly, Rachel blushed and gave herself away immediately.

'Ah, I see I've scored,' Flora said. 'I must say I have wondered. He does seem to spend an awful lot of time at our house, and not just to see me. But I didn't realize you were . . .' she dropped her eyes again, 'intimate.'

'How did you realize that?' Rachel felt relieved, now that she knew.

'I was the last one to come up last night, having gone to the library to select a book to read in bed. I wasn't snooping, I assure you. I saw Bosco go into your room.' She leaned forward. 'Is it wise, my dear Rachel?'

'I think it's very wise,' Rachel replied. 'You say that all your family marry incompatible people. Would you like us to marry?'

'I know he asked you. I didn't realize he still felt the same.'

'Well, I think he does now; maybe not before, and not in between. We've been lovers since the summer. We are, I think you'll agree, very discreet, Flora. We don't flaunt our secret to others.'

'I'm afraid I still can't approve.' Flora shook her head. 'I don't know why. I have no experience of love, either emotionally or physically. Yet, for me, it is not right for two unmarried people to sleep together. I am very surprised at you.'

'I was surprised at myself, I assure you.'

'Then *why*?' Flora clasped and unclasped her hands.

'Desire, love, what you like. Your brother is a very attractive man. I felt, I'll confess, flattered by his attentions like any other silly young woman. I wasn't sure at the time but I believe, now, they are sincere.'

'And would you marry him?'

'What stops us is the reaction of your family, especially if you think, and I do, that Adam and Melanie are not well suited.'

'I like Adam,' Flora said firmly. 'But I think Melanie should have someone more worldly. He hates balls and parties and she loves them.'

'Why did she marry him then?'

'She told me she was anxious to be married again. Many men did not find her very eligible with a young child. Certainly there weren't as many around as before her marriage to Harry.'

'So Adam was a kind of second best?'

'Well, let's say he was there. He loved her and she thought love might follow for her. She told me all about it. I confess I did warn her not to go ahead, but she quite rightly asked: who was I to give advice? I hoped she might change her mind, but she didn't and she never confided in me again. Nor will she now. Somehow I think they will make a go of it, sticking to proprieties. I think Adam will be a famous man. He has the dedication and the talent. But you, dear Rachel,' Flora rose and, going up to the bed, took her hand, 'please take care. For, much as I love Bosco, and you, I cannot help asking myself if you really are right for each other, or fair to each other in acting like this. Bosco is a man and has little to fear; but you have a reputation to consider. Once lost, it can never be regained. That's all I have to say.'

Blowing her a kiss she walked out of the room leaving Rachel dejectedly lying in bed, thinking.

CHAPTER 12

Arthur, Viscount Gore, was not at all intimidated by the accusing stare of the Earl of Crewe and Carstairs. He had known him since he was a small child and been dandled on his lordship's knee. Now that he was married to his daughter he was no more in awe of Lord Crewe than he had been at a tender age. It was almost as though Arthur Gore had been born with too much self-confidence – more than was good for any man because, among other things, it seemed to render him insensitive to the needs of others, including his wife.

At the age of twenty-eight Arthur Gore was a tall man, though not as tall as his father, and growing a little corpulent because of his fondness for good food and drink, though it was the kind of corpulence that, because of his height, makes a man big rather than fat. He had what one might call a commanding presence, well equipped to assume one day the rank and duties of one of England's premier earls. The Earl and the Viscount had been talking for half an hour in one of the majestic drawing-rooms of Crewe Castle on the borders of Wiltshire and Berkshire. It stood on a hill, overlooking acres of English pastureland, contentedly grazing sheep and cows, and the horses that played such an important role in the life of the Crewe family.

Arthur had come to get his wife back and George Crewe was explaining why she didn't want to come. She had, he said, been married for three years and in that time she had miscarried four times and produced one small daughter, now sleeping in her nursery two floors away from where they were standing. He said that his daughter knew her duty, like any well-brought-up English girl, but this she felt she had more than adequately performed. It was not her intention *not* to return to her husband – she would certainly return some time if he still wanted her – but she wished to rest with her family, seeing that Lord Gore would not give to his wife the consideration in marital matters that she expected. It was all very delicate and personal and caused the two English gentlemen a good deal of embarrassment in discussion.

'You mean I am to leave her alone entirely?' Arthur expostulated.

'Unless you can find ways to prevent conception, yes. And there are ways, my dear boy.'

'I find such matters disgusting,' Arthur said, wrinkling his long, thin, aristocratic nose.

'Nevertheless . . . I can quite see Frances's point. We are not in the Dark Ages or even in the midst of the last century when a woman was bound to obey her husband.'

'Do you not think that the case?' Arthur crossed one leg neatly over the other, tapping his cigar ash into a large glass tray. 'I must confess I do. The marriage vows say "love and obey". Frances promised that. I believe in the sanctity of those vows and Frances's place is by me – unless she wants a divorce?' Arthur thrust out his chin aggressively and even Lord Crewe, sixth Earl and Minister of State in His Majesty's government, flinched.

'No one was talking about divorce.'

'Let Frances come back to me then, or I shall divorce her for deserting me.'

'You are quite set on that, Arthur?'

'I am, Uncle George.' Although the Crewes and Askhams were not related the children of each family had always addressed the parents of the other by these courtesy family titles. 'I will see my solicitor unless she consents to return – and soon.'

'Then I must put it to Frances and let you know what she says. It seems a very serious business to me.'

'Losing one's wife is a very serious business,' Arthur insisted. 'She has been here over six months. Do you think I could see her and make this point to her myself?'

'I will put it to her on your behalf if I may. I think your attitude might distress her.'

'At least let me see my daughter then.' Arthur rose and dusted himself with his hands. 'Or she will be forgetting all about her father.'

The point put forcibly to Frances by her father that Arthur wasn't play-acting but would set about divorcing her settled the matter quite quickly. Neither Frances nor the Crewe family could face the idea of such a scandal. As a divorced woman Frances would lose her position at Court, her status in society, and even being Arthur's wife was preferable to that.

So, after a certain amount of mutual skirmishing – each side striving for the best position – she was returned in some state to Askham Hall a week later accompanied by her mother and father and with her baby in the care of its nurse. There was a luncheon, polite talk before and afterwards and the Crewes finally left in the later afternoon amidst a lot of jolly laughter and without the seven months' separation ever once being referred to. In fact from the way that everyone behaved it would be possible to think it had never happened.

As for Arthur, his lawful position over his wife having been well and truly established, he lost no time in putting it into practice again with the result that Frances was again pregnant in the spring of 1903. Once more she had to face a long period confined to her room; once again she was advised to rest as much as possible and stay in bed, but this she refused to do.

Dulcie begged her, her mother pleaded with her, Lord Askham said it might be a good idea, though he knew nothing about those things, and Arthur ordered her, but she took no notice. She even went riding.

'I have obeyed him by returning to him,' she announced, 'and now I am going to do what I like.' She didn't add that with obedience went the sort of hatred for her unfeeling spouse she could never have imagined possible.

For many months it seemed that the whole family and everyone near them, Askhams and Crewes, relations and close personal friends, were caught up in the drama concerning Frances and Arthur, taking one side or the other. The men almost solidly sided with Arthur. Even Adam thought he had his rights; but the women could see Frances's point of view even if they didn't all say so. Lady Askham, as one who knew her duty and had always done it, tended to side with the men. On the other hand she was so fond of Frances that she didn't come down firmly on one side or the other but remained, as it were, sitting on the fence.

Flora's thoughts still dwelt somewhere in the ancient world in the second century before Christ, but Rachel was quite sure where her loyalty lay: with Frances. Only Frances wasn't at all interested in what she thought because she didn't believe in feminism; nor did she think this was a feminist issue. It was simply a basic reaction to being used by her husband, made repeatedly pregnant and missing her sport.

Rachel only rarely saw the Askhams *en famille* and only one member of it was of any real concern to her at all, apart from her brother and his wife. That person was Bosco.

The year 1903 was a crucial one in the fight for women's suffrage, though even the participants didn't realize quite how important it was to be, because it marked the beginning of the campaign of passive resistance. The main activities of the campaign hitherto had been centred in Manchester around Mrs Emmeline Pankhurst, the widow of a Liberal barrister Dr Pankhurst, and her daughters Christabel and Sylvia. The tough working women in the cotton mills of Lancashire who had been admitted to membership of the trades unions in the 1880s had played leading roles in the campaign for the vote. So, instead of being primarily an activity of enlightened ladies of the middle classes, with their meetings in one another's drawing-rooms, and their circulation of pamphlets, the matter became of universal concern among women of all classes.

Rachel Bolingbroke, an unpaid organizer of the movement, travelled around the country, talking and addressing meetings in church halls, in drawing-rooms, even on windy street corners. Much of her time was spent with the Pankhursts and their circle in Manchester who, disappointed with the Labour Party's procrastination, were making plans to form a new society dedicated to the suffrage: the Women's Social and Political Union. Rachel was in the forefront of this initiative, and one of the rooms in the house in George Street became her office which was entirely devoted to her activities in the movement and her work for various charitable causes.

But, apart from these interests, whenever she had the time, she had her secret life: her illicit affair from which she drew strength and purpose for the Cause. If Bosco thought his relationship with a suffragist was in any way extraordinary he didn't say so. His army life and the events and activities that went with it were as important to him as Rachel's were to her. The Lancers as a regiment were very fond of sport and devoted much time to the cultivation of physical excellence. When they weren't engaged in duties, which were largely ceremonial, they were taking part in equestrian events, polo tournaments, shooting matches, boxing bouts and athletics of every kind. Bosco was an all-round athlete and sportsman, revelling in putting his fitness to the test in every possible way.

This obsession with sporting prowess had been more pronounced since the Battle of Omdurman. It was as though Bosco wanted to prove to himself that, by exhibitions of physical skill, he was indeed a man – a soldier, a sportsman, an athlete. It was as though he wished to expunge from his memory for ever that dark side he had revealed to himself on the battlefield – that part that was not quite an officer, a sportsman and a gentleman.

Although the memory of that day gradually receded from his mind and he was probably not even aware of doing things for the reason he did, Bosco, for all his self assurance, all his elegance, splendour and popularity, often felt inside himself that he was only half a man. Someone who lived with the knowledge that, once in his life, he had committed a shameful deed; a deed unworthy of himself that he could never completely forget.

He also attended all the balls, dinners and parties expected of him, but the hopeful young women found him more elusive than ever. Lady Hesther, in despair lest she should be left on the shelf, became engaged at the end of her third season and was married with great ceremony at St Margaret's, Westminster, the wedding of the year with, naturally, the King and Queen present.

Dulcie couldn't understand her younger son, but her own life was enlarged and complicated even further by her appointment to the Court as lady-in-waiting to Queen Alexandra; and her social engagements became more important, more pressing than ever.

In the summer of 1903 Melanie gave birth to a daughter and Lady Gore miscarried yet again due, said her husband and doctor, to her refusal to take care of herself. It was even suggested that if she continued with her pregnancies she would perhaps permanently damage her health and be forced to lead the life of an invalid.

1903, in fact, was a busy year for everybody. In Paris the King initiated the *Entente Cordiale* and was fêted everywhere and in Paris Pierre Curie announced his discovery of the properties of radium.

In India, where the Askhams' friend Lord Curzon was Viceroy, a splendid Durbar was held in Delhi in honour of the King's coronation the previous year; and at home Joseph Chamberlain began his campaign in favour of Imperial Preference which was to prove the death knell for many years of the Conservative and Unionist Party.

Flora went again to Egypt and left Rachel on her own in the house in George Street to which Bosco repaired as often as he could.

'Our affair is two years old,' he said one night in the winter when he had prised a reluctant Rachel from her study. She was off to Manchester the following day. 'Don't you want me to make a respectable woman of you?'

'You would really like to get married?'

'Wouldn't you?'

'Ah, but do you think your mother is ready for it, and what *would* the Queen say?'

'The Queen is a very nice old stick. I like her.'

'I hardly think she'd like being referred to as an "old stick".'

'She's a very human person, Alexandra, tolerating her hoary old man like she does.'

'But she has her own "friends", has she not? Rather like your mother?'

'Exactly, her admirers. Not a word of scandal there, though. Well, what about us? Don't change the point.'

'I think *if* we married,' Rachel said carefully, 'it might be the undoing of us. We have very different interests,

Bosco. You would become more involved in my life and I, inevitably, in yours. I would hate society. And you're not really very interested in my activities.'

'But aren't you jealous of me going alone to all the dances and parties?'

'Not a bit. You have freely chosen me, so why should I be jealous?'

'I am in love with you, Rachel.'

'I know it and I want you to remain in love with me. I think you like the excitement of a liaison like this. How dull it would be to see each other all the time!'

'I believe you mean it.' He kissed her brow. 'You're a most extraordinary woman. I've never met anyone like you.'

'*And* all the dances, the parties and the balls with the officers! Ugh! I'd hate it.'

The sudden peal of the doorbell downstairs interrupted this conversation and Rachel sat up in bed while Bosco stared at her.

'Are you expecting someone?'

'Of course I'm not. I'd hardly be here if I were.'

'Maybe they'll go away.'

'But Mary will answer the door.'

'Oh hell, I'd forgotten about her. What does she think, by the way, we do up here?'

'I hope she's far too discreet even to speculate. As my office is next door to my bedroom maybe she thinks I'm busy converting you to the suffrage.'

She sprang out of bed and, putting on her robe, listened at the door.

'It's Adam!' She turned and stared at Bosco, her face very red. Just then she could hear Mary's footsteps on the stairs and, opening the door, she called out: 'Don't come up, Mary. I'll be down in a minute.'

She shut the door and hurriedly dressed while Bosco lay on the bed stifling his giggles with the sheet.

'Why is it so funny?' she enquired tersely, tugging at her hair in the mirror.

'Caught *in flagrante delicto*. Shall you tell him I'm here?'

'Your coat is in the hall.'

'Oh God.'

'I'll go down and talk to him, and you come as soon as you can.'

'But what will he say? He might challenge me to a duel.'

'Perhaps it's time he knew. Or maybe he already does.'

Rachel opened the door and hurried downstairs to find Adam warming his hands by the fire. He greeted her with a look of puzzlement on his face.

'Is Bosco here?'

'Yes.'

'Then where is he?'

'He's upstairs.'

They looked at each other and then Adam sat down abruptly. 'Oh God,' he said. 'Mel told me something like this was going on.'

'Didn't you guess?'

'Such a thing would never enter my mind. I wouldn't think either that you . . .' he shook his head.

'But you *would* think that Bosco . . .'

'He's a man.'

Rachel sat opposite him, her expression stern. 'Adam, don't you think a woman should have some pleasure too, even if she's not married?'

'I'm glad you call it that,' he didn't hide his bitterness. 'Melanie hates it.'

'Oh, Adam . . .'

'She submits, endures . . . Sometimes I feel like a criminal. Why must it be that women seem to find it a crime in marriage and a pleasure outside it?'

'I don't know. Maybe not all do.' She got up and came to sit by him, but he pushed her away.

'Please don't.'

'Am I unclean?'

'No, of course not! Still, I can't . . . quite get used to it. It doesn't seem right.'

'I see.'

They were sitting silently, stiffly, avoiding each other's eyes when Bosco entered looking decidedly sheepish.

Rachel looked at him. 'He knows.'

'Knows or knew?'

'Knows. I just told him.'

'And he doesn't approve, I can see.' Bosco sat down, helping himself to a cigarette.

'Why don't you marry my sister?' Adam stared at him with the air of an injured parent.

'I would marry her tomorrow, but she won't marry me.'

'That's absurd.' Adam turned on Rachel. 'What do you mean you won't marry him? Don't you love him?'

'To distraction.' She flung back her head, smiling at Bosco in such a way that Adam felt envious.

'Well then?'

'We like things as they are.'

'That's nonsense.'

'You just said, may I remind you, Adam, that women inside marriage didn't seem as happy as they did outside.'

'What on earth do you mean?' Bosco looked from one to the other.

'We were talking about the intimate side . . . apparently Melanie . . .'

'Oh please . . .' Adam held up a hand. 'I can't discuss this with the pair of you together.'

'I see.' Bosco, man of the world, nodded his head understandingly. 'Another teaser, like Mama. I should have warned you, after Harry.'

Adam stood up and, with his back to the fire, put his hands in his pockets.

'I'd prefer not to discuss my marital affairs, which I

regard as personal, but this business between the two of you – I am really concerned about it Bosco. I cannot condone a liaison of this nature with my sister. If people get to know about it she will be ruined.'

'No one has got to hear about it and it has been going on for two years.'

'Does Flora know?'

'Of course!'

'And she condones it?'

'On the contrary,' Bosco said. 'She ignores it. She feels as you do, but there isn't anything she can do. We don't flout it when she's here. Anyway most of the time she isn't.'

'But the maid . . .'

'We're very careful with her too.'

'But supposing I'd been someone else?' Adam looked at them gravely. 'Bosco's coat was in the hall. You're both upstairs. Supposing I'd been one of Rachel's political friends?'

'Most people don't come unannounced,' Rachel shook her head. 'All right, Adam, it *is* a little hole in the corner . . .'

'*Little* . . .' he expostulated.

'We don't exactly like that part.'

'But do you like the secrecy?'

'In a way we do,' she smiled, again, at Bosco. 'You see, we lead such dissimilar lives. We feel if we married it would put a strain on what we have. Besides Lady Askham hates me.'

'Well, she doesn't like me, but that didn't stop me marrying her daughter.'

'But it helped to stop us,' Bosco said. 'Really. Our romance started officially when you and Mel were on honeymoon. We thought, then, it might make Mama ill. Now, two years later . . .'

'It's a long time.' Adam's voice was stern.

'Well, we like it this way.'

'Don't you want children?'

Rachel and Bosco exchanged glances and then looked away.

'We're not saying that we will never marry, but not yet.' Rachel's tone was firm.

'Don't you think, if it comes to that, that Bosco might not want to marry you? Might he not despise a woman who gave herself so easily?'

'Oh Adam, you are being old-fashioned and preposterous!' Rachel burst out. 'You really do surprise me. Knowing Bosco, you should know what sort of man he is. Please now let's change the subject.'

But after Adam had gone and Bosco had been pacified and too sent on his way, she wondered.

Just how *did* a man feel about his mistress, and what would she do if Bosco, after all, turned out like so many others?

The thought didn't haunt her, but it worried her and it introduced a note of uncertainty into their relationship that hadn't been there before. She wondered if he really saw her as a scarlet woman, or if he loved her as much as he said; if he respected her. Respect meant an awful lot, in and out of society.

Rachel tried to put the matter from her mind, going busily from one function to another, plotting with Millicent Fawcett, Mr and Mrs Pethwick-Lawrence and the Pankhursts whenever they could meet together, and all the other helpers, ordinary working women as well as people like Rachel and academics like Flora. The movement became divided. Some wanted more vigorous action and some wanted to achieve their goal by persuasion. But the increasing number of militants began to ask where persuasion had got them so far. The answer, clearly, was nowhere. Bills introduced by sympathetic members into the House of Commons were defeated by that most effective means of all – laughter. The women were derided and patronized, their aspirations minimized and mocked. It made them very angry.

Rachel was among these militant spirits. She yearned for action, for a means of demonstrating in a more active and vigorous fashion her frustration about the slow progress of the Cause.

One of Rachel's political friends was a lady called Betty Osborne, whose husband was a city businessman. She was one of the last people one would have expected to find engaged in such work because she was a very feminine, slight little creature ostensibly greatly in awe of her husband. Yet the Cause attracted women of all kinds and Betty was a devoted worker. The Osbornes had a large house in Devonshire Place, not far from George Street, and Rachel was a frequent visitor there, though only during the day. She was never invited to dine or to evening parties because, like so many other of Mrs Osborne's suffragist friends, she was single.

One day Betty Osborne asked her why she wasn't married. 'You could contribute so much more to the movement if you were.' Mrs Osborne and Rachel had spent the afternoon addressing envelopes, and were taking a break for a cup of tea in Mrs Osborne's elegant drawing-room.

'I don't see how.' Rachel flushed despite herself.

'Surely you have an admirer? You're such an attractive girl.'

'I do, as a matter of fact.'

'Oh I knew it! Splendid!' Betty Osborne clapped her hands together. 'When is the wedding to be?'

'I'm not engaged.'

'Oh?'

Rachel carefully placed her cup on a table and gravely regarded her friend. 'You know, Betty, I like you so much but I find this the most ridiculous conversation.'

'Why, dear?'

'Because I find it very old-fashioned. To say that I must have a husband in order to participate in the movement strikes me as absurd.'

'I'm just saying, dearest Rachel, what other people think and say. Mrs Fawcett is married, Mrs Pankhurst is a widow. To be married or to have been married gives one status, my dear. Like it or not, it's a fact.'

'I don't like it,' Rachel said, 'and I'm afraid I don't agree with you.' She suddenly felt less friendly towards Betty than before.

'Does your admirer not *wish* to marry you?'

'Yes . . . I think so,' she added.

'*Ah* . . . you only *think* so?' Betty Osborne looked at her sympathetically and brushed the crumbs of cake from her lap, energetically pushing the tea table to one side. 'Well, now, let's get back to the envelopes. I'm sure your affairs are no concern of mine, dearest Rachel, and please, please don't take offence. Put it from your mind that I ever brought the matter up.'

But Rachel found it hard to put from her mind. Not only whether, in the interests of the Cause, she should marry Bosco, but whether, in fact, he really wanted to marry her.

In the spring of 1904 Lady Gore, in an effort to give the Askhams their much desired heir, was once again pregnant. The matter was a little more pressing than before because in the course of the very cold and wet winter just passed Lord Askham had sustained a severe attack of bronchitis which had taxed an already weak heart.

Lord Askham had not been asked by Mr Balfour to continue in his advisory position at the Foreign Office when he formed his new administration. The Earl was quite happy to leave the burdens of government to others and retire to his estates as a country gentleman. In addition to land the Askhams had invested money in a number of lucrative business activities – gold mines in South Africa, diamonds in South America and cattle and wheat in the United States and Canada. Lord Askham was a director of half-a-dozen large concerns, and his son Arthur actively engaged in a dozen more in addition to his duties as MP for Askham.

Frederick Askham, never having asked much from life – it had all come to him without his asking – nevertheless got a great deal from it. In a way he was a very simple, straightforward man who loved his wife and children, his family inheritance, his great houses and estates, the people who served them, and the country he served. If he'd had mistresses no one knew of it and it was unlikely that he had, because he was the kind of man who found enough satisfaction in a reasonably happy marriage and whose interest in so many things provided sufficient outlets for his energies.

At the age of sixty Lord Askham was quite happy to take a back seat and enjoy the fruits of life's garden, which he had cultivated so assiduously and diligently since he was a young man.

Dulcie got back from a tour of waiting one day in April, just as the patina of winter in the grounds of Askham Hall was beginning to give place to the emerging buds and early flowers of spring. The London social season was about to start and she only planned to have a few days at home before the official opening of Askham House for all the parties and dinners she intended to give in the next few months. Of course, Askham House remained open all the year round with its full complement of staff for the use of the family, and for the political functions which Lord Askham gave before his retirement. But at the end of winter the house was closed for cleaning, some repainting and necessary repairs, and when it was open again the season had begun.

Dulcie sensed, as soon as she arrived at the Hall, that some kind of crisis was afoot not only by the fact that none of her family came to greet her, but by the abnormally sombre countenances of the servants – as though they were hiding something from her – who unloaded her bags from the carriage, took them upstairs and served her tea while her maid unpacked. Lord Askham, she was informed, was 'somewhere' on the estate; Lady Gore was resting and Lord Gore was writing letters and would join his mother later. Lady Melanie had arrived unexpectedly, too, and was also in her room.

'What a lot of "resting",' Dulcie said, opening her post. 'I didn't realize everyone was quite so tired.'

The butler poured tea and withdrew and, for half an hour, Dulcie was busy with her correspondence, discarding this letter and that brochure into the wastepaper basket; pencilling notes on others and getting genuine enjoyment from only one or two.

Arthur found her laughing at some joke made by one of her more literate friends when he came into the drawing-room and asked if there was tea for him.

'Of course, dearest boy. How *are* you?' She held her cheek up for his kiss. 'I didn't think you were due until tomorrow. Is Frances all right?'

'It is about Frances I am here, Mother,' Arthur gravely accepted the teacup his mother gave him and selected a cake.

'Oh dear, I hope she's not unwell?'

'Not yet,' Arthur carefully creased his trousers and sat down. 'A state of affairs unlikely to continue . . . if she goes on as she is, that is.'

Dulcie's attitude of studied interest assured him she was all ears.

'The fact is, Mother,' Arthur said solemnly, 'she has

been warned by the obstetrician, Sir Charles Bullington Hyde, a man of the utmost eminence, as you know, that if she does not rest she will miscarry and permanently damage her health. He says there is no need for it, if she is careful.'

'And what does Frances say to that?'

'What do you think?' Arthur sipped his tea, looking at his mother over the rim of his cup.

'She's a very silly girl,' Dulcie took up the letter she'd been reading. 'Franny Hetherington says that if we go up to Scotland in August there . . .'

'I am not going to Scotland in August, Mother. I shall be in America.'

'Oh?'

'I shall be going in June and returning in September. I have just told Frances this which is why you might have noticed a rather subdued air in the house when you came in. I'm afraid she had hysterics and threw things about, a most disgraceful display – news of which will have been conveyed to those few servants who didn't hear it.'

'That can't have been good for her.' Dulcie eyed the cakes but decided to resist on account of her figure which everyone said was so admirable. Working for a queen who had such an enviably trim figure was a marvellous encouragement. Hector had recently written a poem to Dulcie beginning: 'Oh Fair One with the gracious curves . . .' It was certainly a warning to one to keep away from the cakes.

'I would never have thought Frances capable of such behaviour,' Arthur tenderly felt the back of his head. 'She hit me with a book end.'

Dulcie looked startled. This was, indeed, serious. 'But *why* should she object to going to America? I don't understand.'

Dulcie reluctantly folded Lady Hetherington's interesting letter in her lap.

'I've told Frances I shall go alone. She is newly pregnant and can't possibly travel with me.'

'Oh, I don't see why. It's not an illness, after all.'

'I don't want her to, Mother. It is her punishment for her behaviour.'

'But Arthur, she's not a little girl . . .'

'She is, the way she carries on.'

'She has *had* a very difficult time. Try and understand.'

'No more than other women.'

'But she *loves* America and has so many relations there. Surely she will be all right if she takes it easy and stays with them. That aunt with the lovely house in Vermont . . .'

'My mind is quite made up, Mother. I don't want her.'

'But Arthur, she's your wife.' His mother rose and, pulling a chair near him, sat down, a hand on his arm. 'And I'm your mother. I do beg you, darling, not to be so severe with poor Frances. Try, just try and give her a little more tenderness and understanding . . .'

'I give her all I can,' Arthur said stiffly.

'Darling, I do think this baby business has ruined your marriage,' Dulcie sighed deeply. 'After all, Bosco . . .'

'Has no children. Anyway I want *my* son to succeed, not his. Do you realize, Mother, that if I don't have an heir and Bosco doesn't marry the title will be extinct?'

'Yes, I know it, dear, and it *is* a worry, but not at the risk of you and Frances . . .'

'Our marriage is in name only, Mother. Please understand that. Oh yes, we go through the necessaries in order to try and produce an heir, but all affection has gone. Frances thinks I'm selfish, even brutal, she tells me; and I can't forgive her for her own particular kind of selfishness – as though she doesn't *wish* me to have a son. I tell you, Mother, if I could I would divorce Frances . . . if she would give me grounds I would do it tomorrow.'

'Unthinkable,' Dulcie took her hand sharply away and

stood up. 'An Askham in the divorce courts? It would kill your father, and I should have to resign my place at Court. What the dear Queen would say I *dare* not think.' Dulcie put a hand to her head as if summoning another of her headaches.

'I know all that.' Arthur bowed his head. 'And Frances knows it would upset her family, too. It is, as you say, unthinkable . . . Only I do think it.'

'Then, dear, if you only have each other,' Dulcie said practically, 'why not try and make a go of it together? Please? For the family?'

But, whether for the family or themselves, Frances and Arthur remained on terms where they were not speaking to each other for the next few days, while Dulcie anxiously made preparations for the season. Even Lord Askham was affected and mooched about his estate. Only Melanie was cheerful. She was a very devoted mother, doting on her two children; she was away from her dreary husband with his obsession about the law and his increasing obsession with opposing Chamberlain in favour of free trade, thus allying himself more firmly with the Liberal Party. Above all she was free to devote herself to plans for the season, discussions with her dressmaker – a dear little woman, a wizard with a needle – summoned from Winchester. She was also able to write a number of little *billets doux* to the increasing number of young men who vowed that they were in love only with her. Daily Melanie came more and more to resemble her mother.

The crisis came to a head the night before Dulcie was due to return to London as the family gathered in the drawing-room for drinks before dinner. It was obvious that Frances had been crying and Lord Askham, who was fond of his daughter-in-law, had taken Arthur to one side to have a word with him, while the ladies awkwardly sat on the edges of their chairs, their feet tucked neatly together under them.

'What a dreary day it's been,' Dulcie said, by way of making conversation.

'Brown says we'll have rain for weeks,' was Melanie's contribution, Brown being the head gardener, while Frances just looked apathetically towards the window, saying nothing, her face very pale, her eyes unnaturally bright.

Arthur and Lord Askham, drinks in their hands, wandered over to the fireplace, and Lord Askham stood in front of the fire and cleared his throat.

'Frances wants to return to her family.'

'Out of the question!' Dulcie stamped her foot on the floor. 'I *thought* it was something like that.'

'Arthur has told her there will be a divorce if she does.' Lord Askham pointed at Frances. 'Hence the tears.'

'Oh dear, and after I spoke to Arthur the other day,' Dulcie said crossly. 'I begged him to make an effort.'

'Ask *her* to make an effort,' Arthur snapped, not looking at his wife, as though he were talking about a third party.

'But, dear, Frances is in a condition that . . .'

'She is like that whether pregnant or not,' Arthur said. 'I can do nothing with her.'

'Oh, I did so hope it wouldn't get to this,' Dulcie sighed dramatically. 'All the servants will know.'

'That's all you care about, isn't it, Mother?'

Her father, about to intervene, stared at Melanie. 'What do you mean by that, Melanie?'

'Mama only cares about appearances, not about whether Frances and Arthur are happy or not.'

'Of course I care. What a cruel thing to say.' Dulcie looked as though she was about to burst into tears.

'Oh Mama, it's "not in front of the servants". I think it's a tragedy, myself, that two people shouldn't sink their differences for a common cause.'

'And what is that?' Arthur thrust his chin imperiously in the air.

'The family, an heir, the shame of divorce. Do you think I'm so happy with Adam?' She looked around, immediately aware of the impact of her words. 'Not very. We have absolutely nothing in common. Mama was right. He *is* middle class and boring, and so afraid of being thought to have married me for my money that he works himself to death. Yet he is clever and successful and people say he will become a great man. I can't see it myself, but, for the sake of our family – the Askhams not the Bolingbrokes, of course – I am going to stay with Adam; don't worry about that. We go our own ways. Why can't Arthur and Frances do the same, instead of making all this fuss? Adam and I aren't very important, really; but as Father's heir Arthur has a duty to avoid scandal and, as she married him freely of her own choice, Frances has a duty to stay with him.'

'It's not quite that simple, unfortunately, dear,' her mother looked apologetically at her daughter-in-law. 'Poor Frances has spent most of every year since she was married being pregnant. You and Adam are fortunate in that you can have children quite easily.'

At that, instead of oil being poured on troubled waters, Frances burst into tears and Melanie rushed over to apologize and comfort her while Arthur poured himself another drink. His father, sighing deeply, sank into a large chair, holding out his glass to Arthur for a refill.

'I'm sorry, I shouldn't have said that,' Dulcie was beside herself. 'I chose the wrong words. Really, I'm just upset by all this family misery. Frances, if Arthur takes you with him to America would that make you feel better?'

'She's not going,' Arthur said. 'My mind is made up, my plans made. I've told her that, which was when she said she'd go back to her parents, for good this time.'

'But supposing Frances had a son, Arthur, and he grew up estranged from his father?'

'Oh, he wouldn't,' Arthur replied airily. 'I'd have him made a ward of court and returned to me. She wouldn't be fit to bring him up.'

'There's no need to talk like that!' Lord Askham's face, to Dulcie's concern, looked quite grey. 'It would never come to it. I'm sure you and Frances will see sense and sort out your differences. This divorce business is quite nonsense.'

'But people do, nevertheless, get divorced, Father, and if Frances and I do I shall be able to marry again, hopefully to a more amenable lady who will think it her duty to give me a son.'

'Don't worry, I'd never divorce you,' Frances's tears were now quite dry and her brittle voice went with the harsh expression on her face.

'But if you left me I would divorce you – for desertion.'

'Then I won't.' Frances sat back and, for the first time, the colour returned to her cheeks and she smiled, quite gaily. 'I will remain a thorn in your flesh, Arthur Gore, for as long as you live, and it will give me great pleasure. I will *never* let you marry another woman. You can be quite sure of that.'

At that moment the butler came in to announce dinner and there was an awkward pause until he exited again after being instructed by Lord Askham to close the door.

'I see,' Lord Askham said. 'Well, that's clear enough. Which brings us back to Bosco. If he doesn't marry, what then?'

'He'll have to marry Rachel.' Melanie's face had on it a bright, felicitous smile as though she were making some singularly happy announcement.

'Rachel?' Lady Askham moved so violently that she spilled a drop of sherry on her dress. 'Not that . . . girl.'

'My sister-in-law,' Melanie said sweetly.

'But what on earth has *she* got to do with this? Why

should he marry her? I thought all that was over and done with years ago!'

'She's been his mistress for nearly three years.' Melanie took a thoughtful sip of her drink. 'It's a wonder to me that nobody else has guessed. You're all most frightfully slow. He's utterly faithful to her. It's either Rachel Bolingbroke or bachelordom, believe you me. He adores her. He'll never ever marry anyone else.'

CHAPTER 13

Arthur Gore felt very much at home in the Vanderveld mansion on Cape Cod. This was a graceful structure, faithfully copied in the manner of Palladio with huge Doric columns supporting an equally enormous arch surmounting the porch. The imposing front of the house was recessed between two wings which jutted out towards the sea. Smooth, well-tended lawns and carefully laid out gardens surrounded the house, and the whole was enclosed by an intricate wrought-iron fence with a majestic pair of gates copied from the Château at Versailles.

Though only started twenty years before when Arped Vanderveld had made his first million dollars, the house, nevertheless, had the style and harmony of a much older Georgian mansion. Much of the stone had, indeed, been shipped across the Atlantic from a similar house, which an enterprising Victorian entrepreneur had had pulled down in order to construct something much more modern in the then fashionable style of red-brick Victorian Gothic.

In scale, it was even larger than Askham Hall with its elegant, well-spaced rooms with a view of the sea and the mass of coloured servants to look after the family and their guests. Arthur had come there for a few days after hectic weeks in Chicago, New York and Philadelphia attending mainly to family business but also spending quite a lot of the time socializing. An English lord without his wife was a most attractive proposition to any hostess and Arthur was fêted, dined and made the principal guest at a number of fashionable parties and dances given in his honour.

The Askham family had long-standing business connections with the Vandervelds, and Arped Vanderveld II looked after many of the Askham interests in the financial world, investing dollars earned in America on the New York stock exchange, increasing the family fortunes even further.

The elder Vanderveld would have liked Arthur to have married his daughter, Rosalie, who, in fact, was still single after rejecting the offers of a number of young men her father thought either insufficiently rich or beneath her socially.

Like the Crewes, the Vandervelds were a good breeding family, having numerous branches and offspring scattered throughout the eastern states of America. Many of them had their own grand houses on Nantucket Island or Martha's Vineyard or near the family mansion on Cape Cod itself, overlooking the swirling waters of the Atlantic.

Arthur had seen a good deal of Rosalie Vanderveld during his stay in America. She was about the same age as Frances and had very much the same tastes and interests. They even looked a little alike with their dark hair and equine faces with superior expressions; only Arthur hadn't been married to Rosalie for four years as he had to Frances so that he failed to see the resemblance and consequently found her attractive, desirable and congenial.

Maybe, if the divorce with Frances could be brought about . . . A number of rich American girls had married into the English aristocracy and to Rosalie's undoubted physical attractions and, hopefully, fecundity (surely lightning couldn't strike in the same place twice?) would be added a substantial dowry. This the Askhams certainly had no need of, but neither would they turn their noses up at it – greed being endemic to the already wealthy.

Arped Vanderveld senior, aware of the mutual attraction between his daughter and Lord Gore, had done his best to bring them together because he had the additional advantage of knowing something of the state of the marriage between Arthur and his existing wife. It was for this reason that he invited him for a few days to the family mansion, arranging fishing and boating trips, with Rosalie, naturally, in the party and a good many dinners, sporting and social functions besides.

In August of that year, despite the welcome cool sea breezes, it was very hot on Cape Cod. It had been absolutely stifling in Chicago and New York and Arthur was very glad of the opportunity for rest offered by the Vandervelds coupled with the chance to see even more of their eldest daughter.

After several days in Cape Cod Arthur was due to return to Philadelphia and go from there to Boston to take a boat home.

But, despite his desire for rest and enjoyment Arthur had felt very tired, almost unwell, as though he had influenza, during the few days he'd been there. He found the late parties and fishing trips something of an ordeal which was surprising in one normally full of energy, like his mother, little given to such human frailties as tiredness and weakness. The night before he was due to leave for Philadelphia he surprised the company at dinner by excusing himself and asking leave to go to bed early.

Rosalie accompanied him alone to the hall to say goodnight. 'Are you sure you're all right?' She knew how unlike Arthur it was to seek his bed before midnight.

'I have been extraordinarily tired,' Arthur said rather irritably. 'It's most unlike me.'

'But you feel all right otherwise?' she enquired anxiously. 'Would you like to see the doctor?'

'Oh, good heavens no!' Arthur managed a laugh though he didn't feel at all humorous. 'I can't remember when I last saw a doctor. No, a good night's sleep is all I need. The heat hasn't helped either.'

Rosalie felt disappointed. She'd hoped for a quiet stroll

in the gardens after dinner, when the sight of the foam-crested Atlantic waves breaking on the seashore beneath the full moon could play all sorts of tricks on those of a romantic disposition. As it was she got a chaste kiss on the forehead, a squeeze of the hand from Arthur, and, sorrowfully she watched him go slowly upstairs to his room. Somehow she felt this abrupt departure, this lack of any desire to linger with her, marked the end of her chances with him. He stood at the top of the stairs and looked down at her.

'I'll be as right as rain in the morning,' he said, trying to sound more cheerful than he felt. 'See you then.'

But Arthur woke well before morning and lay drenched in sweat aware of a feeling of panic, a rapid pounding of the heart, pain and stiffness in the limbs, difficulty in breathing. He lay there for a moment almost engulfed by the fear and then, when he tried to lift an arm to turn the light on, discovered he couldn't move. He tried his legs and he couldn't get out of bed. He knew then that this was a nightmare and that when he woke he would be perfectly all right. He couldn't even turn his head to see the clock which ticked irritatingly away on the table beside him.

He knew when he woke he would be fine, right as rain . . . but he lay there as dawn slowly broke over the horizon, light flooded the room, and then the sun came out. Still he couldn't move. He couldn't cry out or ring a bell. He tried to call Frances's, or his mother's name, but no sound came. He thought that this was some sort of punishment for his behaviour and silently he begged for the forgiveness of a wife he had mentally and physically abused so often. If only he got better he would love her and care for her even if they never had a son.

Then he knew that he was very ill indeed.

Arthur wasn't discovered until halfway through the morning. He'd been missed at breakfast but it had been decided to let him sleep, knowing how tired he'd been the night before. Maybe he wanted to delay his trip to Philadelphia and would resent being called.

It was Rosalie Vanderveld who finally got anxious, pacing the hall to see him when he came down. She sent a servant up at eleven o'clock and it was he who found the Viscount paralysed from head to foot, unable to speak, as he had lain for, possibly, the past six or seven hours.

Two days later Arthur Gore died from the poliomyelitis that he had contracted, it was supposed, in Chicago where the disease in the hot summer months was always prevalent. Or perhaps he had got it in New York or Philadelphia, no one could say. He wasn't moved from his room, slowly lapsing into unconsciousness as his paralysed rib-cage laboured for breath. He died there without speaking, without sending messages to his family or seeing a beloved, familiar face again, except that of Rosalie, permanently by his side, and no one knew whether or not he really loved her. What thoughts he had are not recorded. It may be hoped that he was too ill to have many as he died in a foreign land, far from the home and lands he had one day, with every justification, expected to inherit.

It is not difficult to imagine the shattering effect of the news of Arthur's death on the members of the Askham family scattered throughout England that summer of 1904. Lord and Lady Askham were at Balmoral with the King and Queen, Dulcie in waiting on the Queen, taking picnics with the ladies; and Frederick stalking deer or salmon-fishing with the King and a party of like-minded companions. Bosco was also in Scotland staying with his mother's family, the Kittos, who had a lodge on the Borders doing, with his uncles and cousins, very much the same sort of thing as his father and the King were doing further north: a fair amount of killing.

Melanie, having decided to get her duties by her husband over with quickly, was pregnant again and, with

Adam, staying with Bolingbroke friends in Yorkshire. Flora was in Devon with Frances and her family who always took a large draughty house by the sea for the summer months so that the endless number of young Crewes, the progeny of numerous brothers and sisters, could have the benefit of the sea air. It was Flora who broke the news to Frances that she was a widow.

Arthur was buried in Cape Cod. There was no question of bringing a body infected with a particularly virulent form of poliomyelitis back to England in that hot summer. No boat would have taken it, no doctor allowed it to go. So the heir to the great earldom of Askham was buried in America, his funeral attended by all the monied nobility of Cape Cod and the surrounding countryside. People travelled from New York, Boston, Philadelphia, Chicago and even further afield to do honour to one so cruelly cut off in his prime on their shores.

The Vandervelds felt a personal responsibility for Arthur's death, although everyone said they could not possibly have known or done anything to prevent it. The germ was there when he'd arrived. Polio killed either very swiftly, or maimed, or some victims recovered completely. It was the sort of haphazard thing that could only be attributed to an act of God.

Rosalie Vanderveld in particular felt bereaved, having narrowly missed, she thought, being the successor to the present Lady Gore. Two servants in the house also caught the disease but both survived. As they were black no one cared very much whether they recovered or not. It was the loss to the Askhams that was considered irreparable.

In October all the Askham family, a full complement of Crewes and Kittos, and Arped Vanderveld II who had come over for the occasion, foregathered at the church of St Margaret's, Westminster, where Arthur was married, for a memorial service. It was attended by all the people who attended big Askham events including the Queen, the Princess of Wales and Princess Victoria, the unmarried daughter of the King and Queen kept close to her mother's apron strings. In addition there were members of the diplomatic corps, politicians from both Houses of Parliament, family retainers from the two Askham houses and, well at the back, a liberal sprinkling of the business community with whom Arthur had been connected.

Technically Bosco had succeeded his brother as Viscount Gore and was now entitled to be called 'your lordship'. However, as Frances was expecting a child in two months' time, Bosco's title hung in the balance in the event that the child was a boy, in which case he would become heir to the earldom of Askham, all its lands, wealth and possessions that would, in the fullness of time, have accrued to his father.

Bosco, accordingly, made it known that for the time being he would continue to use the family name of Down, and would not assume the viscountcy until his brother's child was born. Bosco, and his parents, devoutly hoped it would be a male.

Frances did not attend the memorial service because, since the birth of a normal full-term baby was now so vital, she had taken considerably more care of herself since the death of Arthur than she had previously, and remained quietly with her in-laws at the manor house in Wiltshire.

Rachel did not attend the service either. Since her liaison with Bosco had been made known to the family, Lady Askham had refused to receive her, and Bosco also shared the opprobrium of his mother and father. Whereas no one would have minded – indeed, would have expected – that a young man might discreetly visit a brothel from time to time, or keep a mistress of an inferior class, his affair with a middle-class girl, his brother-in-law's sister, was considered outrageous and put both him and her beyond the pale.

But Rachel didn't care what Lady Askham thought

about her. As far as she was concerned it wouldn't grieve her if she never saw her ladyship again. Her work in the increasingly active and militant women's movement made her world and that of the Askhams seem more apart than ever. Their only link was Bosco, and her main concern now, as the months of waiting passed, was that if Frances did indeed have a daughter she might lose him for ever. She was firmly convinced that her world and that of the Askhams could never meet, never be shared.

'It was a horrible year,' Dulcie Askham sighed, turning from her contemplation of the bare trees in the park, the thin sheet of ice covering the lake. 'God grant I never live to see another like it.'

Frances got up and, walking towards her mother-in-law, encircled her waist with her arm and led her to the sofa.

'There, Mama, you must keep cheerful for me, for yourself, for the family. We all need you.' She kissed her gently on the cheek.

But Dulcie, weighed down with worry, found it hard to be cheerful. The family still wore black in mourning for Arthur, and the Queen had excused her duties at Court until the mourning period was over, so that she could spend more time with her daughter-in-law. Dulcie pressed Frances's hand, entwining it in hers.

'You're so brave, my dear. God knows you've had a year too. I know you and Arthur were estranged, but no one would have had this terrible thing happen.'

'Not estranged, Mama.' Frances had only called her mother-in-law by this familiar title since Arthur's death. Since that dreadful news came, in fact, they had been closer than ever. 'I think that, in time, Arthur and I would have become friends again. We had a lot in common and I own, now that it is too late, that I was very selfish, thinking only of myself. You once spoke to me of my duties as his wife and these I forgot in my reckless pursuit of my own comfort and pleasure. I see now – how much time have I not had to reflect on it – that I should have tried to understand Arthur better, to appreciate his very real concern lest we could not produce a son.'

'It's so easy to say that now, dear,' Dulcie dabbed at her eyes with a handkerchief edged with black lace. 'But I know how unpleasant these demands can be to a woman of refinement. Men are like strangers. Sometimes they can seem only brutish beasts. We women are quite unprepared for marriage and some never do get used to it. It was only after I had had my children that I felt more relaxed and loving towards my own dear husband. I think that would have been the same with you and poor dear Arthur. But you mustn't reproach yourself, Frances, never.' She stared mournfully at her daughter-in-law whose heavy and ponderous figure was also encased in black. There seemed nothing sadder, at that moment, than a widowed woman awaiting the birth of a child.

'But I do reproach myself, Mama, and I always will. To think that he died away from me . . .'

'But, dearest, had he taken you with him you would have been near him. That wasn't your fault. Indeed, I often think that frightful thing might never have happened had you accompanied him. I don't know why.'

'But Arthur left me at home for my own good, Mama, for mine and that of our child. What might not have happened had I continued this hectic pace in America, or maybe some accident during a storm at sea? I see now how wise dear Arthur was and, to the end of my life, I shall continue to reproach myself that he never lived to hear me ask for forgiveness, to acknowledge that he, my lord and master, was right. You may say men are beasts, Mama, but I think they are cleverer than us, and wiser too. They are indeed the strongest sex.'

'Stronger only in some ways,' Dulcie gave Frances's

hand a final pat and got up again. She felt restless and kept looking anxiously out of the window for Frederick and Flora, who had gone riding. These days she seemed full of unease, of dark forebodings, riddled with the fear of sudden accidents, unexpected misfortune. She wanted to have her loved ones round her, to protect them and be protected by them.

'I think I'll go up and rest now, Mama,' Frances got heavily to her feet.

'Are you all right, dearest?' Dulcie put an anxious hand to her mouth, her handkerchief with its black border fluttering slightly.

'Oh perfectly all right, Mama. But any day, any minute now, you know . . .'

Frances smiled wanly and went slowly to the door, bent and somehow dejected like a very old lady, as though carrying her grief for her husband along with the burden of her unborn child.

Later, at dinner, Dulcie, who had eaten very little, drew back her chair with a sigh. 'Poor lamb, she's so very brave. She was talking to me today of her veneration for dear Arthur.'

'Hrrumph,' Lord Askham growled and refilled his glass from the decanter in front of him. 'Too late to talk about that now.'

'Oh, dear, don't be so unkind. She loved him really, you know.'

'She says it now,' his lordship drank from his glass and wiped his moustache on his napkin, 'when nothing can be done about it. She gave Arthur years of misery.'

'I think that is a very unjust assumption, Frederick. Frances was, is, a young spirited woman. Arthur wanted so desperately to have an heir that he was not always as thoughtful in his approach to Frances as he might have been. I know we love him and miss him so much now that we forget; but that was the truth. Oh, I know you sided with him. What man would not? Men don't understand the feelings of the weaker sex.'

'I must say the more I know, the more pleased I am I've remained unmarried.' Flora sipped water from her glass, it still being expected that a woman should not drink wine at table, though Dulcie had defied this convention for some years.

'But let us hope it will not always be so, Flora dear,' her mother smiled at her somewhat reproachfully. 'You are but thirty. There is plenty of time yet.'

'Mama, you know no man has ever looked at me with the eye of romance, nor have I ever been proposed to. Is it likely to happen now?'

Dulcie studied her plain daughter who now wore her gold-rimmed spectacles permanently as her weak eyes worsened due, her mother reasoned, to too many hours of study. Hours when a young woman of title and fortune should be out and about enjoying herself, cultivating the company of young men. Melanie, unfortunately, cultivated such company without discrimination regardless of her own condition and the fact that she was married. No, it was not likely, Dulcie decided, that Flora would marry and she put her own glass of wine thoughtfully to her lips.

'Having the views you do, Flora, I wonder you can continue to share a house with that . . .' Dulcie appeared to choke on her wine, though the gesture was contrived, 'that harlot.'

'Mama, a harlot is a woman who receives payment for . . .'

'I am quite well aware what a harlot is,' her mother snapped. 'And, whatever you say, that woman, whose name I cannot bring myself to pronounce, *is* a harlot. Any woman who gives herself so wantonly to a man in that way outside marriage is, in my opinion, a whore.'

'I agree,' Lord Askham said. 'She has ensnared Bosco,

no doubt with an eye to marrying him should he succeed to the title.'

Flora flung her napkin on the table and jumped up, the flickering lights of the candles gleaming against her glasses, obscuring her eyes.

'I don't know how you can speak like that, Papa! It is *quite* untrue. Bosco has, to my knowledge, twice asked Rachel to marry him and she has refused.'

'Wait until he succeeds,' her father said wryly, '*if* he does. It will be different then. She is nothing but a fortune-hunter, like her brother. When that family became involved with ours a rot set in, believe me. That fellow Bolingbroke hardly does a stroke of work, receives few briefs and trots around after his fellow Liberals ranting against giving protection to the countries of our Empire. What, if not to protect its interests, is an Empire for?'

'I beg your pardon, Papa, but Adam does work – very hard. He still only devils in his chambers and, it is true, his remuneration is low. As for protection, as many Conservatives agree with the Liberals as oppose them.'

'No matter what you say, my dear,' her father sat back in his chair twiddling the stem of his glass, 'these people – these people have different standards, whatever you say or think, and I believe that, in your heart, you think as we do.'

'Well, I don't!'

'Well, you should, and pray, Flora, don't stand there looking at me so defiantly with such impertinence or, whatever your age, I shall send you to your room.'

'Please, Fred,' Dulcie looked anxiously from husband to daughter as the pair glowered at each other. 'I shall have one of my heads,' and she put a trembling hand to her brow.

'I tell you, my dear, I won't have it,' Frederick persisted. 'Don't we have enough trouble in this household, this family, without my elder daughter being insubordinate? We gain an indifferent son-in-law, we lose a responsible, beloved son. We have a threat of an irresponsible, immoral, younger son as my heir . . . Believe me, the day Bosco succeeds to the title will mark the end of the Askham family.'

'Ah, that's what's really in your mind, Papa, is it?' Flora sank on to her chair, her hands tightly clasped on her lap.

'Yes, it is.' Her father, disregarding the conventional rules, lit a cigarette. His face was very red and his breathing stertorous. 'You know I have always been nervous of Bosco, apprehensive on his behalf. He is always headstrong and weak . . .'

'Weak he is not, Father . . .'

'I don't mean physically weak. He is brave, and a soldier he should remain. It's all he's good for – that, and womanizing. But weak, morally, he is and please don't argue with me.' His lordship went even more puce in the face and started coughing. Flora noted with concern how breathless he was, and had been that day after riding. He had gone to his room to rest before dinner. She was seized by a sudden foreboding, a feeling of anxiety and, reaching over, took his hand.

'Please forgive me, Father, and don't distress yourself. I would not for the world argue with you did I not believe you to be wrong. Bosco is a very good, gentle person, and a responsible one.' She held up a hand as her father started to snort again. 'Further, a womanizer he emphatically is not. Girls may chase him, but he doesn't run after them. He genuinely loves Rachel and if their behaviour is reprehensible – and I do agree with you it is – they are both of age.' Flora looked appealingly to both parents. 'These are modern times. Queen Victoria is dead and her son, our beloved King, never famous for his own fidelity. I'm sorry, Mama, but you know that to be the case. Rachel is not alone in giving herself to a man without the security of a wedding ring.'

'Indeed she's *not* alone . . .' Dulcie, her lips pursed, started to intervene.

'*Please*, Mama, let me finish. She is not a harlot or a whore or anything you say. She is a very dedicated woman, devoted to her good works and sincere in her belief that women are unjustly treated because they do not have a voice in political affairs. The works of charity she undertakes, not sparing herself for an instant, would amaze you if you knew their extent. She is also an excellent speaker, a good writer and a thoughtful person. She did not marry Bosco – it is still my belief she would like to – because of how you would react.'

'How *I* would react?' Dulcie barked the question in astonishment.

'Yes, Mama. She knows you don't like her.'

'I hate her,' Dulcie said calmly.

'Yes, hate,' Flora nodded her head. 'She knows that too.'

'I am always *most* polite to her, I'm sure,' Dulcie sounded offended in the way people often are when their own duplicity is revealed.

'Yes, but your feelings betray you, Mama. They are too obvious. As she and Bosco are of age, they could have married at any time, but she fears it would affect your love for him.'

'I feel little for him anyway,' her mother said. 'The way he behaves.'

'That's not true, Mama. You know you love him. You love him too much even if he is, in your eyes, the lost, stray sheep. That shows too. Rachel does not wish to appear as a rival for your affections.'

'That is quite ridiculous!' Dulcie stood up and started agitatedly to pace the room. 'I should think that girl scarcely ever considers me. You wait and see what a scheming little thing she turns into if Frances is unlucky enough to produce a . . .' she paused, not wishing to pronounce the dreaded word 'girl'.

'I assure you she is not scheming, and she is in some real misery because of her love for my brother. She has denied herself the security and comfort of marriage, the joy of children, because she doesn't wish to alienate Bosco from his family. I tell you that if Bosco does inherit she will be a very unhappy woman and make him a very unhappy man because she will certainly not marry him. She has no wish for this kind of life.'

'She should consider herself fortunate to have the chance,' Dulcie said haughtily. 'I, certainly, would *dread* to see her in my place. She wouldn't have the slightest idea of how to run a gracious home, no idea of how to entertain the set of people we move amongst. The Court would be barred to her . . .'

'Why?' Flora felt angry again, her desire to placate her parents flagging.

'Well . . .' Dulcie shrugged her shoulders and looked at her husband, who had lit a second cigarette and sat slumped red-faced in his chair, breathing heavily like an angry bear.

'You mean you've told the Queen about this?'

'Her Majesty, I am honoured to say, is my great friend as well as my Sovereign.' Dulcie thrust out her bosom importantly. 'I was so upset at the time of Melanie's revelation, and Her Majesty, so wise and perspicacious, perceiving something was amiss, drew me to one side and enquired what that might be. Of course I told her and, I may say, received comfort from her.'

'Used as she is to that sort of situation,' Frederick mumbled, to receive an indignant look from his wife.

'Don't be vulgar, Fred, please. Her Majesty is glad that the King has the company of pleasant people like Mrs

Keppel and thoughtful Agnes Keyser. They are companions for him and relieve him of much tedium.'

'Oh Dulcie,' her husband glanced at her. 'Who *are* you deceiving?'

'It is not a matter I wish to discuss with you or anyone, dearest Fred,' Dulcie said coldly. 'But I will say this: what the King does is one thing. As far as I am concerned his august station in life makes him a law unto himself. What my son and his shameless paramour do, however, is quite another. God grant . . .'

What it was that Dulcie wished God to grant will never be known because, simultaneously, two things happened that were to alter the fortunes of the Askham family irrevocably. For as she spoke her husband clutched at his chest and, with an agonized expression on his face, fell forward; and at the same moment Frances's maid, opening the door without knocking, rushed into the room crying:

'Oh come quickly, please, my lady. Lady Frances has started the most sudden and shocking pains. Screaming her head off, she is.'

Dulcie, white with horror, her eyes on the supine body of her husband writhing across the table, was too paralysed to move and it was left for Flora to say:

'Quickly send Jervase for Dr Fraser and say my father, too, is ill. He should send for the obstetrician from Winchester, but not to delay himself and come at once. And pray hurry, Drinkwater. Hurry, hurry, hurry.' Then she knelt beside her father, an arm round his back, and put her other hand to his chest.

Huddled together in Trafalgar Square, shoulders hunched against the cold, there were, Rachel estimated, about four thousand people, the majority of them unemployed, which was what the demonstration was about. There were the usual clusters of the more affluent, like, she had to confess, herself, who kept off the chill of the December day with mufflers and scarves, fur collars pulled well up over the backs of their necks.

Unemployment was the highest it had been since the 1870s and Balfour's ineffectual government, locked in internecine strife about tariff reform, seemed largely unaware that such people existed. All attempts at legislating to ameliorate their lot were thwarted by vested interests backed by politicians.

No one could call these members of the House of Commons corrupt; they were not motivated by bribes or overwhelming desires directly to line their own pockets. But their fortunes and those of the owners of industry coincided. Both were concerned to retain the *status quo*, all those things which, in their opinion, had made Britain such a great power in the nineteenth century that was just past. This was why they were called Conservative and Unionist, because they wished to conserve the past and preserve the union which made Ireland a part of Britain.

The one hope, in the opinion of many, was that the Conservatives would be defeated and the Liberals, under Sir Henry Campbell-Bannerman, would come to power with such able men in their ranks as Edward Grey, Winston Churchill and Lloyd George, all also and incidentally sympathetic to the cause of women's suffrage.

Since the foundation of the Women's Social and Political Union the year before the Cause had struggled on, the growing passive resistance campaign a source of constant irritation to the government. During this year alone, 1904, nearly thirty thousand summonses for non-payment of dues had been issued and many women had been imprisoned, some two or three times. There were also men active in the Cause, ready to go to prison too. But, as yet, the campaign had really to emerge as an effective political force because it was considered such a dubious issue, even among the most enlightened.

Rachel had spent the year becoming increasingly frustrated with the ineffectiveness of the campaign, urging more active and violent tactics in a manner which alienated her from a good many of her friends. The Pankhursts, however, were with her, also other leading lights of the movement such as Eva Gore-Booth, Esther Roper and the Manchester working girl Annie Kenney. But the more conventional demurred at non-payment of taxes and the split in the movement grew wider.

Unlike Mrs Pankhurst, Rachel had not yet lost faith in the power of the Labour Party to bring about reform, and she maintained her friendship with Keir Hardie, Ramsay MacDonald, Philip Snowden and others, through whom she became more involved than ever in campaigns against all kinds of injustice: low wages, child poverty, poor medical care, the education of the poor and, naturally, the extent of unemployment in a land where there was no system of insurance other than poor relief and its attendant humiliations.

Rachel was with a group of her friends in Trafalgar Square listening to the speeches which concluded the demonstration. Her arm was tucked into that of Betty Osborne on one side and, on the other, a girl called Madge Wilkinson, who was a university student studying classics, introduced to her by Flora.

'Where is Lady Flora today?' Madge asked as they made their way up Charing Cross Road when the meeting was over.

'She went home to see her family. She won't be back until after Christmas.'

'And what are you doing for Christmas?'

'I'm staying here. My father is coming up to visit my brother and his wife and we'll all meet up on Christmas Day. I shall be glad of the chance to do some reading and catch up on paperwork.'

'I do admire you, Rachel,' Madge said, sighing enviously. 'I wish I had your dedication.'

'But you have surely?' Rachel looked surprised. 'And you're so young, not yet twenty. I'm twenty-seven.'

'Don't you ever think you'll marry?' Madge glanced at her furtively. They were alone because Rachel wanted to borrow a book from Madge who lived in Gower Street and Betty and the others had dispersed in other directions.

Rachel laughed. 'You mean because I'm so old?'

'Well,' Madge looked embarrassed. 'No, I didn't mean that.'

'I think you did,' Rachel said gently, glancing at the pretty, dark girl beside her, her bonny face quite rosy in the cold of the December afternoon.

'I mean you're so attractive. I don't know why you aren't married.'

'What do you think would happen to all my interests if I married? Wouldn't my husband and, perhaps, subsequent family take up too much of my time?'

'Oh, is *that* why you don't marry?'

'Don't you think it's a good reason?'

They reached St Giles's Circus and continued straight past it up Tottenham Court Road. On the seedy fringes of Soho a number of tramps, all their possessions contained in one ragged bundle, made their aimless way, they knew not where. Rachel shivered. It was a very cold day, and would be a very cold night on which to have nowhere to sleep.

'I hope I shall marry,' Madge said, 'though my parents said the odds were stacked against me if I became a bluestocking.'

'They didn't want you to study?'

'No, they did not. My mother wept all night after I told her I had been accepted at London University. They think I shall be a teacher and a spinster.'

'There could be worse things,' Rachel said. 'You could be a very selfish, idle and overrich married woman like some I know.'

'Do you? Do you know those sorts of people?'

'Unfortunately I do,' Rachel said, thinking of Lady Askham and her friends.

'Oh, who?'

'Never mind,' Rachel smiled. 'As you don't know, it's better you remain in ignorance or else you might come to despise them as I do.'

Rachel didn't want to tell this young, susceptible girl that Flora, someone she admired, was a member of the same family too, though she didn't include her in her strictures. Oh, no: certainly not gentle Flora who remained an understanding, if incurious, friend, whatever her mother thought.

'I would like a husband, and I would like children,' Madge said simply. 'But not yet. I want to get my degree and work, perhaps teach, and then . . .'

Rachel was fond of Madge so she said no more, sparing her her thoughts on female emancipation. Going with her to her lodgings, she borrowed the book she wanted and walked back along Mortimer Street and Wigmore Street towards home, thinking about their conversation. To be unmarried was still to be considered somehow second-rate. Even the prison of marriage was better, in most eyes, than the freedom of spinsterhood.

If she had thrown herself into her work this year she knew it was partly because of Bosco, and the attitude of his family after they found out about their relationship. Bosco had immediately wanted them to marry to make it respectable, but Rachel, again, refused because she felt it would be giving in to his mother.

'Always my mother,' Bosco had raged. 'I think you're obsessed by her.'

'She's obsessed by me,' Rachel had retorted. 'Her mind is quite distorted by hatred of me. Adam said she nearly had a stroke when she heard the news.'

'Melanie had no right to tell her. It was disloyal.'

'Oh, it's because of your brother and the question of the

heir. They have nothing else on their minds. They're ruining the life of a young woman, Frances, just so that she can produce a boy. Well, I hate it and all that it stands for!'

She'd stared at him defiantly and then, seeing the hurt in his eyes, she'd apologized and they'd embraced.

But, since that time, matters between Bosco and herself had not gone smoothly. It was true that she saw very little of him. There had been the death of his brother in which she was almost powerless to comfort him because it was a family matter and she was not part of the family. He went on manoeuvres with the army and to various country houses for holidays in the summer, parties and weekends where he must continually meet a number of nubile, suitable young women who she knew vied with one another for his attention.

Would she lose him? Did she not deserve to? Should she perhaps not give him up, free him so that they could pursue their lives along different paths? Theirs, after all, was an unnatural, clandestine relationship, frowned upon by society. Her own friends would be every bit as shocked as his family if only they knew.

So why did they go on? For pleasure alone? For the delight they had in each other's bodies, the tenderness of their embraces, the intimate secrets they alone shared, the delicious little meals taken *à deux* in the privacy of the house in George Street into which she now let herself, glad to be home because it was dark. The lights were on in the first-floor sitting-room and she hurried in, wondering if Flora had come back, or if the maid had merely turned them on when she stoked the fire to provide a welcome and warmth against the bitter winter's day.

Bosco was sitting in the chair by the fire, his legs crossed, reading the paper. He put it down as she came in and for a moment they stared at each other, she guilty because of the thoughts she'd entertained, and he as though he were surprised by her solemn expression.

'Is anything the matter?' He got up and came slowly towards her. She hastily took off hcr hat and gloves and coat, putting them on a chair, and shook her head.

He put his arms around her and cradled her head against his shoulder.

'I need you,' he said.

'Oh Bosco,' she nuzzled her face against his and then their lips met in a long, lasting kiss.

'You're terribly cold,' he said at last, rubbing her hands between his.

'It's terribly cold outside and I stood for hours in Trafalgar Square.'

'What a funny place to stand for hours.' He led her gently to the fire and, stooping, jabbed it with the long iron poker.

'There was a demonstration,' she looked at herself in the mirror and quickly tucked the stray pieces of blonde hair into the soft bun at the back of her head, 'against unemployment. Do you know it is the highest total for more than twenty years? And what does the government do? Nothing.'

'But what can *you* do, my darling?' He gently took her in his arms again and looked into her eyes. 'Don't you wear yourself out by these meetings and demonstrations, and where does it get you or them? You look terribly tired.'

'I am tired.' Rachel freed herself and sat down. 'I'll get Mary to bring us some tea.'

'She's gone out. She was just about to go when I came and I said she could.' He looked at her meaningfully, his eyes sidling towards the door.

The house was empty. It was too good an opportunity to miss.

It was bitterly cold in her unheated bedroom, and they huddled close together beneath the bedclothes giggling rather breathlessly because they'd undressed so quickly and jumped into bed. His strong warm body, his urgent desire, seemed to infuse her with life and she felt a desperate need for him as she entwined her legs around his as though to imprison the precious part of him inside her for ever. He kissed her eyes and her mouth, and then pulled hungrily at her breasts as if there were nourishment there for him, sustenance against the cold and damp of the day.

They lay for a long time after making love still entrapped within each other, conscious of each other's heartbeats. Only the lamp from the street outside illumined the room, casting a soft, seasonal radiance.

'I love you, Rachel,' Bosco said at last.

'And I love you. I love you but . . .' She wriggled free and gently pushed him away, turning on her side so that she could gaze at him in the dusk.

'But what?'

'I wondered if we should free each other?'

'But we are free, my darling,' he put a finger on her nose and gently squashed it. 'Don't you feel free?'

'We're really imprisoned by our love. We can't go forwards and we can't go back.'

'We can go forwards any time you like, but backwards, no.'

'Supposing you're the heir?'

'Ah.' Bosco sat up and, heedless of the cold, crossed his arms over his legs. 'That's it, is it?'

'The baby is due *very* soon.'

'It would make no difference.'

'It must.'

'It can never separate us.'

'Do you really not think so?' Rachel turned and lay on her back resting her head on her arms linked on the pillow. 'I think it will make the most enormous difference to you. You will be even further from me socially than now.'

'But I'm not distanced from you now, you silly girl. Any distance we have is maintained by you.'

'It's because I'm not suitable. I'd stick out like a sore thumb in your crowd.'

'And what of Lady Warwick, formerly the King's mistress, and one of the richest women in the land? She's a socialist.'

'Yes, but everyone thinks she's eccentric. Besides, she was born to it and can behave as oddly as she likes. No one takes her very seriously. If you're part of that society you're accepted by them. I'm not. People would think I married you because of your money and position.'

'That's rubbish when you think of Adam.'

'What about Adam?'

'Well, he married Melanie and no one says it was for her money.'

'I should think your mother says it was. Anyway, that marriage is hardly the greatest success, which would seem to prove the point that people of different classes shouldn't marry.'

'That's not because of class,' Bosco said solemnly. 'It's because of this.' He looked at her.

'What?'

'This. Making love.'

'How do you know?'

'My sister throws out too many hints. Adam was a virgin and she too impatient to teach him. At least *this* will be all right in our marriage.'

'It's all that would be all right. Some say it isn't enough to live on. They would still think that I wished to better myself socially and, perhaps, financially. I *am* terribly poor, by the way.'

She gazed at him rather archly, the way lovers do and, reaching out, he stroked her face with his cold hand.

'Knowing you no one would think that.'

'Your mother thinks it. I must say I dislike that woman as much as she dislikes me.'

Bosco sighed and, albeit unwittingly, by moving slightly away from her seemed to convey to Rachel his disapproval of this slight to his mother.

'Mama has had a very bad year, Rachel. I don't make excuses for her, but she is devastated about the death of Arthur, the uncertainty over Frances and the baby. I have never seen Mama so tired or so low. Sometimes I feel really worried about her.'

Rachel clasped his hand, still resting on her cheek. 'I'm sorry. That's where I'd never make you a good wife. I'm too intolerant. I'd not understand people like her.'

'My greatest wish for 1905 would be that you and Mama should get on, and become friends.'

'It will never happen, I'm afraid. I'm . . .'

She stopped and looked at Bosco as the sound of rapid footsteps up the stairs penetrated their conversation. There was a sudden banging on the door and the voice of Flora called:

'Rachel?'

'I'm here,' Rachel cried. 'I . . .' but before she could finish the door was flung open and Flora stood on the threshold, gazing at them myopically through the gloom. Rachel quickly drew the bedclothes over herself and felt Bosco cower beside her.

'Are you there, Rachel? Are you not well?' Flora advanced across the room and then stopped as, her eyes becoming accustomed to the dusk, she made out two figures in the bed instead of the one she'd expected. 'Is it Bosco with you?'

'Yes,' Rachel replied guiltily. She was always very careful not to receive her lover when Flora was about, out of respect for her views.

'Thank God,' Flora drew off her gloves and reached for the switch by the side of the door, suddenly flooding the room with a hard, garish light, throwing into relief the small bed, the patterned William Morris wallpaper and the heavy mahogany furniture, much of which had come from an unwanted store at Askham Hall. 'Please don't be embarrassed,' Flora said practically, standing beside the bed and gazing down at them as though she was accustomed to this sort of spectacle. 'This is no time for prudery.'

'What's the matter, Flora?' Bosco, cross and embarrassed, glanced at the clock by the bedside. 'Can't you see that . . .'

'Bosco, I have some very bad news for you. Papa has been taken seriously ill. He had a sort of seizure and collapsed. It's his heart.'

Flora, forgetting the proprieties, sat on the bed beside her brother and Rachel. 'I thought he was dead but he has made some recovery. He is still seriously ill and Frances . . .' she stared at him and then looked at Rachel, her eyes going from one to the other. 'Frances has had a baby . . . a fine, healthy baby. It's a girl.'

PART III

1908–1913: Innocence Lost

CHAPTER 14

Rachel walked slowly along the path leading to the wood which Askham Grange shared with the big house on the other side of the lake. The western tip of the lake bordered on Grange property, and she liked to sit by the water's edge in a special seat which her husband had had constructed for her. Now, on a hot July day in 1908, she made for this favourite spot again, a parasol in one hand protecting her head from the sun and in her other a copy of Morley's *Life of Gladstone*, a recent best-selling biography and a present from Adam.

As the ground sloped towards the lake Rachel went even more slowly, treading very carefully over the small stones littering the path, reaching out to steady herself, a hand on the wooden fence that marked the boundary between the grounds of the Grange and those of Askham Hall. Finally she reached the spot she sought, protected by the overhanging branches of a laburnum tree which bent over the lake, sweeping the smooth surface of the water. Thankfully at last she sat down, slightly breathless because of the heat and the exertion of going down the steep, pebble-strewn hill.

From where she sat she could see the Hall very clearly now and, on the other side of the lake, the seat where Bosco had told her all those years ago that he loved her.

Love for Bosco; it had transformed her life, and as her gaze lingered on the seat beside the rhododendron bushes her mind roved over the years since they'd sat there under the watchful eyes of his mother, especially of the last three tranquil, gloriously happy years of their marriage. She closed her eyes and leaned back, surrendering herself to an emotion now quite commonplace – happiness.

After their wedding in the spring of 1905 Bosco had resigned from the Lancers and had thrown himself with enthusiasm, with unexpected pleasure, into the position vacated by his late brother. This involved not only the management of the Askham estates but also participation in the various business enterprises that ensured the security and prosperity of the family. His father had made a good recovery from his heart attack but, because of poor circulation, remained a semi-invalid. He was not bedridden but forced to take life a lot more quietly than he had before.

But the transformation was greatest for Rachel, forced, almost reluctantly, to the altar by fear of losing the person who meant most in the world to her. She married Bosco for love, not for his wealth or title; but there were many who thought otherwise, and the hostility of Lady Askham was, and remained, implacable. According to her, and her friends, Bosco's mistress had held off until he could offer her the security and status that she would not have enjoyed as the itinerant wife of a younger son, a mere captain in the Lancers. Lady Askham never forgave Rachel for having been Bosco's mistress, for the conditions she imposed about the marriage but, above all, for being herself – independent, warm-spirited, middle class – a woman who had her own opinions and voiced them.

The conditions Rachel imposed before she agreed to the wedding were that she and Bosco should live completely separately from his parents, with their own town house and their own country residence. The Grange, which had been lived in by Frederick's mother, also a woman of independent views, had fallen into dereliction since her death in 1890. It was a little too near the Hall for Rachel's liking, but to turn it down would have been stupid. It was not a large house, but it was a compact and beautiful old building which remained largely a Tudor mansion, having escaped the rebuilding fervour of the sixth Earl who tore down all the Elizabethan parts of the Hall and constructed in its place the noble, neo-classical building that stood there now.

For a town house they moved into property in Berkeley Square which also belonged to the Askhams, but had been let for many years and conveniently fell vacant. It was rather like the house in St James's Square, only on a smaller scale, with ten bedrooms, reception and dining-rooms, servants' quarters and a mews at the back for the horses and carriages which now made up the retinue of the heir to the earldom.

But Rachel's greatest transformation, and her greatest sacrifice, but also her greatest pleasure, was in deciding to throw herself into motherhood as soon as she could, and to give up all active involvement in the suffrage movement which gathered momentum every year. On her desk upstairs she had a letter from Mrs Pankhurst, who had been sentenced to six weeks in prison earlier in the year, urging her to lend her name in support of the movement now that she was a woman of position and importance. But she knew how she would reply; the draft lay by the side of the letter:

My dear Emmeline,

Much as I would like to do as you ask I cannot. I am the mother of two young children and expecting a third, and one of the understandings I have with my dear husband is that I will not bring the Askham name into prominence associated with the Cause, because of the distress it would give his invalid father.

I am so sorry about this, but, believe me, it remains very close to my heart and, were circumstances other than they are, I would do differently.

As ever, with affection,

Yours sincerely.

Rachel could visualize the scorn on the beautiful face of her former friend who would probably tear the letter up and put it in the wastepaper basket.

It was one of the things she'd promised Bosco. They agreed that they should sink as many differences as they could in the interests of marital harmony, because, as neither of them could live apart from the other, their life together had to be a compromise. But only for the time being, Rachel had promised; and she remained devoted to charitable causes, especially the care of destitute children, contributing in the only way she could, with money, to ameliorate their lot.

But the last three years seemed to have been a continual pregnancy. Her first child, a boy, Ralph, had been born in the spring of 1906 and their second, Charlotte, a year later. The new one was due any day which was why she had moved so slowly, conscious of the heat and the burden she was carrying, grateful to find shelter on the seat under the laburnum which Bosco, with his usual thoughtfulness, had had made for her.

Bosco infused her with his love, his care, his consideration. The mantle of the country squire, the man of affairs, had seemed to fall very easily upon him, as though he had been unaware of hidden resources, abilities and desires. He had not become staid, bumptious or boring like Arthur; but he had become responsible, concerned for his tenants and their welfare. He showed a degree of perspicacity in business affairs that no one knew he possessed, and he developed skills in knowing what parts of the vast Askham estates to develop and which ones to sell off. Altogether he became a rounder, happier man and almost overnight the image of the dashing Lancer officer vanished and, with his assumption of the viscountcy and its duties, he became almost a different personality. But, who knew whether it was because of that, or his final conquest of the woman he had first fallen in love with in those wintry months of the year 1899?

Rachel had fallen asleep in the sun, her parasol and the unread Morley biography lying at her feet. Then, like the princess in the story, she was awakened by a kiss and her Prince Charming, seated beside her, smiled into her eyes.

She blinked, accustoming her eyes once more to the light. 'Bosco! How long have you been there?'

'I just arrived, my darling.'

Rachel laughed and ran her hand over her stomach. 'I wonder that any man wants to kiss me looking like this.'

'Darling, I love you even better, if that were possible – and it isn't – when you are pregnant. You have no idea how truly beautiful you are. I shall keep you like this for ever.'

'Oh no you won't!' Rachel retorted, shifting to ease her bulk. 'One more after this and that is it.'

'Supposing we have a boy and then a girl. Won't that be clever?'

'Your mother did it, so I don't suppose she'd think it very clever.'

Bosco's smile vanished.

'Ah, Mama. I'm afraid I have news that mightn't please you. She is coming for lunch and may even be at the house now. But a nice surprise is that my cousin, Constance Kitto, is visiting her and lunching with us too. Besides, Mama complains that she never sees her grandchildren.'

'That is quite untrue. I'd be delighted to meet your cousin, but Ralph practically lives with your mother. I'm sure she'll alienate him from me.'

'Dearest, don't remind me.' Bosco pressed her hand. 'My greatest joy would be if you and Mama . . .'

'Oh I know, don't say it. My greatest joy would be if she could be nice, for once, to me instead of making all the cutting remarks she does: "I'm sure it was never like that in *my* day, Rachel dear" and so on. I don't think anything ever is as it was in her day. . .thank goodness.'

'But still, my darling, you do bridle when you see her. Your attitude changes at once.'

'How would *you* feel if someone hated you, constantly belittled you? Told everyone you married her son for his money and position?'

'You know she doesn't say that.'

'But she does. She thinks it and says it. She also told Melanie I was a whore.'

'Well, Melanie had no right to repeat it. Anyway, you're a respectable whore now.'

He bent towards her again but she pushed him away, the change in her mind from tranquillity to anger showing in her face.

'Please don't speak like that, Bosco! It offends me. You know that Melanie deliberately makes mischief. She does enjoy it. She gets more like your mother every day. . . and a string of young men as well, I hear.'

'No harm there, like Mama, though I wish that Captain Eldon would stay away. He annoys Papa no end. Hector Lafaire he finds a likeable idiot, but the overt masculinity of Eldon offends him. I must say, it offends me too.'

'But your mother will never change, my dearest.' Rachel, restored to good humour, patted his cheek. 'She will always be a flirt and she will always be vicious to my brother and me. I should think her great longing is that I die in childbirth.'

'Oh darling, don't say that!' Bosco put his cheek to hers.

'I shan't, don't worry. Dr Fraser said I was the strongest woman he had ever delivered. Strong as an ox, he said. Very good breeding people, we Bolingbrokes.'

'Thank God for that anyway.' Bosco consulted his watch. 'We have no problems like poor Arthur and Frances; that helped to destroy their marriage.'

'Still, we have others, though God help they don't wreck ours. Your mother is certainly one and I fear the influence she will have on our children because her personality is so strong, so formidable.' She glanced at her husband, now solemn and disturbed by her speech, and brushed his lips with hers. Then she put a hand on his arm. 'Now help me up, my love. It takes me ten minutes to get up that path and I should hate your mother to see me in anything but the pink!'

'You really are very *large*,' Lady Askham said rudely, staring at Rachel's midriff. 'Are there by any chance twins in your family, Rachel?'

'No, Lady Askham.' Rachel withheld, with difficulty, a further retort.

'Well, there are in ours.' Lady Askham crumbled her bread thoughtfully on her plate. 'My brother Bosco was a twin, but the other half died when he was two.'

'Well, if we have a boy and a girl then I shan't have need to have any more children.' Rachel smiled sweetly at her mother-in-law and rang the bell for the second course.

She kept a small staff at the Grange, preferring to live as simple a life as possible with Bosco and their children. No livery was worn and the maids and footmen doubled up so that many of them grumbled at having more duties than those at the big house. Rachel had introduced middle-class ideas of economy into the housekeeping finances and the running of the two houses, not all of which found favour with the servants brought up on Askham standards and Askham largesse.

Rachel, however, was a modern woman and she had seen too much real poverty, not only in London but near them in the country, to want to encourage waste and profligacy in her household.

Accordingly only one maid served the lunch, and there was only one cook in the kitchen. The two footmen in the house shared all their normal duties between them as well as those of the steward and the butler who would normally be employed in a noble household. The Gores had a butler in London, where Bosco did a lot of entertaining, but the staff in the country had been reduced to a minimum.

The food was frugal, too, consisting of meat and vegetables produced from the home farm, freshly baked wholemeal bread from the kitchen and water only drunk at lunch-time, never wine.

The regime suited Bosco who, when he was in the country, was out all day inspecting the property on the Wiltshire estate or closeted with the estates manager in an office in the big house. He often lunched alone with his mother and father and, today, having Lady Askham for lunch was unusual. Nevertheless, her ladyship was given the simple fare the Gore family were used to for the midday meal.

'Do you plan four children?' Lady Askham enquired after the maid had served the main course and withdrawn again.

'Bosco would like a very large family, but I think four is enough.' Rachel poured herself more water. 'I don't intend to spend my whole life breeding.'

'What do you intend to spend it on then?' Lady Askham stared unsmilingly at her daughter-in-law. 'Doubtless you'd be busy demonstrating on the streets of London and getting yourself thrown into prison again.' Lady Askham peered at the meat on her plate as though it had something crawling over it. She disapproved of almost everything about the parsimonious way Rachel ran the Grange, including the culinary aspect of simple, wholesome fare.

'I have *never* been in prison, as your ladyship well knows.' Rachel's tone was dangerous. 'Nor was I accustomed to demonstrate on the streets.'

'Well, all your friends are there. Was not that awful Pankhurst creature a friend of yours?'

'Have you met Mrs Pankhurst, Lady Askham?' Rachel felt her lip trembling and, underneath the table, clenched her fists, one hand into the other.

'I have not.'

'Then how do you know she's awful?'

'The woman is a gaolbird! She attacks the very foundations of our society.'

'Mama, in front of Constance, do you think?' Bosco intervened, looking at his young cousin.

'But Constance must know these things in case she becomes infected too.'

'Are you for the women's vote, Constance?' Rachel said gently, ignoring her mother-in-law.

'I haven't thought about it,' Constance looked nervously from one angry lady to the other.

'Constance is *much* too young,' Dulcie put a protective hand on her niece's arm. 'And I hope when she is old enough she will have the sense to realize that this country has grown into the greatest in the world through the achievements of its men backed by the love and help of their women.'

Rachel gave a little splutter, coughed and apologized, looking around her and patting her chest.

'Oh, forgive me, Lady Askham, but I haven't heard anything so old-fashioned since my own poor mother told me I must never go out alone, when I was thinking of travelling all over Europe by myself.'

'Your mother was quite right. Things have not changed and, if they have, they are for the worst.'

'This conversation is getting nowhere.' Bosco patiently,

neatly put his knife and fork together. 'Mama and Rachel simply do not agree. They both have a point of view which I respect and I'm sure Constance does too. Now, can we talk of something else?'

'I was *actually* going to say, Lady Askham, before you rushed to draw your own curious conclusions,' Rachel glanced severely at her mother-in-law, 'that I would like time to give Bosco more help visiting tenants and seeing if I can help to improve their lot. We have many poor people on our lands whom we could do more to help. But, more importantly, I want to spend more time with my children while they are young so that they know me and I am not a remote figure to them. I assure you I shan't be on the streets of London – not for the moment anyway.'

'I was not aware there were many "poor people" on our estates,' Dulcie sniffed huffily. 'If there are you can be sure it's their own fault, because there is plenty of work for them to do. As for being a remote figure to one's children I never was, I'm sure.' She stared at Bosco who, however, shook his head smilingly as if to mitigate the effect of what he was going to say:

'Mama, I must confess I don't remember much about you until I was quite old, and that's the truth. We used to be taken to see you and Papa twice a day when you were at home, and mostly you weren't. Our children are about the house the whole day, or will be when they are older, and they will always accompany us to London.'

'What thanks a mother gets for sacrificing her life,' Lady Askham lowered her voice, a stricken look on her face. 'I only hope your children will be as grateful to you, Rachel. What do *you* think, dearest Constance, you must feel very left out?'

Constance Kitto had played a very small part in the conversation so far, and felt rather unnerved not only by her aunt's forthrightness, which she knew, but by her cousin's wife's vigorous defence of herself as well as her willingness to confront Aunt Dulcie, a woman much older than herself. Constance, raised in an Edinburgh academy for young ladies, taught that respect for her elders was a *sine qua non* of existence, was both rather amazed and appalled by Cousin Bosco's wife.

'Really, Aunt, I have only been here for half an hour. I can hardly give an opinion, nor would I wish to in such a short time. But Lady Gore's children do look awfully well, however they are brought up.'

'Were it left to me . . .' Lady Askham began, but Rachel abruptly cut her short.

'I assure you it won't be, Lady Askham. I would never ask you to do anything for my children. I can't think it would be good for them.'

'Rachel!' Bosco threw his napkin on the table and stared at her. 'How *can* you speak like that to Mama?'

'How can your mother speak like she does to me?' Rachel's normally pleasant voice seemed to have lowered half an octave. 'She insults me in my own house. She does nothing but belittle and demean me with her sneers and her criticism . . .'

'I assure you, dear Rachel . . .' Lady Askham, who had kept her hat on at lunch, as though to reassure herself that her stay was of a temporary nature, adjusted the pert, modern little scrap of veil over her eyes.

'And I assure *you*, Lady Askham, that I am mistress in my own house and shall do as I please. You are welcome here, but not with your constant sneering and carping. If you can contrive to put a little sweetness on your busy tongue we might get on better.'

Lady Askham quivered, stared at her plate, put her knife and fork neatly together and stood up.

'I shan't stay here for a *moment* longer. Constance.'

She beckoned imperiously to her niece who half stood up as though wondering what to do and then sat down again. The Edinburgh academy so ill-equipped young ladies for situations such as this. She was a guest of her aunt's, yet a guest of Rachel's so – what to do?

'Mama, *please*,' Bosco got up too, and went over to his mother, trying to get her to sit down again, but she pushed him away.

'I assure you, Bosco, I am going and I shan't set foot again in this house until your wife apologizes to me.'

'I apologize?' Rachel too threw her napkin on the table and made an attempt to rise but, like Constance, thought better of it, only for a different reason.

'Yes, you!' Dulcie's frantic fingers flew to her triple row of pearls which she twirled round and round on her neck, symbols of her agitation. 'You strumpet; you who ensnared my son, who have no manners, no idea of running a large house with your mean-minded middle-class ways. You should hear what the servants think of it all. Not much, I can tell you!'

'I'm surprised you, of all people, listen to servants' gossip, Lady Askham.' Rachel's pallor, considering her condition, was alarming. 'And, *as* for being a strumpet who ensnared your son – '

'Mama didn't mean that,' Bosco looked agonizingly from wife to mother, mother to wife.

'Oh yes I did!' His mother's aggression switched to him. 'How can you possibly trust a woman who gave herself so freely to you outside marriage? How do you know you can trust her now? That her children are really yours and not those of some half-baked, half-educated member of the Labour Party?'

'Mama, I really must escort you home.' Bosco seized her arm and steered her to the door. 'I can see you're beside yourself. And as for Rachel, she is very near her time and will be ill if this continues.'

'Good!' Dulcie said, looking over her shoulder: 'Constance. Come at once!'

'I prefer to stay here, Aunt, and see that Rachel is all right.'

'I see her attitude of disobedience is catching,' Dulcie began, but Bosco led her into the hall shutting the door of the dining-room firmly behind him.

Under the anxious eye of Constance, Rachel made a determined effort to recover; but she was trembling so much, and the pounding of her heart made her so uncomfortable that she felt short of breath. She took a long draught of water to steady herself.

'Are you all right?' Constance enquired anxiously.

'I mustn't let her win,' Rachel gritted her teeth. 'She would like to see me dead. I'm sorry, because she's your aunt.'

'I didn't realize there was such animosity.'

Rachel looked out of the window, as if making sure that Lady Askham would not bob back again.

'Lady Askham developed an antipathy towards me as long ago as 1898 when we met in Cairo. She disliked my brother too, but me particularly. Bosco once told me he imagined she thought I was dangerous, and that she had a premonition how closely our lives would be linked. It is a strange, irrational feeling, that of your aunt, for a woman who never wished her any harm. Nor did I, then, desire her son.

'I have done my best to placate her for his sake, but I can't; so I no longer try. But today was the most serious quarrel we have ever had and it distresses me you should have been here to witness it as I know you must admire your aunt.'

'I never heard anyone speak to Auntie like that,'

Constance's eyes gleamed admiringly. 'Mama is mortally afraid of her. She never raises her voice in her presence. Wait until I tell Mama *this*!'

'She may not be too pleased.' Rachel slowly rose to ease the tension in her legs, the nagging pain in her back. She walked up and down the dining-room, stretching and rubbing that spot at the base of her spine where the ache came from. Inside her the baby jumped and kicked so ferociously that she did wonder, not for the first time, if there were indeed two. She turned to her young guest and smiled:

'Do forgive me, dear, if I go upstairs to rest. I have to face Bosco when he comes back. He won't be pleased. You'll find the children in the garden with their nurse; or you can take a book, or just sit.'

'I think I should get back to Auntie now,' Constance said nervously. 'I'd hate her to send me home.'

After resting in the afternoon Rachel went into the garden and was lying idly on a swing when Bosco arrived. Little Ralph played a few yards away under the watchful eyes of his nurse and baby Charlotte sat in a wooden pen with some bricks, but kept reaching with her chubby little hands to try and get out of her pen.

For a while Bosco ignored Rachel, the sunny, loving mood of the morning gone, and played with the children, pretending to run races with Ralph and alternately lifting Charlotte out of her pen and throwing her gently back into it again, while she squealed with laughter and raised her arms asking for more.

Rachel watched them with the pleasure she always had when seeing Bosco with his children whom he adored. One of the surprises was what a good father this previously carefree bachelor made, spending much more time with them than was common even in that enlightened post-Victorian age, when too many fathers were still inclined to the firm opinion that children should be seen and not heard. When he came over to her at last she smiled and held out her hand but he didn't take it. His face remained severe.

'Oh Bosco, don't let your mother upset you.'

'I am upset,' he said, squatting on the grass beside her. 'I am terribly upset. How could *you* say to her the things you did?'

As Rachel sat upright the swing tilted dangerously.

'*I* say the things I did! What about your mother, pray? She called me a prostitute.'

'A strumpet is not quite the same thing.'

'Then I don't know what it is because I always thought it was. To me a strumpet and a whore are synonymous. In front of your cousin, a girl of eighteen I scarcely knew, and in my own home she insulted me in a way that not only threw opprobrium on me but also on herself. I think I was most restrained.'

'*You* restrained?' Bosco's laugh was humourless. 'My mother doesn't think that. I thought she was going to have a heart attack. She had to lie down as soon as I got her home. My father is most upset.'

'And what about me? I am on the point of giving birth to a child. Did no one think of that?'

'Oh, you're as strong as an ox, Rachel. You said so today yourself. Really you must be more temperate with my mother. She is not as young as you are, nor as resilient.'

Rachel snorted. 'Your mother is just as tough as me, certainly not old, and equally resilient.'

'You are too alike.'

'Alike? Your mother and I? What an insult.'

Bosco began to pluck at the grass on which he was

sitting. 'Really, Rachel, if you knew how your attitude to Mama distresses me I'm sure you would try and do something about it. My mother is my mother and has my love and respect. You are my wife and I love and respect you too. It is a terrible dilemma for me to be between two such strong women, always at war. You would think that for my sake you would try and present an agreeable aspect of yourself to my mother, control your temper. You will have to apologize to Mama or she will never come here again or, she says, receive you at the Hall, whether you are my wife or not. My father too has taken her side and is sending you a letter.'

'And you?' Rachel stared at him in disbelief. 'What's your attitude?'

'I . . . well,' Bosco threw a handful of grass towards Ralph who toddled over, pursued by his nurse who realized his parents wanted to be alone. 'I think Mama is right. You are a younger woman and should apologize. Then she is willing to overlook today.'

'Never. If she hadn't called me a prostitute I might, just might, for your sake have sent her a note but, after that? You must think I'm mad.'

'I assure you she didn't mean it.'

'Then neither did I mean what I said.'

'Well, tell her.'

'No.'

Rachel pursed her lips and stuck out her chin and Bosco, knowing that she meant what she said, sighed heavily and, getting up, strolled slowly across the lawn and back again. He stood for a while looking at her, his hands in his pockets, his expression very far from that of the lover of the morning sitting beside her on the bench by the lake.

'Rachel, sometimes I wish . . .'

'Yes?'

'Never mind.'

'That you hadn't married me? Is that what you were going to say?'

'How could it be what I was going to say! You know I adore you.'

'Then what was it?'

'I just wish that . . . maybe you had been brought up differently. You would never have dreamed of being so offensive to an older woman.'

'Really?' Rachel pretended to be amused. 'Have you, by chance, ever heard the way your sisters address their mother? Both of them? "I won't do this" and "I won't do that"?'

'Yes, but it's not quite the same thing. A row is a row. You and Mama are continually bickering when you're together.'

'Then I shan't see her.'

'That looks like happening anyway, but what will be the effect on our family?'

'No effect as far as I can see. You will continue to see your parents, the children their grandmother and grandfather and I shall, happily, be spared the pleasure of setting eyes again on your mother.'

'You can't mean that?'

'I do.' She stared at him coldly. 'Once Lady Askham realizes that I am Viscountess Gore, your wife, and not some woman of the streets the wind blew in there may be a change, but not until then. Your mother has always hated me, you know that. Was she not the main reason I resisted marrying you for so long? Well now, sometimes, I wish I hadn't.'

'How can you *possibly* say that when you were so upset at thinking I meant it a moment ago? How *can* you?'

Rachel hung her head, biting her lip, knowing she'd

gone too far, but feeling, also, that it was too late to retract.

'She *is* a blight on our lives, Bosco. Of course I don't mean I wish I hadn't married you. Do you realize that whenever we see your mother the atmosphere between us changes? Yet when we are together our happiness is perfect.'

'My mother says you're jealous.'

'Jealous? Of who?'

'Of her, of course. She feels pity for you, she says.'

'Does she now? How very gracious. And how revealing, Bosco, it is of your own character to know that you take notice of every little bit of tittle-tattle your mother says against your wife.'

'I don't. I'm merely reporting what she says.'

'And what did you say?' Rachel stared up at him feeling at a distinct disadvantage, lying horizontal in her hammock like a stranded whale. 'How did you answer your mother when she said that?'

'I said . . . Oh, I said that . . . Oh, I can't remember what I said, Rachel, if anything. I try to keep my Mama off the subject of you. But I do wish, my dearest wife, that for once in your life you'd remember the "obedience" part of the marriage vows. You promised to obey me and I wish to God you would. If even once in a while you'd do as you're told, as women had to of old, we'd all be very much happier.'

'Oh, would we indeed? Thank you, Bosco, very much. Those are certainly words I'll never forget.' Resenting her bulk, Rachel got carefully off the hammock and stood looking at her husband.

Then, slowly, she went into the house, along the corridor and into her sitting-room to her desk where the draft of the letter to Mrs Pankhurst still lay. Tearing it up she took up her pen, drew a fresh sheet of paper towards her and wrote:

Dear Emmeline,

Thank you so much for your letter. Nothing would give me greater pleasure than to lend my name to the Cause and, as soon as I can, to participate as much as I can. How proud I am of you and those of my fellows who are risking financial ruin and imprisonment for their beliefs. May I soon join them, and you.

I am expecting a child very shortly but, as soon as I am able, you will hear from me again.

With every good wish.

She put down her pen, read through the letter twice, addressed an envelope, put the letter in and sealed it. Then, in case she should change her mind, she sent quickly for a maid to take it to the post. But after she had gone Rachel sat for a long, long time at her desk strumming her fingers on the top.

Lady Melanie Bolingbroke accepted another small cake covered with icing sugar and multicoloured hundreds and thousands and then, looking at it critically, said that, really, she shouldn't and put it reluctantly back on the plate again.

Lord Denton Rigby asked why ever not, and offered her the plate once more, holding it enticingly under her pert, aristocratic little nose.

'Because of my figure,' Melanie fleetingly outlined her slim waist with the palm of her hand, smiling at him artfully.

'Your figure's beautiful, Melanie,' he dutifully said but Melanie pushed the plate away. It was a delightful game; the kind of silliness she enjoyed.

'I want to keep it that way, Denty darling. The women in our family have a tendency to run to fat. Oh, not Mama, or Flora who is as thin as a beanpole, but I've hundreds of very fat aunts. Lady Kitto, my mother's sister-in-law, is huge,' and Melanie opened her arms as wide as she could, as though she would embrace the whole of the Ritz Hotel and Green Park besides. Denton's eyes duly boggled.

'I assure you, Melanie, I can't ever see you anything but as slender, as lovely, as bewitching as you are now.'

'No cakes, Denty,' Melanie protested and sipped her cup of weak China tea instead, looking teasingly at him over the rim.

Tea with a swain, or lunch, or sometimes dinner was a commonplace part of every day taken either at the Ritz or Brown's or Gunter's or, sometimes when she was sure Adam wouldn't be home, even more intimately at the little house in John Street.

Melanie's social whirl dominated her life. Not that she wasn't a good mother to her three children: Bobby, the first-born, still doted on by his grandparents; Susan who had been born in 1903 and Christopher who followed in 1905. Both Adam's children spent a lot of time with their half-brother in Manchester Square because the John Street house was, in Melanie's opinion, so tiny, so unsuitable for the upbringing of the young.

'And yet Adam's so *mean*,' she confided her predicament to Denton, after the matter of the cakes had been settled and the tempting plate removed by a waiter who was asked to bring fresh tea instead. 'It's not that I haven't the money or that the Lightermans wouldn't buy us a much larger establishment anywhere we wanted. They feel they owe it to the memory of poor Harry; but Adam won't accept.'

'I can understand that,' Denton said loyally. 'A man doesn't want to be kept by his wife, or the parents of her first husband.'

'It's not a question of *keeping*, Denty dear,' she lightly pressed his nose with a white, beautifully manicured finger, an intimate gesture that would not be lost on anyone happening to glance at the smart couple taking tea in the elegant surroundings of the Ritz one hot summer's day in the year 1908. The windows looking on to Green Park were open and the heavy fronds of the trees, the fragrant smells of summer, almost offered the illusion that they were in the country. 'It's a question of just having a little more space, a little bit extra. Adam has never quite got over being poor and marrying above his station.'

'Oh Mel, that's a hard thing to say.' Lord Denton swept a hand across his well-kept moustaches, brushing them up into a twirl at either side of his red cheeks. He was a well-built man in his thirties, handsome in a heavy, rather florid sort of way, as though he spent a good amount of his time out of doors, which he did whenever his duties at the Foreign Office would allow. He was forever hacking and hunting and playing polo, which was how Melanie had met him; one day at Askham he had formed part of the ex-army team that Bosco had got together to play a scratch team of amateur country gentlemen.

Of all the men she met, and there were quite a few, Melanie was rather nervous of Lord Denton Rigby, son of the Marquess of Cadcaster who spent most of his life in the West Indies. Unlike the Askhams he had let his estates and fortune dwindle so that his heir, Lord Filment, and all his younger sons had actually to work. Yet his duties at the Foreign Office sat very lightly on the broad shoulders of Lord Denton who had a number of friends in high places concerned with the governing of the country, and able to dismiss his many absences on other matters.

Melanie was nervous about Denton because he was high-tempered and she thought him dangerous – as though she were playing with fire. He was not only more manly, but more persistent than the rest: he actually wanted to go further than tea at the Ritz or dinner at Quaglino's, and made his intentions clear. He wanted to get her to bed and have a full-blown affair, but Melanie's abhorrence of the physical side of love had not changed since her second marriage or the births of two more children, as Adam knew to his cost.

It was so hot in the Ritz that after tea they strolled through Green Park and the Mall into St James's Park where even the birds looked tired and stood rather listlessly around the edge of the lake, very few of them actually bothering to fly, so that a heavy stillness hung across the park on that August afternoon. Denton took Melanie's arm, steering her towards a bench.

'Mel,' he said sitting close to her, his heavy breath hot on her cheeks. 'I have this flat in Pimlico . . .'

'Oh, Denty, darling, don't go on about that sort of thing *again*! It's such a bore.'

Melanie was wearing a singularly pretty, natural-waisted dress of white poplin overprinted with huge white and blue tea roses and a wide flat straw hat on her head with large artificial roses cleverly matched to the colour of her dress. She looked far younger than the twice- married mother of three that she was. She was only twenty-eight but looked, nevertheless, not much more than the nineteen years of age she had been when she was first married. Her beautiful auburn hair had just a little artificial aid to bring out its natural highlights and her pale, ethereal complexion, her large blue-green eyes conveyed an enticing combination of innocence and allurement. Denton Rigby was head-over-heels in love with her.

'But, Mel, you'd never leave Adam?'

'Leave Adam? Of course I'd never leave Adam! What an idea. We Askhams don't believe in divorce.'

'Well then?' Rather sportily dressed himself in a grey very fine hound's-tooth check suit with a soft-collared white shirt, and a pale grey tie, Denton looked dashing and elegant as he rested his hands over the top of his silver-topped cane and looked at her.

'Well what, Denty dear?' She fluttered her long eyelashes in a simulation of innocence. 'You know I'd never dream of an *affaire*.'

'But why not? I thought all married ladies had them?'

'I am not one of those,' Melanie said haughtily. 'And if you think I am . . .'

'Oh no, I assure you, I don't.'

'Then why do you suggest it?'

Her tone, from being girlish and winsome, was now rather high-pitched and sharp and she looked at him with the sort of expression, part amusement and part horror, that had made her mother famous in circles where men congregated to talk about women.

'Mel,' Denton reached out a hand, attempting to take one of hers, 'I'm a man and you're a woman . . .'

'Quite obvious, dear Denty.'

'I can't just exist on tea. I want you for my own. I want to be your lover.'

'And what do I get in exchange for that, pray?'

'I thought, felt, hoped, you might love me too.' His look, for a man of his temperament, was verging on the pitiful.

'You want me to risk everything, my home and reputation, just to go to bed with you?'

'I assure you there won't be any risk.'

'My husband is a Member of Parliament, an increasingly eminent lawyer. What would happen to him if a story about his wife's infidelity got around?'

'But it won't.'

'You can't be sure. Besides,' she hung her pretty head in a rather artificial gesture of submission. 'It's not the sort of thing I'd ever be tempted to do. I don't like it.'

'It?' His face was puzzled.

'It,' she looked at him archly. 'You know. "It."'

'Ah, "it", I see.' His face went even redder. 'You're such a flirt, I would have thought you would.'

'Well, I don't, and both my husbands have been aware of this.'

Denton tried reassurance. 'But it's just what I'd expect from a well-brought-up woman. You don't *have* to like it, dearest. Most women don't, unless they're whores. It would give me so much pleasure that that would be your reward. And I would be *very* gentle.' He licked his lips quite lasciviously as if at the very thought and, somehow, Melanie couldn't imagine him being gentle at all. In his blustering way he reminded her a little of Harry. He would be all pushy and forceful, lacking finesse.

'I feel you're spoiling the day, Denty,' Melanie sulkily looked first at the sky then at her watch. 'If you want to go on seeing me like this, all right. If not, don't.'

'Oh, but I do.'

'Then you can escort me to Manchester Square and say no more about this silly subject ever again.'

Denton jumped up, his hopes temporarily rebuffed. He felt sure that this was her subtle way of encouraging him, inflaming his desires. It was an expected part of the game. He knew women too well.

Mabel Lighterman had hardly changed with the years except that she had grown even stouter. But her hair was still that brilliant blonde, her face – in an age where make-up was a rarity and frowned upon – deeply encrusted with powder, rouge, mascara and all the artifices with which she endeavoured to keep young. In dress she still tried to be in the height of fashion, but managed to look years behind it.

Melanie adored her as much as ever and flung herself into her arms as she and Denton were led up to the first-floor drawing-room with its view of the Square, now leafy with thick midsummer foliage. Most of the rooms they had passed on their way up were covered with sheets because the Lightermans were preparing, like all London at the end of the season, to go to the country for the hunting and shooting parties that they still kept up in their efforts to attract the cream of society.

'Bosco is coming next week,' she said after offering them tea which they refused. 'I do hope you can prevail upon Adam to come too, Mel dear. He looked so tired when I saw him last.'

'If he's tired it's his own fault,' Melanie said in an offhand manner. 'No one asked him to be a Member of Parliament.'

'But they did, dear. I heard Mr Asquith himself suggest Bisley to him when the seat fell vacant after the death of . . . I can't remember what his name was, the previous Member.'

'Asquith suggested it to a number of young men and Adam may have been one. The Liberals were so keen to flood the Commons to get rid of the Unionists.'

'I don't approve of Adam being a Liberal,' Denton stroked his moustaches again.

'Oh, don't you, Denton? Well, he is,' Melanie yawned, artificially, pretending to hide her mouth and her dainty even teeth with her hand, as though the subject were just too boring. 'How I agree with you. Father said we have never had anyone in the family in the House who wasn't a Tory in the old days, or a Unionist. Adam is into all those dreary subjects like reform of the poor law, education, something called National Insurance and, of course, women's suffrage which he gets from Rachel.'

Denton burst into laughter at the thought of such amusing antics.

'The day women have the vote I'll emigrate,' he said.

'That's what Sir Robert says too,' Mabel replied comfortably, 'though I do think they have a point, poor dears. They are certainly very sincere.'

'They merely make a wretched nuisance of themselves and demean their sex. All these demonstrations, the number mounting daily. If I were their husbands I'd take a whip to them.'

'But most of them *haven't* husbands, Denton,' Melanie said as though explaining a point to an idiot. 'That's the point. They are frustrated spinsters like my sister Flora who has decided to embrace the Cause for some strange reason. Having kept her nose for years in the ancient world she suddenly emerges and sticks it right into the twentieth century. Whereas my sister-in-law Rachel, having been such a firebrand, has gone off it completely.'

'Too busy with her babies,' Mabel said smilingly. 'Beautiful babies too. And twins.' She clasped her hands, closing her eyes in a brief moment of surrogate ecstasy, 'A boy *and* a girl. Isn't that the cleverest thing? I'm dying to see them. I hear they're perfect angels.'

'Dear little things,' Melanie nodded her head briefly. 'She says she won't have any more now. I wonder she wants to come to your place with the twins just a month old.'

'She isn't. Bosco's coming alone.'

'How odd. They always go everywhere together.' Melanie looked at her thoughtfully and then her gaze strayed towards the window, resting on the waving branches of the tall plane trees. 'I've never known them apart since their marriage. I wonder if anything's wrong?'

'I don't expect so, dear. Bosco loves polo and he's just coming for a day or two. He'll want to rush back to Rachel and those babies, believe you me. I never saw two people so much in love after being married so long, to say nothing of what went on before.'

'What was that?' Denton suddenly looked interested, wiping his thick red neck with a large white handkerchief because of the heat.

'Oh, nothing,' Melanie shot Mabel a warning glance and then with her most sugared smile said: 'Why don't you ask Denton as well, Mabel, if Adam can't come? He simply *adores* a game of polo.'

CHAPTER 15

The Lightermans' house on the Thames was what many would have called a rich man's folly, but some admired as the pinnacle of Victorian architectural magnificence. It had been built by Sir Robert on virgin land cut out of a stretch of forest and so was surrounded on all sides by trees. The huge gabled, turreted red-brick house was surrounded by acres of formal gardens and broad verdant lawns sweeping down to the river anchorage at which were row-boats, skiffs, punts and various types of craft belonging to Sir Robert.

In 1908 Sir Robert Lighterman was seventy-five but boasted he had never had a day's illness in his life; his tough, rough origins, he claimed, having both helped to protect and preserve him, like old port benefits from many years in cask. He did walk with the aid of a stick, but this he attributed to gout caused by an overfondness for the said port, also for brandy and Madeira wine. The stick, in fact, gave him an air of benign authority, rather like that wielded by a bluff, eighteenth-century squire of the type portrayed in the plays of Congreve or Richard Brinsley Sheridan.

Like his wife Mabel, Sir Robert loved parties, filling his house with people, some of whom he had never previously met and most of whom he hoped had never done a day's work in their lives. To him that was still the sure sign of aristocracy and breeding, qualities that, for all his wealth, Sir Robert had never been able to buy and never would and still envied. Of course the army was an exception; it was not regarded as work and nor were the diplomatic service or any branch of the Foreign Office – duties lightly undertaken and usually occupied by young scions of just the kind of families that Sir Robert liked to encourage to visit his homes.

Despite the patronizing attitude of the Askhams to the Lightermans – they were scarcely ever asked to visit either St James's Square or Askham Hall – Sir Robert and his wife were proud of their connection with that ancient, noble family: the fact that they shared a grandson with an earl. Sir Robert was leaving no stone unturned, no pound that he could usefully place unspent, to try and secure for himself before his demise a heritable honour like a barony that he could pass on to his great joy, the pride and love of his life: his grandson Bobby.

The polo teams were made up of young Oxford graduates and undergraduates, soldiers from Sandhurst at nearby Camberley, and a remnant of Bosco's ex-army team which he called the Gore Irregulars. Bosco was delighted to welcome his old acquaintance Denton Rigby, even if he was surprised to see him one of the company.

'I didn't know you knew old Lighterman?'

'I know your sister, though.' Denton looked at him and lit a cigarette. The two men were inspecting their horses, which had arrived that morning, in the stables at the far end of the polo meadow behind the house.

'Adam too, of course.'

'Of course.'

'Adam is my best friend,' Bosco said with a warning note in his voice, not quite liking the familiar, rather jocose glance that Denton had given him, 'and Melanie *is* my sister.'

'Look, old fellow,' Denton gave his bluff, ex-army laugh. He had been briefly in the Grenadiers, before deciding that soldiering was not for him, which was how he'd met Bosco. 'I know that! No need to sweat, is there? No harm in it; no harm at all.'

'Melanie, I hear, has a little coterie of admirers in London and I don't like it. I didn't know you were among them. Remember she's a married woman with three children. They, her husband and her home, should be enough to take up most of her time.'

'I'm sure they do. But he neglects her, you know. Surely you know that?'

'I know nothing of the kind. He's busy carving a career for himself, and very commendably too. Adam adores Melanie and all he does he does for her. He wants to be someone to make her proud of him. Can't you see that, Denton?'

'A bloke can carve out a career without neglecting his wife. Anyway, there's nothing in my relationship with Melanie. She wouldn't consider it for one thing.'

'Have you asked her?'

Denton turned away and ran a careful, practised hand over the flank of his horse.

'Have you asked her?' Bosco said again, seizing him by the shoulder. 'Answer me, Denton.'

'It's no concern of yours.' Angrily Denton brushed his hand away.

'It *is* my concern,' Bosco raised a fist and shook it under Denton's nose. 'And if I ever hear . . .'

'My dear Bosco, I should think you've heard an awful lot already and that's nothing to do with me. Melanie's quite well known in Town, you know.'

Bosco hit him squarely on the chin and Denton, taken by surprise at this sudden and unexpected attack, fell back, saving himself by clutching at the stall holding his horse. Bosco was about to lurch at him again when a rather frightened female voice called out:

'Oh I say! What *are* you boys up to?' and Melanie, a

vision in pink-and-white tulle with a wide hat made of stiffened rose organdie, stood at the entrance to the stable gazing at them solemnly, turning her parasol idly over her head.

Denton righted himself, feeling his chin with his hand, and Bosco smoothed back his hair.

'Bosco, did you *hit* Denton? Shouldn't that sort of thing be saved for the polo field, darling? Or is this just a little preliminary skirmish?'

'Something like that,' Bosco said, dusting himself down. 'Stay away from Denton, Melanie, or I'll hit him much harder next time round.'

Melanie, flinging her open parasol on the ground, rushed up to Denton and put a hand on his chin.

'Am I the reason? Oh, you silly boys.'

'I told him that,' Denton flushed as her hand remained caressingly against his cheek, relishing the concern in her eyes. 'I said that I admired you, but nothing more.'

'He also said you had quite a name about Town.' Bosco glowered at his sister.

'Oh, did you say that, Denty? How naughty of you. Quite untrue. If I have a few, a very few, admirers, is that not the prerogative of an . . .' She paused momentarily as though in search of the right words, words that should not give offence, '. . . of an attractive woman?'

'All that sort of thing has gone out, Melanie,' Bosco snapped. 'It went out in the nineties when women had the idea of themselves as the playthings of men. Well, they weren't and they're not. You should have more dignity.'

'You're frightfully stuffy, Bosco,' Melanie said derisively. 'You're beginning to sound like Rachel. Just because Rachel is plain and continually pregnant so can't have any admirers . . .'

'Melanie, I forbid you to speak like that about my wife,' Bosco thundered.

'Lady Gore is certainly not plain.' Denton looked apologetically at Bosco.

'Might you fancy her yourself then?' Melanie, clearly in a dangerous mood for mischief, looked at him slyly, while Bosco clenched his fists again as though his next victim would be her.

'I would never *dream* of casting glances at Lady Gore.' Denton had gone quite pale.

'But I am fair game?'

'This is getting quite out of hand,' Denton's tone was brusque. 'I think I'd better leave.'

'Leave? Leave here? Oh you can't do that! The Lightermans would be terribly offended.'

'I can plead an engagement.'

Melanie shook her head. 'They know quite well I asked you because of Bosco. Now look,' she held out both hands in an attitude of supplication, looking bewitchingly appealing and pretty. 'Let's forget this silly business and be friends. You men are quite ridiculous when you talk about women as though we were, indeed, your playthings. After all, Adam is here, is he not?' She glanced at Bosco. 'You can be quite sure all the proprieties will be observed.'

'You'd no right to call Rachel plain,' Bosco took out his case and lit a cigarette, angrily blowing out the match and tossing it away after he'd lit it.

'I apologize. That *was* nasty, and wrong. I was a little piqued. Rachel is a decidedly handsome woman even if she is a bit like Caesar's wife. Above reproach, you know. Now are we friends?' The broad gesture of her arms included both antagonists. 'Friends?'

'Friends,' Denton looked nervously at Bosco who, however, said nothing and turned away. Taking up a brush he began to groom his horse in the next stall, even though it already glistened like polished chestnut.

* * *

Dulcie Askham, though avoiding the company of the common Lightermans when she could, enjoyed, nevertheless, a fuss being made of her; being the centre of attention; being surrounded by young and amusing men. In the frenzied Victorian gothic folly of Robertswood by the side of the Thames she found all three. It was also nice to get away from her ailing husband, whose demands increased as he got weaker. There was the additional advantage that her detestable daughter-in-law would not be there and thus she could, for once, have her son to herself.

Indeed it was rather like a family reunion because Flora had unexpectedly accepted an invitation for the house-party, and Melanie and Adam she knew would be there. Delectable Denton Rigby was an added bonus.

'Dear Denton,' she said, passing him a plate of sandwiches across the small table they shared on the lawn for tea later that afternoon. 'What a lovely surprise to find you here. I didn't know you knew the Lightermans.'

Not wishing to risk a recurrence of what had happened in the stables a few hours before, Denton carefully omitted to attribute the introduction to Melanie and made up some other excuse instead.

'Your *father*?' Dulcie exclaimed in surprise. 'I would have thought him the last kind of man to hobnob with a person like' – she looked over her shoulder but Sir Robert was nowhere in sight, 'him. I thought the dear Marquess was much too grand to know someone quite so lacking in gentility.'

'I should have thought the Earl of Askham too,' Denton nibbled a cucumber sandwich and balanced, as delicately as he could, a very thin porcelain cup with a tiny handle between the fingers and thumb of a massive hand. Dulcie shrugged.

'In these days one has to mix with all kinds, alas.

Melanie made that first frightful marriage,' she raised her eyes to the heavens and, with an expressive shrug of her shoulders, gestured around her. 'This is the result: the Lightermans, and their vulgar house. It looks like St Pancras Station.'

'It is nevertheless quite a remarkable place. And their house in Manchester Square! *That's* like a museum.'

'So I hear. I resist all invitations to go there, I'm glad to say, so far successfully. The little I am obliged to see them is quite enough. We share a grandchild, but he always comes to me. It's bad enough to have that and the atrocious "Mabel" – what a name – referring to me as a friend. She once asked me to present her at Court! *Quelle horreur!* I told her she was much too old and would look ridiculous. Well, one has to be frank, *n'est-ce pas*, Denton? I am only here this time to be a little alone with my children. It is so seldom I have them to myself. Adam I heard was not to come and now he has,' Dulcie flapped her hands again in a vague gesture of despair, leaning confidentially towards him. '*Another* marriage like the first . . .'

'Really?' Denton responded eagerly. 'I understood Lady Melanie was very happy.'

'From whom did you understand that?' Dulcie gazed at him, her eyes unnaturally large.

'From herself. She says she is a little lonely . . . that Mr Bolingbroke is on his way up, a successful man.'

'I'll believe it when I see it,' Dulcie sipped her tea.

'You don't think he'll be successful?'

'I don't think he has the push. Now Bosco. There is a man who will be successful. The way he has thrown himself into managing the estates, understanding all the nuances of poor dear Arthur's business interests, is remarkable.' Denton fingered his chin, saying nothing. 'We all underestimated my younger son, considering him good for little else than playing at soldiers, though we were, and are, proud of his record at Omdurman. But he is twice the man I thought him. Now if he were not lumbered with that wife of his . . .'

'Lumbered?' Denton sat up and scratched behind his ear. He knew that Dulcie loved to gossip and, as he did too, he had purposely sought out her company for tea. 'Do I hear you right, Lady Askham?'

'You do indeed. "Lumbered" is the word I used and "lumbered" is what is meant. She is like a stone round his neck. She, of course, is no lady and never will be. She is a scheming adventuress. I dread to think what will happen to the Hall when I and my poor husband are no more. She will probably fill it full of beggar children and their unwed mothers and gaolbirds connected with the women's suffrage movement.'

'I see you're disappointed in your children.' Denton asked if he could smoke and Dulcie nodded her head.

'Of course you may and, yes, I am disappointed not in my children but in their choice of marriage partners. Melanie has made a fool of herself twice over, and Bosco, who could have had *any* woman he wanted . . .'

'I don't suppose you remember me, Lady Askham,' a voice behind her shoulder interrupted her and, turning, she looked up at the speaker whose whole demeanour was deferential, his angular body leaning almost awkwardly to one side. Dulcie frowned, screwing up her eyes.

'I'm afraid I don't.'

'Egypt, my lady, in 1898. Adrian Hastings.'

Dulcie put down her cup and looked at Denton, shaking her head. 'I'm afraid I still can't recall the occasion, Mr . . . but please, do sit down.'

Hastings perched nervously on the garden chair beside Dulcie. He was in his early forties, with pleasant bland features, his thinning hair, of a nondescript colour, parted in the middle.

'You may recall we went on a picnic to Sakkara. I'm a newspaper journalist. I don't know why but I was invited to be one of the party. You remember Achmed Asher . . .'

'Oh!' Dulcie gave a little shriek and held up both hands as though to prevent him from continuing. 'Please don't mention the name of that awful man, that terrible occasion . . .'

'I must admit it *was* rather uncomfortable. The flies in the desert.'

'I wasn't thinking of the flies,' Dulcie's guest was suddenly unwelcome. 'I was thinking of that horrible little man and that perfectly disgusting woman with him.'

'Madame Hassim?'

'If that was her name. I can't remember.' Dulcie fanned herself vigorously with a white glove and commented on the state of the weather in an effort to change the conversation but Hastings, like a greyhound, or rather newshound, on the scent, bent forward.

'She is living in London now.'

'Who?'

'Madame Hassim.'

'Good gracious. How awful. I hope I never see her.'

'I'm sure your paths are unlikely to cross, Lady Askham. How, may I ask, is Captain Down?'

'You're very out-of-date, young man,' Dulcie looked at him dismissively. 'My son is now the Viscount Gore, heir to my poor dear husband who, alas, does not enjoy good health.' Dulcie looked sadly into her empty teacup as though wishing to divine from the few tealeaves scattered on the bottom what the future might bring.

'I'm very sorry to hear that.'

'For a reporter you're out of touch, my good man. Did

you not know my son Arthur died of the poliomyelitis in America a few years ago? There was a raging epidemic in Chicago.'

'I didn't hear about your son, Lady Askham. I mainly deal with . . . well, trivia. It used not to be so but, alas, it is now. I came back from Egypt in very poor health . . .'

Dulcie was not the least interested in Mr Hastings or his state of health. He was the sort of insignificant-looking man she abhorred.

'My son's death was certainly not trivial. It was a most tragic event. Everyone knew about it. There was a huge memorial service at St Margaret's, Westminster. Were you there, Denton?'

'I was indeed, Lady Askham, sorrowing a few rows behind you with my family,' Denton said insincerely, having had, in common with a number of people, little time for the self-important Viscount Gore.

'Ah yes, your mother was so fond of dear Arthur. Do you know Lord Denton Rigby, Mr . . . er?'

'Hastings, my lady,' Adrian said loudly, in case she was deaf.

'I must remember the Battle,' Dulcie smiled at her own wit.

'I of course know of Lord Denton by name.'

'Trivia, I suppose,' Denton said, laughing heartily, despising the little creep. 'What paper is it you work for, Mr Hastings?'

Adrian Hastings mentioned the name of a well-known Fleet Street paper and Denton asked how he came to be here.

'I write about gossip,' Hastings said, 'or society, if you prefer. What could be more "in" society than an occasion graced by Lady Askham and her family? Are Lady Flora and Lady Melanie well? I was very sorry to hear of the death of Lieutenant Lighterman.'

'She married again,' Dulcie said brusquely. 'Now, there is something for you to gossip about. Her new husband is a leading politician and member of the Bar. Why don't you run along, Mr Battle, and find him?'

Realizing he was outstaying his welcome – something he did frequently – Hastings stood up and removed his hat.

'I would enjoy meeting Lady Melanie's new husband, Lady Askham. Alas, I do not think his activities in Parliament or the Bar would furnish me with the kind of material I specialize in. I do hope I see you again. Good day.'

'Good day, Mr . . .' Dulcie began but already Adrian Hastings had strode huffily away.

'What a curious man,' Dulcie peered at the plate of shrimp sandwiches, turning up the edges to see if they were quite fresh. 'Vulgar, don't you think?'

'Very,' Denton refilled her ladyship's cup. 'I can't think how he came to be of your party.'

'Neither can I,' Dulcie thanked him and placed her cup on the table, shivering realistically. 'The whole excursion was a complete disaster and I must confess that, if he was there, I can't remember him at all.'

But Achmed Asher she did remember and the memory left a very bitter taste in her mouth.

'I'm not awfully good at punting,' Adam said to Flora, pushing the boat away from the riverbank. 'But anything to get away from the mob.'

Melanie, who had been about to accompany them until she spotted Denton Rigby on the lawn having tea with her mother, gave the boat a little shove with her foot and then sped off to join them calling: 'Have a good time' with a wave as she did.

Adam grimaced. 'Hope you don't mind just me.'

'Of course I don't mind just you,' Flora opened her

parasol against the heat of the sun, then trailed a hand in the water as Adam did, rather inexpertly, manoeuvre the craft out into the water.

'I haven't punted since I was at Cambridge,' Adam paused to mop his brow. The punt tilted dangerously and he staggered uneasily in the stern of the boat, grasping the pole and sticking it firmly on to the soft mud on the riverbank. 'I don't think we should go too far out.'

'No, stick to the bank,' Flora felt rather alarmed but didn't want to undermine his confidence. 'I don't know why you wanted to punt at all.'

'I thought it might amuse Mel,' Adam sighed, leaning heavily on the pole. 'She finds me a very dull fellow. I only came to please her and now I rather wish I hadn't.'

'Why?' Flora lay back, grateful for cool water on her hand.

'This isn't my sort of party. I don't know any of these people, do you?'

'Only a few. I don't like it much either.'

'Have you noticed how Denton Rigby follows her about?' Adam looked again towards the lawn where about a dozen couples sat at little individual tables having tea.

'Well, Melanie *is* a bit like Mama. She likes company. She means no harm.'

'She likes young *men*. Don't you think I don't know.'

'In that case I think they're both rivals for Denton!' Flora laughed, trying to brush it aside. 'He follows Mama about too. There's safety in numbers, Adam. You have no need to worry on that score.'

Adam put down the pole so that it rested alongside them in the boat and sat opposite her, letting the punt meander gently with the tide. Soon the house was out of sight and they drifted along by the heavily wooded slopes of the bank.

'I do worry about Mel,' Adam got out his case, selecting a cigarette, lighting it and blowing smoke into the air. 'She has no interest in my work. She thinks I'm a boring man and I am.'

'You're not. I'm very proud of you.'

'You are?' He looked at her with amazement.

'Of course I am. You're still young and yet you've made a great success. Your last speech in the House on the women's vote was magnificent. It was very brave because you had so much opposition, even from your own party – *especially* your own party.'

'You heard it?'

'Oh yes. I was there in the gallery listening to you.'

'But why didn't you tell me? We could have had tea on the terrace afterwards.'

'Next time I shall.'

'I didn't know you were interested in politics.'

'I'm a lot more interested since I knew Rachel. I used to laugh at the idea of women's suffrage but now I take it quite seriously.'

'It's not a laughing matter,' Adam said looking anxiously towards the deep water into which they were heading.

'I realize that now. It is not mere feminism but the awakening of a truly new consciousness of the rights and dignity of women. I am sure Rachel will be interested in it again too now that she's had her babies.'

'I thought she was happy with domesticity?'

'She is; but she feels guilty too. The movement is so active and she feels called upon to play her part.'

'Your mother won't be pleased.'

'I don't suppose Rachel cares. She and Mama have not spoken to each other since the row before the twins were born.'

'It was as serious as that?'

'Oh yes.' Flora looked worried. 'I'm afraid it upset Bosco too. His loyalties are so divided between Mama and Rachel, but I told him his wife should come first. He's afraid, though, she'll get herself sent to prison and disgrace the family. Since he became the heir Bosco is much more conscious of the family dignity and his responsibilities. Anyway Rachel isn't going to do anything just yet until the twins are older.'

'I'm glad of that.' Adam got up again and, seizing the pole, jammed it into the water but could find no purchase in the riverbed. 'We're too far out!' he cried.

Next to her foot Flora espied a small paddle and, grasping it, she began vigorously to paddle on the side of her that was nearest the centre of the river and, gradually, the small craft turned towards the bank.

'I can feel the ground again,' Adam said, jabbing his pole into the water. 'Well done, Flora.'

'Push firmly towards the bank,' Flora instructed him. 'We can leave the punt there and walk back. I don't think you are a very good punter after all.'

She felt a little alarmed by the incident; though she'd never felt they were in danger, her hand on her paddle was moist.

Between them they manoeuvred the punt to the shelter of the bank and seizing the branch of an overhanging tree she pulled until they were fast on the mud.

'There. We're safe now.'

'I think I worried you, didn't I?'

'A bit. Not much. We could always have shouted for help and I'm sure the valiant Denton Rigby would have dived in and saved us.'

'His help I can do without.'

'Not if we're drowning. I can't swim.'

Flora smiled and suddenly Adam sat down in the boat again facing her, his hands linked.

'I do like you, Flora. You're a good, sensible girl. Now Mel would have panicked in a situation like that.'

'But Mel is beautiful. Beautiful ladies can do as they like. I can't. They are *expected* to be in situations where they need rescuing. I have to make friends by being sensible.'

Adam got out another cigarette and tapped it on his thumb before putting it in his mouth and lighting it.

'You underestimate yourself, Flora dear. You always have.'

'How have I underestimated myself?' She twirled her parasol over her head, her face half hidden by the wide brim of her functional and eminently plain straw hat, without frills, bows, pieces of fruit, feathers, or even just ribbons. With her hair tightly screwed back into an unfashionable bun at the nape of her neck and her glasses perched on the end of her nose, making her look more short-sighted than she was, she did, indeed, look like a prim Victorian school-teacher on a day's outing.

'You're a very fine, intelligent woman, a Doctor of Philosophy in Ancient Egyptian studies.'

'Oh yes, I know I'm very clever,' Flora's voice was bitter. 'I make up for my lack of beauty with my brains. But sometimes I envy the Melanies and Mamas of this world who don't have to try so hard. Don't try at all, in fact.'

'But are they any happier?' Adam searched her face trying to divine her true thoughts.

'I don't know,' Flora studied with exaggerated care the pattern on her silk parasol. 'I must say I love things of the mind but, perhaps, I would like to have married and had children.'

'*Have*! It's not too late!'

For answer Flora gave him a wry look, saying nothing.

'It isn't,' Adam insisted. 'There must be any number of intelligent men who like your company.'

'Not enough to marry me. I intimidate them, I know it.

They like my brain but not my body. If you want to know, Adam, I'm jealous of my sister; of her looks, her gaiety, which I can never attempt to emulate, and her conquests. Isn't that despicable?'

'It's not despicable. Perhaps it's understandable; but it's certainly not necessary. You know, Flora, if you let your hair loose, had it dressed more fashionably, wore becoming clothes and maybe tried to manage without wearing your spectacles all the time you could be just as attractive as Mel. You have a lovely colouring and your hair is very fine. There,' Adam flushed and looked away, 'I've said too much.'

'No, no, you're very kind,' Flora leaned eagerly forward. 'I mean I do appreciate what you say, but you see I despise trying to be something I'm not, using my looks to entrap men. Now Rachel I admire. She is herself and she is not afraid to use her brain. Rachel isn't strictly beautiful, but she makes the best of herself without being false. To many people she's lovely. To me she is, in many ways, the ideal woman and I am proud to have her for a sister-in-law.'

'And I'm proud to have *you* for a sister-in-law, believe me.' Adam leant forward and gently grasped her hand.

'Oh dear, we must get back,' Flora said, suddenly flustered by the intimacy of the gesture. 'Everyone will think we've sunk.'

'I don't suppose "everyone" cares.' Adam stood up, jumped on to the bank and, extending his hand, helped Flora out. But, unexpectedly, he didn't let her hand go. He held on to it, gazing into her eyes:

'I do mean what I say. I am proud of you. Don't let Mel or anyone else ever make you feel inferior. Do you promise me?'

'I'll try,' Flora hurriedly removed her hand, bending awkwardly towards the boat to make sure it was secure upon the bank.

When they returned to the house by a path through the woods it was true that no one appeared to have missed them. The lawn was deserted and from the field at the back they could hear the sound of galloping hooves interrupted, intermittently, by cheers.

'Polo,' Flora said. 'I forgot there was a game.'

'And Denton Rigby no doubt,' Adam said ruefully, taking her arm and steering her along a path that led round the back of the house to the large field which was now thronged with spectators, the ladies seated on chairs, the men, most of them sporting college or military blazers and boaters with striped ribbons, standing behind them.

Lady Askham, as usual, held court; the little throng of chattering admirers around her obscuring her view of the game in which, in any event, she had no interest. On the periphery Adrian Hastings stood chatting to Melanie who, observing Flora and Adam, beckoned to them, loudly calling out as they approached:

'Did you get a ducking? Bosco said Adam couldn't punt for toffee.'

'I can't,' Adam admitted.

'We saw you struggling in the middle of the river and Bosco was about to commandeer another craft and row to your rescue. But then we saw brave old Flora seize a paddle and save you both!'

'Yes, she saved our lives,' Adam said drily, looking at his wife.

'Trust you, Adam, to get in a mess.' The scorn in Melanie's voice was so withering, so loud, that those nearest to her stopped their own conversations to listen while, to one side, in the field the polo ponies with their doughty riders galloped furiously up and down in search of a tiny white ball.

Flora was about to reprimand her sister but thought

better of it. She gave Adam a sympathetic smile while, nervous about the diversion she'd created, thinking, perhaps, she'd gone a little too far, Melanie lowered her voice and said in a more friendly and gentle manner:

'Adam, do you recall Mr Hastings who was with us that time we went into the desert to visit the pyramids of something or the other? I must say I couldn't remember him at all.' Taking Hastings by the arm, she gently drew him forward. Hastings removed his hat and bowed.

'I didn't realize you were Lady Melanie's second husband, Mr Bolingbroke. I do congratulate you, late though it must seem. Your mother-in-law was only telling me at tea this afternoon how very successful you had become.'

'How do you do, Mr Hastings?' Adam shook his hand, too polite to add that he didn't, in fact, remember him either. 'Nice to see you again.'

'It was a long time ago, sir, ten years.'

'My goodness it is as long as that, isn't it? And you recall Lady Flora, my sister?'

'Of course I remember Lady Flora,' Hastings, with a sycophantic grin, took her hand. 'Just as charming, if I may say so.'

'You may, Mr Hastings, but I don't think it's strictly true.'

'Always belittling herself,' Melanie stifled an artificial yawn. 'I think, in a way, dearest Flora hopes to draw the attention of others by always denigrating herself.'

'Which *you* have no need to do, my dear,' Flora sweetly replied, while Adrian Hastings, writer of gossip, pricked up his ears.

'Three children, I hear, Lady Melanie? What an achievement.'

'Were you introduced to my brother?' Melanie said, as

though her own family were of little importance. 'He has four, including a set of twins.'

'Indeed, I've been watching Lord Gore on the field. I don't wonder he got a medal for his charge with the Lancers. He is a very fine horseman. Do you not play, Mr Bolingbroke?'

'No, I'm cerebral,' Adam replied ruefully. 'I was never such a good mount as Bosco, although I did at one time play polo with the Regiment.'

'What a fool you'd make of yourself if you did now.' The cruelty of Melanie's words was belied by the sweetness of her smile. 'Almost as much of a fool as you looked trying to punt on the river.'

'Really, Melanie,' Flora said irritably. 'Who's denigrating who now?' And her reproachful look implied the unspoken words 'in front of strangers, too'. Melanie ignored her and applied herself in earnest to a study of the field.

Mentally Adrian Hastings was making notes. Maybe he would have something for his gossip column after all. Family tensions among the aristocracy. Well, well.

Half-time was called in the polo match and the players cantered off the pitch in search of refreshment. As soon as the bell rang double doors at the back of the house, which led to the dining-room, were thrown open. From these a team of servants bearing trays issued and started circulating among the guests offering tea, soft drinks, champagne, and tiny sandwiches made of cucumber, potted meat, egg, sardines or shrimps. The sun, now lower in the sky, filtered from the west through the branches of the thick chestnut, plane and oak trees surrounding the green, well-kept, carefully mown pitch. It was a perfect English occasion: tea on the lawn during a polo match. The ladies, their parasols shielding them from the late afternoon heat, ate from white-painted iron tables scattered about while the men squatted on the grass, some carefully sitting on their blazers, boaters by their sides.

The players gave their horses into the hands of their grooms and sauntered around the field in search of friends and supporters. The first to reach Lady Askham was Denton Rigby who arrived peeling off his gloves, his thick black hair sprouting through his open-necked shirt, his ruddy face gleaming with rude health and the pleasure of success. He had scored for his team in the previous game and they now led the side captained by Bosco. With Denton were Sir Harold Ashby, Martin Parkinson-Harvey and Major Ferdie Hudson of the Guards, who was also on the list of those fortunates privileged to take Melanie to tea at the Ritz.

As the group of sweating players gathered round Dulcie, the aesthetes, dandified hangers-on and other lesser fry hurriedly made room for them. There were a few churlish glances and muttered complaints including a distinctly irritable whine from Hector Lafaire, clad from head to foot in immaculate white save for a large spotted blue cravat, who had been busy composing a poem: 'To a Fair Lady on a Summer's Day.' He removed himself and his notebook to a less crowded spot where he immediately crossed out all that he had written and began again: 'To My Fair Lady Who Spurns Me'.

Few took any notice of the ardent poet except Adrian Hastings who was busy making notes of another kind.

'My golly, it's hot,' Denton exclaimed in a loud voice, mopping his brow and running his hands through his thick wet hair. He was approached by a deferential waiter with glasses of champagne on a tray and, taking one, drank it down in a gulp and then took another.

'Haven't you a tankard of this stuff, man? Thirsty work out there on the field.'

The servant, looking nonplussed, returned to the house for instructions.

'Denton!' Dulcie trilled. 'Your chukka was magnificent. You will clear the field. And you too, Ferdie dear.'

Dulcie, in the shade of her parasol, gazed admiringly at all the sweating, thirsty men and turned animatedly to Ferdie Hudson patting him once or twice on the head. The others squatted on the ground beside or in front of her, and Denton edged his way towards Melanie who sulkily watched him from beneath the wide brim of her striking organdie hat with its huge pink bow trailing across her slim bare shoulders. He raised his glass to Flora and smiled at Adam, standing slightly behind her, arms akimbo, looking at him coldly.

'You made it back to base, I see,' Denton said laughingly. 'We were about to dive in and rescue you.'

'There was no need, I assure you,' Adam continued his glacial stare. 'We were never in any danger.'

'Not used to a punt, I see.'

'Adam isn't used to anything,' Melanie gave her patronizing smile. 'Except making speeches. He does a lot of that.'

'Well, I can't make speeches,' Denton said placatingly. He didn't particularly wish to antagonize Melanie's husband, although it was amusing to see her making much of him and little of her husband in public. As a servant approached him carrying a large silver tankard on a small tray, he took it without saying thank you and put it to his lips.

'If *you* get drunk, naughty Denton, you won't be able to play any more of that excellent polo.' Melanie gave him a flirtatious glance.

'Won't I just though! Wait and see.' Denton took another deep draught and grinned at her, his lips shining with champagne which trickled over his chin and dripped on to his chest. 'Don't you play any games at all, Adam?'

'Not any more. I used to. But those days are behind me now. As Melanie says, I'm too busy speechifying and trying to change the laws of the country.'

'Why should they need changing? Isn't it a fine country as it is?'

'Some of us think there could be improvements.'

'I bet you're one of those fellows who wants the vote for women?' Denton wagged a reproving finger at him.

'As a matter of fact I am. Does that distress you?'

'It distresses me to think of pretty ladies worrying themselves with matters that have always been the proper concern of men.'

'Why?' Flora moved closer to Adam as though to indicate her solidarity with him.

'Why what, Lady Flora? I don't quite understand?'

'Why are they no concern of theirs? Of ours?'

'Because the proper place for women is in the home, isn't that what you're saying, Denton?' Melanie looked at him archly, twirling her parasol above her head.

'Well, not in the home exactly, Melanie, but that sort of thing.'

'Or maybe, Lord Denton, you think that our brains are smaller?' Flora's eyes, behind her glasses, narrowed accusingly.

'I just know what I think, Lady Flora, and my opinion is shared by a good many others I know.'

'I wonder if *they're* worth knowing, though?'

'Are you saying *I'm* not worth knowing, Lady Flora?'

'I'm not sure about that.' She glanced at Adam who had begun to smile his approval.

'Denton, you're ignoring me,' Dulcie called over her shoulder, beckoning to him. 'I can hear you arguing. What are you arguing about?' She turned in her chair and, just as Bosco approached from where he had been inspecting one of the hooves of his horse, he saw both his mother and Melanie gazing with rapt attention at his rival on the field. Bosco felt hot and annoyed, suspecting his horse might be going lame, and was wiping his damp hands on a cloth.

'Arguing?' he said catching his mother's words. 'Who's arguing?'

'Have a glass of champagne, dearest,' his mother counselled him smiling sweetly. 'That's if Lord Denton has left any for you to drink.'

'We're not arguing, Bosco,' Denton passed him a glass from a tray that had been left on a table beside Dulcie's chair. 'We're just having a discussion.'

'Denton thinks women's brains are smaller,' Melanie giggled.

'I do not!'

'You never answered Flora's question.'

'Of course I don't think they're smaller.'

'You said you didn't know.'

'As a matter of fact there *is* some evidence that the brains of women are smaller,' Adrian Hastings intervened smoothly. 'I remember reading something about it.'

'What utter rot,' Bosco looked angrily at him, clearly having no idea who he was.

'I see you don't remember me, Lord Gore,' Adrian produced a card from the case he'd taken from his pocket and passed it to him. 'Adrian Hastings.'

Bosco looked at the card, then at him.

'Your face is familiar.'

'Cairo, Lord Gore, in 1898. I had the pleasure of joining you and your family on a picnic in the desert . . .'

'Oh that!' Bosco looked in outrage at his mother who lowered her head.

'And, subsequently, I tried to get to the front, but

without success. I was stuck in Berber with the fever but I heard of your exploits. I must congratulate you.'

'Thank you. It was some time ago.' Bosco tucked the card in his shirt pocket, looking like someone trying to recollect an event long past that had ceased to interest him. 'I must say I don't remember you very well.'

'Poor Mr Hastings, no one remembers him!' Melanie gave him a pitying smile. 'How awful to be so anonymous.'

Indeed Adrian Hastings was very anonymous. He had the inability to wear clothes well that characterizes a lot of people who are hard to remember. He was a very ordinary man, thin and quite small of stature. His own mortification at being remembered by no one in that fashionable party long ago may be imagined. Because, with his journalistic flair, his passion for collecting facts, he remembered each one of them minutely.

'I think you have changed a good deal, Mr Hastings,' Flora said kindly. '*I* recall you perfectly well, but your face is thinner.'

'And my hair,' Adrian pathetically fingered his pate, balding in the middle with what few strands he had in the front carefully combed out on either side to give him a semblance of a parting. 'I was very ill. The desert didn't suit me at all.'

'How come you to be here?' Bosco was only one of many to ask the question and Adrian explained why he was.

'Well, don't write any gossip about us,' Bosco said, a note of warning in his voice.

'Only nice things, I'm sure.' Dulcie waved a friendly hand in his direction, not wishing to offend this man whom she vaguely felt to be dangerous. A sense of menace had suddenly obtruded itself into the friendly concourse on that quite beautiful summer's day. She felt an unaccustomed tremor of unease. The Cairo connection disturbed her, as she could see it did Bosco. Could Hastings *possibly* have remembered the incident that caused the party to split up at Sakkara? She felt, in fact she knew, he did. He had a rather conical shaped head which she was sure contained a good brain and narrow, inquisitive eyes indicative of a retentive memory. 'You must sit next to me, Mr Hastings, and watch the next half.' She looked sharply at Ferdie Hudson, an unspoken command to vacate the chair on which he was sitting.

'Plenty of time, Ferdie,' Dulcie said as he rose, '*after* the match has begun. Bosco, you will have to be very clever to defeat Ferdie and Denton. They have the upper hand.'

'Only in the first half, Mama.'

'But Denton's getting drunk on champagne. He will probably fall off his horse.' Melanie's jibe continued to amuse her.

'I am not getting drunk!' Denton angrily thumped his tankard on the table, the liquid spilling from it showing that the pot was still half full.

'Dutch courage,' Bosco said, clearly enjoying his discomfiture. 'Some people need it.'

'I'll thank you to take that back, Gore.' Denton glared at him and suddenly everyone in the little party, aware of the tension, stopped talking and gazed at the two protagonists.

'It was only a joke . . .' Melanie began but Denton interrupted her.

'I did resent the implication, Melanie, that I drank to give me courage to lick that feeble side, and I *would* like an apology.'

'You're much, *much* too serious, Denton,' Dulcie looked nervously from him to her son. 'This is a lovely, sunny afternoon and the occasion a merry one. Why can't we all merely enjoy ourselves?'

'Merrier if Denton's drunk,' Melanie could not resist

saying and Adam took her arm as if to shake her, hissing in her ear: 'Be quiet!'

'I *do* apologize, Denton,' Bosco said with obvious insincerity. 'I assure you I meant no offence and if you need to drink to give you strength for the second half, I can't say I blame you.'

Bosco, raising his own glass to his lips, nonchalantly drained it. Denton however turned his back on him and strode angrily to where the panting, chafing horses, watered and now rubbed down, waited to be remounted. At that opportune moment the bell rang for the second half.

'Are they ancient enemies?' Adrian Hastings, with an obsequiousness that seemed part of him when in the presence of the aristocracy, took the seat vacated by Ferdie Hudson next to Dulcie.

'Not at all! What can you mean?' Dulcie eyed him in consternation, turning to Melanie who now sat on her other side.

'I thought there was an unpleasant kind of atmosphere. Not sporting at all.'

'But they are rivals in sport,' Adam, standing behind Melanie, watched the players walking their horses on to the field. The sun was almost obscured, low on the horizon behind the trees, and quite a few people had left the spectacle, maybe to rest before changing for dinner. Mabel Lighterman sat with a few intimate friends some yards away from Dulcie and her party, and waved to her as the crowd around her dispersed.

'You're very popular,' she called. 'The young men don't come to me!'

Dulcie inclined her head and smiled back saying, under her breath: 'Vulgar woman.'

'I beg your pardon?' Adrian bent his head towards her.

'Nothing. Some people are just permanently envious.'

'I think she envies your success with men, Lady Askham. I see there are only ladies gathered round her while here, except for your daughters, there are only men. I remember you had the same success in the desert . . .'

Adrian looked at her and Dulcie, half avoiding his eyes, felt herself blushing so much that she was forced to wave at her face vigorously with her mauve, scented glove. Her ensemble for the day was in that colour, exceptionally muted and pretty – a tight-waisted dress, high-necked with leg-of-mutton sleeves, topped by a flat straw hat decorated with large artificial peonies and roses, also in mauve.

'They are all great friends of my son, I assure you, Mr Hastings. Why ever should they gather round little me?'

Adrian momentarily achieved some ascendancy by shaking his head, smiling and saying nothing.

Bosco remounted his horse, feeling ruffled and irritable. Ever since the row between his wife and his mother he had not been the same person at all. His normal good humour, his tranquillity, were deeply disturbed and he felt they would not be restored until the two women he loved best in the world were speaking again. Even speaking without friendship was better than this acrimonious silence.

He had decided to come to the Lightermans alone in order to try and speak to his mother who, these days, was always in London or visiting friends in the country, her duty to her sick husband taking second place to her long list of social engagements. Not that Lord Askham wasn't well looked after; he was surrounded by devoted servants and Bosco or Rachel went over to see him at least once a day, or invited him to the Grange. But it wasn't the same as having the company of one's life companion in one's declining years, and Bosco knew his father felt it. But he also knew that, whereas Lord Askham was now an old man, his wife, not so many years junior to him, felt young.

But the opportunity to talk to his mother alone had not

so far arisen. She never moved without having people around her, and even when he'd gone to her bedroom the previous night she hadn't been there. Bosco adored his mother, but part of him bitterly resented her and a part – a very small part – was actually ashamed of her. He loved and admired her beauty, he was proud of her youthful appearance, though she was well past fifty, but he did think that she drew too much attention to herself and made an ass of herself into the bargain. Today was one of those occasions.

Now she was apparently a rival with his sister for the attention of one particularly asinine and stupid man. Bosco had never really cared for Denton Rigby whose duties at the Foreign Office seemed a mere formality. He wondered such people were allowed to be employed there, with their penchant for a good time and ineptitude for work. They had been flung together at drinking parties, or polo matches, but Denton was not the sort of person Bosco would ever choose for a close friend – he was not cultured like Adam, or warm and loyal, as Harry had been.

Bosco rode slowly on to the field and took up his place for the chukka seriously worried and disturbed by what had happened during the break: the way Melanie taunted Adam; the discomfiture and humiliation of his best friend; and the perfect fool she made of herself in appearing to compete with her mother for the approval of one singularly smug and unpleasant man – a byword in London for his womanizing and his conquests, the subsequent downfall of susceptible ladies.

As the little ball bounced along the field and the players converged on it, Bosco looked out for Denton who towered on a magnificent black mare, two hands taller than the other horses. The black horse seemed to suit Denton who now, in Bosco's mind, was a blackguard of the first order. Denton kept on crossing his path, swinging his stick with, Bosco thought, a threatening gesture towards him, his dark eyes gleaming. As the game progressed and Denton's side won another chukka Bosco felt the anger and rage in his heart turning to hate. Despite the fact that he was younger and more mobile than his adversary, Denton seemed to have the best of him in the game, swinging at the ball and following it through down the field with unerring craftsmanship to score yet again.

Bosco, overwhelmed by the heat and the flying grass, the clods of earth as the ball appeared and disappeared, found himself seeking out Denton, regardless of the rules, ignoring the rest, and he was twice cautioned by the referee. In his mind the vision persisted of his mother and Melanie, heads inclining towards Denton, almost lost in admiration, as that great slobbery oaf quaffed from a huge tankard of champagne as if to show how puny were the men drinking from glasses. The foam-flecked mouth seemed to grin evilly at Bosco and those white flashing teeth incited him to recklessness.

If he, Bosco, didn't play well, however, the rest of his team did and the score was even before the last chukka of the game. As Bosco waited for the start he looked over at his mother and Melanie and raised his stick in salute, but they seemed to ignore him, both their heads bent in attention to the squirmer Adrian Hastings.

There was another ass, Bosco thought, swinging his stick for the off, a dangerous little snipe too with his memories of that picnic in the desert. What mischief was he plotting as he sat listening to his mother and Melanie, doubtless spilling gossip into his ears and making fools of themselves once more?

The ball passed him and Bosco charged after it, swinging his stick, took aim and was about to hit it straight for goal when another stick became entangled with his own and the player, freeing his, knocked the ball and put it in the opposite direction from the one followed by Bosco, who looked up and saw Denton grinning down at him. Denton mockingly touched his cap and charged after the ball towards the goal of the opposing side.

Bosco, chasing after him, then felt the hatred flood through him, and as the horses' hooves of the other players attacking and defending pounded on either side of him, his mind suddenly went back ten years to the pounding of horses along a brown, sandy desert and the flashing teeth of the Dervish enemy as they jumped up to attack him and his men from the *khor*. Treacherous, dangerous savages. He raised his stick and struck out for the ball as if it were a sword in his hand with which to cut down the enemy, and once again his move was foiled by a player leaning towards him, half off his horse, attempting to rob him yet again of the ball and victory. And, yet again, it was none other than the captain of the opposing side: Denton Rigby. Bosco, now beside himself with rage, his eyes almost blinded by the throbbing blood whirling about his brain, lifted his stick above his head and, as he did, he pressed his stirrups into the flank of his mount, bringing his stick sharply down on its rump, and pushed it right against Denton's, crushing the man between the two horses.

A whistle blew, all the spectators at the edge of the field flung up their arms and cried: 'Foul!' But Rigby, one foot alone remaining in a single stirrup, was dragged along the ground as his petrified horse ran on, and everyone else rushed after it. Finally it was left to a young groom watching the match to dive on to the field, stop the horse and probably save its rider's life.

As Denton lay on the ground beside the panting horse, there was a silence in the crowd and then everyone started forward at once. Dulcie, with her hand to her mouth, had watched the whole incident, anticipating almost every move Bosco made. From the very start of the second half she had wanted to rush out and warn him as if aware of what was in his mind, conscious of his hatred of Denton. But why, why? Not blessed with insight, she simply didn't know.

Now she sat alone with Melanie while Adam and Adrian Hastings joined those gathering by the body at the far end of the field.

'Is he dead?' Dulcie whispered.

'Bosco looked as though he meant to kill him.' Tears had sprung to Melanie's eyes.

'Oh no! Why should he mean to kill him?' Unknowing, the two women looked at each other in surmise.

'Did you see the way he raised his stick? He meant to bring it down on Denton's head. He moved and struck the horse instead.'

'Denton was playing *very* unfairly. He cheated several times. Bosco was right to feel annoyed.'

'Mama, it was not the game that upset Bosco.'

Mother and daughter looked at each other again and then up at Adam, who came walking back apparently unruffled.

'Amazingly, he seems all right, shaken but not dead as I thought he was at first. He may have broken something, and he'll be sore for several days the way he was dragged. Several weeks maybe.' Adam squinted into the distance where they could see Bosco standing beside Denton and stooping as if to talk to him. 'He's lucky to be alive.'

Some distance away from the group on the field stood Adrian Hastings once again busily scribbling away. He wanted to record the events as soon as he could, while all the images, each juicy incident, every scandalous word, were fresh in his mind.

CHAPTER 16

Lord Brancaster, proprietor of *The Sentinel and Echo*, looked at the card his secretary had just brought in.

'Lord Gore? Bosco Gore?'

'He seems very angry, my lord.'

'Well, show him in. Don't let him stand there!'

The secretary had scarcely reached the door when Bosco thrust past her and, without the courtesy of a greeting, threw a page of newsprint before Lord Brancaster on his desk.

'I want that man sacked!'

'My dear Bosco, do sit down,' Lord Brancaster, a fellow Etonian and long-standing friend of the Askham family, rose from his chair and leaned over to shake Bosco's hand. 'Please ensure we aren't disturbed, Miss Carter.' Miss Carter, looking very alarmed and not a little indignant, shut the door quietly but firmly behind her.

Jeremy Brancaster came from behind his desk and, taking a box of cigarettes from it, offered one to Bosco who shook his head.

'You won't mollify me, Jeremy.'

'First let me see what it is that disturbs you.'

The newly ennobled press baron resumed his own seat and, putting a pair of reading glasses fussily upon his nose, perused the paper before him after looking at the top to check the date. He read:

All society was assembled Saturday last at the Thames-side home of SIR ROBERT AND LADY LIGHTERMAN, the main event of the pleasant summer's day being a polo match

between a visiting team from Oxford and members of a scratch team put together by VISCOUNT GORE and known as Gore's Irregulars. Watching the match was LORD GORE's mother the legendary hostess LADY ASKHAM and her beautiful daughter LADY MELANIE, there with her husband MR ADAM BOLINGBROKE, the Member of Parliament for Bisley in Yorkshire. Also present was LORD DENTON RIGBY, son of the MARQUESS OF CADCASTER, who caused some light-hearted merriment by his chivalrous attentions to both the ladies much to the obvious irritation of LORD GORE and the discomfiture of MR BOLINGBROKE who, only an hour before, had nearly capsized the punt in which he unsuccessfully attempted to steer his sister-in-law LADY FLORA DOWN upon the river. It was no doubt fortuitous that, at the end of the match which his side was losing VISCOUNT GORE – known as Bosco, a hero of Omdurman – collided with LORD DENTON causing him to fall off his horse and sustain quite severe injuries, as he was dragged along by his steed before it was brought to a halt by an able stable lad who probably saved his lordship's life.

LORD DENTON was carried off the field to the consternation of LORD GORE who did everything he could to revive him, and to LADY ASKHAM and LADY MELANIE who ran after the injured polo player into the house.

LADY LIGHTERMAN, who was herself once a nurse, administered first aid to the injured nobleman who is still resting at Robertswood, the Lighterman home, recovering from his accident on the field. Some, seeing LORD GORE pursue his opponent, recalled the famous charge of the 21st Lancers at Omdurman and wondered if his lordship thought that LORD DENTON RIGBY and his team were a crowd of Dervishes to be similarly and summarily dealt with.

'Ha!' Lord Brancaster took off his spectacles, laid them neatly on the desk before him and looked at Bosco. 'I'm afraid I didn't see this.'

'Would you have stopped it?'

'Most certainly I would. But I have an editor and I never see the paper until it appears. I missed this item completely.'

'A funny way to run a newspaper,' Bosco sat down and

crossed his legs. 'So if I sue this man I sue you too, is that it?'

'Sue?' Jeremy Brancaster looked in alarm towards Ludgate Circus which lay directly in his view between his imposing office and Blackfriars Bridge. 'You'd actually sue?'

'With all the implications in that smear, and my mother at Court? Of course I'll sue. My brother-in-law, Adam Bolingbroke, says we have a very good case. The insinuations not only involve Denton Rigby, a family friend, but myself, my mother and sister too. There must be a retraction, an apology, and that fellow Hastings, who wormed his way unwanted into the Lighterman household, sacked.'

'But if his facts are right?' Lord Brancaster's head turned from the window to his unwelcome visitor.

'The facts are wrong; not only wrong, but libellous. I'll sue you for such a sum of money, Brancaster, that it will bleed you to death.' Bosco stood up. 'Do I have your word?'

'I can't give it, I'm afraid.' Brancaster rose too. 'If I sacked everyone who offended my readers I'd have no staff left. This is popular journalism today, Bosco, pioneered by Harmsworth with the *Daily Mail* and the *Daily Mirror*. They have set standards we have to keep up with.'

'No standards at all, if you ask me. This is gutter talk. Do you think the Queen wishes to be surrounded by ladies who are the subjects of uncouth speculation in the pages of the gutter press? How do you think it affects my old, sick father? My mother is beside herself with worry.'

'I am sorry about that. In future this sort of thing will have to be cleared by me. I'll certainly speak to Hastings.'

'But you won't sack him?'

Lord Brancaster stared at his desk, pressing his fingers very firmly upon it so that they made a momentary impression on the soft, embossed leather.

'I can't sack him until I've made an investigation. If everything is made up I might think again. But, if you like, I'll apologize if a misleading impression was given.'

'No, not good enough. People will ask us why we didn't sue. Actually Bolingbroke would love the case. It'll make his name.'

'Sue then,' Lord Brancaster, ineffably polite, showed his guest the door, 'and thank you for calling.'

'Sue?' Rachel exclaimed. 'Is it wise?'

'It's the only course. I would have been content if that man were sacked and put out of circulation for good.'

'But you wouldn't do that, Bosco. You'd only make him angry.'

'Let him be angry.'

'He could do more harm. You know,' Rachel, who had been doing her accounts when Bosco burst in, pushed her chair back from her desk, 'I remember him quite well in Egypt. He said very little and read a lot. He was such a mild little man. That's why no one could remember him. Maybe that made him vicious. But I do recall him quite well because I wondered why he was there. He didn't know any of us and he seemed so out of place.'

'I don't think you'd recognize him now. I didn't. He said he'd been very ill.'

'Poor man.'

'Poor man, my foot,' Bosco flung himself on the sofa in the room Rachel kept as her sanctuary, his arms spread out along the back, his fingers agitatedly tapping the pretty, flowered chintz covering it. The room was so like Rachel, peaceful and imbued with a deep sense of calm, flower-filled on this autumnal September afternoon.

Bosco worried Rachel. His new sense of unease seemed to have its origins in the row about his mother; one which, now, she deeply regretted. But things done cannot be undone and much of what she had said she meant. She was not a person who said things she immediately wanted to withdraw. Even if she said them in the heat of the moment she invariably meant them, and what she'd said about her mother-in-law she'd thought and brooded over for years. But Bosco had become more volatile, rather as he was when she first knew him. The affair between herself and Dulcie had unsettled him deeply, and this latest disaster at the Lightermans, seemed positively to have unhinged him. He had done nothing but rage and talk about it since the event ten days before.

'What is the latest news of Lord Denton?' Rachel enquired, trying to keep her concern about him out of her eyes. They telephoned daily for news of the invalid.

'He's still kept in bed, but no permanent injury, nothing broken which I consider well-nigh miraculous. He was dragged along for about a hundred yards by his horse. The injury seems more to his self-esteem, though he says I deliberately pushed him which I didn't.'

'Didn't you?'

'Push him? Yes, but I didn't do it deliberately.'

'Oh.'

'You too think it was deliberate?' Bosco half rose from the sofa, his face suffused with one of his sudden, violent moods of temper. In recent years he had grown a thick moustache and, in his angry moments, looked not a little like Denton Rigby because he had also put on weight. He was not fat, but he was now a well-built man as his father had been before his illness. A man of wealth, of responsibility, a family man and man of affairs. The lithe, quick captain of the Lancers seemed decades ago.

'It certainly appears that *some* people who saw it,' Rachel chose her words with care, 'thought it might have been deliberate. That's why Adam thinks you'd be so unwise to sue.'

'Oh, you've talked to him, have you?'

'Of course. He's my brother and he's concerned. He felt you lost your temper with Denton, not without cause. He was angry too because Denton obviously flirted quite deliberately with Mel. Oh, I *wish* I'd been there. I might, somehow, have prevented the whole thing were I not so anxious to keep away from your mother. Adam and Melanie, by the way, are coming over for dinner.'

Since the affair at the Lightermans, Melanie had been staying at Askham Hall because Dulcie had been so put out by the newspaper report that she had been ordered complete rest by Dr Fraser, that ever-vigilant custodian of the Askhams' health. As Rachel was not wanted and Flora was engaged in work in London it had fallen to Melanie to be put in charge of her mother which she gladly did, taking her three children with her. Adam had joined them for the weekend.

'Sue?' Adam shook his head at dinner that night. 'Not a chance. You'd have to prove he was lying and he wasn't. Some of us who'd heard the quarrel between you and Denton thought you went for Denton deliberately. Had I been in your place I would have myself.'

'You're all frightfully silly and serious about this,' Melanie tossed her head. 'There was absolutely nothing between me and Denty at all. As for Mama . . . why, he is about twenty years younger than she is. The whole thing has prostrated Mama with grief. I certainly think the Hastings person quite rightly *should* be sued, if only to teach him a lesson not to offend his betters.'

'Would you give evidence?' Adam asked.

'In court?'

'Yes.'

'Why?' Melanie put a hand on her breast, clearly put out. 'I don't know. I don't suppose so. Anyway the quarrel was between Bosco and Denton. It was about polo, not me.'

'It was all about you, you know that – polo or not. There was an undercurrent of intrigue. Everything about that afternoon would come out. You may be called upon to swear that you never saw Denton alone. That there was nothing in the least flirtatious between you . . .'

'And I would swear that,' Melanie met the challenging look in his eyes. 'Willingly.'

'I told Brancaster we'd win if we sued, that you'd said so,' Bosco smiled at Adam, seeming to find it a good joke. 'Bluff, of course. Well, if we can't sue – and it seems it would cause more problems than it would solve with family secrets laid bare, and so on – there is only one thing for me to do.' Bosco leaned back, fingering the glass of the good wine they served when they had guests. Rachel may not have been up to his mother's exacting standards, but she could excel as a hostess when they had company, creating original dishes in the kitchen by herself. She was an accomplished woman; a woman of many parts. He looked round the table, meeting the interested, alert expressions on the faces of his listeners. 'I must buy the paper.'

'What a lovely idea, Bosco,' Melanie clapped her hands. 'We'd make it a leading paper for women's fashions.'

'We'd make it a leading paper for women's suffrage,' Rachel also smiled with amusement. 'But really, it's a preposterous idea, darling.'

'Why?'

'You have enough to do. Besides, do you really want a paper?'

'Yes. Newspapers are the thing, there's no doubt about that. Brancaster's right about popular journalism of the kind that Harmsworth has done so successfully. There's a lot of money in it too as well as power, though I must say the aspect of power appeals to me more. I would like to be a powerful man. Do you know that, Adam?' He looked with affection at his brother-in-law. 'It appeals to me, and what is more powerful than the printed word?'

'But wouldn't acquiring *The Sentinel* be an act of revenge?'

'Yes, and good business too. It is a successful newspaper with a good circulation, not too old, founded only a few years ago. It has very good premises in Fleet Street and there are lots of other ideas I have too.'

'How long have you had them?' Rachel rang her little bell to summon the maid and footman who waited on them only when they had guests.

'I developed them instantly in the cab as I drove up Fleet Street after seeing that idiotic and timorous fool, Brancaster, whose fag I actually was at Eton. I never admired him even then, though I doubt if he remembers I ever fagged for him. He greeted me most civilly, I must say.'

'Would he sell?'

'That I don't know. I called a meeting of the Board of Askham Developments in Berkeley Square yesterday and put this idea to them. Everyone was most enthusiastic, including my father whom I told last night.'

'But not me,' Rachel said.

'You're not enthusiastic, dear?' Bosco leaned forward.

'I mean you didn't tell me.'

'I wanted it to be a surprise for this evening. Look, the thing is that businesswise priorities are changing. I want to get out of coal because oil is becoming a more important and accessible source of energy, and the miners are all heading for trouble over wages and so on. With the motorcar, oil and petroleum will become prime commodities and so will newspapers because of the power of advertisements. We are becoming an increasingly prosperous and acquisitive society, more women are working and so have more money to spend. Fashions, yes, and women's interests will be of importance to them.'

'I see you've thought about it fairly seriously,' Adam sat back as the maid removed his plate, shaking his head when the footman offered him wine. 'And I think maybe you're right; but will Brancaster sell? Why not Harmsworth?'

'Harmsworth is much more developed and he's a more serious businessman. He has two Fleet Street papers already and is a professional. Brancaster, in my view, is a mere dabbler. I think if we made him a very good offer he would sell. Or we might see how the shares are constituted to buy him out. I have all sorts of plans, you'll see.' Bosco lifted his glass to toast the table at large, one after the other, in a happy, ebullient mood.

Afterwards in the smoking-room Adam said: 'You really are serious, aren't you?'

'About the paper? Oh yes, I seldom do anything on impulse, Adam.'

'Unless it is to knock Denton off his horse. You must have meant that.'

Bosco snicked off the end of his cigar and took his time lighting it. The smoking-room was at the back of the house with French windows leading on to the garden which, on this pleasant mid-September night, were half-open. It was furnished with leather armchairs, a billiard table and smaller tables scattered with books and newspapers. It was a homely room, oak-panelled and smelling of tobacco and whisky. Bosco regarded it as his den and spent a good deal of his time alone in it when he was at home.

'Do you know I hardly remember it?' he said, satisfied when his cigar was alight. 'It's true I was very angry with Denton, who kept on attacking me personally in the game. He made numerous fouls which no one saw to get my ball. There was a personal element in it that inflamed me, as it was meant to do. Also I do remember thinking of the charge which was what so annoyed me about that idiot Hastings. He got it right.'

'But you never mentioned that to him afterwards?'

'I didn't speak to him at all. I was too anxious about Denton . . . Oh, Adam, do you think me a villain?' Bosco collapsed into one of the chairs, hanging his head, forgetful of the lighted cigar between his fingers, suddenly conscious of his actions, his thoughts, his motives.

Adam stood in front of the fireplace in which a small fire glowed low in the grate because, although the days were mild, the evenings were cool. Then he raised his head and puffed at his cigar, looking out into the garden softly illuminated by the lights from the house shining through uncurtained windows. 'You will never allow yourself to forget Cardew will you?'

'I will never forget Cardew and now I won't forget Rigby. They were both cads, but no matter. I am jealous through and through of men who flirt with the women who belong to me, and they prompt me to reckless action.'

'But Melanie belongs to me, and your mother to your father – if we can talk in such an old-fashioned way.'

'No, they belong to me too. They're my family. I hated Cardew and I hate Denton. I hate the type of man they represent. Denton was so vicious on the field and I remember thinking to myself "he's a rogue and a cad, let him have it!" The next thing I knew my horse had cannoned up alongside his, almost crushing his body, causing him to fall to try and save himself. I was quite horrified at the result of my actions, I assure you. I was also overcome instantly with the same feeling of remorse I had all those years ago in Omdurman. I am no good, Adam. I'm a man tormented by my passions.'

Bosco's voice broke and Adam, drawing up a chair, sat opposite him and put his hand on Bosco's arm.

'You're a tempestuous man, Bosco, but you're no villain. If you like, I felt like murdering Rigby too, with his sly glances at my wife and his belittling remarks made to me in her presence. His jokes about my predicament on the river and so on.'

'Well, that was rather funny, seeing you wobbling there in the middle. I laughed with Denton. No harm meant there, I assure you.'

'I didn't find it funny myself, even in retrospect. We were never in any danger, even without the paddle; we should simply have floated downstream towards the bank. Denton *is* a thug. He takes delight in the weakness of others. Doubtless he's a coward himself.'

'I can't think how I ever liked him, even a little.'

'I hate him.'

Bosco looked up at Adam with surprise. 'Really?'

'Oh yes. He does take Melanie to tea and dines alone with her at home when I'm away. Had I been you on that horse I'd have done the same. Oh Bosco, I am such a failure with Mel and yet I love her so much. If only you knew how much I loved her.' His expression as he looked at Bosco was not only forlorn but hopeless, as though his cause was lost.

'I know that, old man,' Bosco was glad to forget for a moment his own troubles.

'And yet I don't make her happy. We were and are ill-suited.' As Bosco didn't say anything he got up and walked over to the billiard table taking up the cue and making some imaginary shots. In the light of the single lamp hanging over the table his gaunt, pale face seemed not only sad but unmistakably resigned. 'You knew that, didn't you? You thought Flora would suit me best and, I must say, the more I know her the more I think you were right. And she *is* a beauty, you know, if you look into her eyes, imagine her with her hair loose about her shoulders.'

'And do you?' Bosco's expression as he rekindled his cigar was startled.

'Sometimes. I did that day on the river and we spoke of our mutual admiration . . . oh, nothing too personal or intimate, I assure you, but my feelings did surprise me, I confess. She comes to hear my speeches in the House which Mel can never be bothered to do. She is thoughtful in so many little ways.'

'But it's too late,' Bosco said, getting up and leaning across the table, hands joined, to look at his friend.

'Oh, but I love Melanie,' Adam protested, 'make no mistake about that. I love her as ardently and with as much passion as I am able, or she lets me. But it is difficult to feel at one's ease with a woman you know despises you – who prefers hulking great empty-headed bullies like Denton Rigby and Ferdie Hudson and how many more? Does she go to their beds? I don't know. I feel like a man with a big, unhealed wound inside him, aching with a love for Melanie that is forever unsatisfied. No, my dear friend, I understand hate, believe me I do; and jealousy and the wish for revenge and, if you are a murderer in your heart then, believe me, I am too.'

Melanie tapped lightly on the door, anxiously looking over her shoulder along the corridor to be certain she was unobserved. There was no reply and, without tapping again, she turned the handle, half opened the door and popped her head round. The large room was bright with sunlight and in the huge bed which occupied its centre even the bulk of Denton Rigby managed to seem quite tiny. He lay on his back, head propped up on the pillows, an unopened book on his lap as if he had thus fallen asleep. Melanie crept towards him, a single yellow rose in her hand which she had surreptitiously taken from a vase on the table in the hall, and, when she got close to the bed, she put it beside him on the pillow gazing down at the strong, handsome face, now unusually pale.

'Denton,' she whispered, not sure whether he was really asleep or pretending. His eyelids flickered, not altogether convincingly and, as he opened his eyes, she stood back from the bed, her finger pressed against her lips. 'Shhh,' she said. 'I'm not meant to be here.'

'Melanie.' Denton struggled to sit up, his sleek black hair falling across his face to make him seem more saturnine and sinister than ever. She shivered a little, now that she was alone in his presence.

'No one knows I'm here,' she sat gingerly on a chair beside the bed, 'and I mustn't stay long. I just had to see how you were. Mabel says you're better, but tired. Poor, poor Denty.'

'But how did you come to be here?' He reached to the table by his bedside and took a sip from the glass of water standing on it. Then, seeing the rose, he held it to his nose, sniffed it and lay back, a smile of anticipation on his face as he said softly: 'Thanks, Mel.'

'I've come over with Bosco and Rachel, I've brought my children to see Mabel. Bosco has a new motorcar and it's just too deevy for words, very fast. Do you know we got here in under three hours?' Melanie wore a tweed costume and a sensible hat, high-heeled laced-up boots.

'What sort of car has Bosco got?' Denton asked with interest, settling himself comfortably on his pillows, playing with the stem of the rose.

'A Daimler Phaeton, the very latest model. Bosco wants to go into cars and was trying it out. He's come to talk business with Sir Robert. He wants to buy the paper.'

'What paper?'

'*That* paper, the one with the horrid story. Bosco wants to punish the odious Hastings.'

'Isn't that rather a drastic, expensive way to do it?' Denton chuckled.

'Bosco wants a paper anyway, he says, and by buying it he can also get that creature sacked. It's very like Bosco.' Melanie giggled. 'Very dramatic. How *are* you, Denty darling?' She reached over and took his hand, and he eagerly grasped hers, bringing it to his lips.

'Oh, Mel, I've been lying here dreaming of you. You look like a vision, an answer to prayer.'

Melanie, rising to the compliment, ran her hands over her waist as though to emphasize its trim line. She took off her hat with its neat little veil and shook out her hair, which she now wore parted in the centre and puffed out at either side in its new, neat Marcel waves.

'These are only my travelling clothes, Denty. Bosco said we had to wrap up because the speed of the car makes it so cold inside. Little Bobby loved it. The poor little angel's being sent away to school and he does so hate the idea.' Melanie patted her hair. 'Sir Robert's paying for everything, of course.'

'And Adam?' Denton enquired, a note of unease creeping into his voice.

'Oh, Adam's up in London doing important things, something ridiculous to do with the suffrage. They're planning a new campaign, can you believe it, and even Rachel says she's going to join in. Bosco's furious. But then Bosco seems furious about everything since "that day" – you know the one I mean – and Adam scarcely ever talks to me. I tell you, Denty dear, when you get well you'd better go abroad. They're awfully cross, and they'd be *mad* if they knew I was actually seeing you. Bosco thought you'd gone back to town.'

'I'm not afraid of your husband or brother. Besides, the injury was done to *me*.'

'People do argue it was Bosco's fault,' Melanie said guardedly, 'but not done deliberately, though some of us think otherwise. You were very rough in the game.'

'He wanted to kill me,' Denton's voice rose. 'I saw it in his eyes as he rode towards me.'

'He hated you flirting with Mama. He's so jealous, so possessive.' Melanie undid the buttons of her costume jacket to reveal a plain cashmere jumper and a single row of pearls. She looked very smart, very chic and, inwardly, Denton groaned. 'I was a teensy bit annoyed too, Denty dear, flashing your great big eyes first at me *then* at Mama!'

'But how could I possibly have eyes for your mother! She's years older than I am. It's you I want, not her.'

'Yes, but Mama likes young men, everyone knows that. She encourages them and I think you took advantage of that to annoy me.' She gazed at him with just the right amount of reproach tempered, he thought, with a gleam of encouragement in her lovely eyes, so that his heart turned right over. Melanie wanted him; he knew it.

'But why should it annoy you, dearest heart, if you don't want me?'

'Because . . .' Abruptly Melanie got up and started to pace about the room, almost deliberately in and out of the sunbeams which danced upon her chestnut hair, so that, in the eyes of her infatuated beholder, the slender form of Melanie, his heart's desire, seemed like a torch aflame. She paused and regarded him gravely. 'Because, maybe I do – one day.'

'Oh Melanie!' Denton threw back the covers of his bed and jumped out, demonstrating his fitness if nothing else, but also shocking Melanie who had only ever in her life seen her two husbands, occasionally her father and brothers, in their night attire. As Denton strode towards her, she panicked and fled to the far corner of the room where he caught up with her, pinioning her against the wall.

'Melanie . . .'

'Denton, *don't*.' She put up her hand to push him away but he caught it, pressing forward, putting both his arms around her and crushing her small head against his heaving chest. Then, still up against the wall, he kissed her full hard on the mouth forcing her lips open with his tongue until his teeth ground against hers. She struggled and when at last he freed her she squealed: 'Denton . . . I . . .' but he ignored her pleas and, scooping her up, carried her over to the bed, throwing her on it and then himself on top of her.

Melanie began to fight, clawing at Denton, but her fury inflamed him further and he pulled up her skirt, revealing her long, boned corset, the suspenders attached to the tops of her white silk stockings and, overall, a pair of long woollen drawers edged with lace.

'Denton, I warn you . . .' Melanie said hysterically, puce with shame, but Denton knew women. Many a game begun like this had ended in submission, followed by hours, weeks, if not months of pleasure as the victim, once overpowered, became his slave and wanted more – furtive meetings, hurried appointments, until one or other of them tired. Denton usually tired first, because there was never just one, but always another, and another waiting to be taken.

He was thus unable to believe that her protestations, her kicking and her sobs, were anything other, in reality, than pleas for more, cries of pleasure.

Sir Robert had listened for a good hour to Bosco, and even his seventy-five-year-old veins seemed to course with fresh, healthy new blood as all the plans and schemes were outlined before him. They sat in Sir Robert's study overlooking the lawn sweeping down to the river and, from time to time, they saw Rachel and Mabel walk past, deep in conversation, while Melanie's three children played near the water's edge under the watchful eye of their two nannies. It was a calm, domestic scene, enhanced by the beauty of the autumn day. The gentle breeze caused wave upon wave to run upon the water; it sighed through the multicoloured leaves upon the trees, bringing some fluttering to the ground, and others to be swept along by the current of the river.

The men had returned to the study after lunch and, by three o'clock, Sir Robert knew all that he needed to about the plans of Askham Developments, a company that Bosco had set up a few years before to gather together all the different threads of the various businesses begun by Arthur.

'Arthur would indeed be proud of you,' Sir Robert said, raising his glass to toast his guest. 'Your father too, I warrant.'

'Father's very pleased,' Bosco held up his glass in a reciprocal toast, 'and very surprised. He felt I had no head for business, or the management of the estates. Nor for marriage either,' Bosco's eyes travelled to where he could see Rachel sauntering down the path with Mabel.

'And you see, you have a gift for all three! You have a solid business, four fine children and a lovely wife. She's a credit to you, Bosco, a woman of intelligence. Mabel and I always liked Rachel, from the day we met her.'

'I know it,' Bosco sighed and put down his glass. 'How I know it, how I wish Mama liked her as much as you. There is an enmity between them that casts a gloom upon our whole lives.'

'You must not let your mother interfere with your

marriage,' Robert said sternly, leaning forward in his chair as if counselling the son he had lost; and, indeed, he loved Bosco as a son. 'My Mabel would interfere with the lives of our girls if she could, but I won't let her.'

'But Mama *hates* Rachel.'

'Mabel isn't over-fond of our sons-in-law, believe me, but . . .' Sir Robert pointed a warning finger. 'A woman's jealousy is hard to control, and all mothers are jealous of the people their offspring marry. You are married to Rachel, Bosco, and, good woman that she is, Lady Askham has no part in that marriage. She is your mother, but Rachel is your wife and that's what matters.'

'Thank you, Robert,' Bosco said after a moment's pause. 'That's good advice which I shall be sure to try and heed. But since Arthur died and my father became ill I have meant a lot to Mama.'

'And that's quite right and proper,' the old man patted Bosco's knee. 'But she mustn't run your life, or your wife. Remember that, if you wish to be married for as long and as happily as I've been.'

'You're a very wise man, Robert,' Bosco looked at him gratefully, 'and I shall try and follow your advice.'

'Now let me see,' Sir Robert leaned back in his comfortable chair, his gouty legs spread out before him resting on a small tapestry stool, and glanced again through the papers Bosco had given him.

'The motorcars I like. Though some people say they're not here to stay I think they're wrong. They're noisy, smelly, they're faster than the horse – not so fast as the train, mind – but progress is being made all the time and that fellow Ford in America is a genius. His new "Model T" will be, they say, a people's car. Soon everyone will be able to afford one, not just rich fellows like you and me, though I intend to stick to the horse-drawn variety of carriage until the day I die. Much more reliable; they don't break down. But the motorcar is exciting, and if you can link up with Ford and produce cars like his here . . . Well, who knows . . . ?'

'I thought "The Askham" would be a fine name for a model, but I have yet to meet the right engineer. Arthur was actually dealing with Ford when he died. He had been to his works in Detroit and left a very full report in the papers we found after his death. Our agent there, Vanderveld, is looking around for me at the moment to find some bright inventive fellow who wants to come to England. I don't just want to import Henry Ford's cars and sell them here. I want our own.'

'To "The Askham",' Sir Robert raised his glass again, refilling it when he'd put it down. In his old age, besides the company of the young and the companionship of his beloved wife, his chief solace was in brandy and fine cigars. 'Now the one thing I'm happy about is oil; happy about disposing of the shares in the coal mines, because the miners will cause nothing but trouble if these labour fellows ever get in. But I'm not very happy about the paper. Why a paper?' Sir Robert glanced at the documents on his knee and glared at Bosco over the rim of his glasses. 'Or rather, why that paper?'

'I don't think Harmsworth would sell. He's expanding.'

'And Brancaster will?'

'We've looked into his finances and they are much shakier than Harmsworth's. In fact I think he needs money, and would probably be glad to sell outright.'

'No other motive?'

'Would it matter if there were?'

'I seem to recall a very nasty little report a week or two ago. In fact Rigby's still not completely fit, though I do wonder if he's not extending his convalescence unnecessarily long. It's very comfortable here,' Sir Robert added, as an afterthought.

'Yes, it has to do with that,' Bosco said. 'I'll admit it gave me the idea that I wanted to punish Hastings. Having money has that effect on me. It's to do with power. But, once I'd thought of it, I liked it and now I don't really care about him at all. He is a person of no importance whatsoever, though it would give me satisfaction to give him his comeuppance. And I shall, one way or the other. I'll either get him in the courts, or I'll lose him his job, or I'll beat the daylights out of him with my bare hands. He won't go unpunished.'

'I'd be glad to see his downfall too,' Sir Robert said angrily, 'worming his way into the house under false pretences. Anyway let's not talk about him. I doubt if either of us will ever see him again.'

'I don't want to see him and I'd better not read a word against me or my family . . .'

'You think, anyway, the paper is sound?'

'Oh very,' the mean, vengeful look left Bosco's face as suddenly as it had come, and he smiled. 'I would like to influence world opinion. Why not?'

'Why not indeed?' Sir Robert nodded agreement. 'I'll drink to that. Now, Bosco, to practical matters. You are telling me all this, figures carefully set out and the facts well presented, not just to inform me. Am I not right? You want advice, or what?'

'I want advice but also I want money.' Bosco put his glass carefully on the table and, taking his cigarette case from his waistcoat pocket, extracted a cigarette and carefully lit it. 'Since Arthur's tragic death I have had not only to learn the business but also I wanted to know exactly how much we were worth. Quite a lot,' he blew smoke into the air. 'But, if I sell the coal-mine shares and dispose of the others we have in textiles and so on, risk industries, I will have plenty, but not soon enough to raise the cash for the paper.'

'How much do you think you'll need?'

Bosco named a sum that made Sir Robert whistle and, leaning back, he gazed at the ceiling as though seeing imaginary balance sheets.

'As much as that?'

'With a seat on the Board of Askham Developments and, of course, Bobby's future bound up with ours even more intimately than now.'

'Ah, now you have me.' Sir Robert's wrinkled old face broke into a smile that was almost youthful, and he gazed fondly out of the window where he could see his nine-year-old grandson ordering his half-brother and sister about on the lawn. 'You know that little chap is my life. I want him to be a man as fine as his father, and he will be. Finer. I want the world to be his oyster and so it shall. He will have my houses and my fortune, every penny, but I don't want him to be an idler and waste it, Bosco. If I give you the money and I accept a seat on the Board I want you, in turn, to promise me that you will keep my Bobby's interests on a par with those of your own children. That you will look after him and see to his welfare when I'm gone. That you will be a second father to him.'

'I will of course. I already love him as one of my own and, in memory of dear Harry, his claims to my time will always be paramount.'

'Let's shake on that,' Sir Robert extended a trembling hand which Bosco seized, imprisoning it between his as though it were a treasure beyond all price – even the price of a newspaper.

Bosco found Rachel and Mabel sitting on the grass while Bobby in a boat was trying to show the two younger ones how grown-up he was. Susan who was five and Christopher, three, were regarding him with a certain amount of awe and their nurse hovered anxiously while Roger, the boatman, kept a hand firmly on the prow of Bobby's boat. Bobby was a tall, dark child resembling his mother, except that his hair was black like his father's. But he had inherited much of Melanie's beauty as well as her charm, and was almost too good-looking for a boy – pale skin, straight black hair and enormous dark brown eyes. Susan was a rather solemn little girl with straight hair – of the colour known euphemistically as 'ash' and unequivocally as 'mouse' – caught up in a wide pink bow. Melanie worried about her lack of looks and consequently fussed about her and overdressed her as though to make her feel even more uncomfortable and out of place. Susan was a tomboy who liked the company of her brothers and she strove very hard now to get into the boat with Bobby. On the other hand, in the strange unfair way that nature has of playing tricks, Christopher had Melanie's thick auburn hair and, like Bobby, was a pretty child, pale and blue-green-eyed. A certain delicacy in his constitution since birth showed in a rather apathetic attitude to life, a dispositon to worry and fuss about himself. He didn't try and get into the boat, but remained gravely on the bank, his hand in that of his nurse, watching Bobby and Susan.

'Where's Mel?' Bosco said, sitting on the rug on the grass beside the ladies.

'I thought she was with you?' Rachel looked at him and then glanced around.

'No I've been talking business with Robert. We are to be partners, Mabel.'

'Oh, that's splendid now,' Mabel grasped his hand. 'It will give him a new interest in life.'

'He really wants it for Bobby, for him to have security and a stake in the joint family fortunes. He wants Mel's permission to let me keep an eye on Bobby's fortune after his death.'

'I'm sure that will be readily granted. Where is she then? I'll go and look for her. You take care of these babies, mind.' She shook a finger at him and Rachel, who smiled and leaned back upon her hands. Making sure that no one was looking, Bosco leaned forward and kissed her cheek.

'I love you,' he said. Rachel also looked round and put her hand over his.

'That's nice.'

'I love you very, very much. I couldn't take my eyes off you as you were walking in the garden. Our children have given you an extraordinary beauty.'

'I think that's contentment not children,' Rachel said prosaically. 'I am, or was, very content.'

'Was?' Bosco's eyes clouded with concern.

'Well, just lately, since the quarrel with your mother, I thought you were less in love with me.'

'How could I ever be less in love with you!' Bosco protested, kissing her again. Then freeing his hands sat up, his arms joined round his knees. He didn't look at Rachel but ahead of him towards the river and the children playing beside it, Bobby swaying and laughing in the boat, repulsing the determined attempts of Susan to get into it with him. 'I agree, the question of the differences between you and Mama have been deeply unsettling to me. I feel a special responsibility for Mama since Arthur died. But Robert has just given me some very good advice, besides agreeing to pay £200,000 cash into Askham Developments . . .'

'You need as much as that?'

'We need at least that, unless we are to sell all our assets at a loss. Oh, don't worry, we have plenty of money, but it is all tied up in stocks, shares and mines. We want to generate more capital by selling when the time is right, not because we have to.'

'And this is all to buy the paper in order to get your own back on Adrian Hastings?' Rachel looked at him incredulously.

'Oh no, not at all! I don't need anything like £200,000 to buy the paper. But, with the paper, I want the building, a prime site in the centre of London. That will set us back £100,000 if we are to make the offer soon. I also want money free to invest in the motor industry, have our own engineer and plant maybe somewhere near Askham. Call it Askham Motors.'

Rachel snuggled up against him.

'It all sounds very exciting. And what was the other good advice he gave you?'

Bosco bent his head to look at her. 'He said I should put you before Mama.'

'I'm glad to hear it. That is very good advice indeed.'

'He's right. I do put you before her, but I don't make it clear enough. We postponed marrying because of Mama and I think we have both to some extent always been a little afraid of her.'

'*I'm* not afraid of your mother,' Rachel indignantly sat up and dusted herself. 'I was afraid of hurting you, and I was right. She has hurt you and the reason is because of me.'

'Well, that's all over now, my darling.' Bosco pinched her chin between his fingers and kissed her lips. 'I shall never again reproach you for your attitude to Mama and I shall make it very clear to her where my loyalties lie, even though I remain her loving and devoted son . . .'

Bosco let go of Rachel and lay back on the rug, his hands under his head. Above him tiny wisps of cloud scudded about the sky bringing, it seemed, a promise of rain later in the day, and a sudden gust of wind made him pull his jacket tightly over his chest.

'It's getting colder. I think we must go soon,' he reached

for her hand and put it to his lips. 'How happy I am. Do you know that? How very very happy.'

As Rachel bent over to return his kiss he grasped her playfully and tried to bring her down on the ground beside him, but she shook herself free putting a hand to her hair.

'Darling, someone will see us and think it most unbecoming for two aged parents of four children to be cavorting like spring lambs.'

'The children can't see us,' Bosco raised his head and looked towards the rise in the ground that obscured them from view before it sloped towards the water.

'Who knows who can see us from the house?'

'Who cares? I don't. Robert is having his afternoon snooze and Mabel is somewhere scouring the place for Melanie. I wonder where she is?'

Rachel's hand suddenly flew to her lips and she looked anxiously up at the house.

'Oh, I do hope she hasn't gone to see . . .'

But before she could finish a sudden ear-splitting scream rang out that sent her hurtling towards the water expecting to see an overturned boat. However, the children, safe and all visible with their nannies, were also looking with consternation towards the house when another scream rang out and then another. Christopher started to cry and his nurse raised him up in her arms while Rachel ran back to join Bosco who, however, had started a fast sprint towards the house.

Mabel was just walking up the broad staircase of Robertswood, which had been copied from one in the Château of Chambord on the Loire, when she heard the first scream. Having an inkling of where Melanie might be, a search of the grounds and the downstairs of the house having failed to find her, she was on her way to Denton's room. Denton was supposed to have left a week ago and the party hadn't known he was there, otherwise, Bosco said, they wouldn't have come. Mabel thought Denton was lazy and idle and he had not grown in her estimation since being a guest under her roof. When she heard the scream she ran up the stairs as fast as her chubby legs would carry her and, during the second and the third, was running along the corridor, her heart palpitating, already feeling out of breath.

She paused outside Denton's room to try and compose herself and then without knocking she threw open the door. She had not, after all, been a nurse in the slums of Victorian London for nothing, but even then the sight appalled her. Melanie lay on her back on Denton's bed with her legs lewdly spread apart and between them lay Denton, naked from the waist down in what looked like the final moments of copulation. Melanie's white face wore an agonized expression and her mouth was wide open as if in the act of emitting another scream, her eyes staring wildly at the ceiling. Incongruously she still wore her fashionable high-buttoned boots, but her stockings were wrinkled over them and on the floor were her corsets, her warm woollen drawers and Denton's pyjama trousers all together in an unsightly heap.

As Mabel ran into the room Denton arched his back, gave a long low groan and then lay supine on top of his obviously unwilling partner, breathing as stertorously as Mabel.

For a second Mabel stared, appalled, at the primitive scene being enacted by two members of the nobility in her own house and then, looking towards the half-open window, she ran back to the door and locked it. If she'd heard the screams so clearly everyone else would have as well, including the children. She pocketed the key and went over to the bed not knowing as she did exactly what she would do.

Melanie didn't scream again but lay as she was, her white face with its open mouth and staring eyes causing Mabel to wonder for a moment if she were dead.

'Melanie,' she called putting a hand on her forehead, and gradually the staring eyes refocused and gazed at her with horror. The tears on Melanie's cheeks were still fresh and a large globule of saliva dripped from her mouth.

'Get up, Denton,' Mabel said authoritatively, making a grab for his shoulder. But Denton didn't seem to hear her. The sweat was running from his brow and his breathing was so sharp it sounded rasping, painful.

'Denton,' Mabel said again, more loudly. 'Get up and get into the dressing-room before this room is full of people. Melanie's screams were heard all over the house and garden.'

Denton slowly raised himself from Melanie's body, his expression dazed, as Mabel swiftly covered her nudity noting, as she did, that there were streaks of blood on the sheets.

Rape. Mabel shuddered and, as Denton, whisking his pyjama trousers from the floor, scuttled into the dressing-room, she sat on the bed and stroked Melanie's white brow, also covered with perspiration.

'There,' she cooed in her most nursy voice, 'there, there.'

Melanie shut her mouth and closed her eyes and, from under her lids, a fresh stream of tears coursed forth. She started to tremble violently and Mabel took off her own comfortable knitted cardigan and put it across Melanie's shoulder, pulling the bedclothes right up to her chin. At least the tears were better than the open mouth and staring. At least she was alive.

'Melanie dearest,' she crooned. 'It's your old Mabel, your old friend. Speak to me, duckie.'

But Melanie's shaking increased, as did the tears welling from still tightly-closed eyes.

'You should never have got yourself in this situation, dearie. But you did and that's it. Shame on his lordship, I say, but no real harm done except to your bruised soul, I hope.'

Melanie had such difficulty in forming her words that a very short sentence took a long time to utter.

'How . . . c . . . cc . . . oul . . . d . . . h . . . h . . . he? How c . . . could . . . heeeeeee . . . Oh Mabel?' Melanie reached up and threw her arms round Mabel who held her in her arms like a baby. Then she put a finger under her chin and looked into her face.

'You were unwilling?'

Melanie's eyes flew open and, though they were still drowned in tears, they were surprisingly clear.

'*Of course* I was unwilling! I just c . . . came up to s . . . see him. I brought him a flower, a rose. I was sorry for him. He misunderstood me.'

Mabel had already noticed the crushed yellow rose lying on the floor. Giving a man like Denton a rose was an open invitation to seduction. How naïve Melanie still was, despite her two marriages, her three children and her sophistication.

'He certainly misunderstood you,' Mabel grunted disbelievingly.

'But h . . . h . . . how co . . . uld . . . he . . . he . . . mis . . . under . . . stand. I fought.'

'I can see that all right,' Mabel stared at the considerable disorder not only on the bed, which looked as though it had been subject to a whirlwind, but around the room. 'Maybe it was his idea of loveplay. Some men like him do, I'm afraid, and yet they call them "gentlemen".'

'Oh Mabel, dear good Mabel,' Melanie clung to her pathetically but, gradually, the trembling was subsiding. 'What shall I do? Everyone must have heard.'

Just at that moment, as if in confirmation, there was a

banging on the door and Bosco shouted: 'What the hell is going on? Open up. Denton, are you there?'

'I'm here, Bosco,' Mabel called out soothingly.'Everything is all right. We shan't be a minute.'

'A maid said the screams came from this room. Where's Denton? Where's Mel?'

Mabel let go of Melanie and ran as lightly as her fifteen stones would let her across the room, putting her mouth to the door.

'Bosco, go away! Everything is all right, I tell you. I'll be down directly. Now the door is firmly locked and it is made of good solid oak so kindly do as I say. I'll explain everything.'

'You'd better.' Bosco's voice was angry and frustrated and she could hear his footsteps thudding along the corridor as he hurried away.

'Now then,' Mabel said briskly, going back to the bed and standing looking down at Melanie. 'Are you badly hurt . . . there.' As tactfully as she could, she pointed her head to the middle of the bed. 'Do you want to see a doctor?'

'Oh no! Of course I was very unwilling and he was very violent. Yes, I am hurt.'

'You'd better let me see,' Mabel said and, seeing Melanie's hesitation, she smiled at her kindly but authoritatively.

'Remember I'm a nurse. I've seen it all before. Didn't I help when Bobby was born too?'

Melanie reluctantly allowed her kind, concerned, experienced friend to administer to her; to assure her that there was no harm done, and to sponge with warm water and soap the bruises on her thighs. But the hurt was more to her soul than her body, to her pride and self-esteem and, as she climbed disconsolately out of bed, Mabel thought she had never seen such a bedraggled, miserable, pathetic specimen of humanity even in working-class Brixton in the old days.

'I'll bring these,' Mabel scooped up the discarded garments. 'No one will see us if we run along the corridor. Quick now.'

She unlocked and opened the door just as Rachel was about to knock on it. She stood back looking at Melanie in dismay.

'Oh, so it was . . .'

'Quick,' Mabel said. 'We're taking her to her room. Then I want to go downstairs and see Bosco while you look after Mel. There's a dear.'

Rachel, quickly apprehending the situation, nodded and, with her arm round Melanie, steered her towards the room she normally occupied at the far end of the corridor, and which was always kept ready for her.

Bosco said: 'I'll kill the bastard.'

'You won't do any such thing. I want you to leave straightaway, now, with Rachel and let Melanie stay here. I'll see that "Lord" Denton' (she scornfully emphasized the 'lord' as if to denigrate his nobility) 'is despatched swiftly back to London tonight. He should have left before, but said he was not quite better. Huh! The laziest man I ever saw and, hopefully, I'll never set eyes on him again.'

'But I can't just leave him!' Bosco was enraged. 'After raping my sister . . . I want to kill him.'

'I'm not saying it was "rape" exactly,' Mabel said wisely. 'You know your sister, Bosco. I believe she flirted with him, led him on and then . . .'

'But he made her scream . . .'

'She screamed when she realized it was too late. She inflamed him if you ask me. She had all her clothes off, or most of them. I don't think he could have got them off unless she really wanted . . .'

'Wait until Adam hears of this. I don't give sixpence for that man's chances of staying alive.'

Mabel put a pudgy hand firmly in the middle of Bosco's chest and pushed him into a chair.

'Now listen to me, Bosco Gore. Adam must never ever get to hear of this. Do you understand me? Melanie won't tell him and Denton sure as anything won't. I certainly shan't and nor will Robert. This must be a secret, a family matter between us because if Adam does hear about it his marriage to Melanie is as good as over and disgrace for her will surely follow. I'd hate his fine career to be ruined by a man like Denton Rigby. Adam's worth ten of him.'

Bosco beat his fists against his forehead as though to try and relieve his agony of mind. 'I can't let it go, Mabel. I can't. I must see him. He cannot be allowed to get away with this.'

He was about to rise, but Mabel gave him another firm push back into his chair again.

'See here, Bosco. If you go to that man you'll kill him. I know you. I'm going to get Rachel now and tell her to take you home straightaway, this moment. If necessary I will keep you away by force.'

'Oh, how?' Bosco laughed despite himself.

'I'll get two of our strong manservants. They'll keep you here. I don't wish you, on any account, to see Denton Rigby in my house today. Do you understand that? I don't want any more carnage. You owe it to us as your hosts, to Robert who is an old man – and who has just promised you a lot of money incidentally – and may . . . God, I pray that he may not have heard Melanie's screams if he was fast asleep, as he sometimes is at this time of day, after a good lunch and a few brandies. He hasn't stirred, even with all this commotion going on. Now, you sit here and I'll get Rachel and as soon as she's ready you must go. You can leave Mel here with her little ones. I'll look after them. Denton will be gone in an hour or two.'

Suddenly Bosco loved this wise old woman, whom his mother called 'common', with her shrewd practicality and cockney common sense. He reached up for her hand and kissed it.

'You're the salt of the earth, Mabel. I'll do as you say.'

She smiled at him tenderly, patted his head and bustled off and, as he saw her go, he thought, with amazement, that she was really quite happy being busy and needed, despite the tragedy of what had happened. She was, indeed, the salt of the earth.

Soon afterwards Rachel came in, pale but composed, dressed already in her hat and coat. Mabel almost pushed them out of the house and stayed watching them in the drive when, after kisses and farewells, Bosco put the heavy Daimler motorcar into gear and furiously drove away.

Adam said: 'Melanie's pregnant.'

'That's splendid news,' Bosco didn't look up from the figures he was poring over on his desk. 'I'd never have thought Brancaster would have taken less than £100,000 for *The Sentinel* and building, but he has. He's a fool!' He looked up with the gleeful expression of one businessman who has done down another. For the first time, then, he saw the expression on Adam's face and it surprised him. 'Aren't you pleased about the baby?'

'No.' Adam walked towards the window and looked on to the bare trees in Berkeley Square, blowing and bowing in the winter's sleet which drove against the window-pane as though the trees themselves were weeping. He pressed his head against it, seeking relief from the cool glass. 'I'm not the father.'

Bosco neatly capped his pen, placed it on top of the balance sheet and joined his hands, his face grave and sympathetic, his voice, when he spoke, low and warm.

'Are you sure?'

'Quite, quite sure.' Adam's face as he slowly turned and came back into the room was as grey and bleak as the weather outside. 'Melanie and I have not had intercourse for many months. She told me she disliked it so much, that we now had the children I wanted, so I have left her alone. It is not in my nature to enforce my marital rights against my wife's wishes.'

How Bosco loved his friend. How, at that moment, he detested his sister who failed to appreciate a man of such worth and nobility of character. He got up and put his arms around Adam's shoulders, leading him to a deep armchair upholstered in black leather, one of several he had in his large comfortable study from which he ran the operations of his business activities, now expanding and multifarious since his talk with Sir Robert three months before.

'My dear Adam,' he said, offering him a cigarette. 'This is the most terrible shock for you, and you have my very deep sympathy and also my respect. Will you divorce Melanie now?'

'Not unless she wants me to – or rather, I would let her divorce me. I asked her if she wished to marry the father and she told me that she didn't.'

'Did she tell you his name?' Bosco, guessing who the culprit was, lowered his eyes. His mind was on Denton Rigby who shortly after the incident at Robertswood had left the country to visit his father in the West Indies.

'No. She wants to get rid of the baby.'

'That's very dangerous.'

'I simply won't allow it. She is so distraught and sad, Bosco. You know, I think she really loves me.'

'I'm sure she does,' Bosco lowered himself in the chair opposite his friend. 'She will need you now if you can be magnanimous enough to forgive her.'

'Oh, I forgive her,' Adam leaned his head wearily back against the chair and closed his eyes. He looked, now that Bosco saw him relaxed, as though he hadn't slept for days. 'You see, I still adore her. I will, of course, accept the child as my own; but if I ever find out who the father is, who is the creature who has brought so much unhappiness on my darling, I might kill him.'

'Better then that you don't know,' Bosco said, 'and thus end a fine career.'

'You're right.' Adam opened his eyes but still his gaze seemed sightless. 'He is obviously some cur who took advantage of her – she said he did in a moment of weakness, when she had unwittingly compromised herself. She said she was most unwilling, was caught by surprise, that it was almost rape. For that alone I'd be prepared to kill. And all these months she has suffered without telling me. I knew she was unwell, but not why. The thought simply never occurred to me that she was pregnant. I wanted her to see a doctor, and then she told me. Well, thank you, Bosco, my good friend,' Adam rose and, going over to Bosco's chair, shook his hand. 'You are not only my brother-in-law, but the best friend I have.'

'And you're mine,' Bosco said keeping Adam's hand in his. 'Between us, I think we're invincible.'

CHAPTER 17

Lady Askham was not only seldom ill, she disliked illness in others. It interfered with her sense of security, her optimistic insistence that all was right with the world. The normal illnesses of her children, when young, had hardly concerned her. The nasty, messy or painful aspects had been taken care of by Dr Fraser and the ministrations of the nursery nurse, the under-nurses and reliable old Nanny Hudson, now living in comfort in a cottage on the estate. The long illness of her husband had thus been a hard ordeal for a woman who was basically selfish, wrapped up in herself, but whose energy and natural ebullience were as legendary as her beauty, as deceptive as her elegance and charm.

In the very hot summer of the year 1911, a year when the tar melted on the streets and all sensible people took to their country homes or, if they did not have them – as most ordinary citizens who were unfortunate enough to live in London did not – trips to the open spaces of suburbia, the seaside, the river or the parks, it was particularly trying for Dulcie to watch the steady, debilitating decline of her husband without being able to do anything to arrest it.

She was still lady-in-waiting to dear Queen Alexandra, now Queen Dowager upon the death of her husband, beloved Edward, the previous year. She had attended Her Majesty at the coronation of her son George in June, and then she had gone down to Askham to await what seemed the inevitable demise of her spouse of thirty-eight years.

Yet Frederick, tenth Earl of Askham, was reluctant to

go even though he would leave his estates, his titles and properties in good hands. Coughing, unable to walk any distance, save a few steps, he spent most of his days wrapped in a rug on the terrace of Askham Hall, facing the lake and watching the steady stately progression of a new race of swans and ducks along the even stretch of the water. The summer heat was particularly difficult for Lord Askham because, even though his face ran with perspiration, his blood was so thin that his body remained cold, and he sat huddled in his rug wishing not for death but for peace.

It was thus that Bosco found him one day in August when he walked over from the Grange on one of the many visits he made to his father. Over his trousers and open-necked shirt he wore only a thin linen jacket and this he thankfully removed and put over the back of the chair next to his father.

Lord Askham stirred and his eyes flickered open.

'Is it you, Dulcie?'

'It's I, Father. Mother is upstairs resting.'

'Arthur, is it?' The old man slowly turned his head, his dim eyes taking in the figure of his son bending forward and slipping his hand in his. These days he dwelt frequently in the past and no one had told him that his old friend and contemporary, the late King, was dead. Somehow he would never adjust to young Georgie being King, even though he had succeeded to the throne as a respectable, staid married man of forty-five with six children of his own.

'It's Bosco, Father.'

'Bosco? Are you not at the war?'

'The war is long over, Father.'

'You covered yourself with glory. We were very proud of you, my boy.'

Bosco gently shook his father and the old man jolted himself as if waking up completely.

'Ah, Bosco of course. I was dreaming. I dreamt of Arthur. Poor Arthur. Why did we ever let him go to America? He would still be alive.'

'Maybe, Father, maybe not. Not for us to stop him anyway.' Bosco pressed his hand, his eyes filling with tears. Any day now, he thought . . . and was he himself ready? He had had enough time of preparation. Seven years, but still he didn't feel quite fit enough to assume that ancient title, those awesome responsibilities. 'Frances is here today with the children. You haven't seen Frances for a while, Father.'

'She should have stayed here with us. Your mother was always very fond of Frances.' The old man closed his eyes as if in a reverie or as if, tired with the effort of waking, he wanted to sleep again.

Frances came and went but she had her own home in London, and when she was in the country she lived in a wing of Crewe Castle which had been specially prepared for her. Her two daughters were quiet, correct little creatures, docile and obedient, strictly brought up by a mother who taught them to venerate the memory of their father and constantly to mourn his loss. They were never allowed to forget it. In his death Frances loved Arthur more than she ever had in life, as if all those sorrowing, troublesome years of marital disharmony and constant pregnancies had never happened.

'You've done very well, Bosco,' Frederick murmured, his eyes still closed. 'I have no worries about leaving Askham and its inheritance to you. You were a wild lad once, but that has all changed . . . thanks to that good wife of yours. I like her, but your mother never has.'

'I know that, Father. Still, they tolerate each other better than they did before.'

'Rachel's a good, sound woman, good for you, a worthy successor to your mother if she could only see it.'

'That won't be for a long time yet, Father,' Bosco said caressing the thin fragile hand, the skin almost as transparent as paper.

'Soon, very soon now. I don't want to go, yet I will have peace. Peace,' and the Earl's chin sank upon his chest and he slept again. Bosco thought that death was indeed kind if it took people gently, without pain. Better like this than on the battlefield.

That night Lord Askham died, his last coherent words having been spoken quietly on the terrace of the home where he was born to the son whom he loved.

There seemed to have been too many funerals – the King's, various lifelong family friends, Lord Kitto, Dulcie's brother, now succeeded by her nephew who was considerably younger than her son the new Lord Askham.

Bosco led the mourners at the simple ceremony at which his father was laid to rest in the family vault, his mother on one side of him, Rachel on the other. Queen Alexandra, ever gentle and considerate, came to be with her friend Dulcie and this gave the occasion an aspect of pomp and formality the family would prefer not to have had, except that to be honoured by royalty was a singular mark of favouritism.

The Queen came by train for the funeral and shortly afterwards went back to London the same way, with her lady-in-waiting and other members of the nobility who had travelled down to Wiltshire with her.

Dulcie sat in the drawing-room after they had all gone except for close family: the Kittos, the Crewes and her own children, now especially precious. On the very fringe were the Lightermans, who she would never ever consider family, however good they were to Bosco or Melanie, however kind to her. Mabel hovered about, the eternal nurse and comforter, seeming rather to relish the occasion as people of that kind do, at their best when needed.

In widowhood, in grief, Dulcie looked magnificent. Black became her and she kept her funeral dress carefully in mothballs in the wardrobe, taking it out for one funereal occasion after the other, more so, recently, she found as one got older. She had first worn it for the death of her mother-in-law in 1890 and it hadn't needed a stitch or tuck since.

'I can't believe he's gone,' she said from her solitary, stately high-backed chair placed, like a throne, in the centre of the room. 'Part of my life, my soul.'

Frances pressed her hand, Frances who had hardly ever left her side since the old man died. Frances not only looked well in black, but she liked it. She enjoyed reading about death and going to funerals. It became her melancholy disposition; the grief and guilt that had overtaken her since the death of Arthur and dominated her life. But for that she would be Lady Askham, her daughters Ladies too instead of mere Honourables. But for that horrible stroke of misfortune they would be with her now in the family home instead of rootless as they were, not quite belonging, not penniless but nothing like as rich as they would have been – heiresses, both, when they grew up. Their futures certainly didn't look very auspicious – dull, prim little girls growing up always in the lengthening shadow of a distant death, yet always made more immediate to them by their mother.

Frances stared at the new Lady Askham, unable to keep the envy from her face though she had spent so many years becoming adjusted to widowhood, to loss and grief.

Rachel too looked well in black, tall, dignified, her hair very blonde, especially this summer because of spending so much time out of doors.

Rachel loved gardening; it was her favourite hobby apart from writing articles on the suffrage and political affairs for Bosco's paper *The Sentinel* which was now overtaking the circulation of all the other Fleet Street newspapers combined. She loved her husband, her children, her garden and her work in that order. She was fortunate in being, at the age of thirty-four, a very happy, fulfilled young woman whom so many people admired and many envied including, now, her sister-in-law.

Rachel busied about the large drawing-room, saying goodbye to local mourners, making sure that arrangements for putting up the family who had too far to travel were complete.

'You can see she's taken over,' Frances murmured to her sister Lady Leander, 'she's probably been preparing for this for years.'

Sophie Leander pressed Frances's hand, knowing quite well the mixture of envy, grief and, perhaps, malice which now suffused her soul. She had, after all, been born a Lady, a member of the august Crewe family, and Rachel was nothing. It was most unfair. Frances, once so striking, had allowed herself to become colourless, rather dowdy. Instead of making a new life for herself when Arthur died she seemed to have died with him for reasons no one quite understood.

'Bosco told me they won't move into the house unless Lady Askham, Dulcie that is, wishes it.'

'And believe me she doesn't,' Frances said. 'She hates Rachel with a deep and abiding passion.'

'Still?' Sophie murmured, smiling at Lady Kitto who was passing. 'I thought that was all resolved?'

'It will never be resolved for Dulcie. She never forgave her for being Bosco's mistress. You can't blame her – her son marrying a woman like that!' Frances sniffed, her narrow nose, as if always on the search for the prurient, the unbecoming or the vile, the stench of unwholesome things, quivered accusingly. 'To see her in this position now is very hard for her to bear.'

'It must be.' Sophie nodded at Flora who had been supervising all the young children scampering about in the playroom below. As members of the family they had all been expected to attend the funeral of their grandfather except the very youngest, Jordan Bolingbroke, Adam and Melanie's new son, who was only two.

'Are they all well?' Frances enquired sweetly. 'I hope my two are being good and responsible.'

'As always, Frances dear,' Flora said, bending to scoop up an empty glass. 'I have never known them anything else.'

'Poor girls,' Frances sighed. 'Fatherless, and now without a grandfather.'

'Bosco will always love them and look after them, you know that, Frances, despite his responsibilities.'

'But he will never be like Arthur, or Lord Askham,' Frances said sorrowfully. 'He can never, never replace them.'

'Of course, he can't, but what he can do he will. And so will Rachel,' Flora said firmly, knowing that her sister-in-law shared the hostility towards the new Lady Askham with her mother.

'Little Jordan is the dearest boy,' Sophie Leander observed, daintily pecking a rather tired-looking sandwich left over on her plate. 'Not a *bit* like the other two. I wonder where he got those dark good looks from?'

'Don't you think he's like Bobby?' Flora said mildly.

'But Bobby, I understand, though I never met him, looks like Harry. Who does Jordan look like?'

'Harry too,' Flora said enigmatically and used the excuse of saying goodbye to her father's aged sister who had come from Winchester for the funeral to take her leave.

Finally, when everyone had gone, there was a small dinner-party for the family who remained. It was still very hot and all the windows were wide open, though the curtains were drawn because of the insects which swarmed in profusion that summer, being attracted by the bright electric light. The heavy, sombre mourning clothes both for men and women made the evening hard to bear – and all longed for their bedrooms and the chance to shed some clothes.

Dulcie repeated over and over that she couldn't believe Frederick was dead and, once again, the various members of the family recorded aspects of his life they remembered best. It was all very dismal, very Victorian, very Askham.

Melanie was particularly upset by the death of her father who had always had a soft spot for his younger daughter. She had noticeably clung to Adam that day, as though he were the last thing left to her, and now she sat by his side listening and, occasionally, weeping.

At family occasions Bosco had taken the head of the table now for a number of years, so the position was not unusual to him and, as usual, Rachel sat halfway down the table and not at its head, a seat reserved for his mother. Rachel was next to Lord Kitto and his brother, the Honourable Ralph, Dulcie's nephews. The new Lord Kitto was unmarried and regarded as a great catch among the young lady hopefuls in London. Like Bosco he was also a Lancer, thus continuing a cavalry tradition in the family. Indeed, he had a look of Bosco about him and although fourteen years separated them, the two men got on well.

After dinner the men went into the billiard room to smoke, the ladies remaining in the drawing-room where the talk inevitably returned to interminable reminiscences about the merits of the late Lord Askham. Such, really, is the function of mourning and, as with primitive tribes and more modern ancestor worshippers, it was well played out at Askham Hall that night. Rachel sat with Flora and Constance Kitto, whom she hadn't seen since the summer of 1908 just before the twins were born.

Constance was a militant suffragette activist and the latest scandal in a family which had seen a good many of them. She also dressed eccentrically, wearing mannish clothes and divided skirts like that other notable eccentric, Lady Harberton, leader of the Radical Dress Movement. But today she looked quite normal in a neat black dress and, for the funeral itself, a small black felt hat with a veil.

Many in the Kitto family regarded Constance's fall from grace to date from the time she stayed with Dulcie in the summer of 1908 and met Rachel. Up to that time she had been quite apathetic about the women's movement. They thought it most singular that the change had come about just then.

'*The Sentinel* doesn't go nearly far enough,' Constance was saying. 'Why don't you really come out in favour of the militants?'

'Because sometimes I think they go too far,' Rachel replied. 'They're alienating the people. The Pethwick-Lawrences think so and so do I.'

'But I thought you were for us,' Constance said angrily. 'Even if you never have the courage to appear yourself.'

'You know I gave Bosco my word I would avoid militancy?' Rachel lowered her voice. 'It was the compromise we had, the understanding.'

'Mrs Pankhurst said you wrote to her . . .'

'That was before Bosco bought the paper. I have walked in processions and I have spoken on platforms. I have barracked the House of Commons and demonstrated in Parliament Square, but I have never broken the law. Because of his position I never could and I never wanted to. Now I think burning houses and setting fire to pillar boxes goes too far. I say so in *The Sentinel*.'

'And there are many who hate you for it.'

'The movement has become too full of hate,' Rachel said sadly. 'We have lost the spirit of comradeliness that so pervaded those early years. Some of the members of the movement even hate one another. You cannot build on hate.'

'But you *can*, Rachel,' Constance's tone had the thin, steely whine of fanaticism. 'For forty years women have tried to get the vote by reason. Now there is only one way left to them: violence.'

'You have brought great dishonour on the family,' Dulcie, who had overheard part of the conversation, deemed it time to add her own observations. 'Particularly you, Constance, with your name always in the papers, but Rachel as well. I wonder both of you don't put your talents to better use.'

'Such as what, Lady Askham?' In view of this sting, Rachel forgot her vow not to quarrel with Bosco's mother, or to refuse to be provoked by her.

'Such as writing stories or articles about what you do well; gardening, something suitable of that nature,' Dulcie said loftily. 'But you put your oar into something you know nothing about. What woman can expect to know about politics?'

'No *lady*,' was Frances's opinion.

'You only breed dissent and antagonism,' Dulcie continued. 'I wonder the Queen was good enough to make the journey today.'

'But it wasn't my funeral, Lady Askham,' Rachel said icily. 'Doubtless you wish it had been.'

'I call that impertinent!' Dulcie thrust out her majestic bosom like a strutting pigeon. 'No doubt you think you can talk to me as you like, now that you bear the same name as I.'

'On the contrary,' Rachel swallowed hard, 'I would never dream of being impertinent to you and I apologize if you thought I was.'

'I most certainly do.'

'Mother!' Flora said urgently. 'Please desist. Don't mar this sacred day by a family quarrel.'

'I will never quarrel with Lady Askham, I assure you,' Rachel rose from her chair. 'If I over-reacted, once again I apologize, and now I must go and see that all is in order for our guests.'

'"Our guests" indeed, is it?' Dulcie's voice throbbed with emotion. 'In *my* house? I thought they were my guests, or do you intend to move in tonight? Am I to be put on to the streets?'

She began to sob theatrically, dabbing her eyes with her black-edged handkerchief, one of half a dozen or so that had seen so much use on other occasions, being kept neatly in a drawer in mothballs, like the dress.

Flora went over to her mother and took her arm. 'Mama, I beg of you, come to bed now. You know Rachel and Bosco have said, even when Father was ill, that they would *never* move into the Hall unless you wanted to move out. They said it again when the will was read. It's very unfair to say otherwise.'

'Ah, but do they really mean it now that it's legally theirs?'

'Of course we mean it, Lady Askham,' Rachel answered. 'We want you to live as long as you wish in your own home. I was just trying to be helpful.'

Mabel thought it her turn to bustle over.

'Now, Dulcie, you must *not* upset yourself. Rachel and Bosco only wish what you wish. Go to bed now, like a good girl, that's a dear. Flora will take you. You've had an exhausting day and tomorrow we will discuss plans for you to come over to Robertswood and have a good rest.'

Dulcie, suppressing a shudder at the very idea, allowed herself to be led away by Flora while all the ladies present stood up as she passed, as though she were royalty.

Pausing dramatically at the door she said mournfully: 'Send Bosco to me. I want to see him before I go to sleep. Who knows how much longer I shall have to live?'

The months that followed Lord Askham's death were not easy. Despite the fact that he had left a will that was neat, clear and legal, that all his affairs were in order, there was much to be done. The injured attitude of the widowed Lady Askham was an obstacle to many other matters Bosco and Rachel would have liked to have done with and cleared up.

It was plainly ridiculous that Dulcie should remain in a huge mansion that Bosco, the man of business and now influential newspaper owner, would like to have occupied. The Grange was so much more suitable for her and had, indeed, been the dowager's house until the death of Frederick's mother. But Dulcie would not hear of her place being usurped by Rachel and no one liked to insist on it. So she lived on in the great, bare house like a ghost, suitably accompanied most of the time by Frances. They could thus spend hours and hours together discussing their late husbands and the supposed machinations of the wicked Rachel.

There were other complicated matters involving family trusts that had to be unravelled and settled, more money for Flora and Melanie, and legacies for the grandchildren, each of whom became wealthy young people though they couldn't touch their money until they were twenty-one. Bobby Lighterman, now twelve and going up to Eton the following year, was a considerable heir and looking after even part of his fortune was quite a task for Bosco to undertake, together with all the other duties and responsibilities he had inherited.

Accordingly he spent more and more time in London and Rachel, reluctant as ever to be parted too long from her children, remained in the country writing her articles, tending her garden and longing for the days when Bosco could be home with her.

Despite the advantages the Hall had over the Grange Rachel was not sorry that they didn't live there. Her garden was her joy and she had transformed it from a wilderness into the sort of showplace that local people talked about and asked to visit. She was Chairman of the Askham and District Horticultural Association and considered an expert in dahlias which she was asked to judge all over southwest England. She supported the new Girl Guide movement that had been set up by Lady Baden-Powell and was Patroness of the local branch. She was not a mere dispenser of charity, but took a real and sympathetic interest in all the people who came to her for advice and causes which needed her help.

Dulcie Askham had always been considered very grand in the district, a figurehead, much admired and respected but regarded by the local population with the sort of awe that she considered right and proper. She kept her distance. She would distribute prizes at the annual prize days of the various schools and associations in the area, and she gave generously and ostentatiously to charity without doing anything practical, because at heart she was a true Conservative who believed in the virtues of thrift, hard work and self-help. She thought the poor were largely poor because they had chosen to be, and the sick owed their situation to the fact that they had not taken sufficient care of themselves. She was not regarded with the love that her mother-in-law had been, previous occupant of the

Grange, nor with the devotion that her daughter-in-law came to earn during the years when she lived in the Grange first as Lady Gore and then as Lady Askham, heir to the great house itself.

One night Bosco, after a day's hard work, took himself off alone for a stroll around the Square and then across Piccadilly towards Quaglino's, where he had an engagement to meet Flora, Melanie and Adam and afterwards to go to a theatre. He arrived at Quaglino's shortly before eight and sat in the foyer drinking a pink gin and studying the menu, waiting for the others. When they arrived the head waiter took them to their table, booked well in advance. It was Christmas-time and many people took wives, sweethearts and family or business friends to that famous restaurant to celebrate the festive season where not only could they eat and drink well, but dance into the small hours of the morning.

'What a pity Rachel can't be here,' Melanie said, her feet tapping to the music of the small orchestra. 'I don't think you see enough of her, Bosco.'

'I don't,' Bosco agreed. 'But she doesn't wish to live in London while the children are small.'

'I can't say I blame her,' Adam lit a cigarette, 'I hate it myself.'

'Adam, you *don't* hate London,' Melanie chided him. 'Especially as we are getting a lovely new house.'

'Oh, where?' Bosco gazed at them over the top of the menu and, as he did, his eyes were suddenly mesmerized by the face of a woman sitting only two tables away from him, who was looking earnestly in his direction. As their eyes met she smiled and, in an instant, Bosco was transported across the years and saw, with startling clarity, those eyes close to his, the bed in the huge heavily scented room, as if it were yesterday. Nimet. A lump rose in his throat and he quickly looked away again, not daring to believe what he saw.

The house was in St John's Wood, a part of London that Melanie regarded as almost as good as being in the country, only across the park and not too far to walk home, should one so wish, from the centre of town. She was describing it in great detail – its size, its proximity to Lord's, which Adam loved, the spacious grounds, everything which she could now afford since the legacy from her father had been made over to her.

But Bosco – in another world, a different era – didn't hear a word. He smiled, nodded his head, drank another gin, smoked another cigarette, ordered from the menu and every two minutes he looked once again in her direction just to be sure; and there she was, she really was, smiling at him just as familiarly as ever. She was with a man, but Bosco didn't care. She looked older but twice as ravishing, sophisticated, glamorous in a chiffon evening dress with a low décolletage and her hair fashionably lacquered, puffed out at either side of her face and curving over her forehead. She smoked a cigarette through a long jade holder, holding it away from her, even more enticing seen through the swirling smoke.

When she got up to dance with her partner Bosco's eyes followed her, noting the slim curves of her hips, the fact that her bust had filled out a little in the twelve years since he'd seen her. If it had, not much else had changed. She looked just as alluring as she had when she was a girl of, what? Nineteen, twenty-two? He had never really known her age.

'Bosco, you've suddenly gone all broody,' Melanie said sharply, rapping on the table. 'I don't think you've heard a thing I said. Have you seen someone you know?'

'No, shall we dance,' Bosco held out his hand, anxious

to be in the proximity of a woman who, he realized, still fascinated him no matter what she'd done.

'Oh, all right. Let's dansare, darling,' Melanie said in the current idiom, trying not to appear bored at being faced with the uninteresting choice of dancing either with her husband or her brother. He took her arm and led her through the crowded tables, the waving palms, on to the dance floor, where he immediately began looking over her shoulders for Nimet.

'Do you want to dance?' Adam gazed at Flora who shook her head.

'I'd rather be here with you.'

Adam felt under the table and touched her hand, but she drew back because, although they were in love, flesh was forbidden to them because of the degree of relationship. Flora felt that there was something positively evil in loving one's sister's husband, even knowing the truth about Jordan and the lovers Melanie had had since his birth. Or maybe they were lovers in the sense that Adam was, beloved but distanced, never fondled or kissed. Unlikely, and certainly not as tender, noble or as selfless. The love of Adam and Flora was cerebral and showed itself in devotion to the causes Adam, and now she, held dear: the Liberal philosophy of compassion and welfare, the urgent but still hopeless cause of women's suffrage.

Since Asquith had succeeded the sick Campbell-Bannerman in 1908 Adam had held office first in Home Affairs and now at the Treasury. Unimportant, minor offices where his worth was insufficiently regarded because he was felt to be not quite politically sound, too much of a rebel. The previous year there had been two elections over the issue of reform of the House of Lords, legislation which some alleged had hastened the death of King Edward. Each time the government was returned with reduced majorities. Yet it was still strong, though not strong enough to implement its original 1905 promise to enlarge the franchise to include women; and thus it had lost many of its original supporters. There were those who had felt that as soon as a Liberal government came to power women would have the vote. How betrayed they felt now.

But Adam remained firm in his original Liberal faith. He knew one day they would win, just as they would introduce a National Insurance Bill, in the face of stiff opposition, not least from the medical profession, and as they had finally reduced the power of the Lords over the question of the People's Budget. Meanwhile he worked untiringly for the Cause, campaigning for it in Parliament and defending the women in the courts.

One lamentable consequence of this was that Adam was no wealthier than he ever had been. His MP's salary was only £400 a year, and he was often not paid for his work at the Bar. He had resisted, as long as he could, giving up the house in John Street but now that Melanie's own fortune was so substantial he had had to give way.

But he remained a poor man, surrounded by wealthy people whom he loved, but could not help resenting. Bosco was a millionaire and Flora, dear Flora, was wealthy too, but gave so much of her money to the Cause: her money to the Cause and her love to him.

Just to sit opposite each other, looking at each other, was enough. To be alone, even in a crowded room, was paradise.

'Sometimes I think Adam wishes he'd married Flora,' Melanie said, humming under her breath to the catchy tune of the dance orchestra. 'Look at them just sitting ogling each other.'

'He admires her, that's all,' Bosco said. 'You know he adores you.'

'I can't think why. I'm not very nice to him.'

'You're unworthy of Adam,' Bosco gave her a twirl. 'I don't know why he stands by you, but he does.'

'At least he's acknowledged Jordan as his son. That was the decent thing.'

'A lot of men wouldn't have. The divorce courts and ignominy it would have been for you with another man, madam.'

'Would *you*, darling?' Melanie, in blue translucent taffeta sparkling with sequins, feathers in her hair, smiled naughtily at him.

'No. I would certainly have divorced you.'

'He couldn't marry Flora anyway. Aren't there degrees of matrimony which are forbidden?'

'Yes. The Reformation in England took place because Henry VIII married his brother's wife. The Church said he shouldn't and Henry said he should.'

'Yes, but we're not Catholics. I'm sure it's different now.'

'I think you have to have a special dispensation. Ask Adam.' Bosco smiled and twirled her around again. Then he saw Nimet, and also that she seemed to be encouraging her partner to drift in their direction.

'Are you *sure* you don't know that woman?' Melanie with a movement of her head indicated Nimet, now clearly in view. 'I'm sure she's giving you the eye.'

'Her face is vaguely familiar,' Bosco said, trying to sound offhand. 'Cairo, I think, in 1899.'

'My, that *is* a long time ago. Look, they're coming over. I knew she recognized you. What a good-looker!'

'Hello,' Nimet said as the music stopped and the couples on the dance floor changed, some returning to their tables and others taking up positions on the floor. 'I wondered if you'd recognize me. Bosco Down, isn't it?'

'That was a long time ago,' Melanie laughed. 'You're now speaking to the Earl of Askham.'

'Am I indeed?' Nimet smiled. Her skin was still smooth and youthful, her eyes dark, limpid, inviting – heavily ringed with black kohl. She looked decidedly Oriental, quintessentially exotic. Other men were admiring her too. 'I must congratulate you.'

'My father died earlier in the year,' Bosco said huskily, as though there were something sticking in his throat. 'So it's no real cause for congratulation.'

'I'm sorry to hear that.' (Oh, the soft voice of the siren.) 'May I introduce Count da Ponte? He's from Rome.' Melanie had been busy eyeing the handsome man who bowed, draping himself, Italian-style, over her hand. 'Is this your wife, Bosco?'

'My sister,' Bosco answered her, clearing his throat again. 'My wife's in the country. My sister, Lady Melanie Bolingbroke. Nimet El-Said,' he said as Melanie slyly glanced at him, wagging a finger.

'Oh, then, you *do* remember her? You even remember her name.'

'It suddenly came to me,' Bosco said dishonestly and, as the music started again, he held out his hand. 'Would you care to dance?'

'Nothing pleases me more,' Nimet slipped into his arms and Melanie, too, seemed quite pleased with the exchange, accepting the arm of the Italian Count.

For some moments Bosco felt as though he were in some kind of dream from which he would soon be awakened, perhaps violently. He couldn't believe that her body was again in his arms, that her lips almost brushed his ear and that that fragrance of oriental perfume was just the same – subtle, indefinable, mysterious, with a hint of menace.

'Do you forgive me then, Bosco?' Her tone of voice was softly suggestive.

'I must, mustn't I?' Bosco gazed solemnly into her eyes, in which he already felt himself lost.

'I thought so much about you. I wish you'd written to me.'

'I couldn't then. I was very angry. I was a young, impetuous man and I felt betrayed.'

'Madame Hassim was so cruel. She was greedy. I didn't want money from you . . . only love.' The room seemed to rotate before him, the couples dancing on the floor, the busy diners, heads together, laughing, talking, the swift-footed waiters running up and down between the tables. 'Is she really your sister, or your mistress?' Nimet indicated Melanie, lost – as if to provoke her husband – in the Count's arms.

'I have no mistress,' Bosco whispered. 'Yes, she is my sister.'

'You are faithful to your wife?'

'Yes.'

'How very singular.'

'She's a very singular woman. Just now she's in the country.'

'Have you children?'

'Four.'

'Four!' Nimet pretended amazement. 'Quite an old, old man. *And* an earl.' Lowering her voice she spoke into his ear. 'You haven't altered at all you know, Bosco. I recognized you instantly, even with the moustache. Maybe a little broader, but still the same, dear Bosco. The one man I never forgot.'

'Nimet, I must see you again,' Bosco said urgently, anxious not to quench the flame, the old flame that had risen between them, binding them, soldering them together as of old. 'How can it be arranged?'

'Your wife is in the country, you say?'

'Yes.'

'You have a house in town?'

'Thirty-five, Berkeley Square.'

'Then I'll come there.'

'What about the Count?'

'I can easily dispose of him – perhaps to your sister?'

'Later tonight?' Bosco ignored her insinuation, aware only of her, desiring only Nimet.

'Tomorrow would be better.'

'Would you like to go out to dine?'

'I don't think I dare,' her voice suggested danger. 'Not just yet. It's a bit like Cairo, you know. One has to be careful.'

'Are you married?' As he looked mystified she quickly put her finger against her lips and shook her head.

'I'll tell you everything tomorrow night. Say eleven?'

'Eleven,' Bosco said feeling his pulse quicken, his head swim; that rash, thoughtless mood of Cairo overpowering him yet again; suspending wisdom, common sense, his ability to question, his better judgment.

CHAPTER 18

To imagine the house in St James's Square in the spring of 1873, when Dulcie had first come there as a bride, was not, after all, so difficult. Very little had changed in the Square itself. Maybe the trees were taller, leafier; the shrubs and bushes thicker; the flowers, certainly, seemed more profuse. But, surely, the birds sitting on the branches watching her curiously as she gazed out of the large window on the first floor were the children, grandchildren, maybe great-grandchildren of those who had lived there forty years before? Sparrows, blackbirds and pigeons, after all, had their ancestral homes just as earls and countesses did. Dulcie was sure that generations of the same families of pigeons had nested in the eaves under the roofs, in the apertures along the back wall, on the windowsills, and by the drainpipes running into the well of the courtyard from whence the smells from the kitchen wafted continually skywards.

And, just as the outside and the surroundings had scarcely changed at all, neither had the inside, Dulcie thought, leaving the window and walking slowly back into the drawing-room. Frederick's mother, a considerable heiress in her own right, one of the Mountacres from Mountacre Park in Staffordshire, had cast a connoisseur's eye over the contents of the whole house and thrown out all the heavy, ornate carved mahogany which had been the vogue for most of the nineteenth century. She had replaced it with sideboards, cabinets, dressers, desks, tables and chairs made of pinewood, satinwood or polished oak, with rectilinear forms and gilded mouldings, or inlaid Wedgwood plaques and marquetries of coloured woods designed by Philip Webb, Bruce Talbert or William Burges. The last two were masters of the new Gothic style, one of whose pioneers was William Morris. There was Morris wallpaper in some of the bedrooms; and wardrobes, cupboards, and a huge four-poster bed by E. W. Godwin who was considered a genius for his clever adaptations of many styles – Greek, Egyptian, Renaissance and Japanese.

But as well as modern English furniture, with its use of bevelled glass, canopies, painted and inlaid decoration and slender supports, Phyllida Askham had bought pieces from the time of Louis XV, or French Early Empire, and delicate chinoiserie and ormolu, porcelain and silver, from the masters working in Vienna a hundred years before.

The same ruthless reappraisal happened to the Askham art collection, now judged priceless with its unrivalled paintings by Gainsborough, Constable and the major English watercolourists of the eighteenth and nineteenth centuries. She had restored, revarnished, rehung and bought, again from the sale rooms and privately from many of the great houses in the land, including royalty.

Yes, Askham House was a treasure house as well as a family home and what dramas, occasions, joys and sorrows had it not witnessed since the days when its first occupier, William, second Earl of Askham had brought his young bride to the place in the way that Frederick had brought Dulcie.

Dulcie sat in one of the early Chippendale chairs to await the arrival of her son and his wife. She had decided to relinquish the house and give it entirely over to them. She no longer wished to live there, to sleep alone in the great empty bed, the servants upstairs and the creaking of the long, deserted corridors giving rise to numerous fancies and fears. Bosco had offered her Berkeley Square, but she had accepted a grace-and-favour apartment in St James's Palace where she would be near not only the Queen Dowager and her frequent calls of duty, now that she had time on her hands, but also her family and friends.

A number of brides had been brought here by the Earls of Askham and their heirs, Dulcie thought, but not Bosco's. He had now been married seven years and fathered four children, his wife rigorously excluded because of Dulcie's disapproval. Had she been right? She looked at herself in the long Sheraton mirror that reflected the Square and saw a woman still slim, some even thought beautiful, who dressed with care, choosing her clothes from the fashionable houses. Was she formidable too? Yes, too formidable, her eyes told her; too unkind to Rachel just because she had shared Bosco's bed before their marriage. Or had that just been an excuse? It was difficult to know because, over the years, her various prejudices had become blurred to such an extent that they were often interwoven.

She had never, she recalled, liked Rachel from the Cairo days. She remembered looking at her when they first met and thinking that she was a girl unlike those she was used to: unconformist, iconoclastic, bold. It wasn't just that she was middle class, she had a curious quality of classlessness and was therefore uncontrollable. It was easy to see, even then, that she would never be impressed by the fact that the Askhams were members of an ancient aristocracy, or allow herself to be enclosed within the bounds of Askham proprieties.

And she was right. It was almost as though she knew, then, what a danger Rachel would be. How she and her brother would obtrude their unwelcome presence into her family and disrupt it as, indeed, they both had.

No, it wasn't just the fact that Rachel had been Bosco's

mistress. Awful though that fact was in itself it was an excuse; besides, even if she *had* liked Rachel and if it were true, was it right to condemn in others a weakness one had never felt oneself? She, whose only passionate affairs were conducted in public, who liked men solely for the glory their admiration shed on a woman; for what was a woman without a man? Nothing, emptiness. But for her, Dulcie Askham, admiration was the end in itself, the thing most eagerly sought. She had never allowed a single admirer to be alone with her for too long, or be permitted the intimacy of the bedchamber. In all her life she had only slept with one man: her husband, though it would have surprised a good few people to learn this.

'Lady Askham, my lady.' The butler, coming quietly into the room bowed, and Dulcie, startled, looked up from her reverie. She could still not get used to hearing the detested woman being addressed by her name.

'Is Lady Askham alone, Bromwich?'

'Yes, my lady.'

'Show her in.'

Dulcie remained where she was, her grey pleated dress falling in folds to the floor, her handbag over the arm of the chair. She wore a hat with a large turned-up brim trimmed with grey feathers and, already, she felt a visitor in her own home. As Rachel came in she inclined her head and the feathers bobbed beckoningly over her eyes. She did not rise.

'Good morning, Rachel,' she said. 'Is Bosco not with you?' She extended a hand which Rachel shook, aware of the cold, icy touch. They did not kiss. They never did.

'Bosco will be here later, Lady Askham. He had some meeting in the City.'

'Do sit down, Rachel,' Lady Askham graciously pointed to a chair. 'Please feel at ease in your own home.'

Rachel was elegant, too, in a green costume, the skirt

narrowing from knee to ankle, the high Directoire waistline accentuated by a wide sash under her bosom, her cutaway coat trimmed with a darker shade of green braid. Her hat, high on her head, was made of bands of plum-coloured velvet, cleverly swathed together and ornamented with a clutch of dark green feathers at the back. Dulcie nodded approvingly.

'You look very nice. You must tell me the name of your couturier.'

'Thank you.' Rachel, nervous, perched on the rim of the seat. She did not feel at ease in her own home at all as, she knew, she was not meant to.

'There's no need, really, to show you round, is there?' Dulcie came straight to the point. 'I'm sure you'll wish to make many changes. Though my mother-in-law, Phyllida Askham, had such perfect taste, tastes do change.'

'I'm sure I shan't change a thing, Lady Askham. You have kept the house most beautifully. Bosco, I know, wants it to remain as his grandmother and you have made it.'

'That's nice of him,' Dulcie sniffed. 'Though I say it myself, *my* taste has also always been considered impeccable.'

'It is, Lady Askham. I could never hope to emulate it.'

Well, the girl was trying. Dulcie looked at her suspiciously. 'Do you intend to entertain a lot, Rachel?'

'I expect so. In the season. But please don't think we're going to introduce a vast number of changes. And you will always be welcome here, you know that. Any time.'

'That's very civil of you. I'm obliged.' Dulcie rang the little silver bell on the table by her side. 'Will you take tea or coffee? Then I'll introduce you formally to the staff.'

'Coffee please, Lady Askham.'

Bromwich entered, bowed and, as Lady Askham was about to order coffee, said: 'There is a gentleman downstairs, my lady, asking for Lord Askham.'

'Who is he, did he say? Has he a card?'

'He merely asked if his lordship was in. I said he was expected, and he asked if he could wait.'

'Did he give you his name?' Dulcie looked at Rachel. 'Are you expecting anyone?' And, as Rachel shook her head, Bromwich continued:

'He says he is from Egypt, my lady.'

'From Egypt?' As Dulcie looked at the footman astonishment registered on her face. 'What sort of person is he?'

Bromwich frowned and shuffled his feet.

'A curious personage, if I may say so, my lady. Not quite a gentleman.'

'In that case you'd better show him out.' Dulcie's voice was firm. 'Kindly ask him to write a letter to make an appointment. His lordship is a very busy man.'

'I told him that, my lady, and he insisted on waiting.' Bromwich looked embarrassed and Rachel smiled reassuringly.

'Lady Askham, would you mind if Bromwich asked him up? He may be a friend of Lord Cromer or someone Bosco knew in Egypt. It might be rather rude to send him away.'

Dulcie was about to refuse and then thought better of it. After all, Rachel was officially the new chatelaine of Askham House.

'Show him up then, Bromwich,' she instructed, 'but say it is only for a few minutes. And only two cups, Bromwich. We don't want to encourage the creature to stay. Do we?' She looked pointedly at Rachel.

'We don't know until we know who he is,' Rachel replied. 'It may be a friend.'

'*Friends* usually give their names.' Dulcie gave her a withering glance before resting her eyes firmly on the door.

When Achmed Asher walked in a few minutes later

Dulcie had no difficulty at all in recalling him, as had not been the case with the unfortunate Adrian Hastings. No, her memory of him was very vivid indeed and, in her imagination, she was swiftly transported to a hotel room in Cairo fourteen years before. This sinister little man had not changed one iota except that he wore an immaculate double-breasted grey suit, and the tarbush was replaced by a stiff Homburg hat, of the kind introduced into this country by the late King, which he carried in his hand. His thinning hair was parted in the centre and his moustaches were just as stiffly waxed as they had been all those years ago.

As Dulcie stared at him he stared back. Rachel, fascinated, looked on.

'Do you remember me, my lady?' Asher bowed very low.

'I should think I do. What impertinence, this time, makes you come to my house?'

'I asked to see Lord Askham, my lady,' Achmed, perhaps a trifle put out, shuffled from one foot to the other.

'Lord Askham is not here. What is your business?'

'It's of a personal nature, my lady.'

'Then I think you had best be gone before he gets here. Neither I nor Lord Askham have very pleasant memories of you.'

Asher raised his eyebrows. 'But Lord Askham does not know me, my lady.'

'Oh yes he does. Lord Askham is my son, whom you knew as Lieutenant Down, and this is his wife.'

Dulcie jerked her head towards Rachel, who neither smiled nor frowned but continued to keep a pleasant, anticipatory expression on her face.

'I think you do not remember me, Mr Asher. I was on the picnic to Sakkara as Rachel Bolingbroke.'

Without being asked Asher looked round for a seat and

abruptly sat down, nervously, rapidly passing the brim of his hat through his hands. It was just the sort of rude behaviour Dulcie expected of a creature of his kind and she looked disgustedly away.

'*You* are Lady Askham?' Asher said unbelievingly. 'Lord Askham is dead?'

'My husband has been dead for over a year. Lieutenant Down, as you knew him, is the new Earl of Askham. You thought my husband was still alive?'

'Yes.' Asher looked furtively across at Rachel.

'Then you have no business with my son?'

'No . . . yes, that is, if I may see you alone for a moment, Lady Askham.' As he recovered his composure, gazing solemnly at her, Dulcie momentarily felt fear.

'What you have to say to me you can say in front of my daughter-in-law,' she said. 'And you had best say it quickly and be gone.'

'Ah . . . well . . .' Asher stood up and placed his plainly new hat on a nearby table. Then he put his hands behind his back and gazed at the ceiling. 'What I have to say, Lady Askham, can only be said to you alone.'

'I'll wait outside the door,' Rachel rose and signalled to her mother-in-law by raising her eyebrows. 'I'll be within earshot if you want me.'

'I'm sure what Mr Asher has to say won't take a minute,' Dulcie said crossly. 'Please don't go too far away.'

'I shan't.' Rachel didn't look at Asher as she left the room, and when the door was shut behind her she carefully stationed herself close to it so that she could hear what went on inside.

'Now, Asher, state your business and be brief.' Dulcie took a handkerchief from her dress pocket and kneaded it nervously in her hand which she found, to her annoyance, had suddenly become moist.

'Well, it does concern Cairo, as I think you suspected.'

The tone of Asher's voice had changed from an unpleasantly obsequious politeness to one of insolence. 'The fact is, Lady Askham, I have fallen on very bad times these past few years . . .'

'That is no concern of mine,' Dulcie interrupted him, 'and if you have the temerity to refer to that matter in Cairo again, which is long since past and buried, I will have you horsewhipped.'

Achmed's tone grew unctuous: 'I think not, Lady Askham, when you hear what I have to say – distressing news that might affect not only *you* but your son.'

'How can it affect my son?'

'Because it concerns him *too*, my lady. You will recall on that delightful occasion when we picnicked in the desert an . . . how shall I put it . . . incident occurred between you and Captain Crystal?'

'No incident occurred between me and Captain Crystal.' The tone of Dulcie's voice was like low, subterranean thunder.

'Well, a lot of people thought so, including your son. I have it on the best authority that he killed Captain Cardew and disguised it as an act of war during the Battle of Omdurman.'

As Dulcie stood up her handbag clattered to the floor, spilling its contents.

'That is a wicked falsehood. That is *monstrous*.'

'Nevertheless there are those who would swear to it. An enquiry by Lords Cromer and Kitchener was hushed up. Now I, you may imagine, dear Lady Askham, am quite prepared to forget this distressing matter if . . .' he looked furtively over his shoulder.

'If I should pay you a few thousand pounds, I expect!' Dulcie's voice bristled with contempt.

'Exactly. I didn't wish to distress you with this news, of course.'

'Of course you did. You monster! You wanted to blackmail my husband and maybe by it destroy my marriage. I am thankful that the Great Reaper came to our aid and removed the poor man from your scheming machinations, though I doubt whether he would have received you, let alone listened to you. You would have been ejected into the Square.'

Asher shrugged his shoulders and when he spoke his voice had acquired a wheedling tone which was even less pleasant than before.

'Alas, being a poor man, I have no alternative but to find money where I can.'

'Making it the way you know best. Criminally.' Dulcie stretched out her arm and pointed a quivering finger at the door. 'Out!'

'Are you sure, Lady Askham?' Asher's face assumed a look of cunning.

'Quite sure. You cannot harm me any more.'

'But *Lord* Askham?'

'No one would believe that story. It's rubbish.'

'But if I assure you that it's perfectly true? Lieutenant Down at the time admitted it.'

'And what do you suppose *you* can do about it now?'

'Tell the King?' Asher suggested. 'Queen Alexandra, whom I understand your ladyship is close to? Not a nice story, even after fourteen years.'

'And how do I know we will be rid of you this time?' Dulcie felt her heart fluttering and dabbed at her brow with her crumpled handkerchief.

'Only on the promise of a gentleman.'

'A gentleman!' Flinging back her head Dulcie emitted a sound that was hardly a laugh – more like a roar – but which Bosco heard as he hurried up the stairs to find the double doors to the drawing-room closed and his wife standing behind them, her ear pressed close to the woodwork.

'What's going on?' he whispered and Rachel drew him aside and explained what had transpired as quickly as she could.

'Asher!' Bosco boomed as Rachel put a hand to her mouth, but it was too late. With a bound Bosco flung open the doors and strode into the room to find his mother and Asher confronting each other as if in the terminal stages of a mortal combat.

Asher scarcely had time to turn before Bosco had grabbed him by the back of his collar and started twisting it like a tourniquet, practically lifting the small man right off the floor as he did.

Asher's hands began to flail the air as his face slowly changed colour before Bosco freed him, but not until he had shaken him again, like a dog.

'What are *you* doing here, Asher, I say! What are you doing here?' His voice grew in volume with every word until, on the last one, it seemed to reverberate round the room like thunder: 'here, here, here' growing gradually fainter, like an echo. 'As if I didn't know,' Bosco continued, before the unfortunate man could speak. 'Up to your blackmailing tricks again, are you, your lies? When did they let you out of prison?'

'Prison, Lieutenant Down?'

'*Lord Askham*, if you don't mind.' Bosco began to shout again. 'You miserable, snivelling little dungheap of humanity, how dare you come here and threaten my mother? How dare you darken the doors of my house?'

'He needs money,' Dulcie said, breaking down at last, and Rachel running over to her took her hand and said:

'Come with me, Lady Askham, and rest. Bosco will deal with this creature.'

Weakly, tremulously, Dulcie, without a word or a backward glance allowed herself to be led away by Rachel whose comforting arms were about her shoulders. She didn't feel herself at all. She felt like an old woman. As soon as the door was closed Bosco's arm shot out for Asher's throat again and he began viciously to knot the tie under his thyroid cartilage.

'See here, Asher. If I kill you now on these premises no one will ever be the wiser.'

'The servants . . .' Asher gasped, as with a dying breath.

'Are my servants,' Bosco interrupted him. 'They would never betray me for the likes of a weasel like you. And kill you I shall unless I hear from your unsavoury lips that you will leave this country immediately – God knows how you came to be here – and never, ever let me hear of you or see you again.'

As he removed his hand, the tie, once of an immaculate grey silk but now reduced to the substance of a rag, flopped across the front of the wretched man's crumpled shirt.

'Yes, Lord Askham,' Asher gulped and, seeking the refuge of a chair, staggered across the room and sat down, breathing heavily. 'I am not a well man, Lord Askham.'

'I should think not. You don't look well. Gaol fever no doubt. How *you* had the temerity to come here after all these years. You could have sent my mother to her grave after my father who you thought still alive – you're ignorant too! *Then* I would have killed you.'

'You're a violent man, Lord Askham.'

'Only to snivelling, creepy little curs like you. I tell you, I'd cheerfully despatch you here and now, and defy the laws of the land, were it not for the distress it might give my mother and my wife. Now Asher, I'm going to kick you down the stairs unless you run . . . fast . . . now.'

As Bosco advanced menacingly upon him, Asher, with a loud squeak, leapt out of his chair and ran like a rabbit for the door leaving his shining new hat behind him.

Bosco stood at the top of the stairs listening, and when he heard the front door shut, he went quickly to the window and watched Asher dive across St James's Square as though he had been peppered with gunshot.

'I would enjoy it if I didn't hate him so much,' he said broodingly to Rachel, who had quietly come to stand by his side. 'How's Mama?'

'Recovering. I was just about to go in and do what I could when I heard you. Thank God you came.'

'But how came the rogue to be here? That's what surprises me.'

'I suppose he can travel freely like anyone else.'

'No, not freely. As an ex-gaolbird he'd be watched. He shouldn't be allowed into this country. I must get on to the Egyptian Office about him.'

'I'm very sorry your mother heard about Crystal.'

'So am I,' Bosco clenched and unclenched his hands. 'That business will follow me, one way or the other, to my grave. It's as though Cardew remains to haunt me.'

Rachel encircled his neck with her arm and kissed his cheek.

'No, it won't. It's all over and forgotten.'

'Except by him.'

'Anyway it's not true.'

'But why did it resurrect itself again – after all these years, and how did *he* hear it? That's what I want to know.'

Nimet lay for a long time in silence after Bosco told her about Asher's visit, recreating for her, in vivid detail, the drama in St James's Square several days before.

'Would you have killed him?'

'Probably.'

Nimet wound her arms around him and nestled her head against his. 'I like strong, violent men.'

'You're a tease,' Bosco laughed and kissed her. The room was dark and only the lights from Berkeley Square flickered like shadows on the ceiling, reminding him of Cairo and the incense-laden smoke curling up towards the ornamental drapery.

'How did your wife react to him?'

'She was bewildered by the whole thing, but calm. That's Rachel. Mama was the worst. I had to send for the doctor to administer a soporific. Afterwards she asked me about Cardew. I said I felt guilty for his death but, of course, I hadn't killed him.'

Nimet turned to him, her face worried.

'Do you know, when you told me you had in Cairo I thought it was true.'

'I had it very much on my mind then. I think I felt it *was* true.'

'Other people may have thought so too. Did you tell many people? Maybe that's how Achmed heard it.'

'But why does he only come up with it now? I can't understand it.'

'Maybe he was in prison all these years?'

'Maybe.'

Bosco kissed her again and let his hand travel along her slim, naked body next to his. He didn't feel guilty about Nimet because she was so different from Rachel. It was like making love to a dream; a dream that reminded him of his youth, of long, hot Egyptian nights, and not of his present existence as a man of title and substance, a family man, a father. With Nimet he lived in a past which seemed to bear no relevance to the present or future. She was like a tale from *The Arabian Nights* – evanescent, fictional.

She was still a mystery to him. Where she lived or what she did he didn't know. She came to him late at night and left him before dawn. Everything about Nimet was shadowy, ephemeral. He didn't know anything about her, how she came to be in England, where she lived, or what had happened to the Count da Ponte.

'I thought he was your lover, that you lived with him.'

Nimet had shaken her head and smiled.

'Why all these mysteries still, Nimet?'

'Why not?' she'd said. Nothing had changed since Cairo. Nothing. But, as in Cairo he had deliberately avoided knowing the truth, the same thing happened to him yet again. He felt that if he knew it he would like it as little as he had then, and that once again he would lose her. He couldn't bear to lose her now. Not after four months of only the kind of love – passionate, sensual, forbidden – that Nimet could offer.

Had she been married? First she had nodded her head, then she shook it and he knew that he would never ever know the truth. Never know the truth about Nimet.

'When you have St James's Square I won't be able to come here,' she said after the talk about Asher.

'Yes, you will. I'm making it into the headquarters of my company. I shall keep a furnished flat on top. For you.'

'But won't your wife be in London more often?'

'Never you mind about that. We'll meet just the same. I'm never going to lose you now.'

He never talked to her about Rachel and the questions she asked were very few. It was as though they both respected Rachel's place in their lives without even letting consideration of her come between them. To Nimet she was a figurehead, statuesque. She might not exist because, in many ways, Nimet felt she had preceded her in Bosco's affections. She knew, and loved, him first. Nimet had told him she'd always loved him, always remembered him, had never forgotten him and he knew now that the same was true about himself. There was always a small part of Bosco that had never belonged to Rachel; one that the sensuous, hedonistic wiles of Nimet fulfilled instead. He wondered whether, if he'd rescued her in Cairo all those years before, anything would have been different. Would he have presented her in London as his wife? Difficult to know. What would his mother have said? Easy to guess that, but all too late now.

Nimet never complained. She never had. They could still never be seen together because, although the circumstances were very different to the ones prevailing in Cairo where Nimet, the alleged daughter of a wealthy sheikh, told Bosco she could never be seen, it was he now who was so well-known in London that the capital would soon be filled with rumour if he were seen in public with a woman like Nimet.

But Bosco liked things as they were: not one wife, but two; not one bed but a choice; not one love but different kinds.

He felt he was a very fortunate man, well contented with his life and the abundance thereof.

The house in St John's Wood, though large, was not large enough for Melanie. As soon as they had moved into it she started looking for somewhere bigger. There were those among her friends and acquaintances who felt she wouldn't even be satisfied with the house in Manchester Square and its museum-like proportions, if and when her son Bobby inherited it.

Melanie was a disappointed woman, never satisfied; always craving the unattainable – more beauty, more money, bigger houses, deeper love. The care and devotion Adam had given her over the birth of Jordan remained unappreciated and unrewarded. Guilty at first, she soon took his sympathy for granted and ended up despising him for giving it. A husband who could be so complaisant must indeed be a fool, Melanie reasoned; and soon she continued with her flirtations in the same manner as before, inheriting the mantle of her mother who was now rather a staid and respectable lady, constantly in the company of the dowager Queen. Indeed, Dulcie's day was now past. A woman nearing sixty, she had enjoyed beauty, the admiration of men, for forty years and gracefully, with dignity, she yielded her place to another. The author of the poems to his Fair Lady had fled to France to compose them in honour of someone else, and all those ardent young captains and subalterns, out of place at the Court and St James's Palace, gathered round Melanie Bolingbroke instead.

Melanie's disappointments in general extended, in particular, to her children, especially her daughter whom she didn't consider beautiful enough, and her husband who wasn't sufficiently successful. After a bright, auspicious start Adam had not proved to have enough ambition to satisfy his wife. He was an idealist, accepting legal cases where the remuneration was poor; dropping out of the government because of a disagreement with Asquith, who had turned venomously against the vote for women.

After ten years of marriage, therefore, Melanie found herself an admired beauty, a much sought-after woman about town with a substantial income of her own, but with a husband whom she neither loved nor respected because she felt he was only half a man, and who had failed to achieve either fame or riches to justify his promise.

On a day in the spring of 1912 Melanie took her accustomed long time over her toilet in preparation for a call on Rachel, who had moved into Askham House after a little redecoration, a few replacements of the furniture which she otherwise left in exactly the same position that the revered Phyllida had wanted it and the formidable Dulcie had left it. Rachel felt that probably her daughter-in-law would do the same, such was the power of tradition in the Askham family.

Rachel wanted to be in London because her interest in journalism was turning into a full-time occupation. She enjoyed being at the heart of things, taking part in union meetings in Clement's Inn, or discussions with the rival Women's Freedom League formed by Mrs Despard and her associates.

St John's Wood, true to its name, was a leafy part of the metropolis with well-spaced houses and broad roads that had gained popularity in the middle of the nineteenth century, because it was near enough to the centre of London yet sufficiently far from it too. Between it and the narrow city streets was the broad, green lung of Regent's Park where, daily, the children's nurses took them for walks, meeting other nurses with similar charges – all well-heeled, well-paid minions of the wealthy.

At thirteen Bobby had gone to Eton, and the others were at home: tomboy Susan and nervous Christopher, and the baby Jordan who seemed to everyone, for some reason no one could quite explain, neither kith nor kin with the others. Jordan was a very beautiful child, vigorous and alert, yet it was clear that his mother detested him and his father had very little time for him. Because he was constantly seeking attention by being naughty, his nurse despaired of him, Nanny was always devising ingenious punishments for him, and all this despite the fact that he was only three years old. Nurse Horner would tell Nanny Stewart that Jordan was bad; bad blood there somewhere and nothing good would come of him. Nanny, for no clear reason that she knew, was inclined to agree.

Melanie, standing in front of her mirror, was putting on her hat when Adam came into her bedroom.

'Couldn't you knock?' Melanie enquired brusquely, looking at him over her shoulder.

'I'm sorry.' Adam stopped as though he'd been caught trespassing.

'You're always sorry, that's your trouble.' Melanie gave her hat a sharp twist bringing the curled brim over the centre of her forehead, her fingers sweeping along the large ostrich plume at the back.

'I wondered if I could give you a lift into town? I'm just leaving.'

'Oh?' Melanie considered the matter.

'Or may I not know where you're going?'

'I'm going to see your sister, Lady Askham, as a matter of fact. I must say, though, that I can never get used to calling her by that title.'

'Why?'

Melanie glanced scornfully at him. 'She doesn't deserve it, does she? Who is she? Nobody.'

'Why visit her then? You're beginning to sound just like your mother.'

'Well, my mother was right. Rachel is getting too big for her boots. She practically runs Bosco's paper . . .'

'He seems quite pleased by that . . .'

'Ah, but is he?' Melanie drew on her gloves, gazing critically at herself once more, turning her head this way and that to see the new hat at a different angle.

'Oh, you mean the woman's place; in the home?' Adam put his hands in his pockets and swayed back on his heels.

'Don't be absurd, Adam. You know I don't mean that.' She looked at him sharply and walked towards the door.

'You said it once to Denton Rigby. At the Lightermans'.'

Melanie turned swiftly on her heels and stopped. 'And, please, never, *ever* mention that name to me again. Never, do you hear?'

Not for the first time Adam wondered why.

Adam had little skill at doing physical things. He was

clumsy with his hands and, consequently, bad at driving a motorcar. Melanie did it much better, but it would not be done to be seen at the wheel with her husband in the passenger seat. There were things that were done and not done, and this was decidedly not done. A lady was driven – even if she enjoyed driving the car down country lanes where no one could see her. Melanie wanted a chauffeur and constantly bickered and argued with Adam over this minor piece of extravagance. In fact their whole style of living was affected by the gap created between Melanie's demands and what Adam felt they could afford.

'I want to pop in and pick up Flora.' Adam steered the heavy Bugatti, that Melanie had insisted on buying, along Avenue Road towards the park.

'Always "picking up Flora",' Melanie chanted. 'Whatever would you do without her?'

'I sometimes wonder,' Adam reached down the side of the car to apply the brake before turning into Regent's Park.

'You should have married Flora,' Melanie lifted her face towards the burgeoning buds on the trees under which they were passing. In the distance they could see the profusion of purple and yellow crocuses spreading towards the lakeside like a carpet. For no particular reason – for he had seen it many times since – the sight reminded Adam of that foggy night so many years before when Bosco had suggested that he marry Flora, and he had replied by telling him of his love for Melanie. 'Well?' she looked sharply at him when he didn't reply.

'I loved you.'

'I notice the past tense: "loved".' And as Adam kept his hands on the wheel, his eyes firmly on the road again without rising to the bait, she said: 'We can get a divorce if you wish.'

'I don't wish. Do you?'

As he looked at her the car veered slightly off course and he rapidly rotated the wheel to straighten it again.

'I don't know,' Melanie said. 'I have wondered, I must say. We certainly don't seem to get on very well, but the scandal bothers me.'

'Is that all that bothers you? Not four children?'

'Yes, frankly,' Melanie said, her eyes narrowed on the road. 'The scandal bothers me more. They say children can adapt to their parents' separation quite happily. A lot more people are doing it now. I think *we* would be happier living apart; but I would never be received at Court as a divorced woman, and you know that kind of thing is important to me.'

'Well, if it is you are best off as you are. I will certainly never divorce you unless you wish it, as I've told you before. For my part I think the children are important and come first. We can live our lives very well, as they are.'

'That's it then,' Melanie said joining her hands comfortably in her lap, as though it was a pleasant day's outing and she were merely enjoying the view.

When they arrived at George Street Adam hooted, but as Flora did not appear at the window he got out of the car and knocked on the door, which was opened at last by the maid Mary.

'Lady Flora said would you wait for her, sir? She's gone to get a paper.'

'A paper?' Adam said irritably, looking at his wife who was tapping her feet on the floor of the car.

'Something very important she says, sir.'

'I'm not waiting,' Melanie called. 'I'm already late. I see little enough of Rachel, as it is, and she'll be angry to be kept waiting, now that she's a countess.'

Adam looked agitatedly up and down the road as if uncertain what to do. He was by nature instinctively polite, and Melanie's habit of bullying him meant that he either bullied back or conformed. Being a gentleman he rarely bullied. Tired of this customary – as she saw it – vacillation Melanie climbed impatiently out of the car.

'You can *never* make up your mind, can you? Call me a cab please, Mary, or I'll be late for Lady Askham.' And obediently Mary ran all the way along George Street to Baker Street returning in a minute with a hansom, while Adam patiently endured Melanie's taunts about Flora being more important to him than she was.

'Oh, for God's sake be quiet,' he said at last and turning his back on her went into the house, mounting the stairs to the first-floor study where Flora had all her papers and documents stacked as Rachel used to in the old days.

After a few moments he heard Melanie's cab departing, and gratefully he sat back at ease in a large chair to wait for Flora. It was so peaceful here away from Melanie's continual nattering, her complaints, veiled accusations and insinuations. He knew she was a deeply unhappy woman and also, now, that they had never been suited. But too late, too late. As he heard the door downstairs open and Flora's light footfall running up the stairs he experienced a brief flash of happiness that he thought was past long ago. He got up to welcome her with all the enthusiasm of an anxious lover.

'Melanie couldn't wait,' he said as she came through the door.

'No matter.' Flora was somehow unusually brisk and purposeful peeling off her gloves, which she'd donned even for the five-minute walk to Baker Street Station and back. She was still spinsterish, meticulous and precise; but he didn't mind. He loved her. 'There's something terrible in the paper about Bosco.' Flora looked worried. 'Billy Carstairs rang me from *The Sentinel* to warn me. He feels that one of us, you or I or both, should tell

Rachel personally before she hears it from someone else. She will have a terrible shock. Bosco too. Who's to tell him?'

The little group gathered round the fireplace at Askham House was distinctly funereal. Except for the fact that they were not in black they could just have come back from one of the many mournful ceremonies the family graced with such depressing regularity.

'It's Adrian Hastings again,' Adam shook out the badly printed news-sheet and read it aloud for the fourth or fifth time as though, somehow, each time it would sound better. 'I recognize his style.'

'Revenge,' Rachel murmured stooping to poke the fire. Melanie sat stiffly in the corner, still in her coat and chic new hat, her face so grave that one would have suspected the matter was more damaging to her than anyone else. In a way she felt it was, because she cared more than anyone else about appearances.

'Someone will have to tell Mama,' she said.

'Best kept from Mama as long as we can,' Flora commented. 'In fact very few people may see it. Whoever has heard of the *World City Argus*?'

Adam shook his head. 'I never did, I must say.'

'No one will read it. It'll all blow over.'

'Not a chance,' Adam glanced at the paper again. 'These allegations, however obscure, are far far too damaging. Bosco will definitely have to sue this time.' And, as if to himself, he read:

Interesting material comes to your correspondent about THE EARL OF ASKHAM who, until he succeeded his father in 1911, was VISCOUNT GORE. Before that he was LIEUTENANT BOSCO DOWN of the 21st Lancers, a regiment which took part in the magnificent Battle of Omdurman.

All this may seem a very long time ago, but the item is linked with one that appeared some years ago in *The Sentinel and Echo* newspaper where the writer referred to the fascination that DULCIE, LADY ASKHAM, the present Earl's mother, and LADY MELANIE BOLINGBROKE, his sister, had felt for the opposite sex. There was also reference to an incident where the then VISCOUNT GORE, apparently intentionally, brought down LORD DENTON RIGBY on the polo field in retaliation for the attentions he was paying to his mother and sister.

The news that reaches your correspondent is that by curious chance a similar incident occurred during the Battle of Omdurman when the then LIEUTENANT DOWN was responsible for the death of CAPTAIN CARDEW CRYSTAL, on secondment from the Egyptian Cavalry, who had been seen to pay a great deal of overt attention to the Lieutenant's then young and beautiful mother. It is said that LIEUTENANT DOWN confessed to LORD CROMER his culpability in the matter and his lordship ordered an investigation which was subsequently hushed up by LORD KITCHENER OF KHARTOUM, Lieutenant Down's commanding officer, with the connivance of LORD CROMER, both friends of the family.

Isn't life strange?

It was unsigned but appeared as an item of gossip in a section called 'Straggler's Tales'. There were other similarly scurrilous paragraphs about well-known people – actors, actresses, politicians, socialites, but none as damaging as this.

'Yes, sue,' Adam concluded, glancing round, 'punitive damages.'

'But why should he do this *now*?' Melanie moaned. 'What purpose can it possibly serve?'

'As Rachel said, revenge,' Adam replied. 'Bosco got him sacked from *The Sentinel*.'

'But that was *years* ago!'

'He would still be brooding, thirsting for blood. Maybe he just heard it from somewhere.'

'I wonder where?' Rachel went to the fireplace,

thoughtfully pulling the bell. 'I must go to Berkeley Square and tell Bosco myself.'

'Isn't Hampstead too near Lady Melanie?' Nimet enquired, looking down from the top of the tall building to the Square below.

Bosco shook his head. 'It's quite a long way from St John's Wood, in a different direction.'

'And you really like the house?'

'I really love it.'

'I shall go, then.' Nimet came over to him and sat on his knee while his hand caressed the soft rotundity of her stomach. 'You really are happy about the baby, aren't you, Bosco?'

'Very.' Bosco's hand continued its soothing action.

'I thought you'd be furious.'

'I believe it was meant. As long as you can bear it alone, Nimet, I can too. I will give you every support I can . . . short of marriage.'

'I know that. I can't expect marriage and I never have – but a house of my own!' As she clasped her hands her eyes seemed to sparkle. 'That *will* be wonderful.'

Bosco put his arms around her and leaned his head over her shoulder.

'Why don't you tell me the truth?'

'What truth?'

'What you do. Where you live. I assure you I shan't mind.'

'What's the point?'

'But I want to know. I want to know all about you. You tantalize me, Nimet.'

'Isn't that part of my charm?' She glanced coquettishly at him, turning her head slightly so that he could see the gentle slant of her eyes. He knew she was more beautiful than she had been thirteen years before, because maturity, which made some people fade, had brought to her its own special kind of allure. How old was she now? Thirty, thirty-five? Thinking thus he felt fearful for her. How would she cope on her own? Would she be truly well and properly looked after? What consequences were there for her – for him?

A bell connected the hall with the small flat at the top of the house which very few people even knew about. As this rang Bosco felt a tremor of alarm because the butler only ever used it in emergency.

'Yes?' He lifted the mouthpiece to his ear, holding the thick heavy wire in his hand, still gazing at Nimet.

'Lady Askham is just arriving outside the house, sir. She has come by cab and is paying the driver.'

'Thank you. I'll be down directly.'

'Lady Askham?' Nimet rose and impulsively put her hands over her face as if to ward off bad news. 'She knows?'

'Why should she know?'

'But why has she come?'

'That I don't know. It must be something personal if she didn't use the phone.'

'It's about me.'

'We'll see.'

'What shall I do, Bosco? Oh darling, what *shall* I do?'

'Stay here, Nimet,' Bosco's voice was very brisk, yet soothing. 'There is no need at all for her to come up here. She can't possibly know.'

Bosco kissed her and, quickly opening the door that led to the small flight of stairs on to the main corridor of the third floor, he went down them and from there to the first floor where he had his study, just in time to greet Rachel.

As she saw him walk quickly, almost furtively, along the corridor there was something about Bosco that rather disturbed Rachel. His face was flushed and his hair, normally immaculately brushed and neatly parted, was in disorder. He was smoothing it back with both hands as he saw her and even then he looked startled and, she thought, slightly guilty, as though he'd been caught out in something.

'Rachel, what are you doing here?' He quickly lit a cigarette, nervously tossing the match into a tray on his desk.

'Why are you so agitated, Bosco? Have you seen it?'

'What?'

Rachel removed her hat and sat down slowly on the sofa as though she had plenty of time. 'Sit down, Bosco,' she said, patting the place beside her. 'I'm afraid I have something unpleasant to tell you.'

'For God's sake, what is it?' Bosco's tone puzzled her and, as he stood leaning over his desk staring down at her, she looked at him in astonishment.

'Then what *are* you so agitated about?'

'And what are you?'

'This,' Rachel handed the cutting from the newspaper to him. 'From your manner, I thought you'd seen it already.'

Drawing on his cigarette Bosco sat down, crossed one leg over the other and read the paper slowly. Behind him the tall trees in the Square waved gently as if welcoming the spring.

'Adrian Hastings,' he said putting it down before him after a long pause. 'Hastings, for sure. Well, well.'

'Adam says you must sue.'

'Of course I'll sue. But why now?' Bosco went leisurely over to the window and, leaning against it, looked out into the Square. 'Where did he get this stale information from, and why rake it up now?'

'Oh my darling, I'm so sorry.' Rachel quickly rose and, going over to him, put her arms around his neck. As she did she was aware of a faint hint of spice or essential oils, a vaguely oriental fragrance and she pressed her nose to Bosco's jacket, inhaling it.

Some other arms than hers, she felt sure, had been round his shoulder that day.

CHAPTER 19

From the window at the top of *The Sentinel* building it was possible to see up Ludgate Hill to St Paul's surrounded by the narrow little streets on one side and on the other, sloping down to the riverside wharves, merchants' offices and warehouses containing goods of all kinds. These ranged from wines, ropes, tallow, spices, to foods from different parts of the world, and the essential oils used in the making of perfumes and scents.

Rachel was not conventionally religious, except in the sense that, when at Askham, she always went to Sunday church. Nevertheless she often found uplift and inspiration from the sight of that noble monument with its twin turrets, its leaden dome, the single golden cross reaching skywards, as she sat in her tiny office, sucking the top of her pen, planning her articles. Sometimes it almost seemed as though she were praying for guidance to say the right things.

For the cause of women's suffrage was in crisis, a crisis so profound that she despaired of its eventual realization of its goal. It had split into too many little groups and factions and there was a new, disturbing element of violence that not only undermined her faith in the virtue of their ideal but also that of many others. After many years of cooperation, the Pankhursts and the Pethwick-Lawrences had split. Rachel was on the side of the Pethwick-Lawrences who abhorred the more extreme manifestations of violence now embraced with an enthusiastic intolerance by the Pankhursts and their more fanatical followers.

From the disruption of meetings, demonstrations and hunger strikes the militants had now progressed to actual destruction of property; stone-throwing, burning buildings and smashing windows, and even if she were not the Countess of Askham Rachel felt she could never ever condone or follow such anarchic behaviour.

So she applied her pen and her rhetorical gifts to trying to deflect the move away from self-destruction. The suffragettes were increasingly alienating their friends, even those politicians like Lloyd George and Winston Churchill who had once believed in the justice of their Cause. As Mrs Despard, who sided with the Pethwick-Lawrences, had written in *The Vote* the previous March: 'We have not the least respect for plate-glass windows or for the usual British idea of "respectability" and "womanliness", but we care too deeply for our Cause to endanger that chance of success, however slender that chance might be.'

Rachel now took up this theme for her article, and drew a neat line under the heading *The Slender Chance*.

The Conciliation Bill which was recently defeated by a mere fourteen votes in the House of Commons has shown what harm the militants in our movement have done to the suffrage cause. For we women wish only for our rights, not the destruction of society, and if we are to preserve the institutions that we hold dear it is to the House of Commons, with its rich traditions of democracy and fair play, that we must look if we are ever to achieve our aims. The Bill was supported by a Conservative and a Liberal who tried with great skill to disentangle the principle of the justice of our Cause from the harm the militants are doing to it. Yet it was not helped by the disorderly conduct of the member for Oxford University (Lord Hugh Cecil) who shouted down the Prime Minister, thus helping to ensure the defeat of the Bill.

To those who have worked for so long and so hard for the Cause this is a bitter blow; for the spirit of the Mother of Parliaments is turning from support for the Cause to downright antagonism.

When the Liberal government was returned to power in 1906 what high hopes we had. There were over 400 members in the House of Commons who could be said to support the principle of votes for women, yet how have their numbers dwindled. It is true that the government has reneged on its promises, crushed our ideals, but . . .

Sensing a movement behind her Rachel turned and saw Flora looking over her shoulder.

'Sorry, dearest,' she said, her hand on Rachel's arm. 'Am I disturbing you?'

Rachel flung down her pen and stretched, glad of the break.

'I'm just trying to get some sense into the violent militants in the movement; but what can one do? A faint, small voice among so many. If we go on like this we shall never see justice in this century.'

'Oh, we shall,' Flora sat down, smoothing her long grey skirt over her knees, 'I am *convinced* that we shall.'

'But how?'

'War,' Flora said calmly, taking out a cigarette and lighting it.

'War? What kind of war?'

'Between nations. Adam is convinced we shall have war with Germany within five years.'

'Oh, that rumour of war has been going on ever since I can remember. They said when King Edward died that the Kaiser would invade but he never did.'

'He was not strong enough then. But he is getting stronger every day. The German war machine is making such rapid strides that soon its numbers will exceed ours. They will have more ships than we have, more guns and more men.'

'But that doesn't mean to say Germany wants to go to war with England! The Kaiser is a cousin of the King. How close he is to our Royal family. I simply can't believe it.'

'Germany is too ambitious, too envious of England, too greedy for conquest on the continent. Now we have a war in the Balkans, on Germany's doorstep. The whole of Europe is becoming unsettled and, in Adam's view and mine, will soon be aflame.'

'Oh Flora,' Rachel said horrified. 'I don't know how you can talk like that. Bosco and Adam would be involved.'

'Only if they wished it. They will be too old at first.'

'But how will war get us the vote?'

'Because women will show what they can do. You'll see. The whole world will change.'

'Well I, for one, hope that it may be peacefully yet, somehow, this violence of normally law-abiding women does seem like a harbinger of what might come. You've made me go quite cold.' Rachel hugged herself, rubbing her arms to dispel the goose-flesh. 'I can't in my heart believe that we shall *ever* have war.'

'Well, Adam thinks . . .' Flora hesitated, as if aware of the number of times Adam's name came into the conversation these days. It was always what Adam thought or Adam was doing or saying.

Flora's growing reputation as an Egyptologist had almost sunk beneath the weight of the unpaid work she was doing on behalf of Adam and the Cause. Adam's concern about money, his care not to lay a finger on any of Melanie's, made his life style one of the utmost frugality. As a young barrister he was still poorly paid and his unpaid work for the women's movement, his unstinting and unremitting care for his less well-off constituents meant that much of his time was unremunerated. Flora had taught herself to type so that she could act as his secretary for most of his work.

'Adam thinks?' Rachel prompted gently.

'Adam thinks we shall be involved in war and that, at the moment, we are unprepared.'

Rachel rose from her desk and walked to the window,

her head bent in thought. She loved her brother and she loved Flora, but she did not like the fact that, all too clearly, they loved each other. Perhaps she, more than anyone, observing them closely and seeing the amount of time they spent working together, knew the depth and extent of their relationship. But how far it had actually progressed she didn't know.

'Are you and Adam lovers?' she asked, her back turned to Flora, her eyes on the dome of St Paul's, stark and simple in its boldness against the brilliant washed-blue of the spring sky. 'I know it's no business of mine but . . .'

'It *is* your business.' Flora's reply was so soft as to be scarcely audible. 'And the answer is that we are not. But we do love each other.'

'Yes, I know that and – Oh!' Rachel extended her arms and ran over to Flora, hugging her. 'Oh! I'm *glad*. Glad that you have each other but glad you aren't lovers. I know the physical thing may not seem very important,' she looked into Flora's eyes, 'and yet at the same time it is.'

'I know it is, and that's why we aren't lovers. Adam is too fine a man to be unfaithful to Melanie in that way and yet – ' Flora gazed across Rachel's shoulder ' – I know they do not share a bed, and have not for a long time.

'Besides,' she continued, 'anything more between us would be impossible – even were Melanie to die, which God grant she won't, for a very long time. I could never, ever contemplate that kind of physical relationship with my sister's husband, whatever the circumstances.'

She parted from Rachel and, perching against the large oval table littered with papers and books where Rachel worked, went on, 'I am very happy at the way things are between Adam and me. I *do* feel fulfilled as a woman. To be needed by him, and to be able to help him the way I can is of the greatest satisfaction to me. He fills my life with a kind of radiance it didn't have before. See,' she ran her hand through her hair, no longer scraped back into a spinsterly bun, but waved and coiffeured by Melanie's chic hairdresser in Bruton Street, 'I take more care of my appearance because it pleases Adam. I look at clothes with an eye to what he'd like. I only wear my glasses when working – they aren't really necessary, you know.' She removed them with a smile and twirled them about in her hand, the sunlight glancing on the fine gold rims.

Rachel knew how attractive Flora could be if she wished and, in fact, the change had been noticed not only by her but many others in the past year. Flora was thin, her face scholarly, her disposition grave. She would never be another Melanie, nor another Dulcie Askham but, in her own quiet way, she had a grace and dignity, a kind of beauty that neither of the others had.

Rachel went across and, once again, she hugged her.

'I'm so glad we had this talk. May I tell Bosco about it? He will be happy too.'

Bosco too felt content that morning as he prepared to go to the office in Berkeley Street which was nearing completion as the headquarters of Askham Developments. He and Rachel had settled easily and quickly into having the house in St James's Square as their main home – the Grange was kept for weekends and long holidays. The children were in London with their parents too, six-year-old Ralph being tutored upstairs at this very moment, Charlotte and the twins still in the nursery with their nurses and Nanny Mackintosh who had come to them after seeing the Kitto children all grown up.

It was a happy, peaceful family home; the home of a successful man, the activities of whose intelligent wife were much talked about in the different circles among which he moved. The movement for women's suffrage was accepted as one that was not only here to stay but would, inevitably, one day be realized. Even if it took fifty years it would happen, perhaps when they were all dead and their children forced the issue through. But meanwhile, in the madness and confusion brought about by the extremists among the female militants, Rachel's voice was considered a moderating, sensible influence and her column in *The Sentinel*, which dwelt not only on women's issues but other political matters as well, was read with approval and interest.

A woman political commentator was a new phenomenon in the modern newspaper world although it was not altogether new in journalism or literature. But few alive recalled Harriet Martineau and her *Tales of Political Economy* which were trailblazers for thoughtful, intelligent women some sixty years before. There was Mrs Webb and her clever husband, Sidney, supporters of the Labour Party and founders of the Fabian Society to which Rachel also belonged. The Webbs with the Pethwick-Lawrences, the Shaws and Mrs Despard, had been dinner guests only a few evenings before.

How nice it was, Bosco thought, tying his tie and completing his toilet, to be able to entertain the intelligentsia one evening and hard-headed car manufacturers from Detroit another.

Bosco had already read all the papers and been riding in the Row that morning and now, at eleven, he had finished dressing in a new morning suit, black tail coat and striped trousers, delivered by his Savile Row tailors only the day before.

'Very nice, my lord,' his valet, Farrow, said approvingly, brushing the noble shoulders to ensure not a speck of dust remained. 'And that tie does, indeed, suit it very well sir, as her ladyship said.'

'Her ladyship is always right, Farrow!' Bosco laughed

and, after combing his hair and moustache and patting his cheeks with toilet water, tucking a handkerchief in his breast pocket and threading the chain of his gold repeater, a legacy from his father, through his waistcoat button, was ready.

He was about to go to the door, Farrow regarding him not only with approval but some pride as well – for had he not transformed the Earl from a rather raw, careless captain in the Lancers to the elegant man of affairs he now was? – when the butler, Bromwich, after a discreet knock, opened it and seeing Bosco a foot or two away, bowed.

'There is a lady downstairs to see you, my lord.'

'A lady?' Bosco looked interested. 'Who?'

'She would not give her name, my lord. She asked first for Lady Askham and when I said her ladyship was not in she asked for you. A foreign lady, sir,' Bromwich said with a slight wrinkling of the nose as though that somehow made her not quite *comme il faut*.

Bosco's thoughts immediately flew to Nimet who, of course, would not give her name, though why should she ask for Rachel? Why should she come at all?

'I'll see her at once,' Bosco glanced again at himself in the mirror before hurrying downstairs ahead of the stately butler who, needless to say, would never have dreamt of increasing his pace and who thus forfeited his privilege and duty of throwing open the door and announcing his employer.

Bosco stood on the threshold and looked at the silhouette outlined against the window. She wore a long, loose-fitting three-quarter-length apricot-coloured coat, the hem and the collar edged with fur over a hobble skirt slit at the sides and narrow towards the ankle. Her matching felt hat was covered with a spotted veil which completely concealed her face. But still he was able to recognize her immediately. For not by one iota, in face, expression or figure – unless perhaps she was just a trifle stouter – had Madame Hassim changed since he last saw her in Cairo thirteen years before.

'What are you doing here?' Bosco said impolitely, closing the door behind him.

'Really, my lord, is that the way to address a lady?'

'"Lady",' Bosco taunted. 'My God, you call yourself a *lady*?'

'I think you should modulate your voice a little,' Madame Hassim said loftily, advancing slowly across the room like a predatory lizard. 'You might not wish your servants to hear what I have to say.'

'Nor have *I* any wish to hear what you have to say. It wouldn't interest me in the slightest, I assure you. Get out.'

Bosco pointed towards the door, turning to open it, when a gloved hand was placed on his arm, the face of his visitor, only three or four inches from his, wearing an unmistakable look of menace.

'I shouldn't do that, Bosco Down. For it is as Bosco Down I remember you, not the fine, substantial gentleman of obvious affluence you have now become.'

Bosco roughly freed his arm from her odious clasp and leaning against the door, his hand still on the handle, said: 'You were paid off handsomely, Madame Hassim, and undertook never to let me hear from you again. I will have you thrown out of the country.'

'Oh, but I have lived here for some years, Lord Askham. That will not be so easy. It may not be very pleasant for you, either, to have to explain why.'

Knowing that she had his attention she strolled, with as much grace as she could within the confines of her narrow skirt, to a chair and, sitting down, unfastened her bag and produced a long amber holder into which she inserted a thick Turkish cigarette she procured from a case. All this was done with the maximum waste of time and it seemed like several minutes before Madame Hassim addressed Bosco again, pointing to a chair opposite her.

'Do sit down. It will be more comfortable if you hear me out, and quicker too. I don't know when your dear wife is expected home.'

Bosco grudgingly did as she asked, noting the emphasis on the word 'dear' and, as he did, a horrible thought struck him.

'Is that why you asked for her?'

'I asked if she was at home. Of course I would have gone away if she had been. It is not her I came to see.'

'You could have telephoned me or sent a note.'

'Ah, but I knew you would not receive me, Bosco. I know what sort of man you are.'

'I wish you would call me Lord Askham,' Bosco said frigidly. 'I dislike the use of the familiar from a creature like you.'

'Really?' Madame Hassim raised her eyebrows, carefully putting the tip of her cigarette holder through one of the gaps in her veil and sucking at it thoughtfully. Immediately her attitude recalled to Bosco's mind the scene in the house in Cairo where he had first become ensnared by Nimet.

Nimet! At the very thought of her he started inwardly to tremble, knowing how inevitable it was now that there was a connection between her and the visit by Madame Hassim.

'Yes, Nimet,' Madame Hassim nodded removing her holder uncannily, as if reading his thoughts. 'Did you never connect the two of us together in London?'

'Never,' Bosco said and Madame Hassim thought briefly, triumphantly, that she detected a sob in his voice.

'Of course she wouldn't tell you, but then she was never very honest. She hasn't been honest with you now, has she, Bosco?' She made the emphasis on his name sound like insolence.

'So you know all about that?' Bosco felt an agitation in his breast which he had difficulty in recalling ever having experienced before. He had known anger, fear and apprehension but he had never before had the impression of a void opening beneath his feet – a void which would yet reveal things he'd prefer not to know.

'No, *that's* the point,' Madame Hassim said with a shrug of annoyance so that the fine hairs of her fur trembled as though ruffled by a light breeze. 'I didn't know until yesterday, when she informs me that she is not only pregnant but about to leave me. I knew *nothing* of your affair, so skilfully did she hide it from me. I felt her liaison was with the Conte da Ponte and, as she regularly paid me sums of money – got from you, I expect – I had no reason to question that. The Count has his own comfortable establishment in Portman Square. Nimet never liked a number of clients at a time,' she paused momentarily, noting with pleasure the anguish on Bosco's face. 'You have at least that consolation, if it is any. I don't know.'

'Then how did you know it was me?' Bosco's knuckles were white as his hands clasped the arms of his chair, and he strained forward as if about to spring at her.

'I had to beat it out of her, of course.'

'You *what*?' Bosco rose and advanced swiftly across the room, his hands outstretched, finally, for Madame Hassim's throat. When he was within a foot of her she held up a hand as though able, by some magical artifice, to put an impenetrable, invisible wall between them.

'Pray control yourself, Bosco, and listen. Go back to your chair.'

Bosco stared at her and then returned, slumping back into his seat like a whipped, deflated cur.

'I didn't beat her very hard, of course, knowing her

condition. A few strokes of a cane on the palms of her hand were sufficient to show her I meant business. She told me that she had had a liaison with you for a number of months. That she met you by chance one night at Quaglino's and that it was you she visited, not Conte da Ponte, and that the child she expected, and wanted, was yours. She is such a foolish girl.' Madame shook her head and, expelling the stump of her cigarette, fitted a fresh one into her holder. 'Woman, I should say, for she is not as young as she looks. I suppose she didn't tell you how old she was either? It is for this reason she wishes to bear the child, she says, because she might not have the chance to have another. She also said she was in love with you – which I must say I found amusing – and always has been. You were the only man who had apparently ever aroused any real emotion in her heart which, for the whore she is, is quite an achievement, I suppose.'

Bosco felt tears start to his eyes. Tears he had never known since his father died. Fresh, salty tears that stung his eyes and which he brushed quickly away.

'Yes, she is a whore, Bosco,' the Cairene continued mercilessly. 'One of my best. Most men, in time, become infatuated with her. She was, as she told you, a girl of good parentage, but she was illegitimate and neither her father nor mother wanted her. Her father was indeed a sheikh, but he never saw her from the day she was born. Her mother was one of my girls, a very beautiful Nubian who had Persian blood in her, hence Nimet's quite remarkable looks. I must say,' Madame Hassim drew on her cigarette, a nostalgic look on her raddled face, 'I have always had a soft spot for Nimet and she, I think in her heart, for me. She is inventive, imaginative, beautiful, very. But for her lamentable origins she might have had a very good life. Now she feels that as the mistress of an earl she will have one. And do you know,' she looked at him keenly, her dark venomous eyes glinting oddly through her veil, 'I do not begrudge it her. I will allow her her freedom, but you will have to pay.'

'This is not a country where slaves are tolerated,' Bosco said in a thick voice. 'I will not pay you one penny more in blood money. I will have you deported from the country. I will . . .'

'Pray do not bore me with these tedious words,' Madame Hassim put up her gloved hand to stifle a long, artificial yawn. 'You know quite well you will do nothing of the kind. As I blackmailed you before, I am ready to do so again. Never fear. Lord Cromer is still alive and so is Lord Kitchener. You are a member of the House of Lords, I hear. Well, your fellow peers will all hear of this. Everyone will hear of it, if I have my way. And even if I am expelled from the country, which I don't doubt you have the power to do, I will have my revenge. Your dear wife, above all. Does she know?' Looking at the discomfiture on his face she smiled. 'I doubt it. I doubt it very much indeed. *That* will be your downfall, Bosco, and seeing you now, looking at you and this,' Madame Hassim gestured around at the elegant room and its fine furnishings, 'I doubt if that is something you'll enjoy. You already, I understand, have a court case coming up. You will not wish for another.'

'How do you know that?' Bosco demanded, but Madame Hassim laughed and put her finger to her heavily made-up lips.

'Secrets, secrets,' she whispered, 'and now to business.' She glanced at the watch on her wrist and raised her eyes to peer out of the window.

'Is Lady Askham shopping or . . .'

'Hurry up, hurry up,' Bosco said, beset by a feeling of urgency.

'Of course I wish substantial payment to compensate for

Nimet's loss, and also freedom from prosecution. No one must know who I am or what I do. I am not known as Madame Hassim here either, and I will not tell you my name. I came here with a French passport and am known as a respectable Frenchwoman.'

'Respectable!' Bosco scoffed. 'I doubt that. The police are not as silly as you think.'

'They are very silly indeed, as a matter of fact.' Madame Hassim looked at him with surprise. 'It would astonish you to know how silly. My house is run, and managed, very discreetly; it is tucked away in a modest part of London, and no one is at all the wiser, I assure you. I have three or four girls and my business is run decorously.'

'And Nimet was part of all this?'

Madame Hassim smiled. 'You find it incredible, do you not? Do you know, I really think she'll miss me. I hope she will come and see me, with the baby of course, from time to time.'

Bosco raised a fist and shook it at her and she waved at him, as if telling him to be quiet.

'I want five thousand pounds paid in notes of the realm now, and an annuity of five hundred paid, also in notes, in a way I will instruct you after you agree. In exchange I will deliver Nimet to you – for she is my prisoner and has no way of communicating with you now – and that will be that.'

'You will go on and on and on,' Bosco jumped up again, continuing to shake his fist. 'I know you.'

'No, I assure you, with that money I shall be perfectly content. Nimet is not as young as she was, and my other girls are not only prettier but more willing, more adaptable. I am reluctant to part with her because I have had her since a young girl. She grew up with me, and I shall miss her. I hate to make this transaction – a happy event for both of you, I'm sure – sound so commercial, but that is my price for Nimet. My word is my bond.'

She sat back folding her hands on her ample lap and gazing at him with the kind of determination he knew he would never shift.

'How do I pay the money?' Bosco asked.

Yes, Bosco would be happy, Rachel thought, when, an hour or two after she and Flora had parted, she left the building to return to St James's Square. Flora had gone back to George Street to work on the draft of a speech for Adam, and Rachel finished her article. That night there was to be a dinner for some American car manufacturers from Detroit who were advising Bosco on the development of the new Askham motorcar being built at a plant near Winchester, upon which all the available Askham and Lighterman capital was now being directed.

It was nearly noon and, as she hurried along Fleet Street, the clock on St Paul's chimed the hour. The newspaper offices were disgorging their workers into the street for lunch: clerks and office girls, secretaries and typists, typesetters and printworkers who repaired to the cafés and restaurants, the public houses and eating-places which had sprung up in the last ten years since Fleet Street had become the printing heart of the metropolis.

Passing Temple Bar and the Law Courts Rachel thought of the court case which would be held there as soon as the wheels of the law, which could move so slowly, were hurried along. Adam was working on the case in his chambers. He would not be taking part because he was a crucial witness for Bosco, but a leading silk had been engaged. There was some excitement about the case in legal circles because of who was taking part and the fact that it went back so many years. Lord Cromer was being called for Bosco and there was also some surprise that the paper had not agreed to settle because it would be an expensive action and there seemed little doubt who would win. Bosco, with all the Askham money, could well afford to sue, but it was wondered where the seedy *World City Argus* and its down-at-heel reporter could find the money. Some thought that there were sinister goings-on behind the scenes, that money from Cairo was involved, and rumours circulated through both legal and social circles in London that did Bosco no good at all. They were anxious to bring the case to court.

But it was worrying, Rachel thought, as she hurried past the Law Courts into the Strand, and she would be glad when it was called. Bosco appeared unperturbed by the whole thing and went about his business and his many affairs, his engagements and his tours around various Askham properties in the country, with his usual calm and humour. In fact Bosco seemed particularly happy. The days of the tension between herself and his mother were shelved, if not exactly over. A *modus vivendi* had been established by which they saw each other infrequently, and were civil if not warm when they did.

Then they had their happy home, he and she, their four adorable healthy, spirited children and Rachel had her work away from the home which she enjoyed. She was an independent woman, a presence in public life. And finally, and her steps quickened as she thought of this, they had their love and what a firm, strong, enduring bond that had proved to be. What a lucky, fortunate woman she was. As Rachel turned from Pall Mall into St James's Square, having completed her brisk walk in the late spring sunshine in half an hour, she gave a deep, heartfelt sigh of satisfaction.

It was then that she saw a woman hurry down the stairs of Askham House, a woman elegantly dressed, clutching her fashionable coat across her bosom and carrying an expensive lizardskin handbag. When she got to the bottom of the steps she looked, almost furtively, first one way and then another, like a thief, before she walked quickly across St James's Square towards Duke of York Street and disappeared from sight.

Rachel slowed down and walked thoughtfully, almost fearfully, across the Square, having approached it from a different direction from the one taken by the woman. She remembered the faint odour of, she had been sure, perfume on Bosco's shoulder that day in Berkeley Square. As she drew nearer the house she saw Bosco looking down from the first-floor drawing-room window in the direction which the woman had taken. When he saw her he started, made as if to back away but, aware that she had seen him, waved.

Rachel didn't wave back but let herself into the house, gave her coat and hat to Bromwich and walked up the stairs slowly and deliberately, aware of the fast pounding of her heart.

Bosco was still by the window when she walked into the long sunlit room. She had been so richly, contentedly tranquil on that splendid spring day that seemed the harbinger of good things: the season, the parties, the long nights spent dancing, the picnic trips taken by boat with the children along the waters of the Thames from Robertswood.

All this and more seemed to vanish now as though, in a premonition or intimation of farewell to those anticipated pleasures, she stood at the threshold and said in as normal a voice as she could make it: 'Who was that woman?'

Bosco turned slowly, letting the window sash that he held in his hand drop. The dejection and worry on his face so startled her that she wanted to rush up and comfort him but, because of the doubt and suspicion in her mind, she didn't. She remained by the door which she'd now closed, but needed to be near should she wish to escape from some horror, she knew not what.

'I thought you might recognize her,' he sank into a chair, running a hand over his jowl, the hand wearing on the little finger the signet ring she'd given him as a wedding present. The ring on his finger was as symbolic of their union, their trust, as the one on hers.

'Why should I recognize her?' Rachel walked slowly into the room – until she stood in front of Bosco, arms akimbo, gazing at him.

'It was Madame Hassim.'

'Madame Hassim! Oh?' Rachel knelt down on the floor and placed a hand on his knee. 'Oh, what a relief.'

'Relief?' Bosco looked at her with astonishment, clasping her hand in his.

'I thought she might be your mistress!'

'Mistress?' Bosco pressed her hand convulsively. 'Whatever gave you that idea?'

'Some perfume I smelt on you one day, or thought I smelled. It was that day I came to you in Berkeley Square to tell you about the Hastings article.'

'Perfume?' Bosco wrinkled his nose, sad and ashamed that he had to pretend with her, had to hide his guilt. To be so near and yet not to know seemed cruel; but more cruel by far to tell her, and even more difficult to explain how different the two loves were, how complementary to his life, not in conflict with it. He stroked her hand and put it tenderly to his lips.

'I thought your coat smelled of perfume. I was disturbed. There was something about the house . . .' She shook her head. 'But now it seems silly.'

'It was probably some new toilet water I was using.' Bosco brushed his hand again over his chin.

'Yes, that would be it. Certainly I don't think Madame Hassim could be your mistress.'

'That she certainly would not,' Bosco said, almost light-hearted with relief, forgetting his guilt as well as the deep wound she had left.

'But whatever did she want? Was it something to do with the trial?'

Bosco let Rachel's hand fall and, getting up, wandered towards the window, one hand in his pocket, the fingers of the other lightly touching the window-frame as he gazed out again on to the Square.

'She wanted to do me harm, that's all I can tell you. Do you know, my darling,' turning slowly he gazed at her, 'I think that woman really means one day to destroy me.'

'Not while you have me.' Rachel got up and walked over to him, clasping him in her arms. 'I will never, never let her or anyone else bring harm to you. I'm sorry I was suspicious,' she leaned her head against his shoulder. 'I love you so much, frequently thank my good fortune I have you. God knows, with your love and all else that you have given to me I never, never had any reason to doubt you.'

Bosco buried his face in her shoulder and, for the second time that day, his eyes once again filled with tears.

CHAPTER 20

As one progressed up East Heath Road from Belsize Park by carriage, motorcar or on foot, the Heath was on the right side and, to the left, a number of small attractive, narrow streets seemed to dive down into the bowels of Hampstead itself eventually converging, one way and another, on the High Street. These angular passages, leafy cobbled streets with iron horse posts at regular intervals along the uneven pavements, bore such names as Well Walk, Willow Walk, Flask Walk and so on. Hampstead, because it was high, narrow and very old – being, for many years, a village on the outskirts of London – was a place for walking, the width of its streets being sufficient to discourage the carriage or the motorcar.

Not one of the houses in these streets resembled its neighbour, a blessing that was beginning to be appreciated as the century advanced and urban planning, with its dull uniformity, became a symbol not only of wealth but of increasingly rising standards. There were tall houses; fat, rather squat houses; elegant houses with arches and porticoes; and a few cottage-type dwellings clothed in wisteria, honeysuckle, clematis and variegated ivy, approaching which one might imagine oneself to be in the heart of the country.

It was in such a small cottage set back from the cobbled lane and protected by a high hedge, so that one had to stand on tiptoe to see over the top, that Madame Seder lived with her baby, a nurse to help look after it and a maid to do all the housework, including the cooking. Even then the nurse had to sleep with the baby because the little house was so tiny.

Bosco had bought it for Nimet not because he was mean about money but because, as they were on their way down Well Road to view a much larger house, they had passed this delightful habitation, tucked away behind its high privet hedge, which was for sale, and Nimet had immediately decided it was for her or, rather, them. Somehow its very aspect, pink-walled, covered with ivy and honeysuckle, suggested a love nest. She had now lived there for six months, ever since the summer, moving in three months before her baby, Hugo, was born.

Bosco's grandfather had been called Hugh, but a Frenchwoman, newly arrived from France, would surely call her son Hugo? And Madame Seder, obviously wealthy with her good taste and her French maid, was able quickly to merge into being part of the landscape, the anonymity which even a village like Hampstead was able to offer.

She seldom went out, she seldom walked on the Heath or drove to town. Few of her neighbours had ever seen her and not many the gentleman who often came to call, leaving his motor parked in a street a few minutes away from the cottage.

Bosco lay on his back in Nimet's bed listening to the sounds of Hugo crying in the next room. One of the disadvantages of the size of this cottage was the proximity of everything, the noises that travelled, such as the baby's cries, which a man used, as Bosco was, to large rooms and long corridors and privacy whenever he desired it, found very strange.

When one of his children had cried the green baize door between the nursery suites and the rest of the house was shut, drowning the sound from parental ears, and not opened again until they had ceased.

'Is he all right?' Bosco looked anxiously at Nimet who

was braiding her hair in the mirror. She often went around the house with her long hair flowing but, when Bosco came, she braided it into a coil that she twisted round her head in a style part-Grecian but also part-Egyptian, as though she was still reluctant to be parted from those familiar roots.

'Of course he's all right. Have you never heard a baby cry, Bosco?'

'Not often,' Bosco smiled. 'I realized how spoiled I've been, and what I've missed.'

'Missed?' Nimet turned round to look at him, her fingers still in her thick hair.

'Well, Rachel has done her best, but the children were always rather kept away from us. I mean, we see them more than most parents but, still, I don't recall much about their babyhood.' Bosco looked out of the window to where the heavy branches of the magnolia tree in the centre of the small lawn were weighed down by thick frills of January snow, like a Christmas decoration. Bosco's thoughts flew to the Christmas just past which he had spent with a large family party in Wiltshire, while Nimet had been here all alone except for the baby and her small staff, without personal friends.

'Do you feel very lonely here, Nimet? Cut off from the world?'

She went on braiding her hair, her nimble fingers dextrously weaving in and out as she spliced the heavy strands of hair, but her eyes, reflected in the glass, were looking straight at him.

'I'm lonely, but content. I always look forward to seeing you.'

'But you have no friends, no family. I feel very guilty about you, Nimet.'

'Well, you shouldn't.' Nimet finished her hair and walked slowly over to him, sitting by his side on the edge of the bed. 'You have given me so much that I never expected to have – a house of my own, a child. What sort of life did I have with Madame Hassim?'

'You should have contacted me as soon as she brought you to England.'

Nimet tossed back her head, a bright, fixed smile just managing to hide a sarcastic twist of the lips.

'Oh, I would never have *dared*! Besides, I didn't know where you were, how to find you, or what your reaction would have been if I had. It was only when I saw you in Quaglino's that I knew that, despite the past, you and I had never ceased to love each other.'

Bosco drew her down beside him on the bed. 'A year ago, my darling Nimet. What a happy year for me. A happy, successful year blessed with the birth of little Hugo. And yet it is you I worry about, you I feel guilty about. You all alone here . . .' Bosco shook his head and kissed her cheek inhaling that lovely fragrance, that subtle, Arabian essence that for him would always be part of her.

'Do you think it will be forever like this?' Nimet, sinking on to the bed, leaned her head against his shoulder.

'Like what?'

'This, just the two of us? You visiting, me waiting.'

Bosco scratched his head.

'My brother-in-law thinks there'll be war with Germany.'

'War?' Nimet's head flew up and she gazed at him with dark, serious eyes.

'That's what he thinks. Who knows what any of us will do if there's a war? I'm a bit old, but I'll volunteer.'

'Oh, don't *talk* of it!' Nimet put both hands over her eyes. 'I can't bear to think of me here, alone, without you.'

'Don't worry, I'll come back.' Bosco kissed the slim arch of her neck. 'I may not even go away.'

But it was true, the feeling that there would be war between Germany and England began to grow, owing largely to the nature of the conflict in the Balkans and the fear that it would spread to Europe. Winston Churchill warned that if it did, it would have much greater repercussions than were supposed; but when he spoke he envisaged a conflict between Austria and Russia and insisted that the monarchy was the bulwark of peace in Europe. Even he, a visionary in many ways, lacked the power to predict the future.

Despite the ominous rumblings, violence among the suffragists grew as though reflecting the prevailing industrial unrest and discontent among the low paid. Of seven million workers 60 per cent got under thirty shillings as a weekly wage.

There were many who said the aims of the Liberal government had failed, even though the passage of the Contributory Pension Scheme, Lloyd George's great reform, had at last been put into practice despite the attempts of so many with vested interests – including the doctors who didn't think they'd be paid enough – to prevent it.

The preparations for the libel trial against World Argus Newspapers and Adrian Hastings had now been dragging on for nearly a year. Bosco's counsel delayed, feeling it should never be allowed to come to court because, although he was clearly innocent, the publicity would do him no good. As the other side, however, continued to refuse to offer an apology, the case was set to be heard at the High Court of London in March 1913 with a stack of impressive witnesses lined up for the plaintiff. Those in the know thought that it would be one of the shorter libel trials in English legal history and that Bosco would receive the punitive damages his counsel would demand.

Rachel was nervous about the trial, nervous these days about everything. She was worried about unrest in the Balkans and the persistent rumours of war, and she was worried about the extreme course taken by some of the suffragettes and the subsequent excessive prison sentences, even though the women had gathered a certain amount of sympathy by the repugnance most people felt for forcible feeding.

But, more than anything, Rachel was worried about Bosco; about the fact that, in a way she couldn't pin down, he seemed to have become more remote from her, not less loving but less . . . Had she been questioned about it she wouldn't have been able to think of the right word to describe it. It was as though Bosco, though bodily present, had his mind continually somewhere else. At times looking at him sitting there so self-contained, present and yet not present, she wondered what he was really thinking. At these times she felt afraid.

'Penny for them,' she said one day as Bosco walked restlessly up and down the drawing-room at the Grange, glancing at his watch as though he was late for something.

'What, darling?' he paused and looked at her.

'What are you thinking?'

'Of all the thousand things I have to do. I wish I were not so busy, Rachel.'

She came up to him and he put his arms around her, but only briefly, not even a momentary caress.

'Oh Bosco,' she said clinging to him. 'You are so precious to me. You do know that, don't you?'

'Of course I do, my darling.' Bosco gently pushed her away. 'I think Baker will be here now with the car. The new Askham will be ready in about a year. Isn't that exciting?' He finished putting some papers into his case and snapped shut the lock, smiling as though he were pleased to be going.

'Very exciting,' Rachel replied without enthusiasm. She didn't want to be a nagging, discontented wife, so she tried to make all the right noises and smile at all the right times. But she wanted to seize him by the arms, hang on to him and say: 'Where are you *going*? What are you *doing*? Who are you *seeing*, Bosco?'

Instead she did none of these things and, as Ralph and Charlotte were brought in to say goodbye to their father, she turned to take them by their hands and bring them forward for the customary kiss. The twins were with their grandmother who was at Askham Hall with Frances and her two children.

'Goodbye darlings,' Bosco kissed them affectionately, first one and then the other, taking Charlotte's little head between his hands and squeezing it. 'Take care, precious.'

'When . . .' Rachel began but Bosco was already at the door without turning to wave goodbye, without, even, having kissed her.

'But where did Madame say she was going?' Bosco, feeling unnaturally and unusually anxious, shouldered his way past Amélie, the French maid, into the hall.

'She didn't say, sir.'

'And she took the baby *and* the nurse?'

'She packed her cases and I got a cab in the High Street.'

'Perhaps she's gone to France?'

'Perhaps, sir.' Amélie looked doubtful and rather anxious, Bosco thought, as if she didn't believe she had.

'No one came? There was no one here?' Bosco looked around as if a face, or a figure, would suddenly appear from behind the door.

'No one came, sir!' Then Amélie appeared to remember something and her pale, apathetic face became briefly animated. 'There was someone here, but he didn't come in. He asked for Madame and gave her something. She appeared surprised, she took it and it was a day or two after that she decided to go away.'

'What did he give her?' Bosco by now was genuinely alarmed.

'A document of some kind, sir, a paper. I didn't hear what he said to her because after I opened the door I went into the kitchen to make coffee. But he was only here a minute, standing on the threshold of the door.'

'Did Madame say what he wanted?'

'No, sir. She never mentioned him, so I soon forgot about it. I saw her reading the paper and, now that I recall, she did appear unhappy about it.'

Amélie, though blessed with common sense and a docile personality, was not over-endowed with intelligence. Bosco couldn't see Nimet discussing anything really important with her.

'Madame will certainly be back,' Amélie said as though wishing to end on a cheerful note. 'She has left most of her jewellery and all her nice clothes, and wages for me for two weeks. She only packed one or two small cases to take with her.'

'Tell me exactly what she said, try and think now.' Bosco made one last effort to uncover some clue.

'She said,' Amélie went through the motions of careful thought, 'Madame said: "I will be gone a few days, Amélie. Goodbye."'

'I see. Well, if she gets back tell her to telephone me straightaway.'

'I will, sir.'

Amélie bobbed, showed him to the door and watched as he walked slowly along the garden path towards the gate. It would serve Madame right if her lover left her, she thought, wrinkling her nose with the contempt underlings have for those supposed to be their betters, but whose behaviour they consider foolish.

A woman like Madame Seder, who didn't have much in life, would soon, in Amélie's opinion, be losing what little she had.

As everyone had predicted, it looked as though the trial for libel brought by the Earl of Askham against World Argus Newspapers and Adrian Hastings would soon be over. Witness after witness had been called to testify to the bravery of the Earl as a young man at Omdurman and to his character since.

But Sir Augustus Claremont, KC, who led for the plaintiff, was saving his best witnesses to the end. Even then he expected that the defence lawyers would consult with their clients and give in. Why, one had only to look at the Earl of Askham, a large, formidable man, sitting in the well of the court with his elegant wife, a distinguished journalist, to know that he could never have been guilty of cowardice or malice however long ago. The jury, twelve good men and true, dressed in their best suits, were clearly both enthralled and impressed.

The trial was in its second day and even the Judge seemed to think it wouldn't go to a third. His bias was plain. He was excessively polite to Sir Augustus and his witnesses and rude or disparaging to Mr Fothergill Harper when he rose to cross-question them. Mr Harper had only recently taken silk and was observed, despite his previous reputation, to be ill-at-ease, as though the pressure of attacking a nobleman of such eminence and so many men of importance in the dock were too much for him, and he left most of the work to his junior.

The junior, Mr Seymour Phillips, was a clever young man whom Adam knew well. In his opinion he was cleverer than Harper, but Adam had no doubts at all about the outcome of the trial. The only issue would be if the defence would give in before the Judge's summing-up and thus try and settle for less damages than they might otherwise be awarded.

Lord Cromer in the dock was an older, but just as imposing a figure as he had been when Bosco remembered standing in front of him as a young man. They met occasionally now in the House of Lords, but infrequently socially because his lordship was a leading antagonist of the women's suffrage, had indeed formed a league of his own against it, and Rachel hated him. She sat glowering at him as he stood now, being questioned by the nimble Seymour Phillips.

'But how *well* do you recall that occasion, Lord Cromer?'

'As though it were yesterday,' his lordship glanced affably at Bosco from the witness box.

'Really? And yet it was fourteen years ago.'

'I have a very good memory,' his lordship said looking contemptuously at the young barrister, as though doubting his competence. 'There was a story that Captain Crystal had been killed at Omdurman and that young Down, Lord Askham here,' he glanced again at Bosco, 'had something to do with it. Lieutenant Down himself told me he felt very guilty about it because he had tried to save his, that is Down's, life. But his guilt was excessive and misplaced, coming about as the result of his over-compassionate nature, and the rigours of war. There were too many people in the charge who saw what actually happened to know that any other verdict is ridiculous.'

'But the chief witness is dead, is he not, Lord Cromer? Lieutenant Lighterman died in the charge.'

'Lieutenant Lighterman was already dead when the incident happened. Lieutenant Down, who was very attached to him because he was not only his friend but his brother-in-law, didn't know this and risked his own life to try and save him. Crystal of the Egyptian Horse, also coming up at the last minute, did the same thing, but it was useless. At that point Crystal was killed, I think by a Dervish spear. I have looked up my notes and there is no doubt about it. No doubt at all. The character of a great Englishman has been cruelly sullied.'

Lord Cromer folded his hands over the ledge of the witness box and glared at Phillips who, saying he had no more questions, sat down and began hurriedly to confer with his senior. The court was then adjourned for lunch.

'I think they will call a halt this afternoon,' Adam said, spooning his soup, and looking at Bosco across the table. 'Cromer had them grovelling, I heard.'

'He was very convincing.'

'Well, it's me this afternoon, if it does continue.'

'I wish Mama didn't have to go into the dock,' Bosco crumbled his roll into his soup. 'I wish she could be spared that.'

'I think your mama is rather looking forward to it.' Rachel glanced out of the window at the Fleet Street traffic. 'She's ordered a new dress.'

Adam thought for a few moments, as though debating within himself as to whether or not to break bad news, and then said: 'I hear they have a private detective sniffing round.'

'A private detective?'

'An unsavoury man called Rupert Crosby. He is usually used on divorce cases and has a nose for anything unpleasant. There's nothing unpleasant in this, is there, Bosco? Nothing you haven't told us?'

'Of course there's nothing I haven't told you!' Bosco said angrily. 'What secrets should I have from you?'

Adam shook his head and leaned back as the waiter

took his plate. 'I just wondered. That aspect I didn't like very much. They're an uninspiring crowd anyway – even the counsel are second-rate.'

'Anything associated with Hastings would be sordid,' Bosco said shortly. 'He's a very sordid man. After this I expect him to leave the country, because no paper in Fleet Street will employ him.'

After lunch Bosco and Rachel went back to the court while Adam, who had yet to be called, waited outside with all the photographers who, as soon as Dulcie arrived, leapt forward to take pictures of her. Dulcie was accompanied by Flora and Melanie and their pictures were in every newspaper in the land that night and the following morning under the heading: DOWAGER COUNTESS TESTIFIES AT TRIAL: FAMOUS BEAUTY IN THE BOX.

If Dulcie was nervous she gave no sign of it as she stepped into the witness box and bowed to the jury and the Judge, Sir Lawrence Henshaw who, in common with most of the judiciary, was an old friend of hers.

'Would you like to be seated, Lady Askham?'

'No thank you, my lord.' Dulcie and the Judge exchanged glances of mutual admiration again and Sir Augustus, smiling and bowing, rose to examine her.

'Your name is Dulcie, Lady Askham, and you are the widow of the tenth Earl of Askham and mother of the plaintiff, the eleventh?'

'I am,' Dulcie inclined her head, the grey ostrich feathers on her new hat waving like a salaam.

'And do you recall, Lady Askham, those days in Cairo in the summer of 1898 which form the substance of this trial?'

'I do, Sir Augustus. My younger daughter was married to Harry Lighterman and they remain very vivid to me indeed.'

Dulcie wore a walking-out costume the colour of muted

squirrel, chosen carefully to give an impression of modesty, with a three-quarter-length caped coat tied at hip level by a large black bow. Her brown felt hat tipped over her forehead and, attached to its curling brim, was a spotted veil which covered her face completely. She wore long brown leather gloves and carried a large leather handbag. The protection of her veil gave her more confidence than she had felt when she came into the witness box. This was reinforced by the deference of the Judge, the presence of so many agreeable men in the court, young and old, who could scarcely conceal their admiring glances, and the tone of Sir Augustus which was positively unctuous as he addressed her again:

'It is therefore very unlikely, Lady Askham, that a lady such as yourself, mother of four grown-up children, would form an attachment for a much younger man, the age, say, of your son-in-law?'

The silence of the court was interrupted by a ripple of coughs and murmurs of incredulity as Dulcie, drawing herself up, her hand firmly on the edge of the witness box, replied: '*Extremely* unlikely, Sir Augustus. Indeed, it did not happen. Captain Crystal was merely one of a number of friends of my son and son-in-law whom I met that year in Cairo. I have always been fortunate in counting among my friends many of the opposite sex, but merely as *friends*. I was happily married to the late Lord Askham, and remained so until the day he died.'

'Thank you, Lady Askham,' Sir Augustus bowed so low that his spectacles nearly fell off. 'You have answered me perfectly.'

But Seymour Phillips, unimpressed by this show of chivalry, the sleeves of his gown flying, was not a bit subdued by the social distinction of the woman in the box.

'Is it not true to say, Lady Askham, that, over the years, you have encouraged young men to pay court to you?'

Again there was a murmur which the Judge had to silence by banging his gavel on the bench.

'Not at all,' Lady Askham snapped. 'If I am surrounded by friends of my children, am I supposed to retire?'

This time there was laughter which the Judge joined in, then everyone composed themselves and the laughter and coughing ceased.

'There was *no* occasion during that picnic in the desert when you were alone with Captain Crystal?'

Bosco looked at his mother and then exchanged glances with Rachel, whose hand crept over his.

'Yes, certainly I was alone, maybe for a few minutes. We went for a walk as it was so hot, but we expected, if I recall, Mr Bolingbroke, now my son-in-law, to follow us. We were soon joined, in any event, by my son and daughter Melanie who had walked in the other direction.'

'Do you recall Mr Hastings on that picnic, Lady Askham?'

'No I don't,' Dulcie peered arrogantly into the court as though looking for a beetle. 'I have no recollection of that "person" at all until I saw him at the home of Sir Robert Lighterman, where he had no business to be incidentally, and he reminded us who he was.'

'Thank you, Lady Askham. No more questions, my lord.'

Sir Lawrence and Dulcie exchanged smiles again and Sir Augustus bowed. Dulcie paused as she left the witness box, gazing around, as though she expected a round of applause to break out, before she joined Rachel and Bosco on the bench behind counsel.

Melanie was called next and dealt summarily with the suggestion that her mother and Captain Crystal had a relationship. She had had her mother in sight all the time, she said, as she followed her down the path through the forest.

Such was the sense of complacency that afternoon, the air of injured innocence, of a wrong done that would soon be righted pervading the court, that it is doubtful if even Melanie realized she was lying.

The last witness in the afternoon was Adam who had to answer a number of questions about Crystal and the charge. Adam was a good witness, used to asking and answering questions in court and he went quickly, easily and convincingly through his evidence.

It was true, he admitted, that Bosco didn't like Crystal because he made a bit of a nuisance of himself and hung around his mother. But after that they scarcely saw each other, because Crystal was in a separate regiment and only joined the charge at the last moment.

Sir Augustus made much of this as proving that Bosco could not possibly have wanted to kill him because he did not know he would be there. Adam, too, had been present when Crystal was killed and Bosco, lying wounded on the ground, could not possibly have killed him.

'It is a question of *luring* him to his death, Mr Bolingbroke.'

Even the ebullient Mr Phillips by this time seemed dejected and when Adam replied 'Rubbish' in a loud voice he sat down again shaking his head.

At the end of the day the Judge invited leading counsel to his chambers and asked why the defence wanted to waste everyone's money and the court's time and continue the trial.

Both Mr Harper and Mr Phillips were quite adamant they wanted to continue because they had witnesses who would swear differently to the evidence so far produced in court. This fact disturbed Sir Augustus who was a very busy man, though always relishing the limelight a trial of this kind afforded.

'Is there *any* reason why they should wish to continue the trial, Lord Askham?'

Bosco sat with Sir Augustus in his chambers in the Inner Temple as mystified as his counsel; but he was also oppressed by a feeling of apprehension even though, so far, everything had gone so well.

'Not that I know of, Sir Augustus.'

'There is nothing you haven't revealed to me?'

'Nothing at all.'

'I shall examine you very carefully in the box tomorrow.'

'And I shall be ready,' Bosco said, getting up and taking his top hat from Sir Augustus's clerk. 'Good day to you, sir.'

That night Bosco couldn't sleep and Rachel, aware of his agitation, asked him if anything were amiss.

'Nothing,' Bosco said, 'except that, of course, I wish this was all over. I didn't like seeing Mama in the box.'

'She was magnificent. I think she even enjoyed it. *And* the praise in the evening papers. COUNTESS PUTS COUNSEL IN HIS PLACE.'

Bosco smiled, but he didn't look happy. Ever since he'd been to the Hampstead house four days before and found Nimet missing he had been worried. He couldn't help feeling, indeed knowing, that her absence was connected with the case. But how? He knew he hadn't killed Crystal and no one could prove that he had. But where had she gone and why? To be got out of the way? But then, again, why?

Even after Rachel made him a strong whisky and soda he couldn't sleep and lay awake until dawn.

But when called next day as the last witness for his side he was convincing, to the point and, apparently, truthful.

He was taken through the events of that summer up to the charge and was in the witness box all morning.

'What did you mean when you told Lord Cromer and others that you felt guilty, Lord Askham?'

'I felt guilty that my friends, my brother officers, were dead and that I was alive. I felt guilty I hadn't done more to save Harry, or Cardew.'

'But what more could you have done, Lord Askham?' Sir Augustus enquired gently.

Bosco's face bore a look of anguish. 'I don't know, but one always thinks one could have done more.'

'Mr Bolingbroke has testified that you wept when Captain Crystal died. Is that true?'

'True,' Bosco said, lowering his voice, hanging his head and, as he did, the memory of that day came flooding back and he apologized to Cardew, once again, silently in his heart.

'You never wanted Captain Crystal dead?'

'Never,' Bosco said emotionally. 'I didn't like him, but I didn't want him dead.'

'But why didn't you like him, Lord Askham? Was he not your friend?' Sir Augustus looked anxiously at his junior, Mr Jocelyn Allardyce.

'He was never really a friend, just one of many people we met in Cairo. He hung around one a lot, and got on our nerves. I didn't see him again after the picnic at Sakkara and I never expected to see him in the charge. He was in a different regiment.'

'Thank you, Lord Askham.'

Sir Augustus sat down, mopping his brow, and Mr Harper rose to cross-examine.

'An element has been brought out, Lord Askham, it seems to me that was not here before. You didn't actually *like* Captain Crystal?'

'I didn't actually *like* him,' Bosco agreed, 'but I didn't

want to kill him. Most people that I have actively disliked in my life, and I am nearly thirty-eight years of age, are still alive.'

The court was prevented from fresh laughter by a warning look from the judge.

'You were never actually jealous of Captain Crystal?'

Bosco went on holding his ground convincingly and was in the witness box until the close of the session in the afternoon. Although he had stuck to his testimony, and was an ideal witness, some of his replies excited the press who the day before had thought the Askham case, though interesting, was all sewn up.

LORD ASKHAM UNEASY IN THE WITNESS BOX, said one.

LORD ASKHAM NOT SO SURE HE DIDN'T 'HATE', screamed another.

Suddenly, it seemed that the outcome of the trial was not as clear-cut as it had once appeared. The atmosphere seemed to affect the participants as, late that afternoon, they streamed out of the court into the Strand with newsboys crying: 'ASKHAM CASE. ASKHAM CASE. LATEST. LORD ASKHAM ALL DAY IN THE BOX. GRILLED BY COUNSEL.'

'We will destroy their witnesses tomorrow,' Sir Augustus said with, Bosco thought, less conviction than he had shown the day before. 'I may have to recall you. I wish you hadn't said you didn't like Crystal.'

'But it was true.'

'Still you could have phrased it differently.' Sir Augustus sighed. 'I only hope there are no surprises from the other side.'

The next day Bosco was briefly recalled by his counsel to clarify what he meant by not liking Crystal. He said that he didn't automatically like everyone he met, even brother officers. He just didn't find Crystal a particularly interesting fellow.

'He was an irritant, in other words?'

'Exactly,' Bosco said. 'He was a very dull sort of chap, really. But harmless.'

Getting just the answer he wanted Sir Augustus sat down, concluding the plaintiff's case.

Almost immediately the defence rose to state its case briefly and, just before lunch, Adrian Hastings was called. Everyone looked at him with interest, wondering how such a mild, nondescript person could have caused such a furore. Hastings, dressed in a suit that had seen better days and a faded crumpled tie which he fingered uneasily, looked an uninspiring, even pathetic, figure and his evidence was delivered in such a quiet voice that the Judge, who had obviously made up his mind about the issue, kept on barking at him to speak up.

Once again he recounted the details of the picnic, but admitted he didn't see Lady Askham and Captain Crystal go off alone; or rather, he *thought* he had, but he knew that all the other members of the party were missing too. He kept on using the words 'I thought' which irritated the Judge who interrupted him more than he had any other witness. As Sir Augustus rose to cross-examine, the feeling was that he would make short work of this witness, and the defence itself.

'Tell me, Mr Hastings,' Sir Augustus said, clutching the edges of his gown. 'In what circumstances do you find yourself now?'

'How do you mean, sir?' Hastings looked nervously at the Judge, only to be met by an equally unsympathetic stare.

'Are you a rich man, poor man? What?'

'I am not very well off, sir.'

'Doubtless, then, you will not have any pennies to spare if Lord Askham wins his case.'

'No, sir,' Hastings hung his head.

'Why, then, did you not agree to settle? Could you

really afford to bring this matter to court? Are you not wasting everyone's time?'

'I don't think so, sir.'

'Are you not, in fact,' Sir Augustus swept on like an unstoppable tide, 'a mean-minded, poverty-stricken little man motivated solely by revenge because Lord Askham had you fired once before for this tittle-tattle that you pour forth from your poisonous pen?'

'I am not motivated by revenge.'

'I find that hard to believe.'

So did Sir Lawrence, to judge from his indignant nod as he folded his arms and leaned back in the high judicial chair.

'I think,' Sir Augustus stabbed the air, 'you felt angry and humiliated by that previous incident and your one wish was to humiliate Lord Askham and his family in turn, regardless of what happened to you. For a man of his eminence to waste his time in this court because of the likes of you seems to me the grossest impertinence.'

Mr Hastings' counsel stood up and objected and the Judge reluctantly agreed with him and directed Sir Augustus to limit himself to the facts.

Sir Augustus then went on to expound the facts and said that, though it was singular and unusual that Mr Hastings had been one of the party in the desert picnic so many years before, he had not been at Omdurman or anywhere near it and didn't know what he was talking about. All this evidence was based on hearsay, and the case should be thrown out.

The agile Seymour Phillips leapt to his feet at this point to say that he would produce witnesses who did know more about it, and would say so. Sir Augustus made an attempt to get the trial stopped on the grounds that the sole evidence against Lord Askham was hearsay and therefore inadmissible; but Mr Phillips assured them that before very long they would hear direct evidence itself. He seemed to relish the thought and rubbed his hands together when he sat down, a gesture that worried Bosco.

As the next witness was called, Bosco was aware of the sweat in the palms of his hands which he surreptitiously wiped on the back of his trousers. The loathing he felt for this creature as once again he had to look at her almost overwhelmed him by its strength and forcefulness. He felt that she emanated evil and corruption like a Stygian force and her apparent equanimity as she stepped into the box amazed him. One with such a lot on her conscience should, he felt, be bowed and remorseful. But not Madame Hassim, who gave a pleasant smile as once again the details of the picnic were gone over with her counsel and, she said, she thought Lady Askham and Captain Crystal had gone off alone, but couldn't be sure. She said the whole business of the picnic had been very sad because she and Mr Asher had gone to such trouble on behalf of Lady Askham and her family, trouble which they felt was not appreciated. Mr Harper sat down.

'Asher?' Sir Augustus said, rising and peering at her above the rims of his spectacles. 'Who is this "Asher"?'

'He is my brother, sir,' Madame Hassim dropped her voice. 'My half-brother. He is half-English, but I am pure Egyptian. We had the same mother.'

Bosco bent forward to whisper to Mr Allardyce who, after listening to what he had to say, tugged at the sleeve of Sir Augustus's gown. Sir Augustus asked for a moment's delay and then went into a huddle with Mr Allardyce and Bosco.

'I am instructed to say,' Sir Augustus stood up and cleared his throat, 'that Lord Askham has had dealings both with this Mr Asher and Madame Hassim who, it appears, is living here under another name. He had no idea that she and Mr Asher were related.'

'Does it matter?' the Judge enquired.

'Lord Askham thinks it does matter, sir, because the witness's evidence is suspect.'

'Is Mr Asher to be called?'

'Mr Asher is not in the country, my lord,' Harper intervened. 'His whereabouts cannot be ascertained.'

'Continue with the cross-examination,' the Judge said tersely and Sir Augustus continued, taking Madame Hassim not only through the events of the picnic but over much of her life as well, though he left out some very important parts, to Bosco's relief. He thought it was almost impossible to believe that so many half-truths, including his, could be spoken in a court of law; but imagined this must always be the case, people wishing to present only their best sides in public.

Bosco leaned back against his bench staring at the witness. The old fear had returned, not now of Cardew, not of the consequences of the trial, but of something much deeper, indefinite. She knew too much about him and she must know where Nimet was. Maybe she had . . .

He sat up and gripped the back of the bench in front of him, staring hard at his hated foe in the dock who was coming to the end of her evidence, during which enough doubt had been thrown on to her as almost to destroy the value of her testimony. As, flustered, she left the witness box, the Judge could be seen making notes, after saying that there were a number of unsatisfactory aspects of her presence in this country which he would be asking Scotland Yard to look into.

Bosco watched her go and then he sank back against his seat and closed his eyes, opening them at last only to see Rachel staring anxiously at him.

'Are you all right?'

He nodded his head but already he knew as, after a

little huddle between Hastings' counsel, the next witness was called in a loud clear voice by the clerk.

'Call Mrs Seder . . .'

'Call Mrs Seder . . .' the echo reverberated around the court, through the doors and along the marble corridors of the High Courts of Justice. Bosco sprang foward as the door opened and Nimet, dressed in black, her face so pale that she looked like a wraith, slowly entered and was led by an usher into the witness box. She appeared to have been crying and, as she took the oath, Mr Harper stood up and said:

'There has been a certain amount of difficulty with this witness, my lord, and we must declare her hostile. But her evidence is crucial.'

As the Judge leaned forward Bosco could be seen speaking urgently to Sir Augustus who, with a startled expression, brought his junior into the conversation. When Mr Harper, with a smug expression on his face, rose to examine, Sir Augustus stood up, clearly perturbed, and interrupted him.

'My lord, could we have a word with you?'

'Approach the bench,' the Judge said, beckoning to the two leading counsel and, as they went up to confer with him, a little buzz of speculation ran round the court. Rachel, ashen-faced, sat there staring at Nimet, who was gazing at the floor. Melanie had a hand to her mouth and was speaking quietly, but rapidly, to Adam. The Judge announced that the court would be adjourned and, looking very annoyed, left the bench. As he did all the court reporters made a movement *en masse* for the doors.

ASKHAM CASE ADJOURNED, MYSTERY WITNESS IN THE BOX, screamed the lunch-time papers.

LORD ASKHAM CONFRONTED BY A MYSTERIOUS WOMAN WITNESS. CASE ADJOURNED.

* * *

'I *asked* you to tell me the truth,' Sir Augustus thundered, snapping his jaws shut like a guillotine as if, given sixpence, he would bite off Bosco's head.

'I did tell you the truth. I had no idea she would be called.'

'And she is your mistress *now*?'

'Yes.'

'Well, what can she do? She is already hostile. How can she harm you? What can she say?'

'I think she will say that in Cairo I once told her I had killed Cardew. I still felt very emotional in those days – it was only a year later – and my guilt was as real as if I actually had. I think she believed me and told Madame Hassim, who was in her confidence. Asher – who we now know is Madame Hassim's brother – hated me because he tried to get money from me a year or two ago and I threw him out of the house. He and Hastings knew each other, obviously kept in touch, and so you have the sequence of this whole horrible business; and how it could happen that I am destroyed not by a deed of murder but by my temper and my contempt for these low, unworthy creatures. I cannot have Mrs Seder examined in the box, even if hostile. I cannot allow my wife to be humiliated more than she is already.'

'Really, Lord Askham, seeing that that woman had disappeared you might have known what had happened.'

'I couldn't believe it of her.'

'*If* she was subpoenaed she had no choice.'

'She could have told me. You'd think she would have trusted me. I think Madame Hassim made her a prisoner. That woman has had an evil influence on her all her life.'

'Well, whatever's happened you'll do yourself no good at all, if we don't continue.'

'The trial *can't* continue, Sir Augustus.' From the windows of the Inner Temple Bosco could see the trees along the embankment, the grey, leaden sky between. 'I want to end the case.'

'But you're mad. It's tantamount to an admission of guilt.'

'No matter.' Bosco turned and looked at him. 'I am not guilty, but I will not have Nimet subjected to this in court, nor my wife having to sit there and listen to her. Our relationship will be told to all the world.'

'They will know anyway,' the lawyer said sourly. 'People will guess. If we go on I *might* be able, just *might*, to turn the tables by discrediting this Nimet too.'

'I can't have it. End the trial.'

'You will have to pay all the expenses, yours and the defendant's. It will amount to thousands and thousands of pounds.'

'I will pay them.'

Sir Augustus angrily took off his gown, throwing it across a chair in front of his desk. Then he went up to Bosco and, standing two or three inches away from him, looked as though he was about to clasp him by his lapels and shake him, but he changed his mind. Instead he stuck a finger under his nose, a finger that shook with indignation.

'My dear Lord Askham, you might lose a mistress and, possibly, a wife if you continue with the case; but if you don't you'll ruin yourself. Your position in society will be finished. The speculation and innuendo will never stop. You will be labelled a murderer.'

'Let people say what they like.' Bosco put his hat squarely on his head, glared at the distinguished counsel and, turning, marched out of the door without saying 'good day'.

Bosco stepped outside the ancient building which formed part of the venerable Inner Temple and standing for a moment, hands in his pockets, sniffed the air. It was almost as though he could smell the ominous whiff of disaster, the news that would rapidly circulate around the courts, down Fleet Street, across London and into the world at large that the Askham case had been called off because a slim, dark-clad woman of Middle Eastern appearance had appeared briefly in the witness box.

Hastings, Madame Hassim, the wretched Asher had not only won, they had, indeed, conquered. The power of evil could, and apparently did, triumph over good. They might not be a penny richer, but perhaps they felt the wealth in their hearts: that poverty, ignorance, treachery and duplicity could succeed where all the power and money that noble birth could bring, failed.

It was very cold in the Temple gardens and Bosco's thin coat provided little protection against the wind. He walked slowly through the gardens and on to the Embankment, then he stopped as though wondering which direction to take. Did he have a choice? He looked this way and that. One way lay oblivion, forgetfulness, the end of everything. That way was towards the river. Another way lay eastwards to flight and anonymity; a disappearance that could be easily arranged with, perhaps, a sea trip to Africa or the Americas.

The way westwards, the right, hard way, led home. It led to an acceptance of the *status quo*, except that things were no longer as they were and perhaps could never be again. In time people would forget about the trial and the Askham name would rise from the ashes; maybe at the end of his lifetime or not until the next generation. But, certainly, as long as he lived there would always be people about to say, 'Askham? Surely that was the fellow who . . . ? Funny business. No one ever knew the truth.' Maybe if war did come it would blot out everything. The way westwards was the way back to his family, his children and the wife whom he had so criminally mistreated, whom he had lied to, cheated and deceived. For that, if nothing more, he deserved punishment.

He walked slowly along the Embankment, the mellow lights that had just come on seeming to point the way through the gloom not only on this cold March day, but in his life. Along a path that had been ordained for him since the day Arthur died, and which he must follow. He went past the Adelphi, Somerset House, through Trafalgar Square and into Pall Mall.

He could already hear the journalists baying like dogs outside his front door as he stepped into the Square, but he dodged up King Street into the mews and through the back door of Askham House. He sniffed the kitchen smells and walked slowly through the door that divided the house into those who served and those who were served. Bromwich was standing in the hall peering through the narrow stained-glass window that ran by the side of the front door at the mass outside. He turned as he heard Bosco and with his mouth open held out his hand.

'My lord, I . . .'

'Did her ladyship reach home all right?'

'She did, my lord. Mr Bolingbroke and Lady Melanie, divining what would happen, returned before the news broke. Your sister and brother-in-law have left, but her ladyship is upstairs.'

Bosco gave him his hat and coat and, standing in front of the hall mirror, ran his hands through his hair. As he was about to mount the stairs Bromwich, clearing his throat, said: 'May I say, Lord Askham, how *very* sorry I am.'

'That's very good of you, Bromwich,' Bosco said with an appreciative smile. 'This sort of thing will soon blow over.'

Bosco swiftly climbed the stairs two at a time, trying to feel that he had just come home from a normal day's work, or from his club or an outing to Askham. Rachel was standing by the fireplace, warming her hands, her back to him, and the first words she uttered as he came in quietly, closing the door behind him, were:

'It's so cold, isn't it? Have you had tea?'

Bosco didn't reply but walked quickly up behind her and then stopped, not daring to touch her. It seemed so incongruous – the pair of them preparing to take tea on a cold afternoon against the continuous background murmur of reporters kept at bay downstairs by the faithful Bromwich. Oh, were it otherwise, Bosco thought, feeling such nostalgia for the times that had been and were no more that it almost hurt. If only . . . if only . . .

Slowly she turned and gazed at him. 'She's your mistress, isn't she?'

Bosco nodded.

'Apparently I'm the last to know. They say it's always the case.'

'No one knows.'

'Well, they do now.'

As Bosco sat down, his head in his hands, Rachel poured the tea waiting for them on a tray as though it were just another normal day.

'And Melanie knew. She was there the night you met her. She knows everything about her. Boofie da Conte told her. Apparently she was a prostitute in Cairo. You've known her for years . . .'

Rachel stopped and waited; maybe hoping, trusting, Bosco would deny it all, but he nodded his head.

'I've known her for years, but she's only been my mistress for a year. I did know her briefly in Cairo, before you and I started any relationship. I met her again at Quaglino's and I couldn't resist her, Rachel. I'm sorry. I'm sorry because I love you . . .' Bosco looked up at her and held out his hand. 'I really do. I'm sorry that I've hurt you . . . It's so hard to explain.'

'*Hurt* me! You've ruined my life, Bosco, and yours. It will take people years to get over this. But I can't promise that I ever shall. Didn't you *know* she'd be called?'

'I think I guessed, but rather too late in the day. Maybe I had a premonition the night before, which was why I couldn't sleep. She wasn't at her home. Now it is clear to me, but it wasn't then.'

'If only you'd *told* me, it was something we could have faced together. But to find out like that . . .'

'How *could* I tell you? I couldn't tell you. I hoped it wouldn't happen. It was only when I saw Madame Hassim, that evil witch, in court that I knew it would.'

'If you'd told me. If I'd known,' Rachel's face remained pale despite the hot tea, 'I would have stood by you. The examination could have gone ahead. Now I know about your mistress. The whole world knows, or guesses, and we are all ruined. Adam thinks Sir Augustus could still have pulled it off and saved the day, particularly as your . . . she . . . that woman, was hostile, appearing against her will evidently.'

'I would never have allowed it. I couldn't allow it because of you and Mama, and everybody else. I couldn't face it. Let people think what they like. I knew she'd destroy me, Hassim. I think she put a curse on me years ago. I have always known that the Egyptian connection, that sinister link, would be the undoing of me, and it has.'

Bosco got up and, going over to the fireplace, leaned his hands against the great marble mantel gazing into the flames.

'Shall you divorce me, Rachel?'

'Do you want to marry . . . this woman?'

'No.'

'Then I won't, not yet anyway. This is Melanie and

Adam all over again, isn't it? You really are quite a pair for infidelity – brother and sister. It must run in the family.'

'I was never unfaithful to you. I was in the grip . . .' he looked upwards as though trying to find the right words '. . . of something I couldn't control. Nimet was a dream, a vision, unreal. She was Egypt and my youth. She never ever competed with you. Like all illicit pleasures it was a dangerous one, and how I'm paying for it now. Rachel, I am so sorry. I swear I'll never see her again.'

As he turned round he saw Rachel standing regarding him dispassionately, her arms akimbo.

'Your mother may not think much of me, Bosco, but I have decided what to do. I'll carry on as though nothing had happened, in public that is. I'm sure she'd approve of that. If I leave home everyone will be at you like a pack of wolves. We share too many things for me, hurt though I am, to wish to hurt you more. So, if you wish it, I shall continue to live in this house with you, and do all the things we used to do, be seen in public and so on, except for one thing.'

'And that is?' Bosco said, knowing.

'I won't sleep in your bed. I won't now, and I don't know that I shall ever return. Shocked as I am – I really can't think straight – I'm sure I'm doing the right thing now. But in every other way, and for as long as you want, I will support you and be your wife . . . in name only. Not in the spirit and not, definitely not, in the flesh.'

PART IV

1913–1915: Innocence Regained

CHAPTER 21

The aftermath of the sensational Askham libel trial was pretty much as everyone had predicted. For whatever reason, Bosco was considered to have been guilty, if not of murder or cowardice, then of some misdemeanour or other. Much was made of the appearance of the mysterious woman, but no one could find Mrs Seder or anyone who knew anything about her. Indeed, the witnesses against Bosco at the trial soon made themselves scarce, even Adrian Hastings who probably thought he'd done enough harm to a family whose only initial fault had been to forget that he'd accompanied them on a picnic into the Egyptian desert long ago.

Although much was made of the case in the press, the laws of the country prevented too much speculation on the reason for ending the trial in case another libel case should ensue. Bosco still had his interests jealously guarded by his legal representatives, even if he had let them down.

Both Bosco and his immediate family noticed at once the effects the trial would have on them. He was cold-shouldered at his clubs, in the House of Lords, wherever he went, except by men of business who always have had the wisdom to put money before anything else; and the Askham wealth, despite the enormous costs of paying for both sides at the trial, was still considerable. The number of social invitations sharply declined and Dulcie offered to retire from the Court, a request the compassionate Dowager Queen properly refused although she did agree that a period out of the limelight, for Dulcie's sake, might be a good thing.

So, for the time being – no one knew how long it would last – the great Askham family were cast into limbo, disgraced, finished, and all because of one jealous man and an indiscretion or two committed many years before.

But maybe of all the Askhams the socialite Melanie felt the ostracism most keenly and bitterly because doors previously flung open were closed; red carpets laid out for the Earl's sister were rapidly rolled up again. She ceased to be at the top of the lists of leading London hostesses, and invitations from gallant and blueblooded young officers stopped abruptly. Only one swain remained faithful, who was not affected by the prejudices of the English upper classes because he was not one of them. Stefano da Ponte's door in Portman Square was always open, his purse ever ready to shell out, however much of his family's fortune was required to keep Melanie happy in jewels, flowers, outrageous and expensive forms of entertainment. His optimistic Latin temperament was just what she needed to maintain her *amour propre* in those long hard months before the Askham case gradually receded from the public mind.

The Count had fallen in love with Melanie the night he met her at Quaglino's fourteen months before and scarcely a day had passed since then when they had not met. Of course when Melanie went down to Askham, or to the Kittos on the Scottish Borders, Stefano was missing; but not when she went to the country for the weekend to the many parties that her friends gave and to which she and her husband were invited, or had been before the trial.

Stefano, whose family was as old as the very first Medicis, merchants of Florence, was always invited too. Adam had come to regard him as a sort of second husband, an unofficial one who kept Melanie at least partially happy because no single man was able to do that entirely. Melanie liked almost everything about da Ponte: his generosity, his kindness, the fact that he adored her, his looks. But there was one displeasing aspect: she did not like the fact that he was Italian. German, yes; French, yes; Austrian, yes; Russian, yes; Spanish, well almost; but Italian . . . no. There was something faintly comical about the Italians, the notion of the Latin lover, and as far as Melanie was concerned they were in the same boat as Greeks, Bulgarians, Rumanians, Hungarians, Serbs and vaguely Ruritanian nations of that kind.

Even the fact that Stefano's family had huge estates the length and breadth of Italy, that his mother was a princess and his uncle a cardinal, and the family was related to at least two former popes, didn't help. In fact they made it all a bit worse because of the connection with that awful, shame-making institution, anathema to all good Protestants, however insincere their beliefs, the Roman Catholic Church.

No, Stefano was Italian and he was Catholic and Melanie heartily wished he were neither – just good simple old Boofie, the Anglicized diminutive she quickly adopted for him to try and minimize the Italian link; 'Boofie' being short for beautiful. So handsome, robust Stefano became an inspired Englishman, willingly reduced to the level of a lapdog by the mistress he adored.

Curiously enough Boofie da Ponte did look very English. He had blond hair and blue eyes, a florid complexion, a huge walrus-type moustache. He was rather large, not stout but substantially built; not thin and dark and sinister – the stereotype of the Latin lover, or the kind of brigand connected with murders in dark Venetian alleys – but bluff, genial and English-looking.

Boofie had been educated in England, and had never lost the habits acquired at his English public school including, with an impeccable English accent, an in souciance, a sense of the ridiculous, beautiful manners and a flair for wearing casual country clothes.

It may be wondered why this paragon was in the arms of a lady of doubtful reputation the night that Melanie met him. The answer is as simple, or as complex, according to how one sees it, as it was to try and explain what that true blue member of the English aristocracy, Bosco Askham, was doing in Nimet's bed. Stefano didn't know the truth about Nimet either and had met her in Quaglino's some weeks before. She was with a party, he subsequently realized, that had included Madame Hassim and some people he didn't know, but who affected to be languid English gentry entertaining friends from Cairo. It was only later, when he knew her a little better, when he knew what a liar she was, that he found out more about her. Now he felt that, had he done all he should have done, he would have saved Bosco from the shame and disgrace of the trial.

'Boofie darling, you couldn't *possibly* have known.' Melanie said a few weeks after the trial in her usual, weepy way after she had collapsed on the sofa in Boofie's drawing-room allowing herself to wallow, as was customary, in recrimination and grief. 'I didn't know. No one knew.'

'Yes, but I didn't see her after that, and then I knew she'd left the address where she lived.'

'But none of us thought that Bosco had another woman! He was supposed to be pots in love with Rachel. How could *anyone* know he'd bought her a little house in Hampstead and there they were as cosy as two bugs? Not Mama, Boofie dear, not Flora, certainly not Rachel and not you and me.'

'I wonder what's happened to her now?' Boofie gazed at his beloved through the haze of cigarette smoke which surrounded him almost permanently, like a pillar of cloud. 'I would like to find out.'

'I think if I found her or saw her again I would kill her,'

Melanie said. 'I don't think I'd hesitate if I had a gun or a dagger. I'd shoot her there or stab her there,' she thrust her arm into the air and Boofie, rising from his chair, crossed the room and fell to his knees beside her.

'I do adore you, *cara*. I would never, ever let you do such a thing. Melanie,' he took her hand and entwined it in his. 'Can we be married? Can't we stop this pretence?'

'What pretence?'

'The pretence that you are married to Adam. He knows it's pretending too. He loves your sister, and you love me.'

'Yes, but he and Flora would never marry. It's not that sort of carnal thing at all.' Melanie looked nervously at Boofie because, as far as she could, she kept their relationship from being carnal too. 'Flora said it never would be and, knowing her and Adam as I do, I think she's right.'

'But I want to marry you, my darling, and live openly with you. Please, Melanie,' he took her fingers and kissed them one by one.

'I would *never* be a Catholic,' Melanie said with alarm, stalling as she always did.

'You wouldn't have to be, my darling. I am only nominally Catholic and if I married you I couldn't be either because you already have a husband and four children, so there would be no grounds for annulment, I'm afraid.'

'I'll think about it,' Melanie said leaning back, her eyes wandering, as they so often did, over the luxurious furniture and hangings in Boofie's drawing-room. He had so much taste and polish, so *much* money. Instead of pretending to be poor all the time with Adam, living in the poky house in St John's Wood, she could live where she liked with glorious long holidays on one of Boofie's Italian estates. Luxury at last. Melanie stretched out her arms like a cat and let him kiss her.

* * *

The other person who felt the effects of the case, but for a different reason, was Rachel Askham. She felt it so angrily, so bitterly, that she thought it would colour her life for good; that she would never again be the person she was before it happened. She would never be the same, or sane again. But her bitterness wasn't directed against society, for which she didn't care a fig. It was directed against Bosco, her husband, her lover, who had betrayed her and demeaned their love.

It didn't matter that the whole world knew it, but that she knew it; it had happened not to them but to her. She was the deceived wife who had shared her bed, her body, her love with another woman; a prostitute from Cairo who had insinuated herself into her husband's affections. And he, Bosco, the noble, the beloved, had allowed himself to be seduced.

Rachel had lived with this bitterness and hatred for so long that she could never imagine it leaving her. She couldn't rise above it. Although nominally she was Bosco's wife they were hardly ever together. They did very little socializing or entertaining, so she was not required to be seen in public with him, and at home she hardly spoke to him. The children were sent to the Grange to get what peace they could in the country, away from the stares of the curious, the ostracism of other nannies walking their charges in the park.

But the inhabitants of Askham gathered around their lord to protect him and his family from the prying curiosity of the world. What reporters came down to snoop around quickly went away rebuffed by this wall of solidarity and support that Bosco's dependants gave him. In fact one paper went so far as to write a grudging, flattering article about it: THE VILLAGE THAT GRIEVED WITH ITS LORD. Even a journalist managed to be impressed.

But Rachel didn't go to Askham and hide herself. Her

place was in London; not beside Bosco, but in the offices of *The Sentinel*, with which she was becoming more involved, encouraged by Rathbone Collier, a northerner who had edited the paper since Bosco bought it and sacked the previous editor.

It was Rathbone who exercised his authority in Fleet Street to find out the name of the Argus writer, to confirm it was Hastings, and it was the joint efforts of Rathbone and Bosco combined that ensured Hastings would never be offered another job, even a freelance one, in Fleet Street. And if Hastings went to the provinces and started up again there they would follow him; with money, with threats, with writs. They would follow him to the end of the world to stop another line being printed against the Askham family.

For in his way Rathbone had become, like the villagers of Askham, intensely loyal. Bosco had lifted him up from the Fleet Street mill and made him editor. He was a socialist and he was allowed to state his own views. He was allowed to write about the plight of the poor, the iniquities of privilege in one of the richest countries of the world. He supported not only the suffrage but all other restrictions on the freedom of women. Rathbone loved the Askhams passionately. He was one of Rachel's sturdiest supporters in the weeks and months that followed the trial, suggesting subjects for her to write about, places to visit to take her mind off what had happened. He was one of the few who really knew the state of affairs between herself and Bosco.

But Rathbone had an even closer link with the family, though they weren't all aware of it. He had loved Flora for almost as long as he'd worked on the paper; but had never dared show the extent of his love, not because she was an earl's daughter, his employer's sister, but because of Adam. In his solid working-class, non-conformist tradition Rathbone was a moral man, and believed that people should stay married and be faithful to their wives even if those wives deceived them. He knew how correct Adam and Flora were in disguising their love, and how very difficult it would be for him to break up such a selfless relationship.

On a warm day in July during that summer of 1913, Rathbone was working in his office when Rachel, dressed in black, came into his room waving a purple iris in her hand. She looked tired yet her face was flushed and, as she sat down in the large shabby chair by Rathbone's desk, he thought that, for the first time since the trial, that sad expression had left Rachel's face and once again she was happy.

'How was it?' He put down the pencil with which he wrote his articles and lit a cigarette.

'Oh Rath, it was marvellous! It was inspiring. Mrs Pankhurst's empty carriage followed the hearse. She was arrested just before she stepped into it and everyone cheered. Some people said it was the greatest funeral procession the city has seen since that for Queen Victoria. Yet for me, who saw the late Queen's funeral pass, it was even more splendid. There were literally *thousands* of women dressed in black, purple or white and carrying irises, laurels or red peonies. There were the hunger strikers, women doctors and graduates, even the clergy, and a great brass band banging away at the end of the procession. Emily's body was reverently followed all the way from Victoria to King's Cross. I could never have imagined anything like it! You can have the whole of the front page tomorrow.'

'You look as though you'd been to a wedding, not a funeral.'

'But it was *joyous*, Rath! It was *joyful*. I think Emily, by her sacrifice, has done the Cause the greatest service yet.

Who else would throw themselves in front of a horse for the movement? Who else has deliberately died for it?' As she saw the look of scepticism on Rathbone's face she hurried on. 'Oh, I know many people thought Emily was rather mad. She was the first to use fire; she threw herself down the stairs at Holloway prison, and she was, indeed, a fanatic. One of the banners said: THOUGHTS HAVE GONE FORTH WHOSE POWER CAN SLEEP NO MORE. VICTORY, VICTORY.

'Emily Davison's death and her funeral today have made me one with her. I am going to be a militant too!' Standing, Rachel waved the wilting iris over her head just as Flora, also dressed in black, came into the room with her cousin, Constance Kitto. Both girls, Rathbone noticed, also had rapturous faces and, crossing through the article he had just written, he decided on the spur of the moment to write another. 'FROM TODAY, THE WOMEN CAN NEVER GO BACK.'

'A militant, did I hear?' Constance, dressed in purple – a colour that little became her stout frame – leapt about enthusiastically. But Constance, as unconcerned about her looks as she had ever been, enjoyed dressing strangely. She liked being fat because she despised those silly women who corseted themselves, suffering pain, solely to attract men. She lived in the same boarding-house as Rathbone in Islington, although she spent most of her time in and out of gaol. She was unconventional, warm-hearted, fanatical, arrogant because of her aristocratic lineage which she used quite ruthlessly to gain any advantage for the Cause. Like Emily Davison and so many others she was borne aloft by an ideal that was not religious, but which seemed to have little relationship to reality. She was unscrupulous, cunning and passionate. If the women ever got the vote she would have to find another cause to keep her going. Such people invariably needed to, and did.

She rushed now to embrace Rachel: 'Oh Rachel, are you really, darling? One of us?'

'One of you,' Rachel said clasping her.

'Where will the fire be?'

As she saw Constance's eyes gleam, Flora put her flower on Rathbone's desk and leaned against it, her face grave. 'Don't be silly, Rachel. Don't you think we've had our names in the papers enough?'

'So?' Rachel stared at her sister-in-law, dear Flora whom she loved so much, but who sometimes seemed too good and noble for this world. 'Don't you think I've been silent for long enough? Well,' she sat down in the chair and stuck out her legs. 'That is so no longer. The Earl of Askham is ruined; he has ruined himself. Many people even consider him a murderer, at the least an adulterer.'

'Rachel, I *beg* of you, dearest!' Flora started angrily away from the desk, but Rachel held up her hand.

'In many ways he *is* a murderer, though not in the way they think. He has murdered me and our love, our marriage. That is what I care about; not the family name, nor the parties and receptions, the balls and weekends we are, thank God, no longer invited to. I care about my husband and what happened to him, what he did to me. And because of him I have been silent. I have not thrown stones or set fire to houses or thrown myself under horses. Well, now,' Rachel struggled to her feet waving the crushed iris bravely over her head, 'I intend to. Lead on, Constance!'

'Rachel, really!' Rathbone, looking perplexed, lit a fresh cigarette. His fingers and beard were permanently stained with nicotine. 'You mustn't go mad now. You have been so strong, so good, so *right*. Your behaviour has been admirable and I agree with Flora. You will only hurt yourself, and maybe Bosco, even more. Even you think he's suffered enough. Whatever you say, you have done valiant service to the Cause by keeping your head clear, your voice calm above the rabble. I beg you, don't weaken, don't give in now.'

'Weaken? On the contrary I believe, at last, that I'm becoming strong. Come, Constance,' Rachel went to the door and held out her hand, 'let's go up to my room and hatch a plot.' Constance, giggling like a mischievous schoolgirl, clasped Rachel's hand and willingly allowed herself to be pulled out of the room.

'I must go and stop them,' Flora said, but Rathbone took hold of her arm and drew her back.

'When Rachel thinks about it she will see sense. She won't do anything. I've never known her like this. She's drunk on the funeral procession.'

'It was very moving.' Flora removed her glasses and, as she began to clean them, blowing on both sides and polishing them with her handkerchief, Rathbone, not for the first time, thought how attractive she could be if she tried. She had a very fine bone structure and the deprivations of her life, the added wisdom of years had honed her looks away from and beyond mere beauty. Rathbone occasionally took Flora out, but he knew that she felt unfaithful to Adam, so she talked about him all the time instead: his work, his dedication, his wasted talent. Thus it was not surprising that, finding herself alone with him now, she added: 'Adam was there, of course.'

'Of course.' Rathbone sat down at his desk and sighed, crossing through his article again. 'Flora, when will you realize . . .'

'That I will get nowhere with Adam?' She replaced her glasses neatly back on her nose, tucking the wire ends over her ears, and smiled. 'I know, I know, I know; but can't a pure love like ours be fine? I feel refined.'

'Pure love like yours is sterile when someone else loves you, Flora. Or so it seems to me.'

Rathbone, as though shocked by his own words, exhaled smoke so hard that his head was swathed in it and Flora almost lost sight of him. He waved the smoke away coughing and, as he did, he saw her face, open-mouthed, gazing at him. 'Sorry, I made a mess of my proposal,' he vainly tried to smile, watching the vapour thin out towards the window.

'*You* are proposing to me, Rathbone Collier?'

'Yes.' Eyes filled with tears from the smoke, Rathbone ground out his cigarette before it could provide camouflage for him again. 'I have loved you, Flora, for years. I know I'm the most unworthy of mortals to ask an earl's daughter to marry me, but I would hope, I would *try* to make the best of husbands.'

'Oh Rath,' Flora held out her hands and, as he seized them, his eyes were lit by hope. 'Oh Rath, that is the kindest, nicest thing that has ever happened to me – well almost, apart from Adam telling me he loved me too. And you see, it is because of that, Rath, that I can't. I am his.'

Rathbone let her arms fall and stamped his foot on the uneven boards of the floor.

'But Flora, you are *not* his! You never can be. You told me you don't want to be. Not in that way.'

'But I am, Rath, in the way that is really important. If I married you I think Adam would kill himself.'

'But Adam has no right to kill himself, would have no right! He has a wife, four children . . . Don't you think he has enough?'

'Exactly.' Flora, unperturbed by the commotion obviously taking place inside Rathbone's large breast, nodded vigorously. '*That's* why Adam needs me. In time I will have to be a surrogate mother to those children because Melanie, who used to be an excellent mother, is so no longer. She neglects them for Boofie da Ponte, just to humiliate Adam even further. Why, if I were to marry you what would happen to Adam?'

'Let him come and live with us!' Rathbone shouted, beside himself with frustration and vexation. 'I tell you what, he can have a bed in the same room. He . . .'

Flora coldly drew herself up, even more daunting than she was before. Her glare made him far more ashamed than any words could.

'I apologize,' Rathbone hung his head, 'that is no way to win you.'

'Indeed it is no way, and I hope we can remain friends, Rath, but on the same basis as now.'

'Yes.' Rathbone wearily sat down. 'Yes, of course; but, Flora, I will never ever understand how a woman as intelligent as you, as gifted as you undoubtedly are, can make herself so subservient to the needs of one man. You stand against everything that women are trying to achieve.'

'I?' Flora looked at him with amazement. 'How can you say that of me?'

'Because it's true. You are Adam's helpmeet, his secretary, his dogsbody. Adam has only to whistle and there you are, bright and cheerful, ready to please, like any Victorian woman, a mere creature to her mate. And yet, Flora, you are an important, substantial person in your own right. How is it you prefer to have no existence outside a man who can't even marry you, make love to you, be your equal – for he is no equal. In a way you are Adam's appendage just as if you were a housemaid on whose services the cleanliness of the house depended.'

'That is a very unkind, unfair, untrue thing to say,' Flora said in a low, angry voice. 'I am not Adam's servant. I just happen to believe in the things he stands for. I happen to think he is a very fine person who deserves not only better from his wife, my sister, but in his life. In many ways Adam has failed because of his altruism and nobility of character. Unless he applies himself to the law, currying briefs and doing as he is told, he will never be a KC; and unless he toadies up to Asquith, Churchill and Lloyd George he will never achieve office in Parliament. He has very little money, yet never touches a penny of Melanie's and will take none of mine. I admire him.'

'Oh, I know you admire him. But don't you want to be your own woman, Flora? Don't you?'

'I am my own woman,' she replied crossly. 'How can marriage change that, the general status of married women, property laws and so on being as they are?'

'You know you will always be equal with me. I will respect everything you are and everything you own. I will never, ever subject you to anything that displeases you because of the laws of this country. Like Mrs Pethwick-Lawrence you could add your name to mine. How would you like that? That's equality for you! And Flora, you are a woman well into her thirties. Well, I am thirty-eight. I would like children . . . wouldn't you?'

He tried to look into her eyes but she turned away.

'I like children,' she said after a while, 'of course I do. But my own? I'm not sure. I am aunt to a good many, ten nephews and nieces of my brothers and sister and many other relationships from our numerous family. In that way I am quite fulfilled.'

'Will you at least think, Flora, when you go out of here today? Will you at least turn it over in your mind?'

Flora slowly picked up the crushed iris from his desk and twirling it around in her fingers gazed at him.

'I will turn it over in my mind of course, Rath, and thank you enormously. No one has ever proposed to me before, so this is a big day in more ways than one. But I am certain I know what the answer will be. And I think you do too.'

* * *

The lights at the corners of the buildings in Covent Garden flickered, casting little illumination on the narrow passages that ran between Bow Street and the Opera House on one side and Kingsway on the other.

It amused the conspirators to meet in the proximity of the magistrate's court of which so many of them were already graduates. Constance Kitto boasted that she had been in every cell in the building.

There were ten of them because they didn't want to attract too much attention to themselves as, one by one or, at most, in twos and threes they left the meeting-place in the flat of one of their working-class colleagues, who lived in a Covent Garden tenement, and went down either Drury Lane or Bow Street to the Strand. Clutching their rocks they walked along, still in diffused groups, before gathering outside the Athenaeum Club in Pall Mall, that bastion of male privilege and reaction.

'VOTES FOR WOMEN!' Grace Featherstone cast the first stone and the others followed, but almost all went wide as the windows of the club were angrily flung open and servants began to pour down the stairs through the open door.

Rachel was one of the last to leave Covent Garden, with Constance to give her courage, because she had nearly decided not to go. As she passed the Opera House she recalled the many times she and Bosco, arriving in their chauffeur-driven motorcar, had been greeted by the manager at the door before being shown up to their box in the grand tier. The last occasion had only been a few weeks before the trial, and she had worn a new evening dress sewn with hundreds of tiny sequins which was Bosco's Christmas present to her as well as a choker of diamonds to wear with it. And how splendid Bosco had looked that night, she vividly recalled, as he always did in formal dress. How she had loved him, how proud she was to be his wife. What an ideal life it had seemed, one she had never ceased to be grateful for, perhaps because she had a premonition that one day it would suddenly be curtailed.

Now, as she crept past like a fugitive, hugging her shabby black coat that concealed a fistful of stones, a woollen hat on her head, the contrast seemed so marked, so bitter, so ironic that she almost faltered in her steps.

'Come on!' Constance urged her. 'You can't go back now.'

No, never go back. She clutched Constance's arm as they hurried through the market to the Strand.

When they got to the Athenaeum the first stones had been thrown and the advance party of women was in full flight along Pall Mall. Rachel and Constance, without crossing the street, without the chance to throw a stone, ran after them, turning the corner into St James's Square, lit up with the lights from the houses of the wealthy, including that large mansion on the west side of the Square, Askham House.

At the sight of it Rachel's nerve once again failed her and she tried to turn back, but Constance held on to her.

'You *said* you'd do it,' she said. 'You said you'd stone your own home. Think of the Cause. Think of Emily.'

Rachel paused, trembling, then took a deep breath and thought of the Cause: of Emily Davison, Constance Lytton, the Pankhursts, Annie Kenney and of all the women in and out of prison because of the iniquitous new Cat and Mouse Act. She reminded herself of all the women up and down the country who daily and nightly fired houses, barns, churches, mail boxes, anything. She thought of those who failed to pay their taxes because of the principle, as old as democracy, of no taxation without representation – a mistake which had cost England America and was now costing her the support of half of her population. Standing outside her own home Rachel looked through those familiar windows, knowing behind which was what room – that the large drawing-room, that the dining-room, that Bosco's study, and that the bedroom they had shared until a few months before.

As she stood there gazing at it, reliving memories, she could sense the faces of her comrades turned expectantly on her and then, suddenly, resolutely, she withdrew her hands from her pockets, raised one over her head and shouting: 'VOTES FOR WOMEN!' flung the largest stone she had right through the first-floor drawing-room window. Even as she heard the panes crack and the splinters fall to the ground, the others raised their arms and did the same.

The magistrate looked with impartiality at the ten women in the dock before him as the clerk of the court read out the charges: 'You are charged that you wilfully damaged the windows of the Athenaeum Club on the night of 17 September 1913 with possible danger to life, and on the same night you did also wilfully damage the windows of Askham House, St James's Square, with the same intent.'

When asked how they pleaded they all said 'Guilty', including Rachel Askham and Constance Kitto, whereupon there appeared some confusion in the box as the accused looked at each other, some shaking their heads.

At that point Adam Bolingbroke, in the well of the court, stepped forward addressing himself to the clerk, who approached the magistrate.

'I understand you represent Lady Askham, Mr Bolingbroke?'

'Yes, Sir.'

'He does not,' Rachel spoke clearly from the dock. 'I wish to represent myself.'

Brother and sister stared at each other and the magistrate, a patient man, leaned across the bench. 'As I understand, Lady Askham, it is your first time in this court, I strongly advise you to accept the offer of Mr Bolingbroke whom, I am told is also your brother.'

'Thank you, Your Worship, but I don't wish for his services.'

At this a policeman stepped forward, saying to the magistrate: 'It is my instruction, Sir, that Miss Kitto and Lady Askham were not present when the stones were thrown at the Athenaeum Club, but arrived a few minutes later, joining their comrades directly in St James's Square.'

'Are there witnesses to this, Constable?'

'Yes, Sir. Two of the waiters at the Athenaeum are acquainted with Lady Askham, as her husband Lord Askham is a member of the club, and they saw her arriving as they were giving chase to those who had thrown the stones. Her ladyship and Miss Kitto were on the other side of the street. I should add, Sir, that the police wish to offer no evidence in this case concerning Lady Askham, as the property in question concerning the second charge in St James's Square is her own home.'

There was a buzz in the court and some laughter which was promptly stopped by the magistrate.

'Lady Askham,' he said without looking at her, 'you may stand down. You are discharged.'

'But I wish to plead guilty, Sir,' Rachel said firmly, hanging on to the edge of the dock to stop herself trembling, avoiding looking at Adam.

The magistrate leaned across the bench again and this time gazed at her severely.

'Lady Askham, it is not for *you* to tell *me* what you plead when the police do not wish to prosecute on the reasonable grounds that, in the first place, you were not present at the Athenaeum Club when the damage which the prosecution said had occurred was caused by the throwing of stones and, in the second, that the property in question is yours. Please stand down.'

Rachel looked as though she was about to refuse, but the girl next to her, Margaret Prudence – who was not well named, being one of the most persistent and recalcitrant of militant offenders – whispered to her: 'You'll have to do as he says, Rachel. They'll get you for breach of the peace and that's no fun because you're only bound over. We'll do something like this again.' Margaret gave her a friendly nudge and, as a policeman opened the door, Rachel, scarlet-faced with humiliation, feeling she had let down her friends, left the dock.

As Adam came over to take her arm she furiously shook him off, marching out of the door without a backward glance at the friends she had so wished to join.

But as she walked down the steps of the court a clutch of reporters rushed towards her and, suddenly afraid, Rachel looked round to find Adam close behind. Now she allowed him to take her arm, clinging to him as he pushed through the mass of reporters and hailed a passing cab. The press swarmed about the cab as they got in, asking for a statement.

'Why did you do it, Lady Askham?'

'Is it because of your husband, Lady Askham?'

'Has it anything to do with the libel trial?'

'What has your husband said about it, Lady Askham?'

Rachel sat tight-lipped at the back of the cab and Adam shut the door and told the driver to take them to George Street.

'Why George Street?' Rachel asked as they turned the corner.

'Because they won't think of looking for you there. You've done it now, Rachel.'

'Done what?'

'You've made yourself a household name.'

'Bosco did that already at the libel trial. Everyone knows that I'm a deceived wife.'

Adam put his hand over hers and held it all the way to Marylebone.

'I knew that girl would be the death of me,' Dulcie murmured weakly. 'One day I knew she would kill me, and now she has.'

'Mother, you're not dying.' Bosco leaned over her bed, gently stroking the damp hair back from her forehead. 'Dr Fraser says it was only a fainting attack caused by strain.'

'*Only* a fainting attack? I have never fainted before in my life,' Dulcie said, recovering some of her old spirit. 'My constitution has always been remarkably sound. Fancy, her name all over the papers . . .' Dulcie let a white hand flap by the side of the bed and looked wanly at her son.

Of course he knew she was exaggerating, but in a way she had reason. Both he and Rachel had given her more cause for worry in a single year than she had had in most of her sheltered life. For a woman who was as proud as she was, to see the Askham name blazoned all over the papers in a defamatory way was as great a humiliation as if it had, indeed, happened to her. What affected one Askham affected them all.

'I'm only glad your poor father is dead or this would have killed him,' Dulcie said with magnificent disregard for logic. 'Better to have died peacefully in his bed than die, as I shall, of shame.'

'Mama, Rachel was discharged. She will not be fined or go to prison.'

'She will if she does it again, and it looks as though she's going to. She's out of hand – mad, as I always thought she was. When I think what the Kitto family went through on account of poor, silly Constance . . .' Dulcie put her hands over her eyes and started to shake.

'Mama, you must *not* carry on like this, or you will be

really ill,' Bosco said anxiously. 'You *must* rest and try and forget it. Adam has talked to Rachel and begged her to see sense. Everyone has – Flora, Melanie, Rathbone Collier. And Rachel herself was shocked when all the newspapermen tried to jump into her cab. She realized then that she is not as the other women, however much she'd like to be. Their names are unknown and subsequently quickly forgotten, unlike hers. So far as I have any influence with her I shall plead with her myself. Yet, so far she has avoided me.'

Bosco got up from the chair by his mother's bed and went to the window, gazing into the park and across to the Grange where Rachel was soon expected.

He had not been at home when the stones had been thrown but in Berkeley Square where, since his estrangement from his wife, he spent an increasing amount of time. Work now was all that Bosco felt he had to live for. Work and the children, and little enough he saw of them. He knew that he and Rachel spent their time covering up for the children, keeping them in ignorance of the terrible events that seemed continually to be overtaking the family. Terrible, and shameful. His mother was right.

Dr Fraser had been sent for when Dulcie fainted after reading the morning paper. At first it was thought she'd had a heart attack or a stroke, but there seemed to be no damage to the brain or the heart. She was simply exhausted, Dr Fraser had said, and needed to be as much protected as the children from this unwelcome notoriety, so new to the family.

'It comes to a pretty pass when you cease to have influence over your wife,' Dulcie said in ringing tones, forgetting that she was supposed to be ill. 'I suppose it's all over that woman . . .'

'Oh, please don't mention that again, Mother.' Bosco looked at his watch. 'It is all over and done with. People have forgotten now about the trial and, in time, I hope Rachel will forget about it too.'

But would he forget, and would she? Bosco gently drew the bedclothes up over his mother's shoulders and, telling her to rest and that he would be back, he went downstairs to telephone Frances to see if she would come and look after her mother-in-law.

Dearest Bosco, my darling,

Won't you come to your Nimet? Why don't you ever answer my letters? You know how sorry I am, but until I can tell you myself I shan't feel forgiven.

Remember before you spurned me when I wrote to you in Cairo and you lived to regret it. Please don't regret it again, my darling. Hugo sends tender kisses to his papa.

Your sorrowing Nimet

Bosco read the letter again and then tore it into small fragments and put it in the fire. Soon after the trial Nimet had written a letter to him explaining about the subpoena, that they had told her she had to testify and that she had no choice; how she dared not face him. But Bosco hardened his heart to any pleas from a mistress who had so injured him, and that heart remained as hard as stone. He answered through his lawyers, settling money on her and saying that any communication had to be through them. He could never forgive her, and any feelings of tenderness towards little Hugo, innocent victim, he brushed to one side. He would ensure that he was taken care of, well educated and, maybe, one day in time when the wound had healed, he would see him again. But he never wanted to see his child's mother.

Bosco was a sorrowful man and the expression on his face, the fresh lines of suffering, even moved Rachel as she came slowly into the room to find him sitting by the fire. When he saw her he jerked as if he'd been asleep, but he did not get up and she remained close to the door.

'I'm sorry about your mother,' she said. 'How is she?'

'She's very tired and weak, but not seriously ill.'

'I suppose she blames me,' Rachel perched on the arm of a chair by the door.

'Well, she had a shock. She fainted when she saw the headlines in the paper: LADY ASKHAM ARRESTED. After all, she's Lady Askham too. She thought of the Queen, who's been so good, and her friends at Court. The shame was for herself, for her name, as much as for you. You can't blame her.'

'I am genuinely sorry about your mother, that's why I came. But how people do use illness as a weapon, while the rest of us have to continue as if we were made of steel.'

'You have the advantage of years over my mother,' Bosco said bitterly. 'Sometimes I think you *are* made of steel.'

'And you? What are you made of, Bosco?'

'Flesh and blood.' Bosco jumped up. 'Needing the support and love of my wife. I'm a man and I need a woman . . .'

'I'm surprised your mistress doesn't satisfy those needs,' Rachel said coldly. 'Surely her loving arms are always open to you? Or do you lie to her too?'

'I never see her. I told you that. I made you that promise and I've kept it. She was a weakness, a folly, and it is over. I have told you a dozen times of my repentance for that folly, Rachel, and still you can't forgive me. Now this,' he looked towards the daily paper lying on the table. 'You are just putting a knife in the wound and twisting it. Surely, much as I've hurt you, I didn't deserve all this? Just when the public is forgetting? You were never a militant. What made you change your mind?'

'Emily Davison's funeral.'

'It was I who made you change your mind.' Bosco's hand thumped against his breast. 'I. By stoning Askham

House you were stoning me; by attracting banner headlines in the paper you're crucifying us all. The effect of that far outweighs any good you did, any service to your Cause, which I supported too.'

'All you can think of is the Askham name.' Rachel's scathing tone showed how unmoved she was by his words. 'Well, I don't care a fig for the Askham name. I can tell you this, Bosco,' she slowly rose to her feet and stood facing him, smaller than he was, slender in her white blouse and straight black skirt, 'I never wanted to be Lady Askham and I don't feel like Lady Askham. I don't wish to be Lady Askham. I never have. I never felt a lady in that sense, a woman of title, and I have never become one. I feel as far from your mother, from your grandparents and your ancestors as it is possible to feel. I married for love, not to be an Askham, and now that the first and most important has gone, I don't wish for the other. I don't feel at home in Askham House nor in Askham Hall, though I love the Grange, because it is a home. Nevertheless I feel now that the time has come for us to part.'

'Divorce?' Bosco could hardly pronounce the word.

'Separation. I know you won't want more headlines for the time being. I could go and live with Flora, come down here when you are away. I've thought about it very carefully in the train. I find it so hard to live with you, as we are now. I think it's warping me. I loved you passionately; but I didn't want to marry you and I never should have, because you have made me into something I didn't wish to be.'

'I beg you to rethink all this, Rachel,' Bosco said desperately. 'You have said you'd live with me and you have, without the true bonds of marriage. This strange, unnatural life I have accepted because it is better than not to have you at all. But, please, for our children's sake, don't go away, don't leave. Stay with us.' Bosco's voice broke and he held out a hand; but Rachel remained where she was, a frozen statue of wounded love, of despair. She lowered her head, at last, listening as Bosco continued:

'I love you, Rachel, I love you still. I realize how badly I wronged you and I have done penance for it. I have never seen Nimet again and I never shall. I have only room in my heart for one person and that is you, and whatever happens I will love you all my life.'

As Rachel gazed at him it was as though her heart wept; but she remained dry-eyed. She felt frozen in grief and fear because what she wanted most in her life remained unattainable, despite all that had happened – their marriage, their children, their love.

But between them now was the shadow of Nimet, and always would be. The shadow of the past – past and present irreconcilable, offering no future.

CHAPTER 22

Rathbone Collier put down *The Times* on his knee and placed his reading glasses on top of it.

'There's going to be a war,' he announced.

'Between who?' Rachel seemed to have been hearing this prognostication for years from various people, so she didn't look up but continued with her article:

The violence of certain members of the women's suffrage movement, and I must emphasize it is still only a tiny minority, does a disservice to us all. Damage to a great masterpiece like the Rokeby Venus; to the Sargent portrait of Henry James and, now, the senseless placing of a bomb under the coronation chair which could have damaged one of our priceless national institutions, Westminster Abbey, is beyond the bounds of reason and common sense . . .

'All over the world,' Rathbone said when at last she stopped writing and looked at him. 'The Archduke Ferdinand has been murdered in Sarajevo.'

'How can that possibly cause a war affecting us? Who knows who the Archduke Ferdinand is, except a few people?'

'He is the heir to the Emperor of Austria and there has already been war in the Balkans for two years. I tell you, this will be the tinder to the fire.'

'Adam said that years ago,' Rachel's eyes were on her work, 'and it hasn't happened yet.'

'Germany has been rearming for years too and, I tell you, it will. No one has that amount of armaments without wanting to use them. Germany is bristling with arms and all kinds of new weapons that will make Omdurman seem like a primitive game.'

'Ask Bosco about that!' Rachel laughed, her eyes running over her column. 'There, I think that's just about right!' She signed it with a flourish, looking pleased.

'You're not really taking any of this in are you, Rachel?'

'Any of what?' Rachel enquired.

'Anything about Archduke Ferdinand and the rearmament of Germany. It's very serious.'

'I don't see the connection.' Rachel put her copy in the basket for the copy boy, then stretched. 'Well, I feel very good today. I don't know why. Do you know, it is just over a year since Emily's funeral and still we have made no real progress. So why should I feel good?'

'Tell me.'

'I don't know. It must be the summer. It *has* been a lovely summer, hasn't it?' She gazed out of the window. 'One to remember.'

Rathbone got up from the chair in Rachel's room where he had been sitting, in companionable silence, as she worked and, coming over to her desk, perched against it.

'Has it really been a lovely summer for you, Rachel?'

'Well, weatherwise I mean.'

'I don't think you've looked happy for months, not really happy as you used to . . . as you used to look before the libel trial. You were radiant then.'

'Well, that changed things, didn't it?' she said crisply. 'A lot changed after the trial.'

'But how much of that was your fault and how much Bosco's?'

'It was all Bosco's!' Rachel said indignantly. '*I* didn't have an affair with someone else.'

'But couldn't you *ever* have it in your heart to forgive him?'

'No, I couldn't, and I never did.'

'I wonder why that was.'

'I should have thought it was quite simple.' Rachel screwed the cap on her pen. 'Have you ever had someone be unfaithful to you?'

'Yes,' Rathbone nodded, and Rachel looked at him with surprise.

'Really?'

'Yes. I was married once. My wife was unfaithful to me.'

'I didn't know.'

'And look at Adam. His wife's unfaithful to him. I have reason to know that, and regret it, because of Flora.'

'Well, Flora's just a silly girl. I think she likes being hurt.'

'You're very hard at times, you know, Rachel.'

'*I*? Hard?' Rachel's affronted expression made Rathbone wonder if he'd gone too far. But he was a persistent man and, doggedly, continued:

'You don't think you are, but occasionally it's true. I know how much Bosco loves you, how much he regrets the past. He is my employer and my friend and I know him a good deal better than you think.'

Rachel leaned her elbow on the desk and cupped her chin in her hands.

'Did he put you up to all this?'

'No, he didn't! He *never* talks to me about you except with affection and love, and regret. I know that you just live together, ostensibly as man and wife, for the sake of appearances.'

'How do you know that?' Rachel said sharply.

'I know it, never mind. Bosco didn't tell me, but I know about your bargain: until the children are old enough you will stay together and, for his sake and theirs, you desisted from further militancy in the movement as long as he left you alone.'

'Flora told you?'

'I can't say who told me, but I *know*; and a lot of other people know and regret it, because they think of you and Bosco as a fine couple who really love each other and should be together. You should forgive Bosco, Rachel, and forget. He has done his penance. Have you ever thought that there is an element of selfishness in all this as far as you are concerned? And I speak as a friend.'

'How do you mean, selfish?'

'The marriage vows included the good things and the bad.'

'They didn't include infidelity, as I recall.'

'No, but for better or for worse. Bosco didn't desert you, go off with this woman. He was tempted and he fell. She nearly destroyed him, and in these lonely months since everyone deserted him he has been bereft of your love as well. Doesn't it pain you to see how unhappy he is? Does it surprise you he would welcome a war to escape?'

'Why are you telling me all this today?' Rachel tapped her fingers on her desk as if she were impatient to finish.

'I just thought it was time someone, who has both your interests at heart, said something. An affair is a sad betrayal but need not be a mortal wound. I loved my wife, even though she was unfaithful to me, and I forgave her.'

'And what happened?'

Rathbone smiled. 'She was unfaithful again, and that was too much. Bosco will never be unfaithful to you again. He hates himself for what he did. Why not be magnanimous, Rachel? Why not swallow your pride and take him in your arms, before it is too late?'

'Too late? What do you mean, too late?' Rachel frowned as Rathbone tapped the newspaper now in his hands.

'Because there *is* going to be a war. It will not be like Omdurman. All Europe will be on fire, and I happen to know that Bosco is trying to enlist. *That* is why I spoke today.'

Rachel felt as if someone had thrown iced water over her. 'Enlist?'

'In the Lancers. He's trying to rejoin his old regiment.'

'But how do you know this and not I?' Rachel stood up angrily.

'Because, maybe, you don't talk any more. Do you?'

'We live together. Of course we talk.'

'Yes, but intimately, like husband and wife, sharing. Do you talk like that?'

Rachel flung back her head and stared at him. 'We don't talk like that, but I would have expected to be told something like this. I wish you'd tell me who told you. Did Bosco?'

Rathbone shook his head and, coughing, lit a fresh cigarette, the last one hardly cold in its tray.

'Another sad man told me. Another unhappily married husband. Adam is trying to do the same thing. They both want to go to war, maybe they want to get killed.'

Rachel threw open the door of Askham House and looked wildly around so that Bromwich was concerned to discover what was amiss.

'Did someone chase you, my lady?'

'Is his lordship here, Bromwich?'

'He just left, my lady.'

'Where to? Where did he go?'

'I think he was walking to Berkeley Square, my lady. He said he would not be in for dinner.'

Rachel flew out of the door, down the stairs and across the Square, up Duke of York Street and along Jermyn Street, looking frantically at the backs of the people walking along the street ahead of her. Which way would he go? This seemed the logical way; through Burlington

Arcade. Or would he go into Berkeley Street, or up Albemarle Street?

She stopped and realized she didn't know. He could go in almost any direction. He could have taken a cab. It didn't really matter, because she could find her own way to Berkeley Square, but the panic that had overtaken her in the office refused to go away. She would lose Bosco. She had lost him already. In the time it had taken to get from Fleet Street to St James's Square by cab she had completed a self-examination whose conclusions rather appalled her. Instead of seeing herself as a victim she suddenly had the insight of Rathbone, or Flora or Adam. She became not a victim but a monster of selfishness who refused to forgive, who, as Bosco had once said, twisted the knife in the wound. Well, she had suffered, but so had he. How she had made him suffer! How drained of revenge she felt now in this frenzy of remorse, this desire for reconciliation. She stopped in the street feeling so dejected and disconsolate that she could have openly wept, and one or two people passing glanced curiously at the unhappy-looking woman standing in the middle of the pavement, looking this way and that.

'I do beg your pardon,' the gentleman, emerging from Turnball and Asser with a parcel under his arm, said politely as he almost collided with her. Then, looking again, he stopped and exclaimed: 'Why, Rachel.'

'Oh Bosco!' Rachel threw her arms around him, regardless of the glances even more numerous and curious. She drew back and looked at him.

'What's the matter?'

'Nothing, I thought . . .'

Bosco's expression of politeness – he had doffed his hat almost instinctively before realizing who she was – slowly gave way to bewilderment. 'But what did you think? Where were you going?'

'I was looking for you.' She stared back at him not quite knowing what to say.

'But, my dear, has something happened? The children?' Anxiously he seized her by the arm and gently, silently steered her down the street and home.

Bromwich, who had been hovering by the door, let them in, observing that her ladyship appeared even more agitated than when she had left a few minutes before.

'Send tea to my study, Bromwich, and some brandy,' Bosco said without further explanation, his arm still tenderly round Rachel's shoulders.

Bromwich bowed and Bosco led her, still wearing her coat, up the stairs to the small room next to the main drawing-room where he worked when he was at home. Though it was a warm day she was trembling.

Bosco sat her down in a chair and half filled a balloon glass with brandy that he had in his study.

'I fear something terrible has happened, Rachel. Is it Mama? Please tell me.'

Rachel shook her head and, now that they were alone, she put it between her hands and wept openly.

'It's about . . . you.'

'*Me*?' Bosco looked surprised and poured himself a brandy too. 'Then it can't be so bad.'

'I've just heard that you're enlisting in the Lancers.'

'Ah!' Bosco nodded and sat down, content with the explanation. 'Melanie told you?'

'Rathbone told me. He said you and Adam were two unhappily married men who wanted to join up.'

Bosco smiled and sipped his drink. 'Perhaps something like that.'

'Why didn't you tell me?'

'Because, my darling Rachel, I didn't think you would care very much.'

'Oh Bosco.' Rachel flung herself out of her chair and

knelt by his side. 'When Rathbone told me I suddenly knew that you would go to the war that you have always said would happen, and that it would be my fault.'

'No, it's not your fault.' Bosco gently stroked her hair back from her head. 'I want to enlist anyway. I always enjoyed soldiering, and if there is a war they will want experienced men. That's what I thought anyway, but I was wrong.'

'They *don't* want you?' She smiled, relieved.

Sadly Bosco shook his head. 'They say I'm too old; but I really think they don't want a disgraced officer who might have murdered somebody to lead their fine body of men. The Guards – all regiments – turned me down too. I am *persona non grata*, it seems, even in the army.'

Rachel took his hand and nudged it with her nose.

'You have suffered terribly, haven't you? In every way?'

As he nodded and smiled she realized with a shock how little she had really looked at him these past months. His hair was quite grey at the sides and his face was, surely, prematurely lined for a man under forty?

Rachel felt such pity and remorse at that moment that she was in danger of feeling more sorry for herself than for him: her victim. The victim of her failure to realize that a greater love is required when one has experienced a great wrong – that life is rather like a series of proportions, requiring different amounts at different times.

'I have been a very bad wife to you, Bosco,' she said sadly.

'Is this just because I want to enlist, this concern?'

'You are right to be sceptical, but it came to me today how selfish I'd been. You lost not only your reputation, your friends, the love and support you needed from me, but your self-respect as well. Rathbone helped me realize my own culpability and to see how rejected you've felt.'

'I have been rejected, it's true, but I knew that would pass. It's passing already. Someone smiled at me in the Reform the other day, and Mr Asquith shook my hand in Parliament Square. People *do* forget. But the Lancers and the Guards, well, it's true that hurt a bit. They don't want me, not because of my age, but because of my past.' He gazed at her sadly, continuing to stroke her head. 'But I have paid for it all – my debt to society and to you. I am a scandal; maybe a murderer, certainly a fornicator. I am a lonely man and, sometimes, I do think that my life really isn't worth living.'

'Is it too late for us?' Rachel said, kissing his hand.

'Are you ready to forgive me?'

'If you don't go away, but stay with me. Let's make a bargain. Let's begin again.'

Bosco leaned back in his chair, his eyes smarting with tears. 'We can begin again, with what time we have.'

'We have all the time. You have no need to enlist.'

'I have a need,' Bosco said. '*If* my country is at war – and there's no certainty we will be – I want to go too.'

'Not if I plead with you?'

'Not even if you plead with me, my darling.' He leaned forward, taking her head between his hands, his eyes alight with tenderness. 'Believe me, this day you have made me the happiest of men if you mean to restore our love. We have both, in this past dreadful year, learned a lot about ourselves we didn't know before. We have learned a lot about others, too, and who our friends are. With this self-knowledge – and our love which, I feel, has never died – we can help each other. But I shall not think myself worthy of you if others are fighting while I stay at home. Anyway, no one might take me. I am trying now for a line regiment which is where all the fun will be.'

* * *

It was not much fun. It was certainly nothing like Omdurman – that small, almost cosy little battle that had lasted two hours. This one not only had all the casualties and the violence of the Sudan, but the unspeakable mutilations caused by the modern weapons of a new kind of war.

Looking at Omdurman in perspective now was like looking at Waterloo. This war was not only sharp and fierce, brutal and unrelenting, it was also going to last a long time. Bosco, who had crossed with the Middlesex Regiment almost at the beginning and heard the talk about the war being over by Christmas, knew now that they were all wrong. The British army, faced with the overwhelming superiority of well-trained, well-equipped and prepared, disciplined German forces, who had several times nearly conquered them, knew that if it did not end in defeat for the British as the Germans quickly pressed on to Paris it would last a very long time indeed.

If the Germans had been able to do what they wanted when they crossed the Belgian border, and had streamed on to Paris, the war might well have been over before Christmas. But the assembled British and French armies staked out in hastily dug narrow trenches in Flanders and Picardy somehow, miraculously, prevented this, despite the setbacks at Mons, Le Cateau and the Battle of the Marne. The vast German army failed in its attempts to push them back into the sea and, despite the horrific losses, the Allies hung on.

It was not a clean war – a quick sabre thrust, a lance in the arm, a neat rifle bullet through the head. It was a dirty, vicious, frightful war, the troops permanently weary, muddy and soaked to the skin and, as the winter advanced, the conditions worsened.

Bosco had enlisted under the name of Down and was given his old rank of Captain. He was older than most of the other captains and, indeed, than most of the men with whom he fought. The ages of some of the young recruits appalled him; but their stamina and enthusiasm, at least in the beginning, were inspiring, and so was the overall order and discipline in the ranks of an army most of whose members had never seen action before.

Bosco never felt nostalgia for the cavalry because this was not a war for horses, but for howitzers, bombs, machine guns, rifles, knives and, too often, bare hands as the troops tore at the barbed wire that stood between them and the enemy trenches. As part of the 8th Infantry Brigade Bosco fought in all the major battles up to Christmas 1914. He was twice slightly wounded, once in the arm and once, more seriously, in the thigh when he had to be taken to a field hospital and laid up for several days before he was ready for action again.

In August, General Smith-Dorrien's 2nd Army Corps, of which Bosco's division was part, had numbered 37,000 men; by the middle of October, when Bosco got his thigh wound at La Bassée, it had lost 25,000 of them. By mid-October they had fought night and day with scarcely any sleep – or what there was broken by the rain. They were constantly penetrated by the cold and half-blinded by the fog, to say nothing of the continual fear engendered by the possibility of enemy patrols lurking behind every narrow piece of scrub or thorn hedge.

Yet as late as the end of October the 2nd Corps, or its remnants, supplemented by men hastily drafted from England, were in action again at the Bois de Biez near Neuve-Chapelle when twelve enemy battalions tried to rush their trenches. In the darkness they were pushed back, with heavy loss of life on both sides, by the Gordon Highlanders and the Royal Scots who almost lifted the enemy out of their trenches on the points of their bayonets.

The Middlesex Regiment fell in to man the trenches.

Bosco, recovered from his thigh injury but still feeling the effects of exhaustion, was back again with his troops, raised now to the rank of Major because of the heavy loss among senior officers. But on 26 October Sir John French strengthened the Smith-Dorrien Corps with the 2nd Cavalry Division and three Indian battalions. Nevertheless the Germans were still able to entrench themselves in the village of Neuve-Chapelle, near the centre of the British line, inflicting heavy losses on the Royal Fusiliers.

On 28 October a fresh assault was made on the village by Smith-Dorrien's troops and by the 29th it had been evacuated, although only temporarily, to be reoccupied later by the Germans.

For such was the minute progress made by both sides in the war – a few hundred feet of ground, lost, recaptured and lost again. It must have seemed to an invisible beholder – were there one – like a busy line of ants going again and again over the same ground, retreating, reconquering and then beginning all over again.

At the end of October, General Mackenzie, who had succeeded General Hamilton, killed by a stray burst of shrapnel, was invalided home and Bosco's 3rd Division fell under the command of General Wing. The 2nd Army Corps had lost 360 officers and 8,200 men since the middle of the month when they had crossed the La Bassée canal.

On 29 October they were taken out of the front line, and Bosco and many others were promised leave for the first time. Bosco's thigh wound had not healed completely, and he was taken to hospital in Boulogne and given a week's rest and treatment. He was then asked if he wanted to be sent home on leave, but, hearing how hard pressed the 2nd Corps were – the bulk of them having been sent north to assist the defenders in the first Battle of Ypres – he asked to be returned to the trenches. There his brigade, the 8th, remained with General Maude's 14th

Brigade and the Indian Battalions still manning the trenches south in La Bassée. Bosco made many bold sorties in and around Ploegsteert and the Plygon and the Nonnenboschen woods, leading small parties of volunteers to flush out the enemy, an activity requiring skill, which he had in plenty, and selfless daring which, together with so many of his fellow officers and men, he possessed in full measure.

On 17 November the battalions of the 2nd Corps were active south of Ypres on the Menin road with Lord Cavan's Guardsmen on their right, and the cavalry to the right of them. This day Bosco nearly lost his life capturing an enemy trench with a small party of his men. He was separated from the body of the troops and had to lie where he was, surrounded by vigilant Germans, until dark when, bleeding from cuts all over his body from thorns and barbed wire, he made his way back to the line with a wounded fellow officer, Lieutenant John Daley of the Guards.

By this time both armies, the Germans and the English, were tired and there was a lull until 23 November when the Germans attacked eight hundred yards of trenches near Armentières held by the valiant Indian troops. The Germans caused havoc with their *minen-werfers*, small mortars projecting enormous bombs, some weighing as much as 200 pounds. The Germans were repulsed, the fighting lasting well into the night with the Gerwhalis Indians gleefully cutting enemy throats with their fearsome knives, and a small party of Wilde's rifles causing carnage with hand bombs.

On 14 December Bosco was back with the 8th Brigade and in action again with the Royal Scots and the Gordons. By this time he had accumulated a considerable reputation, and whenever he asked for volunteers there was no shortage of men willing to come forward and follow him.

He was fearless, selfless, brave and yet showed extraordinary thoughtfulness to his troops, never risking a life unless it was absolutely necessary and the objective clear. Already he had become a legend, and his name, although he didn't know it, figured regularly in despatches flashed back to headquarters. In the army Bosco appeared once again to have found himself. He loved the life, the comradeship with men of all kinds, the eternal presence of danger. He liked sleeping in his clothes in the muddy trenches, eating out of tins and slopping around in the wet, edging through the fog peering forwards towards one knew not what.

In those days he ceaselessly thought of Rachel and his family and of a past which now, confronted with this monumental danger, seemed trivial. What was it to lose one's reputation in a court of law, however ill-deserved, when one hourly went in danger of complete annihilation? Fundamentals such as those through which he now lived made everything else unimportant. But it restored to him a joy and adventure in living which he had largely forgotten.

The important things, apart from war, were the family and the various manifestations of love: love for his wife, his mother, his legitimate children, his sisters, his dead father and brother and love for . . . little Hugo? Bosco thought about him a great deal because he realized he was now more ashamed of this than anything else, depriving a small innocent boy of the love of a father. One day, he thought, he would make it up to him. One day, if he could.

In common with many others – he knew because they frequently talked about it – Bosco never thought of death as applying to himself. He saw others around him die continually, sometimes in the most appalling manner, yet he was sure that there was no bullet, no bomb or stray piece of shrapnel marked for him. This knowledge enabled him to increase his acts of harassing the enemy behind their own lines; to perform astonishing feats and take risks, because he knew that his name had not appeared on death's chariot yet.

On 14 December the task was to take possession of the Petit Bois at Wytschaete which had been unsuccessfully attacked by the Lincolns a few days before. The big guns were turned on the wood as the members of the Brigade swarmed ahead and, the Royal Scots in the lead, drove the Germans to the far end and established machine-gun positions. The Gordons, under Major Baird, dashed forward and gained ground; the Middlesex with Bosco in the lead following up. Bosco, seeing that Major Baird could not maintain his position, called for a small party of volunteers to help him destroy the deadly German machine guns which were now in action.

Immediately a sergeant and three troopers came forward, and they crept beneath the undergrowth and began to hurl hand bombs at the enemy position.

Bosco saw his sergeant rise to lob a bomb and, as he did, he was caught in the chest by machine-gun fire and fell bleeding to the ground. Instructing his men to retreat Bosco crept forward to his sergeant and, catching hold of his legs, began to drag him slowly to safety. As he did so a solitary sniper, rising unseen from the ground, raised his gun and killed the sergeant – if he was not dead already – with a bullet that went through his body and into Bosco's right arm, momentarily paralysing it. The blood spurted into Bosco's face and, thinking his jugular had been severed, he reached for his lanyard to try and make a tourniquet. One of his men, Private Rose, charging forward in a lull, lifted him right off the ground and hurled him among the ranks of the Gordons who were slowly retreating.

'You're lucky to be alive,' Major Baird said. Then, eyeing him doubtfully, added, 'that's *if* you live.'

Bosco lived, bruised, cut, his arm surprisingly only broken by the swift, clean passage of the bullet. He was taken immediately to the field station where his skill in applying a ready-made tourniquet was praised by the casualty officer: 'I seem to have seen you a lot before. Isn't it time you had a rest? Well, you'll have no choice with this. Back to England, my lad, for you.'

Bosco then allowed himself the luxury of fainting. Maybe it was with pain or because he knew that a job well done had to have its own reward.

Lying in bed at the Grange he found that the abnormal quiet got on his nerves. He listened with an eagerness Rachel couldn't understand for the sound of the children scampering up the stairs and along the corridor to see him. What amazed her about Bosco was that, incredibly, he was alive.

His body was lacerated with bullet grazes, cuts made by knives, bayonets and barbed wire. The old wound in his thigh constantly suppurated and must have frequently caused him pain, and his arm, though mending well, looked as though it had been almost severed at the joint. Dr Fraser, on one of his frequent calls, looked at him with satisfaction.

'Well, you'll not go back now. I think you have earned a desk job, Lord Askham.'

'If I had a desk job I'd shoot myself,' Bosco said. 'You've no idea how exciting it is out there, Dr Fraser! A man never has a moment to feel bored, though we're all weary to death. I don't think I ever felt so alive except, maybe, in the Lancers.'

'Are you never frightened?' The doctor, forgetting himself, sat on his lordship's bed.

'Frequently terrified, but then the blood races through the body and the fear literally ebbs away. It is only after a battle that one realizes what nearly happened and then, maybe, one feels a touch of fear. Like this,' Bosco looked sourly at his bandaged arm. 'I tell you, I must be ready soon after Christmas. We've a heck of a job to do out there.'

Rachel, perched on the foot of his bed listening, gazed at Dr Fraser.

'He can't go back, can he? Not ever?'

'Well, he *can* go back, I suppose,' Dr Fraser said doubtfully, 'but I don't know if he can take much more punishment. The army doctors seem quite happy if he has a staff job. They seem to think you'll get a medal for this latest action – one of a long line.'

'Oh, they give medals away like peas,' Bosco said dismissively. 'Every man there is a hero in his way. In one engagement when the staff tried to find survivors to make recommendations for medals, they couldn't because everyone was dead. There are more unsung heroes there than you will ever know.'

'Bosco, I do wish you'd stay, darling.'

After Dr Fraser had gone Rachel moved up the bed and took his hand. 'Like Dr Fraser says, I feel you can't go on like this. It's tempting fate.'

'My dearest,' Bosco drew her to him with his free arm. 'As I'm not dead now I never will be, at least not in this war. I lead a charmed life.'

'But you can't go on through years of this! Besides, there's no need. Surely, surely you've proved your point? They say that more than half the men sent out there are slaughtered.'

'I can go on as long as they can go on,' Bosco began stubbornly, then stopped as a small head appeared round the door.

'Papa, may I come in?'

'Of course you may, darling.' Releasing Rachel, Bosco held out the good arm and Charlotte, his darling, leapt on to his bed, putting both hands tightly around his neck.

'Ralph says when can you come down and play soldiers? He has them all set up in the playroom.'

'Do you still run messages all the time for Ralph?' Bosco tapped her snub little nose. 'What will he do when you're grown up? Will you do it then?'

'Yes, Papa!' Charlotte loved Ralph even more, she thought, than she loved her father. When she was tiny she had followed him around, and now he only had to lift a finger for his orders immediately to be carried out. Bosco thought of his own independent sisters during their childhood, and how odd it was that, whereas they had grown up in the last years of Victorian England when women were much more submissive than they were now, they were so independent and headstrong. Yet these days when women were gaining so much respect for themselves by nursing all over Europe and the Balkans in lonely and dangerous places, or making munitions alongside the men in factories in England, his little tomboy daughter, instead of being independent, was submissive as her aunts, and certainly her mother, never had been.

'Papa can't come down until his arm is better, darling. He may come down for Christmas Day, but not to do anything too vigorous, although God knows I don't want him to get so *much* better that he can go to France again.'

'Are you going away again, Papa?' Charlotte said seriously, creeping into his arms.

'Maybe, in a month or so. We'll see. Lots of time for games before then.'

Bosco loved his children, his home. As he was the ideal soldier so was he also, happily reunited with his wife, the ideal family man. With a lot of effort and string-pulling and help from no less a person than Lord Kitchener of Khartoum, Minister for War, Bosco was home within a week of his injury. Mabel and Melanie were in France with a special mobile hospital unit, and had him whisked from Armentières to Boulogne and then to Dover in no time at all. He was seen by army surgeons at Dover where Rachel met him with an ambulance she'd hired from the General hospital in Winchester and, by 20 December, two days before, he was home.

Later that day the children came up to play in his room, Ralph importantly bossing the others about – Charlotte and the six-year-old twins, the Honourable Frederick and Lady Augusta Down, known as Freddie and Gus.

Rachel left Bosco alone with the children, after telling them to be careful and not too boisterous, because she knew how important it was for him to be with them. She thought, as she went downstairs, that these last few days had been for her the attainment, at last, of a summit of happiness. The realization that her husband was alive, when so many like him had been left behind, dead, made Bosco doubly precious, the marriage doubly secure and the wish to have him home permanently doubly strong.

On Christmas Day Dr Fraser allowed Bosco to get out of bed and be taken over to the Hall to enjoy the festivities, organized by Flora and Frances who were staying with Dulcie. Frances's girls, who were rarely allowed to go to parties, went almost frantic with excitement when they could. Also there was Adam who had briefly come over to see Bosco and was staying at the Grange before going to the Lightermans. There Sir Robert, his two daughters and their husbands and large families, were looking after the four Bolingbroke children and trying to carry on in the absence of Melanie and Mabel.

After a lot of negotiating with his chambers and the

House of Commons Adam had been released, and had been training with a London Territorial regiment due to embark for France some time in the New Year.

Also at the family lunch, held at the Hall on Christmas Day, were Dulcie's sister-in-law Lady Kitto and her daughter Constance who had brought such pain and disgrace to the Kitto family with her constant sojourns in prison, made much of in the newspapers. But Constance thrived on gaol life, and looked now bonny and well and also as fat as though she'd just been on a Mediterranean cruise.

The lunch was held in the enormous dining-room at the back of the house with a view of Askham Forest and the Grange nestling in front of it resembling, from this distance, the little house of Hansel and Gretel in the fairy story. Rachel, quiet for a minute during the festivities and looking about her, listening to the chatter, suddenly vividly recalled the first time she'd eaten here when Bosco was invalided home from Omdurman, and she had come as a visitor and unexpectedly stayed longer. How awed she'd felt in that dining-room that winter's day in 1899 – almost the exact time of year as now – with Lady Askham looking down her nose at her, and Adam and Lord Askham trying very hard to find a topic of conversation of interest to them all. They'd finally decided on Egypt . . . Egypt! How long ago, how far away it all seemed now.

'And yet,' she heard Bosco saying, 'although fought on a completely different scale, the first time I saw the Germans advance last August, spread out over the plain in front of the English trenches, I thought immediately of Omdurman.

'They advanced, not in a shoulder-to-shoulder column as is common in modern warfare, but spread out over the plain during what, in the days of Omdurman, we called twenty-acre formation – a vast crowd scattered at the front and thick at the back. Our men simply waited for them to get near enough and shot them down. It was a massacre on the Omdurman scale, and I could hardly believe it. It was like the Dervishes all over again and, like the Dervishes, they kept on coming.'

After that, though, they'd got more cunning and Bosco spared the company at table, which included the children, many of the obscene details of battle that even he found hard to believe in this elegant candlelit room; the huge Christmas tree behind the table with its beautiful polished twinkling silver, the dusk gathering outside in the late afternoon. Beside them the liveried footmen stood as they had served the Askham family at dinner for generations, and downstairs in the kitchen the chef and his staff would be preparing the delicious dishes, oblivious of war.

'They say the King has given up wine for the war?' Bosco looked at his mother and raised his glass.

'He has, to show an example. 'Life at Buckingham Palace is very austere, more austere than in most humble houses in the country, though you might not believe it.'

'His Majesty came to the front in December. It did the men a power of good just to see him.'

'He was so graciously touched and moved by their devotion,' Dulcie said. 'He told me too, in confidence, that he had heard very stirring reports of your personal bravery and how angry many of the Guard's officers were that you had been turned down by them.'

'One always finds one's friends a little too late,' Bosco said without bitterness. 'I'm proud now to be in the Middlesex, a fine regiment. They are known as "the Diehards" and could not be better named.'

'To the men of the Middlesex.' As Adam raised his glass the reflection of candlelight through the red wine in the crystal reminded Rachel of blood and, suddenly rigid with fear and apprehension on that happy day, she closed her eyes to blot out the sight.

Afterwards, as was the custom, and had been for generations, there were games in the big hall in which the children of all the senior staff and estate workers joined. Rachel wanted Bosco to go back to bed, but he insisted on escorting his mother, who always presented the prizes, sitting next to her with his heavily bandaged arm in a sling. The servants, dressed in their Christmas best, stood around, shoulder to shoulder with the Askham family and its guests in a customary display of the true English spirit of comradeliness and democracy that was as old to the Askhams as their name. The same spirit that Bosco had seen day after day in France where officers and men risked their lives together for the same cause, the same desire for freedom, the same dear country they loved. Bosco fondly eyed his children, who competed in the games with the same skills, disadvantages and fears as the other children, as anxious to win and receive a prize as anyone else there.

Charlotte, like her cousin Susan, was a tomboy and known in the family as Charlie. She was only seven, dark-haired, dark-eyed and always into mischief. Ralph, a year older, was a serious boy, very like Rachel with fair hair that looked, even in winter, as though it were permanently streaked by the sun. He seemed to realize the extent of his future responsibilities, to be very much aware of being young Lord Gore, heir to his father who even now was every day in peril at the war. Ralph was a warm, affectionate boy, a great companion to Rachel since Bosco left, a foil between her and his grandmother who adored him. But he seemed intuitively to sense his mother's position and, although he loved his grandmother, he was never dominated by her.

The twins, Freddie and Gus, were full of energy and charm. Again the boy was fair and the girl dark, thus fulfilling some sort of genetic law that boys resemble their mothers and girls their fathers. All the Askham children were handsome without being as beautiful as Bobby Lighterman or Jordan Bolingbroke. They were even-tempered, jolly, normal sort of children of whom any parent would be proud.

During the party, which went on until nightfall, Dulcie and Bosco chatted together from time to time as if sharing some happy memory of the past, some child they had known in infancy who was now so tall or one who was so clever he had gone to grammar school. Bosco knew them all; in many cases he'd grown up with the parents who came over to him for a word, a clasp of the hand, a comradely pat on the shoulder. It was a happy, nostalgic day, one, Bosco knew, he would frequently return to in his mind when tramping through the Flanders' mud.

During the party Flora and Adam slipped out by the front door and, well wrapped up against the cold, went for a turn round the lake, she slipping her arm through his.

'I wish you weren't going.'

'I'm looking forward to it. Bosco says it's all enormous fun.'

'Fun! Have you seen his wounds? His body is a mass of scars. Rachel said she nearly fainted when she first helped him to bathe.'

'Well, that's fun,' Adam said jovially. 'Bosco likes that sort of thing. All boys love bandages.'

'I must say, apart from that, he looks marvellously well, and cheerful. How I hope he and you come safe home again. So many people we know are already dead. Why should you and Bosco escape?'

'Why not?' Adam said taking her hand and rubbing it gently. 'You know, after the war, Flora, Mel and I will probably get a divorce?'

'Well?' She stopped walking and looked at him. In the

dusk a duck made a last, panicky flight across the water to join its mates, sending up a wash that sent wide ripples on the calm wintry surface.

'Well, will you be thinking about it?'

'About what?'

'Don't be silly, Flora. I'm certain we can marry. There must be a way round.'

'I could never marry my sister's husband,' Flora said quietly. 'I've told you that, Adam. Our relationship is different, finer.'

'Yes, but it's not enough . . . for me.' He looked at her, wanting so much to kiss her; but they had never kissed, their lips had never met. Occasionally they held hands; but anything more intimate was forbidden. Forbidden by Flora.

'In that case, if you feel like that, and I do know what you mean, you'll have to marry someone else.' Suddenly, not knowing it was going to happen, Flora burst into tears and leaned against him, propelled by the violence of her sobs.

'Flora, Flora darling.' In vain he tried to comfort her but for several moments her body shook, the tears from her eyes wetting his lapel and the shoulder of his coat. He raised her chin, gazing at her white face, her eyes scarcely visible now that it was almost dark. 'What is it?'

'It's just . . .' Flora sobbed, 'that i . . . if you . . . m . . . m . . . married someone else I couldn't live.'

'Don't worry, I shan't,' Adam held her closely in his arms, patting her. 'If I can't marry you, I won't marry anybody.'

'That was a lovely day,' Bosco said later that night when he and Rachel were lying together in the big four-poster family bed that had belonged to his grandparents, Phyllida Askham having brought it with her when she moved into the Grange. The children, tired out with the fun of the day, were asleep, and the servants too slumbered happily in their beds, replete with rich food and perhaps, one or two of them, slightly drunk on good draught beer and glasses of crusted port. It had taken Bosco some time to get used to the silence of the nights at Askham; to the fact that one could go to bed and sleep until morning without being woken by sporadic gunfire, the threat of night attacks, or cramp brought about by the cold and damp. Sometimes the peace of the nights was so profound that he could hardly sleep at all. 'It was a real traditional family Christmas,' he continued as Rachel snuggled against him. 'Who knows . . .' he stopped and she edged even closer to him, suddenly aware of the chill of the night outside, remembering the blood-coloured wine twinkling grimly in the glasses.

'Who knows?' she prompted.

'Nothing.'

'You were going to say "who knows when we'll have another?"'

'Well, who does know?' She felt his face turn to her and he chuckled. 'I may not have leave next year, or the war might be over or . . .' he paused again.

'You might be dead,' she whispered, and felt the fierce restraining embrace of his good arm.

'Darling, why do you torment yourself? You might be run down by a bus or a cab as you tear along Fleet Street with your copy. Mama might have the heart attack she's always threatening to have. No one can ever say at the end of one year what's going to happen by the end of the next.'

'Still I do think of it. Flora was reminding us tonight of the people we know who are already dead. You have much more chance of being shot at the front than I have of being killed by a bus in Fleet Street.'

'It's a chance we must take.'

'But it's not *necessary*, Bosco!' Rachel angrily sat up and put on the light by the side of their bed so that he could see by the expression on her face how real was her fear. 'You have already served your country well. You have made your point, the point you wanted to make ever since the trial. You are a hero, not a coward. You may get a medal. You can now quite comfortably take a back seat.'

He saw she was angry, true, but also how lovely she was – her blonde hair framing her face, that grave, very English face with its straight eyebrows, full but sculptured lips and firm chin. It was a face of character, but not humourless. Rachel could laugh, and she could love. Reaching across he put off the light and pulled her down beside him.

'I can never take a back seat. I wouldn't be comfortable in it.'

'You will never forget Omdurman, will you?'

He shook his head, his eyes sad with past memories. 'Never.'

'You weren't a coward *then* and you're not now. But you will never stop trying to prove yourself, Bosco, until . . .' Suddenly, breaking under a strain she had borne for so many weeks, she burst into tears. 'Until you're dead. *Then* you'll want HERO written on your grave.'

Bosco took her gently in his arms and put his hand tenderly behind her head as though he were rocking a baby. 'Darling, don't torture yourself. Believe me, if you were at the front these notions would never occur to you. It may be cold and wet and bloody and, maybe, dangerous, but it isn't all the time. We have many moments of pleasure and good humour. One day I came upon the 12th Lancers. I knew one or two of them and they let me have a mount and we had a race. That was one of the few times it was ever known I was the Earl of Askham, because one of the men I knew had been at Omdurman. The 21st have gone to India, but he wanted to fight. That was a day of good fun and sport, and in the evening we billeted in an old farmhouse and had a wonderful meal cooked by the farmer's wife and several bottles of good wine.

'And then, sometimes, the mornings are marvellous, the larks singing and the sky so blue and clear. I stroll around quite a lot, as though I were walking in the country. I meet a lot of people I know – Lord Carvan is there with the Guards and making a name for himself, by the way, as a bit of a swashbuckler. Some people, knowing me, remember the reputation of Bosco Kitto and call me a chip off the old block. I like the company of men and the comradeship. I really do enjoy myself a lot and I'll be sorry when it ends, though I hate to see good chaps being killed. All this has taken my mind off what happened last year; and when I come back in peacetime the slate will be clean and I'll feel a new man. Sometimes I'm really sorry I left the army because I feel at home there. I would never leave voluntarily so long as I can fight, Rachel, until the war is over so, please, my darling, put it out of your mind for good. Enjoy your life, as I enjoy mine.'

He kissed her tenderly and Rachel, thoughtful for a while, stroked his face, relishing the pleasure of touch, the present gift of life.

'All right, I'll be brave too,' she said. 'I will never refer to it, or ask you for the rest of your leave or ever again. There was a time when I didn't support you, and I should have done. Now I'm going to support you to the hilt.'

'And never refer to *that* again either. That's an order,' Bosco said sternly. 'That was a time that perhaps had to happen between us. It happens to many men and women, husbands and wives. Some never get over it and remain strangers all their lives, like poor Adam and Mel. Thank God we did get over it, and we've known since the kind of love we didn't have before to make up for it. Your daily letters to France are a joy to me and I never close my eyes without thinking of you. That's something, Rachel, isn't it?'

'Yes.' Rachel felt like crying but for him, a soldier, and knowing now how it was to be a soldier's wife, tears were a weakness, forbidden. So instead of crying she smiled. 'Love we never had before and worth having now.'

'Would you like another child?' Bosco said suddenly.

'Why?' Rachel, her mind still on the war and its possibilities, was taken completely by surprise.

'I think it might be rather nice to have just one more.'

'Do you really feel that?'

'Yes.'

She knew he was looking at her even though it was dark. 'Why?'

'A sort of memento, of this. Of our being together, of coming safe home. It's like a souvenir, if you like.'

'What would the children say?'

'I think they'd like it. Freddie and Gus are only six. That's not too big a space.'

'Shouldn't we wait until the war's over?' Rachel said, feeling again apprehensive, whether of motherhood, or the responsibility, or the thought, possibly, of having to bring up a child without Bosco. After all, one had to be realistic. Somehow it seemed like a bad omen, tempting fate, to agree.

'Who knows when the war will end?' Bosco gently began stroking her bare thigh. 'You might be too old.'

'My goodness! Do you mean the war will last another *ten* years? I feel a bit old now at thirty-seven, but it is still possible.'

'Then let's try it,' Bosco kissed her. 'I really would like it. Let's try, while I'm home, for a baby.'

'I hope it won't have a broken arm,' Rachel said, feeling irresponsible, amorous, light-headed; laughing rather helplessly in the dark.

CHAPTER 23

Since the previous October the Flanders village of Neuve-Chapelle had remained in the hands of the enemy. The British trenches stayed as they were, some few hundred yards to the west of the village, behind which were the Aubers Ridge and the great plains of Lille and Turcoing. It was Sir John French's plan to take the village; and Rawlings' 4th Army Corps, together with the Indian Corps, were chosen for the assault upon a front half a mile wide.

The British airmen had done a good job in destroying the railway lines leading to the village, and thus preventing further reinforcements. During the night of 10 March 1915 the troops were brought up to the advance trenches in single file and just before daylight they stood crammed together, smoking and waiting for the signal to mount the short ladders already in position to swarm out over the top.

Through his glasses in the dim light of dawn Bosco could see that the landscape in front of them was a formidable one. There were huge barbed-wire entanglements in front of positions where the well-armed enemy were firmly entrenched and had been for four months. They were rested, well equipped, their morale bolstered by many small victories, the overall failure of the Allied troops to dislodge them. Behind them, too, the outlying farms and houses were like fortresses bristling with guns pointed at an unseen assailant.

But this time the British had the advantage of surprise.

Their airmen so patrolled the skies that no enemy aeroplanes dared approach, and so the latest build-up of troops had been unobserved. The defenders too remained largely without reinforcements or the means to acquire them because of the attack on the railway lines.

Bosco put down his glasses and walked along the tightly packed row of troops, stopping to encourage the young, those whom he knew were nervous, patting the backs of those who looked strong and confident, though appearances could be deceptive. These moments before the men went over the top, although exhilarating, were among the most nerve-racking of the war and having seen what he had seen, the great fences of barbed wire, he felt less exultant and more fearful than usual.

With the Middlesex were the 2nd Scottish Rifles, the 2nd Devons, the West Yorkshires and a regiment of London Territorials among whom, by chance, was Adam awaiting his baptism by fire. Bosco and Adam, joyful at their unexpected reunion, had travelled abroad together the previous week. Bosco had the ribbon of the bar to his Omdurman DSO on his chest, personally handed to him by the King, and the rank of Colonel, plus a new attachment from the 4th Middlesex Regiment to the 2nd. To be together with Adam now was extreme good fortune for them both and, as he hurried along the line, Bosco looked out for his friend among the officers standing in groups talking cheerfully to their men.

He found Adam at the far end of the trench smoking a cigarette, sitting casually on his greatcoat although the morning was bitterly cold. Bosco bent down beside him, tilting back his tin hat. 'Writing a poem?'

'Writing a letter, you idiot. I thought I might as well let Flora have a few last words before I go into battle.'

'They won't be your last words, Adam.'

'It's something to do,' Adam said and, as he looked up,

Bosco realized that his friend was petrified with fear and this nonchalance was subterfuge.

'You'll be all right, you know,' Bosco said, gripping his shoulders, wishing he could infuse him with his own peculiar brand of recklessness. But thoughtful, sensitive Adam would never be reckless.

'Honestly, it's quite all right,' Adam tossed away his cigarette, 'and I'm not afraid to die.'

'You must never think of death when you're here,' Bosco said urgently. 'You must just think of what you have to do as a job, as if you're in court or speaking in the House.'

His words were suddenly drowned by an enormous barrage as, at 7.30 a.m. promptly, the 300 British guns began firing to try and clear the barbed wire in front of the enemy trenches and open a way for the assault of the troops. Bosco released Adam's shoulder. 'Good luck,' he called. 'We'll have a drink when this is all over.'

Adam winked and saluted, getting swiftly to his feet and straightening his tin hat on his head with a hand that, Bosco saw, was trembling. It was all right to feel reckless, but to go over the top feeling panic-stricken was a kind of bravery on its own. Bosco walked slowly back along the twisting, curving line to his own troop who were now gazing as if transfixed by the sight of the top of the trench. Some already had their feet on the bottom rungs of the ladders; but this was the crucial moment when others faltered, thinking of their families. This was the moment when the comforting, jovial word was often important.

'Take it easy, men,' Bosco called. 'Don't go up until the whistle blows. Control your enthusiasm – if you can!'

For half an hour the barrage continued and when it finished and Bosco cautiously raised his head over the parapet he saw that, while to the right of them and in front of the Indian lines the stakes supporting the barbed wire had been torn from the earth, in front of his Brigade, the 23rd, the gunfire had missed the enemy's defences altogether. The barbed-wire barrier remained like a huge impenetrable thicket of bramble and thorns while, beyond, the barrels of the deadly machine guns peeping out over the enemy trenches could be clearly seen. Bosco could see that, as soon as the whistle blew, the way forward for the 25th Brigade would be clear, but the 23rd would be impeded by the mass of tangled wire.

'I'll need half a dozen men to form an advance party with me as soon as the whistle blows to cut through the wire,' Bosco shouted and immediately a dozen volunteers rushed foward. Bosco picked six of the most experienced and also the most nimble, because they would have to run for their lives through the gunfire.

As the men waited tensely for the whistle, Bosco climbed halfway up the ladder in order to be the first over the top. He felt calm and optimistic about the outcome, thrilled rather than afraid, and when, at five minutes past eight the whistles sounded along the line of trenches, he raced for the top and, calling to those behind him, sprinted the few yards to the wire as the fearful assault of the enemy's bullets spattered all round him. The men of the 25th Brigade – the Lincolns, the Berkshires, the 1st Irish Rifles and the 2nd Rifle Brigade – passed straight through the passages made by the guns to clear the enemy trenches, while Bosco and his men started to hack at the grim insurmountable barrier in front of them. Some of them tore at the wire until their hands were raw and then the rest of the Brigade began to do the same. But it was hopeless and all the time the deadly hail of machine-gun bullets continued until the ground was strewn with the dead and dying, many of whom had become impaled on the tangled wire.

'We can't make it, sir,' Corporal Hackett called and, as

Bosco turned to him, the corporal fell, caught in the throat by a spray of bullets. Next to him Colonel Bliss of the Scottish Rifles also lay dead, but 'B' Company under Captain Ferris had made some headway, their bombardiers hurling more bombs to clear a way through the wire.

Yet the Middlesex, nicknamed 'the Diehards', continued to attack the obstacle between them and their goal and every time they were repulsed they would cry: 'Rally boys and at it again' as, once more, they hurled themselves upon the wires.

It was a sickening sight, a ghastly spectacle, but then Bosco saw that what was preventing a further move forward, as well as causing most of the carnage, was a solitary enemy machine gun placed on a knoll higher than the rest. Its barrel was trained on the narrow clearing 'B' Company had found and, as the men crawled through it, they were quickly mown down. The stretcher parties were now all over the field performing their melancholy tasks.

Calling to Sergeant Bramall and Lieutenant Fulwith, Bosco indicated a way through the wire by which they could attack the machine gun from the rear.

'You'll never do it, Colonel,' Sergeant Bramall called, trying to make himself heard above the din.

'Hold the wire up for me and don't argue,' Bosco commanded, even as he lay upon the muddy soil and began to wriggle his way under the wire knowing that at any moment the lone gunner could see him and turn his aim upon him.

When the other men saw what their colonel was doing they rushed foward to hold up the wire, uttering encouraging noises like a party of men on the rugger field. 'At it Colonel Down!' 'Up and on The Diehards!'

'You'll need two of us to do what you're trying to do, sir,' Corporal Mackenzie of the Scottish Rifles called and began to wriggle after him.

The thorns from the wire tore at Bosco's flesh, his clothes, his hair; but still he continued because it was too late to go back and, so far, he could still see the gunner with his back to him, his aim concentrated on one of the narrow passages through which the rest were trying to gain access to the trenches.

Then he found he was clear of the wire and, looking behind him, realized that Mackenzie was still struggling through. He held up the wire for him but Mackenzie was stuck, caught on a barb by the back of his jacket, unable to go forward or back.

'You'll have to run for it, Colonel,' Mackenzie said sourly, knowing what it meant for him. 'I think yon's turning.' His eye indicated the gunner with a grim smile and, seeing that he was indeed beginning to veer round towards them, Bosco, gripping his knife in his hand, ran swiftly along the ground reaching him just as the gunner turned and fired a dreadful volley of bullets on the hapless Mackenzie lying trussed by the wire.

'You bastard!' Bosco shouted and taking a leap forward jumped right into the gunner's lair, kicking him in the face and knocking his gun sideways. Then he stabbed him viciously in the back and, throwing his body off the knoll, took charge of the gun while, below him, the men who had observed his action raised their hands in a cheer.

'Go to it, lads!' he called and turned his gun sharply upon the defending Germans.

He knew it could not, would not, last because already the enemy had seen what had happened and that the powerful weapon was in alien hands. From all sides they began to creep forward firing steadily at Bosco who, ducking bullets, thought that maybe his optimism about the day had been misplaced and that this was, indeed, the end. But still he kept on firing, aware from time to time that some of the bullets being fired at him were reaching their target: in the arm, the leg and, badly, in the foot. He could see the mass of grey bodies slithering through the mud towards him, the plan being, he knew, to converge upon him and take him in a mass attack; but still he kept on. Like Mackenzie before him he knew it was too late to go back.

Bosco felt that if these were his final moments then death, after all, had no sting. He felt no pain from his wounds and no sorrow in his heart except for the loved ones he would leave behind. The exultation that had borne him through the bitter campaign since the summer of 1914 was with him still. He felt charmed, had no regrets, and his only thought at that moment was to take as many of the enemy as he could with him; so he kept up his own deadly, accurate fire.

But, unknown to him, a party of his own men were also approaching from the other side to relieve him, staggering towards the knoll with their own heavy machine gun. With two guns Fulwith had seen they would have superior command of the trench, being able to fire at the enemy in both directions.

The Germans were closing in on Bosco when, behind him, he felt rather than saw a body and someone called loudly in his ear, 'Keep firing, Colonel, relief is at hand' and turning, he looked into the dirty, grinning, welcome face of Lieutenant Fulwith who was not more than nineteen years old.

'Good man,' Bosco said. 'I thought the end was nigh.' He slightly turned the angle of his gun so as to cover the men who were quickly assembling theirs. 'Do you know it was quite sweet? I was surprised.'

'You're *very* badly wounded, Colonel, maybe it is,' Lieutenant Fulwith said with the mournful humour of the trenches. 'You'd better back out to our lines and I'll cover.'

'Back out?' Bosco called, his eyes in the sights of his gun. 'I don't know the meaning of the words "back out".'

'We want you for another day, sir,' Fulwith said, gently taking Bosco's place behind the gun. Bosco only now saw the amount of blood that was pumping from the various wounds in his body. He was also beginning to feel dizzy and, as Private Knole came up in support, he leaned briefly in his arms.

'You leave me, Knole. I don't want to be a burden. I can crawl back on my own.'

'We'll cover for you, sir,' Fulwith called, giving directions to the men who now had the second machine gun in action. 'If you go to the right there is a small passage back to trenches which the enemy have forgotten to cover.'

Bosco waved and started painfully down the hill clutching his arm from which a torrent of blood was pouring. He remembered his skill at making a tourniquet, but felt that if he stopped he would pass out. There were too many inert reminders lying around him of what happened when a man stopped.

He took a deep breath and dropped to his knees, knowing that he was supported by his own fire, and slowly he began to crawl through the mass of tangled bodies, some still caught grotesquely on the wire, wondering now if he could really make it.

Slowly Bosco made his way through the carnage and mud, thinking of very little but making it to the other side. He supposed this was what everyone thought – those who made it and those who didn't. His only regret was that if he did make it back he would probably never be fit enough to return to the front line. He could tell by increasing muzziness in his head and stiffness in his limbs that he was badly hurt, and a new graze over the eye from a bullet caused fresh blood which made it hard to see.

Ahead of him a man, still impaled on the wire, flapped

his arm like a scarecrow, the rest of his body moving with uncoordinated jerks. The more he struggled the more firmly he became enmeshed in the wire. Bosco paused beside him and drew himself up, gently trying to free the soldier's arm from the barbs. The muddy, grimy face looked straight at him in gratitude and Bosco recognized his friend and brother-in-law, Adam.

'My God, man, we must get you out of this,' he said, but Adam gasped:

'I'm absolutely done for, Bosco. I can't get free.'

'You're hit too,' Bosco said.

'In the legs, just as I was about to get through. I saw you with that machine gun and it kept the bastards away.'

'There are two of them there now. I'll get you out of this.' Patiently, as if undoing a complicated piece of knitting, Bosco tried to prise the barbs away from the clothes and flesh of his friend. Yet every time he moved Adam winced with pain until, taking hold of Bosco with his good hand, he said:

'Bosco, I am done for. There is no getting out of this. Leave me and save yourself. You're in a pretty bad way, but I have no chance.'

Bosco saw that Harry's face was smiling as he reached down from his horse, his hand extended.

'Quick, Bosco, take it, take it. You saved me, now save yourself.'

Bosco felt the awful pain in his stomach but, with one hand, reached for Harry's, feeling the warm clasp as his friend and brother-in-law pulled.

Then suddenly Harry sagged forward and fell off his horse beside Bosco, a smile still on his face.

'Harry,' Bosco cried, 'Harry?'

* * *

'I'm *not* leaving you,' Bosco said grimly, one arm protectively round Adam while with his free hand he continued the careful process of separating Adam from his painful and debilitating torment.

Another bullet hit Bosco in the leg but at last he began to detach Adam's body from the wire until it was completely free and Adam clutched at him, his face now streaming with tears.

'We can't get back, Bosco, together. I can't move, even without the wire. I think my leg's broken.'

'Sir,' Bosco felt a hand on his shoulder as Sergeant Bramall, clutching his rifle, knelt beside him. 'We've lost the other gun. You'll have to let me drag you in, or you've had it.'

'Save Captain Bolingbroke and leave me,' Bosco said, pointing to the limp body of his friend.

'He's pretty bad, sir,' Sergeant Bramall looked doubtfully at him and, following his gaze, Bosco saw that Adam's head was lolling, his eyes closed. 'I think he's dead, Colonel.'

'He's only fainted,' Bosco said feeling, for the first time in the entire war, panic-stricken.

'He's *dead*, sir, save yourself.'

'Harry's dead, man! Hurry! Hurry or you'll kill us both.'

But Bosco knew he couldn't leave his friend and brother-in-law to be cut to pieces by the Dervishes in the field. He shook his head at Cardew.

'*Hurry,* sir,' Sergeant Bramall said, tugging at Bosco, but Bosco clasped Adam in his arms.

'Save yourself, Sergeant. I order you to take cover. I'm going to try and get this man behind our lines. He's my friend.'

Sergeant Bramall bent down to help Bosco but Bosco

shouted: 'Better *two* men dead than three, you idiot. Do as I command.'

The sergeant reluctantly let Adam's legs fall and, with a last glance at Bosco, ran for his life towards the safety of the trenches while the bullets spattered after him.

Adam's eyelids flickered and Bosco knew he wasn't dead. He began to try and drag him carefully towards their lines, knowing how hurt he was, when he heard a shout behind him and someone called: 'Take cover.'

Bosco saw the barrel of the captured machine gun train right on Adam's limp body and then, hurling himself across him, he lay upon him, cradling his friend's head in his arms.

'It's all right Adam. We're in this together,' he said, aware of his own ebbing strength. 'You know I'll never leave you, brother. Never, never, never.'

Later they found both bodies lying cheek to cheek, as though the two men had embraced in death.

The letter said:

> My darling, if you read this I shall already be dead and I know how my speaking to you like this must grieve you. I can't foretell the manner of my death and, as I write this, I can't even envisage it, so confident am I, as I've told you, that I shall survive.
>
> With this letter I know I will bring you a double pain, not only because of my death, but because of something I have to tell you that I have hitherto lacked the courage to say.
>
> Before I do I want to tell you, my darling, how much your sweet, serene person has meant to my life, and how even an hour of knowing you is the greatest privilege a man could wish for. As it is I have known you for seventeen years, and been your lover and husband for thirteen of these. If I should die and it is given to me to have one last thought it will be of you, and all the happiness you have brought me. We agreed never to refer again to that unhappy time between us, nor shall I now except to apologize, once again, with all my heart, for the way I hurt you.
>
> Thank you, my darling, and forgive me that I have now left you alone.

I am writing this shortly before going back to the front after the most glorious leave and time spent with you and the children.

It seems we did not make that final baby, my darling, and, if you are reading this letter, maybe it is as well because you have enough to do rebuilding your life without a new child to care for.

But oh, my Rachel, would you do something for me? Can you forgive me, in the nobility and generosity of your heart, for what I am about to ask you?

I had a son by Nimet. His name is Hugo, and he is now nearly three years old. I wanted to tell you this leave about Hugo and my guilt, but I dared not. I thought it might make you too unhappy, even to know of his existence, and spoil what there was between us; and I am too selfish for that.

I wonder now, Rachel, if you would go personally and see the little fellow for me? See that he is well looked after and has everything he needs. My solicitors will give you Nimet's address. Hopefully it will not be too painful for you to see Nimet after all this time. She may even arrange to be out when you call. I feel more peaceful in my mind having asked this favour.

You see, darling, I am a coward after all. Since the trial I haven't seen Nimet, nor wanted to see her but, frequently, I have thought of that little fellow who did not ask to be born and will now be fatherless.

I lacked the courage to do anything about it this leave believing that it is better, at what cost to me though, if I do not see Hugo. If I survive I will make an arrangement to see him and I hope, if I do, that I will have the courage to tell you; you who are all-forgiving and are everything to me.

One day, Rachel, we shall be united in Paradise. I know that, but now writing this I pray that we may have many years together yet to grow old in each other's company.

Rachel, dry-eyed, put down the letter. She had read it many times since it had arrived from his solicitors together with their own letter of condolence. Adam Bolingbroke lived, but just, saved by the body of his friend. He was still in hospital in Boulogne looked after, among others, by Melanie who, like Bosco, had found her own particular fulfilment in the war: a selfish woman who had lost her selfishness in the care of others, and who was very much loved by men of all ranks. Adam was terribly injured, but it was thought he would survive. She sent frequent letters home about his condition and said that all he could say was that he had caused Bosco's death.

That her brother should cause the death of her husband did not seem extraordinary to Rachel because she knew that, finding him as he had, Bosco would never desert him anyway, and she would not have wanted him to. It seemed to her then that her beloved Adam, with his shattered body, was less fortunate than Bosco who, having laid down his life for his friend, had, surely, found peace not only with his Maker, but himself. What future could poor Adam now look forward to with his dreadful wounds, his broken marriage, his memories to keep him company in those long night hours. Such as she had known for the past few weeks?

It was Bosco's way of making reparation for Omdurman. It was the way, maybe, that he had always wished to die.

She picked up the letter yet again and let her eyes run quickly through the closely written pages. To think that he had written them here, in this house. How much it must have cost him to write them, to tell her about Hugo knowing what fresh suffering it would cause.

Rachel, sitting by the open window in her sitting-room, looked at the daffodils and the crocuses that were tentatively putting out their buds to the calm spring air. A year ago she and Bosco had been as strangers. They had only had two months of joy together after their reunion, and another two, that went all too quickly, when he had recovered from his broken arm. She knew he had not been fit to return to the front – his arm was still stiff – yet nothing would stop him. She knew even then, as she said goodbye, and despite his reassurances, that it was unlikely she would see him again.

But now? She got up and leant out of the window, inhaling the fragrant air of Askham, untainted by the smells of war, that had once contained within it everything that Bosco loved – his home, his family, his house, his animals, his lands.

But one thing it did not contain was Nimet or his son by her, and Rachel knew that, with all her generosity of spirit, with all the magnanimity and forgiveness he expected of her, the soldier's widow, she could never ever bring herself to look upon Nimet or the boy Hugo at whatever cost.

The church at Askham was packed, of course, as one would expect for the memorial service to a man who was not only the lord of the manor, but had died a hero's death. The citation for the Victoria Cross had outlined his exploits on that day, 12 March: how bravely he had led his men, how he had captured a German machine gun single-handed and held off the enemy, causing great casualties among them, while sustaining severe wounds until his men were safe. How then he had disregarded all attempts to save him, dragging himself back to his lines alone until he came upon the fallen body of a comrade impaled on barbed wire, and near death. He had refused to leave him, patiently freeing him from his entanglement despite his own mortal wounds and, in the end, he gave his life for him by shielding his body from a hail of bullets which caused his own immediate death.

In the church now the Victoria Cross lay with its purple ribbon on a purple cushion on a bier surrounded by flowers in front of the altar. It had been pinned the week before on the nine-year-old Earl of Askham, Bosco's son, by the King himself in a private ceremony attended by Rachel, Dulcie and her friend Queen Alexandra, who had held her hand. Next to it were his other medals gained in battle – the DSO and bar and the Omdurman medal.

The bright June sun filtered through the stained glass of the window behind the high altar upon the bronze of the cross, made from a cannon in the Crimean War, and the silver of the medals, as the Rector delivered his stirring oration in memory of the late Earl.

Most members of the family were there: Rachel, Dulcie, Flora, Ralph clutching the hand of his mother, with Charlotte on the other side, the twins between Dulcie and Flora.

The Kittos were there. Frances, of course, was there with her tall, plain daughters. The Crewes, the Mackenzies, the Lawfords, the Dugdales, the Lyttons, the Frobishers, were there, the Pardoes, the Hunts and the Smith-Forresters. You could hardly put a name to all the people who had come to Askham parish church that day, three months after Bosco's death. Bosco's relatives and friends from all over the British Isles were there, and many uniforms among them of comrades on leave from the war. The King's aide-de-camp was there and a lady-in-waiting represented Queen Mary, another Queen Alexandra. There were notables from London and Winchester, assize judges and civic dignitaries; and there were the simple, sorrowing people of Askham – Bosco's people.

It was necessary, the Rector said, to remember not only Bosco and his bravery, the men who died with him and among whom he was buried in Flanders' field, but also their enemies.

For in death they were all one in the bosom of their God who was merciful to everyone, friend and foe. The real Christian message was not only thankfulness for the lives of the fallen but forgiveness too.

Forgiveness of their enemies.

At the end the congregation stood for Bosco's favourite hymn: 'He who would true valour see'.

> No goblin nor foul fiend
> Can daunt his spirit.
> He knows he at the end
> Shall life inherit.
> Then fancies fly away.
> He'll not fear what men say,
> He'll labour night and day
> To be a Pilgrim.

and a great swelling chorus finished almost triumphantly on the last words.

In the sunshine afterwards they strolled from the church to the Hall, through the fields where Bosco had jumped his ponies as a boy and along a path through the wood where he had hunted.

The children ran ahead, grateful to be out of the church except for Ralph, who still clung tearfully to the hand of his mother. He had found it very hard to be brave, especially when he had taken up the purple cushion at the end of the service and carried his dead father's medals from the church.

Thoughtful, composed, even smiling at her guests, Rachel walked slowly along the path, with Flora behind her and Mabel on the other side. Mabel who, despite being in her seventieth year, had done such marvellous work organizing the nursing services in France. She had also visited Bosco's grave in Flanders and was able to bring comfort to the family by telling them in what a beautiful spot he lay, in the shelter of a wood she said reminded her of Askham. Despite the fact that the terrain was pitted with trenches and shell holes, they would make it beautiful after the war, she had assured them. When peace had returned it would be such a pretty place.

Mabel had good news of Adam, too, getting better, but

still badly crippled and due to be sent home soon. Melanie cared for him tenderly, though Boofie was always there in the background, an ambulance driver plying bravely between Boulogne and the front. Flora had found it hard to take the news of Adam's injuries and not to be able to be there; but her mother had needed her perhaps even more than Adam who, after all, had Melanie, his wife. She tried not to feel jealous about Melanie, because she had no right. Mabel helped just a little by assuring her that Melanie's devotion was more as a nurse than a wife, and that both she and Adam knew this.

Mabel put her arm through Flora's and, briefly, Rachel found herself alone with Ralph who had pinned his father's Victoria Cross on his lapel, just as the King had done.

Rachel stopped and, looking back, saw that in the stream of mourners behind her Dulcie too was momentarily alone, her head bent, walking very slowly, clutching her black coat to her as though she were cold.

Rachel waited until Dulcie had caught up with her and then she put her arm round her shoulder and drew her gently along.

Dulcie had been in bed for weeks after Bosco's death. No one could quite put a name to what ailed her, but she was still hardly recovered. Rachel had spent hours by her bedside talking about Bosco, going through his entire life – time and time and time again. It was never any trouble for Rachel to be called to see her – night or day, she would always be there. At last, she was needed by Dulcie.

The slender figure looked too thin and her aristocratic beauty had degenerated into an unhealthy sharpness of features; a grey, unnatural pallor. She no longer dyed her hair, but had let it go quite grey. It was very hard now, Rachel thought compassionately, to think of the beautiful, legendary Lady Askham of the Cairo days.

'You should have come by car,' Rachel said, telling Ralph to slow down because his grandmother was tired; but he pulled his mother forward, forgetting his dignity as an earl and wanting to be with his sisters and brother, his many young cousins from all over England. Rachel, laughing, released his hand, allowing him to run after the others, so that the two black-clad women were alone.

'It was a very moving ceremony, wasn't it?' Rachel said.

'Very. But it doesn't bring Bosco back.'

'We have much to be thankful for.'

'Yes, I suppose so, although it is hard to think what,' Dulcie murmured.

'For Bosco's life? For the children?' Rachel suggested and stopped and looked at her mother-in-law.

'For that and them.' At last Dulcie raised her head, her eyes meeting those of her daughter-in-law, and momentarily that haggard, sorrowing face was very briefly illuminated by a tired smile. 'And for you too, Rachel. I realize now how lucky he was to have you. And, although I'll confess I never thought to hear myself say it, I'm grateful to have you too.'

Slowly she slid her hand into Rachel's who clasped it warmly to her side.

'We must all show forgiveness now,' Rachel said, recalling the Rector's words.

We must all show forgiveness.

Rachel stood in front of the little cottage in Hampstead which Bosco had bought for his mistress and their son. The trees in the small garden were in full summer leaf but the rest, though bright with flowers, was overgrown and neglected.

The windows were curtainless and it was obvious that the house had been empty for many months. It looked just like a love nest, she thought; not hating it, but seeing it with a feeling of surprise as though it really somehow had nothing to do with her, which was true. Of the lovers one was dead, and the other . . . where was she?

The FOR SALE notice over the garden gate directed enquirers to Messrs Hardacre, Harris & Hobbs of Camden Town.

Rachel wasn't sure if she was seeing Mr Hardacre, Mr Harris or Mr Hobbs or, maybe, none of them because the man who took her into the small office and shut the door behind them only mumbled his name.

'The cottage has been for sale for well over six months, Lady Askham. Are you interested in making a purchase?'

'I am interested in the lady who was there before, Mrs Seder. She was a friend of my husband's and I wanted to tell her he was dead.'

'I'm so sorry to hear that, Lady Askham,' the man hurriedly leafed through a card index, 'but I have no idea where Mrs Seder is. She left instructions that enquiries were to be made of a Mrs Hussid who lives in Streatham. Curious name, Hussid,' the man said looking at the card. 'I think she's foreign.'

Rachel, pretty sure she knew the real identity of Mrs Hussid, made a note of the address and, thanking the man for his help, gave it to Baker who waited outside the office with the Daimler, and asked him to take her there.

'Streatham, my lady?' Baker wrinkled his nose and opened the door for Rachel to climb in.

Parts of Streatham, south of the river, so fashionable in the latter half of the nineteenth century, were still prosperous, but others had seen far, far better days. The house that Rachel now stood looking at was in a street that had gone quite a long way down in the world. It was a tall double-fronted building with white, badly peeling stucco, the door and window-frames painted a bilious shade of green, maybe quite recently in a hasty and somewhat unsuccessful effort to do the place up. There was a FOR SALE notice outside it too and Rachel, wondering if she was too late, told Baker to wait for her in the car as she swiftly opened the creaking gate and made her way up the cracked, cobbled path overgrown with weeds.

Yet, as she walked she was aware of one of the dingy lace curtains being parted, as someone observed her progress and then, as she knocked, the curtain was let fall and she could hear footsteps behind the door.

'May I come in, Madame Hassim?' she said as it was grudgingly opened, and that acquaintance of long ago poked her head round.

'I must say I'm surprised,' Madame Hassim gaped at her as Rachel, putting a hand firmly on the door, stepped into the hall which was even less prepossessing than the outside of the house. 'You're the last person I would have expected to see.'

It is a cliché to call people 'shadows of their former selves', but that was the only phrase that immediately came to Rachel's mind as she looked at the once elegant creature, wealthy proprietress of a Cairo brothel. She wore a long purple silk dress that looked as though it had made its début in Madame Hassim's better days, maybe Cairo of the 1890s, and had undertaken the journey to England with her. Part of the hem was torn and trailed on the floor, showing a pair of cracked black patent-leather shoes, scuffed and worn down at the heels. Over the top part of the dress, perhaps in an attempt to conceal some dun-coloured stains, because it was a warm day, was a long grey cardigan frayed at the edges, including the sleeves.

Her face had always been raddled, ever since Rachel remembered it, and that was still carefully made up with powder and rouge – perhaps a little more thickly than before to conceal the crevices, deepened by time – and the inevitable heavy, black kohl rings round the eyes. The face was more pitted, however, than Rachel remembered and, whereas too she remembered that Madame Hassim's suspiciously jet black hair had always been luxurious, surely not so luxurious as this? Clearly Madame Hassim had on a very new, but rather cheap, wig.

'I won't keep you very long, Madame Hassim.' Rachel forced her eyes away from the vision in front of her to the closed door painted, like the rest of the hall, in a depressing shade of battleship grey. 'Is Nimet with you?'

'Oh, Nimet?' Madame Hassim could hardly conceal her surprise. 'You've come about *her*, is it?'

'It is. I see her house in Hampstead is for sale.'

'It is, and asking too much for it is the reason it remains for sale, if you ask me.' Madame Hassim contemptuously flung open the door and led the way into a room crammed with old, cheap furniture. There was a heavy flock paper on the walls to which the dust adhered, as barnacles do to rocks, and there was a fearful, malodorous smell of must. 'Who wants to pay £150 for a cottage in wartime?'

'Yes indeed.' Rachel looked around, feeling that she preferred not to sit.

'You better tell me what it is you want, Rachel,' Madame Hassim said sweeping, with a grandiloquent gesture, an under-fed, manged cat, protesting indignantly, from what was obviously the best chair in the room. 'I know I can call you Rachel. I feel I've known you since you were a girl.' Madame Hassim looked at her quite fondly, Rachel thought, as though they'd always been friends. Maybe she scented money.

'I want to know where Nimet is.'

'Well, she isn't here,' Madame Hassim gave that hoarse cackle that Rachel suddenly, vividly, recalled from Cairo days. She wondered if she was a woman who had ever been capable of pure joyous laughter, even when she was a small – very small it would have to be – unsullied girl.

'Will she soon be back? My husband was asking about her.'

'Oh, *was* he?' Madame Hassim said slyly. 'Well, she's gone to Cairo to entertain the troops on their way to the Dardanelles. Maybe he'll see her there?'

'Bosco is dead, Madame,' Rachel reluctantly perched on the edge of the hair-strewn chair vacated by the cat. 'He was killed in March in Flanders.'

'How sorry I am to hear that,' Madame Hassim was instantly passionate concern, her black eyes immediately clouding with grief, and Rachel thought that she had missed her vocation as an actress. Some of the best courtesans had been actresses, and vice-versa. 'He was a good man, a nice man, but very foolish, eh?' She wagged a finger at Rachel and winked suggestively. 'Weak. He couldn't say "no" to women or maybe I should say "a" woman. "That" woman. He always had a weakness for Nimet. She'll be sorry that he's dead. She always hoped he'd go back to her and that's why she hung on. But you hung on harder, didn't you, Rachel? You won?'

'I didn't "hang on" at all, Madame Hassim,' Rachel corrected her coldly. 'Bosco could have been free from me any time he wanted, but he didn't. But if she loved him even a tiny bit she should never have appeared in the witness box. It ruined his life. I even think it caused his death, drove him to the war, because he was so unhappy.'

'Ah, that's what I *knew* would happen.' Madame Hassim carefully, gingerly sat herself down on a chair opposite Rachel, as though fearful it would give way. 'I was against all that from the beginning.'

'Then *why*? Why did they not just come out with it and ask for money?'

'Oh, it wasn't really all money,' Madame Hassim's bright red lips parted in a rueful grin, showing that she had lost two crucial front teeth. 'It was more revenge really, and not from me, I assure you. My brother, Asher, never liked your husband and he was a vengeful man. He never liked Bosco's mother either. He thought they despised us and, I must say, I think they did. You too – all of you English in Cairo. But it was really Mr Hastings who plotted the whole thing, and neither of us ever cared much for him. It seemed a very good idea, though, because Bosco had told Nimet long ago that he had killed Captain Crystal and Nimet, being a simple girl, believed him and told me. I, of course, told my brother.'

'Why did you never say in Cairo that he was your brother?'

'Oh, because he was ashamed of me! He never wanted people to know. He was half-English, whereas his mother, and mine, was a humble Cairene, a girl no better than she should be, a woman of easy virtue. He was always proud of his father, the diplomat!' Madame Hassim gave her coarse laugh again, somehow managing this time to make it also sound obscene. 'I went along with Achmed, but then he was sent to prison and became a very ill man. He came over to England to see me and met Mr Hastings, by chance, once again in a tavern in Fleet Street. He had just been fired from his paper by Bosco who had threatened that he would never get another job.

'Hastings too felt despised by the Askham family, though his skin was completely white. Unfortunately none of you remembered him at a party he went to at Lady Lighterman's, and he had come down in life as well. It made him feel sore: he was a nasty little man. He was a man who drank a lot, and in his drunken moods – which were frequent – he got very spiteful indeed, very mean. Then he saw a way to get his own back by humiliating

Bosco in public, which was why he wouldn't settle beforehand. He thought that Nimet's evidence would be crucial. Achmed had told him about Cairo, of course.'

'He really thought he'd win?'

'Oh yes. Why not?'

'No one else did.'

'But no one *knew* about Nimet. The lawyers thought we would win which was the only thing that persuaded them to take the case, because *we* had no money. We never thought it would end the way it did. It ruined us all. Bosco stopped paying me the money that he'd promised when I released Nimet to go to him – she was one of my best girls, you know. An annuity of five hundred a year and I wouldn't be living in this mess. I can tell you I'm about to sell up and go back to Cairo myself.'

'Well,' Rachel stood up, 'I think there's not much more to say.' She walked across to the heavily curtained French windows that stood open, leading to a small overgrown garden at the back. Her eyes were suddenly riveted by movement and, parting the dirty lace curtains, she saw a small child jumping on and off a wooden box, looking lonely and forlorn the way that neglected, unwanted children do. He wore shabby patched trousers and a darned jumper that looked much too hot for the summer day, and his face had that lost, vacuous expression such as old people have who have been dumped and forgotten.

'Who's that?' Rachel said gesturing.

'Oh, him!' Madame Hassim ambled to the window, arms akimbo. 'That's Nimet's child. I suppose you know about him.'

'That's *Hugo*?' Rachel looked at her incredulously. 'She didn't take him with her?'

'No. She was always going to send for him, but never quite got round to it. That was typical of Nimet. Frankly, I never knew what Bosco saw in her, apart from her looks. I suppose they were all he was interested in, though she got rather fat after she had the baby. I always thought he was very good to her because she was a shallow girl and a terrible liar.' Madame Hassim raised shocked eyes to the ceiling where, in some places, the plaster had parted from the wall. 'Oh, what a liar! No, I can never understand men; and some women, come to that, I can't understand at all. I could never, never understand her going on and on about love when all she wanted was money and security.'

'She must have loved him, surely, to have had his child?'

Rachel couldn't take her eyes off the little boy who had not yet realized he was being observed. Suddenly he crouched down and, picking up a stone, began to scratch something on the box. She thought she had never seen anything, any creature, so lonely and forlorn in her life. She saw too that he was a handsome boy, despite his unkempt appearance, with olive skin, thick black hair and large blue eyes. Madame Hassim followed her gaze.

'I don't think she knew what love was. Girls brought up like that hardly ever do. I was one myself, so I know. No, she wanted a home and, Bosco being a gentleman, she knew that he'd give it to her. The child was an appendage and, honestly, she never loved him.'

'He looks so sweet.'

'Oh, he's very nice.' Madame Hassim swept open the doors wide as though offering a choice item – a person, a thing – for inspection. 'But what I will do with him I don't know.'

'Won't you take him with you?' Rachel looked from Hugo to Madame Hassim in surprise.

'Take him with me?' Madame Hassim cackled wickedly again. 'I should think not. When I've got rid of this house *and* the cottage – probably take a low price to get rid of them both – I shall be off to Cairo. At least I have a little property and friends there. That trial ruined me doubly, because I had a nice little business here, just a couple of girls but clean and easy, and quite a smart clientele. You should have seen this place a few years ago,' Madame Hassim's hands swept fancifully through the air, as though sketching a crystal chandelier here, a mahogany wall cupboard there, maybe a Persian rug or two and a sofa upholstered in scarlet velvet. 'Then the police were after me and threatened me with prison. After what it did to my brother, no thank you!'

'What did happen to him?' Rachel asked more out of politeness than curiosity, seeing that his name kept cropping up.

'He died a year ago, home in Cairo. He had this awful illness, couldn't breathe. Left no money of course. Ah dear me, Rachel, money.' Madame Hassim paused and looked at her speculatively. 'I suppose you've a lot of it now? How would you like to buy these houses? Take them off me, as a friend, for old times' sake. I'll let you have them very cheap.'

'I'll think about it.' Rachel wandered out into the garden and squatted down beside Hugo. 'Hello Hugo!' The little boy, surprised, sat down quickly on his bottom and regarded her gravely.

'He doesn't smile much,' Madame Hassim explained apologetically. 'You couldn't expect him to, really. Not much to smile about, poor little thing. The man from the orphanage is coming tomorrow.'

'The *orphanage*!' Rachel jumped. 'Oh, but you couldn't! He's Bosco's son. Bosco left money for him, he told me.'

'She took everything, you know.' Madame Hassim shook her head disapprovingly and pulled her grey cardigan around her ample body as if she felt a chill. 'She had no conscience. *I* can't take him with me and I can't leave him here. Can I?' Madame Hassim glanced at her, as though from one reasonable person to another.

'Would you let me take him?' Rachel said suddenly and then put her hand to her mouth, as though the words had come out involuntarily, shocking even herself.

'*You'd* take him? Your husband's child by his mistress? You must be mad.'

'Perhaps I am.' Rachel bent and gave a hand to Hugo who clutched at it, staring desperately up at her, as if he knew that his fate depended entirely upon her. She felt so drawn to this little boy, Bosco's child, that she forgot how much she had hated the mother. Forgot entirely who the mother was in that moment of pity and compassion for a little boy whom nobody loved or wanted and who, as Bosco said, was entirely blameless, had never asked to be born. She thought of her own four, happy, well-cared-for children and, bending forward, she took Hugo in her arms, the little hand still tightly clasping hers, as though he would never let her go.

Suddenly he smiled and Madame Hassim clapped her hands together, exclaiming: 'There, he likes you! I've hardly *ever* seen him smile. Little brat.'

Rachel thought that was scarcely surprising considering the sort of life he seemed to have had with his mother and her.

'I'll take him.' She put her arms round him more firmly, as if already he belonged to her. 'I have four other children and he'll easily fit in.'

'I must say I admire you,' Madame Hassim said grudgingly.

'If you can arrange it when you get back to Cairo – and no blackmail mind – I'll adopt him and have the whole thing made legal. It's what Bosco would have wanted, I know.'

'It will cost you something.' That familiar look of cunning returned to Madame's eyes.

'I thought it might,' Rachel said equably; 'but the lawyers can discuss all that. Bosco would have wanted me to give a home to his son; and I'll take the houses too. There.'

Rachel's gesture was not entirely altruistic. She felt that the sooner Madame Hassim had left these shores the happier she would be.

'Well, now, isn't this a happy day, after all?' Madame Hassim looked almost joyful. 'I can see he's taken to you too.' Indeed Hugo wouldn't let her put him down but clung to her as she stood up, that little hand still tightly clenched over her finger. 'Could you let me have some money on account, say, fifty pounds?' Madame Hassim briefly closed her eyes, as if she could hardly, dared hardly, envisage such an amount.

'I could perhaps let you have twenty immediately.' Rachel dug awkwardly in her bag because of Hugo's fiercely clinging arm. She thought if she attempted to free herself he would cry. Producing four new five-pound notes, she held them out to Madame Hassim whose fingers snapped over them like a trap.

'That'll do,' Madame Hassim said eagerly. 'I know I can trust you. And you'll really take the houses?'

'I'll see the lawyer gets in touch with you immediately.' Both Rachel's arms were now around Hugo and she hugged him. 'We'll go now.'

'Don't you want his clothes?' Madame Hassim looked at her doubtfully.

'I think I've clothes for him.' The last thing Rachel wanted was any remnants like the ones he had on. Those would be burnt immediately.

'I can see now you're in a hurry to be off, perhaps before you realize you've made a mistake.'

'I haven't made a mistake, never fear.' Rachel's hands closed comfortingly round the thin little legs. 'I love him already.'

'I must say, you do amuse me, but I remember, even in Egypt, thinking you were an unusual girl. I never thought, either, that you were the type that someone like Bosco would marry. You were never what I'd call strictly pretty; I hope you don't mind me saying.'

'I don't mind at all.' Rachel paused at the door as Madame Hassim opened it for her, and smiled. 'I don't suppose we'll see each other again, Madame Hassim, but I wish you well. Goodbye.'

'Goodbye, goodbye,' Madame Hassim said, waving cheerfully, and bent to try and kiss Hugo who shied immediately away from her, turning his head so that her kiss landed on his back. 'There now, ungrateful for all I've done for him. Just like his mother.'

As Rachel ran swiftly down the path Madame Hassim didn't try again but continued waving, her hand clutching her cardigan across the bosom of her stained dress.

'Don't forget the money,' she shouted as Baker quickly got out to open the back door of the car, 'don't forget it, will you, whatever you do?'

Rachel turned and nodded, devoutly hoping they were the last words she would ever hear from a woman so painfully and inextricably connected with her past.

'Home, Baker,' she said as she settled Hugo on the seat beside her. That well-trained servant knew better than to question his employer, but even he gazed doubtfully at the small human bundle who looked at him with terror, refusing to be budged for a moment from Rachel's side.

As the car left the kerb she felt Hugo relax a little and look back, as though to make sure that Madame Hassim was not coming with them. Rachel glanced over her shoulder too and saw that the sickly green door was already closed. She imagined that Madame Hassim, well pleased with the day's business of selling a child and two houses, had hurried upstairs, hardly believing her good fortune, to begin to pack in case Rachel changed her mind and returned.

'There now, we're alone,' Rachel pressed the small body to hers. 'You'll have brothers and sisters, Hugo, and a pony to ride, dogs and other animals to play with. You'll have a family of your own . . . and a father who loved you, but whom you'll never remember,' she concluded sadly, not knowing how much he understood. He was evidently a bright, alert child, his eyes darting about with curiosity, certainly suppressed excitement, as the car made its way through the dismal streets of South London. She could see how lonely and insecure he'd been because his little hand still clung tightly on to hers, as it had when she first lifted him up in the garden. Young Hugo had chosen his own destiny.

As she held him close to her she was aware of his warm body throbbing with life, with hope. He already seemed part of her as though, in a strange osmosis, he really was hers and Bosco's son, the baby he'd wanted on his last leave and had never had.

Cradling him in her arms as they crossed at last over Westminster Bridge, past the Houses of Parliament where Bosco had sat as a peer and the great Abbey church where the nation would mourn its heroes, Rachel felt at peace for the first time since Bosco's death. A kind of contentment as though, in doing his will, she had at last earned his approbation.

Gazing, then, up at the sky as the car entered St James's Park she thought she saw a familiar profile, a shadowy outline made by the clouds and she wondered if, somehow, Bosco was looking down, smiling on them.

ACKNOWLEDGEMENTS

I would like to thank Lionel Bloch, LL.B, for his invaluable help and advice over certain points concerning the law of libel, and also for reading the chapter containing the trial in the High Court and commenting on it. I am indebted too to Jane Moonman, JP, and Billy Strachan, Senior Chief Clerk to the magistrates at Clerkenwell Court, for advising on the proceedings in Bow Street Magistrates' Court and reading the relevant chapter.

Finally my grateful thanks to Professor Philip Larkin for his kindness in personally agreeing to let me use a line from his lovely poem 'MCMXIV' for the title of my book, and allowing me to quote from it.

Nicola Thorne

BIBLIOGRAPHY

Alice, Princess, Duchess of Gloucester, *The Memoirs of Princess Alice, Duchess of Gloucester* (London, 1983).

Anglesey, The Marquis of, *A History of the British Cavalry 1816–1919*, Vol III 1872–1898 (London, 1982).

Anon, *Letters from Egypt* (Private circulation) (London, 1854).

Baedeker, K. (Ed.), *Egypt: Handbook for Travellers* (London, 1902).

Blake, R. L. V. Ffrench, *The 17th/21st Lancers* (London, 1968).

Buckingham and Chandos, The Duchess of, *Letters from Egypt* (Stockport, 1896).

Budge, E. A. Wallis, *The Nile: Notes for Travellers in Egypt* (London 1905).

Churchill, Winston Spencer, *The River War: an Historical Account of the Reconquest of the Soudan*, 2 vols. (London, 1899).

Dangerfield, George, *The Strange Death of Liberal England* (London, 1966).

Doyle, A. Conan, *The British Campaign in Europe, 1914–1918* (London, N.D.).

Edes, Mary Elisabeth and Frasier, Dudley (Eds.), *The Age of Extravagance: an Edwardian Reader* (London, 1955).

Fulford, Roger, *Votes for Women: the story of a struggle* (London, 1958).

Lamplough, A. O. (Illus.), *Egypt and How to See It* (Guide book) (London, 1907).

Morgan, David, *Suffragists and Liberals: the Politics of Woman Suffrage in England* (Oxford, 1975).

Mosley, Nicholas, *Julian Grenfell: his life and the times of his death 1888–1915* (London, 1976).
Moynihan, Michael (Ed.), *Greater Love: letters home 1914–1918* (London, 1980).
Nowell-Smith, Simon (Ed.), *Edwardian England 1901–1914* (London, 1964).
Penfield, Frederic Courtland, *Present-day Egypt* (London, 1899).
Sackville-West, V., *The Edwardians* (London, 1930).
Steevens, G. W., *Egypt in 1898* (Edinburgh and London, 1898).
Strachey, Ray, *The Cause: A Short History of the Women's Movement in Great Britain* (London, 1978).
Tirard, H. M. and N., *Sketches from a Nile Steamer: for the Use of Travellers in Egypt* (London, 1899).
Warner, Philip, *Dervish: the rise and fall of an African Empire* (London, 1973).
Wohl, Robert, *The Generation of 1914* (London, 1980).
Ziegler, Philip, *Omdurman* (London, 1974).